Bunnies and Burrows

Authors
B. Dennis Sustare, Ph.D.
Scott R. Robinson, Ph.D.

Developer
Bill Webb

Producer
Bill Webb

Editor
Krista Collins

Layout and Production
Elizabeth Stewart

Front Cover Art
Moa Wallin

Interior Art
Darlene, Maggie Vandewalle, Faith Burgar, C.J. Marsh, Claire Rierson, brusheezy.com, vecteezy.com

Cartography
Scott R. Robinson, Ph.D.

FROG GOD GAMES IS

CEO
Bill Webb

Chief Operating Officer
Zach Glazar

Production Director
Charles A. Wright

Creative Director
Matthew J. Finch

Special Projects Director
Jim Wampler

Customer Service Director
Michael Badolato

FROG
GOD
GAMES

Table of Contents

DARLE
©2

Welcome to B&B

Original B&B

Bunnies & Burrows was first published in 1976 by **Fantasy Games Unlimited**. It provided a complete roleplaying game system in a fantasy setting, but unlike prior RPGs, it allowed you to roleplay as an intelligent rabbit rather than a traditional humanoid race (e.g., human, elf, dwarf, or halfling). There were rules for combat and herbalism, and the risks of traps, diseases, and predators. This new edition (2018) has been completely revised and expanded to enhance clarity and playability.

Overview of the New Edition

In this new edition, you can still play as a rabbit, but you also have the option to play as a raccoon, squirrel, chipmunk, skunk, porcupine, opossum, jackrabbit, or armadillo, each with their own characteristics and abilities. Many aspects of the original game have been enhanced here. A full, logical system of herbalism is presented, forming an analogue to the magic systems in other fantasy roleplaying games. Predatory behavior is expanded to include the pursuit phase as well as the final combat. The bestiary we present is greatly expanded over the original version. We have worked hard to provide an ecological feel in the game, and to outline a wide range of habitats to explore. There are introductory adventures included now, and guidance on how to create your own adventures and run a campaign. We provide a good variety of play aids, and have created a series of mini-games that are fun by themselves, but can also be incorporated into the campaign itself. We hope you enjoy it.

Getting Started

Only the Gamemaster who will run the campaign needs to read this entire rulebook, for the players can begin creating characters and starting play without knowing the details, learning as they advance. But all the players will find that they do better with a deeper understanding of the rules, especially those that directly pertain to the profession they choose for their character.

This book is organized into three main parts. **Traits and Characteristics** is a description of the eight traits that form the basis of each player's character, equivalent in a way to the genetic makeup of the character, followed by the skill improvement that comes with experience. In this part you will learn how to create a character, the special abilities of that character, and what role each trait plays during the game. No matter what profession you choose, you will find that all the traits are useful to you during play.

The second part is **Playing the Game**. Here you will learn how the game works, though we urge you to start playing and learn through experience as guided by your Gamemaster. The rules of pursuit and

combat are in this part, as well as sections on food, pests, diseases, and all the other things that are part of the life of rabbits.

The third section is **For The Gamemaster**, which explains how to run a campaign and design adventures. As the Gamemaster, you can decide the form the campaign takes, limited only by your imagination. Where will the rabbits live? What quests or challenges do they face? Will you have a campaign that stresses exploration, develops story lines, or is a continual battle to survive? You can decide, and can tailor your campaign to meet the needs and desires of your players. **Bunnies & Burrows** is equally well suited to experienced roleplayers or to beginners, even those to whom this will be their first RPG endeavor.

The third part is followed by several appendices that the Gamemaster will need as reference material. There is one on herbs, a bestiary, and various player aids.

Part I:
Traits and Characteristics

The Eight Base Traits

Eight genetic Traits help determine the possible development and abilities of a player's character in Bunnies & Burrows. These are set at birth, and do not change during the course of the game. For each profession, one of these Traits will be the Primary Trait, though all may prove important in your eventual success.

Strength (STR)	Primary Trait of Fighters and Bandits.
Speed (SPD)	Primary Trait of Runners and Heralds.
Intelligence (INT)	Primary Trait of Scouts and Spies.
Agility (AGI)	Primary Trait of Mavericks and Burglars.
Constitution (CON)	Primary Trait of Empaths and Guardians.
Mysticism (MYS)	Primary Trait of Seers and Shamans.
Smell (SML)	Primary Trait of Herbalists and Traders.
Charisma (CHA)	Primary Trait of Storytellers and Grifters.

Traits and Experience

Although your genetic makeup is set at birth, you decide how to make the most of what you are given. The development of your character starts with your choice of profession, and thereafter proceeds through experience gained during the game. To mark the degree of development, each Trait has a Level, and the Levels increase based on how you assign your experience to your Level progress. Thus, even if your genetic predisposition is low in one Trait, you may choose to advance Levels in that Trait and make it more useful during gameplay. At the start of play for a new character, you will be Level 0 in all Traits, though choosing a profession immediately advances you to Level 1 in two Traits (your Primary Trait, plus one different Trait of your choosing). Thereafter, you may improve your Levels by spending Advancement Points (APs), though your genetics imposes maximum limits to each Trait's Level.

Base Bonus, Maximum Levels and Trait Ratings

For each Trait separately, your genetic value sets a Base Bonus for that Trait, and limits the maximum number of Levels you may attain in that Trait. These never change for your character during the game, though of course you may start playing a new character with different Traits. The following table lists Base Bonus and Maximum Level for the possible Trait values.

Trait Value	Trait Base Bonus	Maximum Trait Level
6 or less	+0	4
7–12	+0	5
13–15	+1	6
16–17	+2	7
18 or more	+3	8

Your **Trait Rating** is the sum of the current Trait Level plus Base Bonus in the same Trait. Thus, if your Strength (STR) Trait Value is 16 (yielding a Base Bonus for Strength of +2) and your current STR Level is 3 — simply denoted as 16 STR, L3 — your STR Rating (which influences damage in combat) is +5 (2+3). Unlike your base genetic values, Trait Ratings continue to increase as you gain Levels, allowing you to become better and better in relevant abilities. But the highest possible Trait Ratings are attainable only by experienced characters with excellent genetic values.

Advancement Points (AP)

As players complete adventures, the GM will award Advancement Points, typically based on the difficulty of the adventure. Prepared scenarios have suggested APs for completion of certain Acts within the Adventure, though the GM may modify these, if desired. During a campaign, players spend their accumulated APs to advance Trait Levels for their characters. It costs one AP to advance from Level 0 to Level 1, two APs from Level 1 to Level 2, three APs from Level 2 to Level 3, etc. A player may spend APs as they are earned, or save them to spend later. Except for the very first AP spent when creating a character (which must be spent in the primary Trait for the chosen Profession), the player may allot APs to various Traits as one wishes. Thus, you may choose to build up one Trait quickly, or spread the APs around to advance multiple Traits more slowly. Every Trait is valuable to advance; the pattern of advancement that you choose helps determine the type of character you are building during the campaign.

Creating a Player Character

There are sixteen different professions from which to choose for your player character, with each profession limited to one specific type of animal. When you create a character, you roll dice to determine your genetic makeup for each of the eight Traits; how many dice you roll is dependent on which type of animal you will be playing. Traditionally, all characters in the original ***Bunnies & Burrows*** were rabbits, but in this new edition, there are additional animal choices. In addition to your genetics and choice of profession, you also pick a name for your character as well as your gender. Every profession is appropriate for either male or female characters (and our arbitrary use of gendered pronouns in the rules below do not imply a preference for one over the other). There are no gender advantages or disadvantages in combat or other activities. It is also possible to import a character from ***Bunnies & Burrows Light*** (BBL), or to choose one from among your offspring (which will be described under **Reproduction**).

If you wish to create a rabbit (bunny) from scratch, you roll three six-sided dice (3d6) for each of the Traits, in order: **STR, SPD, INT, AGI, CON, MYS, SML, CHA.** You may then adjust these results by either (a) adding two points to one Trait, or (b) adding one point to each of three different Traits. Now your genetic makeup is determined and will not change during the course of the game. You then may choose any of eight different professions available to rabbits, each having a different Primary Trait (shown in the table below). You are free to choose any of them, but it is generally to your advantage to pick a profession in which your initial Trait value is high, since that will give you a higher maximum Trait Level (thus, eventual higher Trait Ratings) and certain advantages in your profession.

Fighter	Runner	Scout	Maverick
STR	SPD	INT	AGI

Empath	Seer	Herbalist	Storyteller
CON	MYS	SML	CHA

The abilities of each profession are detailed in the sections on the properties of Traits, under the Trait that is Primary for that profession. At the time of character creation, you start with two Advancement Points to spend. One of these must be spent on the Primary Trait for your chosen profession, but the other may be spent as you wish, or saved for later.

Creating a non-rabbit player character is similar, though none of them may choose any of the professions listed above. Rather, there is a single profession available to each of the non-rabbit animal types. In addition, the dice rolls vary from those for rabbits, reflecting the different genetic makeup of the other animals. See the section on **Non-Rabbit Species and Professions** for details.

Migrating Rabbit Characters from B&B Light

If you developed a rabbit character in ***Bunnies & Burrows Light***, you may migrate it into this complete game following these guidelines. Note that ***B&B Light*** rabbits may not be more than 3rd level in any Trait. You must remain a rabbit if you migrate a character.

1. Choose a Profession: If you were a Fighter, you may choose either a Fighter or a Runner. A Scout may become either a Scout or a Maverick. An Empath may be either an Empath or a Seer. Finally, an Herbalist may be either an Herbalist or a Storyteller. Your levels in the various Traits do not change no matter which Profession you become.

2. Adjust your Base Bonuses: If any of your Traits had a value of 15, reduce your Base Bonus for that Trait from +2 down to +1. If any of your Traits had a value of 18, raise that Base Bonus to +3. All other Base Bonuses remain the same as in ***B&B Light***. Be sure to adjust your Trait Rating accordingly for those Traits. Note that if your CON Rating is reduced or increased, you must recalculate your Hit Points, and if your CHA Rating is reduced, you have one fewer language; if increased, one more.

3. Note your new Special Abilities: Your Special Abilities are now different. Forget any that you had in ***B&B Light*** and examine these rules to find your new Special Abilities for your chosen Profession.

4. Adjust your Languages: If you knew *Rats*, change that to *Nibblers*. If you knew *Diggers*, change that to *Grubbers*. If you knew *Birds*, change that to one (your choice) of *Raptors, Perchers, Strutters*, or *Waders*. You may not pick any new languages; however, if your CHA Rating increased, you may pick one more from the entire new list. If you had to drop a language due to CHA reduction, you may choose which one to drop.

5. Learn the New Rules: You will find that many of the rules (such as Combat) are quite different from ***B&B Light***. Be flexible, and adjust your play. And remember, the GM is always right.

Rabbit Traits and Professions

In the following discussion of Traits and Professions, some skills and abilities are presented in simplified terms. More detailed explanations, as well as advanced or optional rules, are given in the later sections on **Playing the Game** and **For the Gamemaster**.

Strength (STR)

With great strength, you will be much admired by rabbits. You need physical strength to pull heavy things, jump long distances, and do lots of damage in combat. Some foolish rabbits may talk as though the strong ones look tough but lack in other respects; it is not recommended that you utter this to a stronger rabbit, though.

Jumping

The distance a rabbit can jump horizontally is STR Rating +1 (in rabbit body-lengths, about 30 cm, or one foot). Thus, with only a STR Rating of 1, you can jump across a half-meter stream. However, to jump across a full meter (the width of one hex on a Battleboard) requires at least STR Rating 3. For a vertical jump, the maximum distance is half a horizontal jump. Note that some injuries may affect jumping ability, and some situations may require a STR skill check. Jumping is not allowed underground.

Damage in Combat

Strength is the main factor that determines the damage inflicted during combat. Core damage is based on STR Rating (Level + Base Bonus). See **Combat Rules** for details.

Carrying Another Rabbit and Moving Heavy Objects

It is sometimes necessary to carry a disabled rabbit to safety. To determine if this is possible by a single rabbit, compare the STR Rating of the carrying rabbit to the CON Rating of the disabled rabbit (which is related to the weight of the rabbit). If greater or equal, carrying is possible (though you can travel only at one-quarter speed). Otherwise, it requires two or more rabbits combining their strength to pull the disabled rabbit along. Rabbits range in weight from about 500 gram to 3 kilograms, so as a rule of thumb, each point of STR Rating allows a rabbit to carry about 0.5 kilogram, and to nudge an object three times as heavy. Obviously, carrying a very large animal may be difficult or impossible.

Profession: The Fighter (STR)

Mugwort the Fighter

Clearly the strongest rabbits should rule the Warren, and that is why being a Fighter is the best. Fearlessly we rush into every battle, prepared to give our lives to protect the Warren. There is nothing like the satisfaction of ruthless claws, bites, and rips, watching our foes collapse before our onslaught or flee in terror. We can take on the most powerful foes, secure in our knowledge that our fighting tactics and massive damage are likely to win the day. Why, any mate would be honored to breed with one of us, as our kits are also likely to burst with strength."

A Fighter is a warrior rabbit that guards the warren from intruders. They also often serve to help maintain order within the warren due to their physical presence. At higher STR levels, Fighters have special combat abilities (see **Combat Rules** for details). The Primary Trait for a Fighter is Strength.

Special Abilities

- In Pursuit, Fighters may **Vault** over *Minor* obstacles.
- In Combat, Fighters may **Rip** after a successful Bite.
- At STR Level 3, Fighters may **Vault** over *Major* obstacles in Pursuit.
- At STR Level 3, Fighters may **Double Attack** in Combat.
- At STR Level 6, Fighters may attempt **Killing Blow** in Combat.

Vault

In Pursuit, a Fighter may leap over an obstacle and continue running without hindrance. A vaulting Fighter lands on the opposite side of the hex containing the obstacle and maintains the same facing direction and heading. Although a Vault results in advancing 2 hexes, the maneuver costs only one movement point. All Fighters can vault over Minor obstacles; at STR Level 3, a Fighter also can vault over a Major obstacle. Performing a vault counts as one tactical use during a pursuit.

Rip

In combat, if a Fighter succeeds in Holding her adversary (such as after a successful Bite), the next attack she may use the special attack Rip. This represents bringing up the hind legs to viciously rake the opponent, potentially doing considerable damage. See **Combat Rules** for details.

Double Attack

In combat, a Fighter at STR Level 3 or above may conduct a second attack in place of the movement segment of the round. See **Combat Rules** for details.

Killing Blow

In combat, a Fighter at STR Level 6 or above may attempt what is known as a Killing Blow. This is a special attack that has the potential for extreme damage (possibly killing an already injured opponent), though leaving the Fighter greatly exposed to a possible counterattack if the opponent survives. See **Combat Rules** for details.

Speed (SPD)

With a thousand enemies in the world, speed often decides whether you escape or fall prey. And when in combat, quickness is often your primary defense. With high speed you may choose to lure predators to pursue you rather than a slower warren mate, thus giving slower rabbits time to hide or go underground.

Movement

In normal walking, a rabbit proceeds slowly since she is nibbling on food as she goes. While roving (i.e., outside of combat), an average rabbit can move through two hexes in open terrain in 10 minutes (about 100 meters). Speedier rabbits can add their SPD

Base Bonus to this rate. Thus, a rabbit with a Base Bonus of +2 can move up to 4 hexes (~200 meters) in 10 minutes. Terrain can slow movement radically (see Terrain rules). Although the distances and times are much shorter, the same rates and bonuses apply to running during Pursuit. However, special movement rules apply in **Combat**; refer to that section for details.

Defense Bonus

In combat, the success of an attack depends upon the attacker's Attack Score (AS) compared to the defender's Defense Score (DS). Defense Score is determined by adding the defender's SPD Rating to his Defend die. See **Combat Rules** for details.

Climbing

Most rabbits are not very good at climbing, unless they are going up a slanted surface such as a fallen tree. For more vertical climbing (on a rough surface with clawholds), a rabbit may climb its SPD Rating (in meters) each turn, with a SPD skill check required. For simple climbs (e.g., stone wall, dirt bank), use DV=4 for the skill check. For trickier surfaces, a higher degree of difficulty is used (e.g., DV=6 for brick wall, oak tree; DV=8 for cliff face, pine tree). Failure of any SPD check results in falling. If a rabbit falls, succeed with an AGI skill check or take two HP damage for each meter fallen. Climbing by rabbits is too tricky to attempt during combat.

Swimming

All rabbits know how to swim, but it can be challenging for young rabbits or in fast-moving streams. In still water, a rabbit may swim 1d6 + SPD Rating meters in one turn. If the swimming takes longer than one turn, a skill check must be made for each turn. In rough or fast-moving water, the swim rate is reduced to 1 meter per round, with a skill check each round. It is often better to find another way to cross rough water than to try to swim across it.

Profession: The Runner (SPD)

Speedwell the Runner

The fleetest rabbits have always been honored in all the legendary tales. It is not just that we win all the races, but that we also excel in combat due to great defensive skills. At times, we are called on to lure the predators away from weaker rabbits, confident in our ability to outrun them until they have been led far away and we can then duck into cover. Often, the Warren chooses a Runner as a leader, prizing our speedy nature. If you want your kits to survive to adulthood, you could do worse than choosing a Runner as a mate."

A Runner is a speedster that is often used as a messenger for the warren, or as a lookout in an outpost, including elevated locations. Runners excel at maneuvers and defensive combat. At higher SPD levels, Runners have special combat abilities (see **Combat Rules** for details). The Primary Trait for a Runner is Speed.

Special Abilities

- In Pursuit, Runners may use the **Combo** maneuver.
- In Combat, Runners may **Speed Burst**.
- At SPD Level 3, Runners may **Combine Dodge and Attack** in Combat.
- At SPD Level 6, Runners may attempt **Intercept** in Combat.

Combo

Runners are experts in gait and locomotor skill. As a special tactic in pursuit, a Runner may combine any two basic tactics into a single new maneuver. The effects of the two tactics are combined, but the Combo maneuver only counts as one tactical use.

Speed Burst

In Combat, Runners may take an additional move (using full MP) at any time (not just in their turn), but it costs 1 HP to do so.

Combining Dodge and Attack

In Combat, Runners at SPD Level 3 or above can combine Dodge and any of their Attacks in the same action, thus having much better defense.

Intercept

In Combat, Runners at SPD Level 6 or above can attempt to Intercept an attack on another rabbit. This is done by interrupting the attack and running into the hex occupied by the target rabbit, displacing that rabbit to an adjacent hex chosen by the Runner. To succeed, the Runner rolls 1d6 + SPD Rating vs. the attacker's 1d6 + AGI Rating; the same attack that was being done by the attacker is instead resolved against the Runner, defending with 1d6 + SPD Rating. If the intercept fails, the Runner stops on the last hex before entering the target rabbit's hex and the target rabbit receives a −1 reduction in defense against the attacker's attack due to being run into by the Runner.

Intelligence (INT)

You can be strong, speedy, and tough, but if you are not clever, you will often be surprised by a predator or a trap. Understanding your surroundings — what some have called situational awareness — is very important. A clue to a hazard might be right in front of you, but if you do not recognize it, the clue is useless. A glint of metal, a movement of the grass, a moving speck in the sky: spotting these allows you to give the alert and take protective measures before it is too late.

Spotting Predators

The rabbit in the lead of the party has a chance to passively detect predators, excluding Stalker or Cryptic predators. This is done by the GM secretly performing an INT skill check, adjusted by the lead rabbit's INT Base Bonus. The difficulty is based on a combination of the predator type, terrain, weather, and possible other factors. Scouts at INT Level 3 or higher have a chance to passively detect Stalker or Cryptic predators. If a rabbit stops, posts on hind legs, and declares an active search for predators, the search is adjusted by INT Rating (see **Rules for**

Encounters with Other Animals for details). Any rabbit in the party may declare an active search.

Spotting Traps and Other Hazards

The rabbit in the lead of the party or any Scout has a chance to passively detect trap clues, environmental hazards, or pests. This is done by the GM secretly performing an INT skill check, adjusted by the lead rabbit's INT Base Bonus. The difficulty is based on a combination of the trap, hazard, or pest type, terrain, weather, and possible other factors. Scouts use their INT Rating in this check. If any rabbit stops and declares an active search for pests, their search is adjusted by INT Rating (see **Trap Rules** for details). A declared Scout automatically detects pests upon an active examination.

Freeing Trapped Rabbits

If a rabbit is caught in a trap, it may not escape by itself. But another rabbit may attempt to free it. Your INT Rating is used in the attempt, against a difficulty based on the trap. The method used (and the chance of success) depends upon the trap type (See **Trap Rules** for details).

Profession: The Scout (INT)

Sweetbriar the Scout

Any rabbit with a brain immediately realizes that Scouts are the best profession. Our high intelligence makes us key in recognizing all sorts of threats, be they predators, traps, pests, or other environmental hazards. It is due to this that we are often called on to lead exploratory parties. So it also helps if you enjoy the tinge of a little fear, since we are usually the first to encounter dangers. Our bravery in the face of risks has resulted in our being the heroes in many classic rabbit stories. If you want your kits to be clever, pick one of us for a mate."

A specialist in behavior requiring intelligence, the Scout is a master of detection and interpretation. At higher INT levels, Scouts have special detection abilities. The Primary Trait for a Scout is Intelligence.

Special Abilities

- In Pursuit, Scouts may use **Flash Tail** to Confound.
- Scouts get INT Rating Bonus (instead of INT Base Bonus) for passively spotting ordinary predators, trap clues, or pests. With an active examination, a Scout always detects pests.
- Scouts gain an advantage interpreting scent marks, adding their INT Base Bonus to SML Rating.
- In Combat, Scouts may **Evaluate Opponent**.
- At INT Level 3, Scouts may passively detect Stalker or Cryptic predators.
- At INT Level 6, Scouts may attempt to understand the function of man-things (see **Man-Thing Rules**).

Flash Tail

In Pursuit, a Scout may attempt to confound the pursuer by suddenly flashing the bright underside of its tail. Flash tail is performed while running, making the Scout very conspicuous for a moment. When the tail is suddenly hidden, the rabbit momentarily disappears to the Pursuer. Flash Tail may be used only if the Scout is the principal target of pursuit, and must be used as the Scout enters an obstacle (Minor or Major). The effect of a successful tail flash is for the Pursuer to lose track of the fugitive, forcing it to either switch to a new target to chase, or to stop and remain in the same hex for the next full round to reacquire the original target.

Evaluate Opponent

In Combat, Scouts can use a combat action to gather information about the combat abilities of an opponent. The action must be directed to only one opponent; in return, the Scout learns the STR, SPD, and AGI Ratings and current HP of the opponent. (The Scout can assess these abilities accurately, but remember, only the Player understands the numbers!) In addition, if facing a predator, the Scout can tell the age class of the predator (Juvenile, Young Adult, etc.).

Agility (AGI)

As a rabbit, you do not have the manipulation skills of primates, so your reflexes and agility become even more important. A strong rabbit may inflict grievous wounds in combat, but it takes agility to bite and strike. If you are dexterous, you can use your paws and mouth to accomplish surprising things, such as freeing a companion from a trap, getting through a gate to the garden, or making simple constructions from materials found in your travels. It can even help with concealment, camouflage, and disguise.

Chance to Hit

In combat, the success of an attack depends upon the attacker's Attack Score (AS) compared to the defender's Defense Score (DS). Attack Score is determined by adding the attacker's AGI Rating to her Attack die. Some tactics may modify this.

Carrying Items

A rabbit can carry a small item (such as an herb, berry, or acorn) tucked into its fur, as well as a larger item (such as an apple or a small head of lettuce) in its mouth. The number of items carried in the fur is a maximum of the rabbit's AGI Base Bonus +1. A Maverick can carry its AGI Rating number of small items in the fur. Sometimes rabbits find objects that can be used as containers (such as a discarded bottle or candy wrapper, a fallen bird nest, an old shoe, etc.), allowing them to carry more items by carrying the container. With a lucky find, you might be able to carry a thousand items. (**Note:** rabbits can count only to 4; anything more than 4 is "a thousand".)

Throwing Items

Apart from primates, few non-human animals throw things: a few birds flick small objects with their head and beak, and mongooses hike small objects between their legs like a football. A rabbit in **B&B** also can throw small objects, but not with great accuracy or force. There are two ways a rabbit may effectively hurl a small projectile no larger than a hen's egg: a Forward Toss or a Rearward Punt. To Toss an object, you must stand on both hind legs and hold the object in both forepaws. The object is thrown like shooting a basketball. Tossing is poor for distance, good for accuracy, reaches up to 2 meters, and hits an intended target with a successful AGI skill check (DV=6). To Punt an object, face away from the object and kick it hard with one hindfoot. Punting is good for distance, reaching up to the rabbit's STR Rating in meters, but poor for accuracy, landing somewhere within a 1-meter circle. A third method — flinging an object held in the mouth to one side — is practical only while running, and succeeds in casting the object only a half meter upward or to the side.

Applying Herbs in Combat

A rabbit carrying a prepared herb that can be delivered by eating or simple contact can use it on herself during a battle (as her action during a Pause). If you are attempting to use the herb on yourself, it automatically applies without the need for a skill check. Only an Herbalist can attempt to use a contact herb on an ally or opponent during combat, using the Apply Contact Herb special ability. It

can be used on an ally automatically, but requires an attack check against an opponent (Attack Score vs. Defense Score). If you succeed, the herb takes effect at the end of that combat round. Note that if you fail with the attempt, the prepared herb falls on the ground (Roll 1d6: 1–3 it falls in the hex of the target; 4–6 it falls in your hex). See **Combat Rules** for details.

Disarming Traps

Once a trap has been located, you can attempt to disarm it. The difficulty of disarming depends upon the trap type (and sometimes its location). Each type of trap has a preferred method for disarming. Failing this attempt (or using a poor method) may result in being caught by the trap yourself (See **Trap Rules** for details).

Constructions

Some constructions may be done by any rabbit, such as digging a temporary scrape or permanent burrow. Rabbits can also form plugs to block a tunnel in the warren, and can dig short tunnels to go under a fence. Other types of construction also are possible, such as moving sections of bramble to conceal the entrance to a hole, or figuring out some method of moving objects so as to get into an open window. The GM should determine a difficulty value (DV) for whatever construction the players choose to make. Some constructions may be exceedingly difficult, and require extended effort by multiple rabbits. In such a case, break it down into pieces and assign a DV to each part. The skill check used for constructions is usually based on AGI Rating, but may also need a STR or INT check, especially if dealing with heavy objects (STR) or mechanisms with two or more components (INT).

Camouflage and Disguise

You might want to use camouflage to make yourself difficult to spot in certain conditions. A white rabbit trying to infiltrate a farm at dusk might simply roll in the dirt to be less obvious. The GM should determine the difficulty (though camouflage for a rabbit should be easy), while the player makes an AGI skill check.

Disguising yourself as a different rabbit might also be fairly easy; maybe smearing red clay on your flanks makes it look like you are the rabbit Redflank. Disguise as another type of animal is much trickier, and you usually have to know the language of that animal to pull it off convincingly. This may also require the use of certain props — feathers, patches of fur, colored leaves, acorns in the cheeks, twigs held in the mouth to represent fangs — all of these have been used. The GM should make an INT check for whoever the rabbit is attempting to fool, against the AGI check for the disguiser, with perhaps some adjustment for difficulty (for example, disguise as a woodchuck is one thing, disguise as a specific woodchuck would be more difficult).

Profession: The Maverick (AGI)

Periwinkle the Maverick

Guess what I am holding in my paw? It could be some hard-to-get prime food, a piece taken from a disabled trap, a thorn I could use as a weapon, or a mysterious man-thing. We are the masters of manipulation and construction. We can gain passage through obstacles that no other rabbit can pass due to our extraordinary agility. We are the best way to figure out the workings of man-stuff that was designed for hands instead of paws. And just for fun, we are also skilled in disguise. Your life will never be dull if you choose a Maverick as a mate.

A Maverick can accomplish amazing tasks using just paws, nose, chin, and mouth. At higher AGI levels, Mavericks have special manipulation abilities. The Primary Trait for a Maverick is Agility.

Special Abilities

- In Pursuit, Mavericks may use **Tumble**.
- Mavericks may carry a number of objects equal to their AGI Rating.
- At AGI Level 3, Mavericks may attempt to steal items, including food or herbs, in combat.
- At AGI Level 3, Mavericks may carry an additional item large enough to normally require mouth carry by gripping it against the chest with one paw and walking or running three-legged.
- AT AGI Level 6, Mavericks may grip and handle man-things that normally would require an opposable thumb, though they must use either one paw and their mouth, or both paws, to accomplish this.

Tumble

In Pursuit, a Maverick may Tumble on the ground and dash off in a new direction. The Tumble must be performed at the beginning of the round, before any other movement. After the Tumble, the Scout may move up to its full movement allowance in any direction. A Tumble in Pursuit counts as one tactical use.

Stealing in Combat

At AGI Level 3 or above, a Maverick may steal items in combat. This must be an item carried in the fur, not in a container or in the mouth. This special move replaces a normal attack tactic. Roll 1d6 + AGI Rating for the Maverick, vs. 1d6 + INT Rating of the target. On a success, the Maverick gets the item, and can potentially use it in any subsequent round. On a failure, there is still a one-sixth chance of the item falling to the ground in the hex of the target. In either case, the defense of the Maverick is reduced by 2 for one round. See **Combat Rules** for details.

Moving Three-Legged

A Maverick of AGI Level 3 or above may carry an additional item (above normal limits) by gripping it against the chest with one forepaw and walking or running three-legged. Movement rate is one-half normal while doing this. At any time, the Maverick may choose to drop the item and resume normal four-legged movement.

Grasping Man-Thing

A Maverick of AGI Level 6 or above may grip and handle a man-made object that could be held in a single (human) hand. This includes manipulating simple tools that normally would require an opposable thumb, such as a precise pinch-grip (the way a human might manually turn a screw), trigger grip (the way a human holds a handgun or power drill), or power grip (the way a human uses a hammer). However, use of a human tool that ordinarily requires two hands (such as opening a bottle, turning a large valve, or drawing a bow) would require cooperation with another rabbit. The Maverick accomplishes this with a skillful use of paws, head, and mouth in some combination. See **Man-Thing Rules** for details.

Constitution (CON)

Surrounded by a thousand dangers, predators, pests, traps, accidents, bad weather, and simple rotten luck, you need a strong constitution to survive even your first year. A sound mind in a healthy body, as the saying goes; well, constitution is the healthy body part of that.

Rabbit Hit Points (HP)

Hit Points represent the ability of a rabbit to withstand damage. A starting rabbit (level 0) has eight HP plus CON Base Bonus. With each new level of CON, the rabbit gains an additional five HP plus CON Base Bonus. Thus a rabbit with 13 CON, L3 would have $[(8+1) + 3 \times (5+1)] = 27$ HP as a maximum.

Danger and Death

When damage is taken, such as when a rabbit is hit in combat, the damage is deducted from their hit points (HP). If HP reaches zero, the target is unconscious; if below zero, the target dies within ten minutes unless healed to above zero. Rabbits generally strive to avoid an early death by being cautious, but life for a rabbit is dangerous.

Healing

When a rabbit loses hit points (HP) due to fights, traps, accidents, or disease, he needs to recover by healing. Some herbs can be used to provide healing, and Empaths can also heal as a special ability. In addition to these methods, a rabbit heals at the rate of one HP per CON Rating when it sleeps for 4 hours. It can do this twice in a 24-hour period. Empaths have accelerated healing, recovering two HP per CON Rating per sleep. Healing by any means cannot bring HP above your HP maximum at your CON Level.

Cecotropes

The digestive system of rabbits requires a "second pass" for full nutritional benefit. Unlike cows (that have special stomachs for fermentation, and that chew and re-swallow cud for efficient digestion) or horses (that have poor breakdown of cellulose, and so have to eat large amounts of food that passes through only partly digested), rabbits use a special means for full digestion. They expel two types of material: hard dry pellets (fecal material), and soft moist blobs that form in the cecum and are expelled like the hard pellets but at different times of the day. These blobs are called cecotropes and are rich in vital nutrients, vitamins, and probiotics. Rabbits eat their own cecotropes (a function called "cecotrophy") for extra nutrition; this is important for a healthy diet. You can deposit cecotropes twice a day, several hours after a good feeding. Eating your cecotropes allow you to recover extra HP while healing, up to your CON Base Bonus + 1 per day. Although there is no stigma associated with eating your own cecotropes, it is considered a high insult to suggest that another rabbit eat your cecotropes.

Resisting Disease

You can catch disease from pests or from other rabbits. The best way to prevent disease is not getting it in the first place. Groom frequently and avoid sick rabbits. If in contact with a disease source (either a pest or a rabbit with a communicable disease), you must succeed with a resistance check (1d6 + CON Rating vs. DV of disease) to avoid being infected (see **Diseases**). Continued exposure requires repeated checks. Once diseased, you must recover naturally (for some diseases) or be cured (for example, by herbs or empaths).

Resisting Poison

You can be poisoned by drinking bad water, eating spoiled food, poisonous herbs, or poisonweed, or by certain poison attacks. Be careful what you eat and drink, and run away from animals that can poison you. If you are subject to a poisoning attempt, you must succeed with a resistance check (1d6 + CON Rating vs. DV of poison) to avoid the effects of the poison. If not otherwise specified, the poison DV is 4 for ordinary plant toxins and 6 for animal toxins or poisonous herbs. Upon a successful resistance check, the effects of the poison are reduced by half. Once poisoned, most poisons also continue to damage you unless you are somehow cleansed of it (typically by herbs, empaths, or intentional bleeding). See **Health** rules for details.

Reproduction

The number of kits born to a pregnant doe is affected by the CON Base Bonus. See **Breeding Rules** for details.

Aging

During each winter season, there is a chance you die of weakness or aging. This probability goes up as you get older. To determine the survival difficulty, add one to your age in years (your first year is 1, not 0). Roll 1d6 and add CON Base Bonus; to survive that winter, you must exceed your survival difficulty. Wild rabbits tend to die young; it's a harsh life. (This is an optional rule for GMs.)

Profession: The Empath (CON)

Ragged Robin the Empath

I have always been attuned to other rabbits, feeling their emotions and their pains. I can ease their pain by taking it upon myself. I care about others. Fortunately, my inner strength and health are usually strong. If you wish a nurturing parent for your kits, and for them to have sound bodies, then consider an Empath as a mate."

Empaths have exceedingly high constitutions, and are resistant to diseases and fatigue. At higher AGI levels, Empaths have special abilities to transfer health between themselves and another rabbit. The Primary Trait for an Empath is Constitution.

Special Abilities

- In Pursuit, Empaths may use **Second Wind**.
- Empaths may use **Empathic Heal** (Laying On Paws).
- At CON Level 3, Empaths may use **Empathic Hurt** in combat.
- AT CON Level 6, Empaths may attempt **Restore to Life**.

Second Wind

In Pursuit, an Empath may use Second Wind. This allows the Empath to gain an extra movement of two hexes, but at the cost of one HP for each use. The Empath also can transfer Second Wind to any other Fugitive that is running in the same hex or an adjacent hex during Pursuit. The other Fugitive runs forward 2 additional hexes as the Empath takes 1 HP damage. Both rabbits may continue running during Pursuit as the Second Wind is applied. Each use of Second Wind counts as one tactical use.

Empathic Healing

This is the ability of an Empath to heal another by taking some of the damage on himself. This cannot be performed on one's self, but automatically succeeds (no skill check) when applied to an ally. The ally heals 1d6 HP, but the Empath incurs 2 HP damage. It also can be attempted in combat, with the same healing effect (1d6), but causes 3 HP damage to the Empath. Empathic healing also can stop the ongoing effects of poison on a 1d6 roll of 4–6; the Empath takes on no additional damage for countering poison.

Empathic Hurting

This is the ability of an Empath to directly harm an enemy in combat, and in the process to provide slight healing to himself. It requires a successful attack by 1d6 + CON Rating against adjacent opponent, who defends with 1d6 + CON Rating. (Note the different Rating used in this attack.) Damage = CON Base Bonus to opponent, but if successful, heals self by 1 HP. Note that Empathic Hurt results in physical damage to the opponent, but is not considered a physical attack. Failure results in no damage, and if no damage is delivered, no self-healing occurs.

Restore to Life

Attempting to restore a dead rabbit to life is tough, and dangerous. For Restore to Life to be attempted, the rabbit must be "Mostly Dead," not "All the Way Dead," meaning that the body must be intact, and not partially eaten, dismembered, or decomposed. The Difficulty Value (DV) depends on how long the rabbit has been dead, according to the following table:

Up to 1 minute	1–10 minutes	11–30 minutes	31–60 minutes	Less than a day	Up to 2 days
DV=5	DV=7	DV=9	DV=11	DV=13	DV=15

The Empath may attempt this once every five minutes by rolling 1d6 + CON Rating vs. DV. With each attempt, the Empath takes a number of HP damage equal to the DV, whether successful or not. If successful, the dead rabbit is restored to life with just one HP. Any permanent injuries or diseases are not cured by this success.

Mysticism (MYS)

Sometimes rabbits have funny feelings about things. Naturally cautious, rabbits seem to have a sixth sense about dangerous situations. Occasionally, a rabbit shows special talent with this and becomes a Seer.

Shock

Rabbits may become paralyzed with fear. When suddenly startled, such as by a loud noise, it may go into Shock. When exposed to sudden or frightening events, each rabbit in the party must attempt to save from shock by rolling 1d6 + MYS Rating greater than Shock Value of 4. (Note that some situations may raise this Shock Value.) Once in shock, the rabbit stands motionless and cannot take any action for 1d6 combat rounds (if in combat) or 10 minutes (if not in combat).

Sensing Danger

When an encounter is potentially dangerous, the GM should pick one rabbit at random and make a secret check to sense danger (1d6 + MYS Rating vs. a difficulty value). If successful, give a hint to that rabbit (*"You feel very uncomfortable about that hollow log over there."*). A nervous player may ask for this check at any time. Even if no danger is present, the GM should give a warning with a low check result. The other rabbits may start to ignore a player who does this too often as they are continually warned about nonexistent dangers.

Detecting Falsehood

If you are talking to someone and they attempt to lie to you, the GM can secretly check to detect falsehood (1d6 + MYS Rating vs. 1d6 + CHA Rating of the character who is lying).

Rabbit Riddles

Rabbits love riddles, just as they love stories. For some reason, rabbits with high MYS Ratings are often good at both posing and solving riddles. There is no game mechanic for this, but the GM should encourage those with high MYS Ratings to engage in riddles. Note that the result of a trance by a Seer may be given in the form of a visual riddle or an imagined scent mark. (See **Communication** for more information about scent marks.)

Profession: The Seer (MYS)

Moonseed the Seer

Have I met you before? You look familiar, but we may have never met ... yet. Sometimes I see things that have not come to pass, and sometimes they never do. It is difficult to describe. I will not tell you who your mate will be; you must discover that for yourself."

A Seer can enter a dream state to see visions, though these may be of other worlds, or of past or future times. Often these visions are incomplete or deceptive, and it takes an experienced Seer to interpret them correctly. When a vision is discussed with other rabbits, it is not uncommon for them to totally misinterpret what was told. At higher MYS levels, Seers have special mystical abilities. The Primary Trait for a Seer is Mysticism.

Special Abilities

- In Pursuit or Combat, Seers may **Feign Disease**.
- Seers may enter trances. See **Trance** rules for details.
- At MYS Level 3, Seers may use **Luck**, a number of times a day not to exceed their MYS Rating. See Luck rules for details.
- AT MYS Level 6, Seers may attempt to **Tempt Fate**, once a day.

Feign Disease

In Pursuit, a Seer may act as though he is sick with a frightful ailment. If it is not a normal carrion eater (Coyote, Red Wolf, Rats, Wolverine, Grizzly Bear, Caracara, Bald Eagle, or Raven), a Pursuer faced with a rabbit that is Feigning Disease must either stop to investigate (with no movement for the next full round) or immediately switch to another Target (the GM may determine which). If the Pursuer investigates, the Seer must roll a MYS skill check greater than 1d6 + MYS of the Pursuer for the ruse to succeed. Feign Disease has an effect analogous to Instilling Fear, but does not require language communication; it results in the Pursuer losing interest and switching to another Target. Even on a failure, the enemy pauses in its pursuits; the Seer then may flee again in the next round as the Pursuer continues to hesitate. Regardless of whether the attempt succeeds or fails, Feign Disease counts as one tactical use.

Trance

A Seer may enter a trance to try to get a vision about the answer to a question. The number and complexity of trances you may do each day is limited by your MYS Rating. For example, if your MYS Rating is 3, you can perform 3 one-word trances per day, or one two-word and one one-word trance, or one three-word trance. A trance of any complexity takes ten minutes of motionless total concentration; any disturbance ruins the trance but still counts against your daily total.

First the Seer poses the question, which can have no higher word-count (or trance complexity) than what remains for the day based on your MYS Rating. For example, at Level 3 you could ask "Where is water?" (being a three-word trance, this is the most complex question you can ask at that level).

The GM secretly rolls 1d6 + MYS Rating against a difficulty value; with success, the trance gives a vision based on an answer in the same number of words as the question. So, with the example, if the GM determined the answer to be "Spring beside lilac," the vision might take the form of *"You seem to be standing in the shade, and detect the scent of lilacs."*

If the roll fails, the GM gives a totally obscure answer such as *"You seem to be covered by a warm blanket, made of living squirrels."* Presumably, with experience, the player learns to recognize and discount these false visions. On the other hand, continuing as though they are real could lead to some really amusing situations in the game.

At the GM's discretion, a rabbit with a high MYS Base Bonus may also receive a vision unbidden. Unlike trances, spontaneous visions are immediate and instantaneous and do not count against the limit based on MYS Rating. However, like a prophecy, they always should be couched in vague or ambiguous language, either as a riddle, a strange image, or a scrambled scent mark.

Luck

A Luck reroll is a gift that a Seer can make to another character, or use it herself. The premise is that the Seer had a fleeting vision of a near-future action that involves a die roll, and if the roll was bad, do things slightly differently. Thus, a hint could have been given to another character before they made the disarm trap attempt. Accepting the gift is always optional, but if the character accepts it, the die roll is repeated and whatever the result is, that has to apply. Luck can be applied to reroll any Skill Check, or any combat roll if the Seer is in an adjacent hex. It must be applied immediately after the die roll to be replaced, before any effects are applied.

Tempting Fate

A more powerful effect than Luck is the Tempting of Fate. Here, the Seer tries to actually change something that has already occurred. The effect of Tempting Fate is limited to a single event in which the player characters had some involvement. They cannot change something merely told to them, or turn back time for the whole world. To attempt to Tempt Fate, the GM sets the Difficulty Value (DV) of the desired change. The player is allowed to know the DV before the attempt to Tempt Fate is made. The longer in the past, the larger the scope, or the more unlikely the change, the higher the DV. The Seer makes a Tempt Fate by comparing MYS Rating against the DV. If the attempt fails, not only is there no change, but the GM imposes some sort of appropriate (and creative) backlash upon the Seer, the party, or the home warren. So Fate should not be tempted too often, unless the DV is very low.

Eartick found a truffle, and did not share it with Moonseed, so the Seer did a quick Tempt Fate: It succeeded, so Eartick actually found two, and gave one to Moonseed. Yum!

Smell (SML)

Smell is exceedingly important to rabbits. It allows you to find food, recognize other rabbits, find your way around belowground, and sometimes detect danger or track other animals. Smell is an important part of communication between rabbits, and scent marking is used to establish territories and to leave messages. Scent is also a surefire way to tell if a doe is ready for mating, and also is important so that does can recognize their own kits.

Detecting and Identifying Food

All rabbits can readily find and identify common foods in their presence. These include grass, clover, apples, lettuce, forbs, edible berries, and edible mushrooms. Possible foods that you have not yet encountered require a successful skill check against difficulty (due to rarity) based on 1d6 + SML Rating. Once you encounter and identify a new food, you recognize it if you ever find it again. Note that it is possible that a food identification check may succeed (you think it is edible), but that there are surprises in store. The GM determines if a new food type is tasty or nasty, if it is nourishing or damaging, and just how much energy it provides you.

Detecting and Identifying Herbs

Identifying herbs is trickier than identifying food. Possible herbs that you have not yet encountered require a successful skill check against difficulty to recognize different odor qualities, based on 1d6 + SML Rating. Once you encounter and identify a new herb, you can recognize it if you ever find it again, but still have to identify its odor qualities (see **Herb** rules for details). Sometimes one part of a plant may be suitable for food, while another part is useful as an herb. Generally, if the plant is recognized as an herb, the Source of the herbal odor (the useful part of the plant) is known. Even if you can identify an herb, that does not mean you know how to prepare it or what function it may have. Herbalists are needed for those bits of knowledge.

Identifying Scat and Spoor

Scat, or fecal droppings, often have a characteristic odor. If you encounter scat, you may attempt to identify the animal that dropped it, with a difficulty (set by GM) based on how long it has been there and the terrain in which it is found. Roll 1d6 + SML Rating against the difficulty. Success means you know what type of animal it was (but only if you have encountered that type of animal before), and approximately how long ago it was dropped; otherwise, it is too dried up or disturbed to be able to tell. Only one rabbit in the party may make this attempt. A rabbit automatically recognizes cecotropes, but recognizing who deposited the cecotropes requires a skill check.

Spoor includes all other visual signs and odor traces of an animal passing by. If you encounter tracks, tufts of fur, blood trail, or other spoor, you may attempt to identify it with the same rules that apply to scat.

Marking

A rabbit can scent-mark a location by urination, and can scent-mark an object or another rabbit by chin-rubbing. A rabbit can automatically detect any scent-marking that is less than a day old. Older markings also are automatic if their age, in days, is less than the SML Rating of the rabbit. Successfully detecting a scent-mark can give valuable information about the marker, with the number of clues limited by the SML Rating of the sniffer (SML Rating + INT Base Bonus for Scouts). For an ordinary scent mark, you can learn (listed in rank order): (1) species, (2) gender, (3) age, (4) profession, (5) Primary Trait Level, and (6) reproductive status (recently mated, recently given birth, looking for a mate, etc.). Scent marks also can be used to leave more complex messages that can be read by another animal with a high enough SML Rating. See more details under **Communication**.

Tracking

Tracking involves following the path taken by another animal; to obtain information from tracks, see Identifying Scat and Spoor. One rabbit in the party must be designated as the tracker; any more just confuses the attempt. The base Difficulty Value for tracking depends on how long it has been since the animal passed. DV starts at 0 if fewer than ten minutes have passed; add +1 to DV for each ten minutes that passes. Some conditions adjust the DV. Walking in mud or snow during daytime: −2 to DV. Walking on rocks: +1 to DV. Crossing a stream or man-path (road), or Tracking during high winds: +2 to DV. Following a track in a stream: +4 to DV. Tracking during falling snow: Double the DV. Tracking during rain: Triple the DV. Tracking during freezing rain is impossible. At the start of tracking, and each time there is a change in habitat or terrain thereafter, you must make another skill check of SML Rating against DV to continue. If you fail but want to find the trail again, you must spend ten minutes searching your current location, and can then make another tracking attempt (remembering that adjustment for the ten-minute delay).

Use of Smell Underground

Using touch, sound, and smell, a rabbit can rapidly maneuver in a burrow or tunnel. Scents last longer belowground than aboveground, and scent-marking can be detected automatically (no check required) up to a week after it was marked. Does mark their own kits (and their chamber) so they can easily find them again, and as a warning to other rabbits to leave them alone.

Profession: The Herbalist (SML)

Hawksbeard the Herbalist

I have secret knowledge, passed down through generations, of the diversity of plants and the ways to prepare them. I can produce herbs that protect and heal, as well as those that confuse and injure. Clearly this powerful lore cannot be passed on to every rabbit, due to its possible abuse. My nose is a powerful tool in this endeavor, and also allows me great investigative and tracking skills. If you are ready to cleanse the horrors of the world with precious herbs, take an Herbalist as a mate.

An Herbalist is an expert at recognizing and identifying foods and herbs, and is responsible for the preparation of herbs for use by the warren. At higher SML levels, Herbalists can use advanced methods for these preparations. The Primary Trait for an Herbalist is Smell.

Special Abilities

- In Pursuit, Herbalists may **Disperse Herb**.
- In Combat, Herbalists may **Apply Herbs**.
- At SML Level 3, Herbalists may perform **Advanced Preparation of Herbs** (see Herb rules)
- AT SML Level 6, Herbalists may attempt to **Remodel Herbs** (see Herb rules)

Disperse Herb

In Pursuit, if an Herbalist is carrying a prepared herb that can be dispersed in the air (such as a fungal ball or flower dust), she may cast the herb into the air while running. The herb immediately disperses into the current hex and the 3 adjacent hexes behind the herbalist at the time of the herb's dispersal. The dispersed herb immediately affects all individuals (Pursuers and Fugitives) that occupy or enter one of those 4 hexes in the same pursuit round. Each affected individual must roll a saving throw against the effects of the herb (see Herb descriptions). If a Pursuer is two or more hexes farther back, the GM makes a check based on the Pursuer's INT Rating to see if the Pursuer detects the herb, which allows it to avoid the affected hexes, or if it fails to detect it, which means it continues into an affected hex. The dispersed herb cloud lingers until the herbalist's next pursuit turn. The attempt uses up one sprig of the herb regardless of success or failure. Unlike other special pursuit tactics, Disperse Herb can be used any number of times during the same pursuit, so long as the Herbalist has carried sprigs available. However, the same Pursuer automatically detects the herb dispersal and may avoid affected hexes after the herbalist's first attempt.

Simple Preparation of Herbs

Simple Preparation of Herbs includes all those preps that can be completed in a single stage. Any rabbit may attempt a simple preparation of herbs. See **Herbalism Rules** for details.

Advanced Preparation of Herbs

Advanced Preparation of Herbs include all those preps that require more than one stage for completion. Herbalists of SML Level 3 or above may perform these. See **Herbalism Rules** for details.

Remodel Herbs

Herbalists of SML Level 6 or greater may attempt to Remodel Herbs. In other words, they can try to change an herb so that its effect is different than normal by adding one or more additional preparations to the process. This can also involve research into totally new herbal effects. See **Herbalism Rules** for details.

Charisma (CHA)

Charisma is not just about how attractive you are, whether you are beautiful or if you have a charming personality. Charisma is about how well you communicate with others, both rabbits in your warren and other animals that are friends, or even enemies. Communication is vital in both day-to-day activities and the culture of the warren. Your Charisma determines your capacity to learn new languages and to communicate in other, nonverbal ways. It also determines your ability to relate to others on an emotional level, whether by telling stories or attracting a mate.

Languages

Different animals use different languages. Each animal automatically knows its own language. For each point of CHA Rating, you may learn one language other than your own from the choices shown below. Underlined animals are playable as characters.

- Rabbits (rabbit, hare, jackrabbit, pika) [Automatic for rabbits and all player-characters]
- Dogs (dog/fox/wolf/coyote)
- Cats (house cat/bobcat/ocelot/lynx/puma)
- Weasels (stoat/ferret/polecat/skunk/marten/otter/badger/wolverine/mongoose)
- Chatters (squirrel/chipmunk/ground squirrel/flying squirrel/marmot/prairie dog)
- Nibblers (mouse/vole/rat/packrat/kangaroo rat/gopher/muskrat/porcupine/nutria/beaver)
- Grubbers (armadillo/mole/pig/javelina/wild boar/opossum)
- Ramblers (black bear/grizzly bear/coati/raccoon)
- Hoofers (horse/mule/deer/elk/moose/goat/sheep/pronghorn)
- Raptors (predatory birds: hawk/eagle/falcon/harrier/osprey/owl)
- Perchers (terrestrial birds: sparrow/blue jay/crow/raven/blackbird/robin, etc.)
- Strutters (chicken/turkey/quail/grouse/pheasant)
- Waders (aquatic birds: duck/goose/heron/gull/sandpiper/killdeer, etc.)
- Coldies (toad/frog/newt/snake/lizard/turtle)
- Fishies (all fish)
- Crawlies (insect/spider/scorpion/pill bug, etc.).

Rabbits do not know the languages of bats, worms, or humans.

Communication During Encounters

When an encounter takes place in the game, the GM should assume that any talk by the players is heard by any other animals present in the encounter, assuming a common language between the player characters and the non-player characters. If the player says it, the character says it. Rabbits cannot pass notes to one another.

If the players do not share a common language, the GM may decide that some inkling of what is being said may be understood based on a secret CHA skill check. Alternatively, the GM may allow the players to communicate by pantomime.

For more information on speaking to NPCs or resolving attempts to persuade, threaten, barter, or deceive, see the section on Communication.

Finding a Mate

In the world of real animals, mating and reproduction are a central focus of an animal's life. In the game world of **B&B**, reproduction provides an alternative means of creating new player characters with improved abilities. Finding the right mate is important to ensure that your offspring have the best traits possible. Players may choose the best in the litter as a new character to play.

The Role of Stories

Stories are very important to rabbits, and the players should be encouraged to set their communications in the form of stories where possible. For example, if the adventurers return to the warren and want to tell the others about the encounter with a bear, have one of them tell it in the form of a story.

"We pushed through the raspberry bush and nearly ran into this huge, terrifying animal that stood on its hind legs, towering above us, and roaring loudly enough to shake acorns off the trees!"

Passing on Knowledge to Offspring

Any knowledge you gained through adventuring may be considered to be passed on to your offspring once you have been in their presence at least 20 days during their first two months after birth. Presumably you have been telling them stories during this time.

Profession: The Storyteller (CHA)

Moxieplum the Storyteller

There was once a rabbit who could captivate the warren with tales of adventure, danger, and romance. Such are the carriers of lore and tradition, passed on from generation to generation. Do you wish your kits to be guided by the moral stories, hear of a thousand enemies, fantasize about heroes? Then turn your ears toward a Storyteller."

A Storyteller is a master of communication, both with rabbits and with other animals. They are the primary teachers of young rabbits, through the telling of moralistic fables and by passing on cultural history. The Primary Trait for a Storyteller is Charisma.

Special Abilities

- In Pursuit, Storytellers may **Encourage**.
- Storytellers may learn two languages for each point of their CHA Rating (beyond the automatic rabbit language).
- At CHA Level 3, Storytellers may attempt to **Confuse**, in combat.
- AT CHA Level 6, Storytellers may attempt to **Enthrall**.

Encourage

In Pursuit, Storytellers may encourage others who are being pursued by calling out to remind them of the heroic deeds of fabled rabbit heroes. Encourage affects only other rabbits within 2 hexes of the Storyteller; it has no effect on Non-Rabbit Fugitives. Each encouraged rabbit is spurred to immediately move forward 2 hexes in addition to their normal movement allowance. Of course, this may make the Storyteller more vulnerable, as she does not gain the movement advantage of her own encouragement. Each Encouragement counts as one tactical use.

Confuse

In combat, a Storyteller of CHA Level 3 or above may attempt to Confuse an enemy by calling out some potential distraction. The Storyteller targets one opponent (at any distance) and rolls 1d6 + CHA Rating against their 1d6 + INT Rating. On a success, that opponent may not make any attack in the next round. On a failure, however, one friend (randomly chosen among those closest to the targeted enemy) becomes themselves confused and may not make an attack in the next round.

Hawksbeard shouts, "Watch out! Rattlesnake!" Someone in the battle becomes confused, possibly an enemy, possibly a friend.

Enthrall

A Storyteller at CHA Level 6 or more may attempt to Enthrall when out of combat. For a single target, roll 1d6 + CHA Rating vs. 1d6 + INT Rating. For more than one target, reduce the skill check by two points for each additional target (e.g., for three targets, roll 1d6−4 + CHA Rating). The Storyteller may focus the attempt on a subset of targets if a larger group is present

(e.g., focus on two in a group of six). If enthralled, the target(s) act as a faithful follower when in the presence of the Storyteller until one of the following occurs: (a) the enthralled is reduced to less than half his maximum HP, or (b) the Storyteller or the enthralled goes to sleep or is unconscious. A failure to enthrall has no consequences. The Storyteller must know the language of the target to enthrall.

Non-Rabbit Species and Professions

Creating a Non-Rabbit Character

To create any non-rabbit player character, you must choose the species of animal you wish to be (from the eight possibilities) before doing any die rolls. This is because Traits may require rolls of 2d6, 3d6, or 4d6 depending on the animal and the Trait. Once you select your animal, perform your die rolls in order, using the proper number of dice for each Trait. As with rabbits, you may then adjust these results by either (a) adding two points to one Trait, or (b) adding one point to each of three different Traits; however, there is the added restriction that you cannot add points to any of the Traits that use a 2d6 roll for your animal.

The special abilities of each profession are detailed in the sections for each animal. Base Bonus and maximum Levels are determined exactly the same as with rabbits, based on your genetic Trait values. As with creation of a rabbit, a new non-rabbit character starts with two APs, the first of which must be spent in the Primary Trait of your profession.

Languages for Non-Rabbit Player Characters

Every player character knows the Rabbit language for free; it serves as the common language of player parties. Note that this is not the case in general for NPCs of the same species that you may encounter in the campaign, only for PCs that like to hang out with rabbits. In addition, each non-rabbit character automatically knows its own language, listed below. Any additional languages are learned based on CHA Rating, as with rabbits.

Chatters: Squirrel (Grifter), Chipmunk (Spy)
Grubbers: Armadillo (Trader), Opossum (Shaman)
Nibblers: Porcupine (Guardian)
Rabbits: Jackrabbit (Herald)
Ramblers: Raccoon (Bandit)
Weasels: Skunk (Burglar)

Hit Points for Non-Rabbits

Hit Points (HP) are calculated differently than for rabbits, and differently for each non-rabbit species. The approach is similar to that for rabbits: A starting character gets a fixed number of HP plus CON Base Bonus. For each level of CON, they get a different fixed number of HP plus CON Base Bonus. See the following table for details (Rabbit included for comparison)

Species	HP for Starting Character	HPs added for each CON Level
Rabbit	8 + CON Base Bonus	5 + CON Base Bonus
Raccoon	15 + CON Base Bonus	7 + CON Base Bonus
Jackrabbit	8 + CON Base Bonus	5 + CON Base Bonus
Chipmunk	5 + CON Base Bonus	3 + CON Base Bonus
Skunk	10 + CON Base Bonus	6 + CON Base Bonus
Porcupine	18 + CON Base Bonus	8 + CON Base Bonus
Opossum	10 + CON Base Bonus	6 + CON Base Bonus
Armadillo	10 + CON Base Bonus	6 + CON Base Bonus
Gray Squirrel	6 + CON Base Bonus	4 + CON Base Bonus

Animal	STR	SPD	INT	AGI	CON	MYS	SML	CHA	Profession
Raccoon	4d6	3d6	3d6	3d6	3d6	2d6	3d6	2d6	Bandit
Jackrabbit	3d6	4d6	3d6	2d6	3d6	3d6	2d6	3d6	Herald
Chipmunk	2d6	3d6	4d6	3d6	2d6	3d6	3d6	3d6	Spy
Skunk	3d6	3d6	3d6	4d6	3d6	3d6	2d6	2d6	Burglar
Porcupine	3d6	2d6	3d6	2d6	4d6	3d6	3d6	3d6	Guardian
Opossum	3d6	2d6	2d6	3d6	3d6	4d6	3d6	3d6	Shaman
Armadillo	2d6	3d6	2d6	3d6	3d6	3d6	4d6	3d6	Trader
Squirrel	d6	3d6	3d6	3d6	2d6	2d6	3d6	4d6	Grifter

Raccoon: The Bandit (STR)

Concerning Bandits, Mugwort the rabbit says:

I suppose a Trash Panda isn't bad to have with you in a tight spot, what with long eye-teeth and serious attitude. But all that twittering? And what's with washing their food? Can't they just eat grass like a normal animal?"

The raccoon's Primary Trait is STR (4d6), and limited Traits are MYS and CHA (2d6 each); other traits are each 3d6. There is only one possible profession for the raccoon, this being Bandit. Bandits are very good at getting into things. In Intruder Mode, they receive a bonus (+2 to AGI Rating) for overcoming man-thing obstacles such as trashcan lids or doggie doors; this does not apply to other tasks.

Special Abilities

- In Pursuit, Bandits may **Intimidate**.
- Bandits may use **Intruder Mode**.
- Bandits can climb trees.
- Bandits are good diggers.
- At STR Level 3, Bandits may **Double Bite** in combat.
- At STR Level 6, Bandits may carry a large object or animal while walking bipedally.

Intimidate

In lieu of movement during a round of pursuit, a Bandit instead may suddenly turn around and snarl fiercely at the pursuer. Intimidate may be attempted only if the Bandit is within 2 hexes of the Pursuer (PD<3). A Pursuer facing a snarling Raccoon must either stop to appraise the situation in a hex adjacent to the Bandit (during its regular movement) or immediately switch to another Target (the GM may determine which). If the Pursuer stops, its turn ends; no more movement is allowed until the next pursuit round. If the Pursuer immediately switches to a new target, movement can continue, but the Pursuer must maneuver around the Bandit's hex. A switch in the same round as the Intimidate does not count as a voluntary switch tactic. If the Bandit's Intimidation causes the Pursuer to stop, the Bandit may flee again on its next round of movement (keeping in mind that it now faces toward the Pursuer) or stand its ground (remaining in the same hex without turning away). In the event that the Pursuer stops and the Bandit stands his ground, the Bandit must roll a STR skill check greater than 1d6 + MYS of the Pursuer for the Pursuer to remain Intimidated. On a successful STR check, the pursuer must switch to another target, and the switch does count as a voluntary pursuit tactic. On a failure, the pursuer may move or attack as normal.

Intruder Mode

Outside of combat, Bandits are exceptionally good at "getting into things." In Intruder Mode, they receive a bonus (+2 to AGI Rating) for overcoming man-thing obstacles such as trashcan lids or doggie doors; this special ability does not apply to other tasks such as overcoming natural obstacles, or understanding and using man-things. The player must declare he is doing this, and it would take the place of other types of activities such as scanning for predators or searching for herbs.

Double Bite

A Bandit at STR Level 3 or more may Double Bite in combat. Instead of attack/move, this is a form of double attack, though it may only use Bite as a tactic, and the first Bite must succeed for the second Bite to occur. The intention to Double Bite must be declared before the first Bite is resolved. If the first Bite fails, the second Bite automatically fails.

Jackrabbit: The Herald (SPD)

Concerning Heralds, Speedwell the rabbit says:

As swift as a fox, and a fine boxer. But Jacks lack the finesse of a true rabbit. They are all ears and no nose."

The jackrabbit's Primary Trait is SPD (4d6), and limited Traits are AGI and SML (2d6 each); other traits are each 3d6. There is only one possible profession for the jackrabbit, this being Herald. Heralds are not only very fast, but they can run without tiring.

Special Abilities

- In Pursuit, Heralds may **Jump Kick**.
- Heralds may **Dash Without Tiring**.
- Heralds cannot climb trees.
- Heralds are good diggers.
- At SPD Level 3, Heralds may **Box** in combat
- At SPD Level 6, Heralds may **Jump Kick** in combat.

Jump Kick

In Pursuit, the Herald may attempt to deflect or injure a Pursuer by kicking backward while running. The Jackrabbit may continue to run away, with normal movement restrictions, without slowing down. A Jump Kick may occur at any time during movement if the Herald is in an adjacent hex and is facing away from the Pursuer (i.e., if the pursuer is in any of the three hexes to the rear). The player announces whether the kick is an attempt to hit; if it is, resolve as if in combat (i.e., Herald's 1d6 + AGI Rating vs. Pursuer's 1d6 + SPD Rating). If the Jump Kick is not an attempt to hit, it serves as a feint that causes the Pursuer to flinch, reducing its speed during its next movement by 2 hexes. A successful Jump Kick during pursuit inflicts normal damage (see Combat), but does not automatically initiate Combat. Unlike most other pursuit tactics, Jump Kick may be used any number of times during the same pursuit. At Level 6, Heralds also may perform a version of the Jump Kick as a regular attack during Combat, although the kick counts as the attack phase and the subsequent run counts as movement.

Dash Without Tiring

When not in combat, a Herald can run at full speed without extra energy cost indefinitely. Running does not lead to exhaustion nor stimulate hunger.

Box

Heralds at SPD Level 3 or more may Box in combat. You stand on your hind legs and rapidly box with both paws, somewhat like multiple cuffs, but able to do damage, as well as providing some added defense. See **Combat Rules** for details.

Chipmunk: The Spy (INT)

Concerning Spies, Sweetbriar the rabbit says:

I'll admit the little striped mice are good at getting into cracks and crannies. And they are sneaky buggers. But what are they saving all those seeds for?"

The chipmunk's Primary Trait is INT (4d6), and limited Traits are STR and CON (2d6 each); other traits are each 3d6. There is only one possible profession for the chipmunk, this being Spy. Although Spies can run short distances very quickly, they also excel at moving around unobserved. Spies may carry two additional small items in their cheek pouches.

Special Abilities

- In Pursuit or Combat, Spies may **Quick Conceal**.
- Spies may use **Automatic Stealth Mode**.
- Spies can climb trees, including tree canopies.
- Spies are weak diggers.

- Spies get a **Facing Change Bonus** in combat.
- At INT Level 3, Spies may **Double Jump** in combat.
- At INT Level 6, Spies may **Find Hidden Entry**.

Quick Conceal

In Pursuit, if an obstacle is within two hexes, a Spy can dart into that hex and freeze to perform a Quick Conceal. Quick Conceal must be announced at the beginning of movement, and the Chipmunk must end movement in a hex containing an obstacle (Minor or Major). Quick Conceal results in the Fugitive disappearing as a Target. (The token for the Spy is flipped face down on the Pursuit Board. As in other disappearing acts, the token is not removed from the pursuit board, but is turned face down and remains hidden if it remains in one place. In any subsequent turn, the player may elect to turn the token face up and re-engage in the pursuit by moving.) Quick Conceal does not automatically force the Pursuer to switch to another Target. Chaser and Brute predators persist in searching for the Spy, circling halfway around the obstacle hex for 3 pursuit rounds. Stalkers, Cryptics, and Raptors crouch in an adjacent hex for 2 pursuit rounds, waiting and watching for the Spy to reappear. If the Spy is concealed in a Minor obstacle, she must succeed in an INT skill check vs. the predator's 1d6 + INT Rating to remain concealed; the INT check must be repeated in each round that a predator is nearby. However, if the Spy is concealed in a Major obstacle, she is never found; predators eventually give up to switch to another Target or break off pursuit altogether.

Automatic Stealth Mode

A Spy need not make a skill check to move stealthily. Simply declare to the GM that you are moving with stealth and it is automatic. In addition, you may move at full speed while doing this.

Facing Change Bonus

During combat, the Spy can make a "free" facing rotation (turning to face any direction) at the start or conclusion of movement. In addition, they can make a similar facing rotation for each hex of movement for a cost of one extra MP per intermediate hex (in which they rotate).

Double Jump

Spies at INT Level 3 or more may Double Jump in combat, replacing an action/move combination. If you are not currently being bitten or pinned, you may jump between your current hex and one that is exactly two hexes away if those hexes are not at the same height (e.g., ground level and bush, or bush and tree). You may do this again in your second action/move phase, so that in effect you are moving twice this round instead of taking an attack or other action. One of these jumps may be from tree to ground, but not ground to tree. Jumps between adjacent bushes or between trees with adjacent limbs also are permitted.

Find Hidden Entry

Spies at INT Level 6 or more may automatically find a hidden entry, such as a plug in a tunnel or the camouflaged entry to a burrow, without need to perform a skill check. Note that this ability applies to hidden entries or openings, not to hidden or buried caches. Finding buried caches is a SML-based skill (see *Trader*, below).

Skunk: The Burglar (AGI)

Concerning Burglars, Periwinkle the rabbit says:

> *Oh, I wish I had the fingers of a Stink-Kitty. Those essence peddlers are so good with their hands, they can fiddle a tight, twisty man-thing out of a big, clanky man-thing. Handy to have around, as long as they stay downwind."*

The skunk's Primary Trait is AGI (4d6), and limited Traits are SML and CHA (2d6 each); other traits are each 3d6. There is only one possible profession for the skunk, this being Burglar. Burglars are excellent at opening small containers and removing individual items from containers. They also have a strong defensive maneuver with their spray.

Special Abilities

- In Pursuit, Burglars may **Spray**.
- Burglars have **Manipulation Bonus** (+2 to AGI Rating for opening small containers).
- Burglars cannot climb trees.
- Burglars are good diggers.
- At AGI Level 3, Burglars may **Power Spray** in combat (forward shooting range 3 from handstand).
- At AGI Level 6, Burglars may **Disassemble Man-Things**.

Spray and Power Spray

When being pursued, a Burglar may Spray backward without slowing down. If a pursuer is in that hex or enters that hex in the next round, his speed is reduced by 3 for one round. The Burglar may only do this once per Pursuit.

In combat, a Burglar (AGI Level 3 or higher) may Power Spray as her action. To do this, the skunk stands on her front paws and curls her tail and hind legs forward over her head to spray in the direction she was initially facing. The spray goes forward three hexes in that direction, the three hexes directly in front and then the pair of adjacent hexes behind the second hex in the same direction. The strength of the spray is 1d6 + CON Rating. Each target (friend or foe) tries to resist with a roll of 1d6 + CON Rating. If resistance is successful, the target's speed is reduced by 1 for two rounds; if not successful, the target's speed is reduced by 3 for two rounds, and to-hit bonus is reduced by 1 for that time. A Power Spray may be done no more than one time per combat, or three times per day.

Manipulation Bonus

A Burglar attempting to open a small container gets a +2 to AGI Rating for this task. A Burglar also can reach into containers with openings as small as a beer bottle to retrieve individual items, rather than having to empty the entire container on the ground to find a particular item.

Disassemble Man-Things

A Burglar (AGI Level 6 or above) may attempt to disassemble a man-thing. The GM sets a Difficulty Value (DV) and the Burglar rolls 1d6 + AGI Rating to succeed. Some disassemblies may have very high DV.

> **Example:** The Burglar finds a water bowl tied to a doghouse, and tries to untie it. He succeeds, and then grabs the water bowl in his teeth and carries it away.

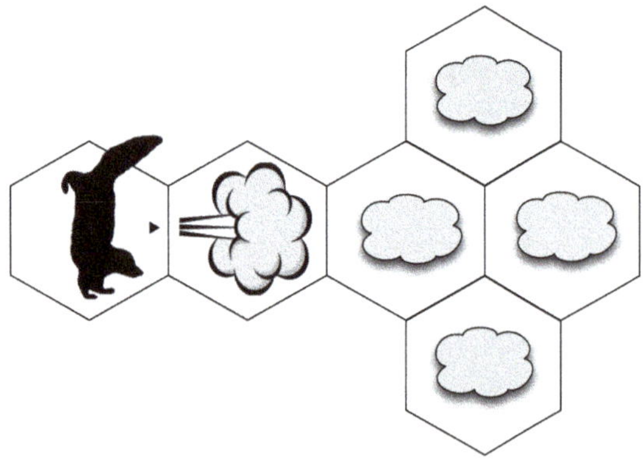

Porcupine: The Guardian (CON)

Concerning Guardians, Ragged Robin the rabbit says:

> *Quill-Pigs are an odd sort. They are slow and clumsy, but good in trees, and I can't think of a better friend to have your back when a Badger visits your burrow."*

"

The porcupine's Primary Trait is CON (4d6), and limited Traits are SPD and AGI (2d6 each); other traits are each 3d6. There is only one possible profession for the porcupine, this being Guardian. Though slow, Guardians are excellent climbers, and their natural defenses make them risky to take on in combat.

Special Abilities

- In Pursuit, Guardians may **Bristle**.
- Guardians can climb trees.
- Guardians are weak diggers.
- At CON Level 3, Guardians may **Throw Quills** in combat (not actually thrown).
- At CON Level 6, Guardians may **Provide Antibiotic** by use of a quill injection to cure disease.

Bristle

In pursuit, a porcupine may abruptly stop at any time during pursuit, crouch down, and Bristle, holding quills out in all directions. The effect is similar to Intimidate by a Burglar. If the Pursuer enters a hex adjacent to the Porcupine, it must either stop to appraise the situation or immediately switch to a new target. If the Pursuer stops, its turn ends; no more movement is allowed until the next pursuit round. If the Pursuer immediately switches to a new target, movement can continue, but the Pursuer must maneuver around the Guardian's hex. As with Intimidate, the Guardian may flee again on its next round of movement or stand its ground. A Pursuer that has halted may choose to attack the Guardian in its next round, but if it enters the hex with the Porcupine, the attacker is immediately stuck by 1d6 quills. If that happens, the attacker takes 2 points of damage (total) before Combat begins, and in any subsequent combat his attack likelihood is reduced by −1 AGI if stuck by 1–3 quills and −2 AGI if stuck by 4 or more quills. An attacker may not remove quills until it quits pursuit and combat.

Climb Trees

A porcupine may climb the trunk of any tree to any height without a skill check.

Throw Quills

In combat, a Guardian at CON Level 3 or greater may replace any regular combat action with an attempt to Throw Quills at one attacker in an adjacent hex. If during that round the attacker tries to bite or claw the porcupine, he is stuck by 1d6 quills, with the result being the same as Bristle in Pursuit (see above). This special ability has no effect on any attacker other than the one the Throw Quills was directed toward. An attacker may not remove quills until leaving the Combat.

Provide Antibiotic

Due to the slight antibiotic chemicals within the quills, a Guardian may attempt to cure a disease by striking an ailing animal with quills. A strike sticks the target with 1d6 quills, doing 2 points of damage (total) as a result of each strike. To cure the disease, make a cure check of CON Rating + the number of quills vs. the GM-determined virulence of the disease. This can be repeated by striking with quills additional times (1d6 quills and 2 HP damage each strike), until the disease is cured or the target takes too much damage to continue.

Opossum: The Shaman (MYS)

Concerning Shamans, Moonseed the rabbit says:

"I have the highest regard for White Dogs. Many think them dim-witted and slow. But I know possums to have a different way of knowing, feeling more than thinking. They should leave their children at home, though."

The opossum's Primary Trait is MYS (4d6), and limited Traits are SPD and INT (2d6 each); other traits are each 3d6. There is only one possible profession for the opossum, this being Shaman. Though not too bright, Shamans can often deduce functions of constructions or objects in a mystical manner. Female Shamans have a large carrying capacity in their pouches (they have two). If they are carrying joeys in their pouches, mental connection with their young increases their MYS Rating by one point.

Special Abilities

- In Pursuit or Combat, Shamans may **Feign Death**.
- Shamans may engage in **Rapid Breeding**.
- Shamans can climb trees.
- Shamans are good diggers.
- At MYS Level 3, Shamans may **Determine Function**.
- At MYS Level 6, Shamans may attempt to **Implant Thoughts**.

Feign Death

In Pursuit, if the enemy is more than two hexes away, the Shaman may fall down as dead, rolling on his back and sticking out his tongue. If the enemy is not a normal carrion eater (Coyote,

Red Wolf, Rats, Wolverine, Grizzly Bear, Caracara, Bald Eagle, or Raven), the Shaman rolls 1d6 + MYS Rating vs. the enemy's 1d6 + SML Rating. On a success, the enemy loses interest and leaves the apparently dead opossum alone. On a failure, the enemy may attack and the Shaman can then attempt to escape again. A Shaman may attempt feigning death more than once in a Pursuit encounter.

Rapid Breeding

After an opossum mates, 3d6 young are born in just 12 days, and they immediately migrate to the mother's pouches. (Opossums have two "hand-warmer" pouches.) The young ("joeys") stay in the pouches, nursing, for about 2½ months, and then may crawl out to be carried on the mother's back or tail. The entire time the joeys are in the pouch, the mother's MYS Rating is one point higher. At five or six months of age, the young are capable of breeding. An adult can have three litters per year.

Determine Function

When encountering a man-thing or any unusual construction, a Shaman of MYS Level 3 or greater may attempt to determine the function of the object or construction. Roll 1d6 + MYS Rating vs. a DV assigned by the GM. If successful, the GM hints at the function in terms that an opossum might understand. Note that understanding an object's function does not automatically explain how to use it.

For example, on finding a dropped cellphone and succeeding in Determine Function, the GM would not identify it as a cellphone, but rather might say, *"It is used so one creature can give a message to another."*

Implant Thoughts

A special ability of a Shaman at MYS Level 6 or higher is to attempt to implant thoughts within the mind of another animal. The Shaman need not know the language of the animal to do this, since the thoughts are in the form of images, aromas, emotions, or urges. The attempt takes ten minutes of concentration, and succeeds based on the Shaman's 1d6 + MYS Rating vs. the target's 1d6 + MYS Rating, with a possible difficulty adjustment by the GM based on the complexity of the attempt implant. The target need not be visible, or even within the immediate vicinity, but should be within 100 meters. Add 1 point of DV for each 100 meters beyond this distance. Note that Implanting a Thought is not the same as Enthrall, which results in an obedient state. The implanted thought can only influence behavior, not dictate it.

For example, a wolf is outside the Shaman's burrow, waiting for him to emerge. The Shaman successfully implants the smell of rotting flesh in the mind of the wolf, who then gives up and wanders away.

Armadillo: The Trader (SML)

Concerning Traders, Hawksbeard the rabbit says:

I'm always wanting odds and ends for working my herbs, and there is nothing like a visit to the nearest Turtle-Rabbit if you need something to trade. And they work for worms! Don't let one run across a man-path, though. It is not pretty.

The armadillo's Primary Trait is SML (4d6), and limited Traits are STR and INT (2d6 each); other traits are each 3d6. There is only one possible profession for the armadillo, this being Trader. It is almost impossible to hide something from a Trader due to their acute sense of smell. A Trader can hold her breath for a long time, which might be useful in an adventure.

Special Abilities

- In Pursuit or Combat, Traders may **Roll Up**.
- In Combat, Traders have **Natural Armor** that reduces damage.
- Traders have an increased ability to **Find Hidden**.
- Traders cannot climb trees.
- Traders are exceptional diggers.
- Traders cannot Bite in combat.
- At CON Level 3, Traders may **Walk Underwater or Raft**.
- At SML Level 3, Traders may **Claw** in combat for double damage.
- At SML Level 6, Traders are immune to diseases and pests.

Roll Up

In Pursuit, an Armadillo may adopt a defensive position that reduces or eliminates vulnerability to attack. The Trader may Roll Up at any time during pursuit, tucking her vulnerable areas inside armor consisting of multiple overlapping plates of bone. Faced with an armored ball, a Pursuer may choose to initiate combat or switch to another Target. However, switching targets does count as a voluntary tactic. Any attack that hits the Trader incurs a damage reduction of 5 HP. Thus, any attack directed at a Trader that is Rolled Up must deliver 6 or more HP of damage or it has no effect. A predator that does no damage to a Rolled-Up Armadillo after two successful hits gives up, and if no other targets are available on the Battleboard, Combat ends.

Natural Armor

In Combat, an Armadillo is protected by its natural armor: a series of overlapping, bony plates covered with a layer of horn.

If the Armadillo chooses to Roll Up, the protection is similar to that in Pursuit (subtract 5 HP from any attack that hits). While Rolled Up, the Armadillo cannot move, use herbs, or take any other action (except to unroll). In regular combat, an Armadillo still receives some protection; subtract 3 HP damage from all attacks that hit an Armadillo that is not Rolled Up. Note that Armor protects only against physical attacks, not against attacks with herbs, Empathic Hurt, etc.

Find Hidden

A Trader has increased ability to find anything aromatic (food, herbs, another animal, etc.) even if concealed, camouflaged, buried, or behind a plug in a burrow. If the Armadillo is just one hex away on a Battleboard scale, the detection is automatic, except in rare cases where strongly scented chemicals have been deployed by men to mask odors.

Walk Underwater or Raft

Armadillos are remarkably capable in the water, but they can use two very unconventional means of moving in water instead of swimming. The armor of the Armadillo increases its density, and by holding its breath, it can Walk Underwater to cross streams, ponds, and small rivers. Underwater walking proceeds at a normal speed; the Armadillo can hold its breath for a number of minutes equal to its CON Rating. (Remember that there are 10 Combat rounds per minute.) To cross larger bodies of water, an armadillo can swallow copious amounts of air, increasing its buoyancy so it floats like a raft. Another animal, with a CON Rating equal to or less than the Armadillo, can be supported on this living raft.

Squirrel: The Grifter (CHA)

Concerning Grifters, Moxieplum the rabbit says:

> *It's a scandal! Simply disgraceful the way those nut smugglers carry on, dashing up a tree to taunt and heckle. They are just fancy rats, I say. Oh, they chatter a good deal, but give me an honest story any day, without all the tail waggling.*

The squirrel's Primary Trait is CHA (4d6), and limited Traits are CON and MYS (2d6 each); other traits are each 3d6. There is only one possible profession for the squirrel, this being Grifter. Not only skilled climbers and jumpers, Grifters can taunt foes and totally distract them.

Special Abilities

- In Pursuit, Grifters may **Tree Dash**
- In Combat, Grifters may **Leap Acrobatically**.
- In Combat, Grifters may **Taunt**.
- Grifters can climb trees, including tree canopies.
- Grifters are weak diggers.
- Grifters get a **Facing Change Bonus** in combat.
- At CHA Level 3, Grifters may **Lie and Cheat** without detection.
- At CHA Level 6, may count to seven (beyond seven is a thousand).

Tree Dash

In Pursuit, if a Major obstacle (presumed to be a tree) is within six hexes with no intervening enemy, a Squirrel may dash and climb the tree in a single round of movement. Tree Dash is similar in its effect to Quick Conceal and other disappearing acts. It results in the Pursuer immediately switching to a new target (unless the predator is a Pine Marten, Ringtail, Goshawk, or Owl); other predators, including good climbers such as cats, cannot catch a Squirrel in a tree. The Grifter may climb back down in any subsequent pursuit round, at which time it becomes available again as a Target.

Leap Acrobatically

If the canopy of one tree is no more than two hexes from the canopy of another tree, a squirrel may leap from one tree to the next without falling or making a skill check. Note that this is twice the distance permitted for tree-to-tree leaps by Chipmunks. The acrobatic leap constitutes the entire movement of the squirrel for that round.

Taunt

A squirrel may taunt a ground-based enemy, whether the squirrel is on the ground or in a tree. Roll 1d6 + CHA Rating vs. the enemy's 1d6 + INT Rating. On a success, the enemy ceases his current activity and makes a full movement in the direction of the squirrel. The squirrel may attempt Taunt multiple times, but cannot repeat a successful Taunt against the same enemy during the same combat. Taunts have no effect on airborne or waterborne opponents.

Facing Change Bonus

During combat, the Grifter can make a "free" facing rotation (turning to face any direction) at the start or conclusion of movement. In addition, they can make a similar facing rotation for each hex of movement for a cost of one extra MP per intermediate hex (in which they rotate).

Lie and Cheat

The normal checks to detect falsehoods always fail if made against a Grifter of CHA Level 3 or above. You probably should not gamble with Grifters. However, this does not mean a Grifter's lies somehow cloud the ordinary senses of another animal. If the Grifter hands a Trader an acorn, and says it is a carrot, the Trader may discount the misstatement, but still treats the acorn like an acorn.

Part II: Playing the Game

What Can a Bunny Do?

Players new to roleplaying games (RPGs) and experienced hands accustomed to outfitting dwarven warriors, elven rangers, or human wizards might be puzzled by a game about rabbits. What, after all, can a rabbit do, except eat, sleep, groom itself, run away from danger, and possibly end its life in the jaws of a fox? Rabbits have been depicted in myths and stories as tricksters and merrymakers, magicians and warriors, with abilities ranging from almost-real-world rabbits (as in the novel *Watership Down* by Richard Adams) to the anxious, waistcoated White Rabbit (of *Alice in Wonderland*) to swashbuckling heroes (as in the *Redwall* novels of Brian Jacques).

Well, our bunnies are closer to natural rabbits than to *The Wind in the Willows*. They may not wield a sword or drive motor cars, but our rabbits can fight (much better than you might expect), spring traps without getting caught, use their wits to outfox a fox or trick a coyote trickster, bargain and persuade other rabbits and even other animals (if they know the language), carry things (tucked in their fur, or in a woven bird nest used as a bag), count (but only up to four), disguise themselves, and tell fabulous stories. Some rabbits may possess more fantastic abilities: they might glimpse events in the future, master the lore of herbalism (the closest thing rabbits have to magic), heal wounds by laying on of paws, and use certain other mental powers. Our own experience has found that the game has a tendency to evolve during play, with rabbits devising new ways to do more complicated things, and thereby becoming more versatile and powerful. Most of all, playing ostensibly small and weak characters such as rabbits, squirrels, and opossums encourages players to use their imagination instead of relying on brute force to solve every problem.

Playing the game starts with players creating their characters, which is described in **Part 1**. It also requires the Gamemaster (GM) to select an Adventure, or to draw up a new scenario, to create the world and define the quests and challenges for the player characters (PCs) to overcome. Here in **Part 2** we introduce the mechanics of running a game, including information that every player should know. To ensure a smooth and enjoyable game, guidelines and tips for the GM are presented in **Part 3**.

Time, Scale & Terrain

Rabbits interact with their surroundings on a scale of a few meters, but they may view habitat features up to a few hundred meters distant, and they may wander over distances of several kilometers. Drawing a detailed map that represents all these different scales is impractical. It therefore is useful for the GM to employ a large aboveground map to chart the various locations and habitats that player characters may visit, and perhaps to draft a few small-scale maps of specific locations, such as the farmer's garden or the burrow system of the home warren. Large-scale maps need not be highly detailed, and the scale may be considered approximate. We recommend that aboveground maps for bunny adventures generally be drawn to a scale with large hexes of about 50–100 meters. An example of a large scale map — depicting the fields and forests of Coneylaeth, the fantasy setting for adventures included with **B&B** — may be found in **Appendix C**. For specific locations, and during encounters with predators or NPCs, it also is helpful to use maps to represent the position and movement of individual PCs and the non-player characters (NPCs) and enemies (such as predators) that they encounter. The Battleboards provided with the game provide one form of small-scale map, using 1-meter hexes to represent a small patch of habitat. Different Battleboards are available for ten principal habitat types and one generic burrow system (with extensions).

Although it is possible to draw up an adventure that takes place in a vast, unchanging landscape, such as a trackless desert, unbroken forest, or post-apocalyptic wasteland, players generally appreciate the opportunity for their characters to visit different kinds of environment. **B&B** provides ten principal habitats that may be distinguished by three physical variables: Moisture, Temperature, and Elevation. Each habitat presents different risks and rewards.

Habitat	Moisture	Temperature	Elevation
Farm	Wet	Warm	Low
Orchard	Wet	Warm	High
Marsh	Wet	Cool	Low
Mountain Stream	Wet	Cool	High
Grassland	Dry	Warm	Low
Rocky Hillside	Dry	Warm	High
Oak Woodland	Dry	Cool	Low
Brushland	Dry	Cool	High
Suburb	Dry	Warm	Low or High
Pine Forest	Dry	Cool	Low or High

Habitats harbor different flora and fauna, available food and water, topography, and microclimates. They also can change markedly between day and night, or in different weather conditions. An oak woodland may seem comfortable and safe in the daytime, but scary on a moonless night. A pleasant mountain meadow bathed in sunshine can quickly pose a threat to survival after a snowstorm. Players should remember that rabbits and other animals survive at the mercy of the elements and must be aware of their local environment.

Dice and Skill Checks

Outcomes of many actions by players are determined by die rolls modified by Trait Ratings, Base Bonuses, or other factors. All die rolls in **B&B** can be resolved with six-sided dice (d6). A Skill Check occurs when a player character attempts an action that is contingent on the PC's abilities for success. Skill checks succeed when a 1d6 die roll plus a Trait Rating exceeds a Difficulty Value (DV) for that task, or the skill check of an adversary. Thus, high die rolls and high Ratings benefit rabbits. In some cases, an attempted action is determined by Base Bonus instead of Rating; this is referred to as a BB check, which is similarly compared to a DV. Difficulty may be prescribed in the rules, or set by the GM with the following guidelines:

Trivial	Easy	Moderate	Hard	Expert	Virtuoso
DV=2	DV=4	DV=6	DV=8	DV=10	DV=12

Combat rolls also add die rolls to Trait Ratings, so higher sums also are better when fighting. Players may perform Public die rolls, where the results are open for everyone to see. In some situations, however, the GM should conduct Private die rolls in secret, such as passive checks for spotting or detecting nearby hidden features or recognizing an unknown herb. The GM may keep the outcome of a Private roll secret (as in a passive check for predators), or limit the information shared with players (for instance, by announcing only that an herb *"smells like an herb"* if the rabbit failed in an attempt to recognize poisonweed).

Ordinary Activities

The rising sun finds you and your friends already emerged from the burrow. Rabbits dot the green meadow as they quietly munch on fresh grass and delicate forbs. Somewhere in the wood a hawk cries out, *"peeeerrr."* Bilberry posts upright to get a better look, but sees nothing. You casually groom, having recognized the call was a poor imitation by a bluejay ...

Real rabbits fill their day with ordinary activities punctuated by moments of stark terror. The lives of rabbits in the game world of **B&B** are a bit more eventful, but typical rabbit behavior still plays an important role. Feeding, grooming, sleeping, and keeping a watchful eye for enemies are crucial for success in pursuit of greater goals.

Movement and Foraging

Normal rabbit movement involves a walking or hopping pace. (A normal rabbit gait technically is termed a "half-bound" where the two front feet step forward independently, then the two hind feet hop.) As rabbits move about their environs, and even when they are purposively traveling from one place to another, they progress in fits and starts, pausing to look about or nibble on blades of grass. Normal movement rate is determined by the rabbit's movement allowance (2 + SPD Base Bonus). On a large map scale, movement thus proceeds at about two large hexes per 10 minutes — or about 10–20 meters per minute. Rabbits with strong SPD Base Bonus can move 3–5 hexes per 10 minutes. Stealthy movement is half speed. Rabbits can run very fast, but running is exhausting and they cannot maintain a

running speed very long. So when players intend to move over large distances quickly, the movement rate may be increased by 2 hexes (i.e., 4 hexes for average rabbits, 5–7 hexes for rabbits with SPD Base Bonus). The same movement allowance applies to Pursuit, although both the map scale is smaller and the time shorter. For movement on a Battleboard, as during combat or in a burrow system, see **Combat**. Although other animals can maintain a faster pace over distance, non-rabbit characters also tend to move more slowly unless pursued; the same movement rates apply. Movement allowances for predators and other animals are listed in the **Bestiary**; the listed values apply both to roving aboveground (hexes per 10 minutes) and to Pursuit on the pursuit board (hexes per round), but see **Combat** for movement rates on Battleboards.

Grooming

There are two kinds of grooming: Protective and Defensive. Protective grooming is performed intermittently, usually when there is a quiet moment or lull in the general flow of activity. It does not serve merely to pass the time; it fulfills an important function. As you will see below, the world is full of pests. Ticks and biting flies and parasites plague the world of rabbits and their fellow animals, and grooming serves a prophylactic function by helping to prevent infestation by such vermin. Protective grooming requires only 1 minute to perform, but removes pests before they can become a bigger problem. In contrast, Defensive grooming is a rabbit's reaction to an existing infestation. Defensive grooming is more labor intensive, requiring 10 minutes to complete. But when covered in mites or leeches, intensive grooming is the first, and sometimes only, line of defense.

Sleeping

Rabbits typically follow a crepuscular activity pattern. Neither truly diurnal nor nocturnal, rabbits can be active at any time of day or night, but prefer to forage and pursue other activities in the hours before and after dawn and dusk. They may sleep, on average, for 8 hours a day, but sleep is divided into two major rest periods in the middle of the day and the middle of the night.

Sleep is restorative. It is the principal time when healing occurs, when memories are archived, when special skills are renewed. A rabbit (or non-rabbit character) recovers from wounds when it sleeps for 4 hours, typically once at midday and again at midnight. Healing is discussed further under **Constitution**.

The midnight sleep is the appropriate time for the GM to update events that transpire over 24-hour intervals. Disease and parasite infestation may grow worse, untreated poison takes its toll, daily limits on certain actions (e.g., luck, tempt fate, trance, spray) are reset, etc.

Scanning and Posting

You may be generally alert for danger, but there are moments when you want to be extra sure. Scanning and Posting are behaviors for Active Spotting of predators or other enemies. Scanning merely involves raising your head and looking around for a few seconds, or rotating your ears to determine the direction of a sound. Posting entails standing upright on hind legs to get a better view. Active Spotting is discussed in more detail under spotting rules, in the section on **Encounters**.

Friendly Competition, Games, and Play

At certain times of year, you may see rabbits chasing each other, then quickly reversing roles, with fugitive becoming pursuer and vice versa. Non-serious activities with reversible roles and flexible rules are the hallmarks of play. The rabbits of **Bunnies & Burrows** love to play games, and much of their social interaction revolves around silly contests, dares, practical jokes, and friendly competition. But play also serves a serious purpose of preparing young animals for serious problems they may face. In the rules that follow, several Mini-Games are offered, which can be played by themselves or in the context of an ongoing Adventure or campaign. When rabbits disagree, or claim the same privilege or prize, the dispute can be settled amicably through a harmless game without resorting to threat or force. Steady Now is a Mini-Game that encompasses a number of simple challenges that can be used in many different contexts in the game. It has the additional advantage of getting players up out of their chairs and sofas to engage in a physical diversion.

Mini-Game: Steady Now

Each in their own way, many different professions take pride in their physical skills. Fighters are strong, Runners are quick, Mavericks are dexterous, Empaths endure. Years of friendly competition have yielded a variety of simple games and contests based on control of the body: the mini-game called **Steady Now**. Some forms of Steady Now are silly. Rabbits also play a terrible version of this, where they challenge each other to be the last one standing in a dangerous situation, such as on an ant nest. As human players of **B&B**, you must NEVER do this. Instead, we restrict the game to safer alternatives, which still test your steadiness and body control. The game is for two or more players.

Setup

Find a safe place to play, where if you fall over, you won't hurt yourself. And where you won't lose dice if you drop them. If you play outside, put a blanket down on the ground. Usually this is played with the players in a circle, so everyone can see each other. Pick one person to issue the first challenge. Then continue clockwise, with each new challenge. Normally, every challenge is different from the last one. Play until one player earns a thousand points (i.e., more than four), or until everyone is giggling so much they cannot go on.

Challenges

We give some sample challenges here, but feel free to add new ones, but only if they are safe for all the players. If there is a challenge that a particular player cannot do, for any reason, it should not be picked. Every player starts the challenge at the same time, and each continues until just one is left. That one wins the challenge and takes a token for score-keeping; the next person then announces the next challenge. When one person has a thousand tokens (more than four), the game ends and that player is the winner. It is fair for any player to say something to get the others laughing, since that might make the game more difficult for them. But you cannot touch another player, nor throw something at them, to make them fail.

Dice on One Finger

Sit down and hold one hand in front, palm down, with your fingers splayed out (not touching). When a player says, "Add one," you each pick up a six-sided die and balance it on top of one finger (that is, on the back of the finger). The die cannot touch the knuckle of your hand nor an adjacent finger. When everyone has their die balanced, say "Add one" and do this again, with a second die on the same finger. It is OK if it touches the first die, but cannot touch an adjacent finger. If your dice fall off the finger, you are out. Keep going until only one player is left, who wins and takes a token.

Dice between Fingertips

Each player extends one finger from each hand, and then, using just the fingertips, holds a die between the left-hand finger and the right-hand finger. When everyone is doing this, someone counts "One." Now put your hands down, and do this again with two dice between the finger tips; that is, the dice will be in a line with the extended fingers. Now slowly count "One … Two." If someone drops his dice once the count starts, he is out. Do this again with three dice, "One … Two … Three," then with four, "One … Two … Three … Four." Finally, if any players are remaining, they do it with a thousand dice between their fingertips. You keep holding the dice until only one player is left, who wins and takes a token. Once you are holding a thousand dice, you don't count; instead, each player (including the ones who have already dropped out) starts calling out silly words in an attempt to get everyone giggling.

Stand on One Paw

This one is simple. All players stand in a circle, not touching each other. When someone says "Start," each player raises one foot off the ground and balances on the other foot. You cannot put the raised foot down on anything, including your other foot. If a player's raised foot touches the ground or anything else, he or she is out. Continue until only one is left, who wins and takes a token.

Dice on Nose

For this one, each player tilts his or her head to one side or the other, so one ear is down and one ear is up. Have your dice where you can reach them without looking. When someone says "Add one," each player at the same time balances a six-sided die on the upper side of their nose, keeping their head tilted so the die does not roll off. Continue adding one die at a time each time a person calls "Add one." You can stack one die on top of another if that seems easier, but you cannot let the dice touch your eyeball or any other part of your face, only the side of your nose. If dice fall off, you are out. When only one player is left, she wins and takes a token.

Feel free to add other physical tests to this game, but you must make sure they are safe to play, and everyone agrees to them.

Detection of Hazards and Environmental Features

All rabbits are able to search for and detect hazards, though Scouts are often best, in the case of detections based on Intelligence (INT). There are three detection situations:

- Catching notice of a clue without searching (passive detection)
- Active searching for clues
- Detailed examination of a location once a clue has been detected

The greatest danger to rabbits is that of predators, but that type of detection is covered in Spotting, in the **Predators** section. Detection and identification of herbs is covered in the section on **Herbs**. There are some special detection abilities of Seers and Shamans (see under those professions). Here we are considering the following types of hazards:

- Detecting pests, which are a nuisance, and can cause disease
- Detecting states of other characters, including disease, injury, and emotions
- Detecting the presence of man-things, including traps
- Detecting potential environmental risks of accident and injury
- Detecting entrances to burrows and lairs
- Detecting tracks and spoor

We present the detection rules for each of these potential hazards, and for each of the detection situations. Note that if a solitary rabbit is close to his home burrow, he notices any obvious change in the environment if the GM rolls 6 on 1d6. A party of five or more rabbits automatically notices such a change without a die roll. (*"That pile of rocks was not there yesterday."*) Close to the burrow means you can see the entrance to the burrow without posting.

Each type of detection is based on clues, which are signs that the hazard is present. Sometimes these clues may be innocuous. For example, an apple on the ground may mean there is a trap present, or that a human passed by and discarded an apple core. It may also just mean you are in an orchard, and this is simply a windfall apple. So each section starts with a discussion of the possible clues for the type of hazard. Usually a way to distinguish one hazard from another is by recognizing the patterns of clues that are present.

Detecting Pests

Typically, pests are small insects or arachnids that can bite or infest rabbits, such as mosquitoes, fleas, etc. Here are some of the clues that can indicate the presence of pests. Chance of passive detection is shown to the right, based on a 1d6 roll by the GM; e.g., [5–6] means the clue is detected without a search if the GM rolls a 5 or 6. [Auto] means automatically detected; the GM just tells you.

- Clouds of flying insects or the sounds of their buzzing [5–6]
- Itching skin [3–6]
- Bites or stings [Auto]
- Small creatures swimming in the water [6, if beside the water]
- Ectoparasites detected by grooming [Auto]

Since parasites of the skin or fur (ectoparasites) are automatically detected upon grooming, players should get in the habit of grooming themselves from time to time, especially in "down time" (when you are not running, in combat, etc., but are just staying in one place to browse on food and talk). With successful passive detection, the GM merely tells you the clue, but not what may have caused it. (*"Something just stung you on the paw."*)

You can also actively search for pests, at which time you automatically detect the clue if the pest is present. (*"I look around for flying insects." "You see a cloud of small gnats or flies hovering nearby. You can hear them buzzing."*)

To specifically identify the pest once you detect the clue, you must make an INT check (1d6 + INT Rating vs. DV). The DV for flying insects or ectoparasites = 4. The DV for pests in the water = 8. If you make the identification, the GM tells you the identity of the pest, but normally does not tell you what to do about it, or what diseases it might cause. You will learn those things by reading the rules or experiencing the effects during the game.

Detecting States of Other Characters

It is often important to notice if another character is wounded, diseased, angry, fearful, in shock, etc. Many such detections are automatic, but others require specific detections. If the other character is not of your species, it can make understanding more difficult. Knowing the language of another creature also helps in knowing the unspoken cues that can be displayed by that creature, as does your having a higher rating in a Trait (that depends on the clue). Here are some of the clues for passive detection.

- Temporary or permanent injuries [3–6]
- Visible wounds or sores [Auto]
- The smell of blood or fear [4–6] (must be downwind)
- Fever [6]
- Red eyes [3–6]
- Moving in an unusual manner [5–6]
- Unusually motionless [2–6]
- Unusual posture [3–6]
- Quilled handicap [Auto]
- Sneezing [Auto]
- Sprayed handicap [Auto] (must be downwind)
- Vulnerable handicap [Auto]
- Patchy loss of fur [3–6]
- Snarls, hisses, roars, alarm calls, etc. [Auto]
- Baring of fangs or other threat or intimidation displays [Auto]

There are some states whose clues cannot be detected passively. These include:

- Confused handicap
- Enthralled handicap
- Fascinated handicap
- Poisoned handicap

You can declare an attempt to actively detect a specific clue, such as *"Do I smell blood on him?"* If the particular clue is present, the GM informs you so automatically, except that clues that cannot be detected passively also cannot be detected actively. You also can make a generic request, such as *"Does anything seem wrong about him?"* In this case, the clue is not automatic, but the GM makes the passive detection roll one more time to see if this time you notice it; this can be done only once for a particular clue.

If you know the language of the other character, you can ask directly (e.g., *"Are you feeling OK? Does anything hurt?"*). The GM decides what clues to provide in the case of Confused, Fascinated, or Poisoned, but the other character will not know if they are Enthralled.

Once you detect a clue, a detailed examination provides more information about the state of the other character, but not necessarily everything you want to know. The DV and Trait being used in the examination varies with the specific state being investigated.

- **Signs of Physical Injury or Disease:** INT check (1d6 + INT Rating vs. DV=6); automatic for Empaths.
- **Smells of Blood/Fear/Sprayed:** SML check (1d6 + SML Rating vs. DV=5); automatic for Herbalists.
- **Signs of Mental Disorder:** MYS check (1d6 + MYS Rating vs. DV=8); automatic for Seers.*
- **Vocalizations and Threats:** CHA check (1d6 + CHA Rating vs. DV=4); automatic for Storytellers.*
- **Signs of Emotional State:** MYS check (1d6 + MYS Rating vs. DV=6); automatic for Seers and Storytellers.*

* If the character being observed is not of your species, add +1 to your roll if you know its language.

Note that evaluating the fighting ability of an adversary in Combat, or judging the relative age of a predator, is a special ability of Scouts.

Detecting Man-Things

If man-things are present, they can offer either opportunity or great risk, so it is important to detect all clues associated with them. Some clues may be indications of man-things, but also may represent natural features in the environment. They are also included here, since wise rabbits tend to be wary. For example, a length of vine may be innocuous, but if there is also the scent of man, it is best to show caution. Also, at a distance, what seems to be a length of vine might prove to be a small snake. Some of these things are very common in the world, and so

might be ignored, which is why they are not all automatic. Here are some of the clues for passive detection.

- Apple, carrot, or other tasty item [Auto if you are downwind; else 4–6]
- Length of vine [4–6]
- Glint of metal [3–6]
- Disturbed earth [4–6]
- Stick [3–6]
- Shaded hex [4–6]
- Man-thing of appreciable size [Auto]
- Scent of man [3–6; Automatic for Herbalists] (must be downwind)

You can declare an attempt to detect a particular clue, and if it is present within one hex, you automatically detect it. Since so many of these are commonly found, you must move about to actively check for them. If you believe a trap is present, you may then attempt to disarm the trap (which may involve moving around to find more clues); see Trap rules for disarming traps (and also play the Trap Snapper mini-game).

Detailed examination is usually needed for information about man-things, which are totally alien to the rabbit consciousness. Examination takes a full, uninterrupted hour, plus successful rolls against both INT level and AGI level (since manipulation is required as well as insight). Two rabbits may cooperate in the examination, each responsible for one Trait. The GM makes die rolls for both Traits at the same time, in each case 1d6 + Trait Rating must equal or exceed the relevant DV for the examination to succeed. A failure on one roll has a chance of either breaking the object or backfiring, potentially damaging the examiner(s). If there is no breakage or backfire, another hour may be spent in examination. A failure on both rolls always results in breakage, backfire, or both, and so no further examination may be done on the object. The GM determines what happens in the case of backfire.

Successful examination of a man-thing reveals something of its nature and function. In most cases, though, rabbits will not be able to use a man-thing in the same way that a person could, since a rabbit is not as large, not as strong, not trained, and has no opposable thumbs. Still, a rabbit (or group) might be able to come up with some use for it.

Detecting Environmental Risks

Many things in the environment (beyond predators and traps) can be risky for rabbits. Bad weather, poor footing, brambles and thorns are just a few hazards that rabbits must watch for. Here are some of the clues for passive detection:

- Mobility impairment (deep snow, mud, sharp fragments on the ground) [4–6 at a distance, Auto if nearby]
- Impending weather change [5–6]
- Thorns and brambles [Auto] (Rabbits watch for these as a possible escape route)
- Fast-moving water [Auto]
- Insecure footing (loose gravel, slick mud, or ice) [3–6; Auto if you step on it]

- Thin ice on a body of water [4–6 if nearby]

For detection of Poisonweed, refer to Herb rules. For crossing thin ice or other treacherous footing, refer to the Ice Crack mini-game.

Declaring an attempt to detect any of these works automatically if the clue is present. This is something rabbits are very skilled at perceiving, but they still might stumble into a problem if not actively searching.

Predicting an imminent weather change depends on how it is attempted.

- **By sight and sound:** INT check (1d6 + INT Rating vs. DV=8; if thunder is heard, all rabbits automatically know a storm is coming)

- **By smell:** SML check (1d6 + SML Rating vs. DV=7)

- **By an ominous sense:** MYS check (1d6 + MYS Rating vs. DV=6)

- **By sensing the future:** (for Seer, requires a successful trance)

Detecting Lairs, Tracks, and Scent Marks

Rabbits are pretty good at spotting burrow entrances unless they are well hidden within vegetation, within roots, or within rock formations. If the party is on the move, the lead rabbit may be able to passively detect tracks that she crosses, but others farther back will not have that opportunity. Here are some of the clues for passive detection.

- Visible burrow entrance [Auto, if within six hexes; daytime only]

- Scent from a burrow [4–6, if downwind of it; day or night]

- Visible tracks on mud, soft dirt, snow, or dust [2–6 for lead rabbit; daytime only]

- Scent from tracks [3–6 if tracks are recent, for lead rabbit; day or night]

Actively checking for scent (burrow or tracks) works automatically if downwind of the source or in the immediate vicinity.

To identify the source of a scent or to identify what made the tracks, or to follow a set of tracks, refer to Tracking rules.

Many animals use scent marks to advertise the boundaries of their territory, announce their social or reproductive status, or stake a claim to coveted resource. In B&B, our rabbits and other animals can exchange messages through the use of scent marks that can be read if one has the nose (a combination of talent and skill). See the section on Communication for more details on reading scent marks.

Health

Finding nutritious food and eating regularly is only one aspect of health. Environmental factors also can exert a profound impact on health, including pests, disease, and exposure to extreme heat or cold. Natural resistance to disease and exposure is based on Constitution. Diminished health from any cause is reflected by reduced hit points (HP).

Food and Energy

Rabbits are herbivores. They eat grass and other green plants, browse on new buds and strip bark from saplings, steal vegetables from a garden and grain from a barn. They may be active day or night, and spend most of their time eating. In the game, it is necessary for you to eat regularly to maintain energy and health. But to simplify game play and maximize time to do things that are interesting and fun (instead of just grazing), record-keeping for energy and nutrition are kept to a minimum.

To simplify record-keeping, the GM checks whether rabbits feel hungry at the same time that he checks for possible wandering encounters. As discussed below, Wandering Encounters occur when rabbits chance upon other animals, including predators. The GM must check whether an encounter occurs by rolling 1d6 every 10 minutes of game time. A roll of 6 indicates an encounter of some sort (see below). In the same die roll, the GM also checks the party's energy status; a roll of 1 indicates the rabbits are feeling hungry. If they are, they must explicitly forage on available food for a full 10 minutes or eat a high-nutrient food (such as a Prized Food). Record-keeping for the GM is simple: write an "H" on a note card; when bunnies become hungry, turn it face (H) up; when they eat, turn it face down. If the rabbits are hungry at the time that another die roll results in a 1, then all bunnies incur 1 HP damage.

Rabbits also gain nutrition from consuming their own cecotropes. Cecotrophy is voluntary but useful; if you deposit and eat cecotropes when hungry, you can both satisfy your hunger and recover 1 HP. Rabbits can deposit and eat cecotropes up to twice per day, requiring 10 minutes. See a more complete discussion under the section on Constitution.

Non-rabbit characters also must eat regularly, but may have different food requirements. Jackrabbits, Porcupines, Chipmunks, and Gray Squirrels are herbivores. Jackrabbits have similar nutritional needs as rabbits. Porcupines will eat green leaves, but prefer twigs, buds, and inner tree bark, especially from smooth-barked trees such as pine, aspen, willow, and cottonwood. These trees may be considered common in Orchard, Pine Forest, Mountain Stream, and Marsh, uncommon in Oak Woodland, Suburb, Farm, and Brushland, and rare in Grassland and Rocky Hillside. Porcupines do relish the same Prized Foods as rabbits, though. Chipmunks and Gray Squirrels prefer seeds and nuts, and catch and eat small insects on occasion. Raccoons, Skunks, and Opossums are omnivores. Roots, nuts, and berries, and catchable insects (beetles, roaches, crickets, grasshoppers, grubs of various kinds) are present in all habitats. Finally, Armadillos eat insects, larvae, and earthworms almost exclusively. Suitable food should be readily available in all habitats except Rocky Hillside, where it is harder to find (uncommon).

Given these food habits, Jackrabbits can satisfy their food needs the same way as rabbits: munching as they move along, with more focused feeding when they feel hungry. They also can deliver and eat cecotropes, unlike all other non-rabbit characters. Other non-rabbit species do not generally forage while traveling, but when food is common in a habitat, they may elect to forage for 10 minutes to satisfy their hunger. If food is uncommon, however, they must forage for 20 minutes to alleviate hunger, and 30 minutes if food is rare. Food limitations thus pose a particular problem for Porcupines and Armadillos.

Effects of Poison

If food is collected and eaten while fresh, it poses no problem. However, if food is retrieved from storage or found in a cache or garbage heap, it may be spoiled. Upon eating a new food that has been stored (other than in a dry burrow) or discarded, roll a toxin resistance check vs. a DV=4. Failure in the toxin check results in the consumer incurring 2 HP poison damage, with no continuing effects. Raccoons and Opossums are immune to spoiled food.

A rabbit may be poisoned by other means than spoiled food. Bites from some animals are poisonous. Other animals have poisonous skin, and transmit the toxin if bitten. Herbs can be poisonous, as can various non-herbal plants that might be confused with edible food. In general, ordinary plant poisons have a DV=4 for toxin resistance checks, and animal poisons or herbs have a DV=6. A successful toxin resistance check reduces the damage inflicted by the poison by half. To stop ongoing effects of poison, the toxin must be removed from the afflicted character's system, either by herbal treatment, empathic healing, or intentional bleeding. A bleeding cure for poison inflicts an additional 1d6 HP of damage, but eliminates further poison damage.

Prized Food and Trade

Although food will not be a limiting factor most of the time, some food items are prized beyond their mere nutritional value. Some foods are sought after as a tasty dish, much as a person might crave chocolate or ice cream. Other foods are considered rare delicacies, more akin to foie gras or caviar. Rabbits and other non-rabbit herbivores and omnivores not only relish these foods, they assume risks, compete, and even fight to get them. Prized food items, along with a few other coveted objects ("shinies"), form the primary basis for trade between rabbits.

Other animals (especially Armadillo or Magpie Traders) also engage in barter, exchanging other items of value (such as banana slugs or nightcrawlers to armadillos, or baubles to magpies) for rabbit currency. The following table presents common prized foods and other items used for trade. "Trade Value" provides an example of an amount a rabbit can understand. (Remember: They can count only to four.) "Currency" lists the equivalent value in acorns (for the convenience of the GM).

Item	Category	Trade Value	Currency
Acorn	standard currency	1 lettuce	1 @
Lettuce, head	prized food	1 acorn	1 @
Blackberry	prized food	1 acorn	1 @
Carrot	prized food	2 acorns	2 @
Cowslip	prized food	2 acorns	2 @
Oats	prized food	4 acorns	4 @
Apple	prized food	4 carrots	8 @
Cilantro	delicacy	4 apples	32 @
Truffle	delicacy	4 cilantro	128 @

Item	Category	Trade Value	Currency
Wiggler[A]	nightcrawler	1 acorn	1 @
Slug[A]	banana slug	2 carrots, 1 acorn	5 @
Lustrous[M]	bottle cap	2 carrots, 1 acorn	5 @
Bright[M]	agate	1 apple, 2 acorns	10 @
Shiny[M]	coin	2 apples, 2 carrots	20 @
Shimmering[M]	steel screw	1 cilantro, 2 apples, 2 acorns	50 @
Glossy[M]	glass bead	3 cilantro, 2 carrots	100 @

A=trade with Armadillo; M=trade with Magpie

Pests and Parasites

Animals are plagued by numerous pests. Ectoparasites (ticks, mites, fleas, and leeches) can sap a rabbit's energy and inflict wounds. Endoparasites (roundworms, flukes, warbles, brainworms) can reduce the value of food, block the effects of herbs, or damage the host. Insects (mosquitoes, biting flies) can attack in swarms, causing confusion and injury. In addition to direct harm, these enemies may transmit disease and can be as lethal as much larger predators.

Rabbits and their followers pick up pests by lingering in habitats where pests are present. If the party stops to forage, rest, or lie in wait away from the home warren, the GM should check for potential pests. A 1d6 roll of 1 indicates that pests are present. Most pests are predictably associated with certain habitats. If pests are present, roll 2d6 and refer to the following table to determine what kind of pest.

Ectoparasites (ticks, mites, fleas, and leeches) initially go undetected, but can be discovered by ordinary grooming. No harm occurs if they are discovered within the first hour of infestation. After one hour, the infestation causes itching and loss of 1 HP per hour until the pests are removed. Ectoparasites may be repelled by various herbs, but must be removed by grooming. However, if not discovered before the onset of itching, the pests may have transmitted disease. On a 1d6 roll of 1 (with a separate die roll for each host), the host becomes infected with a pest-borne disease: Ticks transmit Rabbit Fever to rabbits, hares,

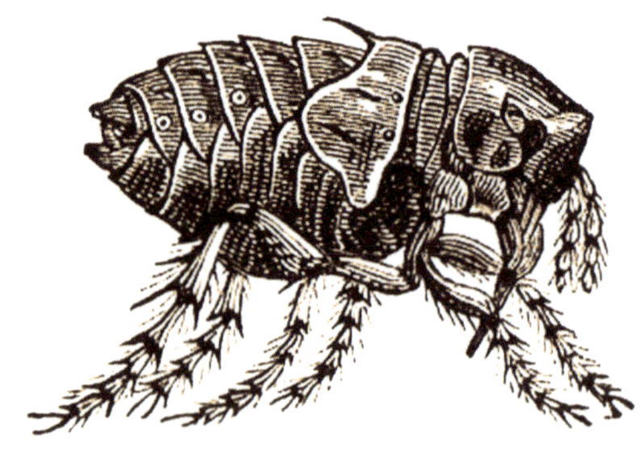

squirrels, and chipmunks; Mites transmit Alopecia to squirrels, chipmunks, and porcupines; Fleas transmit White Blindness to rabbits and hares; Leeches transmit the Shakes to any animal.

2d6 roll	Farm, Suburb, Grassland	Oak Woodland Orchard, Pine Forest	Brushland Rocky Hillside	Marsh Mountain Stream
2–3	Roundworms	Leeches	Flukes	Ticks
4	Mites	Warble Flies	Roundworms	Fleas
5	Ticks	Roundworms	Fleas	Mites
6	Biting Flies	Fleas	Mites	Flukes
7	Fleas	Mites	Ticks	Leeches
8	Warble Flies	Flukes	Biting Flies	Mosquitoes
9	Brainworms	Ticks	Mosquitoes	Biting Flies
10	Flukes	Mosquitoes	Warble Flies	Roundworms
11	Mosquitoes	Biting Flies	Brainworms	Warble Flies
12	Leeches	Brainworms	Leeches	Brainworms

Endoparasites (roundworms, flukes, warbles, brainworms) also go undetected until the onset of symptoms. They cannot be discovered by grooming. After one hour, hosts begin to feel the effects of parasites. Roundworms and Flukes alter host metabolism: food no longer restores energy, and ingested herbs (except for specific curatives for the parasites) fail to have effect. In fact, affected animals may first suspect internal parasites when they notice that eating does not satisfy hunger. Internal parasites must be eradicated by herbal treatment (Pumpkin Seeds or Pestflower).

Warble Flies will be noticed as they buzz around, but do not bite and most likely will be ignored. (The GM should assume that they arouse no suspicion unless a player explicitly investigates.) Warble Flies are nasty creatures that lay eggs on the skin of the host. Multiple eggs will be laid (1d6) on each host that remains within the large-scale hex where they are first encountered, or any of the surrounding hexes, for at least 10 minutes. Protective grooming every other minute is the only way to prevent flies from laying eggs. After one hour, the newly hatched larvae (Warbles) burrow into the skin, causing boil-like lesions. Each warble inflicts 1 HP damage for every hour that it remains alive. The Warbles cannot be removed by grooming, and must be driven out by herbal treatment (Warble Cap) or bitten out. Each warble that is bitten out results in one-half normal damage inflicted by biting (Core Damage = STR Rating of the biter + 1d6). If the Warbles are not removed, adult warble flies emerge from the body of the host (whether alive or dead) and take up residence wherever they may be, including the home warren!

Brainworms enter from larval cysts during normal foraging. They are associated with Raccoons and Skunks, and so may be picked up when foraging near these animals or their home lairs. The larvae enter the bloodstream and migrate through to the brain, where they burrow into the brainstem. The first symptom of brainworm infestation is an involuntary head tilt to the left. Brainworms must be driven out by herbal treatment (Lifemelt Garlic or Pestflower). Fortunately, neither Warbles nor Brainworms transmit any other disease.

Biting insects (mosquitoes, biting flies) round out the list of possible pests. Rabbits and non-rabbits immediately notice their annoying presence, and they begin to bite any mammal, except Armadillo,

after 1 minute. These pests continue to harass their victims until they leave the habitat (not just the large overground hex where they were encountered). Mosquitoes and Biting Flies inflict 1 HP damage immediately, and an additional 1 HP per 10 minutes of exposure thereafter. In addition, bites by Mosquitoes can transmit the Shakes, and bites by Biting Flies can transmit Rabbit Fever. A 1d6 roll of 1 (separately for each host) indicates that the disease has been transmitted.

Diseases

Rabbits and animals are susceptible to a variety of diseases. Some diseases are transmitted by pests such as ticks, mites, fleas, leeches, mosquitoes, and biting flies. Other illnesses may result from infection after injury or exposure to another sick animal. Most diseases can and must be cured by treatment with herbs. Early symptoms show in the first 24 hours. Later symptoms are apparent during the second day of the illness. After 48 hours, permanent consequences may result.

If exposed to a disease vector, roll a resistance check (1d6 + CON Rating). You must exceed the infectivity of the disease (DV) to avoid infection.

Snuffles

Common name for viral illness of any animal

Contracted by exposure to a sick animal. Infectivity DV=4

- **Early symptoms:** Fever
- **Later symptoms:** Sniffles and sneezing, like a common cold
- **Untreated outcome:** No lasting consequences
- **Cures:** Disappears in 48 hours; symptoms may be treated with Willow Leaves

Brainworm

Disease of Rabbits, Hares, Weasels, Grubbers, and Ramblers, including Jackrabbits, Skunks, Armadillos, Opossums, and Raccoons

Caused by brainworm migrating into the brain. Brainworm eggs may infest after host forages near Raccoons or Skunks, or their lairs. Infectivity DV=8

- **Early symptoms:** Head tilt, usually to the left
- **Later symptoms:** Pregnant females abort litters. No other symptoms, except when trying to run. When attempting to run, the victim instead hops in a circle to the left
- **Untreated outcome:** Symptoms do not resolve without herbal treatment
- **Cures:** Brainworms are driven out by treatment with Lifemelt Garlic or Pestflower prepared at twice normal potency (Advanced preparation). If treated before 48 hours, there are no lasting symptoms. After 48 hours, symptoms persist until treated with Lifemelt Garlic prepared at twice normal potency (requires Advanced preparation)

Rabbit Fever (Tularemia)

Disease of Rabbits, Jackrabbits, and Hares, and Chatters, including Squirrels and Chipmunks

Contracted after harm by Ticks or Biting Flies. Infectivity DV=6

- **Early symptoms:** Fever
- **Later symptoms:** High fever, aphagia (refusal to eat)
- **Untreated outcome:** Victim refuses to eat until cured, so failure to eat can lead to death
- **Cures:** Treatment with Willow Leaves prepared at twice normal potency (Advanced preparation).

Rabies

Disease of all animals, but especially Raccoon and Skunk

Contracted by being bitten by an infected animal, often a Bat, Raccoon, or Skunk. Infectivity DV=6

- **Early symptoms:** Fever, fear of water
- **Later symptoms:** Uncontrolled excitement, uncontrolled aggressiveness; death in 72 hours
- **Untreated outcome:** Symptoms do not resolve without herbal treatment
- **Cures:** Treatment with Carcass Flower prepared at twice normal potency (Advanced preparation)

Alopecia

Disease of Nibblers and Chatters, including Porcupines, Squirrels, and Chipmunks

Contracted after harm by mites. Infectivity DV=6

- **Early symptoms:** Loss of fur or quills on the head
- **Later symptoms:** Loss of all fur or quills
- **Untreated outcome:** No other physical symptoms. Porcupines lose quill-based defenses, and the climbing ability of Squirrels and Chipmunks is reduced to that of a rabbit of the same SPD Rating
- **Cures:** Treatment with Lavender Leaf prepared at twice normal potency (requires Advanced preparation)

Bumblefoot

Disease of all animals

Contracted by infection after injury to the foot. Infectivity DV=5

- **Early symptoms:** Sore foot
- **Later symptoms:** Impaired use of legs, especially in walking. Movement reduced by half; SPD Rating temporarily reduced −2
- **Untreated outcome:** If untreated for 48 hours results in permanent lameness, SPD Rating reduced to 0
- **Cures:** Treatment with Dodgeweed prepared at twice normal potency (Advanced preparation)

Leprosy

Disease of Armadillos

Contracted by exposure to an infected Armadillo that sneezes. Infectivity DV=6

- **Early symptoms:** Open sores on legs or tail
- **Later symptoms:** Loss of peripheral sensation in legs, tail, nose, and muzzle
- **Untreated outcome:** Permanent loss of sense of touch
- **Cures:** Treatment with Carcass Flower prepared at twice normal potency (Advanced preparation).

Myxomatosis (White Blindness)

Disease of Rabbits, Jackrabbits, and Hares

Contracted after harm by Fleas. Infectivity DV=6

- **Early symptoms:** Red eyes
- **Later symptoms:** Blindness
- **Untreated outcome:** Permanent loss of sight in one or both eyes. Roll 1d6 for each eye; blindness results on a roll of 1–3
- **Cures:** Treatment with Blind Iris cures disease and restores blindness if administered within 48 hours of infection

Weather

Weather is notoriously changeable, and sometimes poses a threat to well-being. Summer can bring heat waves, drought, and thunderstorms; Winter may see sub-freezing temperatures, frozen rivers, and snow. In spring and fall, sunny skies can shift to bluster and rain in a matter of minutes. Weather should not generally play a major role in the activities and adventures of bunnies. But on occasion, weather may be the adventure.

It is not necessary to follow a strict calendar in **Bunnies & Burrows**, but in any game, the GM and players should know generally what the season is and what range of weather to expect. Rabbits are active at all times of year, in all kinds of climates. But finding food, tracking enemies, searching for herbs, and even crossing a stream may be trivial in sunny weather, and hazardous in ice and snow. Sudden changes in weather conditions may happen as a consequence of hazards that arise from Wandering Encounters. Special weather conditions also may be specified in particular Adventures. But we encourage the GM to consider how a quest or adventure might change under different weather conditions. On days where the GM feels the urge to throw the players a curveball, or when game play seems to lag, consider a sudden rain squall, or blustery wind, a summer thunderstorm, or winter snowfall.

Rabbits are very adaptable. However, they can be susceptible to weather extremes. Prolonged exposure to high heat and direct sunshine without shade can lead to Heat Stroke. With more than an hour of continuous exposure to extreme heat and direct sun, roll a CON skill check vs. DV=6 for each rabbit. Failure results in dehydration and reduction of SPD, INT, and STR Ratings by half (round down). Recovery requires an hour rest in shade or underground and access to drinking water. Conversely, prolonged exposure to extreme cold can lead to Hypothermia. Under conditions that are cold, wet, and windy, roll a CON skill check vs. DV=6 for each rabbit. Failure results in confusion and reduction of AGI, CON, and MYS Ratings by half (round down), with a 33% chance of hallucinating (1d6 roll of 1 or 2). Recovery requires an hour of rest in a warm shelter or huddled with others.

Encounters

As you step into the clearing, a bird cries out a single whistle-like note. You recognize the alarm call and scan the surroundings. A redwing is perched above you, and in another tree you spy the hawk. It has spotted you, too. As it launches into flight, you prepare to dash for cover ...

As the player characters move about, visiting familiar places and exploring new habitats, they are likely to interact with other rabbits, various other creatures, and features of the environment. We refer to such interactions as Encounters. Some encounters are harmless; other animals may pay no attention as a small group of rabbits pass by. Other animals may be predators, eager to add fresh rabbit to the menu. Encounters also may entail interactions with rabbits, other friendly animals, or environmental features such as natural hazards or manmade traps. Encounters with other animals or habitat features are a constant source of danger, but also of opportunity, because encounters offer the chance to learn, to hone professional skills, and to obtain tasty food or useful items.

Planned Encounters may be specified in a particular Adventure, whether it is a unique scenario drafted by the GM or one of the prepared Adventures provided with the game. Planned Encounters occur when player characters approach a mapped environmental hazard, a non-player character (NPC), or the territory of a resident predator. Wandering Encounters take place randomly, as PCs chance upon other creatures in the course of their travels. The GM should keep track of elapsed game time (in the characters' world, not the players'). If no other encounter is specified in an Adventure, rabbits may expect a Wandering Encounter to occur about once each hour. The GM checks for a possible Wandering Encounter each turn (10 min) with a private 1d6 die roll; a result of 1 indicates that the rabbits have come across some other animal or hazard in the vicinity.

The nature of the encounter is determined by the GM in accordance with time (day or night) and location (habitat type). Consult the appropriate table (below) to determine what kind of animal, trap or natural hazard is encountered. However, the mere presence of another animal does not necessarily mean either that it or the PCs have been spotted. If an encounter occurs involving other animals, proceed to Spotting Rules to determine whether the rabbits or the encountered animal(s) see each other.

Encounter Tables

Some animals may wander widely, but most animals may predictably be found only in certain habitats. Activity patterns also differ, with diurnal animals more active in daytime, and nocturnal creatures coming out after dark. The tables below specify which animals are likely to appear during wandering encounters in each of the ten basic habitats during day or night. In addition, encountered animals may vary in number or age. (Important Note: Areas within one large-scale hex of a farm building should be considered a Farm habitat for determining encounters. Areas that represent farm fields or pastures for livestock, but which are not near a farm building, should be considered Grassland.)

Types of Encounters: If a wandering encounter occurs, the GM must complete several more rolls of dice to determine the kind, number and age of the encountered animal. First find the sum of 3d6 and look up the corresponding row in the appropriate table: Diurnal for daytime encounters and Nocturnal for nighttime. If the encounter occurs just before or after dawn or dusk (an activity pattern referred to as Crepuscular), the GM may choose either the Diurnal or Nocturnal table. (Note: In general, nocturnal predators and hazards are more dangerous.)

Because the type of Wandering Encounter is determined by the sum of 3d6, the likelihood of encountering different animals is not constant. For example, encountering a Small Dog (Terrier) in a suburb is nine times more likely than encountering a Peregrine Falcon. For ease of reference, also note that certain results always are associated with the same general class of encounter: 3d6 rolls of 6, 7, or 11 always result in an encounter with a neutral animal; 13 with a trap or natural hazard; 14 with a party of other rabbits; and 18 with a fabulous creature (a Beast of Folklore and Legend). Encounters with various humans are interspersed among predators and neutral animals. If two alternatives appear in the table (e.g., "Sheep/Chicken") the GM may choose or determine which is encountered at random.

To balance for the strength of a party, determine the Party Level by adding the professional level of all characters in the party. For a party of level 10+, subtract 1 for each "1" rolled in the original 3d6, and add 1 for each "6" rolled. For a party of level 20+, subtract 2 for each "1" rolled in the original 3d6, and add 2 for each "6" rolled. The modified result cannot be less than 3 or more than 18.

> **Example:** A party of player characters includes a 4th-level Fighter, a 3rd-level Herbalist, a 3rd-level Scout, a 2nd-level Maverick, and a 3rd-level Bandit (Raccoon); the Party Level is 4+3+3+2+3 = 15. The original wandering encounter 3d6 roll is 12 (2+4+6), but the effective roll is 2+4+6+1 = 13. Consulting the Encounter Table, the GM determines the party encounters a trap or hazard.

Although the GM should check for wandering encounters regularly (approximately every 10 minutes of game time), the encounters don't have to occur like clockwork. GMs should feel free to delay the onset of an encounter by 5 or 10 minutes until there is a natural lull in the action, or to "pile on" an already tense situation. Use a delay to announce a "funny feeling" by one of the characters of imminent danger, particularly if there is a Seer or Shaman in the party.

Wandering Encounters (Diurnal)

3d6	Suburb	Farm	Orchard	Oak Woodland	Marsh
3	Alligator	Caracara	Black Bear	Deer Wolf	Alligator
4	Peregrine Falcon	Bull, young	Bees	Egyptian Mongoose	Red Wolf
5	Dog, huge (Rottweiler)	Red Fox	Red-tailed Hawk	Big Stoat	Snapping Turtle
6	Girl/Robin	Gardener/Duck	Girl/Garter Snake	Picnicker/Butterfly	Birdwatcher/Goose
7	Townie/Crow	Sheep/Chicken	Pig/Blackbird	Wild Boar/Turkey	Muskrat/Pond Turtle
8	Wasps	Dog, large (Retriever)	Red Fox	Ants	Mink
9	House Cat (Persian)	Red-tailed Hawk	Big Stoat	Harris Hawk	Great Egret
10	Dog, small (Terrier)	Dog, med. (Border Collie)	Farm Cat (Maine Coon)	Goshawk	Harrier
11	Tree Squirrel/Pigeon	Cow/Horse	Pigeon/Frog	Tree Squirrel/Woodpecker	Beaver/Gull
12	Polydactyl Cat (Calico)	Polydactyl Cat (Calico)	Gopher Snake	Copperhead	Great Blue Heron
13	Hazard	Hazard	Hazard	Hazard	Hazard
14	Outskirters	Outskirters	Outskirters	Outskirters	Outskirters
15	Boy	Farmer	Boy	Hunter	Trapper
16	Ferret	Farm Cat (Maine Coon)	Harris Hawk	Rattlesnake	Osprey
17	Coyote	Mink	Rattlesnake	Big Stoat	Bald Eagle
18	Caladrius	Whirling Whimpus	Azeban	Jaculus	Lavellan

3d6	Rocky Hillside	Grassland	Pine Forest	Brushland	Mountain Stream
3	Cougar	Python (Burmese)	Wolverine	Black Bear	Grizzly Bear
4	Golden Eagle	Bison	Deer Wolf	Wasps	Cougar
5	Siberian Polecat	Caracara	Red-tailed Hawk	Gopher Snake	Wolverine
6	Hiker/Quail	Game Warden/Grasshopper	Lumberjack/Beetle	Birdwatcher/Walking Stick	Hiker/Butterfly
7	Marmot/Spiny Lizard	Pronghorn/Vulture	Woodpecker/Skink	Ground Squirrel/Racer	Mtn. Goat/Grouse
8	Rattlesnake	Harrier	Stoat	Stoat	Lynx
9	Gopher Snake	Prairie Falcon	Goshawk	Swainson's Hawk	Pine Marten

3d6	Rocky Hillside	Grassland	Pine Forest	Brushland	Mountain Stream
10	Raven	Coyote	Pine Marten	Harris Hawk	Goshawk
11	Goat/Magpie	Prairie Dog/Killdeer	Chipmunk/Blue Jay	Jackrabbit/Pheasant	Snowshoe Hare/Pika
12	Swainson's Hawk	Swainson's Hawk	Red Fox	Raven	Raven
13	Hazard	Hazard	Hazard	Hazard	Hazard
14	Outskirters	Outskirters	Outskirters	Outskirters	Outskirters
15	Sportsman	Rancher	Trapper	Hunter	Ranger
16	Peregrine Falcon	Ants	Copperhead	Prairie Falcon	Golden Eagle
17	Mongoose (Small Asian)	Sandhill Crane	Lynx	Indian Mongoose (Gray)	Gray Wolf
18	Sidehill Gouger	Hoop Snake	Dingmaul	Tripodero	Skvader

Wandering Encounters (Nocturnal)

3d6	Suburb	Farm	Orchard	Oak Woodland	Marsh
3	Alligator	Great Horned Owl	Black Bear	Egyptian Mongoose	Python (Burmese)
4	Coyote	Mink	Great Horned Owl	Deer Wolf	Alligator
5	Polydactyl Cat (Calico)	Red Fox	Gopher Snake	Big Stoat	Snapping Turtle
6	Townie/Mole	Farmer/Gopher	Fruit Bat/Beetle	Javelina/Pillbug	Muskrat/Snail
7	Raccoon/Cockroach	Deer/Mouse	Brown Bat/Millipede	Packrat/Cockroach	Nutria/Newt
8	Dog, large (Doberman)	Rats (Black)	Red Fox	Barn Cat (Black)	Barn Owl
9	Rats (Black)	Barn Cat (Black)	Barred Owl	Great Horned Owl	Mink
10	Alley Cat (Tabby)	Barn Owl	Feral Cat (Bengal)	Gray Fox	Feral Cat (Bengal)
11	Mouse/Brown Bat	Raccoon/Spider	Opossum/Spider	Raccoon/Beetle	Otter/Crab
12	Great Horned Owl	Dog, large (Doberman)	Big Stoat	Ringtail	Big Stoat
13	Hazard	Hazard	Hazard	Hazard	Hazard
14	Outskirters	Outskirters	Outskirters	Outskirters	Outskirters
15	Meezer Cat (Siamese)	Meezer Cat (Siamese)	Barn Cat (Black)	Rattlesnake	Cottonmouth
16	Ferret	Feral Cat (Bengal)	Rattlesnake	Copperhead	Bobcat
17	Boy	Farmer	Boy	Hunter	Trapper
18	Rat King	Chupacabra	Tree Octopus	Azeban	Lavellan

3d6	Rocky Hillside	Grassland	Pine Forest	Brushland	Mountain Stream
3	Cougar	Python (Burmese)	Wolverine	Black Bear	Grizzly Bear
4	Badger	Ocelot	Gray Wolf	Indian Mongoose (Gray)	Cougar
5	Tarantula	Rattlesnake	Siberian Polecat	Black Widow	Wolverine
6	Packrat/Mouse	Game Warden/Beetle	Hiker/Flying Squirrel	Coati/Beetle	Hiker/Flying Squirrel
7	Kangaroo Rat/Beetle	Box Tortoise/Toad	Armadillo/Millipede	Skunk/Mouse	Moose/Newt
8	Great Horned Owl	Alley Cat (Tabby)	Bobcat	Stoat	Stoat
9	Gopher Snake	Barn Owl	Stoat	Gray Fox	Siberian Polecat
10	Rats (Black)	Badger	Barred Owl	Badger	Barred Owl
11	Mtn. Goat/Spider	Deer/Vole	Porcupine/Frog	Packrat/Toad	Elk/Beaver
12	Feral Cat (Bengal)	Coyote	Red Fox	Bobcat	Mink
13	Hazard	Hazard	Hazard	Hazard	Hazard
14	Outskirters	Outskirters	Outskirters	Outskirters	Outskirters

3d6	Rocky Hillside	Grassland	Pine Forest	Brushland	Mountain Stream
15	Rattlesnake	Ferret	Copperhead	Scorpion	Lynx
16	Ringtail	Gopher Snake	Centipede	Coyote	Gray Wolf
17	Sportsman	Rancher	Trapper	Hunter	Ranger
18	Slide-Rock Bolter	Jackalope	Agropelter	Triffid	Flying Wolf

Number of Animals: After specifying what kind of animal is encountered, the GM rolls 1d6 to determine the number of other animals. A roll of 1–5 indicates a single individual, while 6 indicates two individuals. If the Party Level is 10 or more, add one additional animal to those encountered; if the Party Level is 20 or more, add two animals.

Five exceptions exist to this number rule, as follows:

- Rats are always encountered in groups. Roll 2d6 to determine how many. They are represented on the Battleboard by tokens depicting subgroups of 1–4 rats.
- Predators that can hunt with Teamwork are usually encountered in family groups. For Red Wolf, Deer Wolf, Gray Wolf, and Harris Hawk, roll 1d6: 1 = solitary adult; 2 = two adults; 3 = two adults & one juvenile; 4 = two adults & two juveniles; 5 = three adults & one juvenile; and 6 = three adults & 2 juveniles.
- Human Boys and Girls also are typically encountered in small same-sex groups. Apply the same rule as Teamwork to determine how many boys or girls are encountered, although any attack by Boys or Girls will not be coordinated.
- Among neutral animals, Coatis always are found in groups of 1–6.
- Finally, on the rare chance that Flying Wolves are encountered, roll 2d6 to determine how many. For all these exceptions, add two more animals if the Party Level is 10+, and four more animals if the Party Level is 20+.

Age of Predators: As a final step, determine the age of the predator. Roll 1d6 and add the value of the lowest professional level in the party. For example, in a group where the lowest member is a 2nd-level Scout, add 2 to the die roll, then consult the table to determine the predator's age. Note: If the base HP listed for the predator is greater than 50, double the HP Bonus (e.g., +10 for a Mature Adult Stoat, but +20 for a Mature Adult Cougar). If two predators are encountered, determine their age separately. If more than two are encountered, assume that one is a Mature Adult and all the others are Sub-Adults.

Age of Encountered Animals

1d6 + Level	Age	HP Bonus[1]	Pursuit Tactics Known[2]
2	Juvenile	−5	1
3–5	Sub-Adult	0	3
6–7	Young Adult	+5	4
8–9	Mature Adult	+10	5
10+	Apex Adult	+15	6

1 Double for base HP > 50

2 See **Pursuit** section for details

Outskirters / Encounters with Rabbits: If a 14 is obtained on the wandering encounter 3d6 roll, the player characters encounter a party of Outskirters (i.e., rabbits from a warren other than their own). The GM must determine the number and make-up of the outskirters. Some Adventures describe rival warrens that are friendly, neutral, or hostile to the player characters. If a known warren is nearby (within a few hundred meters), the GM may assume that the outskirters come from that warren and draw up the party accordingly. Some Adventures may even include premade scouting or raiding parties for wandering encounters. If a ready-made party of outskirters is not available, use the following table and instructions to quickly assemble a new party of outskirters. Wandering groups of rabbits are rarely made up of more than five rabbits (a leader and the four rabbits he can count).

Roll 1d6 to determine the number of outskirters encountered. If roll = 1, the encountered rabbit is a Scout or Maverick (the GM may choose or determine randomly). On any other result (2–6), the lead member of the other party (not necessarily the leader) is always a Scout. Professions of other outskirters is determined by rolling 2d6 for each member and consulting the following table.

Wandering Rabbits

2d6	Profession
2	Maverick
3	Seer
4–5	Runner
6–7	Fighter
8	Scout
9	Herbalist
10	Empath
11–12	Storyteller

The Party Level of the outskirters should be adjusted to match that of the player characters. As a rule of thumb, divide the Party Level of the player characters by the number of rabbits in the outskirter group. Round the result down to the nearest integer and assign that value as the level of all the outskirters except the one chosen as leader. Assign the remainder to the leader. The party level of the Outskirters now should equal that of the PCs.

> **Example:** A party of five outskirters is encountered by PCs with a party level of 13. The GM chooses a Fighter as leader of the outskirters. The scout and three other rabbits are assigned level 2 (13 ÷ 5 = 2). Because 4 x 2 = 8, the leader is assigned a level of 5 (13 − 8 = 5).

Traps and other Hazards: If a 13 is obtained on the initial wandering encounter 3d6 roll, a trap or natural hazard is encountered. Roll 1d6 and consult the Traps and Hazards table below to determine the type of hazard. On a result of 1–2, refer to the section on Traps for full descriptions of the ten trap types. On a result of 3–6, refer to the descriptions of various natural and manmade hazards below.

Traps and Hazards (1d6)

Habitat	1	2	3	4	5	6
Suburb	Live Trap	Box Trap	Slip & Fall	Heavy Rain	Broken Glass	Auto-mobile
Farm	Live Trap	Snare	Slip & Fall	Hail-storm	Barrel	Electric Wires
Orchard	Box Trap	Net & Sapling	Slip & Fall	Heavy Rain	Tangle of Wire	Falling Branch
Oak Woodland	Pit	Net & Sapling	Slip & Fall	Fog	Spanish Moss	Sinkhole
Marsh	Live Trap	Foot	Fall in Water	Fog	Quaking Bog	Quicksand
Rocky Hillside	Box Trap	Foot	Slip & Fall	Flash Flood	Tangle of Thorns	Rock Fall
Grassland	Pit	Pit & Stakes	Fall in Water	Dust Storm	Foxtails	Stampede
Pine Forest	Net & Sapling	Crossbow	Slip & Fall	Freezing Rain	Pine Pitch	Falling Tree
Brushland	Snare	Bear-tooth	Slip & Fall	Mudslide	Caltrops	Jumping Cholla
Mountain Stream	Foot	Deadfall	Fall in Water	Blizzard	Lightning	Rock Fall

Natural and Manmade Hazards

During wandering encounters, rabbits may be exposed to dangerous events, sudden weather changes, or simple accidents that pose a threat to their health and well-being. The following is a list of hazards that may occur during Wandering Encounters.

Automobile: In a Suburb habitat, or any other habitat adjacent to a road (known to rabbits as a "man-path"), large shiny creatures with circular legs (i.e., automobiles) are a constant threat. They seem to pay no attention to rabbits, neither chasing nor avoiding them. If rabbits encounter an automobile hazard in the vicinity of a street or road, they are caught by surprise while crossing. Select one rabbit from the party at random. Roll 1d6. On a roll of 1, the rabbit is struck by the automobile and incurs 2d6 HP damage. Treat the injury like a critical hit in combat to determine if the rabbit receives a permanent injury. If no road is present, treat the hazard as a motorcycle, farm vehicle, or off-road vehicle, with the same effect.

Barrel: The rabbits discover a large metal object covered in rust (an abandoned steel barrel). The object appears to contain a strange liquid that is leaking from cracks near the base. Determine one rabbit at random who becomes lightheaded from smelling the fumes, and who reports feeling calm, safe, and euphoric. This rabbit must roll a MYS skill check against DV=7. If it fails the MYS check, the rabbit refuses to leave the side of the object. Any other rabbit that remains nearby also must roll a MYS skill check. Every rabbit near the barrel continues to incur 1 HP damage, but reports feeling great, for each minute it is exposed to the fumes. Licking or drinking the toxic liquid immediately results in 2d6 HP of damage.

Blizzard: In a Mountain Stream habitat, a Blizzard can pop up even at the peak of summer. Without warning, the sky darkens and the wind whips up, and the falling snow causes a whiteout. Visibility is reduced to zero. The GM should randomly place a token (representing the party) on the Mountain Stream Battleboard, but keep the Battleboard hidden from the players. PCs may find shelter by reaching the cave or either exit arrow, but must specify movement by number (1–6, with the GM determining which direction is 1, and the others following clockwise); the rabbits cannot see any features beyond the hex they occupy. They may move only at a very slow pace, advancing one hex every 30 seconds. They may stay together or move separately. Unprotected rabbits without shelter from the blizzard incur 1 HP damage for every minute of exposure. (Note: Wolverines and Bears are unaffected by the blizzard.)

Broken Glass: The rabbits come across a patch of broken glass hidden by grass or dead leaves. It looks like a shiny rock, or "hard water." The sharp glass shards injure one rabbit in the foot, resulting in 2 HP damage. All other rabbits nearby must roll an INT check against DV=7 to avoid stepping on a shard and incurring the same damage.

Caltrops: Caltrops are burrs with sharp, hooked spines arranged in a tetrahedron, such that one sharp spike always points upward. Caltrops often go unnoticed until stepped on. Select one rabbit at random to be the first to step on a caltrop; also determine which foot at random. All unaffected rabbits must roll an INT skill check against DV=5 to avoid stepping on a caltrop. The affected rabbit immediately incurs 2 HP damage and loses use of the injured foot until the caltrop is removed. Rabbits with an embedded caltrop have three choices: (a) they may leave the caltrop alone, incurring 1 HP damage each time the affected foot touches the ground or is used for some other purpose; (b) attempt to groom the caltrop out (or allow another to allogroom it out), requiring an AGI skill check against DV=10, with each failed attempt causing 2 HP damage; or (c) bite out the caltrop, causing Core Damage (1d6 + STR Rating of biter).

Dust Storm: A sudden gust of wind raises a cloud of dust, which spawns a dust devil only a few meters from the rabbits. A private 1d6 die roll by the GM determines whether the dust storm advances to the left of the rabbits (1d6 roll = 1–2), straight toward them (3–4), or to the right (5–6). The rabbits must immediately decide to run (left or right) or stand still. They may not run away (it is moving too fast), but individual rabbits in the party may make independent decisions (i.e., running in different directions). Rabbits overtaken by the dust devil incur 1–3 HP damage from inhaling the dust and are blinded for 10 minutes.

Electric Wires: As the rabbits pass near strange things associated with humans, they come across a shiny metal box partially embedded in the ground. One side is open, and inside they can see glistening, shiny things that look similar to the bright stones used for exchange with Magpies and Traders. If any rabbit attempts to touch or retrieve the bright stones (which actually are electrical devices), it receives a severe electrical shock that results in 1d6 HP damage.

Fall in Water: One of the PCs slips and falls into a stream or pond. The GM should not announce the outcome immediately, but wait until the earliest opportunity when one of the characters comes near a stream bank or the edge of a pond. The fall affects only one member of the party, determined randomly if more than one is near a water source. The victim must swim (see Swimming rules) and is swept a short distance downstream in a stream or river before the earliest chance to crawl out.

Falling Branch: As the rabbits pass under a tree, they hear a rustling or crackling noise overhead. If they run immediately, a heavy branch falls to the ground near where they stood. If they don't run, select one rabbit at random and roll 1d6. On a roll of 1, the rabbit is struck by the falling branch and immediately receives 1d6 HP damage.

Falling Tree: As the rabbits pass through the forest, they hear a rustling or crackling noise nearby. The rabbits can choose to run immediately, stand still, or wait to run. If they run immediately, they must specify a direction (1–6). The GM rolls 1d6 and announces the direction of the falling tree. Any rabbit that is running in the same direction (e.g., running and falling direction are both 6) is struck by heavy branches and receives 3d6 HP damage. If running in a direction within 1 of the falling tree (e.g., the tree falls at 6, the rabbit runs at 1 or 5), it is struck by a smaller branch and receives 1d6 HP damage. Any rabbit that waits to run bolts in a random direction (roll 1d6), but excluding the direction the tree is falling; it is struck by a large branch if its direction of running is within 1 of the falling tree, thus receiving 2d6 HP damage. Any rabbit that stands still rolls 1d6; it receives 4d6 damage on a roll of 1, but no damage on any other result.

Flash Flood: A sudden rain squall at a higher elevation results in a flash flood. The rabbits have two minutes of warning; they first hear a dull roar in the first minute, like the growling of a great beast, which grows louder in the second minute. At the beginning of the third minute they can see the wall of water approaching and have one combat round (6 seconds) before it arrives, sweeping everything below a height of 1 meter downhill. Rabbits exposed to flood waters may attempt to hold onto rocks or vegetation with a STR skill check against a DV=8. Rabbits that are swept away incur 2d6 HP in damage.

Fog: Mists rise from the ground and the rabbits are suddenly surrounded by a dense fog. Visibility is reduced to one meter for 10 minutes. At the end of 10 minutes, the GM rolls 1d6 to determine if the fog dissipates; on a roll of 1–3 the fog persists for another 10 minutes; on a roll of 4–6, it vanishes. Continue die rolls every 10 minutes until the fog disappears.

Foxtails: While crossing a grassy area, the rabbits encounter a patch of foxtails. The sharp barbs on the seeds become entangled in their fur, and every rabbit risks having the foxtails become embedded in the skin. Each rabbit must roll an AGI skill check against DV=6 to remove all foxtails without injury. If the AGI check fails, a foxtail becomes embedded under the skin. Rabbits with embedded foxtails have three choices: (a) they may leave the foxtail alone, incurring 1 HP damage per hour for 24 hours; (b) attempt to groom the foxtail out (or allow another to allogroom it out), requiring an AGI skill check against DV=10, with each failed attempt causing 2 HP damage; or (c) bite out the foxtail, causing Core Damage (1d6 + STR Rating of biter).

Freezing Rain: The clouds gather, the sky turns black, and an icy rain falls for 10 minutes. The rain freezes on contact with the ground. Trees and other vegetation offer little protection. If the rabbits do not find solid shelter in the first few minutes, each rabbit must make a CON skill check against a DV=6. Any rabbit that fails incurs 2 HP damage from violent shivering and near hypothermia. For 30 minutes after the rainstorm ends, all inanimate surfaces remain coated with a slippery layer of ice. Walking without falling requires a SPD skill check against a DV=6 each minute. Moving faster than a walk increases the DV to 8. (Note: The frozen surfaces do not affect movement by Stalking predators, Badgers, Wolverines, or Bears, or Chatters and Snowshoe Hares among neutral animals.)

Hailstorm: The clouds gather, the sky turns black, and a rain of large hailstones pounds the earth for 10 minutes. The hailstones are the size of acorns; trees and vegetation offer little protection. Visibility is reduced to one meter. The GM should randomly place a token on the Farm Battleboard, but keep the Battleboard hidden from the players. PCs may find shelter under the bed of the truck, in the doghouse, or at either exit arrow, but must specify movement by number (1–6, with the GM determining which direction is 1, and the others following clockwise); the rabbits cannot see any features beyond the hex they occupy. They may move only at a slow pace, advancing one hex per combat round (6 seconds). They may stay together or move separately. Unprotected rabbits without shelter from the hailstorm must make a CON skill check every turn against a DV=6 or incur 1 HP damage from being struck by hailstones and violent shivering.

Heavy Rain: The clouds gather, the sky turns black, and a sudden downpour drenches everything in the vicinity for 10 minutes. Visibility is reduced to a few meters. The rain affects all members of the party. Trees and other vegetation offer little protection. If the rabbits do not find solid shelter in the first few minutes, each rabbit must make a CON skill check against a DV=5. Any rabbit that fails incurs 2 HP damage from violent shivering.

Jumping Cholla: As the rabbits pass through a brushy area, they enter a patch of jumping cholla cactus. These cactuses possess sharp, hooked spines on limb segments that separate at the slightest touch, seeming to jump from the ground to become embedded in fur and skin. Each rabbit must roll an AGI skill check against DV=5 to avoid any cholla spines. Failure on the AGI check results in attachment of 1d6 spines. Spines can be removed by grooming, causing 1 HP damage for each spine removed.

Lightning: Among the most dangerous natural hazards is a lightning strike during a thunderstorm. The rabbits have warning as dark clouds gather and the sky turns black. The first lightning strike happens at the rabbits' limits of vision, with a delay before thunder is heard of about one second. The next three lightning strikes land in their vicinity. If the rabbits are still aboveground, roll 1d6 for each strike. On a roll of 1, lightning strikes immediately next to the party, causing the ground to erupt or a tree to explode, sending rocks or splinters flying through the air. The rabbit nearest the strike incurs 1d6 HP damage. If the damage = 6, the rabbit also receives direct electrical shock, rendering it unconscious with no breathing. In this state, it must immediately receive curative treatment by an Empath or herbs to avoid death. However, if a rabbit struck by lightning survives, one Trait (determined at random) is permanently increased by one.

Mudslide: An accumulation of rain in past weeks has destabilized part of a hillside. The rabbits have two minutes of warning.

They first hear a dull roar in the first minute, like the growling of a great beast. In the second minute, the ground trembles slightly. At the beginning of the third minute they can see a wall of mud approaching and have one combat round (6 seconds) before it arrives, sweeping everything below a height of 1 meter downhill. Rabbits exposed to the flowing mud may attempt to hold onto rocks or vegetation with a STR skill check against a DV=10. Rabbits swept away incur 2d6 HP in damage. After the mudslide passes, all features within 50 meters are covered by a thick layer of sticky mud the consistency of honey. Movement is slowed to one-quarter speed (25%) until the rabbits leave the area.

Pine Pitch: Pine trees ooze pitch, which gathers on the bark and sometimes at the base of the tree. As the rabbits pass under a pine tree, one rabbit's foot (determined at random) becomes stuck in a puddle of sticky pitch. The rabbit can pull its foot free with a successful STR skill check against a DV=7. However, failure in the STR check results in the pitch spreading to another body part, which also can become stuck to a feature of the environment, including another rabbit. Until free of the pitch, the rabbit is considered immobilized. Once free of the pitch, all sticky patches can be removed by careful grooming for 10 minutes. (Pine Pitch also can be voluntarily gathered by rabbits as a material for construction. Collecting pitch subjects every rabbit to the same risk as accidentally stepping in pitch.)

Quaking Bog: As they walk through a Marsh habitat, the rabbits suddenly find themselves on ground that trembles underfoot with each step. The Quaking Bog extends for 2 meters in all directions. It does not collapse or present any other danger to rabbits, but cannot be distinguished from Quicksand. If any player character warns of "Quicksand," then all PCs must make a MYS skill check against DV=4 to avoid going into Shock.

Quicksand: As they walk through a Marsh habitat, the rabbits suddenly find themselves on ground that trembles underfoot with each step. The Quicksand extends for 2 meters in all directions. The clues for Quicksand exactly duplicate those for Quaking Bog. However, if any PC attempts to jump or run, or engage in any other vigorous activity, he becomes mired in the sand and begins to sink. A rabbit cannot escape Quicksand by itself; it must be dragged free by another, requiring a STR skill check against a DV=6. Failure in the STR check results in both rabbits becoming mired. A rabbit sinks under the sand after five vigorous actions (including attempts to be rescued). Providing a mired rabbit with a tree branch, vine or rope, or other buoyant object prevents further sinking, but does not facilitate escape.

Rockfall: A rock becomes dislodged high on the hillside, causing a much larger rockfall. The rabbits have two minutes of warning. They hear faint clattering in the first minute, like a crow hammering an acorn, which grows louder, like a gathering storm, in the second minute. At the beginning of the third minute, they can see the rockfall rushing down the slope toward them. The rabbits have one combat round (6 seconds) before it arrives, sweeping over everything exposed below a height of 1 meter. Rabbits unprotected and exposed to falling rocks may attempt to dodge large stones. Each exposed rabbit must dodge 2d6 stones. Each dodge requires a SPD skill check against a DV=6. Each failure results in 1–3 HP damage.

Sinkhole: Oak trees produce tannins, which combine with water to form tannic acid. As the tannic acid leaches into the soil, passing through surface layers of sand and clay, it can slowly dissolve limestone bedrock. Over time, the action of weak acid acting on limestone can create caves and undermine rocky foundations of surface soils. When the foundations fail, the surface collapses into a sinkhole. In this hazard, a small sinkhole formed and was covered by twigs and oak leaves. Treat the sinkhole like a Pit trap, with the same clues and consequences (see Traps). If any rabbit falls into the sinkhole, roll 1d6 to determine the depth (in meters). The rabbit that falls receives 2 HP damage for every meter it falls. It is left to the GM's discretion whether the sinkhole leads to a cave system, or merely forms a natural vertical pit like the shaft of a well. The sinkhole has steep vertical walls and cannot be climbed.

Slip & Fall: One of the simplest and most common hazards is to slip and fall down. Animals do this all the time by stepping on a slippery patch, misjudging a foothold, or making some momentary error in judgment. A slip affects only one member of the party, determined at random. Roll an immediate AGI skill check against a DV=7. If the rabbit fails (i.e., AGI Rating + 1d6 ≤ 7), it incurs a minor injury of 1–3 HP. If the accident happens in a hazardous situation (e.g., negotiating a rocky hillside, crossing a stream, climbing a tree), the GM should adjust the outcome for more severe injury or other consequences of falling.

Spanish Moss: While walking under an oak tree, a large mass of Spanish moss falls from the tree and envelops one of the rabbits of the party. Determine which rabbit is affected at random. There is no cost to escape from the tangle, but the effort takes 10 minutes. Until the entangled rabbit fully escapes, it is considered immobile. Although the Spanish moss is not harmful or useful in itself, it may contain useful herbs, poisonweed, or pests. Roll 1d6. On a roll of 1–2, ticks infest the entangled rabbit and any other rabbit attempting to help. On a roll of 3–4, a search reveals what appears to be a Clear or Cloudy herb, but actually is Poisonweed. On a roll of 5–6, a search reveals a true Clear or Cloudy herb (see Herb Search to determine what kind).

Stampede: While crossing a broad open area, something frightens a herd of cattle and causes a stampede. The rabbits have two minutes of warning: They first hear faint clattering in the first minute, like a crow hammering an acorn, which grows louder, like a gathering storm, in the second minute. At the beginning of the third minute, they can see dust rising from the onrushing herd. The rabbits have one combat round (6 seconds) before the stampede arrives. Rabbits unprotected and exposed to the stampede may attempt to dodge individual cattle. Each exposed rabbit must dodge 1d6 animals. Each dodge requires a SPD skill check against a DV=6. Each failure results in 1–3 HP damage.

Tangle of Thorns: Rabbits are at ease pushing through vegetation and brambles. However, they can be caught unaware by a tangle of thorns such as a blackberry bush. By the time the rabbits discover they are surrounded by thorn vines, they risk entanglement. Each rabbit must roll an INT skill check against DV=5 to escape from the tangle. If the first attempt to escape fails, repeated attempts may be made at a cost of 2 HP damage.

Tangle of Wire: The rabbits come across a strange tangle of shiny vines. By the time they discover they are metal wires, they risk entanglement in the wire. Each rabbit must roll an INT skill check against DV=7 to escape from the wire. If the first attempt to escape fails, repeated attempts may be made at a cost of 2 HP damage.

Mini-Game: Ice Crack!

Ice Crack is one of several mini-games that can be played in the course of a regular Adventure or *B&B* campaign, or separately as a fun way to explore natural hazards that bunnies might face. The central premise is that a party of rabbits comes to the banks of a frozen river that they must cross. Although the specific setting for this mini-game is crossing thin ice in winter, it can easily be generalized to other kinds of natural hazards, such as crossing a steep slope covered with scree and loose rocks, negotiating a bog with "quaking ground" of algal mats and floating islands, traversing the fragile ground of a geyser field, scouting a safe path across a patch of forest still smoldering from a recent fire, or even navigating the tunnels of an abandoned burrow system with loose earth on the ceiling of the runs. A special playing board is provided for *Ice Crack* in the back of this book but the hazard field can vary in size, from a few hexes across to a field extending dozens of hexes.

Upon reaching the bank of the frozen river, the bunnies discover the surface is covered by a layer of thin ice. They must carefully cross from one side to the other without breaking through the ice. *Ice Crack* can be played as a solo challenge or by multiple players racing to reach the opposite bank.

Although the ice looks unbroken, the condition of the ice in each hex may change as a bunny enters the hex. Stacked tokens or 6-sided dice may be used to represent ice cracks of increasing severity (1–6), but we recommend simply copying the Ice Crack board and writing tally marks directly on the sheet.

Each bunny starts on on the same side of the river in a hex that overlaps the riverbank. The entry hex has no cracks. Each turn, a bunny can advance one hex in any direction. Entering a hex determines the bunny's new facing direction. Upon entering a new hex (including the entry hex), roll 1d6. Add the die roll to the number of cracks in the hex where the bunny currently stands, then consult the following table to determine how cracks spread out:

Die Roll + Cracks	Adjacent (A)	Forward (F)	Lateral (L)
1	1	0	0
2	1	1	0
3	1	1	1
4	2	1	1
5	2	2	1
6	2	2	2
7	3	2	2
8	3	3	2
9	3	3	3
10	4	3	3
11	4	4	3
12	4	4	4

Cracks propagate ahead of the hex where the bunny stands, based on its current facing direction. Adjacent hexes are the two hexes immediately in front of the bunny and to one side (the side closer to the opposite shore). A Forward hex is two hexes distant, directly in front of the bunny. A Lateral hex is two hexes distant, but to one side (again, closer to the opposite shore).

Example: A bunny already has advanced one hex from shore and stands in a hex with one crack. A 6 is rolled. 6+1=7, so the table indicates 3 cracks should be added to the Adjacent hexes, 2 cracks to the Forward hex, and 2 cracks to the Lateral hex.

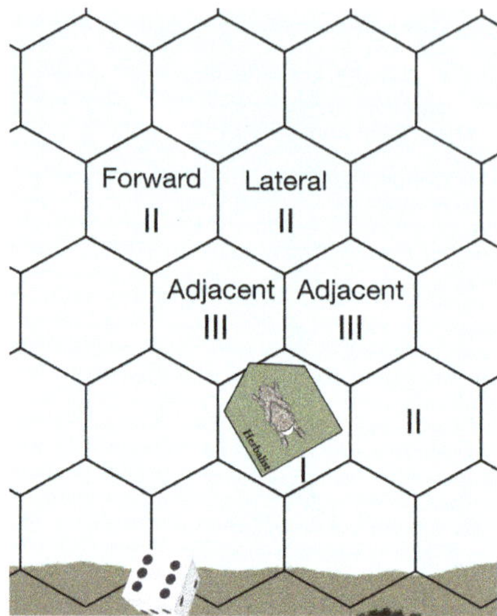

If the Adjacent, Forward, or Lateral hexes already contain cracks, the new cracks are added to the existing total. After the cracks have been indicated, the token may turn any direction and advance one hex. This procedure of advancing, then rolling to determine the spread of cracks, is repeated until the bunny reaches the opposite shore or falls through the ice.

A breakthrough occurs in any hex where the number of cracks exceeds a threshold. A medium threshold is five; in other words, a bunny may occupy a hex with 5 cracks, but may not enter a hex with 6 or more. If there are no hexes remaining that a bunny may enter, it falls through the ice. Likewise, if it is surrounded by breakthrough hexes, with no possible route to either shore, it falls through the ice. However, if the bunny has no possible route to the opposite shore, but can return to the original shore, the game is a draw.

Bunnies may move backward to a hex formerly occupied without penalty. However, the procedure of rolling after movement is repeated, so cracking only worsens in hexes already entered.

Ice Crack also can be played with non-bunny characters. For animals smaller than a rabbit, subtract 1 from the die roll each turn. For animals larger than a rabbit, add 1 to the die roll.

There are several other variant versions of the *Ice Crack* mini-game that may be played:

Multiple animals crossing: If more than one bunny (or other animal) needs to cross, it is better if they do not follow in a line, as the cracks get worse for animals at the end of the line. Instead, they must each find their way across as best they can. Two may cross with the same threshold for breakthrough (6 cracks). If three or four try to cross, increase the breakthrough +1 (7 cracks); if five or more try to cross, increase the breakthrough +2 (8 cracks).

"Capture the Flag" Option: Bunnies start on opposite banks of the river. Each has the goal of reaching the other side first, and preventing the other from crossing. This may be played with two bunnies, or two teams of two bunnies.

Custom Ice Fields: The frozen river depicted on the mini-game board requires a minimum of 12 moves to cross to the opposite bank. But GMs should feel free to explore other configurations with more difficult hazards. Crossing a frozen pond to reach an isolated island, for instance, might require many more moves to reach safety. Safe islands could be provided en route, or certain hexes designated that automatically crack. A time limit might be imposed, limiting the total number of moves before the entire ice field collapses. GMs might keep these options in mind as they devise hazards to customize a game.

Predators

Rabbits are the preferred prey of many predatory animals, including foxes, coyotes, weasels, ferrets, hawks, eagles, and owls. In suburban and farm areas they are chased by dogs and cats. In more exotic settings they may be taken by pythons or alligators or mongooses. And sometimes they fall victim to truly terrifying monsters: mountain lions or wolverines or bears.

In predator-prey relations, physical fighting is preceded by two kinds of tactical interactions. Before an encounter can begin, predators must detect potential prey, and before they can attempt to capture or kill their prey, they must close the distance between them. Encounters thus begin with Spotting, proceed to Pursuit, and may culminate in Combat. These are the three phases of interaction during encounters with predators and, indeed, with any enemies.

The sections that follow provide a comprehensive set of rules governing Spotting and Pursuit. Combat is covered in a separate section. Under Basic Rules, both Spotting and Pursuit can be handled by simple die rolls by the GM and players. Under Extended Rules, Pursuit involves a separate, more-detailed mini-game involving a game board (the Pursuit Board) in conjunction with more detailed movement during the chase and options for tactical maneuvers to evade or thwart pursuers. Rules governing Basic and Extended rules for Spotting and Pursuit are provided below, along with detailed descriptions of tactics available to player characters and the predators that pursue them.

Spotting

The first rule of survival as potential prey is don't be seen. Avoiding detection by an enemy is even more complicated, because different predators possess an array of different perceptual adaptations for sensing prey. A bobcat or hawk may see a rabbit; a fox or owl may hear it. A coyote may track a rabbit by smell. A rattlesnake may detect its unique heat signature in the dark. A mudcat or snapping turtle may not notice a rabbit until it is touched. Regardless of what sensory modality is used, Spotting occurs whenever player characters (PCs) detect a nearby enemy, or the enemy detects the player characters.

When the PCs enter an area with a known predator or NPC, or the GM rolls for a Wandering Encounter, neither the PCs nor the enemies have yet been spotted. The Encounter begins when one side spots the other. There are three logical ways that an Encounter can proceed: the PCs spot the predator; the predator spots the PCs; or both sides spot each other.

The most beneficial situation is, of course, if the PCs spot the predator but are not yet spotted in return. In this case, they can try to hide or sneak away, thereby avoiding Pursuit and Combat.

Basic Rules

Player characters have the opportunity to spot a predator or other enemy whenever they are nearby. "Nearby" is a relative term. In real-world environments, some prey species may spot predators up to a kilometer away in open habitats. But in most circumstances, predators are much, much closer before prey notices them. In B&B, the maximum spotting distance is 100 meters. If the party is moving over a large-scale adventure map (with 50–100 meter hexes), predators are considered nearby if they appear in the same hex or an adjacent hex.

When an enemy is near the player characters, both the enemy and the PCs have an opportunity to spot each other. For player characters, spotting a nearby predator can happen passively, when the party is engaged in other activities, or actively, when players explicitly announce they are looking for danger. Predators also differ in how easily they may be spotted. Refer to the descriptions of different predators, or the predator tables, for the DV associated with spotting that predator.

Passive Spotting

Passive Spotting is determined by a private die roll by the GM. Chasers, Brutes, and Raptors are spotted passively only when the lead rabbit succeeds in an INT BB check (1d6 + INT Base Bonus), which exceeds the predator DV. Scouts use INT Rating for passive spotting. Thus a rabbit with a base score of 14 INT (+1) needs a roll of 4–6 to spot a coyote (DV=4); whereas a 3rd-level Scout with the same base score (INT Rating = 4) would automatically spot a coyote. Stalkers and Cryptics may be spotted passively only by Scouts (INT 3rd level or higher) using the same skill check.

Active Spotting

Rabbits are almost always alert for danger. But players might become wary when characters discover scent clues, tracks, or other spoor, or if local features of the habitat suggest a good place for an ambush. Some rabbits also may have a "sixth sense" of imminent danger (see Seer Rules). Regardless of the reason, Active Spotting occurs only when players announce their character is "scanning" or "posting." Active spotting is not restricted to the lead rabbit or scouts in the party; any player character may attempt to actively spot danger.

The GM may draw a distinction between "Scanning" and "Posting" in resolving a spotting attempt. Scanning (or other descriptors, such as Looking, Searching, Checking, etc.) is useful in spotting the same predators as Passive Spotting. It therefore is effective for any rabbit to spot Chasers, Brutes, or Raptors that were not detected passively by the lead rabbit or Scouts. A Scanning attempt is resolved with an ordinary INT skill check (1d6 + INT Rating) against the predator DV. Posting, in contrast, involves the rabbit standing erect on its hind legs, elevating its head to provide a clearer view of its surroundings. Players who indicate their character is climbing up on a tree stump or rock or some other elevated perch to gain a clearer view should be considered as Posting. When Posting, +2 is added to the INT skill check to spot a predator. As in passive spotting, only 3rd-level Scouts have a chance to actively spot Stalkers or Cryptics by either scanning or posting.

Does the Predator Spot You?

For a predator to spot rabbits or other PCs, it must succeed in a similar INT skill check. The GM rolls 1d6 + predator's INT Rating. If the rabbits are moving normally, this sum must exceed a rabbit DV=6 to spot the rabbits. If the rabbits are moving stealthily, then the predator must exceed 1d6 + INT Rating of the lead rabbit. Searching from the air gives Raptors (and other flying enemies) an advantage in spotting rabbits. Flying Raptors are considered as if Posting; add +2 to their spotting die roll if searching from the air or an elevated perch. All predators automatically decide to hunt if they spot a rabbit. Of course, different predators use different hunting techniques. Refer to the descriptions of specific predators to determine how the predator prefers to hunt.

Safe vs. Close Distance

When any predator other than Cryptics first comes within range of spotting, the GM should conduct a check for passive spotting by the party, as well as determining whether the predator spots the rabbits. If the party detects the predator during this initial spotting check, the predator is considered to be seen at Safe Distance. The predator may spot the rabbits as well, and may attempt to pursue from that distance. But at Safe Distance, the party can attempt to evade the predator altogether (see Basic Pursuit, below).

If neither the predator nor the rabbits are spotted after the first pair of spotting checks, the GM may repeat spotting attempts, at Safe Distance, by both sides. You may assume that predators that have not yet spotted the rabbits continue to wander nearby, remaining within spotting distance of the party for up to five spotting checks. Spotting attempts may be repeated up to five times or until the GM decides that the rabbits are ridiculously lucky and allows the party to pass unscathed.

If a hunting predator spots the rabbits, but the party fails to passively spot the predator at Safe Distance, a second Passive spotting attempt is conducted when the predator has approached to Close Distance. Like the term "nearby," Safe and Close Distance are fuzzy concepts that differ with different predators. Safe Distance for a Hawk may be 100 meters, but for a Cat may be only 20 meters. The GM may assume that Close Distance corresponds to the Initial Pursuit Distance (iPD x 2 meters) listed in the Bestiary. The second spotting check follows the same procedure as the first. If a player declares an Active Spotting attempt after one passive spotting check has been made, the predator always is presumed to be at Close Distance. Note: Cryptics can never be spotted at Safe Distance, even by 3rd-Level Scouts; the only chance to spot Cryptics is at Close Distance.

From Spotting to Combat

When any predator other than Cryptics first comes within range of spotting, the GM should conduct a check for passive spotting by the party, as well as determining whether the predator spots the rabbits. If the predator spots the rabbits, it decides to hunt. This is the beginning of Pursuit.

> An Encounter begins when one or more player characters come in close enough proximity to an enemy (NPC, predator, or human) that they are detected by the enemy. After PCs are spotted, an Encounter consists of two stages: Pursuit and Combat.

Under the basic rules, no formal Pursuit phase of an encounter exists. The player characters and their enemies have the opportunity to spot each other, and spotting can lead directly to combat. When and how combat ensues depends on when the predator is spotted. If the party detects the predator at Safe Distance,

the party generally can avoid pursuit if it chooses. Roll 1d6 for the whole party; on any result other than 1, the party disappears from the predator's view. Note: Some predators such as coyotes and foxes may still attempt to track the rabbits and initiate a second encounter.

If no member of the players' party spots the predator at Safe Distance, then the predator approaches to Close Distance and may initiate Combat. If the party does not detect the predator at Close Distance, the predator begins Combat with surprise. This means that the predator gains a free combat round, with no turn allowed by any target. Rabbits who are not targets also must roll for Shock if surprised. The next round of combat begins with the predator's second attack.

If one of the PCs spots the predator at Close Distance, combat is not avoided. However, neither side gains surprise, and both sides may engage during the first combat round. The predator still strikes first, followed by PCs. The GM may allow players to roll for initiative to determine the order of attacks. Alternatively, the Target is designated as the first among the party to take a combat turn, and the players may determine the sequence of play thereafter.

Pursuit

Extended Rules — Closing the Gap

There are no provisions for actual pursuit of prey by predators in the Basic game; combat begins automatically if enemies approach to Close Distance. Under the Extended rules, predators must close the gap between themselves and their prey before Combat may be initiated. In the real world, most interactions between predators and prey begin and end with the chase. Pursuit, at its core, is about running away. A rabbit engaged in Pursuit ultimately wins if it avoids physical attack. Although there are various tactics that a Fugitive — the one who runs away — can attempt to avoid attack by the Pursuer, nearly all options involve some form of locomotion or maneuver while running. For this reason, the Runner and Herald professions (SPD) are especially relevant to the outcome of Pursuit; Runners have several advantages during this stage of an Encounter.

> **Pursuer:** The predators, rabbits, or other animals that seek to engage in combat with another party (typically the player characters).
>
> **Fugitive:** The rabbits or other characters that seek to avoid combat.

When a predator first appears, either as a planned feature of an Adventure or as a Wandering Encounter, the GM must first determine its approximate position relative to the party. This may be done at the GM's discretion, taking into account terrain features in the overground hex occupied by the party and the surrounding hexes. Alternatively, the predator's position can be determined randomly; roll 1d6 for direction relative to the party. The predator then must approach closely enough to launch its attack.

The GM or players may prefer to skip any approach phase and proceed directly to pursuit. Chasers, Brutes, and Raptors are assumed to begin pursuit at their maximum allowed iPD (as specified by predator type and habitat). Stalkers almost always try to approach more closely. By their nature, Cryptic predators (snakes, alligator, snapping turtle, mink) are rarely seen and pose no threat unless encountered at Close Distance.

The following extended rules for Pursuit apply to encounters with Chasers, Stalkers, Brutes, Raptors, and hostile rabbits. If Cryptic predators are encountered, there is no pursuit; the party is either surprised or not at Close distance; proceed directly to combat.

Approach: During the opening moments of an encounter, after the predator detects the PCs, the predator may remain too far away to begin actual Pursuit. Even at this early phase of the hunt, the predator narrows its focus to improve its odds of success. First, it selects one member among the available prey as the Target. Although the predator may shift its attention to a new target during Pursuit or Combat, it concentrates on the Target during approach, pursuit, and attack. Second, the predator attempts to approach until close enough that a chase is worth attempting. The GM has considerable discretion in how to handle this Approach phase of an encounter. The predator does not begin actual pursuit until it closes to within a preferred distance.

If the party failed to spot the predator at Safe Distance, the predator is presumed to successfully close the gap to the Initial Pursuit Distance (iPD) — the maximum separation between the predator and its target at the beginning of the chase. The preferred distance at which a predator initiates Pursuit varies widely among different species. Refer to the predator tables and descriptions in the Bestiary to find the iPD along with the DV for being spotted for a particular predator. Chasers (dogs, foxes, coyotes) and Raptors (hawks, eagles, owls) generally begin active pursuit farther away and attempt to run down their prey or overtake them with great speed. Brutes (bears, badger) amble at a normal pace in the direction of Fugitives until they approach quite close. Stalkers (cats, weasels) attempt to Stalk to approach more closely without being spotted before beginning a final rush.

Pursuit applies to situations where rabbits, or other PCs, are chased by other rabbits or by predators. Generally the outcome of Pursuit is less certain when rabbits are chased by ground predators such as foxes or cats. When pursued by an aerial predator, rabbits are severely outclassed and the Pursuit stage is very short. Nevertheless, there can be at least one turn of Pursuit even with the swiftest raptor. As an illustration, the average top speed of a rabbit in real life is about 12 meters per second and the top speed of a coyote is 19 meters per second, so a chase is possible despite the coyote's clear speed advantage. But the top speed of a golden eagle is 89 meters per second! The rabbit is never going to outrun the eagle. It can only hope to reach a refuge, evade the eagle by rapid twists and turns, or survive the actual attack.

The iPD also may vary with the presence of cover to conceal the predator's approach, which differs across habitats. The effective iPD when the predator first begins pursuit therefore is the lesser of the iPD value listed in the predator table or the maximum iPD for that habitat. Chasers, Brutes, and Raptors always begin Pursuit at this effective iPD. Stalkers, however, attempt to approach within 5 hexes (on the Pursuit Board) before beginning the chase.

Because predators (other than humans) do not have missile weapons, they must come within attack distance (1 meter) to engage in physical combat. The distance separating a fugitive and pursuer is termed the Pursuit Distance. Pursuit begins when the predator approaches within the iPD dictated by the kind of predator and the habitat, or for Stalkers, when either it approaches within 5 hexes or is spotted by a rabbit. Pursuit ends when the predator (or other pursuer) ends its movement in the same hex as a Target, or when all Fugitives escape.

Setting Up the Pursuit

Pursuit is played out on the **Pursuit Board**. The board is not intended to provide a detailed map of any particular habitat. Rather, it represents the distance separating Fugitives from their Pursuer(s) during the chase. The board is designed to be printed on a tabloid-sized page (11x17") or two connected standard pages (8.5x11"). The green hexes on the left side of the board represent safe refuge; any Fugitives that reach a green hex are considered to have escaped. Small green bush symbols indicate the presence of obstacles that may impede a fleeing rabbit or its pursuer, or offer a temporary refuge. Pursuers and Fugitives can move through any open hex (yellow), including hexes that contain obstacles, but only Fugitives may enter refuge hexes (green). Fugitives may not leave the Pursuit Board

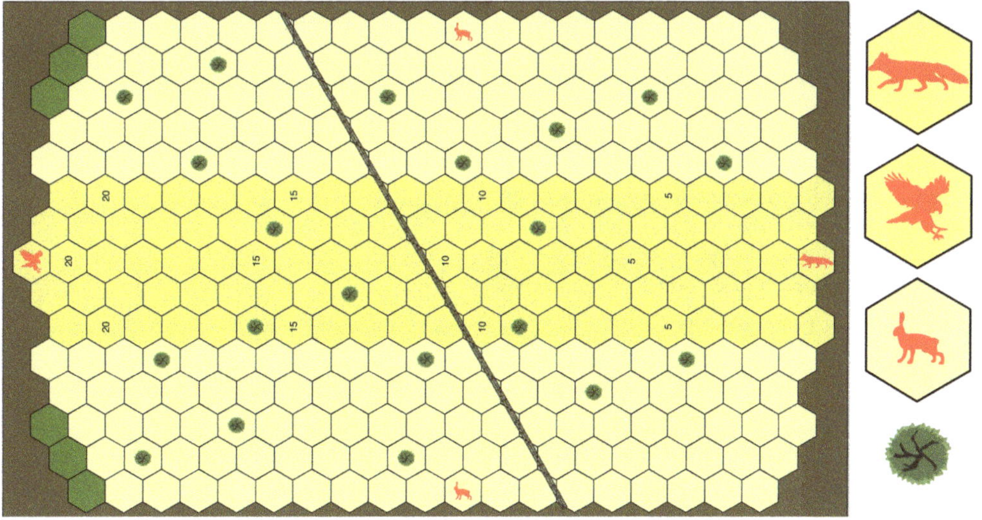

along any brown border, except as the result of a Last Ditch special tactic.

The red icons represent the starting position(s) of the Pursuer(s), whether predators or hostile rabbits. Initial positions of Fugitives (the rabbits and their allies being chased) are determined based on the effective pursuit distance that separates them from their Pursuers at the outset of the encounter. Follow these steps to set up the Pursuit Board:

1. Place Tokens for Pursuer(s): If the Pursuer is a predator (Chaser, Brute, or Raptor), place the appropriate token on the hex containing the red fox icon on right edge of the Pursuit Board. The token should be oriented to face toward the middle of the board. If additional Pursuers are present, they may be stacked together in the same red fox hex. If the predator is a Stalker, place the token face down on any of three hexes with a red fox or rabbit icon, then place two other dummy tokens face down on the other two red icons. (If there are two Stalkers, then use only one dummy token.) If any kind of predator is capable of Teamwork, one token should be placed face up in the hex with the red fox icon and other tokens, at the discretion of the GM, may be placed face down in either or both of the hexes containing a red rabbit icon. The GM also may place a dummy token face down in either of the red rabbit hexes as a ruse. Dummy tokens may be placed even if only one individual is present, if the predator is capable of Teamwork. (The rabbits can never be sure.) After the rabbit's first move, pursuer tokens may, but need not, be flipped face up, facing any direction, and moved separately. However, tokens must be face up to move; dummy tokens must remain in place if remaining face down. If the predator is a Cryptic, there is no pursuit; proceed directly to Combat.

2. Place Tokens for Hostile Rabbits: If the Pursuers are a group of hostile rabbits, place at least one pursuer token on the hex containing the red fox icon. Optionally, the hostile group may be split up; stack other tokens on either of the two red rabbit icons in any combination. Unlike predators acting as a Team, all hostile rabbit tokens should be placed face up. There should be one token for each member of the pursuing group.

3. Place Tokens for Obstacles: There are 20 hexes on the pursuit board that contain small green bush symbols, which indicate the locations of Obstacles. Obstacles may be Minor, consisting of low shrubs, or Major, such as rock piles, dense thickets, or abandoned man-things (rusted automobile or barrel). All habitats have obstacles, but some habitats have more Major obstacles than others. The GM should take a number of obstacle tokens (representing Major obstacles) and blank tokens (Minor obstacles) as specified in the following table. After the tokens are placed face down and thoroughly mixed by the GM, the players may place them all on obstacle hexes on the pursuit board. The identity of the token (Major or Minor) should remain hidden until the first round of Pursuit, after the Fugitive tokens have been placed, when all obstacle tokens are flipped face up to reveal the location of actual Major obstacles.

Habitat	Major	Minor
Grassland	4	16
Marsh	4	16
Farm	5	15
Suburb	5	15
Brushland	6	14
Rocky Hillside	6	14
Mountain Stream	7	13
Orchard	7	13
Oak Woodland	8	12
Pine Forest	8	12

4. Identify a Target: Predators do not attack a whole group of prey; they single out one individual to pursue and attack. At the outset of an Encounter, the Pursuer must identify a particular Fugitive as the Target. For predators with an INT of 3 or less, the Target is selected at random. For predators with INT of 4, the GM must select the rabbit with the lowest CON Rating as the Target. For predators with INT of 5 or more, the GM may select a Target based on any criterion, assuming the predator can accurately judge the rabbits' traits at a distance.

Targets may change during the course of the pursuit, either by an active decision of the Pursuer, or as a consequence of tactics that force the Pursuer to switch targets. If more than one Pursuer is present, all Pursuers must chase the same Target; if one Pursuer must switch Targets, then all Pursuers shift to the same new Target. When the Pursuer(s) are forced to shift to a new Target and no other Targets are available, Pursuit ends and the Encounter is over.

Optional: Players may find it convenient to adopt a small object or figurine such as a rabbit miniature to indicate which player controls the Target. When the target shifts to a new fugitive, transfer the Target idol to the new player.

5. Determine the initial Pursuit Distance: The distance separating the Fugitives from the Pursuer is the pursuit distance. The initial pursuit distance (iPD) may vary with the presence of cover to conceal the predator's approach, which differs across habitats. Habitat effects on maximum iPD are shown in the table below. Each predator also has an iPD value along with a DV for being spotted. The iPD when the predator first begins pursuit is the lesser of the iPD value listed in the predator table or the maximum iPD for that habitat. Note that PD refers to hexes on the Pursuit Board, not to a fixed distance on large-scale maps, and movement allowances of fugitives and pursuers refer to relative, not absolute, speed. Nevertheless, players may think of each unit of PD as about 5 meters in distance.

Maximum iPD

Habitat	Ground	Aerial
Grassland	14	14
Marsh	14	14
Farm	12	14
Suburb	12	14
Rocky Hillside	12	14
Orchard	9	11
Oak Woodland	9	11
Pine Forest	9	11
Mountain Stream	6	8
Brushland	6	8

6. Place Tokens for Fugitives: A token for the Target is placed on the board, facing away from the red fox hex. The Target token is placed on any hex at a distance from the Pursuer (i.e., the red fox hex) equal to the initial Pursuit Distance (e.g., the Target is placed 10 hexes away from the Pursuer if the iPD is 10.) However, the token must be placed within 2 hexes of the midline of the board (demarcated by darker shading on the pursuit board). Numbers on the Pursuit Board are provided as convenient markers of iPD. Tokens for all other Fugitives in the party initially are stacked together with the Target, with the Target token visible on top. In subsequent pursuit turns, they may move separately. When all Fugitive tokens have been placed, turn over the Obstacle tokens. Only tokens representing Major obstacles need remain; blank tokens may be removed at this time.

Tips for Fugitives

Pursuit is played in a series of rounds using a Pursuit Board. Movement is limited by the fugitive or pursuer's movement allowance and by restrictions on turning. Maneuvering is described more fully below, but it is useful for players to keep a few helpful tips in mind:

1. Danger Zone: All of the hexes shown in red in the diagram (right) can be reached by a Fox (movement allowance = 6) in one turn of normal movement. If the Fox begins his turn with a tactical Cut to the right, then he also can reach any of the hexes in orange. Stay out of the Danger Zone!

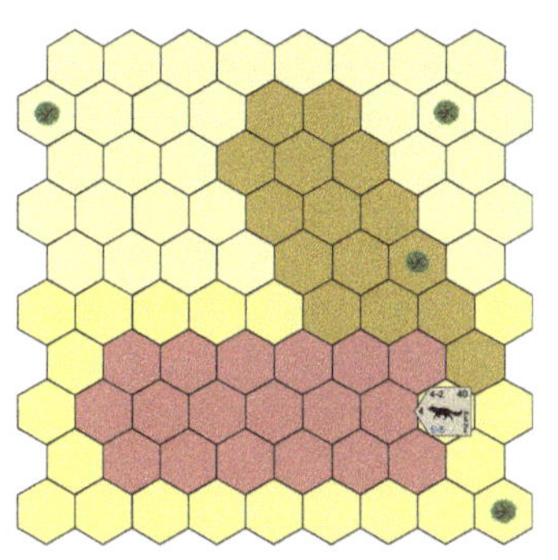

2. Hot on your Heels: If a ground predator is chasing you from directly behind and is within 2 hexes, it will be very difficult for you to escape. Don't let him get Hot on your Heels!

3. Box him In: Tactical maneuvers can be a great help to Fugitives, but Pursuers have tactical skills, too. Force the Pursuer to use up his tactical allotment, or block him from using a tactic in a critical pursuit round. Limit his options and Box him In!

4. Keep your Friends Close: Fugitives are free to run in any direction during pursuit. Scattering in different directions can be an effective strategy for preventing a predator from catching you. But remember, if the Pursuit ultimately ends in combat, the Target must face the predator, and only those other PCs represented by tokens within 2 hexes of the Target may join in. If you want to fight as a team, Keep your Friends Close!

The Chase is On!

Pursuit is played in a series of rounds using a Pursuit Board. In each pursuit round, the Target moves first, then the other Fugitives (in any order decided by the players), then the Pursuers. Movement is restricted to a few basic rules:

- A token can run (change position on the pursuit board) up to its movement allowance each round.
- Most pursuers and non-rabbit characters may pivot once, changing their movement direction by one hexside (60 degrees) while running. Rabbits and a few other animals can pivot through two hexsides (120 degrees).

- Pivoting must occur immediately before the last hex entered, with no further movement beyond that hex.
- If the token halts and remains in the same hex for the entire round without running, it can rotate (change facing direction) one hexside (two for rabbits).
- In addition to normal running and pivoting, the player may elect to perform a tactical maneuver (basic or special). The tactic must be known to the character. Only one tactic can be used by a character during the movement phase of the same round (except Runners using the Combo tactic), although some tactics can be used as an additional, immediate Reaction to the Pursuer. Each character also has a limit (based on SPD Rating) on the number of tactics that may be used in the same Pursuit.
- If any token ends movement in the same hex with its enemy, combat ensues. If a fugitive token enters a green hex, representing safe refuge, then it escapes.

Each player must complete their full movement, including pivots and tactical maneuvers, during their turn. (Exception: Certain pursuit tactics may be applied as Reactions after predator movement.) Full descriptions of options during pursuit are provided below.

1. Obstacles: At the start of the first round of Pursuit, flip all obstacle tokens face up, revealing the location of all Minor and Major obstacles.

2. Movement: During normal movement on the Pursuit Board, a Fugitive or ground predator may Run, Pivot, or Rotate. An aerial predator may Fly, Bank, or Hover. Other patterns of movement also may be allowed under Tactical Maneuvers.

3. Running: The token is advanced through a number of hexes up to its maximum movement allowance. Running advances the token in a straight line, in the facing direction; changes of direction while running require Pivoting. Running is voluntary; the token can move less than its allowance, or not at all.

4. Flying: The token is advanced in a straight line through a number of hexes up to its maximum movement allowance. Like running, flying is voluntary; the token can move less than its allowance. However, Raptors in flight must always move at least one hex, unless using the Hover tactic.

5. Movement allowance: Rabbits have a basic movement allowance of 2 points, plus Base Bonus. Refer to Predator Tables for the movement allowance of different predators. Note that, in general, ground predators have a movement allowance of 3-6, and raptors 8-17. Each empty hex costs one point of movement to enter. Hexes containing obstacles may hinder movement; see below. Note that during normal movement, there is no restriction on a token moving into or out of a hex occupied by another token, including both Fugitives and Pursuers (with the caveat that ending movement in a hex with a Pursuer triggers combat.)

6. Pivoting: During each round of normal pursuit, the token may change direction once. A change of direction while running is a Pivot. The facing direction of the token may pivot one hexside (60 degrees), either left or right. Pivoting is free; no movement points are expended to pivot. However, if the token is moved any distance that turn, then pivoting must occur exactly one hex before the end of movement. That is, pivoting is executed immediately before the last hex entered during normal movement, and the token must be advanced into the last hex. Thus, a coyote with a movement allowance of 9 has many pivoting options: (a) move forward 8 hexes, pivot, then move one last hex; (b) move forward 1–7 hexes, pivot, then enter just one more hex; or (c) pivot before moving, then move just one hex. Note that pivoting before the full movement allowance results in a slowing of pursuit speed; rabbits that carefully follow twisty paths may succeed in escaping from a much faster predator.

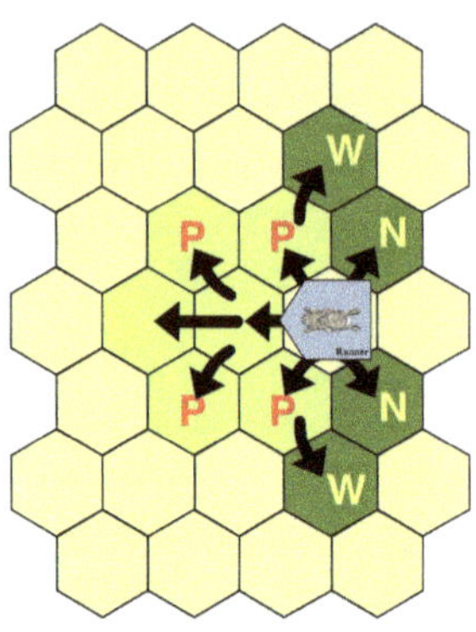

As described above, most animals have a pivoting allotment of one hexside (60 degrees) during normal movement. However, rabbits, jackrabbits, martens, ringtails, and minks can pivot through two hexsides (120 degrees) in the same round. Pivots of two hexsides can be Narrow or Wide. A Narrow pivot involves shifting two hexsides all at once, then advancing one hex. A Wide pivot entails two sequential shifts of one hexside, where the token alters course by one hexside, advances one hex, then alters course in the same direction by one hexside before entering a second hex. Although a Wide pivot looks like two independent changes of direction, the two shifts must occur consecutively, entering adjacent hexes, and thus constitute a single wide curve.

Examples of Pivoting by a rabbit are shown in the diagram at left. All green hexes can be reached in one movement turn by normal Pivoting. Light green hexes marked with "P" can be reached with an ordinary Pivot of one hexside. Dark green hexes require a two-hexside Pivot, with "N" marking Narrow Pivots, and "W" marking Wide Pivots. Note that, like a normal pivot, only one more hex may be entered after completion of a narrow or wide pivot (i.e., after the second hexside).

7. Banking: A Raptor in flight can change direction by Banking, which follows the same rules as Pivoting. Most Raptors can Bank only one hexside, ending movement in the next hex after the Bank. Harriers, Goshawks and Owls, however, can Bank through two hexsides (120 degrees), following the same restrictions as Narrow and Wide Pivots for rabbits.

8. Rotating: If the player elects not to move the token that turn, the facing direction of the token may be rotated one hexside left or right without advancing into a new hex. Ground predators also can Rotate one hexside, but Raptors cannot (see Wheel and Hover tactics). As in Pivoting, rabbits, jackrabbits, martens, ringtails, and minks can rotate through two hexsides if they remain in the same hex.

9. Effect of Obstacles: Each hex containing an obstacle may hinder movement or restrict actions. For player characters and pursuers on the ground: If the hex contains a Minor obstacle, roll 1d6 upon entry; on a result that exceeds the movement allowance for that token, the Minor obstacle does not interfere with movement and the token may proceed up to its full movement allowance. However, a Major obstacle, or a Minor obstacle on a 1d6 roll that equals or is less than the movement allowance, costs all remaining points to enter, which represents the cost of slowing to negotiate bushes, logs, or boulders. No further movement, pivoting, or tactical maneuvers are permitted that round.

Obstacles do not hinder flight for raptors pursuing in the air. Raptors can pass over Minor and Major obstacles without restriction. However, they may not attack a Fugitive in a Major obstacle hex. A Major obstacle is considered to provide complete protection from aerial attack. With the exception of Harris Hawks and Caracaras, which can land and flush out prey on the ground, Raptors must wait for Fugitives to leave a Major obstacle hex before resuming pursuit. Minor obstacles also may protect a Fugitive from aerial attack. Roll 1d6; on a result of 1–3 the raptor may attack, initiating Combat. On a result of 4–6, however, the Minor obstacle provides sufficient cover that the attack is blocked; the raptor must continue in a straight path one hex beyond the obstacle.

When faced with a Fugitive that has taken refuge in a Major obstacle, a Raptor attempts to switch to a new Target (at the cost of one Tactic use). If no alternative targets are available, or if the Raptor has no more tactics to use, it flies to the edge of the board and seemingly disappears. All Fugitives hiding in obstacles must emerge when no Pursuers remain on the board. However, Pursuit has not ended in this special case. Rather, the raptor may re-enter the board at any red icon, including the Hawk icon, on any subsequent turn. The choice of when and where the raptor reappears and its initial facing direction are left up to the GM. This cycle of flying away and suddenly re-emerging continues until Pursuit ends by normal means (i.e., by escape to a green hex or combat).

10. Effect of Fence: The figure that runs diagonally across the board represents a wooden fence. The fence presents no obstacle to movement by rabbits or smaller animals. But animals on the ground larger than a rabbit must expend an extra 1 point of movement to cross a fence. Raptors and other flying animals can traverse a fence line without restriction. However, aerial predators may not attack a Target immediately on the opposite side of the fence. Rather, they must cross the fence into an open hex, then are free to attack a Target in another hex.

Except for Harris Hawks and Caracaras, Raptors may not land on the ground except when attacking a Fugitive. However, any Raptor is free to perch on the fence at the end of their movement, costing one movement point to move from a hex adjacent to the fence to the perch (shown in A). Perching on the fence ends all movement for that turn. The perch is assumed to be located at the point joining three hexes on the fence line (red circle). In the Raptor's next turn, it can launch into any of the three adjoining hexes at a cost of one point, facing any direction away from or parallel to the fence (B), and continue moving from that point. In this way, a perching Raptor can attack either side of the fence in its next turn.

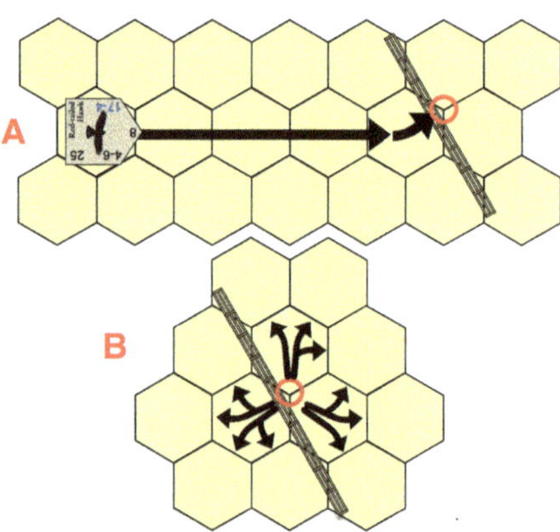

11. Tactical Maneuvers: Rabbits may employ a variety of behavioral tactics to evade a Pursuer. Different pursuit tactics may be executed at the beginning, middle, or end of normal movement. A few tactics enable a Reaction by the Fugitive at the end of the Pursuer's movement; a Reaction counts as a tactical use, but does not count against the Fugitive's next movement turn. The effects and restrictions for each tactic are listed below.

In general, the number of different tactical maneuvers available to rabbits depends on their Trait Ratings. Basic tactics involve sudden changes of speed or direction; rabbits learn the seven Basic tactics as they gain experience in INT or MYS. Rabbits and non-rabbit characters also acquire a unique Special tactic in their declared profession.

During Pursuit, a player may attempt any Basic or Special tactic known to that character. Employing a maneuver, whether during the normal movement phase or as a Reaction to the pursuer, counts as one tactical use. The number of tactical uses allowed during any single pursuit is equal to the character's SPD Rating. A tactical maneuver applies only to the token for that character, not all the fugitives in the same stack (although some tactics act on the pursuer, and therefore may assist all fugitives).

12. Safety: The green hexes along the left edge of the pursuit board represent safe refuges where a Pursuer may not follow. If a Fugitive reaches one of the green hexes during its movement turn, it has escaped and the predator may not pursue it further. Remove the token for that Fugitive from the board; it may not re-enter the board during this pursuit. The Pursuer may never enter a green hex, even to block the movement of a Fugitive. If the Fugitive was the Target of the Pursuer, the Pursuer must switch to a new Target. If no other Fugitives are available as Targets, then the Pursuit ends.

13. Forbidden Zone: The edge (shaded brown) of the pursuit board represents real or perceived barriers to escape. (You may consider brown areas to represent steep cliffs, riverbanks, cyclone fences, impenetrable hedges, or other physical barriers.) If a Token is moved to a hex on the edge of the Board, other than a green hex, the token must change direction and continue movement into available hexes on the Board. It does not escape. Note that one Basic Tactic — Last Ditch — may be attempted only if the token occupies a hex on the edge of the board.

14. Ending Pursuit: If a round of Pursuit ends with a Pursuer occupying the same hex as a Fugitive, Pursuit ends and Combat ensues. This usually occurs when the Pursuer ends movement in a Fugitive's hex, and the Fugitive has no Reaction tactic. It also can occur if a Fugitive ends movement on a hex containing a Pursuer, and the Pursuer does not move in the same Pursuit round. Combat is resolved on a Battleboard appropriate for a given habitat. Combat involves only the Fugitives and Pursuers that occupy the same hex. During the second Combat round, any Fugitives or Pursuers within 2 hexes of the original combat hex at the end of Pursuit may enter the Battleboard at the exit arrows. Any other Fugitives or Pursuers may not participate in this combat.

Players may begin to anticipate how a chase will end and plan accordingly from the outset of Pursuit. However, restrictions on which characters may participate in Combat means that players should start to strategize well before Pursuit ends. Should they stick together to make a stronger fighting unit? Or should they split up, each bunny more likely to escape by itself, but less likely to put up a good fight?

Pursuit Tactics for Rabbits and Non-Rabbit Fugitives

Tactics: Surviving as a Fugitive

Fugitives and Pursuers may employ different tactical maneuvers during a chase that may give themselves an advantage, or create a disadvantage for their adversary. The availability and use of pursuit tactics depends on the Fugitive's Trait Ratings and Profession. Certain tactics also may require the Fugitive to occupy a hex containing an obstacle, or that the predator be closer or farther than a specified distance.

There are two categories of pursuit tactics available to Fugitives: Basic and Special. Basic fugitive tactics may be learned by any rabbit or non-rabbit character. Special Tactics unique to each profession are available only to PCs that have reached Level 3 in their primary Trait.

A pursuit tactic must be known before it can be used, and pursuit knowledge may come with experience or intuition. Rabbits and Non-Rabbit Characters may learn one Basic tactic for every point of INT or MYS Rating, whichever is higher. Characters gain a Special tactic when they reach Level 3 in their declared profession. In the following descriptions of tactics, additional restrictions on who may learn a tactic are listed in parentheses. Some tactics may be restricted to certain species, usually because they depend on anatomy unique to that species. For instance, only rabbits and hares (including jackrabbits) can use Flash Tail, which depends on the Fugitive having a fluffy white tail. If no species codes are listed, then the tactic may be used by any playable animal species.

Unless otherwise indicated, a tactical maneuver may be executed at any time during the player's turn, at the beginning, in the middle, or at the end of normal movement. During any given pursuit, tactics may be used a number of times equal to the character's SPD Rating, up to a maximum of six. (A convenient way to keep track is for each player to place a six-sided die in front of them with the number of pips showing the number of tactical uses remaining. Each time a tactic is employed, turn the die to display one fewer pip. When the last allowed tactic is used, remove the die.)

Use of a pursuit tactic is always voluntary; in most rounds, it is likely that no tactic will be employed. A Fugitive may use a tactic only once during their movement turn. However, a Target also may use certain tactics as Reactions during the Pursuer's turn. The same tactic may be used any number of times by the same Fugitive, up to the maximum number of uses allowed. For example, a rabbit with a SPD Rating of 3 is permitted to use a tactic 3 times during pursuit. The rabbit may perform a Speed Burst all 3 times, or a Speed Burst once, a Jink once, and a Zig-Zag once, and so on. At the end of that pursuit, the number of permitted uses regenerates for the next pursuit.

Basic Fugitive Tactics

Basic fugitive tactics involve sudden changes in speed or direction while running. Successful execution of a Basic tactic usually results in a change of the token's position or facing direction on the pursuit board. Rabbits and non-rabbit characters may learn one new Basic tactic for each point of INT or MYS Rating (whichever is higher). Tactics may be limited to Targets or spatial relation to the Pursuer. "Before" the Pursuer, for example, means any position within 3 hexes that the Pursuer could reach in one turn of normal movement.

1. Speed Burst (Target or Non-Target): An increase in speed while running. The token is advanced one additional hex in the facing direction. The extra hex may be added at the beginning or end of movement, thereby allowing the Fugitive to advance two hexes after a Pivot. Speed Burst also may be played as a Reaction by a Target at the end of the Pursuer's movement. For instance, if the Pursuer lands in the Target's hex, the Target can React with a Speed Burst, advancing to the next hex. A Speed Burst is always successful during normal movement. To succeed as a Reaction, the Fugitive must roll 1d6 + SPD Rating greater than the Pursuer's 1d6 + INT Rating.

2. Zig-Zag (Target only; PD<4): Running in an erratic pattern rather than straight ahead. If a Pursuer is within 3 hexes at the time the Zig-Zag is announced (any time before or during movement), the Pursuer's movement allowance is reduced to only 2 hexes in its next turn.

3. Dust-Up (Any Fugitive before the Pursuer): The Fugitive kicks dust into the air as it runs, momentarily distracting the Pursuer. This can be performed if the Fugitive occupies a hex that the Pursuer could move to during normal movement in the next turn. The Pursuer's lapse of attention prevents it from using any tactical maneuver during its next turn.

4. Jink (Target Only; PD<4): High-speed erratic movement, designed to throw off pursuit. If a Pursuer is within 3 hexes when the Jink occurs, the Pursuer's token is immediately rotated randomly one hexside (60 degrees) to left or right (roll 1d6; turn right on an odd result, left on even). The Jink does not affect normal movement or pivoting by the Fugitive. For example, if the rabbit executes a Jink at the beginning of its movement, causing the Pursuer to alter direction to the left, the rabbit may pivot right during normal movement.

5. Pass Between (Non-Target): If a non-target Fugitive passes between a Pursuer and its Target, the Pursuer might be tricked into switching to the interloper as its new Target. Roll 1d6: on a roll of 1–3, the Pursuer is not distracted and sticks with its original Target; on 4–6, the Pursuer must switch to the new Target, at the cost of one tactical use.

6. Twist (Target or Non-Target): If a Fugitive has a movement allowance of 3 or more, a Twist allows it to turn one additional hexside (60 degrees) during normal movement. The Twist must occur before movement is initiated, as if the token started with a different facing direction, allowing the Fugitive to advance up to its full movement allowance. A twist does not count as a regular pivot, but does count as one tactical use.

7. Freeze (Target or Non-Target; PD<6): Results in the Fugitive coming to a sudden halt. Any pursuing Raptor within 5 hexes misjudge the Fugitive and overfly the Fugitive by one hex in its next pursuit turn. The Raptor can continue normal movement during its turn from that point. May be played as a Reaction by a Target if the Raptor ends movement in the Target's hex, resulting in the Raptor advancing one additional hex beyond the Target. A Freeze during normal movement is always successful. To succeed as a Reaction, the Fugitive must roll 1d6 + INT Rating greater than the Pursuer's 1d6 + INT Rating.

8. Last Ditch (SPD or INT or CON, Target only): Just as every action movie involves a scene where the fugitives jump from a cliff (often into a river), swing across an impossible chasm, run over a rickety bridge, or race in front of a hurtling train, Last Ditch is an attempt to throw off a Pursuer by doing something daring, and potentially stupid. Last Ditch may be attempted only if the token is in a hex on the edge of the pursuit board. This tactic is played by just one player, but the consequences apply to all Fugitives within 1 hex. Last Ditch succeeds on a skill check based on SPD, INT, or CON Rating, DV=6. The Trait used in the skill check must be determined randomly after the Last Ditch attempt is announced; roll 1d6: a result of

1–2=SPD; 3–4=INT; 5–6=CON. If the attempt succeeds, all Fugitive tokens affected by Last Ditch are removed from the pursuit board; the Pursuer must switch to a new Target, if any are available. If the attempt fails, then any Fugitive affected by the Last Ditch is barred from using any Reaction that round, and the nearest Pursuer may be advanced into the hex with the Fugitives to initiate Combat.

Special Tactics available to Rabbits

Available only to declared professions, the effects of Special Tactics may vary with the Trait Level of the rabbit.

1. Vault (Fighter; Target or Non-target): A maneuver where the Fighter leaps over an obstacle and continues running in the same direction. A vaulting Fighter lands on the opposite side of the obstacle facing in the same direction. Although a Vault results in advancing 2 hexes, the maneuver costs only one movement point. All Fighters can vault over Minor obstacles; at STR Level 3, a Fighter also can vault over a Major obstacle.

2. Combo (Runner, Target or Non-Target): As an expert in running, the Runner can combine any two basic tactics into one new maneuver. For example, the Runner may Speed Burst with Dust Up, with the effect of advancing an extra hex while blocking the Pursuer from using a tactical maneuver. The effects of the two tactics are combined, but the Combo maneuver counts only as one tactical use.

3. Flash Tail (Scout; Target only): A maneuver where the bright white underside of the tail is flashed while a rabbit is running, making it very conspicuous, then suddenly hidden, causing the rabbit to momentarily disappear to the Pursuer. Flash Tail must be used when the Scout enters an obstacle hex. When faced with a rabbit that Flashes Tail, a Pursuer must either (a) voluntarily switch to a new Target, or (b) remain in the same hex for the next full round to reacquire the original Target. Switching to a new Target counts as the use of a pursuit tactic.

4. Tumble (Maverick; Target or Non-Target): A maneuver where the Fugitive tumbles on the ground and dashes in a new direction. The token may change direction once to face in any direction (i.e., any number of hex sides), but the Tumble must be performed before any other movement. The Fugitive may move up to its full movement allow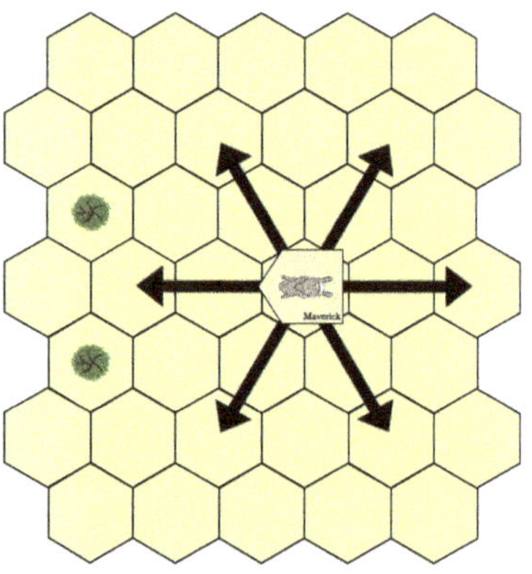ance after the Tumble, including a normal change of direction. Example (right): Movement after a Tumble.

5. Second Wind (Empath; Target or Non-Target): The Empath can summon extra energy to surge ahead 2 hexes beyond the normal movement allowance, at the cost of one HP. Second Wind also can be transferred to any other Fugitive that is running in the same hex or an adjacent hex; the other Fugitive runs forward 2 hexes as the Empath takes 1 HP damage. Second Wind may be applied at the beginning or end of normal movement, so it can extend the number of hexes after a Pivot. Second Wind can be used any number of times during the same pursuit, but the Empath must absorb damage with each use.

6. Feign Disease (Seer, Target only; PD<4): A

distraction display in which the Seer acts as though he is sick with a frightful ailment (e.g., myxomatosis, distemper, rabies). The Seer may attempt to fool a Pursuer into believing that he is "mad" only if the Pursuer is not a normal carrion eater (Coyote, Red Wolf, Rats, Wolverine, Grizzly Bear, Caracara, Bald Eagle, or Raven) and if PD < 4. A Pursuer faced with a rabbit that is Feigning Disease must either (a) stop in a hex adjacent to the Seer to investigate (with no further movement that round, and forcing a raptor to land), or (b) immediately switch to another Target. If the Pursuer stops, the Seer must roll a MYS skill check greater than 1d6 + MYS of the Pursuer for the ruse to succeed. Feign Disease has an effect analogous to Instilling Fear, but does not require language communication; it results in the Pursuer losing interest and switching to another Target. Even if the attempt fails, Feign Disease causes the Pursuer to pause in its pursuit and hesitate, allowing the Seer to flee again in the next round. Regardless of success or failure, an attempt to Feign Disease counts as one tactical use.

7. Disperse Herb (Herbalist, Target or Non-Target): In Pursuit, if an Herbalist is carrying a prepared herb that can be dispersed in the air (such as a fungal ball or flower dust), she may cast the herb into the air while running. The herb immediately disperses into the current hex and the 3 adjacent hexes behind the herbalist at the time of the herb's dispersal. The dispersed herb immediately affects all individuals (Pursuers and Fugitives) that occupy or enter one of those 4 hexes in the same pursuit round. (The herbalist may continue moving, thereby avoiding contact with the dispersed herb.) Each affected individual must roll a saving throw against the effects of the herb (see Herb descriptions). If a Pursuer is two or more hexes farther back, the GM makes a check based on the Pursuer's INT Rating to see if the Pursuer detects the herb, allowing it to avoid the affected hexes, or if failing to detect it, continues into an affected hex. The dispersed herb cloud lingers until the herbalist's next pursuit turn. The attempt uses up one sprig of the herb regardless of success or failure. Unlike most other pursuit tactics, Disperse Herb does not count against the total number of tactics allowed, and can be used any number of times during the same pursuit, so long as the Herbalist has carried sprigs available. However, the same Pursuer automatically detect the herb dispersal and avoid affected hexes after the herbalist's first attempt.

8. Encourage (Storyteller, Target or Non-Target): While running within range of communication, the Storyteller can encourage other rabbits by reminding them of the heroic deeds of fabled rabbit heroes. Encourage only affects other rabbits within 2 hexes of the Storyteller; it has no effect on Non-Rabbit Fugitives. Each encouraged rabbit is spurred to immediately move forward 2 hexes in addition to their normal movement allowance. Of course, this may make the Storyteller more vulnerable, as she does not gain the movement advantage of her encouragement.

Special Tactics available to Non-Rabbits

Available only to playable neutral animals.

1. Intimidate (Bandit, Target or Non-Target; PD<4): In lieu of movement during a round of pursuit, a Raccoon instead may suddenly swing around and snarl fiercely at the pursuer. Intimidate may be attempted only if the Bandit is within 3 hexes of the Pursuer (PD<4). A Pursuer facing a snarling Raccoon must either stop to appraise the situation in a hex adjacent to the Bandit (during its regular movement) or immediately switch to another Target (the GM may determine which). If the Pursuer stops, its turn ends; no more movement is allowed until the next pursuit round. If the Pursuer immediately switches to a new target, movement can continue, but the Pursuer must maneuver around the Bandit's hex. A switch in the same round as the Intimidate counts as a voluntary switch, and therefore reduces the pursuer's remaining tactical uses. If the Bandit's Intimidation causes the Pursuer to stop, the Bandit may flee again on its next round of movement (keeping in mind that it now faces toward the Pursuer) or stand its ground (remaining in the same hex without facing away). In the event that the Pursuer stops and the Bandit stands his ground, the Bandit must roll a STR skill check greater than 1d6 + STR of the Pursuer for the Pursuer to remain Intimidated. On a successful STR check, the pursuer faces the same choice of continuing to face off against the Bandit or switching to another target. On a failure, the pursuer may move or attack as normal.

2. Jump Kick (Herald, Target or Non-Target): An attempt to deflect or injure a Pursuer by kicking backward while running. The Jackrabbit may continue to run away, with normal movement restrictions, without slowing down. A Jump Kick may occur at any time during movement if the Herald is in an adjacent hex and is facing away from the Pursuer (i.e., if the pursuer is in any of the three adjacent hexes to the rear). The player announces whether the kick is an attempt to hit; if it is, resolve as if in combat (i.e., Herald's 1d6 + AGI Rating vs. Pursuer's 1d6 + SPD Rating). If the Jump Kick is not an attempt to hit, it serves as a feint that causes the Pursuer to flinch, reducing its speed during its next movement by 2 hexes. A successful Jump Kick during pursuit inflicts normal damage (see Combat), but does not automatically initiate Combat. Heralds also may perform a version of the Jump Kick as a regular attack during Combat, although the kick counts as the attack phase and the subsequent run counts as movement.

3. Quick Conceal (Spy, Target only): If an obstacle is within two hexes, a Chipmunk can dart into that hex and freeze to perform a Quick Conceal. It functions in much the same way as Flash Tail. When faced with a Target that has sought to Quick Conceal, the Pursuer must (a) voluntarily switch to a new Target, or (b) remain in a hex adjacent to the obstacle for the next full round to reacquire the original Target. Switching to a new Target counts as the use of a pursuit tactic. Chaser and Brute predators are likely to persist in searching for the Spy, circling halfway around the obstacle hex for 3 pursuit rounds. Stalkers crouch in an adjacent hex for 2 pursuit rounds, waiting and watching for the Spy to reappear. Raptors must keep moving, except Harris Hawks and Caracaras, which behave like Stalkers on the ground. All other Raptors abandon the Spy and switch to another Target. If the Spy is concealed in a Minor obstacle, she must succeed in an INT skill check vs. a lurking predator's 1d6 + INT Rating to remain concealed; the INT check must be repeated in each round that a predator is in an adjacent hex. However, if the Spy is concealed in a Major obstacle, it is never found; predators eventually give up to switch to another Target or break off pursuit altogether.

4. Spray (Burglar, Target or Non-Target): When being pursued, a Skunk may Spray backward without slowing down. The Pursuer need not be close for the Burglar to Spray. If the Pursuer is in any of the three hexes to the rear of the skunk at the time of the Spray, or if it enters one of those three hexes in the next 2 pursuit rounds, the Pursuer's speed is reduced to just 2 hexes during each round it is exposed to the spray.

5. Bristle (Guardian, Target only): A porcupine may abruptly stop at any time during pursuit, crouch down, and Bristle, holding quills out in all directions. The effect is similar to Intimidate by a Burglar. If the Pursuer enters a hex adjacent to the Porcupine, it must either stop to appraise the situation or immediately switch to a new target. If the Pursuer stops, its turn ends; no more movement is allowed until the next pursuit round. If the Pursuer immediately switches to a new target, movement can continue, but the Pursuer must maneuver around the Guardian's hex. As with Intimidate, the Guardian may flee again on its next round of movement or stand its ground. A Pursuer that has halted may choose to attack the Guardian in its next round, but if it enters the hex with the Porcupine, the attacker is immediately stuck by 1d6 quills. If that happens, the attacker takes 2 points of damage (total) before Combat begins, and in any subsequent combat his attack likelihood is reduced by −1 AGI if stuck by 1–3 quills and −2 AGI if stuck by 4 or more quills. An attacker may not remove quills until quitting pursuit and combat.

6. Feign Death (Shaman, Target only; PD>2): A distraction display intended to fool a Pursuer into believing that the Opossum has suddenly dropped dead. The Shaman falls down, rolls on its back, and sticks out its tongue. It may be attempted only if the Pursuer is three or more hexes away (PD > 2). Feign Death has an effect analogous to Feign Disease. Success results in the Pursuer first investigating, and possibly abandoning the Target. If the Pursuer is not a normal carrion eater (Coyote, Red Wolf, Rats, Wolverine, Grizzly Bear, Caracara, Bald Eagle, or Raven), the Pursuer loses all movement for its next turn or switches to another Target. If the Pursuer is a regular consumer of carrion, then it is not fooled by the ruse and may initiate Combat. If the Pursuer stops, the Shaman must roll a MYS skill check greater than 1d6 + MYS of the Pursuer for the ruse to succeed. Feign Death has an effect analogous to Instilling Fear, but does not require language communication; it results in the Pursuer losing interest and switching to another Target. Even if the attempt fails, Feign Death causes the Pursuer to pause in its pursuit and hesitate, allowing the Shaman to flee again in the next round. Regardless of success or failure, an attempt to Feign Death counts as one tactical use.

7. Roll Up (Trader): A defensive position adopted by an Armadillo that reduces or eliminates vulnerability to attack. The Trader may Roll Up at any time during pursuit, tucking her vulnerable areas inside armor consisting of multiple overlapping plates of bone. Faced with an armored ball, a Pursuer may choose to initiate combat or switch to another Target. However, switching targets counts as a voluntary tactic. Any physical attack that hits the Trader incurs a damage reduction of 5 HP. Thus, any attack directed at a Trader that is Rolled Up must deliver 6 or more HP of damage or it has no effect. Note that armor has no effect on other forms of attack such as herbs, poison, or Empathic Hurt. These attacks may be played out on the Pursuit board, rather than initiating normal combat. A predator that does no damage to a Rolled-Up Armadillo after two successful hits gives up, and if no other targets are available on the pursuit board, pursuit ends.

8. Tree Dash (Grifter): If a Major obstacle (presumed to be a tree) is within six hexes with no intervening enemy, a Squirrel may dash and climb the tree (or other obstacle) in a single round of movement. Tree Dash is similar in its effect to Quick Conceal and Flash Tail. Chasers (except for Pine Marten and Ringtail) lose one full pursuit round waiting next to the obstacle, then

must switch to another Target. Stalkers and Brutes expend 2 full pursuit rounds attempting to climb after the squirrel, then may switch to a new Target. Only Pine Marten, Ringtail, Goshawk, or Owl may enter the obstacle hex and initiate combat. See special rules for Tree Chases by Pine Martens or Ringtails. The Grifter may climb back down in any subsequent pursuit round, at which time it becomes available again as a Target.

Pursuit Tactics for Predators

Devil take the Hindmost

Predators also have tactical maneuvers available to them during Pursuit. Some predator tactics give them an advantage to close the distance to their Target; others are designed to counter specific Tactics attempted by Prey. Not all pursuit tactics are available to all predators, however. Basic tactics are shared by all predators in the same class. Special tactics are unique to particular predators.

Unlike Fugitive Tactics, which depend on SPD, Predator Tactics are limited by the intelligence of the predator. Any Pursuer may use a predator tactic up to the value of their INT Rating. For example, a Coyote is rated at INT 5; it can use or reuse up to 5 tactics during the same pursuit.

The following table lists 6 Basic tactics known to each predator category. The first tactic in each list is known to Juveniles. For each additional step in age (Sub-Adult, Young Adult, Mature Adult, Apex Adult), 1 or 2 additional tactics are known, in the order listed. Predators may use any tactic they know during pursuit, but only at the time of their normal movement. Unlike Fugitive, predators may not immediately use a tactic as a Reaction during the Fugitive's movement.

Pursuit Tactics Known by Age

Age Class	Chasers	Stalkers	Brutes	Raptors	Cryptics
Juvenile	Switch	Switch	Switch	Switch	No Pursuit
Sub-Adult	Hurry	Hurry	Hurry	Hurry	—
	Spin	Spin	Spin	Drift	—
Young Adult	Cut	Cut	Slap	Hover	—
Mature	Worry	Bound/ Scramble	Bash	Wheel	—
Apex	Bash	Slap	Hurl	Scissors	—

Basic Pursuer Tactics

Basic tactics are available only to the predators indicated in parentheses, but may be limited by Age Class. This list includes only those special abilities that may be used during Pursuit; for special abilities during Combat, see the Combat section.

1. Switch Target (all predators, Juvenile and older): A voluntary change from one Target to another during pursuit. Note that Switch Target, like other predator tactics, may be used a limited number of times during a particular pursuit. Switch Target does not allow a Pursuer to reacquire a Target lost due to Flash Tail, Quick Conceal, or Tree Dash tactics by a Fugitive (see Find Target instead).

2. Hurry (all predators; Subadult and older): A tactic that helps an excited Pursuer to close the gap between itself and a Target. By expending extra effort, the Pursuer can advance one additional hex (2 hexes for a Stalker) at the end of its normal movement. Although a Hurry can cancel the effects of a Fugitive tactic, it may not be used to end movement in the same hex as a Target.

3. Spin (Chasers, Stalkers, Brutes; Sub-Adult and older): The Pursuer spins about to face a new direction. Spin permits the token to remain in the same hex as in Rotate, with no further movement, and turn two hexsides (120 degrees) instead of a normal rotation of one hexside. Martens, Ringtails, and Minks can face any direction (up to 180 degrees) with a Spin.

4. Cut (Chasers, Stalkers; Young Adult and older): A quick counter to an evasive action by the Target, the token may be rotated by one hexside (60 degrees) before normal movement. After the Cut, the token can run and pivot for the full movement allowance. However, a Cut is allowed only in the pursuit round immediately after the Target has employed a Tactical maneuver.

5. Worry (Chasers; Mature or Apex; PD<3): Nipping at a Fugitive when the Pursuer faces the Target and is within 2 hexes of the Target. Worrying prey has the effect of increasing tension and clouding the Fugitive's judgment. The Target that is Worried may not attempt any tactical maneuver and may not pivot more than one hexside during the Fugitive's next round. The effect wears off at the end of the Fugitive's next round of movement.

6. Slap (Stalker, Brute; Young Adult and older; PD=1): Striking with forepaws at a Fugitive that is in one of the three adjacent hexes to the front of the Pursuer. Slapping prey has the effect of increasing tension and clouding the Fugitive's judgment. The Target that is Slapped may not attempt any tactical maneuver and may not pivot more than one hexside during the Fugitive's next round. The effect wears off at the end of the Fugitive's next round of movement.

7. Bound (Cats; Mature or Apex): A maneuver with the same effect as Vault, where the predatory cat (small cat, bobcat, ocelot, lynx, etc.) leaps over an obstacle and continues running in the same direction. Domestic cats (House, Barn, Feral, etc.) can only Bound over Minor obstacles; Bobcats, Ocelot, Lynx, and Cougar can Bound over Major obstacles. Although a Vault results in advancing 2 hexes, the maneuver costs only one movement point.

8. Scramble (Stoats, Ferrets, Mongooses; Mature or Apex): Weasel relatives and Mongooses cannot leap over obstacles like Cats, but they can scramble through obstacles with little or no hindrance. Stoats, Ferrets, and Mongooses can Scramble through a Minor obstacle hex without stopping or checking with a die roll. They can pass through Major obstacle hexes the same way most animals pass through Minor obstacles: roll 1d6; on a result greater than the Pursuer's movement allowance (Stoats), or a roll of 6 (Ferrets and Mongooses), the Major obstacle does not interfere with movement and the Pursuer may proceed up to its full movement. On a result less than or equal to the movement allowance, the Pursuer must stop in the obstacle hex.

9. Bash (all Canid Chasers, Brutes; Mature or Apex; PD=1): Intentional collision with a Fugitive. A Bash may be attempted if the Pursuer occupies a hex adjacent to a Fugitive, but not directly facing the Fugitive, at any point during its normal movement. A Bash may be directed at a Target or Non-Target. The Bash knocks the Fugitive off balance; the Fugitive may move only 1 hex in the next turn.

10. Hurl (Brutes; Apex; PD<4): Hurl allows a Badger, Wolverine, or Bear to fling an object at a Fugitive without slowing down. The Brute merely has to swing a powerful forepaw at a natural object such as a stone, chunk of wood, or clod of dirt to propel the object forward. Hurl may be attempted only if the Pursuer is within 3 hexes of a Fugitive; it may be directed at any Fugitive (not just the Target) within range to the front of a brute. Badgers and Wolverines may Hurl only small objects the size of an apple (100 grams); Bears may Hurl objects the size of a mini-watermelon (3 kilograms). To determine whether the object hits a Fugitive, roll 1d6 + AGI Rating of the Brute vs. 1d6 + SPD Rating of the intended Fugitive. If the Brute's roll exceeds the Fugitive's, the successful hit brings the Fugitive to a full stop for one pursuit round. In addition, a small object causes 1 HP damage and a large object causes 1d6 HP damage. If the object misses, but the Brute's AGI check equals the Fugitive's, then the object hits beside the Fugitive and throws up a cloud of dirt; the Fugitive must roll to check for Shock.

11. Drift (Raptor; Sub-Adult or older): On a long, straight flight path, the raptor can gradually Drift left or right. For every five hexes forward, 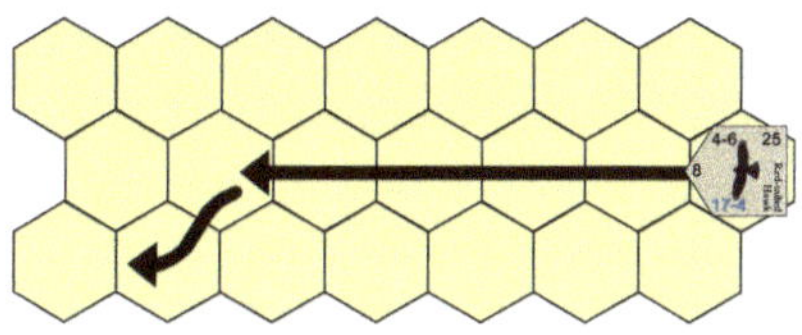the token may be advanced into a 6th hex that is shifted one row to the left or right, maintaining the same facing direction (see diagram). Thus, a Red-tailed hawk with a movement allowance of 17 can drift as much as 3 rows left or right in straight flight from the starting hex.

12. Hover (Raptor; Young Adult and older): An aerial maneuver by a Raptor that permits it to remain flying in the same hex without moving forward. The token is not moved during the turn, but may change facing direction one hexside (60 degrees) left or right as in normal Rotation during ground pursuit. Hover is restricted to Osprey, Harrier, all Falcons, and Barn Owl.

13. Wheel (Raptor; Mature or Apex): An aerial maneuver in which a Raptor banks at a steep angle, allowing it to alter course sharply. The maneuver essentially gives the Raptor the same movement options as a rabbit (or Harrier) making 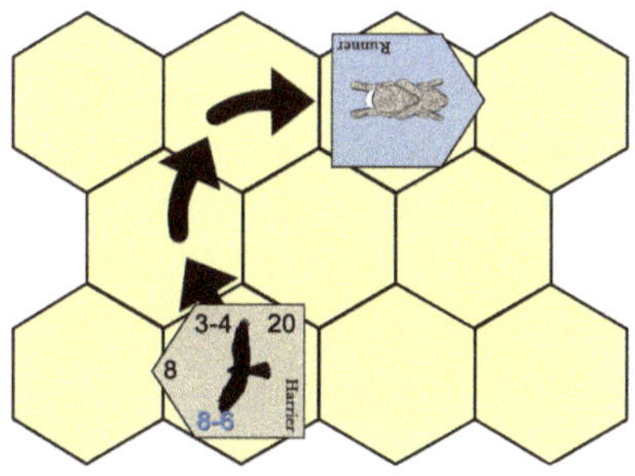a Narrow or Wide Pivot: the Raptor's token may change direction through two hexsides, either in a single 120-degree bank, or in two consecutive 60-degree banks. Harriers, Goshawks, and Owls can completely reverse direction (180 degrees) in a Wheel, but must end movement in a hex that could be reached by Banking (in effect, rotating an additional hexside after a normal Bank). A Wheel must be performed instead of, not in addition to, any other change in direction. Example (right): During pursuit by a harrier, a rabbit runs in the opposite direction. In response, the harrier Wheels, reversing direction 180 degrees, and comes up directly behind the rabbit.

14. Scissors (Raptor; Apex): An aerial maneuver by a Raptor that involves rapid banking left and right, resulting in a zig-zag course in a net forward direction. Movement allowance is reduced by 5 hexes when flying in a Scissors pattern, but the weaving flight counters evasive maneuvers by prey. A Target to the front of the Raptor may not use any Fugitive Tactic in the next turn.

Special Predator Tactics

Available only to specific predators. Special predator tactics are not available to Juveniles, but may be used by all older age classes. As above, this list includes only those special abilities that may be used during Pursuit; for special abilities during Combat, see the Combat section. See specific descriptions of each predator in the Bestiary.

1. Intruder Alert (small or medium dog; PD<3): If a small or medium dog closes to within 2 hexes of any Fugitive, it runs circles around the nearest Fugitive, not attempting to enter the same hex, but barking the whole time; allow small or medium dogs to change facing by one hexside in each hex of movement at no additional cost. (Barking for 5 consecutive turns counts as one Tactical use). If on a Farm, the barking attracts the attention of a Farmer (1d6 roll of 1–4) or Gardener (5 or 6) who approaches at 1 hex/turn from the nearest edge of the Pursuit board. In a Suburb, a barking terrier attracts the attention of 1–6 dogs of various breeds. One additional dog (up to 1d6) arrives at the nearest red icon hex each turn. To determine the breed, roll 1d6 for each: 1=Terrier; 2–3=Border Collie; 4=Retriever; 5=Doberman; 6=Rottweiler.

2. Pounce (Foxes, Coyote, Feral Cat, Bobcat, Ocelot, Lynx; PD<4): If a Fox (Red or Gray), Coyote, Feral Cat (Bengal), Bobcat, Ocelot, or Lynx ends normal movement in a hex with the Target in one of the three adjacent hexes to the front, it may Pounce to advance into the Target hex. Note that Pounce also is a combat tactic with different effects during combat.

3. Shiny (House Cat, Meezer Cat): This tactic is a weakness, not an asset. On any attempt by a House Cat or Meezer Cat to use any other Tactic (including Switch Target), roll 1d6: On a result of 4–6, the Cat is distracted by a foreign object, small bird, or reflected sunlight and turns to run for one turn in a random direction. It may return to any Target in the following turn, which does not count as a tactical switch of targets.

4. Fascinate (Stoat, Big Stoat): Weasels and Stoats are known to employ an unorthodox hunting technique where they engage in crazy antics that disguise their true intention of approaching a curious rabbit more closely. In B&B, Fascinate is a special Pursuit tactic where a rabbit battles between an uncontrollable urge to approach the Stoat and its desire to run away. Roll 1d6 at the end of each turn in which the Pursuer attempts to Fascinate; if the result is less than the Pursuer's INT Rating (4 for a Stoat, 5 for a Big Stoat), then the Target token is moved by the GM up to 2 hexes following rules of normal movement, and the Target is blocked from using a pursuit tactic in its next turn. This Pursuer-controlled movement happens during the Pursuer's turn in addition to Pursuer movement; during the next turn for the Target, the rabbit regains control and can move normally. If the die roll equals or exceeds the Pursuer's INT Rating, the Pursuer's turn ends with no other effect. An attempt to Fascinate counts as one use of a tactical maneuver only on turns where it is successful, and does not interfere with normal movement by the Pursuer. Fascinate plays no role in actual Combat.

5. Tree Chase (Pine Marten, Ringtail): If a Squirrel or Chipmunk flees into a tree pursued by a Marten or Ringtail, or flees into a pile of rocks or rocky slope pursued by a Ringtail, the pursuit becomes a Tree Chase. A Tree Chase is three-dimensional, with Fugitives and Pursuers equally agile moving up and down, out to slender branches, and leaping from limb to limb. Because the tree (or rocks) do not pose an obstacle to pursuit, a Tree Chase is resolved on the regular Pursuit Board, with all other Fugitives and Pursuers removed from the chase. However, a few special rules apply: (a) All obstacle hexes on the Pursuit board are considered leaping sites on different limbs, where a Fugitive or Pursuer may move directly to one of the nearest other obstacle hexes at the cost of 1 movement point. The leap may be attempted only if the path between launching site and landing site requires a change of direction of no more than one hexside (60 degrees); (b) the fence is considered absent from the board; and (c) the only safe refuge, and therefore the only way to escape pursuit, is for the Squirrel or Chipmunk to reach the hex with the red Hawk Icon. This represents a hole in the tree too small to admit the pursuer. All other movement rules apply.

6. Surprise! (Harrier, Barn Owl): Harriers and Barn Owls hunt by coursing low over the ground, taking advantage of swales and other irregularities in the terrain, then suddenly appearing overhead. At the outset of Pursuit, the GM may place extra tokens in the starting hex for the Harrier as dummies. Each extra token counts as one use of a Pursuer Tactic, so the Harrier could, in effect, spend 3 of its Tactic uses to have 3 dummy tokens. All tokens are flipped face down at the start. (Alternatively, use tokens for different raptors, with one secretly designated as representing the true Harrier.) During pursuit, all tokens may be advanced, following normal movement restrictions for a Harrier. A dummy token cannot employ a tactical maneuver during Pursuit, and if the Harrier performs a maneuver other than Surprise then all tokens must be turned face up. When any token approaches within 3 hexes of the Target (PD<4), it is revealed as a dummy token or the true Harrier. Revealed dummy tokens are removed from the board, but tokens that remain face down can continue to move and maneuver.

7. Roar (Black Bear, Grizzly Bear): A loud, bone-chilling vocalization issued during pursuit. A Roar instills fear in Fugitives. Rabbits and Hares must roll for a special Shock check (1d6 + MYS Rating vs. DV=6). (Note: A normal Shock check uses a DV=4.) Failure against the Bear's Roar results in the rabbit stopping and standing motionless for 1d6 pursuit rounds, or until attacked.

Mini-Game: Fox & Rabbit

This mini-game is a way to practice Pursuit of rabbits or non-rabbit characters by various predators. The basic mini-game is designed for two players, but more players can participate by having more Fugitives (and just one Pursuer). If players wish to organize as two teams, then multiple Pursuers may be used as well.

Setup

Players may use their own characters from a B&B Adventure or campaign as the Fugitive they control, or all players may agree on some "standard" Fugitive that all must play (e.g., 3rd-level Runner, 2nd-level any profession, 4th-level non-rabbit, etc.). Unless otherwise specified, a standard Fugitive is assumed to be 3rd level in all traits with a Base Bonus of +1 in their profession and 0 in all other traits. The identity of the Pursuer is determined separately through a process of bidding.

Bidding

The Players agree on a bet. The bet can be prized food such as 4 carrots or 2 apples. The bet also could be for other items of value (herbs, a coveted man-thing) or intangibles such as the promise of a favor to be redeemed in the future. When the bet is established, players engage in bidding to determine who will be the Pursuer. Each player bids by announcing a Pursuer he is willing to face. After one round of bidding, each player has the option of raising his bid or passing. A bid is raised by announcing a different Pursuer, taking care to specify the kind and age class of predator. Bids may only include Chasers, Stalkers, Brutes, or Raptors (Cryptics do not engage in pursuit). Other players may dare a bidder to face more dangerous predators during bidding (and are encouraged to do so), but the bid must be the player's choice. A player who passes has announced that he is unwilling to face a more difficult predator for the agreed stakes. When all players have passed, bidding is over. The player with the highest bid (the most difficult predator) is the Fugitive; the player with the lowest bid is the Pursuer. If more than two players participate, then all intermediate bids also become Fugitives. If the players cannot agree which bid is the most difficult predator, then the Pursuer is chosen randomly from competing bids.

The Chase

The player with the low bid plays the specified predator with stats as listed in the Bestiary. Unless all players agree on a different setting at the outset, the chase takes place in a Farm habitat, allowing 5 Major obstacles and 15 Minor obstacles. The chase follows extended rules for Pursuit, including all basic and special tactical maneuvers. Herbalist fugitives may have a number of prepared herbs of their choice equal to their AGI Base Bonus + 1. The chase continues until a Fugitive is caught by the Pursuer or all Fugitives escape.

The Payoff

If the Pursuer catches any Fugitive, he wins. If the Pursuer fails to catch a Fugitive, then the last Fugitive to reach the safe zone wins (thus providing an incentive to remain on the board and tempt the Pursuer). The winner collects the entire bet. If players wish to play again, either to switch roles or try a different predator, then the process of betting and bidding is repeated.

Other Animals

Many animals in the world that rabbits may encounter pose little or no threat. Some of these are designated as playable species: Raccoon, Jackrabbit, Chipmunk, Skunk, Porcupine, Opossum, Armadillo, and Squirrel. We refer to these and other non-predators as Neutral Animals. Players should note, however, that any particular neutral animal may be a potential ally, casually friendly, aloof and disinterested, or openly hostile. The Bestiary includes a wide variety of the most common neutral animals that rabbits might encounter. However, we encourage GMs to consult field guides to mammals, birds, or reptiles to find descriptions of other species that could be incorporated into the game as neutral animals.

NPCs and Wandering Neutrals

Particular adventures and campaigns drawn up by the GM are likely to include specific characters that are controlled by the GM. These Non-Player Characters, or NPCs, play important roles in advancing storylines and enhancing the richness and color of the game. Some NPCs will be regular fixtures in the game, serving as traders, informants, or mercenaries. However, most neutral animals encountered by players are likely to be one-offs that result from wandering encounters. Unless players simply want to attack or ignore everything they see, interacting with wandering neutrals requires communication skills, which are greatly facilitated by knowledge of the creature's language. Refer to the description of different animal languages under Charisma and to the section on Communication for more details.

For convenience, neutral animals are listed in the Bestiary by language group. Languages roughly follow taxonomic groups of animals such as Chatters (squirrel relatives, in the taxonomic family Sciuridae), Hoofers (ungulates, including cattle, deer, and other large herbivores), and Strutters (chicken-like ground birds). In other cases, unrelated animals with similar habits or life history are lumped together (e.g., Grubbers, which includes Pigs, Moles, Armadillos, and Opossums). Spend a few minutes exploring the Bestiary to get a sense of what animals might be encountered and which languages they use.

In general, neutral animals adopt a live-and-let-live attitude. Many ignore a party of rabbits altogether. Timid species might try to slink away without being noticed. Some can be sly and greedy, and may try to take advantage of a rabbit for personal gain (to steal herbs, for instance). A few, however, are bold and inquisitive, and may approach rabbits out of curiosity. Among the most curious species that may seek out interactions are Otters, Javelinas and Pigs, Coatis and Raccoons, Jays, Crows and Magpies, and juvenile mammals of most species. Most insects and arachnids rarely show any interest in other animals unless they pose a threat, or are attracted to the food they eat, although some spiders (especially Jumping Spiders) may investigate for no apparent reason. Encounters with curious species generally should lead to some kind of interaction.

The reverse need not be the case. Rabbits may find specific utility to developing friendships, or at least working relationships, with neutral animals. Gophers and Moles may be useful for digging, Muskrats or Nutria for exploring underwater, Beavers for felling small trees, or various birds for carrying rapid messages — if you can persuade them. Different species find different inducements most enticing. Many species might value a prized food (other than the foods that rabbits value most highly). Others might have more eclectic tastes. Packrats and Magpies, for example, are famous (perhaps undeservedly) for collecting bright baubles and trinkets. Moose or Elk might be most responsive to herbs that smell like sexual pheromones (But be careful how they respond!). Jackrabbits, Blackbirds, or Turkeys might be goaded by challenging their athletic prowess or self-esteem. Otters, Skunks, Squirrels of all kinds, and Pheasants might be especially attracted to playing games, particularly silly games (such as the Steady Now mini-game), although Pheasants are notoriously bad. Players and the GM should give full rein to their imagination in devising unusual motives and inducements for neutral animals.

Combat

Introduction to Combat

Wise rabbits tend to avoid combat. The world is full of a thousand enemies that wish to make a meal of a plump bunny, and rabbits from other warrens often resent your coming into their territory. Enough hazards exist in the world without going to look for trouble. But sometimes there is simply no alternative to fighting.

In **Bunnies & Burrows**, combat takes place on Battleboards, hex maps that display the features of particular habitats. A battle may start when two parties want to fight each other, or when a predator successfully pursues a target and the final, violent encounter takes place. We first explain basic combat between rabbits (and non-rabbit player characters). This is modified from the same combat that you may have played in **Bunnies & Burrows Light**. It also includes the special abilities of the new professions, including non-rabbit characters, available in the complete game. We next present the combat modifications when fighting predators, or when fighting underground.

Turns and Rounds

A combat turn consists of an action and move of a single combatant, including the resolution of that action. A combat round consists of one combat turn for each combatant, taken in sequence according to initiative. Thus, if there are three combatants on one side and two combatants on the other side, a combat round includes five combat turns, one for each combatant.

Basic Rabbit-Rabbit Combat

When a party of rabbits encounters hostile rabbits, either side may initiate combat; that side is known as the aggressor, and the other side as the target. Note: If fighting underground, there are modifications to some of the following discussion. Combat proceeds as follows:

1. Each side identifies up to three combatants to enter the fight. Any others watch from the side, unless certain options are available.

2. Tokens are placed on the Battleboard to represent the starting location of each combatant. Each combatant player must also place a Combat Tactics Card (CTC) beside their character card to keep track of actions during the battle.

3. Combat proceeds in a series of rounds in which each combatant has a turn to act based upon Initiative, with the aggressor getting an initiative bonus of +1 in the first round. If the aggressor achieved surprise (see Spotting Rabbits), then the first round is free for the aggressor, and combat thereafter begins a second round. Note: Some conditions in combat may temporarily modify your SPD Rating; if so, make an adjustment to your initiative accordingly.

4. Each character in the combat chooses a combat tactic by placing a marker on the CTC. The players may converse during this step, though it must be aloud (no whispers or passed notes), representing communication between the characters. This might be used to coordinate attacks, though it may also provide information to the opponents. If the GM is controlling multiple opponents, she may choose to speak similar communications that they are exchanging, allowing the players to hear, though this is not required.

5. In sequence of initiative, each character in combat takes his or her turn by playing a move/action combination, using the combat tactic they chose in Step 4, and resolving the combat during that turn. Attack and Defend die rolls are made as indicated in combat sequence details described below. Note: Some combat may result in a handicap or injury to a combatant; if so, place the appropriate token on the CTC. This continues until all characters in combat have taken their turn.

6. The next round then begins, using the same initiative, with every combatant choosing new combat tactics at this time. You can conceal your choice until it must be revealed at the round in which you attack or defend. If a combatant falls in battle (unconscious or dead) or leaves the Battleboard (via an exit arrow), there may be a possibility of another combatant entering the board. Combat continues in this manner until (a) both sides agree to stop fighting, or (b) all combatants of one side have died or left the Battleboard.

The Battleboard

Combat is played on a Battleboard, with player characters and their adversaries represented by tokens. There is a Battleboard for each of the various habitats, as well as one for combat within a burrow. There are special rules for underground combat. Descriptions of the Battleboards may be found in Appendix D. A set of tokens for predators and each of the professions of playable characters is provided on separate sheets. Examples of the token sheets also are presented in Appendix D, along with a key to the basic combat stats printed on each token.

Before Combat begins, a target character (always selected by the aggressor side) is placed first in a random location on the Battleboard by rolling 1d6 and placing the token on the numbered hex. An aggressor's token is placed next, on any other numbered hex of their choice. Up to 4 additional combatants, 2 targets & 2 aggressors, may be alternately placed by their controlling player (or GM) on any remaining numbered hexes. Other combatants present in the area but not placed are presumed to hide and watch from the shadows, though certain conditions may allow them to enter the Battleboard at a later time. In the initial placement, each player may choose whichever facing they wish for their character on the Battleboard.

Initiative

Each character of the opposing sides determines when they will act in the combat sequence, based upon their SPD Rating (higher goes earlier). The aggressors each get an initiative bonus of +1 in the first combat round (or the 2nd round if they have surprise). Resolve a tie among player characters by going in order clockwise at the table from the GM's left. If there is a tie between a player character and a character being run by the GM, the player character goes first. On successive rounds of combat, continue to use the same initiative sequence that was originally determined (without the initial bonus for the aggressor), but with adjustments if a handicap in combat temporarily affects your SPD Rating.

Setting Combat Tactics

Before each combat round takes place, a combat tactic is chosen by placing a marker in the selected spot on your CTC. This must be a tactic that you are allowed to use according to your profession, level, and current status in the combat. Note: Some tactics may be allowed only once in a combat, while others may have different restrictions. Some special abilities are also treated as combat tactics; if you have a special ability available, write it on your CTC in the special tactic slot.

Action Turns: Attack and Move

Each turn consists of two actions, either attack then move, or move then attack. Attacking twice or moving twice is not allowed, unless permitted by a special ability. You may not do a partial move, then attack, then complete your move. Attacks may occur only from an adjacent hex unless a special ability allows an attack at a distance. At the end of the combat round, you then choose your combat tactic in preparation for the next combat round. Note: There may be special circumstances in which additional status markers are placed that affect the choice of combat tactic, and these may remain from one round to the next.

Facing

Facing is significant, both for attacks and for movement. Each rabbit token has an indication of the forward facing of the rabbit, and the token must be oriented to point to a hex side of the hex occupied by the rabbit. "Ahead" includes the hex directly in front of the rabbit, plus the adjacent hexes just to its right and left. "Behind" includes the hex directly behind the rabbit, as well as the adjacent hexes to its right and left. Thus, of the six hexes adjacent to the hex occupied by the rabbit, three are ahead and three are behind. Most attacks can be made only ahead of the attacker, and may have further directional restrictions. Some attacks may be made behind, and will be so indicated in the description. If not so indicated, assume the attack is only ahead. Note: You may choose a facing in a direction that you cannot move (e.g., due to terrain restrictions).

Changing facing may be done only during movement, not during an attack (unless a special ability or tactic permits it). Normally, rotation may be done at the start or conclusion of movement, but not during the move. Rotation (to any direction) at the start of the move costs one movement point (MP). If done at the end of the move, rotation to the left or right by one hex side is "free," not costing movement points. Rotation of either two or three hex sides (at the end of move) costs one movement point (total)

and cannot be performed unless there was at least one movement point unused at the end of the rabbit's movement. There are special rules on facing changes during underground combat.

Some animals have special facing change abilities. Chipmunks, Tree Squirrels, Weasels, and Mongooses have a "free" facing rotation (through one, two, or three hex sides) at the start or conclusion of movement. In addition, they can make a similar facing rotation for each hex of movement for a cost of one extra MP per intermediate hex (in which they rotate).

Movement on the Battleboard

Rabbits have a number of movement points (MP) during combat equal to their SPD Rating +2. Different types of terrain on the Battleboard cost differing numbers of movement points to enter. The presence of hostile rabbits, any dotted red line hexsides, and combat handicaps or injuries all may affect your freedom of movement. You may use up to your maximum number of movement points during your turn, unless restricted otherwise. Except for some specific handicaps, you always are allowed to move one hex as a minimum, though you may not be able to rotate your facing at the end of your move. You may move through a friendly rabbit at the normal cost for that hex, but may not end your move in the same hex as that rabbit. You may never move into or through a hex containing a hostile rabbit. (There are exceptions for Hold, whether by predators or rabbits).

Backing

As a special type of movement, a rabbit may go directly back one hex without changing facing. No special moves may be done along with this, and it constitutes the rabbit's total movement for the round.

Terrain Effects on Movement

Unless otherwise indicated, each hex on the Battleboard costs one MP to enter. Some hex types or hex sides have special effects on movement; these are distinguished by graphics on the Battleboard. See Appendix D for further explanation of graphics on different Battleboards.

Hex Type	Graphic Representation	Effect
Bush hex	bush icon in part of hex	may enter on ground; squirrel & chipmunk may climb
Tree hex	small or large tree	Represents two different locations: ground and canopy. Any character in the hex is assumed to be on the ground, unless stacked with "Canopy" token. No character can be in canopy unless a special ability (Climb, Fly) allows it.
Tree Trunk	Yellow bird on perch	Point of access from ground to canopy for Climbers.
Tree Canopy	Branches extend beyond trunk	May be entered from Trunk or adjacent Canopy hex.
Hollow Log	Graphic extends across hex	may be entered at either end; costs one extra MP to enter and one MP to exit; no extra MP to walk on top

Hex Type	Graphic Representation	Effect
Large stream	Hex nearly filled with blue	STR 3+ to Jump across, or all remaining MP to wade
Boulder	Hex filled with boulder symbol encircled by Red Dashed Line	Climb or STR 3+ to Jump on, one extra MP to enter
Impediment	Poor Footing (Rabbit Tracks)	No extra cost to enter, one extra MP to exit; includes hexes with boggy ground, slippery log, or scree

Hex Side Type	Graphic Representation	Effect
Tree trunk or bush	Hex encircled by Red Dashed Line	Costs one extra MP to enter, no extra MP to exit
Hazard	Hex encircled by Blue Dashed Line	Treat as hazard or handicap
Minor obstacle	Single Red Dashed Line	Costs one extra MP to cross either direction
Major obstacle	Double Red Dashed Line	Costs all remaining MP to cross either direction
Blockage	Solid Black Line	Cannot be crossed
Small stream	Blue along hex edge, < 1 hex wide	May be jumped by any character, or 3 MP to wade
Hollow Log	Graphic extends along hexside between two hexes	may be entered at either end; costs one MP to enter and one MP to exit, without occupying either hex to the sides; cannot walk on top
Slope	Slope Arrows (point downhill)	Costs one extra MP to pass up; no MP effect down
Cliff face	Cliff icon along hex edge	Cannot climb up; may jump down for 1d6 damage
Picket fence	White picket	No impediment to rabbit or smaller, costs 3 extra MP to cross up to raccoon, cannot be crossed by large dog
Barrier fence	Brown planking	Cannot be crossed
Wire fence	Red Dashed Line around garden	Cannot be climbed or bitten through; buried 50 centimeters deep

Entering a hex bounded by red dashed lines slows movement. This includes bushes, trees, rocks, etc. Going upslope slows movement. Entering or leaving a water hex greatly slows movement and may cost all remaining MPs (some rabbits may be able to jump across a stream for less cost). Going through a fence may be free, cost 3 extra MP, or be impossible depending on the type of fence. Some hexes with poor footing may cost extra MP to leave the hex. Moving through a series of hexes of this sort thus have costs beyond the 1 MP per hex, which can have important consequences for Combat. Also note that some characters may have special movement abilities that modify these costs.

Terrain Effects on Condition

Moving into or through certain terrain hexes may result in a Handicap being placed on that rabbit. Refer to **Handicap** rules for details of effects.

Ant Hill: If a character stops on an Ant Hill, it receives the Ants Handicap. Any time a character moves through an Ant Hill without stopping on it, roll 1d6: on 1 or 2, it receives the Ants Handicap.

Crossing Fence: When a character crosses a fence, roll 1d6: on 1, the rabbit is snagged in passing; it receives the Bleeding Handicap.

Other hexes represent natural hazards such as Quicksand, or slippery surfaces that risk Slip & Fall. Refer to specific descriptions in the section on Natural and Manmade Hazards.

Effects of Hostile Rabbits on Movement

Moving into a hex that is adjacent to a hostile rabbit incurs the same cost as if that rabbit were not present. Note that if you have sufficient MPs, you need not necessarily stop upon moving adjacent to a hostile rabbit. You may not move into the same hex as a hostile rabbit.

Effects of Handicaps on Movement

Certain combat results may cause handicaps. These include, in part, shock, severe injury, sneezing, sleep, confusion, poison, being held, etc. Some handicaps reduce your available movement points, some result in random movement, and some prevent movement altogether. The description of the specific handicap tells if it affects movement.

Entering the Battleboard During a Fight

If a combatant leaves the Battleboard via an exit arrow, another member of that same side (Aggressor or Target) may enter from the same exit arrow on the subsequent round. The character that enters may not be an individual who fled earlier in the battle. If a combatant dies or falls unconscious, another member of that same side may enter from either exit arrow on any subsequent round. At all times, there remains the restriction as to the number of living, conscious combatants from both sides that may be on the Battleboard simultaneously. (Multiple rats in one hex count as a single combatant.) The new combatant always receives an initiative one less than the lowest currently on the Battleboard. On the round of entry, the character may only move, and not take any other action until the following round.

Attack/Defend Dice

Two dice are used as markers on the CTC, placed in the holders labeled Attack and Defend. In each round of combat, they are rolled and placed the first time your rabbit either attacks or is attacked. Roll two dice and place one in Attack and the other in Defend (your choice).

After your attack is resolved, you remove the die from the Attack holder until it is your turn again, unless you have a special double attack. In that case, reduce the Attack die by two for the second attack; if the die is reduced to zero, then a second attack is not allowed. Remove the die from the CTC after the second attack.

Each time you are attacked, after the attack is resolved, you turn your die in the Defend holder to a value of one less, but still keep it there. In the event it would be reduced to zero, simply remove the die from the Defend holder, and treat the Defend value as zero. There is no way to get a negative value for your Defend die. You will reroll your Defend die when it is your turn again.

There may be a special result in combat that directs you to decrease the value of either the Attack or Defend die; it will say whether the effect is for one round only, or if it is a handicap that endures beyond one round. See that result for detailed instructions.

Conducting an Attack

When it is your turn, and a potential target is within range (either before you move or after you have completed your move), you may conduct one attack using the Combat Tactic you have chosen. This is always optional; even if you have indicated an attack tactic on your CTC, you may choose to not conduct that attack, but you may not change tactics. (The one exception is Flee; if you have chosen that tactic you must attempt to flee, and you may not choose to remain motionless.)

Some tactics allow choices at the time of execution, when a hit succeeds. For example, if you have chosen Claw, you still have the option of switching to Cuff at the instant you hit. Each tactic that allows a choice at execution will show that in its description. Some choices may offer additional possibilities, such as the chance of a critical hit. Others may apply handicaps or benefits to either attacker or target.

Each attack tactic can be used only against a target in the location specified for that tactic. If there is no appropriate target, then the attack is not performed. You cannot switch to a different tactic simply because there is no target for your chosen attack. However, there are tactics for which you yourself are the target, and tactics which have an area as the target (whether or not friends or foes are present in that area). In such cases the tactic may still be used, of course.

To determine the success of your attack, you compare your Attack Score (AS) to your target's Defense Score (DS). If the AS is higher or equal (tied), your attack succeeds; if lower, your attack fails and has no effect. Tactics that are used on yourself always succeed. Tactics that are used against an area succeed, but may be dispersed to a slightly different location than that which was targeted. See description of tactics for details.

Calculating Attack Score (AS)

To determine Attack Score, add the attacker's AGI Rating to his Attack die. If you are attacking from behind your target, using any of the tactics, add 1 to your AS.

Calculating Defense Score (DS)

To determine Defense Score, add the defender's SPD Rating to her Defend die. Certain handicaps will affect your Defense Score.

Vulnerable Marker

Some combat results may place a Vulnerable Marker on a rabbit's CTC. Any attack on a target with a Vulnerable Marker gets a +2 bonus to hit that target. (Multiple Vulnerable markers do stack, and each adds +2 bonus to each AS for an attack on that target.)

Resolving an Attack

For those attacks that succeed, the attack resolution specifies how much damage is done to the target, whether a handicap is rendered, and whether some other status marker must be set for either attacker or target. Determine the result according to the tactic used by the successful attacker, not by the tactic that may have been chosen by the target.

Attack Damage

The core damage done by an attack equals your STR Rating + 1d6. Some tactics may have additional effects, or damage bonuses.

Critical Hits

During combat, some tactics generate the chance of a critical hit. There are three tables for determining critical hits: one for physical attacks from the front of the target; one for rear attacks; and one for non-physical attacks (herbal, mental, etc.). If a Special Handicap is noted, refer to the specific tactic to see what that Handicap is; if no Special is noted, treat that result as 1 HP extra damage.

To determine the result of a critical hit, do a separate roll (1d6 + STR Rating) on the relevant Critical Hit Table below. For some non-physical attacks, a different Trait roll is used when checking for a critical hit. Note: The GM has the option to make permanent injuries into temporary injuries if desired for a less taxing campaign.

Critical Hit Table 1

Physical attack from the front three hexes

1d6 + STR	Result
Any odd number	+1 damage
2, 10	+1d6 damage
4, 12	Special handicap (if none listed, +1 damage)
6, 14	Temporary Injury — Roll 1d6 (1=Ear; 2=Nose; 3=Jaw; 4=Eye; 5–6=Foreleg)
8	Permanent Injury — Roll 1d6 (1=Ear; 2=Nose; 3=Jaw; 4=Eye; 5–6=Foreleg)

Critical Hit Table 2

Physical attack from the back three hexes

1d6 + STR	Result
Any odd number	+1 damage
2, 10	+1d6 damage
4, 12	Special handicap (if none listed, +1 damage)
6, 14	Temporary Injury — Roll 1d6 (1–2=Ear; 3–6=Hind leg)

1d6 + STR	Result
8	Permanent Injury — Roll 1d6 (1–2=Ear; 3–6=Hind leg)

Critical Hit Table 3

Non-physical attack

1d6 + STR	Result
Any odd number	+1 damage
2, 10	Double duration
4, 12	Special handicap (if none listed, +1 damage)
6, 14	Triple duration
8	Permanent until cured

Handicaps

Some special attacks or damaging attacks result in Handicaps, which use tokens placed on the character's CTC as a reminder. The major handicaps (including those from predator attacks) are described below with reference to the "Afflicted" rabbit, and notes when the handicap is removed. If the handicap is not expressly described as having a specific effect on combat or movement, then it has no such effect. Some scenarios may describe handicaps specific to the scenario; these are not listed here.

1. Ants: The Afflicted is being bitten by many ants. This continues as long as the rabbit stands on the ant nest, but diminishes once he moves off. Take 3 HP damage each round on the nest. Once off the nest, damage decreases by 1 HP each round, or stops immediately upon grooming. Costs 1 extra MP to exit. No other effect on combat or movement.

2. Asleep: The Afflicted cannot move or take any action for 1d6 rounds. He will be awakened before that time if he takes a point of damage, including by an ally.

3. Confused: The Afflicted cannot make any attack for one round. He may move, but the direction must be at random (in any direction from starting hex, ignoring original facing), without turning during the move. Final facing is in the same direction as the move. Recovery occurs at the conclusion of the Afflicted's next turn.

4. Diseased: Has the effect of the specific disease. Recovery as described for that disease. Some diseases may lead to a Persistent Disease injury.

5. Enthralled: The Afflicted acts as an ally in the presence of the Storyteller. This handicap remains until the Afflicted (a) falls asleep, (b) falls unconscious, or (c) receives damage until at less than half of his maximum HP. A Storyteller cannot be enthralled.

6. Fascinated: For 1d6 rounds, the Afflicted must move one hex closer to the source of the fascination each round, and may not attack that source. If the source turns away, or if the Afflicted takes any damage, the fascination is immediately broken.

7. Held: The Afflicted is immobilized by the attacker. No movement, and a −2 to success for all attempted actions. Continues until a successful escape, or until the attacker releases the Afflicted. If the attacker moves away from the Afflicted or flees, that also constitutes a release.

8. In Shock: The Afflicted cannot move or take any action, and his DS is zero. In combat, shock lasts for 1d6 combat rounds. Each new round the Afflicted may attempt a saving throw by rolling 1d6 + MYS Rating greater than Shock Value of 4. Removed when the shock runs out, or when the saving throw is made, whichever is earlier. A Seer automatically recovers from shock after one round.

9. Poisoned: The Afflicted immediately loses one movement point. Each round the Afflicted takes 1 point of damage. If the Afflicted drops to half of full HP, he loses one more movement point. Each turn the Afflicted may attempt a saving throw by rolling 1d6 + CON Rating greater than the Poison Value for the specific poison. Removed when the Afflicted is cured, by physical bleeding procedures or herbal cures, or when the saving throw is made, whichever is earlier. An Empath automatically recovers from being poisoned after one round.

10. Quilled: The Afflicted has one quilled marker if stuck by 1–3 quills, and two markers if stuck by four or more. His AGI Rating is reduced by one (if one marker) or two (if two markers), thus reducing his chance to hit in combat. No recovery until the completion of combat, and then recovers by spending ten minutes removing quills (cannot move or eat during this time). An Armadillo or Turtle cannot be quilled.

11. Sneezing: The Afflicted cannot attack, and cannot control movement. Each turn, the GM moves the Afflicted one hex in a random direction. Sneezing lasts for 1d6 rounds.

12. Sprayed: The Afflicted loses three movement points for one round, and gains one movement point back at the end of each succeeding round. Place a −3, −2, or −1 marker under Speed on the CTC. When all those markers are gone, remove the Sprayed marker.

13. Stunned: For one round, the Afflicted is motionless and cannot attack. Full recovery after this time.

14. Vulnerable: The Afflicted has done some attack that leaves him more open to an attack by another. Any attacks on him get a +1 bonus to hit. It is possible to get more than one Vulnerable marker at the same time; in this case, they stack (e.g., three Vulnerable markers would give opponents a +3 to hit). Removed at the start of his next turn.

Injury

A special type of handicap is Injury. This can result from critical hits in combat, traps, accidents, emotional trauma, or disease. A temporary injury heals automatically after 1d6 days (or, if the GM prefers, 1d6 game sessions). A permanent injury never heals. (As a House Rule, the GM may say that all injuries are temporary.) Injuries cannot be cured by empathic healing or herbs. An injury results in reduction of a specific Trait Rating, dependent on the body region that is affected. Each injury reduces the indicated Trait Rating by one point. It is possible to have multiple injuries, and the effects stack.

1. Jaw/Teeth (STR): Damage to the jaw reduces the strength of bites, but also generally weakens the rabbit due to difficulty in eating.

2. Hind leg (SPD): The hind legs contribute more to speed than do the forelegs. A limping rabbit is more likely to attract a predator's attack, and make it more difficult to escape.

3. Eye (INT): Loss of an eye reduces the rabbit's detection ability, as well as its depth perception. Loss of both eyes results in blindness.

4. Foreleg (AGI): Damage to a foreleg greatly affects the manipulation skills of the rabbit, and its chances to hit in combat.

5. Persistent Disease (CON): Being subject to diseases or persistent infestation by parasites can reduce the constitution of the rabbit.

6. Emotional Trauma (MYS): Experiencing great emotional trauma can haunt a rabbit, making him more susceptible to shock.

7. Nose (SML): Nose damage reduces the ability to smell.

8. Ear (CHA): Injuries to the ears affects hearing, and thus communication abilities. It can also be unsightly.

Regular Attack Tactics (available to all rabbits)

Each of these tactics has execution choices. The **preset** [PS] is described first; if an **alternative** [OPT] is not stated by the player at the time of execution, the default is what applies. Once the result of an attack is determined, the player can no longer change the choice that was made. [Roll 6] means a roll of 6 on 1d6 to determine if some extra effect occurs. [Roll 5–6] means either a 5 or 6 succeeds, etc.

Kick [K]:	A Kick may be directed at any of the three adjacent hexes behind the attacker.
[PS]	Core Damage, plus a chance of Critical [Roll 6], Special = defender is Vulnerable.
[OPT] Push Back:	Core Damage, plus a chance to push target away one hex [Roll 6]
[OPT] Hop Forward:	Core Damage, plus a chance to hop forward one hex away from target [Roll 6]

Bite [B]:	A Bite may be directed at the adjacent hex directly ahead of the attacker.
[PS]	Core Damage.
[OPT] Bite and Hold:	Core Damage, plus a chance to Hold [Roll 5–6]; attacker is Vulnerable.
[OPT] Vicious Bite:	Core Damage, plus a chance of Critical [Roll 6], Special = Bleeding; attacker is Vulnerable.

Claw [C]:	A Claw may be directed at any of the three adjacent hexes ahead of the attacker.
[PS]	Core Damage.
[OPT] Cuff:	One point of damage, considered non-hostile. Attacker is Wary.
[OPT] Vicious Claw:	Core Damage, plus a chance of Critical [Roll 6]; attacker is Vulnerable.

Dodge [D]:	A Dodge is defensive in nature; no target is necessary.
[PS]	Increase Defense Score by 2.

Dodge [D]:	A Dodge is defensive in nature; no target is necessary.
[OPT] Use Pause:	The intent is to do something else during your turn, such as use an herb on self, eat, groom, pick up an item in the same hex, drop an item in the same hex, or perform certain special abilities that require non-engagement. If you are not hit at any time until your next turn, this extra action succeeds; otherwise it fails. Increase Defense Score by 1.
[OPT] Flee:	You disengage from the fight and attempt to flee the Battleboard. For the remainder of combat, you may not perform any action, but rather must use your full movement each turn to reach the nearest unblocked exit and leave the board. Increase Defense Score by 3 while still on the board.

Submit [S]:	Much of the fighting between rabbits involves social hierarchy; thus, submission is a valid tactic for rabbits. Generally when one rabbit submits to another, the dominant rabbit stops fighting and does not go on to injure the submissive rabbit. There are some variants available that often have a similar effect.
[PS]	Stop fighting and assume a submissive posture. Submissive rabbit is doubly Vulnerable. However, if another rabbit attacks anyway and the attack hits, submission automatically turns into Flee. This tactic has no effect on predators.
[OPT] Feign Death:	Stop fighting and appear to be dead. May result in some predators ceasing to attack. May attract some scavengers. Some characters get an advantage in Feign Death.
[OPT] Feign Disease:	Stop fighting and appear to be diseased, by markedly unusual behavior. May result in other rabbits fleeing to avoid contamination, and may result in some predators ceasing to attack. However, may attract the attack of certain predators, who cue in on injured prey. Some characters get an advantage in Feign Disease.

Special Ability Tactics

Each of the following tactics is unique to a particular profession. See descriptions of Special Abilities for each profession for more details.

1. Rip [K] (Fighter only, if target is in Hold): If the target is being Held, the Rip may be performed on the same target (otherwise, this attack is ignored, and cannot be switched to another target). Core damage plus an automatic roll for a Critical Hit.

2. Double Attack (L3 Fighter): First attack as normal before moving; whether or not it succeeds, may attempt a second attack in second phase to replace the move option. To indicate this on the CTC, place one marker on Double Attack and a second marker on the type of attack being done (Claw, Kick, or Bite). Both attacks in a Double Attack must be of the same type. The second attack is not required; instead the attacker, after seeing the result of the first attack, may choose to move, but only one hex (or one turn in place).

3. Killing Blow (L6 Fighter): Attempt a double-damage blow to replace a normal attack; if it fails, target takes no damage, and place a Vulnerable marker on the attacker's CTC (to be removed at start of player's next turn). Must indicate the type of attack being done (Claw, Kick or Bite). If the attack is successful, determine its damage and then double it. The Fighter may move normally in this round; that is, this attack counts as a single action (unlike Double Attack), but cannot be combined with Double Attack.

4. Dodge and Attack (L3 Runner): Done like a normal attack, but with an additional marker on the Dodge tactic on CTC. If the attack is successful, increase the attacker's Defend die by one point (maximum 6). If the attack fails, decrease the attacker's Defend die by one point (minimum zero).

5. Steal Item (L3 Maverick): Instead of trying to do damage, the Maverick is trying to take an item from the fur of the target. If the attack is successful, the Maverick gets one item that is being carried in the fur of the target, chosen at random, and immediately can either swallow the item or tuck it into his fur to be carried (if he has room to carry it). If the attack fails, place a Vulnerable marker on the attacker's CTC (to be removed at start of player's next turn). The Maverick cannot steal an item being held in the mouth.

6. Apply Contact Herb: Success is automatic if used on self or ally. If used against opponent, success determined by normal attack roll. Result depends on herb effect. The herb must have been prepared. Can be applied to self by any rabbit. Can be attempted against an opponent only by Herbalist at Level 1 or higher. If attack fails, place a Vulnerable marker on the attacker's CTC (to be removed at start of player's next turn).

7. Apply Area Effect Herb (Herbalist only): The Herbalist throws a prepared area effect herb at a hex directly in front, two hexes away. First determine the accuracy of the throw by rolling 1d6. (1) Lands in 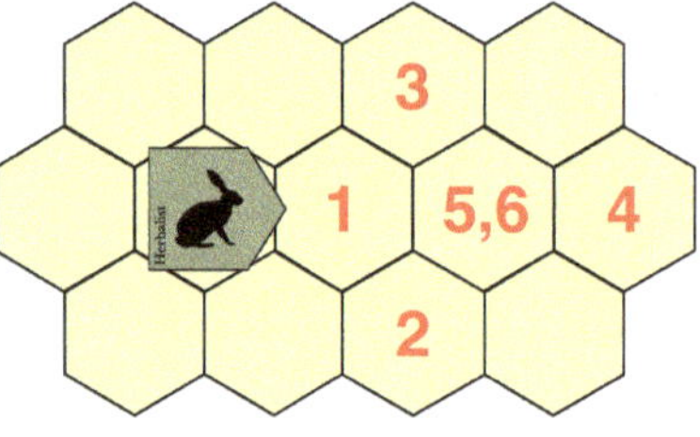 the hex directly ahead, adjacent to the Herbalist; (2–3) Lands ahead and to the right or left; (4) Lands directly ahead, but one hex too far; (5–6) lands in the target hex (see diagram). The herb immediately affects the landing hex plus the six hexes adjacent to it. Note that on a short throw (a 1), this includes the Herbalist in the affected area.

8. Empathic Heal (Empath only): Cannot be performed on self, but automatic on ally. Ally heals 1d6 HP, but Empath incurs 3 HP damage.

9. Empathic Hurt (Empath only): Successful attack by 1d6 + CON Rating against adjacent opponent, who defends with 1d6 + CON Rating. (Note the different Rating used in this attack.) Damage = CON Bonus to opponent, but if successful, heals self by 1 HP. Note: Empathic hurt results in physical damage to the opponent; if no damage results, the Empath doesn't heal.

10. Confuse (L3 Storyteller): Successful attack by 1d6 + CHA Rating against opponent one or two hexes away, who defends with 1d6 + INT Rating. This makes it difficult for the target to distinguish between friend and foe for one round. No attacks by target for that round.

11. Double Bite (L3 Bandit): First bite as normal; if it succeeds, can immediately attempt a second bite (after target defense is decreased by the first attack). Only the successful second bite can be a Bite and Hold. Cannot then take a move or other second action.

12. Box (L3 Herald): This is a double attack by either Claw or Cuff. The first attack is taken as normal; if it succeeds, can immediately attempt the second attack (after target defense is decreased by the first attack and attack die is reduced by two). Cannot then take a move or other second action.

13. Jump Kick [K] (L6 Herald): This is a special attack that incorporates a partial move. It can be used only against a target that is non-adjacent, but is an extra hex away, to any of the three front directions. First move the Herald one hex closer to the target (now becoming adjacent), but without changing current facing, and then carry out the attack as a normal Kick. This does not count as a move; i.e., the Herald may still move either before or after attacking, as normal. If the attack fails, place a Vulnerable marker on the attacker's CTC (to be removed at start of player's next turn).

14. Power Spray [K] (L3 Burglar): Directs a spray in a cone, extending from adjacent hex in front in a cone 3 hexes in that direction (1d6 + AGI Rating vs. 1d6 + CON Rating). If successful, target attempts to flee. Once per day.

15. Throw Quills (L3 Guardian): Directs quills to all (friend or foe) in adjacent hexes to the rear three directions (1d6 + AGI Rating vs. current value of target's Defend die). If hit, target gets quilled with 1d6 quills. Three times per day.

16. Roll Up (Trader only): The Trader rolls into a ball, and is thereby immune to all combat damage unless done by a Brute predator. Cannot attack, and cannot voluntarily move; however, if this is done on a slope, the Trader begins rolling downhill, one hex the first round, two the second, three the third, until leaving the Battleboard or striking a tree, rock, or stream.

17. Armored Protection (L3 Trader): Allows normal movement and attacks by the Trader, but reduces any combat damage taken from physical attacks (not herbs, poison, or Empathic Hurt) by three points per hit.

18. Taunt [D] (Grifter only): Distracts an enemy, who chooses to pursue you (1d6 + CHA Rating vs. 1d6 + INT Rating).

Special Movement Tactics

1. Speed Burst (Runner Only): Runners may take an additional move (using full MP) at any time (not just in their own turn), but it costs 1 HP to do so.

2. Intercept (L6 Runner): If an enemy is adjacent to an ally, and the ally's hex is within movement range of the Runner, the Runner may move to occupy that hex, displacing the ally to any hex adjacent to the Runner but not adjacent to the enemy. No attack may be done this turn, only movement.

3. Double Jump (L3 Spy): A Spy has a special movement, the Double Jump, that permits direction change mid-move. First move as a normal move, up to full movement allowance. Then change facing to any direction and make a second move, again up to full movement allowance. This constitutes the total movement for that turn. No attack may be done this turn, only movement. At the conclusion of the double jump, if the Spy ends in an obscuring hex (bush, tree), consider the Spy to be hidden from friends and foes.

4. Leap Acrobatically (Grifter only): If an elevated terrain feature is within two hexes of the Grifter (such as a bush, tree, or rock), the Grifter may leap directly to that hex without consideration of any obstacles in intervening hexes, including enemies. This constitutes the total movement for that turn. No attack may be done this turn, only movement.

5. Take Flight (Raptor Only): If a raptor is on the ground, it may take flight and move half normal move distance, even if carrying a prey item. All low-terrain obstacles are ignored, but this cannot be done in the direction of a high obstacle (e.g., tree). This constitutes the total movement for that turn. No attack may be done this turn, only movement. At the end of this move, the raptor is in the air, but still low enough to be attacked by opponents on the ground. The following turn the raptor is able to fly higher and be out of range of ground attacks.

6. Dive in Water (Aquatic Only): If an aquatic predator is no more than one hex away from a body of water (i.e., adjacent or one-hex distant), it may move and dive into that water, even if carrying a prey item. This constitutes the total movement for that turn. No attack may be done this turn, only movement. At the end of this move, the aquatic predator is in the water, but not yet totally submerged, and can still be attacked by ground predators on adjacent land hexes. The following turn the aquatic predator swims deeper and is out of range of ground attacks.

Combat with Predators or Neutrals

Fighting Neutrals

Sometimes there may be a fight between rabbits and "neutral" animals (that is, non-predators). Essentially this is played exactly the same as fights involving just rabbits, which were described previously. Some neutrals do have special combat abilities, though. In addition, rabbits have restrictions on the way they fight particular types of neutrals. These restrictions and special abilities are discussed in this section. For stats, please refer to the Bestiary.

Neutral Special Abilities

These neutrals are grouped by languages for convenience. This list includes only those special abilities that may be used during Combat; for special abilities during Pursuit, see the Pursuit section.

Chatters

Squirrels and Chipmunks have special abilities as described for Player Characters (PCs). If fought underground, use the combat rules for burrow combat. For others:

- **Bite [B]:** All Chatters, standard bite only; no claw or kick.

- **Climb:** Chipmunks, Tree Squirrels, and Flying Squirrels can climb trees, including canopy. Ground Squirrels can also climb trees, but preferentially try to run to a burrow. Marmots and Prairie Dogs can climb trees, but not canopy, and they are Vulnerable when in trees.

- **Glide [Pursuit & Combat]:** Flying Squirrel, special move from treetop, canopy, or bush to any destination at same height (if within three hexes) or lower height (if within four hexes). Note that the flying squirrel must Climb to reach a greater height (and can go from treetop to canopy).

- **Alarm Call [Pursuit & Combat]:** Ground Squirrel, Marmot, Prairie Dog. If any of these detects a predator, all animals (friendly, neutral, or hostile) on the board are aware of its location and general identity (ground predator, flying predator, or snake). The predator attacks with a −1 disadvantage (to AS) for 1d6 rounds.

Nibblers

Porcupines have special abilities as described for PCs. For Rats, see the predator section. For others:

- **Bite [B]:** All Nibblers, standard bite only; no claw or kick.

- **Climb:** Mouse, Packrat, and Vole can climb trees, including canopy.

- **Fast Burrow [Pursuit & Combat]:** Gopher. In one round, can burrow into the ground and disappear (but not in rock, mud, water, or pavement); but if damage is taken during that round, it cancels this action.

- **Dive Underwater:** Beaver, Nutria, Muskrat, Otter. If in the water, can go underwater and disappear from non-aquatic predators. While underwater, has full movement allowance. Can stay underwater a number of minutes equal to CON Rating.

- **Serenity:** Voles. Given 10 minutes uninterrupted, a cooperative Vole can empathically induce a state of Serenity, eliminating pain and curing 1d6 damage.

Grubbers

Armadillos and Opossums have special abilities as described for Player Characters (PCs). If fought underground, use the combat rules for burrow combat. For others (none of which can climb trees):

- **Bite [B]:** All Grubbers, standard bite only; no claw or kick.

- **Fast Burrow [Pursuit & Combat]:** Mole. In one round, can burrow into the ground and disappear (but not in rock, mud, water, or pavement); but if damage is taken during that round, it cancels this action.

- **Tusk Gore [B]:** Pig, Javelina, Wild Boar. A special attack with tusks that can be combined with a facing change of one hex side that occurs as part of the attack action; thus, they can make this attack against five adjacent starting hexes (only not against the hex directly behind them at the start of the attack action). Does Core Damage, but always results in a roll on the Critical Table. Their movement points are reduced by 2 on their next move phase (whether in this turn or the next).

Hoofers

All hoofers have the special Hoof-Kick ability. All Hoofers except for Goats and Sheep also have the Stomp attack. Goats and Sheep have the Butt attack. Bulls and Bisons engage in Pursuit, just like predators, and if they catch a rabbit, they may use the Horn Gore attack. Cows, Pronghorns, Deer, Elk, and Moose may also use Horn Gore, but they don't get the +1 to Core Damage.

- **Climb:** Goats can climb trees (not canopy). Goats, Sheep and Mountain Goats can climb rock faces (though Sheep are Vulnerable when doing so).

- **Hoof-Kick [K]:** This tactic can be used against any adjacent target except one directly in front of the attacker. A hit results in core damage plus a chance to stun; roll 1d6: On 4, 5, or 6, the target is stunned.

- **Stomp [C]:** The attacker rears and stomps down on a target that is ahead. A hit results in core damage +2, plus a chance for a critical hit.

- **Butt [B]:** May only be used against a target directly ahead, but is done with an intrinsic move, so the target may be adjacent or one or two hexes ahead. A hit results in core damage, plus a chance to confuse the target; roll 1d6: On a 6, the target is confused.

- **Horn Gore [B]:** May be used against any adjacent target ahead. A hit results in core damage +1, plus a chance of critical hit.

Perchers

All perchers can fly, and can never be attacked by rabbits unless the percher is on the ground. At the least sign of aggression by a rabbit, any percher immediately takes flight. If a Crow or Raven encounters a disabled rabbit (unconscious, or with some handicap that prevents its fighting), it attempts the special Peck Eyes attack. Each success permanently blinds the target in one eye, so after two such attacks the target will be totally blind. A Crow or Raven attempts to kill and eat a blinded rabbit (or other small mammal), unless disturbed by others, in which case they take flight, and watch from a nearby tree for a while. A blinded rabbit remains in shock, and does not fight back.

- **Fly:** Can stay aloft indefinitely, but can also land on the ground or on bushes, treetops (including canopy), or roofs.

- **Peck Eyes [B]:** May be used against an adjacent target that is ahead and not turned away from the attacker. If it succeeds, blind the target in one eye. After each attempt to Peck Eyes, reduce the target's Defend die by one.

- **Alarm Call [Pursuit & Combat]:** Blackbird, Bluejay. If either of these detects a predator, all animals (friendly, neutral, or hostile) on the board are aware of its location and general identity (ground predator, flying predator, or snake). The predator attacks with a −1 disadvantage (to AS) for 1d6 rounds.

Strutters

All strutters can fly, and can never be attacked by rabbits unless the strutter is on the ground. No special combat abilities.

- **Fly:** Can stay aloft for two rounds, but can also land on the ground or on bushes, treetops (including canopy), or roofs. After one round not flying, they can take flight again.

Waders

All waders can fly as well as enter the water, and can never be attacked by rabbits unless the wader is on dry ground. Great Egrets, Great Blue Herons, and Sandhill Cranes have the properties of Cryptics, as well as the special attack of Skewer. Although they normally prey on pond creatures, they may choose to attack rabbits that are nearby.

- **Fly:** Can stay aloft indefinitely, but can also land on the ground or on bushes, treetops (including canopy), or roofs.

- **Enter Water:** Can enter the water from adjacent ground, or can land in the water from flight. Can also take flight from the water.

- **Swim:** Ducks, Geese, and Gulls may swim on the surface. Some Ducks can also swim underwater.

- **Feign Injury:** Killdeer perform a very convincing imitation of a wounded bird; however, it keeps moving (at half speed) to lure a predator away from its nest or young. Can take flight at any time.

- **Skewer [B]:** May be used against an adjacent target that is ahead. A sharp piercing blow with the beak, which is intended to hold the prey. A hit results in core damage. If successful, give the target the Held handicap. Cannot be used against turtles, armadillos, or other armored targets.

Coldies

There are a wide variety of coldies. Some may be aquatic or semi-aquatic, some may go underground, and a few are cryptic predators. Some are poisonous to eat, while some others may deliver poisonous bites. Most have no special combat abilities, except for those that may prey on rabbits (large snakes, snapping turtles, alligators), each of which has special abilities, as shown in the predator section.

- **Turtle Shell Armor:** Box Tortoise, Pond Turtle. Natural armor provides a +2 bonus to DS. May pull into shell for added protection. Any attack that hits the turtle that is pulled in incurs a damage reduction of 5 HP (thus, any attack must deliver 6 or more HP of damage or it has no effect). A predator that does no damage to a turtle after two successful hits gives up, and leaves if no other targets are available. (Exception: See Eagle Beak)

- **Dive Underwater:** Frog, Pond Turtle. If in the water, it can go underwater and disappear from non-aquatic predators. While underwater, it has full movement allowance. Can stay underwater indefinitely.

- **Poisonous Skin:** Newt, Toad. Any successful biting attack on them results in 3 points damage to the attacker (for each attack). Note to GM: Any successful clawing or kicking attack on them results in 1 point damage to attacker (and a bad taste in mouth) the next time the attacker grooms.

- **Climb:** Racer, Skink, Spiny Lizard. May climb trees (including canopy).

- **Tree Dash:** Racer, Skink, Spiny Lizard. In Combat or Pursuit, if a tree (Major obstacle is presumed to be a tree) is within four hexes with no intervening enemy, one of these reptiles may dash and climb the tree in a single round of movement.

- **Autotomy:** Skinks. In Combat, Skinks can autotomize the tail, separating it from the body. The tail continues to writhe and twitch, creating a distraction that may allow the Skink to escape.

Fishies

All fishies are aquatic, and cannot be attacked by rabbits (except for fighting to get free, if a rabbit is caught by a fish). We do not discuss predation by fish, though there are certainly large predatory fish such as large catfish or pike that could attack a swimming rabbit. The GM is welcome to make up special abilities for those fish.

- **Dive Underwater:** All Fishies. Can go underwater and disappear from non-aquatic predators. While underwater, has full movement allowance. Can stay underwater indefinitely.

Crawlies

This is the largest and most diverse of all animal categories. Some are dealt with under Pests. Some are poisonous (e.g., spiders and scorpions) or have very painful attacks (wasps, hornets, bees, fire ants). In general, we have no special abilities for the crawlies, so the GM is free to use her imagination. Also note the Ants handicap, which is triggered when a rabbit stands upon an ant hill.

- **Bite:** Carpenter Ant. See *Bestiary* for details.
- **Poisonous Bite:** Spiders, Black Widow, Tarantula, Centipede. See Bestiary for details.
- **Poisonous Sting:** Acrobat Ants, Fire Ants, Harvester Ants, Wasps, Honeybees, Scorpion. See *Bestiary* for details.
- **Noxious Spray:** Darkling Beetle. See *Bestiary* for details.
- **Roll Up:** Pillbug. If disturbed, this terrestrial crustacean rolls into a ball for protection. This protects these tiny animals from all 1-point attacks (they simply get batted away), but any 2 point damage kills them.
- **Quick Conceal:** Walking Stick. At the end of any move, it freezes and effectively disappears. To detect it once more has a DV= 0.
- **Fly:** Butterfly, Dragonfly, Grasshopper, Honeybees, Wasps. Can stay aloft indefinitely, but can also land on the ground or on bushes, treetops (including canopy), or roofs.

Bats

Always flying except when roosting during the daytime. Rabbits can never fight bats, and ordinary bats will not attack rabbits. No rabbit can speak the language of bats.

- **Fly:** Bats. They only fly at night, and stay in their roosts during the day. They can stay aloft indefinitely, and although they are capable of landing, they almost never do so except at the roost. Bats can even drink water from ponds while in flight.
- **Echolocate:** Bats can navigate and find their flying prey by emitting high-pitched chirps and clicks. This adds 6 points to their AS vs. flying insects at night. However, it has no effect on their defense against owls.

Worms

Always in the earth, and will never attack rabbits. If a rabbit chooses to attack an exposed worm, the worm tries to burrow into the earth. Consider every worm to have just one HP. Earthworms may be collected in the same way as prized food items, and can be used as a trade item ("Wrigglers"). No rabbit can speak the language of worms.

- **Fast Burrow:** If on soil or mud, a worm can burrow into the earth in a single round, if not damaged (and thus killed) during that round.

Fighting Predators

Nearly all predators must succeed with a Pursuit to be able to have combat with a rabbit or other animal. Pursuit is abbreviated under Basic Rules, but resembles a form of combat under Extended Rules. See **Pursuit** for details. Cryptic predators do not engage in the pursuit phase.

If for some reason a party foolishly decides to go out of its way to attack a predator, they must succeed with a stealthy approach (that is, without being detected by the predatory animal). If they fail with this stealth, the predator always runs or flies away rather than confront the party of rabbits. Predators always elect to fight on their own terms. The one exception is if a female predator is protecting her offspring, in which case she always stays and fights. The party may never attack a predator that is currently in the water or in flight. If the stealthy approach is successful, the rabbit party gets a free surprise round of combat, but thereafter the predator may use any of its special tactics, or may simply choose to flee (the usual outcome after a surprise attack on a predator).

Predator Fighting

Unless otherwise stated in the predator description, every predator is initially very aggressive in combat. Most become more defensive if they incur damage at least equal to their CON Rating. In addition, they attempt to withdraw from the fight once they lose half their HP. So a rabbit under attack by a predator need not actually kill the predator, just survive long enough for the predator to withdraw.

Holding the Prey

Most predators seek to subdue the prey after an attack, and this is reflected by the Hold tactic. Upon a success with the predator's primary attack method (either Bite or Claw for most predators), the next round they can attempt to Hold. If successful, the subdued target loses all movement as well as the Dodge tactic. The target can continue to fight back, to either damage the predator and cause it to withdraw, or to Break Free from the Hold. However, any attack by the target (or any other action) while Held incurs a −2 disadvantage.

With the exception of a few predators with an Unbreakable Grip (Golden Eagle, Great Horned Owl, Snapping Turtle), the target character may Break Free from a predator's hold in several ways: (a) if the predator receives 10 HP damage in a single combat round; (b) if the predator sustains effects of an herbal or empathic attack, or other cause of confusion; (c) if the target succeeds in a direct test involving a skill check (STR vs. STR, AGI vs. AGI, or SPD vs. SPD, at the choice of the target). Upon breaking free, the target is placed in an unoccupied adjacent hex, determined at random, with random facing.

Most raptors are not large enough to carry a full-grown rabbit. But a few airborne predators (Eagles, Osprey, Great Horned Owl) have a modification of Hold called Carry, in which they take flight to remove the prey to a safe location, even before the prey is dead. Some aquatic predators (such as alligators) have a modification of Hold called Drag in which they attempt to drag subdued prey to the water, and then the Dive tactic to take the prey into the water, often holding it underwater to drown. Poisonous predators (such as rattlesnakes) never attempt to Hold. Rather, they inject poison then move away for safety, to wait for the poisoned prey to die or become totally immobile, then track and find the prey to consume it.

Although normally no two animals occupy the same hex on a Battleboard, an exception is when a predator succeeds with a Hold. In this case, immediately place the token of the predator on top of the target that is held.

Predator Special Abilities

These predators are grouped by types and languages: Chasers, Stalkers, Brutes, Cryptics and Raptors. This list includes only those special abilities that may be used during Combat; for special abilities during Pursuit, see the Pursuit section. For stats and other details of the individual predators (HP, Trait Ratings, etc.), please refer to the Bestiary.

Chasers

Canids: Dogs and their Relatives

- **Bite [B]:** All Canids can Bite, but none can do a normal Claw or Kick. A hit results in core damage.

- **Shake [B]:** After a successful Bite, in the following round Dogs (all breeds) can attempt to Shake, which does double damage.

- **Intruder Alert:** In place of an attack, a Terrier or Border Collie may take an extra move while barking loudly at any spot in the move. In addition, the Terrier or Border Collie attempts to run circles around an enemy while barking; allow them to change facing by one hexside in each hex of movement at no additional cost. This increases the chance of detection by nearby humans or other dogs, who converge in response. Roll 1d6: on a 6, one human or dog (any breed) enters the Battleboard next round. In addition, if a dog barks in this manner, all rabbits must move one hex directly away from the dog's location at the time of the bark, at the start of their next movement turn.

- **Pounce [K]:** Foxes and Coyotes can Pounce, which is a leaping move/attack that can be made against a target in an adjacent hex ahead, or one hex distant beyond those hexes ahead (in which case the attacker ends up moved one hex ahead). This counts only as the attack portion of the turn, not the move portion. A success does CON Rating of damage, and has a chance to stun. On a hit, roll 1d6; on 6, the target is stunned.

- **Teamwork:** Wolves may engage in teamwork attacks. See *Wolf* descriptions for details.

Pine Martens and Ringtails

Pine Martens have semi-retractable claws that allow them to speedily climb and run along trees and branches. They eat a wide variety of food, though primarily mice and voles. Ringtails are exceptionally agile climbers.

- **Bite [B]:** Pine Marten, Ringtail. A hit results in core damage.

- **Climb:** Pine Marten, Ringtail. Can climb trees, including canopy.

- **Tree Chase:** Pine Marten, Ringtail. Will pursue potential prey into trees, and even along quite small branches. Able to move at their full speed, and can either Bite or Claw.

- **Cliff Chase:** Ringtail. They can ricochet off rocks, climb up angled cliffs, and ascend narrow cracks by chimneying. They can also climb face down at normal speed.

- **Foul Spray:** Ringtail. In addition to normal Bite, Claw, and Kick attacks, ringtails that are caught, or attacked from the rear, scream loudly and spray a pungent, foul secretion from glands near their tail, which applies the Sprayed handicap on all animals behind, up to two hexes distant.

Stalkers

Felids: Cats

- **Bite [B]:** A hit results in core damage.

- **Claw [C]:** A hit results in core damage. Option to Double Claw [C] if no move before or after the attack; hit does double core damage.

- **Shiny:** While a House Cat or Meezer Cat is in combat, if something moves other than its target, there is a chance of distraction. Roll 1d6: on 5 or 6, the house cat runs three hexes in a randomly chosen direction.

- **Hissy:** When an Alley Cat (Tabby) receives any damage during combat, it backs off, arching its back, and hisses loudly. It persists in the combat, but becomes more cautious (larger die in Defense).

- **Mouser:** Barn Cats, Polydactyl Cats, and Farm Cats (Maine coons) receive +2 bonus to AGI Rating when fighting any prey smaller than a rabbit (e.g., squirrels, chipmunks).

- **Pounce [K]:** Feral Cats (Bengals), Bobcats and Lynxes can Pounce, which is a leaping move/attack that can be made against a target in an adjacent hex ahead, or one hex distant beyond those hexes ahead (in which case the attacker ends up moved one hex ahead). This counts only as the attack portion of the turn, not the move portion. A success does CON Rating of damage, and has a chance to stun. On a hit, roll 1d6: on 6, the target is stunned.

- **Nape Bite [B]:** Cougar. Can be done only from rear of target. They can jump on the back of any prey larger than a rabbit and deliver a strong bite to the nape of the neck. If successful, this automatically results in a Hold. Initially does core damage x2; thereafter does an additional 2d6 damage each round (and continues to hold) until the victim escapes (1d6 + victim's AGI Rating vs. 1d6 + cougar's STR Rating) or until the cougar receives damage of at least half its HP.

Weasels:

- **Bite:** Stoats, Weasels, Polecats, Mongooses. A hit results in core damage.

- **Nape Bite [B]:** Stoats, Big Stoats. Can be done only from rear of target. They can jump on the back of the prey and deliver a strong bite to the nape of the neck. If successful, this automatically results in a Hold. Initially does core damage, but thereafter does an additional 1d6 damage each round (and continues to hold) until the victim escapes (1d6 + victim's AGI Rating vs. 1d6 + stoat's STR Rating) or until the stoat receives damage of at least half its HP.

- **Extra Move:** Mongoose. Can move, attack, and then move again in the same round.

Cryptics

Coldies: Snakes

- **Bite:** Gopher Snake, Python, Rattlesnake, Cottonmouth, Copperhead. A hit results in core damage.

- **Constrict:** Gopher Snake, Pythons. After a successful Bite, can attempt to Constrict. If successful, the snake rolls 1d6 + STR Rating vs. prey's 1d6 + CON Rating; if the roll is higher, the prey's heart stops and it must cease all movement and attacks. Death occurs if the prey is not freed within two rounds.

- **Poisonous Bite [B]:** Rattlesnake, Cottonmouth, Copperhead. In addition to normal bite damage, a successful bite injects venom that continues to inflict damage each hour for six hours. The amount of damage depends on the species of poisonous snake (see Bestiary), though a successful toxin resistance check by the prey reduces that damage.

Coldies: Snapping Turtle and Alligator

- **Bite:** Snapping Turtle, Alligator. A hit results in core damage.

- **Drag:** Snapping Turtle, Alligator. If the prey is attacked on land and after a successful Bite, the turtle or alligator drags the prey toward the nearest water at one hex per round.

- **Dive in Water:** Snapping Turtle, Alligator. If adjacent to the water, a turtle or alligator may dive into the water, even if dragging a prey animal. Once in the water, rabbits may not pursue, although a captured prey animal may continue to struggle to escape.

- **Underwater Spin:** Alligator. If an alligator has taken a prey animal into the water, the alligator may spin each round without a die roll. Each spin does an additional 6 points of damage to the prey due to breathing in water.

- **Tail-Slap:** Alligator. Treat like a Kick attack to determine a hit. Can be directed toward any adjacent hex except straight ahead. A successful hit does core damage, and chance of Stun (5–6 on 1d6).

- **Turtle Shell Armor:** Snapping Turtle. Natural armor provides a +2 bonus to DS. May pull into shell for added protection. Any attack that hits the turtle that is pulled in incurs a damage reduction of 5 HP (thus, any attack must deliver 6 or more HP of damage or it has no effect). Like the armor of Armadillos, this protection does not apply to other forms of attack (herbs, poison, Empathic Hurt). A predator that does no damage to a turtle after two successful hits gives up and leaves if no other targets are available. (Exception: See Eagle Beak)

- **Unbreakable Grip:** Snapping Turtle. If the Turtle secures a firm hold after a successful bite, the target cannot Break Free by ordinary means. Escape is possible only if the Turtle voluntarily drops its prey (e.g., after receiving enough damage that it tries to escape).

Waders: Egrets, Herons and Cranes

- **Bite [B]:** Egrets, Herons, Cranes. Does 1 point damage.

- **Skewer [B]:** Egrets, Herons, Cranes. These long-legged waders have strong, sharp beaks. They can use their beak to attempt to skewer the prey. May be used against an adjacent target that is ahead. A sharp piercing blow with the beak, that is intended to hold the prey. Core damage. If successful, give the target the Held handicap. Cannot be used against turtles, armadillos, or other armored targets.

- **Grab and Swallow [B]:** Egrets, Herons, Cranes. Can be attempted only against a prey whose HP is less than one-fourth that of the attacker (rounded up). If successful, the prey is swallowed whole and ceases moves or attacks; prey dies in four rounds.

Weasels: Minks

- **Bite [B]:** Mink. Successful hit does core damage.

- **Drag:** Mink. If the prey is attacked on land and after a successful Bite, the mink drags the prey toward the nearest water at two hexes per round.

- **Dive in Water:** Mink. If adjacent to the water, Mink may dive into the water, even if dragging a prey animal. Once in the water, rabbits may not pursue, although a captured prey animal may continue to struggle to escape.

- **Nape Bite [B]:** Mink. Can be done only from rear of target, or any time if underwater. They can jump on the back of the prey and deliver a strong bite to the nape of the neck. If successful, this automatically results in a Hold. Initially does core damage, but thereafter does an additional 1d6 damage each round (and continues to hold) until the victim escapes (1d6 + victim's AGI Rating vs. 1d6 + stoat's STR Rating) or until the mink receives damage of at least half its HP.

Nibblers: Rats

Unlike other predators, can have multiple rats in the same hex during combat. Resolve attacks once for an entire stack of rats. Rat groups are formed by the GM at the start of combat by rolling 1d6+1 for the size of each group until all rats have been allotted to a group. Thereafter, during that combat, rat groups cannot split or join. If a group's HP are reduced to half of its original amount, that entire group will Flee.

- **Bite:** Rats. A successful bite does 1 point of damage for each rat in the group.

- **Group Attack:** Black Rat. One target is selected, and every group of rats attempts to attack that same target. Remember to decrease target's Defense die by one for each attack.

Brutes

Weasels: Badgers and Wolverines

Badgers and Wolverines are always aggressive; higher die always goes in Attack. Even if wounded, they continue to fight until prey is dead (or they die). Once prey is killed, disengages from combat and retreats to lair with the prey.

- **Bite [B]:** Badger, Wolverine. Successful hit does core damage. Roll for critical (6 on 1d6).

- **Claw [C]:** Badger, Wolverine. Successful hit does core damage +2.

- **Climb:** Wolverine. Can climb trees (not canopy).

Bears

- **Bite [B]:** Bears. Successful hit does core damage. Roll for critical (6 on 1d6).

- **Paw Swipe [C]:** Bears. Successful hit does core damage, and chance of Stun (5–6 on 1d6).

- **Climb:** Bears can climb trees (not canopy). AS −1 while in tree.

Raptors

- **Fly:** All can stay aloft indefinitely, but can also land on the ground or on bushes, treetops (including canopy), or roofs.

- **Wheel:** All can reverse direction at any time, at a cost of 1 MP for the rotation.

- **Aerial Attack [C]:** All Hawks, Falcons, Eagles, Owls. Attack from flight using talons (claws). Successful attack does core damage plus chance of critical (6 on 1d6). Must stay on ground one turn before taking flight again.

Hawks and Falcons

- **Hover:** Osprey, Harrier, Falcons, Barn Owl. Can stay in flight and remain in the same hex. All other Raptors cannot do this, and must move at least one hex each turn to remain in flight.

- **Eagle Beak [B]:** Eagles. Due to its sharp beak and strong muscles, an eagle has a special ability for use with armored prey such as turtles or armadillos. They can reach in to tear out flesh from legs, tail, and neck of the turtle even when it is pulled into its shell. Ignores armor, and does 2 points damage with each successful attack.

- **Unbreakable Grip:** Golden Eagle. If the Golden Eagle secures a firm hold after a successful attack with Talons, the target cannot Break Free by ordinary means. Escape is possible only if the Eagle voluntarily drops its prey (e.g., after receiving enough damage that it tries to escape).

Owls

- **Nightvision:** All Owls can see as well at night as in the daytime. They also use excellent hearing to assist in their perception at night.

- **Unbreakable Grip:** Great Horned Owl. If the Owl secures a firm hold after a successful attack with Talons, the target cannot Break Free by ordinary means. Escape is possible only if the Owl voluntarily drops its prey (e.g., after receiving enough damage that it tries to escape).

Basic Underground Combat

Fighting underground is much like fighting aboveground, with some special modifications. This includes the ability of combatants to change the Battleboard during the combat. Only selected types of predators and other animals go underground, though some predators have special tactics for use in a burrow.

The best way for a GM to handle a burrow invasion is to place the underground Battleboard and ask players to put food and herb caches, kits, and rabbits where they are normally located within the burrow, without saying why. Then keep track of that for later use. This might be used for predator encounters, as well as if pests or diseases are introduced.

Altering the Battleboard

A burrow contains four features: entrances, tunnels, branches, and chambers. An entrance is a connection between the burrow and the surface, and initially the Battleboard displays two entrances, marked by the arrows. This is the only way in or out of the burrow at the start of any combat. A tunnel is a straight or curved passage that is only one hex in width. A branch is a split in a tunnel, such as a Y-junction. A chamber is any group of contiguous open hexes. In between these features are dark brown hexes that represent solid earth. A burrow Battleboard may have hexsides on the edges that permit connection to additional burrow Battleboards; these are shown in light tan (the tunnel/chamber color) rather than dark brown (earth color). If no additional Battleboard is connected, consider these paths non-negotiable.

Some tunnels may ascend or descend one level, and these are marked with slope markers (arrows point downslope). Chambers and branches are colored in one of three colors, with the lightest being the highest (closest to the surface) and the darkest being the deepest. There are no slope changes within a chamber or a branch, only within tunnels.

Plugs

A rabbit may plug a tunnel by digging and pushing dirt into that tunnel from any adjacent connected hex. For sake of gameplay, assume this dirt is removed from top or bottom earth and does not make any changes to the Battleboard other than the establishment of the plug in the tunnel. When a plug is set in a tunnel, it blocks passage through that tunnel. Further, the plug seems like natural earth (rather than a plugged tunnel) unless an intruder detects it as a plug. Rabbits that normally reside in this burrow always recognize it as a plug since they establish a mental image of the burrow and always detect any changes that have been made.

Building a plug requires an attempt that takes an action during a combat round; the rabbit may move either before or after making the attempt. Making a plug requires a STR roll (1d6 + STR Rating) against a DV=4. If successful, place a plug marker in the tunnel. If building a plug in a branch, place the plug marker across one tunnel exit from the branch (it does not block the entire branch). If the attempt fails, there is no change to the Battleboard, and a subsequent attempt would have the same DV. In any given tunnel location, only one rabbit may attempt to make a plug during the entire combat round. Plugs may not be placed in a chamber, and cannot be placed in the entrance arrow, though they may be placed in the tunnel section that connects to the entrance arrow.

A rabbit can remove a known plug with a similar STR check (1d6 + STR Rating vs. DV−4). On a success, simply remove the plug marker from the board. A plug cannot be pushed farther along a tunnel; it can only be placed or removed. Any intruder that is a digger can remove a plug in the same manner, but only if it knows the plug is there. Detecting a plug by a non-resident of the burrow requires success on either of two checks: INT (1d6 + INT Rating vs. DV=6) or SML (1d6 + SML Rating vs. DV=6). As with building a plug, removal takes an action during a combat round, and only one digger may attempt to remove any given plug in a round.

Digging Tunnels

Diggers may attempt to dig a new tunnel in an earth hex or to widen an existing tunnel to form a chamber hex. For a normal digger, it requires two successes to complete this task (some diggers may be able to complete it in a single round). Each attempt takes an action during a combat round, with a STR check (1d6 + STR Rating against DV=6). On the first success, place a Digging marker in the hex; on the second success, replace the half-dug marker with the completed marker, either a tunnel marker or a chamber hex marker. If digging a tunnel between the highest and lowest levels of the burrow, add one to the required number of Digging markers. Assume the dislodged dirt is thrown backward far enough that it does not impede any existing tunnels or chambers behind the digger; an oversimplification, although distributing dirt is a necessary part of underground digging.

It is also possible to dig upward to form a new exit from the burrow. This can be attempted only within a chamber, and requires three successes (four if the chamber is at the deepest level), each with a STR roll (1d6 + STR Rating vs. DV=8). On each success, add a Digging UP marker to the hex. When the third UP marker would be placed (or fourth, if from a deepest chamber), remove the UP markers and place an entrance marker (arrow) in the same hex. Assume that any predators on the surface do not notice the new entrance for 1d6 rounds. Any rabbits may flee through this new entrance in the same manner as the two initial entrances.

Temporary Human Modifications

Humans have a special way to modify the Battleboard: flooding. Pick one entrance where the hose is placed for the flooding, and assume the human does not know of other entrances. Each combat round, extend the flooding one hex in all directions (at same or lower levels) from existing flooding (tunnels and chambers) by adding a water marker to the burrow. For game purposes, note that some parts of the burrow are higher or lower than others; eventually, the entire burrow may become flooded, depending on the layout and relative depths of tunnels and chambers. It is possible to make a plug to block flooding through a tunnel. When all contiguous open tunnels and chambers are flooded, the water cannot proceed farther (there is no seepage through the earth). Other than by this plug method, or if air pockets exist due to changes in depth, the only way rabbits can survive is by leaving the burrow through another entrance. If there is no non-flooded connection to the surface, any rabbits still below in an air pocket take one HP of damage per 10 minutes until they escape (or until the burrow dries out). Once the combat is over, the burrow will be dry again by the next day (or ten hours later).

Each stored item of food or herb that gets flooded must be tested once it dries out. Roll 1d6 for each item: on 1–3 the item is ruined; ruined herbs turn to poisonweed, and may not be obvious to a rabbit.

Carrying During Escape

A rabbit escaping from a burrow system may stop to pick up something to carry with them. Any regular small item may be picked up in the mouth or tucked into the fur as a single action in a round (with an AGI Base Bonus, that number of additional items may be picked up in the same action). The rabbit is still limited to carrying capacity.

Carrying kits to safety is a special case. Any rabbit may carry a single kit in her mouth, but only if no other item is being carried there. Carrying a kit does not slow the carrying rabbit. If kits are caught underground by flooding of a burrow system, they die unless being carried at the time. Carried kits hold their breath and do not need CON checks underwater. They are not exerting themselves, and so use less oxygen. Note that this carrying limitation does not apply to Opossums; smaller young ride in the pouches, while older young cling to mother's back.

Who Can Dig

Rabbits, of course, build and reside in burrows. Some other neutral animals and predators can enter burrows, while others never go underground. Some animals have normal skills at digging, while others are exceptional.

Non-Rabbit Player Characters

Raccoons, Jackrabbits, Chipmunks, Skunks, Opossums, and Armadillos readily go underground. Porcupines and Squirrels will go underground, but prefer to stay in trees at night. Raccoons, Jackrabbits, Skunks, and Opossums are normal diggers. Chipmunks, Squirrels, and Porcupines are considered poor diggers in rabbit-sized burrows; they take twice as long to dig as rabbits (alternatively, the GM may raise the DV for them). Note that the smaller animals are good at digging small tunnels, but simply take longer to make rabbit-sized tunnels. On the other hand, Armadillos are exceptional diggers, and can accomplish a tunnel dig or expansion in a single round without a STR check.

Non-Rabbit Neutrals

Chatters, Nibblers, Grubbers, Coldies, and Crawlies will go underground. Hoofers, Perchers, Strutters, Waders, and Fishies never enter a rabbit burrow.

Predators

Raptors (except for Burrowing Owl) never go underground. Some cats will go underground, but are not diggers; a Bobcat may take over a burrow that someone else has dug. Bears are powerful diggers, but generally will not dig out a burrow for more than a couple of hexes near the surface. Members of the dog family are vigorous diggers, and may spend considerable effort enlarging an entrance to a rabbit burrow, but will not actually enter the burrow (except for certain specialized breeds of domestic dog). They do build limited burrows for their own use, though. Snakes and weasels readily go underground, and are not slowed at all while in a burrow. Most weasels are good diggers, though stoats and the smaller weasels tend to use the burrows of rodents they have killed. Mongooses, Wolverines, and Badgers are exceptional diggers.

Underground Movement

Moving around in a burrow is similar to aboveground movement, with a few restrictions. Raccoons, Jackrabbits, and Porcupines have their SPD Rating (and movement rate) reduced by 2 points (with a minimum of 1). No moves or tactics that involve jumping or leaping may be done underground. A slope, as aboveground, takes one extra MP to go up, but is no different going down. Facing still matters for combat, but an important difference from aboveground movement is that a rabbit may make a free facing change through one hexside for each hex they move at any time during the move. Turning more than one hexside still costs an extra MP, as aboveground. This greater mobility belowground is because there are no clumps of vegetation or other obstacles to rapid turning while running through twisty rabbit tunnels.

Two friendly rabbits may pass each other in a tunnel, but may not stop the round in the same hex as another. Raccoons, Porcupines, and Armadillos may not pass each other in a tunnel, but they can pass a rabbit (or vice versa). A rabbit may pass a Porcupine only from front to back (if the Porcupine permits it), never when approaching from the rear.

If a tunnel or chamber is flooded, swimming must be underwater at a rate of one hex per round (with a SPD Base Bonus that allow an extra number of hexes equal to the Bonus). A CON check must be made each round, 1d6 + CON Rating vs. DV of 8. On a failure, take 1 point of damage. In addition, if swimming in a flooded chamber, must make an INT check each round, 1d6 + INT Rating vs. DV of 8. On a failure, swim one hex in a random direction rather than your desired direction.

Predator Movement Underground

In a number of cases, predators behave differently underground than they would aboveground. With any underground predation (except by cryptics), it is easiest if players and GM all know where every animal is within the border, without detection checks. For a more challenging (and dangerous) game, do not inform the players of predator locations unless they are digging (*"You hear digging in that direction."*), vocalizing (*"You hear loud barks at the entrance."*), or unless a rabbit comes within two hexes of a predator or crosses its path and detects its scent. There are special rules for Cryptics.

Chasers: Foxes, Coyotes, Wolves and Feral Dogs use underground dens only for pupping, though any attacks an intruder that enters their burrow. For game purposes, none of these animals enter a rabbit warren for predation, though they would to rescue a pup. None can turn around inside a rabbit tunnel, and must either back out, or go forward to a chamber in which to turn around. Larger domestic dogs will chase a rabbit to its burrow, but will not enter the burrow. Rather, they bark loudly and dig at the entrance, perhaps for an extended period of time. They may widen the entry tunnel as far down as the first chamber, if particularly motivated; but after eating any kits they find there, they leave and do not dig further, even if they detect rabbit smell farther inside. Dachshunds and small terriers are the only dogs that readily enter a burrow for hunting, and they are quite efficient at that. They can move at full speed underground, and are able to turn around in a rabbit tunnel. They generally will not dig while underground, and so are stopped by a tunnel plug.

Stalkers: Although some members of the cat family will take over another animal's burrow for their own use, consider them never to be underground predators. On the other hand, the weasel and mongoose groups are skilled burrow predators. Stoats, Big Stoats, Ferrets, Polecats, and all Mongooses can easily turn around inside a rabbit burrow. However, if they get a strong grip on a rabbit, they try to back out, pulling the rabbit rather than turning around. Stoats and Big Stoats may surplus kill; that is, even after killing their first prey, if more are present they continue killing, then cache the excess for eating later. With a good sense of smell, they readily detect plugs and can quickly dig through them, though they will not dig new tunnels to reach prey. But a more typical burrow-hunting behavior of the weasel group is to enter a burrow and quickly run through in a search for prey; if they come upon another entrance or double back to the first entrance before encountering any prey, they usually exit and move on to search elsewhere.

Brutes: Although bears rarely search out rabbits for prey, if preparing for hibernation or newly emerged from same, or if they wander near a burrow entrance and smell rabbits within, they may powerfully dig their way in, expanding tunnels to two-hex width as they go, until they get to the first large chamber, where they attack any rabbits they encounter. If in the pre-hibernation period, a bear might decide to use this enlarged burrow (the part they dug out) for their hibernation chamber. In this case, the bear goes out to gather and bring back needled branches and forest duff to line and insulate the chamber. Dispossessed rabbits should just move out and find new lodgings rather than try to displace the bear.

American and European Badgers are quite distinct in behavior. European Badgers frequently dig to expose and eat earthworms, and although they might take over a rabbit burrow for their own use, they usually dig their own. They rarely attack a rabbit, unless the rabbit is particularly annoying. On the other hand, American Badgers are ferocious burrow predators, eagerly going after gophers, ground squirrels, marmots, prairie dogs, and rabbits. They are exceptional diggers, and can enlarge a tunnel to a chamber-sized hex in a single round, without needing a skill roll. They can move full speed through chambers and open hexes underground as fast as they can move aboveground. These badgers are also smart, and may block one entrance with something heavy (or quickly fill it in with dirt), and then go to another entrance to dig down for the prey. They have also been seen to cooperate with a coyote, with the coyote detecting the prey by smell, and standing guard at one entrance, while the badger quickly digs down the other entrance. (For a 3-player variant in the Warren Invasion mini-game, have one player play a rabbit trapped in the warren, another player play a badger, and a third play a coyote, with the two burrow entrances situated at numbered hexes on another Battleboard.)

Wolverines tend to scavenge dead animals during winter, though they can attack and kill even very large animals in deep snow. They dig a den to bear their young during winter, with the entrance tunnel through snow into debris, roots of fallen trees, or between boulders. In the warmer months, they avidly prey on porcupines, marmots, hares, ground squirrels, and rabbits. They are excellent tree climbers as well as exceptional diggers, being able to enlarge a tunnel hex in a single round without a skill roll. They are also so powerful that they can rip open trees and throw aside boulders.

Cryptics: For burrows away from the water, Gopher Snakes, Rattlesnakes, and Rats look for prey underground. If the burrow is in a marsh or pond hex, you may add Minks to that list. If Rats enter, they are searching for cached food or kits, not adult rabbits, though they fight adults if challenged. All Cryptics can turn around within a rabbit tunnel, and can move full speed underground if they choose.

Snakes: At the start, place rabbits, kits, and caches within the burrow, and place six tokens upside down on the numbered hexes; one of these will be the snake and the others are blanks. Thereafter, the GM moves the tokens one hex at a time as she wishes (roll randomly if they are at a branch). If a token becomes adjacent to an adult rabbit (on either's move), turn the token face-up (and remove it, if a blank). If a token moves adjacent to a kit, move it an extra move and remove the kit (even if the token is a blank; this represents a previous attack of the snake that was not detected by the rabbits). A snake can swallow up to 1d6 kits in a single round. If a token moves adjacent to an entrance arrow, remove it. Once the snake token is turned up, remove all blank tokens; thereafter, the snake attempts to reach an entrance and leave, if possible, though it attacks any rabbits it encounters on the way.

Rats: At the start, place rabbits, kits, and caches within the burrow, and place six tokens upside down on the numbered hexes; two of these will be rats (1d4 each) and the others are blanks. Thereafter, the GM moves the tokens three hexes at a time as she wishes (roll randomly if they are at a branch). If a token becomes adjacent to an adult rabbit (on either's move), turn the token face up (and remove it, if a blank). If a token moves adjacent to a kit or food cache, move it an extra move and remove the kit or food (even if the token is a blank; this represents a previous attack of the rats that was not detected by the rabbits). Each rat can kill one kit in a single round, or consume one food item. If a token moves adjacent to an entrance arrow, remove it. Once both rat tokens are turned up, remove all blank tokens; thereafter, the rats attempt to reach an entrance and leave as quickly as possible, though they fight back if attacked.

Minks: At the start, place rabbits, kits, and caches within the burrow. Then roll 1d6 and place the mink adjacent to the closest rabbit to that numbered hex. The mink gets a surprise round. If the mink catches or kills a rabbit, it goes full speed to the nearest entrance arrow to leave the burrow, dragging the rabbit with it, at no diminution of speed. If wounded to less than half maximum HP, it drops the rabbit and flees.

Special Underground Tactics

No tactics may be used underground that involve jumping or leaping.

An Armadillo has a special tactic underground of Block. To do this, he enters a tunnel and wedges himself in, strongly gripping the sides of the tunnel. When Blocking, the Armadillo cannot be dislodged, and has his normal armor protection against attack. To sustain the Block, the Armadillo cannot move or take any other combat action, but may cease the Block during his combat round, if desired. An attacker may dig around the Armadillo, but must successfully widen the tunnel on both sides (to form a chamber hex) to cancel the Block. While digging, the attacker may not make an attack action during the same round.

Area effect weapons (Power Spray, Snuffball, etc.) affect only a single hex if a tunnel, but fill a chamber (up to seven hex size). They do not dissipate if cast in a chamber (place the appropriate marker in the chamber, for the remainder of the combat), but dissipate after one round in a tunnel or branch due to air flowing in the burrow.

Mini-Game: Warren Invasion!

This mini-game is a way to practice combat between rabbits underground, and can also be used to inspire actual warren defense. There are two teams of rabbits, the Defenders and the Raiders. The Defenders set up their warren and their initial placement, and the Raiders then attempt to invade the warren and escape with treasures.

Setup

Choose sides for the game, typically with three rabbits on the Raider side and three rabbits on the Defender side. The players may adjust these numbers to make it easier for one side or the other.

In secret, the Defenders design the warren, with the main warren map in the center and an extension to either side (each extension is placed to connect with a side passage of the main map). The Defenders may select which extensions to place. They may then add up to three warren modification tokens to change the layout of the warren. These tokens are placed face up.

- **New Curved Tunnel:** This token must be placed in an earth hex with one end connecting to a hex in the warren through which a rabbit may move; namely, a tunnel, a branch, or a chamber. If it is possible for the other end to be connected as well, it must be placed so as to do that (though it can be placed even if a second connection is not possible).
- **New Chamber:** This token may be placed on either a tunnel hex or a branch hex to convert it into a one-hex chamber. It may be placed in a hex adjacent to an existing chamber, thus enlarging that chamber.
- **New Plug:** This token may only be placed in a tunnel hex, not a branch or chamber. It serves to temporarily block that tunnel.

Next, they then place their "treasures" in chambers (not tunnels): three food caches, two herb caches, and two nests of kits, as well as two blank treasures. No more than two treasures (or blanks) may be placed in either warren extension (i.e., up to two each), but there is no limit as to how many may be placed in the main map. More than one treasure may be placed in the same chamber. A treasure may be placed in a new chamber. These tokens are placed face down, although the Defenders know what each one is. Note that the treasures have different point values: **Food** (1, 2 and 3), **Herbs** (2 and 3), and **Kits** (each worth 4).

Finally, each Defender places their rabbit token in a passable hex of the warren. The rabbits may be placed in any chamber of the warren, dependent on how they intend to defend it. They may not start in a tunnel or branch. No more than one rabbit may be in the same hex or in adjacent hexes; they also may not be within four hexes of either entrance (i.e., no blocking of the entrance). Otherwise, there are no restrictions on placement. The tokens are placed face up.

The Invasion

Without examining the warren, the Raiders must declare where they are entering; right entrance, left entrance, or a specified combination of the two. At this time, place the Raiders' rabbit tokens just outside the entrances they are using. The Raiders can now see the warren layout (with extensions and modifications), as well as where the Defenders are located. They cannot know what the face down treasure tokens represent. Set up all player CTCs now.

Determine the Initiative for all players; however, the Raiders get a free first move. It is possible for combat to result at the end of even this first move. All combat in the mini-game works just as normal underground combat. The objective for the Raiders is to bypass any Defenders and locate treasures, then to leave the warren with one or more treasures.

Finding a Treasure

When a Raider enters a chamber containing a treasure (or blank), turn that token face up as the Raider first steps in (even if his move is not completed). Any time a Raider is adjacent to a treasure, he may use his attack action to instead pick it up. Any 1- or 2-point treasure may be carried in the fur as a small item. Any 3- or 4-point treasure must be carried in the mouth (thus, a limit of one can be carried per rabbit). Usually, once a

Raider gets a treasure, he attempts to escape the warren with the treasure.

Using a Treasure

A Raider with a food or herb treasure may consume it, and heal twice that number of HP (i.e., a 2-point treasure heals 4 HP). Once this is done, the treasure is removed from the game and cannot be used to score. A Defender may not use a treasure in this manner, nor may a kit treasure be used this way.

Scoring

All treasures removed from the warren by Raiders count toward the score. As usual, if the total is more than four, the score is a thousand. The Defenders are not permitted to remove treasures from the warren to prevent the Raiders from getting them. However, they can carry them to other locations within the warren by picking them up in the same manner as the Raiders. Any time a Defender picks up a treasure, that token must be turned face up, so both sides know what it is. Dead rabbits on either side do not affect the score. And since this is a sort of training game, after its conclusion all "dead" rabbits are back at full strength and ready for the next mini-game (and the Raiders don't get to keep their treasures).

Predator Variant

As a variant, one player may take the role of a predator (one that can invade underground). All the rules are the same, except for the following:

- Do not place any warren modifications
- A predator never takes or uses a food or herb treasure
- A predator that finds a kit treasure may take it or may eat it to gain 8 HP.
- If the predator encounters at least one kit and successfully leaves the warren, it wins. Otherwise the rabbits win (even if a rabbit dies in the defense).

Humans

Humans may be the strangest animals that Rabbits and other PCs may encounter (and see Beasts of Folklore and Legend in the Bestiary for some other strange animals). Humans have hair on their heads like mammals, but walk on two legs like a bird. They cover their bodies with strange colored wrappings that sometimes look like a second skin or a cloak of fur, and sometimes like leaves or bark or snakeskin. They constantly fiddle with objects with their misshapen paws, and carry things about like a bird carries sticks to its nest. They jabber like Crows in a roost, but speak no language understood by any animal (although Ravens and Magpies can mimic them well enough). Humans are truly inscrutable creatures.

Humans come in various forms. See the **Bestiary** for more details.

The most curious thing about encounters with humans, or the places they live, are Man-Things. Man-Things are utterly mysterious objects that sometimes look like something ordinary such as a stick or a stone, but sometimes with strange attachments, folding parts, or contents. Discovering the use of Man-Things is the specialty of Mavericks and Burglars (Skunks), although Bandits (Raccoons) also are adept at manipulating such objects.

Man-Things

Describing Man-Things and Human-related Events

The GM should never use the actual name of a man-thing that has been found. Rather, take care to describe it from the perspective of the rabbit.

Size: Tiny = smaller than a paw; otherwise, describe size in terms of another natural object, such as "apple-sized." Never use dimensions, since rabbits don't use math, or have units of measure (other than counts up to four).

Distance: A short distance can be described as a "hop," with 3 hops to the meter (= 1 foot). Longer distances are likely to be described as a "short dash" (about 10 meters), or a "long run" (about 50 meters). Anything beyond that is more likely to be described as time, as in "better part of a morning" (1 or 2 kilometers), or a "day's journey" (up to 5 kilometers, which at a normal pace would take about 8 hours).

Time: Like distance, units of time are approximate and rabbit-centric: "a heartbeat" or "a long breath" for spans under a minute, a "sunrise" (the time from the first glimpse of the sun to when the full disk of the sun is visible, about 5 minutes in northern latitudes), a "morning" or "afternoon," or a "day."

Shape: Long things may be shaped like a twig, round things like an apple, flat things like a leaf, etc.

Weight: Light = Can be picked up by one rabbit; Heavy = Cannot be picked up by one rabbit.

Surface Appearance: Shiny or dull. Rabbits have limited color vision, so avoid mentioning the colors of an object (although if it is green, you can tell them that). Squirrels and Chipmunks have excellent color vision, however.

Surface Feel: Smooth, rough, bumpy, sharp

Material: Rabbits can quickly recognize natural materials such as stone, dirt, wood, flesh, water. Although decidedly not natural, they also have experience with metal, but cannot distinguish between different kinds of metal. (Metal is still best described as "cold, hard, shiny." Glass is seen as a shiny, clear stone. Plastic is a mystery: chewable, yet bad-tasting and without nutrition.

Smell and Taste: This would be important to rabbits, but may be difficult for the GM to describe since these senses are not as important for most humans. Be creative here, especially by using emotional adjectives.

Moving Parts: Be very careful not to say too much about this, as it could give away to the player what human object it is. You can say something like *"It wiggles on one end when you push it,"* or *"When you try to move it, your paw got pinched."*

An example

A rabbit has found a small screwdriver, which you might describe in this way:

"It's about the size of your ear, light, and cold and shiny at one end. The shiny end is shaped like your front tooth. The other end tastes a little like a root."

Traps

Predators and natural hazards are not the only risks a bunny must face. Traps also may be laid by farmers seeking to protect their crops, hunters looking for easy meat, and trappers collecting soft rabbit pelts. There are 10 kinds of traps that rabbits may encounter, which vary in design and lethality. When your party approaches the location of a hidden trap, the lead rabbit and any Scout in the party have a chance to notice a trap clue with a passive INT skill check (1d6 + INT Base Bonus for the lead rabbit; 1d6 + INT Rating for any Scout) that exceeds the concealment DV of the trap. If the trap is not already specified, determine which trap is encountered by consulting the Traps and Hazards table in the section on **Wandering Encounters**. Roll 1d6 and identify the trap appropriate for the habitat in column 1 (on a roll of 1–3) or column 2 (roll of 4–6). Then refer to the specific trap description below.

If a trap clue is detected, or if a rabbit such as a Seer has a "funny feeling," then place tokens for each rabbit on a Battleboard and allow the player characters to proceed. The trap will be located randomly in one of the 7 hexes centered on one of the numbered hexes on the Battleboard. The rabbits may elect to leave the area (at either of the exit arrows on the Battleboard) or attempt to disarm the trap. In either event, follow the setup and play as outlined in the Trap Snapper mini-game, which follows the trap descriptions.

If the trap is not detected by either the lead rabbit or another Scout, the party enters the area of the trap and risks capture. After the initial passive check to detect a clue, the GM rolls another 1d6 to determine which of 4–6 random hexes is entered by the party. Possible hexes are depicted as green circles in the trap diagrams below. Follow the descriptions for the particular kind of trap to determine if any rabbits accidentally trigger the trap.

Trap Types

Snare

A snare is a loop of wire set near a hedge or undergrowth along a well-used trail. The wire is connected to a wooden peg in the ground, and is concealed with grass and dirt. The trap clue, if detected, appears like a length of vine on the ground. Each rabbit that passes through the 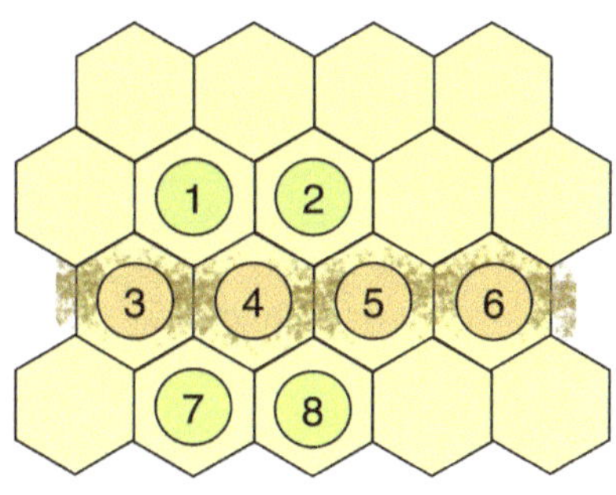

hex with the snare has a 33% chance of being caught (1d6 roll of 1 or 2). Only one rabbit may be caught. A rabbit in the snare incurs 1 HP damage immediately, and 1 HP damage for each additional minute in the snare. (Concealment DV=4; disarm DV=2).

Clue List: Length of Vine (1 and 2; or, 6 and 7). Trap is in 4 (Pull object, either vine).

Live Trap

A live trap occupies hex 4 and an adjacent hex (say, 2). The only entrance to 4 is in 2. The only clue is a bait item (a carrot or other Prized food) in 4. Entering the bait hex (4) triggers the trap. The trap can be disarmed without entering by kicking it from any of the other hexes (1, 3, 5, 6, or 7). There is no damage if caught, but remaining in the trap during extreme heat or cold creates a risk of Heat Stroke or Hypothermia. A CON skill check (DV=6) is necessary to avoid deleterious exposure. A new CON check must be rolled each hour that the rabbit remains in the trap, with the DV increasing by +1 each hour. (Concealment DV=2; disarm DV=4).

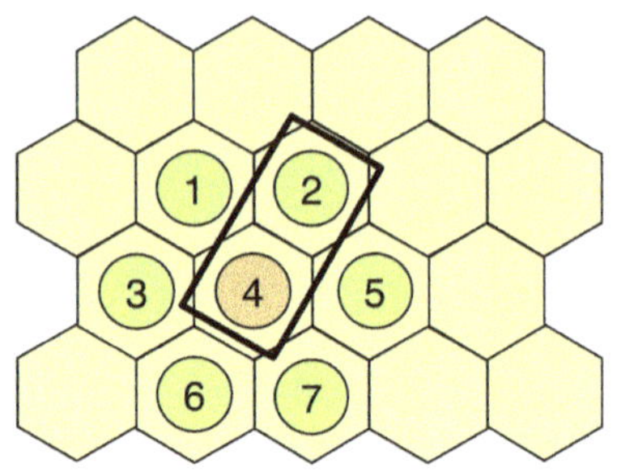

Clue List: Bait Item (4); Shaded Hex (in one of 1, 2, 3, 5, 6, or 7). Trap is in 4 (Kick object from any hex except 4 or the shaded hex; Note: Kicking the bait from the shaded hex also trips the trap).

Box Trap

The setting is as depicted for a Live Trap. A box is tilted up over hex 4 and an adjacent hex (say, 2), with a stick in 4 holding it up. There is a bait item in the adjacent hex. The bait is seen automatically, but the real trap clue, if detected, is the stick in 4. Entering the bait hex (4) or the adjacent trap hex (say, 2) triggers the trap with a 67% chance (1d6 roll of 1–4). The trap can be disarmed by kicking the stick from any of the other adjacent hexes (1, 3, 5, 6, or 7). There is no damage if caught, but remaining in the trap during extreme heat or cold creates a risk of Heat Stroke or Hypothermia. A CON skill check (DV=6) is necessary to avoid deleterious exposure. A new CON check must be rolled each hour that the rabbit remains in the trap, with the DV increasing by +1 each hour. (Concealment DV=4; disarm DV=4).

Clue List: Stick (4); Bait Item (in one of 1, 2, 3, 5, 6, or 7). Trap is in 4 and the hex with the bait (Kick object in 4 from any hex except 4 or the bait hex; Note: Kicking the bait in the bait hex also trips the trap).

Pit Trap

The pit trap is in hex 4. All seven hexes are concealed by leaves or sticks, and bait (carrot, apple) is on 4. The bait is seen automatically, but the real trap clue, if detected, is disturbed earth. The trap may be disarmed by throwing a fairly large weight on 4. Stepping in 4 triggers the trap, but stepping on any of the other six hexes has a 50% chance of triggering it (1d6 roll of 1–3), with the rabbit sliding into the pit in 4. Thus, trying to trip it is hazardous since the rabbit must get close to throw the weight. Alternatively, the GM may decide that 1, 5, and 6 are safe, but 2, 3, and 7 always trigger the trap. There is a small chance (33%, 1d6 roll of 1 or 2) of 2 HP damage if caught. (Concealment DV=6; disarm DV=4).

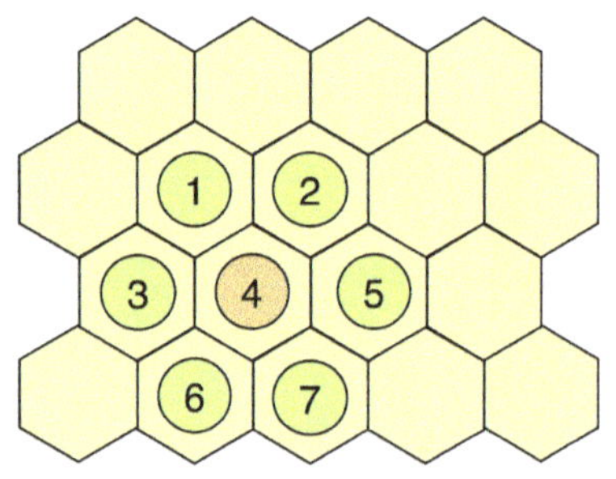

Clue List: Bait Item (4); Disturbed Earth (in two of 1, 2, 3, 5, 6, or 7). Trap is in 4 (Throw rock).

Pit and Stakes Trap

The setting is as depicted for Pit Trap. Similar to the pit trap, but there is no bait, and there are sticks on hex 7, and crumpled grass in hexes 1-6. The trap clue, if detected, is disturbed earth. The trap may be disarmed by throwing a fairly large weight on 7. Stepping in 7 triggers the trap, but stepping on any of the other six hexes has a 50% chance of triggering it (1d6 roll of 1-3), with the rabbit sliding into the pit in 7. Thus, trying to trip it is hazardous, since the rabbit must get close to throw the weight. Alternatively, the GM may decide that 1, 3, and 5 are safe, but 2, 4, and 6 always trigger the trap. If an animal the size of a rabbit falls in the trap, there is a 33% chance of striking a sharpened stake (1d6 roll of 1 or 2), causing 2d6 HP damage. For animals ranging in size from a medium to large dog, the odds are increased to 50% (roll of 1–3) of being impaled. For animals larger than a large dog, the odds are 33% of being impaled by one stake (roll of 1–2), and 33% of being impaled by two stakes (roll of 3–4) for 4d6 damage. (Concealment DV=6; disarm DV=6). An impaled victim is considered held as if by a Foot trap.

Clue List: Stick (4); Disturbed Earth (in two of 1, 2, 3, 5, 6, or 7). Trap is in 4 (Throw rock).

Foot Trap

Assume a dirt trail or runway passes through the habitat, running through hexes 3–4–5. The foot trap is in 4, and a metal peg is in one hex among 1, 2, 6, or 7. The trap is concealed by dirt, and a rope (also under dirt) connects it to the peg. The trap clue, if detected, is a glint of metal at the peg. There may be bait in 3 or 5. The trap may be disarmed by carefully poking a stick into hex 4. Stepping in hex 4 triggers the trap. If caught, the foot trap does little damage (3 HP), but causes injury to the foot, creating risk of infection with Bumblefoot. A CON skill check (DV=5) is necessary to avoid infection. A new CON check must be rolled each hour that the rabbit remains in the trap, with the DV increasing by +1 each hour. (Concealment DV=6; disarm DV=4).

Clue List: Glint of Metal (1, 2, 6, or 7); Bait Item (3 or 5, along trail). Trap is in 4 (Poke).

Net & Sapling

The setting is as depicted for Pit Trap. A Net and Sapling has an apple as bait in hex 4, and rope in all six hexes 1, 2, 3, 5, 6, or 7. The bait is seen automatically, but the real trap clue, if detected, is a length of vine on the ground. If a rabbit touches the apple, all rabbits in these seven hexes are pulled off the ground by the net. Thereafter, an untrapped rabbit can free the others by chewing through the rope found in one specific hex (roll 1d6 to determine which). Finding a rope and chewing it before touching the apple disarms the trap. There is a small chance (33%, 1d6 roll of 1 or 2) of 2 HP damage if caught, determined separately for each rabbit that is trapped. (Concealment DV=6; disarm DV=6).

Clue List: Bait Item (4); Length of Vine (in two of 1, 2, 3, 5, 6, or 7). Trap is in 4, but disarm by chewing rope (Chew vine).

Crossbow Trap

A crossbow is concealed in hex 6, pointing toward hex 3. There is a thin tripline running through 3–4–5, into 6. Any rabbit entering 3, 4, or 5 trips the trap, firing a crossbow bolt. The bolt hits whichever rabbit is closest (i.e., 5; else 4; else 3), inflicting 2d6 HP damage. The trap can be disarmed by kicking dirt into 3, 4, or 5 from hex 1, 2, 7, or 8. (Concealment DV=8; disarm DV=6).

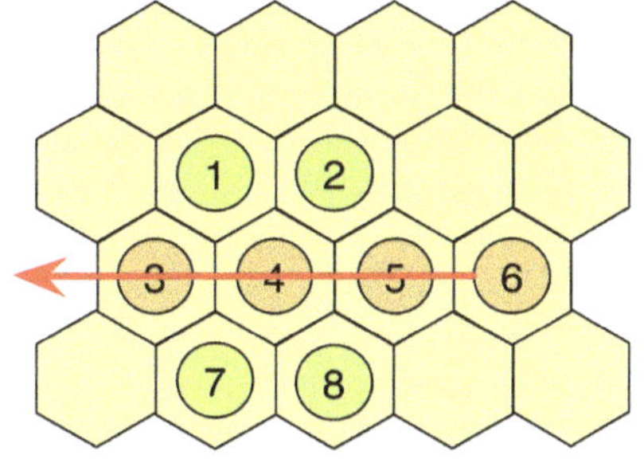

Clue List: Length of Vine (3, 4, 5); Glint of Metal (6). Trap is sprung in 3, 4, or 5; Disarm by Kick dirt into 3, 4, or 5 from 1, 2, 7, or 8.

Beartooth

The setting is as depicted for Pit Trap. The beartooth trap is in hex 4, and a metal peg is in one of the hexes 1–6. The trap is concealed by leaves, and a chain (also under leaves) connects it to the peg. The clue, if detected, is a glint of metal at the peg. The trap may be disarmed by throwing a fairly large rock on the trap, or by finding the peg and pulling that object. Stepping in hex 7 triggers the trap. A Beartooth trap is intended for animals larger than rabbits; triggering one inflicts 4d6 HP damage. If not killed, the rabbit also has the same risk of being infected with Bumblefoot as described for Foot Trap. (Concealment DV=6; disarm DV=8).

Clue List: Glint of Metal (4); Glint of Metal (at location of peg in 1, 2, 3, 5, 6, or 7). Trap is in 4 (Throw rock; or Pull Object at peg).

Deadfall Trap

Assume a log has partly fallen, extending through hexes 3–4–5–6. It is highest from the ground in hex 3. A stick supports the log in 3. The trap clue, if detected, is an upright stick. Any rabbit walking through 4, 5, or 6 has a 50% chance of triggering the trap (1d6 roll of 1–3). A rabbit entering hex 3 automatically triggers the trap. When the log falls, it hits every rabbit located in 3–4–5–6. The trap may be disabled by jumping onto the log from 1, 2, 7, or 8. Deadfall traps may be designed for small animals such as rabbits or for much larger prey. Roll 1d6 for all caught in the trap; the result is the number of d6 dice to roll for damage for each victim. (Concealment DV=4; disarm DV=8).

Clue List: Stick (3); Shaded Hex (4, 5); Log (6). Trap is in 3, but disarm by jumping onto the log from 1, 2, 7, or 8 (Jump on log).

Disarming and Escape

If a trap clue is discovered, one of the rabbits may attempt to safely disarm the trap. An attempt to disarm succeeds with an AGI skill check vs. the disarm DV of the Trap (note the different DV for concealment and disarming). If the rabbit uses a preferred method, then add +2 to the skill check. Success on the skill check means the trap has been disarmed; failure means the rabbit triggers the trap mechanism. However, if the rabbit blunders into the trigger mechanism as the player describes the attempt, disregard the skill check; the rabbit is trapped!

If a rabbit or non-rabbit character is caught in a trap, it cannot escape by itself. Another rabbit may attempt to free it, however, on a successful INT skill check vs. the disarm DV of the trap. Only one rabbit may try at a time. Note the different Trait Rating for escape and disarming. Failure in an escape attempt can lead to several outcomes. For Box, Pit, and Pit & Stakes traps, the would-be Samaritan also is trapped. For Foot, Beartooth, and Deadfall traps, the trapped rabbit incurs additional damage (roll 1d6). There is no additional consequence for a failed escape attempt for other types of traps.

Making Traps

A Maverick with a high AGI Rating may be able to construct traps. See Agility rules for more details.

Mini-Game: Trap Snapper

This mini-game is a way to practice finding and disarming traps. In this game, one player is the Trapper and the other is the Rabbit. In the next round of the game, the roles are reversed. After a chosen number of games, compare the total victory points (VP) of the two players to see who wins.

Setup

The trap setup is done by the Trapper player, out of view of the Rabbit Player. The Trapper chooses a Battleboard and places it on the table. The Trapper next selects a trap type (optionally, it may be chosen randomly), placing its trap grid behind a screen. Note: This must be a trap type appropriate for the habitat of the chosen Battleboard. The trap grid may be rotated to any orientation that can be aligned with the hex layout of the Battleboard (i.e., there are six possible rotations of the trap grid). Place a center number token on the trap grid in any of the seven central hexes on the grid; the location corresponds to a numbered start hex on the Battleboard; the number token should be the same as the number on the Battleboard start hex.

Clue Placement

Find the clue tokens for the trap type and carefully place them, face down, on the corresponding hexes on the Battleboard. For example, if the trap has an apple bait one hex to the right of the center token, put that token one hex to the right of the start number on the Battleboard. Each of the required clues must be placed. Note that for some traps, the particular clue may have multiple possible locations; e.g., there are several hexes for the pit trap where a disturbed earth clue may be found. In such a case, place the clue in any of these possible hexes.

To make the game easier, the Trapper may also place the optional clue. Do not place any of the blank clue tokens in the trap region. When all the clue tokens have been placed for the trap, continue to put the remaining clue tokens (including the blank clue tokens) face down in other locations on the Battleboard, but not in any hex corresponding to one on the trap grid. That is, the Trapper should put them in the vicinity of the other five numbered start areas on the Battleboard so that the Rabbit will not know where the trap is located. Once all clue placement is completed, call the Rabbit player back to the table. Set the turn counter to 1.

Traps and Required Clues

Trap Type	Clue 1	Clue 2	Optional Clue
Snare	Length of Vine	—	2nd Length of Vine
Live Trap	Bait Item	—	Shaded Hex
Box Trap	Bait Item	Upright Stick	—
Pit Trap	Bait Item	Disturbed Earth	2nd Disturbed Earth
Pit and Stakes Trap	Stick on ground	Disturbed Earth	2nd Disturbed Earth
Foot Trap	Glint of Metal	—	Bait Item
Net and Sapling	Length of Vine	Bait Item	2nd Length of Vine
Crossbow Trap	Length of Vine	Glint of Metal	2nd Length of Vine
Beartooth	Glint of Metal	—	2nd Glint of Metal
Deadfall	Upright Stick	Shaded Hex	2nd Shaded Hex

Rabbit Play

The Rabbit starts at either one of the exit arrows on the Battleboard. Each Rabbit turn consists of a move followed by an action.

Movement and Clue Exposure

The Rabbit, regardless of SPD Rating, may move any number of hexes from 0 up to 6, subject to any terrain restrictions of the Battleboard, but ignoring restrictions on facing and rotating. As the Rabbit is moving, the Trapper interrupts in two situations. If the Rabbit trips the trap, the game ends and the Rabbit gets 0 victory points (VP). If the Rabbit enters a hex with a face down clue token, the Trapper turns over the token. If the token is a bait item, the Rabbit gets 1 VP. If the token is an actual clue for the trap, it remains face up; otherwise, it is removed from the Battleboard. To make the game easier, also turn up any clue tokens when the Rabbit moves adjacent to them.

Rabbit Actions

For her action, the Rabbit may do any one of the following:

- Kick dirt to any one adjacent hex.
- Poke stick into any one adjacent hex.
- Throw rock into any one adjacent hex.
- Chew vine in current or any one adjacent hex.
- Kick object in any one adjacent hex.
- Jump onto object in any one adjacent hex (and move to that hex).
- Post: All clue tokens that are one or two hexes away are turned face up.

If the Rabbit action results in disarming the trap, the game ends and the Rabbit gets a number of VPs corresponding to the trap level, plus any time bonus VPs (see below). Once the turn is completed, if the game has not ended, advance the turn counter by 1.

Scoring

If the Rabbit trips the trap (i.e., is caught by the trap), the game is over and the Rabbit gets 0 points. Otherwise, the Rabbit scores according to this schedule:

- **Getting a bait item:** 1 VP
- **Disarming the trap:** A number of VPs equal to the trap level, plus time bonus.
- **Time Bonus:** VPs are awarded for quickly disarming the trap. If disarmed in 1–3 turns, +3 VP; in 4–6 turns, +2 VP; in 7–9 turns, +1 VP; otherwise there are no time bonus VPs.

Herbs and Herbalism

As explained in the section on Traits and Professions, an Herbalist is a rabbit that excels in knowledge of plants and other natural products, and can prepare herbs for use by both herbalists and other rabbits. In the course of play in B&B, you will need some way of redressing the imbalance between bunnies and the greater size, strength, speed, and weaponry of your enemies. In conventional RPGs, the great equalizer is magic; in B&B, that role falls to the use of herbs and herbal knowledge.

Basic Rules: Herbs and Herbalists

There are herbs to cure, herbs to inflict injury, herbs to bolster or sap abilities, and herbs that serve many other useful functions. The Basic Rules provide an introduction to finding, preparing, and using herbs. For those players who want to take advantage of learning and manipulating herbal lore, however, the Extended Rules describe a more complete system of herbal lore akin to alchemy.

Finding Herbs

Finding herbs requires looking in the right places. Herbs of a particular source grow only in certain habitats. The Source is the general location of the herb as a growing thing. There are four herb Sources: Fungal, Floral, Overt, and Covert. Fungal, of course, refers to fungi of various kinds: mushrooms, buttons, caps, balls, boletes, and related decomposers (e.g., Slime Molds). Floral refers to anything derived from the reproductive parts of a flowering plant, including dust (pollen), petals, whole flowers, seeds, nuts, or berries. Overt refers to vegetative parts of a plant aboveground, such as leaves, stems, sap, or bark. Covert refers to parts that grow underground, including roots, tubers, and bulbs. Within each herb Source, there are two herb Types (e.g., Flower and Fruit are considered Floral).

Habitats differ in moisture, temperature, and elevation. Each habitat is optimal for growing particular herbs. If you are looking for a particular herb, you must go to the right habitat to search. The following table summarizes the herb-habitat relationship in two ways: by Herb Source and by Habitat.

Source	Habitat	Habitat	Herb Source
Floral	Orchard	Brushland	**Covert**
	Rocky Hillside	Farm	**Covert**
Fungal	Oak Woodland	Grassland	**Overt**
	Pine Forest	Marsh	**Overt**
	Mountain Stream	Mountain Stream	**Fungal**
Overt	Grassland	Oak Woodland	**Fungal**
	Suburb	Orchard	**Floral**
	Marsh	Pine Forest	**Fungal**
Covert	Farm	Rocky Hillside	**Floral**
	Brushland	Suburb	**Overt**

All habitats contain herbs. A typical overground hex is so large (50–100 meters diameter) that it can be searched many times before the entire area is adequately covered. You may actively search an area for herbs once per hour, using an SML skill check. The difficulty of finding some kind of herb is not hard; the search is successful on any result that exceeds the basic DV=4. Declared Herbalists receive a bonus of +1 in these search rolls (added to their SML Rating). All herbs must be found by active searches; herbs cannot be passively detected. On a failed SML check, or upon request by the player, the search yields the Green herb for that herbal source. (See Extended Rules for more information on Green herbs.)

The Source of the herb is dictated by the habitat, as shown in the table above. The specific result obtained during the SML check determines which of 16 herbs is found. Note that higher SML checks are required to find more complex and powerful herbs, or more different types of herbs.

Herbal Source

SML check	Fungal	Floral	Overt	Covert
< 5	Bracket Fungus	Juniper Berry	Bracken Fern Frond	Ground Pine
5	Poison Mushroom	Fluffyhead	Willow Bark	Slumberlily
6	Snuffball	Razzleberry	Burning Nettle	Mad Iris
7	Bloodcap	Bounceberry Flower	Stinging Nettle	Goldenrod Root
8	Poison Mushroom	Fluffyhead	Willow Bark	Slumberlily
	+ Snuffball	+ Razzleberry	+ Burning Nettle	+ Mad Iris
9	Giant Puffball	Pestflower	Rabbit Weed	Orchid Root
10	Poison Mushroom	Fluffyhead	Willow Bark	Slumberlily
	+ Bloodcap	+ Bounceberry Flower	+ Stinging Nettle	+ Goldenrod Root

SML check	Fungal	Floral	Overt	Covert
11	Poison Mushroom	Fluffyhead	Willow Bark	Slumberlily
	+ Giant Puffball	+ Pestflower	+ Rabbit Weed	+ Orchid Root
12+	Poison Mushroom	Fluffyhead	Willow Bark	Slumberlily
	+ Snuffball	+ Razzleberry	+ Burning Nettle	+ Mad Iris
	+ Bloodcap	+ Bounceberry Flower	+ Stinging Nettle	+ Goldenrod Root

The SML check should involve a private die roll by the GM, so when a search for herbs is successful, the GM should announce only that an herb was found. Of course, because each habitat can provide herbs only of a particular Source, if you recognize a plant or fungus as an herb, you automatically know its herbal Source. However, 16 different herbs are available under Basic rules, four from each herb Source. In addition, a search may find Poisonweed, which exhibits the same properties as a real herb, but with harmful effects. You may either try to recognize Poisonweed to avoid its detrimental effects, or prepare any herb that is found and trust to luck. When an herb search is successful, the GM next determines whether a true herb or poisonweed is found by rolling 1d6: a roll of 1–2 indicates Poisonweed (with odor properties that imitate a true herb); 3–6 indicates a true herb. Another die roll determines the number of sprigs of the herb found (1–6). If more than 4 sprigs are collected, the GM must remember to report the total only as "a thousand." Bunnies can count only to 4.

Recognizing Herbs

When you successfully find an herb, you must identify the properties of that herb before it can be safely prepared and used. Herbs may be distinguished by three odor Properties. Each odor property represents a discernable dimension of the herb's inherent nature. These properties are: Source, Clarity, and Quality. (A fourth odor property — Tone — is introduced in **Extended Rules**.)

> **Example:** Mariposa searches for herbs in an Oak Woodland, a good place to find Fungal herbs. As a 14 SML, L2 Herbalist, her SML check can range from 5–10 (Level 2 + Base Bonus 1 + herbalist bonus 1 = 4 + 1d6 die roll). The GM rolls a 3, and the resulting SML check of 7 indicates she found a Bloodcap. Another die roll (5) indicates that the herb is true, not Poisonweed. One final 1d6 indicates that she found 4 Bloodcaps. The GM tells Mariposa that she successfully found 4 sprigs of a Fungal herb. Now she must perform separate tests to determine the Type (Cap), Clarity (Murky), and Quality (Pungent) of the herbs she found.

You will know the Source of the herb as soon as you find it, but you must examine the herb more carefully to determine its Type. The remaining two odor properties are more esoteric. Clarity refers to the complexity of an herbal odor. If an odor is relatively simple, containing fewer odor components, it is considered to have a greater clarity (i.e., the odor is more pure) than if it contains more odor components. Clarity is the main property that distinguishes useful herbs from other plants. Non-herbs are considered to be indistinct in clarity. Real herbs have one of four odor Clarities: Clear, Cloudy, Murky, or Dense. Herbs of greater complexity generally are associated with more difficult preparation, more powerful effects, and more dangerous unintended consequences.

Quality is a categorical property of herbs. Each quality is distinct and cannot coexist or mix with other qualities. There are four odor Qualities: Minty, Musky, Acrid, and Pungent. These qualities are closely associated with dichotomies of rabbit Traits, which will be discussed at greater length under **Extended Rules**. Like Clarity, non-herbs are considered to be indistinct in odor quality.

Different fungi and plants can mimic the odor properties of a true herb, but have very different, often deleterious, effects. Such false herbs are called Poisonweed. Any rabbit may attempt to identify an herb or distinguish it from Poisonweed, although Herbalists are better at this task. To fully identify the herb, the three odor properties of the herb — Type, Clarity, Quality — must be recognized, and the herb must be distinguished from Poisonweed. However, you may attempt to prepare any herb (or Poisonweed) without fully identifying its properties.

Herb Identity	Source	Type	Clarity	Quality	Preparation	Poisonweed
Bloodcap	Fungal	Cap	Murky	Pungent	Brush	Squeeze
Bounceberry Flower	Floral	Flower	Murky	Musky	Claw	Chew
Burning Nettle	Overt	Leaf	Cloudy	Musky	Chew	Claw
Fluffyhead	Floral	Fruit	Clear	Minty	Lick	Crumble
Giant Puffball	Fungal	Ball	Dense	Pungent	Squeeze	Brush
Goldenrod Root	Covert	Root	Murky	Acrid	Skin	Peel
Mad Iris	Covert	Bulb	Cloudy	Acrid	Peel	Skin
Orchid Root	Covert	Root	Dense	Minty	Crumble	Lick
Pestflower	Floral	Flower	Dense	Acrid	Skin	Peel
Poison Mushroom	Fungal	Cap	Clear	Pungent	Brush	Squeeze
Rabbit Weed	Overt	Leaf	Dense	Musky	Chew	Claw
Razzleberry	Floral	Fruit	Cloudy	Acrid	Peel	Skin
Slumberlily	Covert	Bulb	Clear	Minty	Lick	Crumble
Snuffball	Fungal	Ball	Cloudy	Musky	Claw	Chew
Stinging Nettle	Overt	Stem	Murky	Pungent	Squeeze	Brush
Willow Bark	Overt	Stem	Clear	Minty	Crumble	Lick

As mentioned above, when you find a potential herb, the GM should reveal only the herb Source, such as *"You have found a fungal herb"* or *"You have located a covert herb smell."* Savvy players will quickly learn that even with such meager information, only four herbs are possible in any given habitat. For instance, if searching in an Orchard, only Floral herbs may be found: Fluffyhead, Razzleberry, Bounceberry Flower, and Pestflower. This is why it is important that the GM not announce the discovery of a "berry" or a "flower," but only the herb Source.

You can attempt to investigate the odor properties of the new herb through a series of SML skill checks. Different degrees of difficulty are associated with each odor dimension. Basic recognition of poisonweed or recognition of herb Type involves a DV=4; identifying herb Clarity or Quality requires a DV=6. A complete herbal investigation thus entails four separate SML checks to distinguish Poisonweed, Type, Clarity, and Quality. You can investigate the same herb only once per day (performing any or all four tests). You may use public die rolls for identity tests of Type, Clarity, and Quality. Thus, in each attempt you either learn the odor characteristic of the herb, or know that you have failed the test. Tests to recognize Poisonweed, however, should involve a private die roll by the GM, who announces that it is "Poisonweed" if the test succeeds, but only that it *smells like an herb* if it is a true herb or if the test fails. Note that if you find Poisonweed, the GM will state its apparent herbal Source, but successful recognition of Type, Clarity, and Quality will not reveal that it is not a true herb. The GM therefore should record not only that Poisonweed was found, but what herb it imitates (e.g., "P-Snuffball"). If you try to prepare Poisonweed as if it were a true herb, its contrary nature becomes apparent soon enough.

Preparing Herbs

All herbs that are found growing naturally, and most herbs obtained from Traders or Herbalists, are unprepared and considered "raw." A raw herb must be prepared before use. Player characters of any profession can attempt to prepare an herb, but just as in herb identification, Herbalists have a big advantage in doing so. You do not need to fully identify an herb's properties before attempting a preparation technique. Be forewarned, however, that applying the wrong preparation can ruin an herb, or worse, change it into Poisonweed!

Under the Basic Rules, you may only apply Simple Preparations to prepare herbs for use. There are eight Simple Preparations, as described below. Simple preparations can be conducted anywhere, by any profession, and do not require special materials. Each preparation is appropriate for herbs that exert similar effects, referred to as the herb's Effect Class. When successfully applied, a preparation technique results in a Fresh, which is a prepared herb ready for use.

To attempt preparation of an herb, just announce the preparation technique you want to apply to the raw herb, then roll an SML skill check. This can be a public die roll. Herbs become increasingly more difficult to prepare with increased odor complexity (Clarity): for Clear herbs DV=3, Cloudy DV=4, Murky DV=5, and Dense DV=6. You may prepare as many sprigs of herb as you can count (usually 4) in one preparation attempt, but you may prepare fewer sprigs to allow for failed preparation. Note that if you have not identified the Clarity of the herb, the GM announces success or failure (which provides clues to the herb's actual Clarity). Failure in the attempt ruins the batch of herbs being prepared; ruined herbs are no longer useful for anything (unless you want to trade them to an unsuspecting chump who doesn't know the difference). Application of the wrong preparation technique also ruins the herb, except for one specific technique that converts the herb to Poisonweed (see table). The newly-created Poisonweed appears identical to a prepared true herb, so if you are using a technique that is new to you, be sure to conduct a new attempt to recognize Poisonweed to confirm that preparation was successful. After a successful preparation, be sure to keep a record of the SML Rating of the preparer, which may affect the power of the prepared herb. (**Note to GM**: You may also want to give a label to each batch of prepared herbs of the same kind, to distinguish true herbs from Poisonweed. Players then must specify which batch they wish to use.)

Simple Preparations

Preparation	Effect Class	Poisonweed
Brush	Medicinal	Defensive
Dab	Soporific	Herbal
Lick	Prophylactic	Hypnotic
Rub	Defensive	Medicinal
Scrape	Hypnotic	Prophylactic
Swab	Herbal	Soporific
Whisk	Injurious	Irritant
Wipe	Irritant	Injurious

Brush: Brushing with the backs of the paws is used to prepare Medicinal herbs, but converts Defensive herbs to Poisonweed. Preparation is immediate.

Dab: Dabbing with the nose is used to prepare Soporific herbs, but converts Herbal herbs to Poisonweed. Preparation is immediate.

Lick: Licking with the tongue is used to prepare Prophylactic herbs, but converts Hypnotic herbs to Poisonweed. Preparation is immediate.

Rub: Rubbing with the pads of the paws is used to prepare Defensive herbs, but converts Medicinal herbs to Poisonweed. Preparation is immediate.

Scrape: Scraping with the claws is used to prepare Hypnotic herbs, but converts Prophylactic herbs to Poisonweed. Preparation is immediate.

Swab: Swabbing with the mouth and tongue is used to prepare Herbal herbs, but converts Soporific herbs to Poisonweed. Preparation is immediate.

Whisk: Whisking with the whiskers is used to prepare Injurious herbs, but converts Irritant herbs to Poisonweed. Preparation is immediate.

Wipe: Wiping with the nose and muzzle is used to prepare Irritant herbs, but converts Injurious herbs to Poisonweed. Preparation is immediate.

Using Prepared Herbs

Any rabbit may carry and use an herb, but only an Herbalist or a rabbit of SML level 3 or higher may apply one to an opponent in combat, and only an Herbalist may use an herb during pursuit.

A brief summary of herb effects is provided in the table below. Refer to the complete description of each herb in the *Herbal of Black Adder* in **Appendix A**.

To use an herb, declare your intention to use the herb and how you intend to deliver it. Most herbs simply work if prepared and delivered properly. But some herbs depend on the skill of the herb user. Although nearly all skills associated with herbalism are based on SML Rating, the use of an herb may be based on the Traits associated with that herb.

Methods of Herb Delivery

Each herb is associated with a typical method of delivery (e.g., eating, breathing, contact with skin, rub on fur). Only herbs that are dispersed in air, which exert effects by breathing or skin contact, can be used during Pursuit. Any herb, however, may be delivered by pressing it into an open wound, such as during combat.

Press: All herbs may be delivered during combat by pressing the prepared herb into an open wound, allowing it to make contact with blood.

Eat: Most herbs may be delivered by ingestion, either by eating an herb with solid substance, or by drinking the liquid portion of an herb. However, some herbs are toxic if eaten, but exert other effects when delivered in a different way. Be sure to read the description of the herb and its effects in the *Herbal of Black Adder* in **Appendix A**.

Rub: Herbs that provide protection from foreign agencies such as pests or herbs often are applied to the body surface by rubbing the herb over the fur. In some cases, the herb must be rubbed against a foreign object such as a foot item or another herb. Rubbing employs the same actions as normal grooming behavior and requires the same amount of time as grooming to complete.

Sprinkle: Similar to rubbing, sprinkling applies crumbs or powder from the herb over an external surface, usually a food item or another herb, but in one instance the tongue of the herb user.

Contact: Among the more powerful herbs are those that exert their effects merely by making contact with the skin. Nettles have stinging hairs on their leaves and stems that cause pain and other effects when they make skin contact. Berries also can be applied by smashing them against an enemy and allowing the juice of the berry to contact the skin.

Sniff: A few herbs such as flowers or fungal balls involve self-delivery by sniffing the dust or spores. It is generally unwise to sniff herbs that produce fine particles unless you are confident it is intended to be self-administered.

Breathe: Herbs that produce dust (pollen), spores, tiny seeds with fluffy parachutes (bracts), or other fine particulates may be dispersed into the air, directing them away from the user and toward an intended target. This method of delivery applies to fluffy seed heads, fungal balls, and some flowers that produce abundant pollen. Different herbs have different dispersal patterns that enable the herb user to produce effects over a spatial area, including all viable targets within that area. Fluffy seed heads disperse in a narrow cone extending from the front of the user forward for 2 meters (left). Most fungal balls disperse their spores over a wider front when smashed (middle). Giant Puffballs explode violently, sending spores in all directions, including the hex where the puffball is smashed (right). When an aerial herb is dispersed during Pursuit, however, the dispersal pattern takes the form of a 2-meter cone behind the fugitive.

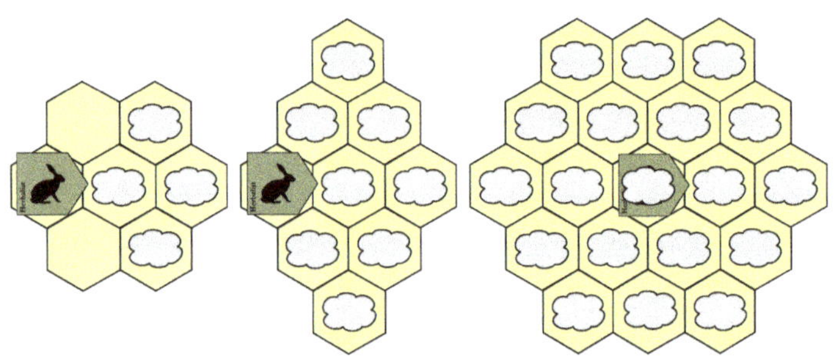

#1	Herb Identity	Effect Class	Trait	Delivery	Effect in Brief (see Herbal for full descriptions)
7	Poison Mushroom	irritant	AGI	eat	internal burning; 1d6 damage
9	Fluffyhead	soporific	MYS	contact	drowsiness; AGI −2
18	Willow Bark	herbal	SML	sprinkle	turns yellow in presence of poison
29	Mad Iris	hypnotic	CHA	eat	attacks at random (friend or foe)
36	Snuffball	defensive	SPD	breathe	causes sneezing; immobile 1 min
45	Razzleberry	hypnotic	CHA	contact	acts upon suggestion 50%
51	Burning Nettle	medicinal	CON	contact	cures wounds 2d6
57	Slumberlily	soporific	MYS	eat	induces sleep ≤ 40 HP
71	Bloodcap	irritant	AGI	eat	wound bleeding; see Combat
76	Bounceberry Flower	defensive	SPD	eat	increases SPD +4
88	Stinging Nettle	injurious	STR	contact	2d6 damage

#1	Herb Identity	Effect Class	Trait	Delivery	Effect in Brief (see Herbal for full descriptions)
94	Goldenrod Root	prophylactic	INT	eat	halts effect of poison
104	Giant Puffball	injurious	STR	breathe	explodes when smashed, 3d6 damage
110	Pestflower	prophylactic	INT	rub	repels all pests
115	Rabbit Weed	medicinal	CON	eat	cures any disease
122	Orchid Root	herbal	SML	eat	protects from all herbs

1 See *Herbal of Black Adder* in **Appendix A** for descriptions of each numbered herb.

Effects of Poisonweed

Attempts to use Poisonweed with the expectation that it is a true herb can lead to contrary, and often disastrous, consequences. Poisonweed may be found growing in nature, or it may be created by faulty preparation or by storing Poisonweed with true herbs. Regardless of its origin, Poisonweed always mimics the odor properties of a true herb, and its effects are dictated by the herb it mimics.

Eating Poisonweed is always toxic, although somewhat less toxic than using a proper poison such as Poison Mushroom. A toxin resistance check is required (1d6 + CON Rating) vs. DV=6. Unless the check exceeds the Poisonweed DV, the consumer incurs 2 HP damage per hour until the toxin is cleared. Using Poisonweed by any other method can produce unexpected effects. Refer to the *Herbal of Black Adder* in **Appendix A** to determine the specific effect of Poisonweed based on the herb that it mimics.

Extended Rules: The Alchemy of Herbalism

You come to me, young rabbit, to learn the secrets of herbal lore. But to gain a deeper understanding of herbs and their uses, you must first look inside yourself to discover the true nature of the rabbit who would be herbalist."

So said Black Adder, the first and foremost of all lapin Herbalists. It is said that Black Adder began life as an insignificant bunny in an insignificant warren. Tormented by bucks that were larger and stronger and faster than he was, Black Adder seized fate and reversed his own ill fortunes through the methodical application of herbs. All animals make use of plants, fungi, insect secretions, and other natural products for purposes other than food to some degree. But Black Adder took the occasional use of sourgrass to relieve a bellyache or willow bark to soothe an injury and transformed it into a profession. It would be more accurate to refer to the Lore of Black Adder as a philosophy than a collection of useful knowledge. To begin to understand herbalism as a practical art, it is necessary first to delve into the underpinnings of herbal philosophy.

The Mystery of the Circle of Traits

All rabbits know of the eight professions and of the eight Traits that define the limits of rabbit skill and personality. But just as herbs may be distinguished by different odor properties, so too can the Traits of rabbits be related to three fundamental dimensions: Body-Mind, Shy-Bold, and Objective-Subjective.

Some professions have skills that are primarily based on physical ability and movement. That is, they depend on the abilities of the Body, such as strength, agility, and endurance. Four Traits are Physical in nature: Strength, Speed, Agility, and Constitution. Other professions have skills that are primarily based on knowledge or understanding, habits of the Mind. Four Traits are Mental in nature: Intelligence, Mysticism, Smell, and Charisma. The Body-Mind distinction defines the first dimension of Traits.

Professions also emphasize skills that reflect basic personality of the rabbit. In nature, some individuals are naturally inquisitive, exploratory, and fearless. Four Traits reflect this Bold end of the spectrum: Strength, Intelligence, Agility, and Charisma. Other individuals are naturally reluctant to explore, more timid in social situations, and more fearful in general. Four Traits reflect this Shy end of the spectrum: Speed, Smell, Mysticism, and Constitution. The Shy-Bold distinction defines the second dimension of Traits.

Finally, Traits and their associated professions have perspective. Some individuals are more focused on outside events, external senses, and objective problems. These represent the Objective end of the spectrum: Strength, Speed, Smell, and Intelligence. Other individuals are more focused on internal events, personal feelings, and subjective problems. These represent the Subjective end of the spectrum: Agility, Constitution, Mysticism, and Charisma. Tension between the Objective and Subjective defines the third dimension of Traits.

Black Adder realized that these three Trait dimensions were interrelated in specific ways. He referred to this set of relationships as forming an endless loop: the Circle of Traits. Because Traits are related to one another in specific ways, and Traits form the basis for rabbit professions, the same set of relationships describes a parallel Circle of Professions (Blue = objective; pink = subjective):

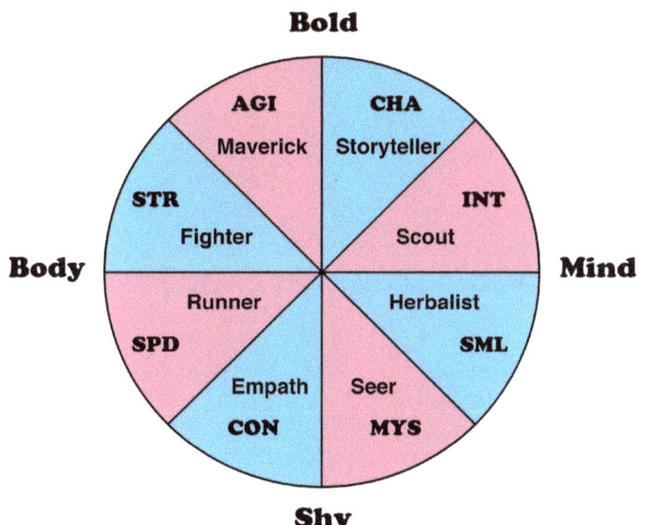

The Spirits of Herbs

Black Adder's most novel insight was that herbs, like rabbits, also had properties that seemed to match the Traits that defined rabbit skills and personality. Other rabbits had long recognized that useful plants could be distinguished by their odors. But unlike other rabbits that simply learned the associations between odors and plants, Black Adder understood that an odor signaled or stood for something that was unseen, just as a footprint in the snow signaled that a fox was nearby. To an Herbalist with a discerning nose, odor properties such as Clarity and Quality served as a sign — as salient as a chin-rubbing — of some animating principle or spirit in the plant. Eventually he identified three Spirits associated with three odor properties. Each of these spirits was, in turn, related to one of the basic dimensions of rabbit Traits.

The relation of herb Temperament, Agency, and Tone to rabbit Traits is summarized in the following table.

Temperament:	Shy				Bold			
Agency:	Mind		Body		Mind		Body	
Quality:	Minty		Musky		Acrid		Pungent	
Perspective:	Subject	Object	Subject	Object	Subject	Object	Subject	Object
Tone:	Fragrant	Putrid	Fragrant	Putrid	Fragrant	Putrid	Fragrant	Putrid
Rabbit Trait:	MYS	SML	CON	SPD	CHA	INT	AGI	STR

Herb Temperament is the spirit related to the Shy-Bold dimension of rabbit Traits. Shy herbs are associated with traits that lie below the midline on the Circle of Professions: Speed, Constitution, Mysticism, and Smell; Bold herbs lie above the midline: Strength, Agility, Charisma, and Intelligence. Shy herbs have an odor Quality of Minty or Musky; Bold herbs have an odor Quality of Acrid or Pungent.

Herb Agency is the spirit related to the Mind-Body dimension of rabbit traits. Physical herbs lie to the left of the midline on the Circle: Agility, Strength, Speed, and Constitution; Mental herbs lie to the right of the midline: Charisma, Intelligence, Smell, and Mysticism. Physical herbs have an odor Quality of Musky or Pungent; Mental herbs have an odor Quality of Minty or Acrid.

A third plant spirit is associated with the **Perspective** dimension of rabbit traits. Objective and Subjective herbs can have any of the four odor Qualities, but can be distinguished by odor Tone, a third fundamental odor property of herbs. There are two odor Tones: Fragrant and Putrid. Odor tone is indicative of perspective, which aids in locating the Type of herb. Fragrant represents the Subjective (S), and Putrid represents the Objective (O).

The last odor property of herbs, **Clarity**, was a puzzle to Black Adder. Unlike the other herb spirits, which were either present or absent, different odor Clarities seem to possess a spirit of greater or lesser complexity, or perhaps, more or fewer simple spirits in number. Moreover, he recognized a fifth Clarity: Green. Some plants or fungi have indistinct odor properties. Odor Quality and Tone seem to be missing altogether, and odor Clarity is simpler even than Clear herbs. Black Adder surmised that Green herbs possess the potential for becoming a useful herb, but have not yet absorbed or developed sufficient herbal spirit to serve as a true herb. Eventually he learned that Green herbs could be converted into useful herbs through proper remodeling. But other plants and fungi that lack a Green odor clarity lack any potential for herbal use.

These associations with rabbit Traits dictate the class of effects produced by an herb. As might be expected, there are eight Classes of herb effects:

Trait	Effect Class	Rabbit Profession	Non-rabbit Profession
STR	Injurious	Fighter	Bandit
SPD	Defensive	Runner	Herald
INT	Prophylactic	Scout	Spy
AGI	Irritant	Maverick	Burglar
CON	Medicinal	Empath	Guardian
MYS	Soporific	Seer	Shaman
SML	Herbal	Herbalist	Trader
CHA	Hypnotic	Storyteller	Grifter

Black Adder's Honeycomb of Herbal Lore

Black Adder discovered many more herbs than the 16 herbs described earlier (under Basic Rules). Some of these herbs may be found growing in nature. Others must be created from raw materials gathered and prepared using advanced techniques. The herbalist with true understanding of the philosophy of herbal lore can even transform one herb into another. The Lore of how to find, recognize, prepare, and use herbs was passed from one Herbalist to another, master to apprentice, down a hundred generations from Black Adder. Much of what had been known has since been forgotten. At present, Herbalists are aware of more than 60 herbs, although new herbs, once thought lost, are rediscovered regularly. The known herbs, their properties, application, and effects, are listed in the *Herbal of Black Adder* in **Appendix A**.

Because there are lawful relationships that bind herbs of different properties and effects together, it is possible to represent the structure of herbal lore. Humans might think of this as a Periodic Table, but the concept of a graphical table is beyond the ken of rabbits. The most organized structure known to bunnies is a honeycomb. This is why the structure of herbal knowledge is known to herbalists as the Honeycomb of Herbal Lore.

Black Adder's Honeycomb of Herbal Lore is shown in **Appendix C**. Rows across the top represent the Temperament, Agency, Quality, and Tone of different herbs. Also shown are the associated Traits and the Effect Class. Columns listed on the left show the Clarity and Source of herbs. Cells within the matrix of the honeycomb list individual herbs, which are described more fully in the Herbal. The numbers in each cell refer to the listing of the herb in the Herbal. Also shown are the four Green plants that lack herbal Clarity, Quality, or Tone, but which hold the potential to become herbs if suitably prepared.

Searching for Herbs

You have two options for how to search for herbs under Extended rules: Quick Search or Rigorous Search. Quick Search is resolved by a few simple die rolls, much like searching under Basic rules. Rigorous Search involves the Herb Scramble Minigame, in which one or more players pit luck, strategy, and perhaps deception against the wits of the GM.

Quick Search

A Quick Search for herbs follows a procedure similar to an herb search under Basic Rules. You may search for herbs in any habitat with a simple SML skill check. Any number from your party may engage in searching. All herbs must be found by active searches; herbs cannot be passively detected. A simple SML skill check (DV=4) for each searcher is used to determine whether a search is successful. The specific result of the SML check specifies which herbs may be found. The Source of the herb is dictated by the habitat; refer to the Source-Habitat table under Basic Rules. The specific result obtained during the SML check determines the Clarity of the herb or herbs that are found.

SML check	Clarity
< 5	Green
5	Clear
6	Cloudy
7	Murky
8	Clear + Cloudy
9	Dense
10	Clear + Murky
11	Cloudy + Murky
12	Clear + Dense
13	Cloudy + Dense
14	Murky + Dense
15+	Clear + Cloudy + Murky

A failed search attempt always results in Green herbs of the appropriate source (i.e., Bracket Fungus, Juniper Berry, Bracken Frond, or Ground Pine). Searchers also can announce their intention to find Green herbs, which is always successful in the correct habitat. Note that a successful search may result in more than one kind of herb found, but only one herb of each Clarity may be found in a given search. Consult the periodic herb table (the Honeycomb in **Appendix C**) to determine which herbs match the Source and Clarity found. The particular herb found is selected randomly from those matching the Source and Clarity.

A search also may yield Poisonweed. You may either try to recognize Poisonweed or prepare any herb that is found and trust to luck. The GM determines whether a successful search finds a true herb or Poisonweed; a 1d6 roll of 1–2 indicates Poisonweed; 3–6 indicates a true herb. The number of sprigs of the herb (or Poisonweed) that are found is determined by a final 1d6 roll (1–6). Remember: Rabbits can count only to 4.

> **Example:** Mariposa searches for herbs in an Oak Woodland, a good place to find Fungal herbs. As a 14 SML, L2 Herbalist, her SML check can range from 5–10 (Level 2 + Base Bonus 1 + Herbalist bonus 1 = 4 + 1d6 die roll). The GM rolls a 1, and the resulting SML check of 5 indicates she found a Clear herb. There are four Clear Fungal herbs: Stumpball, Golden Bolete, Poison Mushroom, and Ruffball. A die roll (1d4, oe 1d6 and reroll on 5-6) determines which of the four herbs was found. One final 1d6 indicates that she found 4 Poison Mushrooms. The GM tells Mariposa that she successfully found 4 sprigs of a Fungal herb. Now she must perform separate tests to determine the Type (Cap), Clarity (Clear), and Quality (Pungent) of the herbs she found.

Searching requires 10 minutes. The same area (large overground hex) can be searched only once per hour. When a search is successful, the GM should announce only the Source of herb that was found and how many sprigs were collected. (Remember counting limitations.)

Rigorous Search

Any member of a party of bunnies may declare that he or she wishes to search a large (overground) hex for possible herbs. Searching requires 10 minutes, and does not guarantee that herbs will be found, even if they are present. Finding herbs depends on the olfactory skills of the bunnies, as well as an effective search strategy.

When the decision to conduct a rigorous search is declared, the GM chooses a Battleboard appropriate for the habitat being searched. The search is restricted to the area of the Battleboard, even though that represents a small proportion of the whole hex. (Aboveground hexes are about 50–100 meters across; Battleboards only show a 9x10 area, about 1% of the large hex.) The GM places the Battleboard out of view of the players, such as behind a visual screen. She then places 13 herb markers on the Battleboard. The search then is conducted following procedures detailed in the Herb Scramble mini-game, which may be found at the end of the section on herbalism.

Recognizing Herbs

Under Extended Rules, when you successfully find an herb, you still must identify the properties of that herb before it can be safely prepared and used. Herbs may be distinguished by four odor Properties. Each odor property represents a discernable dimension of the herb's inherent nature. These properties are: Source, Clarity, Quality, and Tone. (Note the addition of Tone as an odor property, which was not included under Basic Rules.)

The Source of the herb is dictated by the habitat where it was found. The other odor properties can be discovered by a series of SML skill checks as described under the Basic rules. Basic recognition of Poisonweed or recognition of herb Type involves a DV=4. Note that learning the Type of herb also specifies its odor Tone (Fragrant or Pungent). Identifying odor Clarity (Clear, Cloudy, Murky, or Dense) and odor Quality (Minty, Musky, Acrid, or Pungent) requires a DV=6. Refer to the periodic herb table (the Honeycomb in Appendix D) to assist in identifying specific herbs from their odor properties. See Basic Rules for more information on how to investigate herbal properties.

Preparation of Herbs

In the first edition of **Bunnies & Burrows**, herbs had to be prepared before use. Preparation was treated like a form of activation of the herb. It was possible, however, to convert one herb into another herb by treating the activated original with a second herb (e.g., treat Wildroot with Redberry to create Arrow root). However, there was no underlying rationale or system behind these preparations. There was nothing lawful that a player could discern, other than to learn each and every idiosyncratic practice.

In the new herbal system introduced in this edition, herbal practices can be seen as analogous to a kind of alchemy, whereby transformations of one herb into another are possible given the correct kind and sequence of preparation. This is useful for creating herbs that are difficult to find in the wild, herbs with new properties, and herbs with more powerful effects or more effective means of delivery. This goal might imply that some herbs are useful only in the process of preparing other desirable herbs, serving as basic ingredients or catalysts.

Simple Herb Preparations

Simple preparations can be prepared anywhere, by any rabbit, and do not require special materials. Any herb found growing in the wild (including any herb found during an herb search) can be prepared for use using a Simple preparation. Refer to the Basic Rules for a complete listing and description of how to apply Simple Preparations.

Advanced Herb Preparations

Advanced preparations require special materials or locations to complete. They may be attempted by any rabbit, but generally are more difficult for non-Herbalists. Preparation generally takes more time than Simple techniques. Advanced preparations are used to enhance the effects of existing herbs. Before using an advanced preparation, you must first prepare the herb using the appropriate simple technique. There are two Advanced Preparations, each with four variants: Anting and Leaf Pressing.

Ant: Place the herb on an anthill, allowing the ants to swarm over the herb. Anting (as the treatment is called) is appropriate for Fungal (caps and balls) or Covert (roots and bulbs) herbs. By resting on the anthill, the herb is covered by ants, which deposit secretions (formic acid) that alters the chemistry of the herb. The result is a residue that looks like a shriveled version of the original herb. Preparation requires one full day of exposure on the anthill. The effects of Anting depend on the kind of ants, which in turn depends on where the procedure takes place. In general, Anting either doubles the strength of the herb, or destroys it. Anting may be used only once to enhance the effects of a particular herb, but it may be used in combination with Leaf Pressing for cumulative effect. When the process of Anting of an herb is complete, the herb is prepared and ready for immediate use.

There are four kinds of ants that may be used for anting:

- **Acrobat Ant (found in Brushland):** Doubles the strength of Fungal caps such as mushrooms, buttons, and boletes. Acrobat ants destroy Covert herbs, however, and have no effect on Fungal balls.

- **Carpenter Ant (found in Pine Forest, Suburb):** Doubles the strength of Covert roots. Carpenter ants destroy Fungal herbs, however, and have no effect on Covert bulbs.

- **Fire Ant (found in Marsh):** Doubles the strength of Fungal balls such as Puffball or Tuffball. Fire ants destroy Covert herbs, however, and have no effect on Fungal caps.

- **Harvester Ant (found in Rocky Hillside):** Doubles the strength of Covert bulbs such as lilies, irises, and garlic. Harvester ants destroy Fungal herbs, however, and have no effect on Covert roots.

Leaf Press: Place thin pieces of the herb (such as leaves or crumbs) between fresh, green leaves of a tree. Leaf Pressing is appropriate for Floral (flowers and fruits) or Overt (leaves and stems) herbs. When creating a pressing stack, you may arrange multiple layers of alternating leaves and herbs, although you should take care to include only one kind of herb in a stack. When a stack is complete, place a large stone on top to apply pressure through the whole stack. Allow the entire stack to remain undisturbed in darkness for 24 hours, thereby altering the chemistry of the herb. The product of this preparation is a press, which looks like a flattened, slightly dehydrated version of the original herb. Preparation requires one full day pressed between the leaves. The effects of Leaf Pressing depend on the kind of leaves that are used, which in turn depends on where the leaves are collected. In general, Leaf Pressing doubles the strength of the herb or destroys it. Leaf Pressing may be used only once to enhance the effects of a particular herb, but it may be used in combination with Anting for cumulative effect. When the process of Leaf Pressing of an herb is complete, the herb is prepared and ready for immediate use.

Four kinds of tree produce leaves that may be used for leaf pressing:

- **Alder (found by Mountain Streams):** Bark contains salicylic acid. Leaves contain tannins. Doubles the strength of herbal flowers and flower dust. Leaf Pressing with Alder destroys Overt herbs, however, and has no effect on herbal Fruits.

- **Apple (found in Orchards):** Seeds contain amygdalin, a cyanide compound. Doubles the strength of Overt stems, including bark, weeds, sap, and some nettles. Leaf Pressing with Apple destroys Floral herbs, however, and has no effect on Overt leaves.

- **Hawthorne (found in Brushland):** Leaves contain tannins. Can cause cardiac arrhythmia. Doubles the strength of herbal Fruits such as berries and seed heads. Leaf Pressing with Hawthorne destroys Overt herbs, however, and has no effect on herbal Flowers.

- **Oak (found in Oak Woodland):** Leaves contain tannins. Doubles the strength of Overt leafy herbs such as leaves and some nettles. Leaf Pressing with Oak destroys Floral herbs, however, and has no effect on Overt leaves.

Herb Remodeling

Black Adder's deepest insight gave him the power to create new herbs. He speculated that if the nature of an herb is determined by the spirits it possesses, which are signaled by distinctive odor properties, then changing the odor characteristics of an herb might change its effects. This doctrine forms the basis for herb remodeling. An herb can indeed be altered by changing one or more of its odor properties. Each of the three principal odor properties — Clarity, Quality, and Tone — can be modified or replaced by applying the proper remodeling technique. Remodeling can entail adding an odorant that was not present before, a technique called Infusion, or by removing an odorant that was already present, a method called Leaching. The result of subjecting an herb to Infusion or Leaching is a transformation of the Effect Class of the herb without changing its Type. Remodeling creates a new herb — a Secondary Herb — that may not exist in nature, but which may be more useful or more potent than a natural herb.

The Effect Class of an herb is completely determined by its odor properties: Clarity, Quality, & Tone. Clarity is determined by the number of odor color spirits present: 0 = Green, 1 = Clear, 2 = Cloudy, 3 = Murky, 4 = Dense. Odor Quality is determined by the presence or absence of two odor spirits: The Temperament spirit (present = Bold, absent = Shy) and the Agency spirit (present = Mind, absent = Body). Objective or Subjective nature is determined by a Perspective spirit (present = Subjective, absent = Objective). Herbs can be remodeled by adding or subtracting these spirits.

Basic Remodeling Techniques

Four procedures are available to infuse or leach spirits from an herb. Each effectively flips the valence of a spirit, changing its position in the Circle of Traits. Odor properties correspond to the complexity of the herbal odor (Clarity), the temperament and agency of the herb (Quality), and herbal perspective (Tone). Remodeling techniques add or subtract an herbal spirit associated with each property. Because the effects of remodeling are cumulative, a virtually endless variety of herbs may be produced. Remodeling techniques themselves are relatively simple. The effect of a particular technique depends on other materials that are used in the process. Thus, the same technique (e.g., Scenting) can be used to either Infuse or Leach, depending on the essential oil used in the scenting process.

All four remodeling techniques require a beginning substrate and other materials to complete the transformation. The Substrate is the starting material, either an herb that has already been prepared for use, or a Green herb. Other Materials include active components that add or subtract odor spirits, or physical features (tree bark, a concavity to hold a liquid) that facilitate the process. The product that emerges from remodeling then can serve as a Secondary herb, which is already prepared for use, or as the Substrate for further remodeling.

Herb Remodeling Techniques

Method	Spirit	Substrate	Other Materials	Product
Soak	Clarity	Green or Prepared herb	Receptacle, Liquid	mash
Scent	Quality	Prepared herb	Essential Oil	balm
Incubate	Tone	Prepared herb	Nest, Hive	foster herb
Sun-Dry	Tone	Prepared herb	Direct Sunlight	dried herb

Soak: Treating an herb by soaking it in another liquid adds or subtracts an odor spirit, thereby altering its smell and odor Clarity. A concave, nonporous surface such as a depression in a stone, a half-eggshell, or a man-thing open at the top is required as a receptacle to hold the liquid. One of four liquids is introduced into the cavity, and the herb is completely immersed. Soaking in different liquids either leaches or infuses odor spirits, resulting in reduced or enhanced odor complexity. Water is the typical liquid used for soaking, but milk, urine, or blood also may be used to different effect.

To Soak an herb, introduce one of the four liquids listed below into the cavity or receptacle. Then add sprigs of the herb to be soaked. The number of herbs added is limited only by the size of the liquid-holding receptacle, but all must be the same kind of herb. Mixing different herbs results in all herbs being spoiled, so special care must be taken to isolate the herbs if soaking in a natural body of water such as a pond or stream. Allow the herb to soak for 1–3 hours in water, and 1 hour in other liquids. The product of soaking is unusable as an herb for a time after removal from the liquid. The mash, as the product is called, must be allowed to air-dry, not in direct sun, for a period equal to the time spent soaking, after which it becomes a prepared herb of the same type as the original herb.

1. **Water:** Soaking in Water is used to leach Clarity spirit from Cloudy, Murky, or Dense herbs. Catchments of water may be found almost anywhere, but streams and ponds are most easily found in Marsh, Grassland, or Mountain Stream habitats. Each hour of soaking reduces the odor Clarity by one step; thus, a Murky herb that soaks in water for two hours is reduced to a Clear herb of the same Type. However, if allowed to soak beyond the time to produce Clear, the herb is ruined for further use. For example, Soaking Leech Flower in water for one hour reduces the Clarity from Cloudy to Clear, producing a flower with the herbal properties of Mosquito Flower. Soaking Leech Flower for two hours, however, ruins the herb.

2. **Milk:** Soaking in Milk is used to infuse Clarity spirit into Clear herbs and Green substrates. Milk from any animal must be collected fresh and the herb immersed while still warm. Soaking in Milk for one hour increases the odor Clarity by one step, converting a Clear herb into a Cloudy herb of the same type. When applied to a Green substrate, a Clear herb of indeterminate Type, Quality, and Tone is produced, which is suitable only for more remodeling. However, Milk soaking has no effect on Cloudy or Murky herbs, and no additional effect is obtained by soaking for longer than one hour. For example, Soaking Redberry in Milk for one hour increases the Clarity from Clear to Cloudy, producing a berry with the herbal properties of Bounceberry.

3. **Urine:** Soaking in Urine is used to infuse Clarity spirit into Cloudy herbs. Urine must be collected fresh from any animal and the herb immersed while still warm. Urine soaking for one hour increases the odor Clarity by one step, converting a Cloudy herb into a Murky herb of the same type. When applied to herbs other than Cloudy, Urine soaking has no effect, and no additional effect is obtained by soaking for longer than one hour. For example, Soaking Wild Garlic in Urine for one hour increases the Clarity from Cloudy to Murky, producing a bulb with the herbal properties of Blind Iris.

4. **Blood:** Soaking in Blood is used to infuse Clarity spirit into Murky herbs. Blood must be collected fresh from any animal and the herb immersed while still warm. Blood soaking for one hour increases the odor Clarity by one step, converting a Murky herb into a Dense herb of the same type. When applied to herbs other than Murky, Blood soaking has no effect. For example, Soaking Purpleberry in blood for one hour increases the Clarity from Murky to Dense, producing a berry with the herbal properties of Bitterberry.

Scent: Scenting adds another odor cue to an herb, thereby transforming its smell and its odor Quality. The common substances used for scenting contain essential oils, but do not themselves have herbal properties beyond their use in remodeling. All odor Qualities can be altered by Scenting with one or two essential oils. There are four kinds of essential oils, each corresponding to an odor Quality: Minty, Musky, Acrid, and Pungent. The product of scenting is a balm. The process requires one hour.

To Scent an herb, place sprigs of the herb on a hard surface. Dip your paws or chin into an essential oil, allowing your fur to absorb a good amount. Then rub the oil into the herbs with your paws or chin, taking care not to damage the herbs in the process. After all parts of the herb are coated with the oil, let them rest for one hour, allowing the oil to seep into the herb. When the process is complete, excess oil may be licked from the herb without harm. The product of Scenting is a prepared herb of the same type as the original, which is ready for immediate use.

1. **Musk Oil:** Used to leach Agency and Temperament spirits from Minty or Acrid herbs or balms. Musk Oil is obtained from the Scent glands of dead stoats, ferrets, or minks. Squeezing the leaves of Skunk Cabbage, which may be found in Marshes, also yields Musk Oil. The result of scenting with Musk Oil is a balm that smells like a Musky herb of the same type. For example, a Fluffyhead scented with Musk Oil produces a seed head with the herbal properties of Redberry. The resultant herb still can be delivered like the seeds of a dandelion, but produces the Medicinal effects of a redberry.

2. **Mint Oil:** Used to leach Temperament spirit from Acrid and Pungent herbs or balms. Mint Oil is obtained by squeezing the stems of Dead Nettle, which unlike other nettles does not sting. Dead Nettle may be found growing as a weed in Orchards and Farms. Wild Mint, found near Mountain Streams, also yields Mint Oil. The result of scenting with Mint Oil is a balm that smells like a Minty herb of the same type. For example, Leech Flower scented with

Mint Oil produces a flower with the Herbal properties of Falseflower dust.

3. **Acrid Oil:** Used to infuse Agency and Temperament spirits into Musky or Pungent herbs or balms. Acrid Oil is obtained from Rosemary leaves (which contain camphor) or from Pear blossoms. Rosemary bushes can be found in herb gardens on Farms. Pear blossoms can be found during spring and summer in Orchards. The result of scenting with Acrid Oil is a balm that smells like an Acrid herb of the same type. For example, Willow Leaves scented with Acrid Oil produce leaves with the Hypnotic properties of Locoweed.

4. **Pungent Oil:** Used to infuse Temperament spirit into Minty or Musky herbs or balms. Pungent Oil is obtained from the scent glands from skunks, or bulbs from wild onion, which can be found along Mountain Streams, or Marigold flowers, which are found in Farm gardens. The result of scenting with Pungent Oil is a balm that smells like a Pungent herb of the same type. For example, Burning Nettle scented with Pungent Oil produces Biting Nettle, an herb that inflicts damage rather than curing injury.

Incubate: Incubating in an appropriate environment infuses Perspective spirit to an herb, thereby altering its smell and odor Tone. The incubating environment must be warm and nurturing, rich with the Subjective spirit. Common incubation sites include active bird or mouse nests, honeybee hives, or the fur-lined birth chamber of newborn rabbits. Herbs must incubate for one full day to absorb the Subjective spirit, converting its Tone to Fragrant.

To Incubate an herb, you first must locate a good incubation site. The site must be currently active to be effective. Weave sprigs of the herb, using only one kind of herb, into the construction of the incubation site, so they become part of the nest or hive. Allow the herbs to remain in place for one full day before retrieving them. The product of Incubation is a Foster herb of the same type as the original, which is prepared and ready for immediate use. For example, Tickweed incubated in a bird's nest for one day produces a weedy stem with the herbal properties of Locoweed. The resultant herb now has the effect of inciting irrational behavior.

Sun-Dry: Exposing an herb to direct sunlight leaches Perspective spirit from the herb, thereby altering its smell and odor Tone. Sun-drying removes moisture from the herb, driving out the Subjective spirit. After drying in direct sun from dawn to dusk, or on two successive half-days, the herb Tone is converted to Objective.

To sun-dry an herb, you first must locate a good spot in the bright sunlight to place the herbs. Allow the herbs to remain in place for one full day before retrieving them. The product of sun-drying is a Dried herb of the same type as the original, which is prepared and ready for immediate use. For example,

a Bitter Mushroom allowed to Sun-Dry for one day produces a fungal cap with the herbal properties of Tuffball. The resultant herb still must be delivered by ingestion like a mushroom, but now has the effect of enhancing STR instead of AGI.

Changing Herbal Type

The three basic remodeling techniques can change the Clarity, Quality, and Tone of an herb, but they do not change the Source. A fungal herb remains a fungus, an overt herb remains overt. The Type of the remodeled herb also remains unchanged, although an incubated fungal ball can take on the herbal properties of a mushroom. To transfer the herbal properties of one Type of herb to an herb of a different Source requires a different kind of remodeling.

Imbue: Imbuing transfers the herbal properties of one herb into the physical form of another, typically of a different Type. Imbuing is an advanced remodeling technique that combines the effects of other methods. Two substrates must be identified. The first is a prepared herb with the odor properties and effects that you wish to imbue into another form. The second is a non-herbal plant of the Kind that you wish to be imbued with herbal properties. This non-herb is referred to as a shell. Harmless fungi and plants of all kinds may be found in most habitats that have the physical attributes of herbs and can serve as a shell. These include fungal caps and balls, weeds with stems, leaves, roots and bulbs, harmless flowers, and edible seeds and fruits. A listing of common non-herbs and habitats where they can be found is provided in the Herbal of Black Adder in Appendix A.

The first step of the process is to create a mash by soaking the prepared herb. Note that the Soaking process alters the Clarity of the herb. Because the herbal properties of the mash, not the original herb, are imbued, it may be necessary to start with an herb that has greater or less Clarity than the desired herbal properties, or to subject the mash to a second round of Soaking to restore its original properties. Either way, it is the herbal mash that is needed for Imbuing, before it has been allowed to dry.

The next step of the process is to bury the mash together with the non-herbal shell. Ideally, the shell should be completely surrounded by the herbal mash. Burial should take place in loose soil or dead leaves and humus. The aggregate must remain buried for one full day. Upon exhumation, the remaining mash may be removed; the shell will be transformed into an herb of the same kind, having the herbal properties of the mash.

Accidental Remodeling

Prepared herbs stored in direct contact with one another may be accidentally modified by exchanging spirit. The alteration is always in the direction of losing spirit, from Bold Temperament to Shy, from Mind Agency to Body, from Subjective to Objective, and to a lower Clarity. Green herbs require no preparation, but lacking any odor Clarity, Quality, or Tone, still can leach the spirit from other herbs. Roll 1d6 for each day that prepared herbs remain together, or with a Green herb, in the same container (man-thing or woven bag) or piled together in the same burrow chamber; a roll of 1 indicates loss of spirit. If herbs are buried together, the effect is heightened; a roll of 1 or 2 indicates loss of spirit. Note that, as a consequence, Burying in soil or dead leaves can be used as an intentional remodeling technique, especially for inducing specific changes from Fragrant to Putrid, Acrid to Minty, any other Quality to Musky, and simplifying the odor profile to reduce Clarity. The process of Burying is simpler, but less efficient, than Scenting, Water Soaking, or Sun-Drying. Also see Imbue as an advanced remodeling technique that involves burying.

Storage of any prepared herb with Poisonweed also can result in conversion of the whole collection to Poisonweed. Roll 1d6 for each day that prepared herbs are stored in direct contact with Poisonweed (of any kind). A roll of 1 indicates all the herbs have become Poisonweed.

To avoid accidental remodeling, herbs may be inactivated, reverting them to an unprepared state. Herbs that have not yet been prepared for use, or intentionally inactivated, can be stored indefinitely without harm. Paradoxically, inactivation involves the same process as accidental remodeling. Sprigs of a prepared herb are stored together with unprepared sprigs of the same herb. After one day remaining in direct contact, all prepared herbs revert to an unprepared state (no die roll required). They may be prepared again in the normal fashion.

Important Notes on Herb Remodeling

As in other preparations, failure at any step in herb remodeling results in ruining all sprigs of the herb being processed.

If the substrate that is the target of the process is an herb, it must be prepared using the normal method (simple or advanced), making it ready for use before it is subjected to remodeling. Attempts to remodel an unprepared herb produce Poisonweed.

The product of a Simple preparation can be used as the substrate for an Advanced preparation or Herb Remodeling. However, any attempt to apply a simple preparation to an herb that is already prepared ruins the herb for further use.

A Green substrate must start as a Green substrate. If leaching of an herb strips its odor Clarity, it is ruined and cannot be reconstituted as an herb. Attempts to do so produce Poisonweed.

Green herbs lack any discernible herbal spirit. Therefore, transforming a Green substrate into a usable herb requires extra steps. First, the Green substrate must be soaked in Milk to raise its Clarity to Clear. Then it must be remodeled to infuse it with Temperament, Agency, and Perspective spirits. At the end of this process, the herb becomes a Clear Hypnotic herb, positive for all three kinds of spirit. Further remodeling is necessary to leach one or more of these spirits from the herb to produce herbs of other Classes.

Remodeling of a Green herb is a way of producing a useful herb that may be difficult to find growing naturally. Remodeling a Bracket Fungus, for instance, does not create a Bracket Fungus with the herbal properties of a Puffball or Bitter Mushroom. It creates an actual Puffball or Bitter Mushroom.

Successful Preparation or Remodeling

Herb preparation and remodeling are skills, and thus are markedly affected by relevant experience. The primary trait relevant for herbalism is SML. Successful preparation and each step of remodeling is determined by an SML skill check. The difficulty varies with different techniques: DV=4 for simple preparations; DV=6 for advanced preparations; DV=8 for basic remodeling techniques (Soaking, Scenting, Incubating, or Sun-Drying); DV=10 for imbuing. Remember that any rabbit may attempt simple preparations, but only Herbalists can use advanced preparations or remodeling. Herbalists also receive a +1 bonus to SML skill checks; fighters (their opposite on the Circle of Professions) incur a penalty of −1. Thus, even a beginning Herbalist with a +2 Base Bonus could attempt basic remodeling (SML Level 1 + 1 for Herbalist +2 for Base Bonus = 4; plus a 1d6 roll of 6 would exceed the required DV=8 for successful remodeling.)

Herb Effects and Interactions

Remember to record the SML Rating (excluding the Herbalist bonus, but including any herb-induced enhancements) of the character that prepares an herb for use. The power of the herb's effect in some cases is partly determined by the SML Rating of the preparer, not of the ultimate user. For example, Burning Nettle prepared by an Herbalist with a SML Rating of 5 who was using Truebark Dust at the time (+2 SML) cures 1d6 + 7 HP damage from an injured character.

Many herbs can modify the effective trait rating of the user or victim. Some temporarily enhance the rating, while others (or Poisonweed) may cause the rating to decrease. The same herb cannot be used to produce further increases or decreases in trait ratings, although herbs that cause injury or cure wounds certainly can be used repeatedly for effect. Different herbs that have the same kind of effect, however, can be stacked, increasing the effect over the use of either herb alone. For example, Ruffball increases STR +1, and Tuffball increases STR +2, but use of both Ruffball and Tuffball at the same time has the additive effect of increasing STR +3. Similarly, different herbs that have opposite effects can act to cancel the effects of each other. Quickberry has the effect of decreasing AGI −3, but treatment with Heart Leaf, which increases AGI +3, can reverse the effect. Herbs with opposite effects typically may be found in the same column of Black Adder's Honeycomb of Herbal Lore in Appendix D.

Customizing Extended Herbalism Rules

For GMs and players that want the diversity of herbs offered under Extended Rules, but prefer to avoid the complexity of the Advanced Preparation and Herb Remodeling rules, it is possible to strike a balance. You can adopt all the herbs listed in the periodic table of herbs (the Honeycomb) and in the Herbal of Black Adder, relying on the methods of preparation and delivery described there. Extended rules should be used for Quick Herb Search. Other Extended rules are optional.

Mini-Game: Herb Scramble!

Herb Scramble is a mini-game designed for players to explore the extended rules for searching for herbs. It may be played as a solo challenge, as a cooperative game, or by 2–5 competing players. The game can be used as an actual protocol for searching for herbs during an Adventure or Campaign game, or it may be played as a separate, stand-alone exercise. If played during an Adventure or Campaign, players should announce whether they intend to search cooperatively or competitively. It is left to the discretion of the GM whether any herbs actually found in Herb Scramble as a mini-game are available to players during regular roleplay.

Setup

Players decide which habitat they wish to search, which determines which Battleboard to use as the game board. Choice of habitat also determines the herbal Source that might be found (Floral, Fungal, Overt, or Covert).

A neutral party (such as the GM) sets up the appropriate Battleboard behind a screen (for example), out of sight of the players conducting the search. She then places 13 markers face down on the Battleboard. Tokens are provided on the mini-game token sheet for this purpose, but any tokens may be used. The markers represent herbs of four odor Clarities: Clear, Cloudy, Murky, and Dense. As discussed in the section on Herbalism, herbs at the Clear end of the odor spectrum are more common and have simpler effects; herbs closer to the Dense end of the spectrum are rarer and more valuable, and often have more powerful effects. Six markers represent a Clear herb, 4 markers represent a Cloudy herb, 2 markers represent a Murky herb, and 1 marker represents a Dense herb. The Clear herb markers must be placed in a circle of 6 connected hexes. The Cloudy herb markers must be placed in a connected string of 4 hexes; they may be oriented in a straight line, angled, or jagged. The Murky herb markers must be placed in 2 adjacent hexes. The Dense herb marker may be placed anywhere. Markers of different herbs may not be placed in the same hex. Other than these configurations, the GM is free to position the 13 markers anywhere on the Battleboard, irrespective of terrain features.

The Search Routine

Once herb markers have been placed, the players determine which bunny goes first by rolling 1d6 (high number goes first). If players are using their own characters from a B&B game, their searching is limited by their SML Rating. Each bunny searching solo, or in competition with other bunnies, may search a number of hexes equal to his SML Rating + 2d6. If two or more bunnies are cooperating in the search , the total number of hexes searched equals the sum of all the searchers' SML Ratings + 2d6. Thus, a single 3rd-level Herbalist (with a Base Bonus of +2) may search 3+2+2d6 hexes (= 7–17 hexes), but three 2nd-level Scouts (Base Bonus +1), searching cooperatively, may search 3x(2+1) + 2d6 hexes total (= 11–21 hexes). If the searchers are not using established characters and no stats are available, then a solo bunny may search 12 hexes, and two or more bunnies may search 6 hexes each.

Searching then follows the following steps, with players taking turns searching individual hexes:

1. A player declares which hex is searched.

2. If the hex contains an herb (of any clarity other than Green), the GM publicly announces that two sprigs have been found of a particular herbal Source and Clarity. (e.g., *In Hex 36, you find two sprigs of a Fungal herb that is Murky.*)

3. If the hex does not contain an herb, but an herb is located in a hex adjacent to the one searched, the character detects an herbal scent. No information on direction, type of herb, or number of adjacent hexes with herbs should be conveyed. The GM simply (and privately) shows the player a card that reads "Herbal Scent."

4. If the hex does not contain an herb, and no herbal scent is detected, the GM shows the player a card that reads "No Scent" (or left blank).

If an herb is found, the GM should record the removal of the herb from that hex (remove the token or strike out the listing on the GM's search map).

Players continue to search, identifying hexes with herbs, until all allowed searches are expended. If the Herb Scramble was conducted as part of a larger game, the total time to conduct the search is 10 minutes. Players that are not satisfied that they have found enough may choose to expend an additional 10 minutes to continue the search. In this case, the same number of search turns is allowed again, and searching picks up where it left off. No new herbs are placed on the board, and the original markers remain where they were originally placed. However, if players decide to suspend searching, go on to other business, and later return to search again, the search procedure starts over from the beginning. (It may be assumed that the bunnies are not searching in exactly the same place.)

When the search is complete, the players may attempt to identify what kind of herbs were found. Each hex that yields an herb provides two sprigs of that herb. Remember counting limitations when tallying the total number of herbs found.

If played as a separate mini-game, each player receives 1 acorn for each hex that contained a Clear herb, 1 carrot for each Cloudy herb, 2 carrots for each Murky herb, and 1 apple for a rare herb. The player with the greatest value of Prized Food wins.

Herb Search Map

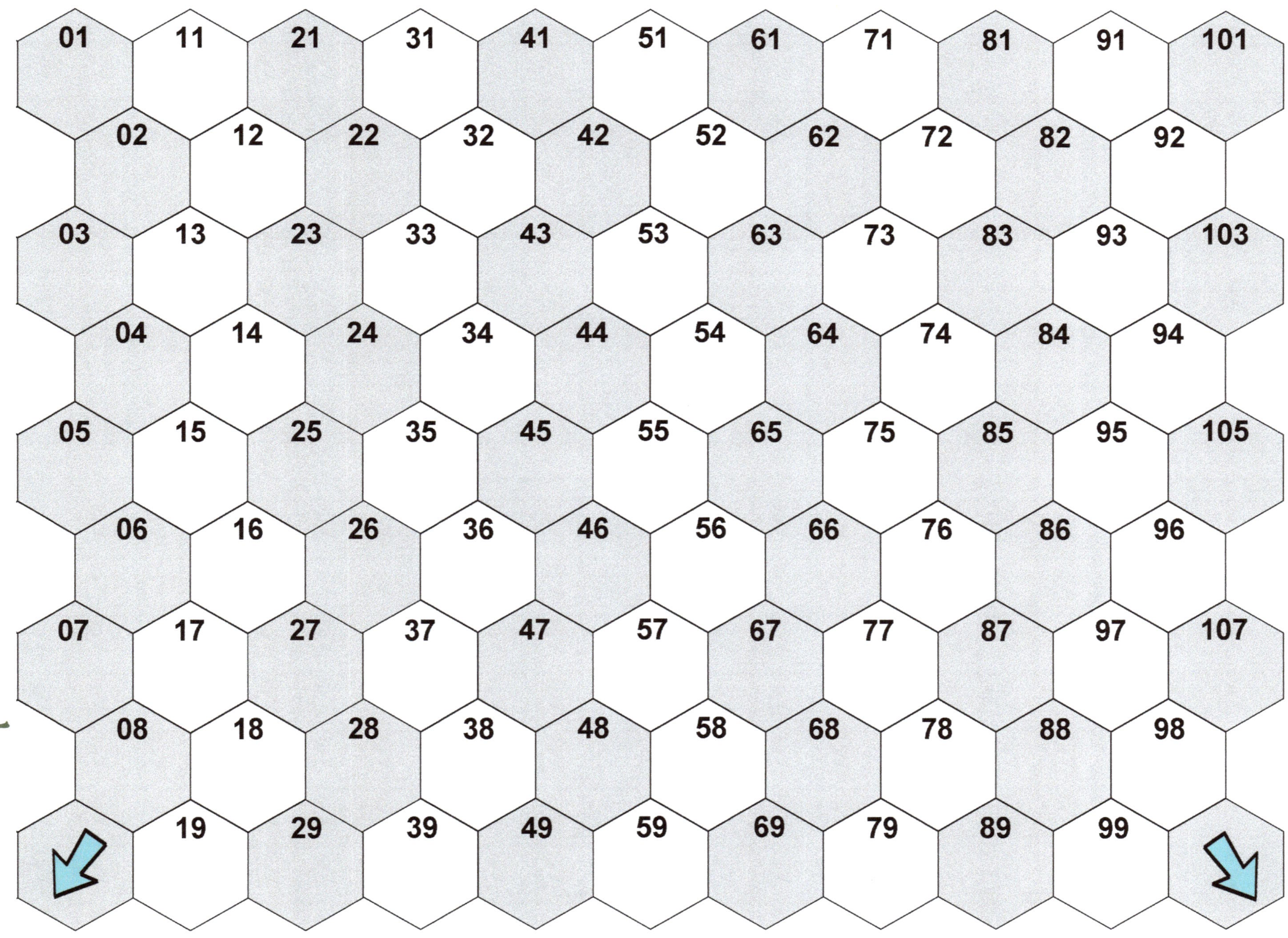

Communication

Persuasion, Threat, Barter, and Deceit

Avoiding and fighting enemies is a familiar part of all roleplaying games, but player characters in B&B can have a wide variety of other encounters with other rabbits, neutral animals, predators, and even humans. When interacting with NPCs, characters may turn to methods other than outright combat to settle differences, defuse tense situations, and resolve conflict. Communication often is a more prudent, and effective, course of action than force.

For rabbits to verbally communicate with any other animals, they must speak the same language. The number of languages any character may speak is limited by their CHA Rating (see Charisma). If there is a language barrier, the GM should encourage players to use nonverbal signals and expressions to act out their intended messages.

Sometimes communication is about information exchange. If the other party is reluctant to cooperate, however, communication may be used to persuade, coerce, barter, or deceive to achieve a desired aim. Before any attempt to seek cooperation, the GM must first determine whether the target, such as an NPC, is friendly, neutral, reluctant, or hostile.

Persuasion depends on the CHA Rating of the character attempting to persuade. The attempt is resolved with a CHA skill check, using a DV=4 for friendly targets, DV=6 for neutral, DV=8 for reluctant, and DV=10 for hostile. The GM should adjust difficulty values based on the context of the exchange. If the persuader offers trade items, valuable information, or flattery, the DV may be reduced by 1–3 points. Conversely, if the persuader is abrasive, insulting, or otherwise offensive, the DV may be increased by 1–3 points. If the first attempt to persuade fails, the same PC, or a different character, may try again. However, the DV increases by one point in each subsequent attempt.

Coercion is a form of persuasion in which compliance is obtained by threat of force. A threat attempt is resolved with a STR skill check, using the same DV values as persuasion. The PC issuing the threat may reduce the DV by 1–3 points by demonstrating a feat of strength, at the GM's discretion. As in persuasion, the DV increases by one point after each unsuccessful attempt to threaten.

Barter attempts to obtain cooperation by exchange of goods or services. If the PC offers trade items such as prized food then the price of cooperation equals twice the DV values, as listed above. Thus, bartering for information from a reluctant NPC would cost the equivalent of 16 @ (16 acorns, 8 carrots, or 2 apples).

Finally, rabbits value trickery and deception, and PCs may attempt to deceive to obtain compliance. The GM must exercise her judgement in attempts to deceive, because the player must describe what the character does or says in their attempt to deceive. Successful deceit is determined by a contest between Charisma and Mysticism. The deception succeeds if 1d6 + CHA Rating of the deceiver is greater than 1d6 + MYS Rating of the character being deceived. As in other forms of persuasion, the GM may add a bonus of 1–3 points to the target's MYS Rating to allow for neutral, reluctant, or hostile NPCs. If the attempt to deceive occurs in front of more than one NPC, then use the highest MYS Rating of the group.

Scent Marks: The Writing of the Hedgerow

Real animals can't speak, let alone write. But they can leave surprisingly complex messages for others to read hours, days, or even weeks later in the form of scent marks. Scent marking of some form is important to most mammals, who use scent marks to advertise the borders of their territory, announce their social or reproductive status, or stake a claim on a coveted resource. In B&B, scent marks serve as a kind of community bulletin board that can be read by any animal with the nose.

In Adventures or campaigns designed by the GM, scent marks can provide clues to important features of the environment, homes of NPCs, or hidden treasures. Depositing a message in a scent mark is a function of SML Rating: The mark can contain the informational equivalent of one word per rating point. Reading the scent mark also depends on SML Rating (one word per point), with Scouts receiving a bonus of one additional word per point of INT Base Bonus.

> **Example:** A scent mark was deposited by a high-level Herbalist (SML=8). The message reads: "Herb cache under white stone beware deadfall trap." Another hardy adventurer — a 3rd-level scout — comes by the scent mark later. His rating (SML=4) + INT Base Bonus (+1) only permits him to read the first five words: "Herb cache under white stone." Looking about, he sees the white stone, and in his attempt to retrieve the cache, is squashed by the deadfall trap that he didn't realize was there.

As the example illustrates, the GM and players should take care in composing scent marks, because animals with lesser SML Ratings are able to decipher only as many words as their rating points permit. This can lead to confusion or intentional misinformation. In fact, a better sequencing in the example would be: *"cache herbs under stone white beware trap deadfall"*. In this reworded message, each word significantly adds to the information available to the reader.

Scent marks do not last long. They disappear after a number of days equal to the SML Rating of the animal that deposited the mark.

Mini-Game: I Never Forget a Face

Storytellers pride themselves on a good memory. This mini-game is a way to see how good a memory you have. It can be played by two or more. The first player to reach a thousand wins, though you may continue playing until all matches are made. Remember, rabbits can only count to four, so if they score more than four, their score is a thousand.

Setup

Place a Battleboard on the table or floor. Take two each of all the different tokens that can represent player characters, including both rabbits and non-rabbits. Turn them all face down on the

Battleboard and mix them up. Then position the upside-down tokens so that each one is in a different hex on the board.

Play

Players take turns trying to match tokens (two tokens that have the same image). The youngest player always goes first, then go clockwise. Select any facedown token and turn it face up on the same hex. Then select any other facedown token and turn it up. If they match, the player takes them off the board and keeps them in front of herself. If they are not a match, turn both face down again, in the same hexes. All players may see the tokens as they are turned up.

If your character has a CHA Trait Bonus, this gives you an advantage. After you turn up your first token, you may get additional looks, one for each point of CHA Trait Bonus. So, if your CHA Bonus is +2, you get to look at three tokens for your second move (1+2), rather than just one. If you make a match to the first token with any of these, you keep the match and turn the others face down again. Note that if your bonus peeks turn up two of the same image, you don't get to keep those; only if one you turn up matches the token you turned in the first part of your round. So using your bonus might actually help the person playing next.

The first player to collect a thousand matches (i.e., more than four) wins, but usually you will continue playing until all matches are made.

How Rabbits Play

In the warren, rabbits play a little differently. One rabbit enters a chamber to set up the game by placing pairs of items around the chamber, covering each one with a leaf. These might be different-colored pebbles, tiny twigs, pieces of pinecone, and so forth. That rabbit then calls in the others (usually young rabbits) to play. The one who set up the game does not play, but watches as a referee. Note that using smell is against the rules, and any rabbit seen sniffing at a leaf is disqualified, and laughed at by the other rabbits.

Mating and Reproduction

The activities of mating and reproduction are greatly simplified for the purposes of the game, although GM's are free to elaborate these rules for greater realism. For example, we do not consider social hierarchies, though this is very important in actual warrens, with dominant bucks and does breeding more successfully than those farther down the social ladder. Even though these rules are simplified, we have tried to make them as true to life as possible within the constraints of efficient game play.

When you create a rabbit for the first time, we do not consider the genetics of your parents, but rather simply roll dice as described in Creating a Character. If later in the campaign you choose to create a new character, either because your current one died or became seriously injured, or you simply want to try a new profession, you may always use the same dice-rolling method. However, there are two alternatives available, if approved by your GM.

Identical Sibling

If your rabbit dies within the first year (either calendar year or campaign year), you may assume that your litter contained an identical sibling that has an exact genetic match to your first rabbit. You may also assume that the sibling has spent Advancement Points in just the same way, so that not only are all your base Traits just the same, but your Levels in each Trait also are the same. Therefore, you can replace your dead or injured rabbit with this new one. It is the same gender as your first rabbit, but of course will have a different name. It starts out without injuries, but also starts without any of the possessions that your last rabbit had; consider them lost or destroyed. Since it is unlikely that you had more than one identical sibling, this can be done only once in the campaign for any rabbit you rolled up and then lost.

Mating

Your rabbit may attempt to find a mate. For game purposes, in any one season assume that no rabbit may breed with more than one other rabbit; that is, a buck-doe pair bonding occurs. (In future years, different pairings may occur.) Rabbits are unable to force mating, since it takes the cooperation of both rabbits to successfully inseminate. So your only option is to find a rabbit of the opposite gender who chooses to become your mate. This may be between two rabbits that are player characters, or between one player character rabbit and one NPC rabbit controlled by the GM. No rabbit is ever compelled to take a mate.

It is to your advantage to mate with a rabbit with the highest available Trait base values, as you shall see. Thus, you are not advised to simply mate with the rabbit of a player who you like in real life; rather, consider your options carefully and try to find a superior mate for breeding. Of course, the other rabbit will be trying the same strategy, so if your Traits are not so hot, you might find you have to settle. Once two rabbits have chosen to mate, simply inform the GM of your bonding and that will remain a bond for this year, even if one of you dies.

Forming a Litter

Once a pair is formed, mating may occur during the breeding season (March through September in the northern hemisphere). After mating, gestation is 30 days, and then birth occurs. Determine the offspring according to the following rules (simplified for game purposes):

1. **Determine litter size:** Roll 1d6 and add the doe's CON Bonus (thus, from 1 to 9 in the litter). Note that the GM has the authority to declare that existing conditions (harsh weather, scarcity of food, infestation by pests, rampant disease) may reduce litter sizes in any given breeding season.

2. **Determine the genetics of each rabbit:** For each Trait, in order, roll 1d6; if odd, take the buck's Base value for that trait; if even, take the doe's Base value for the same trait. You can now see why choosing the partner with the highest traits is advantageous. A lucky kit might turn out to have better traits overall than either parent, but equally, an unlucky one might get the poorer genes. You can also see that the larger the litter, the higher the odds of an exceptional kit being born.

3. **Determine the gender in a similar way:** Roll 1d6; if odd, the kit is male; if even, female.

4. **You may declare the appearance of each kit as you wish:** You may also name the kits at this time, if you wish.

5. **Starting Traits:** All of the new kits start at Level 0 in all Traits.

6. **No points for the kits:** Unlike rolling a new character, you do not get to add any points to the traits of the kits determined in this way. But if you pick one of the litter to play, you can choose the best one.

Choosing the New Rabbit to Play

You may choose to retire your current rabbit and start playing a new one from a litter. If you do so, you must choose from the rabbits born this year (or in the last breeding season if it is now winter). If you choose from your own litter, you may pick any one of the kits to play. If you want to play a kit from another pair's litter, they choose the one for you to play. So you have more options from your own litter, typically, than from another pair's litter.

Once you choose the new kit to play, you must pick a profession. As usual, you then automatically become Level 1 in the Primary Trait for that profession, and you have one additional AP to spend as you wish. Also, if you are retiring a rabbit to play this new one, and the retiring rabbit is present in the warren, you may pass on any of your possessions to the new kit unless the GM declares otherwise.

Retiring a Character

Sometimes your character may have acquired permanent injuries during a campaign, or you may simply wish to play a different profession. You also may want to start playing one of your kits. At any time you may choose to retire your character. When you do this, you have several options.

Become an NPC

Inform the GM that your character is retiring, and may be used as a non-player character (NPC) in the GM's campaign. The GM gets your active character sheet and you receive a copy marked "Retired." Thereafter, the GM has total control of your character, although the wise GM continues to play the character in the style that you favored when you were in control.

Go on Hiatus

Inform the GM that your character is taking a rest from the campaign while you play a new character. This can be done only at a time when you are at your home burrow. Assume your character hangs around the burrow, perhaps helping out with tasks there as directed by the GM. During the hiatus, your character does not change (except that any temporary injuries eventually heal), and does not earn APs. At some later date, if your new character dies or you wish to retire him, you may start playing your old character again. The GM first makes an Aging check, regardless of the current season, since you might have been exposed to disease or other stresses during hiatus; you must survive this Aging check to be able to start playing the character once more.

Totally Remove the Character

If you do not choose to have the character played any more, either by you or the GM, you may simply terminate him. You may decide his fate, if you wish. Perhaps a peaceful death of old age (admired and loved by the warren)? Just did not return one day and fate unknown (caught by a predator or left over the far mountains)? Or a dramatic end concocted between you and the GM (a tale to be told by Storytellers over generations)?

Part III: For the Gamemaster

Designing an Adventure

Adventure Overview

To design your own adventure, you need to first imagine the overall story and objective (the main quest), and decide the appropriate party size, character levels, and how much experience with **Bunnies & Burrows**' rules that the players have. If the objective is to drive the family of brown bears out of the valley, this cannot be done by two 1st-level rabbits (and maybe not by a mid-level party); but if the goal is to steal carrots and lettuce from Farmer Matilda's garden, this might be ideal for a starting party. Decide on the setting and about how long you expect the adventure to take (in terms of game session hours). We find it best to explicitly write out this overview before beginning the design, and then to refer to it as you develop the adventure.

Storyboards

The next step is to storyboard the adventure. Can you break down your overall story into several acts and scenes, or is it best run as a one-shot, able to be completed in a single game session? With experience, you will get a good idea of how long battles take, how long it takes the party to get from Point A to Point B, how often random encounters might occur, and if players spend much time interacting with NPCs or simply talking over strategy among themselves. It may be that you incorporate side quests, some shorter story that the party may decide to do but that is not essential to completion of the main quest. For example, if they decide some snuffballs really help in the boss fight, they may need to venture over to where they can find those herbs, and possibly encounter traps or cantankerous NPCs that complicate things. In the storyboard, briefly sketch out the various stages of the adventure and give them names for your own convenience.

As part of your storyboarding, you might want to think in terms of 2-hour or 3-hour game sessions. Even if an RPG normally meets for five or six hours in a night, breaking into shorter play segments is useful to allow for restroom breaks, snacks, or just standing up and walking around some. When you are writing out the adventure, keep this in mind and incorporate handy cliffhangers: *"On this slope, the snow you are walking across suddenly starts sliding down the hill, and you are being carried towards the cliff."* So, in this case, a literal cliffhanger where the GM can say, *"We'll take a ten-minute break now. Let's have those corn chips and salsa."* Even if your adventure is broken into acts and scenes, the GM might not want to stop at the end of an act, but just barely get the party into the start of the next act, and cliffhang it there. This way, between sessions, the players can think about and discuss what is coming up next.

Setups

Now you should write setups for the start of the adventure, as well as for any separate acts and scenes or side quests within the adventure. Assume the players will not have access to your adventure document, only the GM. A setup is a description (for the GM) of what happens during an act or scene, including a summary of planned encounters and an overview of NPCs that will be met; these may be friendly, hostile (but not predatory), or planned predator encounters. The setup also includes passages for the GM to read to the players. In B&B, it is ideal if these can be framed as a story, as told by a rabbit or neutral animal. Such passages, in setups or elsewhere in the adventure, should not be overly long. Players get bored if the GM is spending a half hour just reading out the setup passage to them. If the party needs important background knowledge and it would take too long to read, designate it as a handout that can be given to players ahead of time. The GM should permit the players to reference such background handouts during the course of play, as they wish. If you intend to have your adventure printed, be sure you lay out these handouts in a manner conducive to printing.

Encounters

Primary NPCs

Your adventure will have a number of key non-player characters (NPCs) that the party can expect to encounter, and who either help or hinder their quests. Each one of these should be designed in detail. This includes the name, species, profession, physical description, personality traits, motivations and objectives, and "stats" (Trait Bonuses and Ratings, Hit Points, etc.). Describe any unique special abilities or possessions they might have. This is especially important for Traders whose current inventory of items to trade must be kept up to date. If they have henchmen or minions, describe them as well. And be sure to tell the location of their home base or lair, and some indication of the range in which they could be encountered. If they have "treasures" (something of value to the party if they are defeated), mention those; this might be food items, herbs, artifacts, etc. Examples of NPCs can be found in the Adventures included in this rulebook.

Minor NPCs can be described in the course of the adventure, as they are encountered. In general, these need much briefer descriptions.

Primary Encounters

Now you have the background information to start writing the main encounters, the ones that will provide the big challenges to the players or are important for achieving the main and side quests. Usually you will write each encounter with an explanation to the GM as to what is happening, but also with descriptive passages for the GM to read to the players as things progress. The passages may use much different language. For example, if they come upon some human artifact, a "man-thing," you can tell the GM exactly what it is, but the descriptive passage will inform the players in terms of rabbit perceptions, which may give only hints as to its identity and purpose.

There may be random elements in the primary encounters. If so, you should tell the method by which the GM determines them. For example, if there are turtles basking on the rock that the party must cross, you might describe this to the GM as *"There are 2d6 turtles basking on the large rock."* Of course, if there are more than four, the GM tells the party, *"A thousand turtles are basking on the rock."* In some cases, you might want to indicate a choice of possibilities based on the level of the party; a small party might encounter three turtles, but a large party might meet eight of them. Don't leave it up to the GM to decide; your adventure should be helping the task of the GM, not making it more difficult. If you are the only GM who will run the adventure, you can leave the details looser. We encourage you to use only d6s for random rolls.

If there are primary NPCs in the encounter, identify them and say what they will do. Does the NPC act one way if the party is friendly, and another way if they are aggressive? Are they willing to be bribed by special foods, herbs, or items? Will they run away if injured, or fight more furiously? Again, explain such things directly to the GM, but also through passages to be spoken to the players at appropriate times in the encounter.

The heart of the adventure lies in the primary encounters, so they should be carefully designed and written. If they work well, the players will probably appreciate the adventure; if not, it could be disastrous. Try to design each primary encounter so that it is not only possible for the party to prevail, but likely, if they play their characters sensibly and skillfully. If the intent of an encounter is for the party to run away and use some other approach, the GM should be guided so that outcome is likely. Not every encounter needs to be solved by brute force. And if an encounter takes the form of a puzzle where the players need to use their wits to succeed, we advise you to either make it a very easy puzzle or have more than one way to solve it. Some players love puzzles and excel at solving them, while others just want to get the story moving and dislike being delayed by puzzles. But a good puzzle is one thing that makes an adventure truly memorable, and should be encouraged.

Random Encounter Tables

You may simply choose to use the encounter tables in these rules and reference them within your adventure. But there may be times when you want to make up your own tables. For example, let's say your adventure involves derailing the circus train. In that case, there may be a chance of the party encountering animals that are not in the regular B&B tables: monkeys, a giraffe, or maybe a tiger. If you are introducing such creatures and are not describing them as primary NPCs or in your primary encounters, but they could be met by the party randomly, be sure to give brief descriptions of their appearance, behavior, and stats beside your random encounter table.

Similarly, you might introduce special foods, herbs, pests, or traps. For each of these that you include, you also need descriptions sufficient to allow the GM to game the interaction. For a new food, what might its trading value be? For a new trap, what happens to a rabbit that gets caught, how can it be detected, and what is needed to free a rabbit or disarm the trap?

Filling in the Gaps

Now you need to add connective tissue between the meat and bones of your primary encounters. Describe what happens as the party proceeds from one part of the adventure to the next. If they are following the streambed, describe it, along with what they might encounter there. If there is more than one way to get from one encounter to the next, describe both of them. Include mentions of the types of predators or traps they might find so the GM can work them into the session. If they might have to rest and heal after one encounter, be sure you have designed a place for them to do that. If they will need to replenish their herbs, have some locales where that might happen. For the most part, not much game time will be spent in these interludes, but it is still important to include them in your adventure. It is also a way to set the mood for the next encounter, to provide omens or warnings, to leave hints and clues, and to just provide some psychic breathing time for the players before the next intense confrontation.

You may also need to have a brief description of what happens after the final encounter or boss fight. Does the warren welcome them back as conquering heroes? Is there some ominous suggestion of bad effects from what they did? Do you want to leave "hooks" for future adventures?

Wrapping Up the Adventure

Run a spell check and grammar check on your document. Check everything over for consistency; for example, do you call it "Dark Cave" in one place and "Deep Cave" in another? Make sure all the gaps in your tables are filled in. Give the adventure a title, and perhaps an "elevator pitch" (a sentence or two that describes it, that one could use to attract people to play it at a convention). At the end, you will want to add a short section giving a guideline as to how much experience the characters should get after completing the main quest and the side quests. This should be in terms of Advancement Points (APs) that the players can use to increase Trait Levels for their characters (though GMs, of course, may choose to award APs differently).

Publishing Your Adventure

Once you finish designing the adventure, it's time to playtest it. GM it for your own players, run it at a convention, give it to someone else to GM to see if it makes sense. Once it has been playtested and you have made any necessary corrections, you might try publishing it. The easiest way is to offer it as a pdf through a fan site, blog, or a site such as DriveThruRPG.com. If your intent is for others to enjoy it, offer it for free or "pay what you want." Offering it for a small amount of money such as 99 cents is possible, but fewer people will get it. Print versions are more difficult, although you can print it yourself and then distribute it. If you are an established designer, especially if you can also illustrate it, you might be able to get it published through a company such as Frog God Games. We are hopeful that many fans of **Bunnies & Burrows** will design modules and offer them through one means or another.

Running a Campaign

Although **Bunnies & Burrows** contains combat and conflict, and can involve some serious moments, it was designed to feature the fun and imagination involved in true roleplaying. As the GM, it is your responsibility to flesh out the roles not just for one character, but for many NPCs. In pre-made adventures, look over the character descriptions for each of the major NPCs and think about how you might give each of them a distinct personality and voice. And remember that your function as the GM is not to serve as the opponent for the players, but to guide them through a story that is cooperatively constructed. Listen to your players and serve as a fair referee, not a stern enforcer of the rules. Look for small ways to reward players for faithfully staying in character. Feel free to add new NPCs or add new features to the game map. It is your world now. Make it your own.

Rules

Whether you are using a pre-made adventure or designing your own campaign, you need to establish the rules before running the campaign. In many places you have options of simpler or more complex rules to follow. The clearest example of this is the choice between the Basic and Extended rules. Do you want to move directly on to combat, or play out the pursuit by a predator? Do your players prefer a simplified set of herbs and their uses, or will they appreciate the challenge of preparing and remodeling their own herbs? You are the best judge of the experience and attitude of your players, as well as how comfortable you are with your understanding of the rules. It certainly is possible to use simpler rules early in the campaign, then gradually switch to higher complexity as both GM and players are ready to do so. To avoid confusion, be sure that your players know when, for example, you begin using more advanced combat or herbal rules.

House Rules

Feel free to make up any new rules if you wish that are for your own campaign. In the old-school spirit, the GM can deviate from the written rules, as long as this is always made clear to the players. You can change encounter tables, give professions new special abilities, create new habitats. Do you think it would be fun if a player could have a gerbil as a character? Fine, create the stats for the gerbil and give it a profession, either an existing one or a totally new idea.

There is no limit to what you can do with home rules, including crossovers with other types of games. Do you want to introduce zombie rabbits, shape-changing rabbits, vampire rabbits, or mutated rabbits? You are in charge of your campaign, so enjoy it (for as long as you think your players will also have fun).

Player Characters

We have generally found that a mix of professions among the player characters leads to the greatest success in a campaign. Players like to be able to decide what species and profession they will play, so you have an immediate dilemma. Of course, as GM you could say that the party can have only one raccoon, but if two players really, really want to run raccoons, that can lead to ill will. In our experience, it is best to let the players decide the makeup of the party however they want. If they want a party of six Herbalists, so be it. They will find some tasks very difficult with such an approach, but may also come up with some highly creative solutions. It is somewhat like a fantasy RPG; if a party wants all magic-users and no fighters or healers, they might not survive for long, but if they are enjoying themselves, that is what matters.

Special consideration needs to be given when a new player is joining an existing campaign. If most of the current player characters are 4th or 5th level, then a brand new rabbit will be challenged by higher-level encounters that might be met. Personally, we have no problem with mixed levels of characters. If you feel differently as the GM, you could give the new character extra APs to spend to catch up (to a degree) to the older characters. But this is certainly not necessary. And in any case, some character will die in an ongoing campaign, and then that player may choose to start playing the rabbit's kit as a new character, so there will naturally be a divergence of levels in the party. It can be part of the fun to have new characters and experienced characters in the same party, and it possibly works out better in B&B than it might in some other RPGs.

Another possibility is for a character to retire from play. The GM might keep that character around as a non-player character (NPC), remembering the style of play that was used by the original player. Remember that it should always be the final decision of the player whether a retired character turns into an NPC or simply fades away. While some players are happy to let the GM take charge of their old character, others may not be willing for that to happen.

Campaign Map

You should have a regional map for your campaign, either by using a published map or by creating your own from scratch. If you are designing your own map, we encourage you to make it geographically and ecologically probable. One option is to begin with a real-world setting and modify it to suit your campaign needs. In fact, creating a realistic campaign map is a good way for you to learn more about the natural world. If prevailing winds are from the west and there is a mountain range in the western portion of your map, and if those winds are likely to contain much moisture by coming across the sea or a large lake, then consider that precipitation will be higher on the western slopes of the mountains as the winds ascend. Similarly, conditions will be drier on the eastern side after dumping the rain on the western slopes. So it would be reasonable to have rainforests to the west of the mountains and grasslands or desert to the east. If it is winter and the winds come over a large lake, you get extra lake-effect snowfall to the side where the winds exit the lake passage.

Figure out the rationale for your geography. Rivers flow downhill, and get larger as more streams are gathered together. If a river is flowing over very flat land, it may change its course from time to time as it meanders about. A river flowing into the sea may be depositing silt to build up a delta. At higher latitudes (in the Northern Hemisphere), or at higher elevations, new plant communities form.

As the GM, everything you do need not make sense environmentally. If you think it is fun to have a patchwork of suburbs, deserts, and marshes with no other habitats, feel free to do so. But we tend to emphasize the natural conditions for rabbits in B&B, so making it more realistic makes sense to us.

Details

On your campaign map, you need to devise the scale of the map. Is one hex a mile across or 50 meters? Do you think each hex should be one and only one habitat, or is there a mixture in each hex? Have you named the various geographic features on the map? Remember, even if you are adapting a real locale for your campaign, the names given to features by human geographers will not be the same as the names assigned by rabbits.

If some areas are particularly important, you may want to also draw up detailed maps. If a number of encounters are likely to occur around one location such as Old McDonald's farm, draw up a map of that farm and its immediate surroundings. You might draw up burrow maps for each warren located on the campaign map. On the other hand, you might skip such detailed maps and just use the relevant Battleboard when you need to have an encounter. Some GMs love drawing maps, some don't. And other people may draw maps that you could use in your campaign.

If you do use detailed maps, placing herbs, food sources, traps, and predator lairs and ranges can be useful. If you do this, we like to have two versions of the map, one with these locations shown for use by the GM, and another with them absent for reference by the players. You might just give the players a copy of that map on which they can make notes as they explore and have encounters. If you want to limit information until players explore a certain area, consider dividing your complete map into sections and distributing each section only when players venture that far.

Laying Out Herbs and Traps

You may just place herbs and traps randomly, but it is more satisfying if you take care to place them logically. The section on Finding Herbs discusses basic rules of thumb for where different kinds of herbs may be found, and each herb description lists the habitats where it grows. So you should not place any herbs in other habitats, except in cases where another animal may have carried and cached some. Most herbs tend to grow in demes, local patches where the herb is common, often having grown outward from one original plant. So instead of placing herbs evenly throughout the habitat, it is better to have one or a few locations where a number are all together. As a gentle hint toward conservation, the GM could use the following rule for regrowth: if the party takes some, but not all, of the herbs in the patch, then after a week of game time they can grow back; however, if the party takes every last herb from the patch, they do not grow back. Another suggestion is to have seasonal differences in

herb abundance, though this can make play more difficult for the player characters. The herbal does not list seasons of growth for the herbs, but the GM can decide that Sunflower Dust and Pumpkin Seeds are available only in the Fall, that Razzleberries are on the plant all Winter, and that Snowcaps appear at the very start of Spring.

In a similar manner, certain types of traps are placed carefully by humans to accomplish particular goals, and with consideration for local conditions. A person would not build a pit trap in a marsh since it would just fill with water. If the farmer's daughter wants a pet rabbit, she might set a live trap or box trap near her garden. A beartooth trap would not be set for rabbits, but rather to catch a larger animal for fur or to remove a nuisance. A deadfall will be set only in an area where there might be a fallen tree. Snares can be set along small trails that have track evidence, or perhaps at the exit from a culvert. If you give some thought before you place the trap, it can add great realism to the campaign. And don't overdo it with traps; you are not trying to kill all the player characters, after all.

Artifacts and Man

A dropped "man-thing" could be found anywhere, though if you think about what the person might have been doing in a certain location, you can make the dropped item more plausible. Pruning shears might be dropped in an orchard, a keyring or phone dropped in a suburb, a bandana in a crop field, a fishing hook next to a pond, or a carabiner along a mountain trail. Whenever you want to add an artifact to the game, decide the most likely place it could be found. You also need to consider the condition of the item. If it is iron and has been there for years, it might be rusted with no moving parts. But if it is an electronic toy that was dropped just this morning, its battery might still be working. As with traps, you generally don't want to overuse the placement of human artifacts, though it is surprising how many items you will find in real life if you start looking around. There is an amazing number of arrowheads still in the environment today, and people who are skilled at spotting them can find some nearly every time they take a walk near a freshly plowed field. Pieces of broken glass or pottery can be found nearly everywhere, as can debris such as candy wrappers, plastic bags, cigarette butts, soda cans and the like. Finally, we have found it best to stick to simple objects and to avoid complex tools or machinery. A rabbit might find an interesting use for a lug nut or a license plate, but is unlikely to drive a working automobile. Remember that it doesn't take much of an artifact to provide a skilled Maverick with opportunities; a simple rubber band can be very utilitarian in the hands of a clever rabbit.

Record-Keeping

An important part of managing a campaign is the record-keeping, but you can make the GM's workload easier by careful organization and by relying on the players. If you have printed out an adventure, then as things change you can make notes right in the text. For example, the party has disabled the trap next to the woodpile, so you can mark that to indicate it. Of course, the trap might get reset, so you could also note when that happens.

Character Sheets

The players need their character sheets during a game session. Between sessions, should the GM take them back, or should the players keep them? This depends on you and your players. If the players are likely to forget to bring them next time, it is better for the GM to keep them. This also permits a player to run someone else's character if that other player fails to show up (though this should be done only if the players agree to it). On the other hand, some players like to keep their sheets to think over how best to use their advancement points and how to manage their possessions. If the players keep their sheets between sessions, it is useful for the GM to have made a copy for reference. This can be handy in planning an upcoming encounter, for example. At the least, the GM should keep a record of any herbs or useful objects stored in a burrow or hidden elsewhere on the map. One rabbit's personal cache is another rabbit's treasure.

If the party has its own version of a local map, with annotations, it is best for the GM to keep that between sessions, to ensure it is available at the next game.

Food and Herbs

It can be a nuisance for the GM to remember exactly how many herbs or food items remain at a particular location, and some prefer to ignore this, simply deciding that every time the party returns there, that the total count of herbs (or food) is present once more (unless the party takes every last one, so the site is exhausted). But if you are running a campaign that severely limits access to herbs, then you may choose to keep track of them all. If you are running the campaign from your laptop, you might have a spreadsheet for recording this.

We have simplified the rules for energy to minimize record-keeping by use of the Hunger (H) token. There may be other ways the GM can reduce records; if you have a good idea about this, please let us know.

Advancement Points

As players gain APs, they may want to spend them immediately to gain levels, or they may save them up so as to be able to spend a larger amount for a higher level. If you can rely on your players to do this accurately, the easiest method is for them to simply write the number of unused APs on the character sheet, then change the total as used. But we have found that sometimes players forget to spend them, or even to record them, until some day when they realize that, even though everybody has played in every game session during the campaign, that some characters are at much higher levels than others. So it is useful for the GM to have an ongoing record of how many APs have been given out. This also is a check against players who mistakenly spend more APs than they have earned.

Carrying Items

The way we prefer to handle this during a game session is to have tokens for containers, food and herbs, and a marker for items being carried in the fur or mouth. Whenever the party leaves the home warren, each player places the items being carried on the container token or if carried in fur or mouth. As items are used or new ones found, adjust this accordingly. Since containers can tear or be dropped, and items can be stolen or damaged during encounters, this makes it easier to determine what happens during the adventure. But an alternative method is for each player to simply write down notes on a card to keep track of items.

Handicaps

During combat, handicaps are indicated with markers placed on the Combat Tactics Card (CTC). This method is perfectly adequate for temporary conditions and injuries. Permanent injuries must be recorded on the character sheet, however, with an indication of what effects they have on the rabbit. The GM should keep her own record of permanent injuries since these may be important in determining what happens in encounters. Also note that predators may deliberately choose obviously injured rabbits as targets for their attacks.

Sandbox vs. Storyboard

Some GMs like the security of a Storyboard approach to a campaign. A main quest carries the plot along from adventure to adventure, and the GM can easily plan for the next game session. The players know what to expect, and are motivated to continue pursuing the main quest, though there may be side quests along the way that provide assistance in the main quest by providing knowledge or materials. Many computer-based RPGs use this approach, and certain milestones must be met before going on to a new area in the game. When designing your Storyboard campaign, you should devise the series of adventures but also provide the "hooks" that direct the party from each adventure to the next. And let the players advance at their own pace. They may need to gain levels before taking on a final "boss" in the ultimate adventure of the campaign. An easy way to accomplish this is by having recurring challenges in some of the earlier adventures. Yes, they can get more snuffballs by going back to the oak woods, but they are likely to get into another fight with the hostile warren when they do so.

But some players like the freedom provided by a Sandbox approach to a campaign. In this setting, the players can proceed as they wish, without feeling forced along a path by a Storyboard

main quest. In each game session, the party might make any random decision: Should we see what is on the other side of the mountains, or do we go try to fight those wolves, or do we explore that unknown area to the south of us? This can be much more of a challenge to the GM. Do you design your entire world in detail, so no matter where they go you are prepared for them? If you have lots of time on your hands, this can certainly be enjoyable, akin to the fun fantasy GMs have in designing mega-dungeons. But it can also be frustrating, if you draw up a really cool encounter in the Dismal Marsh, but the party never goes there.

So there are two other ways to handle a Sandbox campaign. If you are an experienced GM who feels comfortable improvising on the fly, you can just make up things as you go along. Many of the most famous old-school GMs were masters of this improvisation, and never bothered with published scenarios at all. If you are not comfortable with that approach, but don't want to spend the time to populate an entire continent, there is a third way. Design mini-encounters that have no fixed location. For example, perhaps you have an encounter centered around the python's burrow. Just have this in reserve, and when the party moves into an area that you have not prepared, they can suddenly find themselves near the python's burrow, and everything is ready for them. Then you simply mark that location on your campaign map, and it becomes fixed in space thereafter.

There is also a fourth method that works best if you play infrequently. Just end each game session with a cliffhanger as the party discovers something about the next encounter but ends play before dealing with it. Then you, as GM, have time until the next game session to actually design the encounter and be ready to run it when you next meet. *"As you come to the top of the ridge, you see something most bizarre. There are rabbits running around down below, and each one of them seems to be wearing a little jacket or hat. We'll stop here, and continue next week."*

So, Storyboard or Sandbox; ultimately, it is your choice. As always, do what provides the most fun for both the players and the GM.

Roleplay

As with all roleplaying games, getting into character is important. But unlike most RPGs in which the players take the role of humanoid characters, in B&B you are playing animals. Animals that talk, admittedly. If you are a human in an RPG, you are familiar with human emotions, mannerisms, dialects, and gestures. But how do you play so as to distinguish an armadillo from a porcupine? Do porcupines have a Midwestern accent, or armadillos a Texan accent? Even understanding how an animal perceives the world is tricky. Owls have good hearing and night vision, while dogs rely strongly on scent. So if your character has a high Smell Rating, do you sniff a lot when roleplaying your character? Does your chipmunk talk rapidly in a high-pitched voice?

We strongly encourage players to explore the roleplaying possibilities of the various animals in the game. This is not to suggest that you become "furries" in order to play properly, but that you try out different tones of voice and patterns of speech during play. If you feel that you have mastered a particular animal in the game, please consider posting a video to show the rest of us. In some of our adventures we have described the speech patterns of some NPCs to give you some ideas.

Another suggestion is to watch nature videos of the animal you are going to roleplay. This may give you hints as to how to approach its behavior. When we first published B&B, there were few quality films of many animals, even relatively common ones. Now, however, there is an abundance of great videos online, including all of the non-rabbit species you can play. And watch lots of videos of rabbits, both wild ones and house rabbits. GMs should also watch videos of as many different predators as possible, so that you can best decide how encounters are likely to occur. (But be a little more forgiving when running the game for the well-being of your players!)

Experience

Although published adventures may suggest how many APs should be awarded for certain milestones or accomplishments, ultimately this decision rests with the GM. Only you know how often your games meet, how long the campaign is likely to last, and how fast you want your player characters to gain levels. Players like to advance and feel like they are making progress toward being more powerful and gaining more abilities. But if you advance them too fast, it may wind up unbalancing the game for the particular encounters of your adventures. Nevertheless, it is up to you and your players. If you all enjoy playing super rabbits, then we have no problem with that (though in our experience, slow progress and managing to overcome obstacles at low levels can be great fun, and very satisfying).

Catching Up

Sometimes the GM has a new player come into an existing campaign in which the current player characters are mid-level. The GM might wonder if the newbie should also start at mid-level, thinking that the challenges being presented in the campaign are too tough for a beginning rabbit. This decision depends on the game philosophy of the GM. If the GM wants the new player to "catch up," there are a couple of ways to do this. One method is to do a normal creation of a new character, but then give the player more APs to spend (instead of the usual starting 2 APs). For example, you could have the new player character start with 20 or 30 APs to put into levels right away. This is not the method we recommend, since the new player will not know what Traits are best raised until actually experiencing combat and other situations in the game.

So we prefer to have the new player start a character at 1st level, the regular way, and begin play. Then, if the GM wants him to catch up, simply double the number of APs the new player gets after each session; if the other characters finish a 2 AP adventure, give the new player 4 APs instead. This way, he gains on the others, but at a slower pace than simply giving all the extra APs at the start. He has more opportunity to learn the value of the various Traits by playing through adventures since in fact every Trait level gain is advantageous in some way or another, regardless of your profession.

But a catch-up plan is not even necessary. We have found no problem with mixed-level parties in B&B, and it can be fun to play low-level characters even if others around you are higher level. This causes less difficulties in B&B than it might in some other RPG settings.

Appendix A: The Herbal of Black Adder

Among rabbit herbalists, the lore of using herbs is attributed to a figure of lapin legend: Black Adder, the first Herbalist. What is known about different herbs, their attributes, preparations, transformations and uses, is passed from one generation to the next as an unwritten tradition known as the Herbal of Black Adder.

In the following listings, herbs are listed by their periodic number in the Honeycomb. In general, this proceeds from Green herbs to herbs of increasing odor Clarity. Refer to the periodic table of herbs (the Honeycomb) for more information.

Some of the entries in the current Honeycomb remain blank. These represent herbs that are unknown at the present time. Nevertheless, because of the lawful nature of the periodic table, many of the characteristics of these undiscovered herbs are known. All that remains to be learned about them is their Method of Delivery, the Effects they produce, and their effects when acting as Poisonweed. Entries for unknown herbs are included in the listing below to allow creation of new herbs with new effects, either by ourselves or other authors in future supplements or adventures, or by individual gamemasters running local campaigns. Feel free to be creative, but guard against making any particular herb too powerful!

The herbal also includes ordinary fungi and plants that do not possess herbal qualities. These either represent prized foods that are highly sought after and can be used in trade, or plants that have the same botanical features as a true herb, making them suitable as non-herbal shells for herb remodeling (imbuing).

Prized Foods

Acorn

- **Value:** Not particularly favored as food by rabbits, but prized by Nibblers such as Tree Squirrels and Chipmunks, as well as Jays and certain Woodpeckers. A standard unit of trade = 1@, equal to one lettuce.
- **Habitats:** Common in Oak Woodland.

Lettuce

- **Value:** A standard unit of trade, equal to one acorn = 1@.
- **Habitats:** Common in gardens on Farms.

Blackberry

- **Value:** Equal to one acorn when fresh, = 1@.
- **Habitats:** Common in Brushland, Farm and Mountain Stream.

Carrot

- **Value:** Equal to two acorns, = 2@.
- **Habitats:** Common in gardens on Farms. Wild carrots may be found in Mountain Stream.
- **Other Uses:** Carrots may be used to eliminate infestations of intestinal worms.

Cowslip

- **Value:** Equal to two acorns, = 2@.
- **Habitats:** Common in Grassland and Rocky Hillside.

Oats

- **Value:** A small amount, enough to fill an eggshell, is equal to four acorns, = 4@.
- **Habitats:** Common on Farms, often stored in the barn.

Apple

- **Value:** Equal to four carrots, = 8@.
- **Habitats:** Common in Orchards.

Cilantro

- **Value:** One of the most valuable trading commodities when fresh. One sprig is equal to four apples, = 32@.
- **Habitats:** Edible cooking herb grown in Farm gardens.

Truffle

- **Value:** The most valuable trading commodity, apart from certain shiny stones. Equal to four sprigs of Cilantro, = 128@.
- **Habitats:** Uncommon in Oak Woodland.

Non-Herbal Shells

Although lacking in herbal qualities when found in nature, non-herbal shells may be used through a process of Imbuing to create new herbs.

Blackberry

- **Class of Effect:** Non-herbal fruit
- **Description:** A delicious fruit produced on thorny blackberry vines. A prized food that also can be used as a shell for

herbal berries.

- **Habitats:** Common in Brushland, Farm, and Mountain Stream.

Burdock

- **Class of Effect:** Non-herbal flowering plant
- **Description:** A leafy plant that grows a long taproot. The root is edible and can be used as a shell for herbal roots. The seeds of burdock can produce annoying burrs that become tangled in fur.
- **Habitats:** Common in Grassland and Brushland.

Daisy

- **Class of Effect:** Non-herbal flower
- **Description:** A simple flower. Can be used as a shell for herbal flowers, flower dust, and flower sap.
- **Habitats:** Common in Grassland, Marsh, and Suburbs.

Dandelion

- **Class of Effect:** Non-herbal weed
- **Description:** A common weed that produces a fluffy seed head. The greens are good food. The seed head can be used as a shell for herbal seeds such as Fluffyhead and Fluffneedle, and the greens can be used as a shell for herbal weeds.
- **Habitats:** Common in Oak Woodland and Pine Forests.

Dead Nettle

- **Class of Effect:** Non-herbal flowering plant
- **Description:** A nettle with no herbal properties. The nettle hairs cause only a mild tingling when making skin contact, but the stems or leaves can be used as a shell for herbal nettles.
- **Habitats:** Common in Grassland and Rocky Hillside.

Dwarf Puffball

- **Class of Effect:** Non-herbal fungus
- **Description:** A fungal ball with no herbal properties. Edible and can be used as a shell for herbal balls such as Snuffball and Giant Puffball.
- **Habitats:** Common in Oak Woodland and Pine Forests.

Maple Leaves

- **Class of Effect:** Non-herbal tree
- **Description:** Leaves from maple trees. Non-toxic, but not particularly edible. Can be used as a shell for herbal leaves.
- **Habitats:** Common in Oak Woodland (big-leaf maple), Pine Forest (vine maple), and high Mountain Streams (sugar maple).

Maple Tree Bark

- **Class of Effect:** Non-herbal tree
- **Description:** A rough bark from a maple tree, similar to the herb Willow Bark. Sugar maple is known for producing a sugary sap. The bark can be used as a shell for herbal bark.
- **Habitats:** Common in Oak Woodland (big-leaf maple), Pine Forest (vine maple), and high Mountain Streams (sugar maple).

White Mushroom

- **Class of Effect:** Non-herbal fungus
- **Description:** A fungal cap with no herbal properties. Can be used as a shell for herbal caps, mushrooms, buttons, and boletes.
- **Habitats:** Common in Oak Woodland and Mountain Stream.

Wild Onion

- **Class of Effect:** Non-herbal flowering plant
- **Description:** Produces an underground bulb. The bulb is edible and can be used as a shell for herbal bulbs, lilies, irises, and garlics.
- **Habitats:** Common in Brushland. A cultivated version may be found in gardens on Farms.

Herb Descriptions

The Five Clarities

Useful herbs may be distinguished by their odor clarity: Clear, Cloudy, Murky or Dense. A fifth clarity — Green — also is recognized as an indicator of growing things that have the potential to become useful herbs.

Green Herbs

Although lacking in herbal qualities when found in nature, Green herbs may be altered by the application of herbal lore to become powerful herbs.

Bracket Fungus

- **Class of Effect:** Latent herb; Fungal Source.
- **Odor Properties:** A Fungal Source with no other odor properties, but capable of incorporating herbal odor properties through remodeling.
- **Habitats:** Common in Oak Woodland and Orchard.

Juniper Berry

- **Class of Effect:** Latent herb; Floral Source.
- **Odor Properties:** A Floral Source with no other odor properties, but capable of incorporating herbal odor properties through remodeling.
- **Habitats:** Common in Rocky Hillside and Suburb.

Bracken Fern Frond

- **Class of Effect:** Latent herb; Overt Source.
- **Odor Properties:** An Overt Source with no other odor properties, but capable of incorporating herbal odor properties through remodeling.
- **Habitats:** Common in Grassland and Brushland.

Ground Pine (clubmoss)

- **Class of Effect:** Latent herb; Covert Source.
- **Odor Properties:** A Covert Source with no other odor properties, but capable of incorporating herbal odor properties through remodeling.
- **Habitats:** Common in Pine Forest and Mountain Stream.

Clear Herbs

Clear herbs have the simplest odor clarity, reflecting their purity of essence and singularity of purpose.

1. Unknown Herb

- **Class of Effect:** Soporific
- **Associated Trait:** MYS
- **Habitats:** Oak Woodland, Pine Forest, Mountain Stream

Odor Properties:

Source	Type	Clarity	Quality	Temperament	Agency	Tone
Fungal	Cap	Clear	Minty	Shy	Mind	Fragrant

- **Preparation:** Lick
- **Poisonweed:** Crumble
- **Method of Delivery:** _______________
- **Effects:** _______________
- **Poisonweed Effects:** _______________

2. Stumpball

- **Class of Effect:** Herbal
- **Associated Trait:** SML
- **Habitats:** Oak Woodland, Pine Forest, Mountain Stream

Odor Properties:

Source	Type	Clarity	Quality	Temperament	Agency	Tone
Fungal	Ball	Clear	Minty	Shy	Mind	Putrid

- **Preparation:** Crumble
- **Poisonweed:** Lick
- **Method of Delivery:** Breathe spores
- **Effects:** Causes nasal congestion, reduces SML −2. Can be used against multiple opponents; aerial dispersal fills 2-meter front (8 hexes).
- **Poisonweed Effects:** Backfires and rebounds on user, to same effect.

3. Unknown Herb

- **Class of Effect:** Medicinal
- **Associated Trait:** CON
- **Habitats:** Oak Woodland, Pine Forest, Mountain Stream

Odor Properties:

Source	Type	Clarity	Quality	Temperament	Agency	Tone
Fungal	Cap	Clear	Musky	Shy	Body	Fragrant

- **Preparation:** Chew (wet chew)
- **Poisonweed:** Claw
- **Method of Delivery:** _______________
- **Effects:** _______________
- **Poisonweed Effects:** _______________

4. Unknown Herb

- **Class of Effect:** Defensive
- **Associated Trait:** SPD
- **Habitats:** Oak Woodland, Pine Forest, Mountain Stream

Odor Properties:

Source	Type	Clarity	Quality	Temperament	Agency	Tone
Fungal	Ball	Clear	Musky	Shy	Body	Putrid

- **Preparation:** Claw
- **Poisonweed:** Chew (wet chew)
- **Method of Delivery:** _______________
- **Effects:** _______________
- **Poisonweed Effects:** _______________

5. Golden Bolete

- **Class of Effect:** Hypnotic
- **Associated Trait:** CHA
- **Habitats:** Oak Woodland, Pine Forest, Mountain Stream

Odor Properties:

Source	Type	Clarity	Quality	Temperament	Agency	Tone
Fungal	Cap	Clear	Acrid	Bold	Mind	Fragrant

- **Preparation:** Peel
- **Poisonweed:** Skin
- **Method of Delivery:** Eat
- **Effects:** Enhances confidence, increases CHA Rating +2 for 1 hour.
- **Poisonweed Effects:** Toxic. Inflicts 2 HP poison damage per hour until cleared. DV=6 for toxin resistance check.

6. Unknown Herb

- **Class of Effect:** Prophylactic

- **Associated Trait:** INT
- **Habitats:** Oak Woodland, Pine Forest, Mountain Stream

Odor Properties:

Source	Type	Clarity	Quality	Temperament	Agency	Tone
Fungal	Ball	Clear	Acrid	Bold	Mind	Putrid

- **Preparation:** Skin
- **Poisonweed:** Peel
- **Method of Delivery:** _______________________________
- **Effects:** _______________________________
- **Poisonweed Effects:** _______________________________

7. Poison Mushroom

- **Class of Effect:** Irritant
- **Associated Trait:** AGI
- **Habitats:** Oak Woodland, Pine Forest, Mountain Stream

Odor Properties:

Source	Type	Clarity	Quality	Temperament	Agency	Tone
Fungal	Cap	Clear	Pungent	Bold	Body	Fragrant

- **Preparation:** Brush (remove dirt)
- **Poisonweed:** Squeeze
- **Method of Delivery:** Eat
- **Effects:** Internal burning if eaten; inflicts damage as a toxin, 1d6 HP per hour. DV=8 for toxin resistance check.
- **Poisonweed Effects:** Toxic. Inflicts 2 HP poison damage per hour until cleared. DV=6 for toxin resistance check.

8. Ruffball

- **Class of Effect:** Injurious
- **Associated Trait:** STR
- **Habitats:** Oak Woodland, Pine Forest, Mountain Stream

Odor Properties:

Source	Type	Clarity	Quality	Temperament	Agency	Tone
Fungal	Ball	Clear	Pungent	Bold	Body	Putrid

- **Preparation:** Squeeze
- **Poisonweed:** Brush (remove dirt)
- **Method of Delivery:** Eat
- **Effects:** Fills subject with renewed energy; increases STR Rating by +1 for 1 hour. Dissipates if dispersed beyond user, so cannot be applied to multiple subjects.
- **Poisonweed Effects:** Opposite effect, decreasing STR Rating –1. Effect can be delivered to opponent, however, if smashed on opponent's face.

9. Fluffyhead

- **Class of Effect:** Soporific

- **Associated Trait:** MYS
- **Habitats:** Orchard, Rocky Hillside

Odor Properties:

Source	Type	Clarity	Quality	Temperament	Agency	Tone
Floral	Fruit	Clear	Minty	Shy	Mind	Fragrant

- **Preparation:** Lick
- **Poisonweed:** Crumble
- **Method of Delivery:** Skin contact with seeds.
- **Effects:** Seeds disperse like a dandelion head; causes drowsiness; reduces AGI Rating –2 for 1 hour. Can be used against multiple opponents; aerial dispersal in 2-meter cone (4 hexes).
- **Poisonweed Effects:** Backfires and rebounds on user, to same effect.

10. Unknown Herb

- **Class of Effect:** Herbal
- **Associated Trait:** SML
- **Habitats:** Orchard, Rocky Hillside

Odor Properties:

Source	Type	Clarity	Quality	Temperament	Agency	Tone
Floral	Flower	Clear	Minty	Shy	Mind	Putrid

- **Preparation:** Crumble
- **Poisonweed:** Lick
- **Method of Delivery:** _______________________________
- **Effects:** _______________________________
- **Poisonweed Effects:** _______________________________

11. Redberry

- **Class of Effect:** Medicinal
- **Associated Trait:** CON
- **Habitats:** Orchard, Rocky Hillside

Odor Properties:

Source	Type	Clarity	Quality	Temperament	Agency	Tone
Floral	Fruit	Clear	Musky	Shy	Body	Fragrant

- **Preparation:** Chew (wet chew)
- **Poisonweed:** Claw
- **Method of Delivery:** Eat or skin contact with juice.
- **Effects:** Cures wounds, 1d6 HP
- **Poisonweed Effects:** If Skin contact: Opposite effect, inflicts 1d6 HP damage. If Eaten: Toxic. Inflicts 2 HP poison damage per hour until cleared. DV=6 for toxin resistance check.

12. Unknown Herb

- **Class of Effect:** Defensive
- **Associated Trait:** SPD
- **Habitats:** Orchard, Rocky Hillside

Odor Properties:

Source	Type	Clarity	Quality	Tempera-ment	Agency	Tone
Floral	Flower	Clear	Musky	Shy	Body	Putrid

- **Preparation:** Claw
- **Poisonweed:** Chew (wet chew)
- **Method of Delivery:** ______________________
- **Effects:** ______________________
- **Poisonweed Effects:** ______________________

13. Unknown Herb

- **Class of Effect:** Hypnotic
- **Associated Trait:** CHA
- **Habitats:** Orchard, Rocky Hillside

Odor Properties:

Source	Type	Clarity	Quality	Tempera-ment	Agency	Tone
Floral	Fruit	Clear	Acrid	Bold	Mind	Fragrant

- **Preparation:** Peel
- **Poisonweed:** Skin
- **Method of Delivery:** ______________________
- **Effects:** ______________________
- **Poisonweed Effects:** ______________________

14. Mosquito Flower

- **Class of Effect:** Prophylactic
- **Associated Trait:** INT
- **Habitats:** Orchard, Rocky Hillside

Odor Properties:

Source	Type	Clarity	Quality	Tempera-ment	Agency	Tone
Floral	Flower	Clear	Acrid	Bold	Mind	Putrid

- **Preparation:** Skin
- **Poisonweed:** Peel
- **Method of Delivery:** Rub on body surface
- **Effects:** Repels mosquitoes for 1 day
- **Poisonweed Effects:** Attracts mosquitoes in every habitat all day.

15. Joint-Pine Cone

- **Class of Effect:** Irritant
- **Associated Trait:** AGI

- **Habitats:** Orchard, Rocky Hillside

Odor Properties:

Source	Type	Clarity	Quality	Tempera-ment	Agency	Tone
Floral	Fruit	Clear	Pungent	Bold	Body	Fragrant

- **Preparation:** Brush (remove dirt)
- **Poisonweed:** Squeeze
- **Method of Delivery:** Eat
- **Effects:** Enhances concentration and focus, increases AGI Rating by +1 for 1 hour.
- **Poisonweed Effects:** Toxic. Inflicts 2 HP poison damage per hour until cleared. DV=4 for toxin resistance check.

16. Lemonberry Flower

- **Class of Effect:** Injurious
- **Associated Trait:** STR
- **Habitats:** Orchard, Rocky Hillside

Odor Properties:

Source	Type	Clar-ity	Quality	Tempera-ment	Agency	Tone
Floral	Flower	Clear	Pungent	Bold	Body	Putrid

- **Preparation:** Squeeze
- **Poisonweed:** Brush (remove dirt)
- **Method of Delivery:** Eat whole flower
- **Effects:** Inflicts damage, 1d6 HP
- **Poisonweed Effects:** Toxic. Inflicts 2 HP poison damage per hour until cleared. DV=6 for toxin resistance check.

17. Unknown Herb

- **Class of Effect:** Soporific
- **Associated Trait:** MYS
- **Habitats:** Grassland, Marsh, Suburb

Odor Properties:

Source	Type	Clarity	Quality	Tempera-ment	Agency	Tone
Overt	Leaf	Clear	Minty	Shy	Mind	Fragrant

- **Preparation:** Lick
- **Poisonweed:** Crumble
- **Method of Delivery:** ______________________
- **Effects:** ______________________
- **Poisonweed Effects:** ______________________

18. Willow Bark

- **Class of Effect:** Herbal
- **Associated Trait:** SML
- **Habitats:** Grassland, Marsh, Suburb

Odor Properties:

Source	Type	Clarity	Quality	Temperament	Agency	Tone
Overt	Stem	Clear	Minty	Shy	Mind	Putrid

- **Preparation:** Crumble
- **Poisonweed:** Lick
- **Method of Delivery:** Sprinkle on food or herbs
- **Effects:** Turns bright yellow in the presence of poison, or Irritant or Injurious herbs that inflict damage; does not alter poison; does not respond to Poisonweed
- **Poisonweed Effects:** Ruins food or herbs.

19. Willow Leaves

- **Class of Effect:** Medicinal
- **Associated Trait:** CON
- **Habitats:** Grassland, Marsh, Suburb

Odor Properties:

Source	Type	Clarity	Quality	Temperament	Agency	Tone
Overt	Leaf	Clear	Musky	Shy	Body	Fragrant

- **Preparation:** Chew (wet chew)
- **Poisonweed:** Claw
- **Method of Delivery:** Eat
- **Effects:** Reduces pain; cures snuffles. At twice normal potency (requires advanced preparation), cures Rabbit Fever.
- **Poisonweed Effects:** Toxic. Inflicts 2 HP poison damage per hour until cleared. DV=6 for toxin resistance check.

20. Unknown Herb

- **Class of Effect:** Defensive
- **Associated Trait:** SPD
- **Habitats:** Grassland, Marsh, Suburb

Odor Properties:

Source	Type	Clarity	Quality	Temperament	Agency	Tone
Overt	Stem	Clear	Musky	Shy	Body	Putrid

- **Preparation:** Claw
- **Poisonweed:** Chew (wet chew)
- **Method of Delivery:** ______________________________
- **Effects:** ______________________________
- **Poisonweed Effects:** ______________________________

21. Locoweed

- **Class of Effect:** Hypnotic
- **Associated Trait:** CHA
- **Habitats:** Grassland, Marsh, Suburb

Odor Properties:

Source	Type	Clarity	Quality	Temperament	Agency	Tone
Overt	Leaf	Clear	Acrid	Bold	Mind	Fragrant

- **Preparation:** Peel
- **Poisonweed:** Skin
- **Method of Delivery:** Eat
- **Effects:** Incites irrational behavior, causes subject to act contrary to intentions
- **Poisonweed Effects:** Toxic. Inflicts 2 HP poison damage per hour until cleared. DV=6 for toxin resistance check.

22. Tickweed

- **Class of Effect:** Prophylactic
- **Associated Trait:** INT
- **Habitats:** Grassland, Marsh, Suburb

Odor Properties:

Source	Type	Clarity	Quality	Temperament	Agency	Tone
Overt	Stem	Clear	Acrid	Bold	Mind	Putrid

- **Preparation:** Skin
- **Poisonweed:** Peel
- **Method of Delivery:** Rub on body surface
- **Effects:** Repels ticks for 1 day, but does not eradicate tick infestation.
- **Poisonweed Effects:** Attracts ticks in every habitat all day.

23. Scritchweed

- **Class of Effect:** Irritant
- **Associated Trait:** AGI
- **Habitats:** Grassland, Marsh, Suburb

Odor Properties:

Source	Type	Clarity	Quality	Temperament	Agency	Tone
Overt	Leaf	Clear	Pungent	Bold	Body	Fragrant

- **Preparation:** Brush (remove dirt)
- **Poisonweed:** Squeeze
- **Method of Delivery:** Eat
- **Effects:** Causes itching; reduces SPD Rating –2 for 1 hour
- **Poisonweed Effects:** Toxic. Inflicts 2 HP poison damage per hour until cleared. DV=6 for toxin resistance check.

24. Prickly Nettle

- **Class of Effect:** Injurious
- **Associated Trait:** STR
- **Habitats:** Grassland, Marsh, Suburb

Odor Properties:

Source	Type	Clarity	Quality	Tempera-ment	Agency	Tone
Overt	Stem	Clear	Pungent	Bold	Body	Putrid

- **Preparation:** Squeeze
- **Poisonweed:** Brush (remove dirt)
- **Method of Delivery:** Contact with skin
- **Effects:** Painful contact with nettle hairs inflicts damage, 3 HP.
- **Poisonweed Effects:** No effect.

25. Unknown Herb

- **Class of Effect:** Soporific
- **Associated Trait:** MYS
- **Habitats:** Farm, Brushland

Odor Properties:

Source	Type	Clarity	Quality	Tempera-ment	Agency	Tone
Covert	Bulb	Clear	Minty	Shy	Mind	Fragrant

- **Preparation:** Lick
- **Poisonweed:** Crumble
- **Method of Delivery:** ___________________________________
- **Effects:** ___________________________________
- **Poisonweed Effects:** ___________________________________

26. White Snakeroot

- **Class of Effect:** Herbal
- **Associated Trait:** SML
- **Habitats:** Farm, Brushland

Odor Properties:

Source	Type	Clarity	Quality	Tempera-ment	Agency	Tone
Covert	Root	Clear	Minty	Shy	Mind	Putrid

- **Preparation:** Crumble
- **Poisonweed:** Lick
- **Method of Delivery:** Sprinkle on the tongue
- **Effects:** Mildly toxic, causing 3 HP damage (DV=4 toxin resistance check); however, after sprinkled on the tongue, an Herbalist may identify the odor Clarity and Quality of raw herbs by licking them; effect lasts one hour. If toxin is drawn out with use of Sunflower Dust, White Snakeroot becomes powerful curative, cures 2d6 HP
- **Poisonweed Effects:** If sprinkled on tongue: Toxic. Inflicts initial 3 HP damage, then 2 HP poison damage per hour until cleared. DV=6 for toxin resistance check.

27. Woodsorrel Bulb

- **Class of Effect:** Medicinal

- **Associated Trait:** CON
- **Habitats:** Farm, Brushland

Odor Properties:

Source	Type	Clarity	Quality	Tempera-ment	Agency	Tone
Covert	Bulb	Clear	Musky	Shy	Body	Fragrant

- **Preparation:** Chew (wet chew)
- **Poisonweed:** Claw
- **Method of Delivery:** Eat
- **Effects:** Soothes irritation; counters effects of Irritant herbs
- **Poisonweed Effects:** Toxic. Inflicts 2 HP poison damage per hour until cleared. DV=6 for toxin resistance check.

28. Quickberry Root

- **Class of Effect:** Defensive
- **Associated Trait:** SPD
- **Habitats:** Farm, Brushland

Odor Properties:

Source	Type	Clarity	Quality	Tempera-ment	Agency	Tone
Covert	Root	Clear	Musky	Shy	Body	Putrid

- **Preparation:** Claw
- **Poisonweed:** Chew (wet chew)
- **Method of Delivery:** Eat
- **Effects:** Causes subject to randomly jerk from side to side; increases SPD Rating of subject by +2, but decreases AGI Rating by –2 for 1 hour
- **Poisonweed Effects:** Toxic. Inflicts 2 HP poison damage per hour until cleared. DV=6 for toxin resistance check.

29. Mad Iris

- **Class of Effect:** Hypnotic
- **Associated Trait:** CHA
- **Habitats:** Farm, Brushland

Odor Properties:

Source	Type	Clarity	Quality	Tempera-ment	Agency	Tone
Covert	Bulb	Cloudy	Acrid	Bold	Mind	Fragrant

- **Preparation:** Peel
- **Poisonweed:** Skin
- **Method of Delivery:** Eat
- **Effects:** Causes subject to attack a random target, without regard to friend or foe
- **Poisonweed Effects:** Toxic. Inflicts 2 HP poison damage per hour until cleared. DV=6 for toxin resistance check.

30. Flea Root

- **Class of Effect:** Prophylactic

- **Associated Trait:** INT
- **Habitats:** Farm, Brushland

Odor Properties:

Source	Type	Clarity	Quality	Tempera-ment	Agency	Tone
Covert	Root	Clear	Acrid	Bold	Mind	Putrid

- **Preparation:** Skin
- **Poisonweed:** Peel
- **Method of Delivery:** Rub on body surface
- **Effects:** Repels fleas for 1 day, but does not eradicate flea infestation.
- **Poisonweed Effects:** Attracts fleas in every habitat all day.

31. Unknown Herb

- **Class of Effect:** Irritant
- **Associated Trait:** AGI
- **Habitats:** Farm, Brushland

Odor Properties:

Source	Type	Clarity	Quality	Tempera-ment	Agency	Tone
Covert	Bulb	Clear	Pungent	Bold	Body	Fragrant

- **Preparation:** Brush (remove dirt)
- **Poisonweed:** Squeeze
- **Method of Delivery:** _______________________
- **Effects:** _______________________
- **Poisonweed Effects:** _______________________

32. Unknown Herb

- **Class of Effect:** Injurious
- **Associated Trait:** STR
- **Habitats:** Farm, Brushland

Odor Properties:

Source	Type	Clarity	Quality	Tempera-ment	Agency	Tone
Covert	Root	Clear	Pungent	Bold	Body	Putrid

- **Preparation:** Squeeze
- **Poisonweed:** Brush (remove dirt)
- **Method of Delivery:** _______________________
- **Effects:** _______________________
- **Poisonweed Effects:** _______________________

Cloudy Herbs

Cloudy herbs have a sophisticated simplicity that transcends the Clear, without the complexity of more arcane herbs.

33. Unknown Herb

- **Class of Effect:** Soporific
- **Associated Trait:** MYS
- **Habitats:** Oak Woodland, Pine Forest, Mountain Stream

Odor Properties:

Source	Type	Clarity	Quality	Tempera-ment	Agency	Tone
Fungal	Cap	Cloudy	Minty	Shy	Mind	Fragrant

- **Preparation:** Lick
- **Poisonweed:** Crumble
- **Method of Delivery:** _______________________
- **Effects:** _______________________
- **Poisonweed Effects:** _______________________

34. Unknown Herb

- **Class of Effect:** Herbal
- **Associated Trait:** SML
- **Habitats:** Oak Woodland, Pine Forest, Mountain Stream

Odor Properties:

Source	Type	Clarity	Quality	Tempera-ment	Agency	Tone
Fungal	Ball	Cloudy	Minty	Shy	Mind	Putrid

- **Preparation:** Crumble
- **Poisonweed:** Lick
- **Method of Delivery:** _______________________
- **Effects:** _______________________
- **Poisonweed Effects:** _______________________

35. Jelly Button

- **Class of Effect:** Medicinal
- **Associated Trait:** CON
- **Habitats:** Oak Woodland, Pine Forest, Mountain Stream

Odor Properties:

Source	Type	Clarity	Quality	Tempera-ment	Agency	Tone
Floral	Cap	Cloudy	Musky	Shy	Body	Fragrant

- **Preparation:** Chew (wet chew)
- **Poisonweed:** Claw
- **Method of Delivery:** Eat
- **Effects:** Cures Shakes
- **Poisonweed Effects:** Toxic. Inflicts 2 HP poison damage per hour until cleared. DV=6 for toxin resistance check.

36. Snuffball

- **Class of Effect:** Defensive
- **Associated Trait:** SPD

- **Habitats:** Oak Woodland, Pine Forest, Mountain Stream

Odor Properties:

Source	Type	Clarity	Quality	Temperament	Agency	Tone
Fungal	Ball	Cloudy	Musky	Shy	Body	Putrid

- **Preparation:** Claw
- **Poisonweed:** Chew (wet chew)
- **Method of Delivery:** Breathe spores
- **Effects:** Spores cause uncontrollable sneezing; renders subject incapable of any other action, including movement, for 1 minute. Can be used against multiple opponents; aerial dispersal fills 2-meter front (8 hexes).
- **Poisonweed Effects:** Backfires and rebounds on user, to same effect.

37. Unknown Herb

- **Class of Effect:** Hypnotic
- **Associated Trait:** CHA
- **Habitats:** Oak Woodland, Pine Forest, Mountain Stream

Odor Properties:

Source	Type	Clarity	Quality	Temperament	Agency	Tone
Fungal	Cap	Cloudy	Acrid	Bold	Mind	Fragrant

- **Preparation:** Peel
- **Poisonweed:** Skin
- **Method of Delivery:** _______________________
- **Effects:** _______________________
- **Poisonweed Effects:** _______________________

38. Unknown Herb

- **Class of Effect:** Prophylactic
- **Associated Trait:** INT
- **Habitats:** Oak Woodland, Pine Forest, Mountain Stream

Odor Properties:

Source	Type	Clarity	Quality	Temperament	Agency	Tone
Fungal	Ball	Cloudy	Acrid	Bold	Mind	Putrid

- **Preparation:** Skin
- **Poisonweed:** Peel
- **Method of Delivery:** _______________________
- **Effects:** _______________________
- **Poisonweed Effects:** _______________________

39. Bitter Mushroom

- **Class of Effect:** Irritant
- **Associated Trait:** AGI
- **Habitats:** Oak Woodland, Pine Forest, Mountain Stream

Odor Properties:

Source	Type	Clarity	Quality	Temperament	Agency	Tone
Fungal	Cap	Cloudy	Pungent	Bold	Body	Fragrant

- **Preparation:** Brush (remove dirt)
- **Poisonweed:** Squeeze
- **Method of Delivery:** Eat
- **Effects:** Enhances concentration and focus, increases AGI Rating by +2 for 1 hour.
- **Poisonweed Effects:** Toxic. Inflicts 2 HP poison damage per hour until cleared. DV=6 for toxin resistance check.

40. Tuffball

- **Class of Effect:** Injurious
- **Associated Trait:** STR
- **Habitats:** Oak Woodland, Pine Forest, Mountain Stream

Odor Properties:

Source	Type	Clarity	Quality	Temperament	Agency	Tone
Fungal	Ball	Cloudy	Pungent	Bold	Body	Putrid

- **Preparation:** Squeeze
- **Poisonweed:** Brush (remove dirt)
- **Method of Delivery:** Sniff spores
- **Effects:** Fills subject with renewed energy; increases STR Rating by +2 for 1 hour. Dissipates if dispersed beyond user, so cannot be applied to multiple subjects.
- **Poisonweed Effects:** Opposite effect, decreasing STR Rating –2. Effect can be delivered to opponent, however, if smashed on the opponent's face.

41. Poppy Puff

- **Class of Effect:** Soporific
- **Associated Trait:** MYS
- **Habitats:** Orchard, Rocky Hillside

Odor Properties:

Source	Type	Clarity	Quality	Temperament	Agency	Tone
Floral	Fruit	Cloudy	Minty	Shy	Mind	Fragrant

- **Preparation:** Lick
- **Poisonweed:** Crumble
- **Method of Delivery:** Breathe fluff from seeds
- **Effects:** Seeds disperse like a dandelion head; induces sleep in subjects up to 25 HP for 1 hour. Can be used against multiple opponents; aerial dispersal in 2-meter cone.
- **Poisonweed Effects:** Causes sleep, but only for 1 minute.

42. Falseflower Dust

- **Class of Effect:** Herbal

- **Associated Trait:** SML
- **Habitats:** Orchard, Rocky Hillside

Odor Properties:

Source	Type	Clarity	Quality	Tempera-ment	Agency	Tone
Floral	Flower	Cloudy	Minty	Shy	Mind	Putrid

- **Preparation:** Crumble
- **Poisonweed:** Lick
- **Method of Delivery:** Breathe dust (pollen)
- **Effects:** Causes subject to mistakenly perceive true herbs to be toxic poisonweed and vice versa; 1 day. Can be used against multiple opponents; aerial dispersal fills 2-meter cone (4 hexes).
- **Poisonweed Effects:** Backfires and rebounds on user, to same effect.

43. Bounceberry

- **Class of Effect:** Medicinal
- **Associated Trait:** CON
- **Habitats:** Orchard, Rocky Hillside

Odor Properties:

Source	Type	Clarity	Quality	Tempera-ment	Agency	Tone
Floral	Fruit	Cloudy	Musky	Shy	Body	Fragrant

- **Preparation:** Chew (wet chew)
- **Poisonweed:** Claw
- **Method of Delivery:** Eat
- **Effects:** Fills subject with feeling of renewed vigor; increases CON Rating by +2 for 1 hour
- **Poisonweed Effects:** Toxic. Inflicts 2 HP poison damage per hour until cleared. DV=6 for toxin resistance check.

44. Cacomistletoe

- **Class of Effect:** Defensive
- **Associated Trait:** SPD
- **Habitats:** Orchard, Rocky Hillside

Odor Properties:

Source	Type	Clarity	Quality	Tempera-ment	Agency	Tone
Floral	Flower	Cloudy	Musky	Shy	Body	Putrid

- **Preparation:** Claw
- **Poisonweed:** Chew (wet chew)
- **Method of Delivery:** Eat whole flower
- **Effects:** For the purpose of climbing only, increases SPD Rating by +4 for 1 hour. Named for cacomistle, a relative of ringtails renowned for its climbing skills.
- **Poisonweed Effects:** Toxic. Inflicts 2 HP poison damage per hour until cleared. DV=6 for toxin resistance check.

45. Razzleberry

- **Class of Effect:** Hypnotic
- **Associated Trait:** CHA
- **Habitats:** Orchard, Rocky Hillside

Odor Properties:

Source	Type	Clarity	Quality	Tempera-ment	Agency	Tone
Floral	Fruit	Cloudy	Acrid	Bold	Mind	Fragrant

- **Preparation:** Peel
- **Poisonweed:** Skin
- **Method of Delivery:** Eat, or skin contact with juice
- **Effects:** Causes confusion; subject acts upon first suggestion by herb user (50% likelihood; succeeds on 1d6 die roll of 4–6); herb user must speak the language of the subject.
- **Poisonweed Effects. If skin contact:** Juice splashes on user during delivery, causing user to act on first random suggestion by anyone on a 1d6 die roll of 1–3. If eaten: Toxic. Inflicts 2 HP poison damage per hour until cleared. DV=6 for toxin resistance check.

46. Leech Flower

- **Class of Effect:** Prophylactic
- **Associated Trait:** INT
- **Habitats:** Orchard, Rocky Hillside

Odor Properties:

Source	Type	Clarity	Quality	Tempera-ment	Agency	Tone
Floral	Flower	Cloudy	Acrid	Bold	Mind	Putrid

- **Preparation:** Skin
- **Poisonweed:** Peel
- **Method of Delivery:** Rub on body surface
- **Effects:** Repels leeches for 1 day, but does not eradicate leech infestation.
- **Poisonweed Effects:** Attracts leeches in every habitat with open water all day.

47. Lemonberry

- **Class of Effect:** Irritant
- **Associated Trait:** AGI
- **Habitats:** Orchard, Rocky Hillside

Odor Properties:

Source	Type	Clarity	Quality	Tempera-ment	Agency	Tone
Floral	Fruit	Cloudy	Pungent	Bold	Body	Fragrant

- **Preparation:** Brush (remove dirt)
- **Poisonweed:** Squeeze
- **Method of Delivery:** Eat, or skin contact with juice

- **Effects:** Causes itching blisters; inflicts 1 HP damage per minute for 10 minutes
- **Poisonweed Effects:** If skin contact: Juice splashes on user during delivery, causing same itching blisters in user. If eaten: Toxic. Inflicts 2 HP poison damage per hour until cleared. DV=6 for toxin resistance check.

48. Unknown Herb

- **Class of Effect:** Injurious
- **Associated Trait:** STR
- **Habitats:** Orchard, Rocky Hillside

Odor Properties:

Source	Type	Clarity	Quality	Tempera-ment	Agency	Tone
Floral	Flower	Cloudy	Pungent	Bold	Body	Putrid

- **Preparation:** Squeeze
- **Poisonweed:** Brush (remove dirt)
- **Method of Delivery:** ___________________________
- **Effects:** ___________________________
- **Poisonweed Effects:** ___________________________

49. Unknown Herb

- **Class of Effect:** Soporific
- **Associated Trait:** MYS
- **Habitats:** Grassland, Marsh, Suburb

Odor Properties:

Source	Type	Clarity	Quality	Tempera-ment	Agency	Tone
Overt	Leaf	Cloudy	Minty	Shy	Mind	Fragrant

- **Preparation:** Lick
- **Poisonweed:** Crumble
- **Method of Delivery:** ___________________________
- **Effects:** ___________________________
- **Poisonweed Effects:** ___________________________

50. Truebark

- **Class of Effect:** Herbal
- **Associated Trait:** SML
- **Habitats:** Grassland, Marsh, Suburb

Odor Properties:

Source	Type	Clarity	Quality	Tempera-ment	Agency	Tone
Overt	Stem	Cloudy	Minty	Shy	Mind	Putrid

- **Preparation:** Crumble
- **Poisonweed:** Lick
- **Method of Delivery:** Sprinkle over surface of herb
- **Effects:** Turns bright orange when it comes in contact with Poisonweed

- **Poisonweed Effects:** Turns bright orange when it comes in contact with a True Herb.

51. Burning Nettle

- **Class of Effect:** Medicinal
- **Associated Trait:** CON
- **Habitats:** Grassland, Marsh, Suburb

Odor Properties:

Source	Type	Clarity	Quality	Tempera-ment	Agency	Tone
Overt	Leaf	Murky	Musky	Shy	Body	Fragrant

- **Preparation:** Chew (wet chew)
- **Poisonweed:** Claw
- **Method of Delivery:** Contact with skin
- **Effects:** Cures wounds, 2d6 HP
- **Poisonweed Effects:** Inflicts serious wound, 2d6 HP.

52. Dodgeweed

- **Class of Effect:** Defensive
- **Associated Trait:** SPD
- **Habitats:** Grassland, Marsh, Suburb

Odor Properties:

Source	Type	Clarity	Quality	Tempera-ment	Agency	Tone
Overt	Stem	Cloudy	Musky	Shy	Body	Putrid

- **Preparation:** Claw
- **Poisonweed:** Chew (wet chew)
- **Method of Delivery:** Eat
- **Effects:** Fills subject with renewed energy; increases SPD Rating by +2 for 1 hour. At twice normal potency (requires Advanced preparation), cures Bumblefoot.
- **Poisonweed Effects:** Toxic. Inflicts 2 HP poison damage per hour until cleared. DV=6 for toxin resistance check.

53. Black Snakeroot

- **Class of Effect:** Hypnotic
- **Associated Trait:** CHA
- **Habitats:** Grassland, Marsh, Suburb

Odor Properties:

Source	Type	Clarity	Quality	Tempera-ment	Agency	Tone
Overt	Leaf	Cloudy	Acrid	Bold	Mind	Fragrant

- **Preparation:** Peel
- **Poisonweed:** Skin
- **Method of Delivery:** Eat
- **Effects:** Toxic, inflicts 1d6 HP damage; however, after incurring damage, the subject becomes extremely attractive to the opposite sex, arousing female sympathy if the user

is male, or male protective compulsion if user is female; increases CHA Rating by +4 (only for opposite sex) for 1 day.

- **Poisonweed Effects:** Toxic. Inflicts 2 HP poison damage per hour until cleared. DV=6 for toxin resistance check.

54. Mite Weed

- **Class of Effect:** Prophylactic
- **Associated Trait:** INT
- **Habitats:** Grassland, Marsh, Suburb

Odor Properties:

Source	Type	Clarity	Quality	Temperament	Agency	Tone
Overt	Stem	Cloudy	Acrid	Bold	Mind	Putrid

- **Preparation:** Skin
- **Poisonweed:** Peel
- **Method of Delivery:** Rub on body surface
- **Effects:** Repels mites for 1 day, but does not eradicate mite infestation.
- **Poisonweed Effects:** Attracts mites in every habitat all day.

55. Unknown Herb

- **Class of Effect:** Irritant
- **Associated Trait:** AGI
- **Habitats. Grassland, Marsh, Suburb**

Odor Properties:

Source	Type	Clarity	Quality	Temperament	Agency	Tone
Overt	Leaf	Cloudy	Pungent	Bold	Body	Fragrant

- **Preparation:** Brush (remove dirt)
- **Poisonweed:** Squeeze
- **Method of Delivery:** ______________________________
- **Effects:** ______________________________
- **Poisonweed Effects:** ______________________________

56. Biting Nettle

- **Class of Effect:** Injurious
- **Associated Trait:** STR
- **Habitats:** Grassland, Marsh, Suburb

Odor Properties:

Source	Type	Clarity	Quality	Temperament	Agency	Tone
Overt	Stem	Murky	Pungent	Bold	Body	Putrid

- **Preparation:** Squeeze
- **Poisonweed:** Brush (remove dirt)
- **Method of Delivery:** Contact with skin
- **Effects:** Painful contact with nettle hairs inflicts damage,

1d6 HP

- **Poisonweed Effects:** No effect.

57. Slumberlily

- **Class of Effect:** Soporific
- **Associated Trait:** MYS
- **Habitats:** Farm, Brushland

Odor Properties:

Source	Type	Clarity	Quality	Temperament	Agency	Tone
Covert	Bulb	Clear	Minty	Shy	Mind	Fragrant

- **Preparation:** Lick
- **Poisonweed:** Crumble
- **Method of Delivery:** Eat
- **Effects:** Induces sleep in subjects up to 40 HP for 1 hour
- **Poisonweed Effects:** Toxic. Inflicts 2 HP poison damage per hour until cleared. DV=6 for toxin resistance check.

58. Unknown Herb

- **Class of Effect:** Herbal
- **Associated Trait:** SML
- **Habitats:** Farm, Brushland

Odor Properties:

Source	Type	Clarity	Quality	Temperament	Agency	Tone
Covert	Root	Cloudy	Minty	Shy	Mind	Putrid

- **Preparation:** Crumble
- **Poisonweed:** Lick
- **Method of Delivery:** ______________________________
- **Effects:** ______________________________
- **Poisonweed Effects:** ______________________________

59. Wild Garlic

- **Class of Effect:** Medicinal
- **Associated Trait:** CON
- **Habitats:** Farm, Brushland

Odor Properties:

Source	Type	Clarity	Quality	Temperament	Agency	Tone
Covert	Bulb	Cloudy	Musky	Shy	Body	Fragrant

- **Preparation:** Chew (wet chew)
- **Poisonweed:** Claw
- **Method of Delivery:** Eat
- **Effects:** Antitoxin; halts the continuing effects of poison and cures injury caused by poison, 1d6 HP. Also can be used to eliminate infestation by liver flukes.
- **Poisonweed Effects:** Toxic. Inflicts 2 HP poison damage

per hour until cleared. DV=6 for toxin resistance check.

60. Unknown Herb

- **Class of Effect:** Defensive
- **Associated Trait:** SPD
- **Habitats:** Farm, Brushland

Odor Properties:

Source	Type	Clarity	Quality	Temperament	Agency	Tone
Covert	Root	Cloudy	Musky	Shy	Body	Putrid

- **Preparation:** Claw
- **Poisonweed:** Chew (wet chew)
- **Method of Delivery:** ______________________
- **Effects:** ______________________
- **Poisonweed Effects:** ______________________

61. Unknown Herb

- **Class of Effect:** Hypnotic
- **Associated Trait:** CHA
- **Habitats:** Farm, Brushland

Odor Properties:

Source	Type	Clarity	Quality	Temperament	Agency	Tone
Covert	Bulb	Cloudy	Acrid	Bold	Mind	Fragrant

- **Preparation:** Peel
- **Poisonweed:** Skin
- **Method of Delivery:** ______________________
- **Effects:** ______________________
- **Poisonweed Effects:** ______________________

62. Warble Root

- **Class of Effect:** Prophylactic
- **Associated Trait:** INT
- **Habitats:** Farm, Brushland

Odor Properties:

Source	Type	Clarity	Quality	Temperament	Agency	Tone
Covert	Root	Cloudy	Acrid	Bold	Mind	Putrid

- **Preparation:** Skin
- **Poisonweed:** Peel
- **Method of Delivery:** Rub on body surface
- **Effects:** Repels warble flies for 1 day, but does not eradicate warbles.
- **Poisonweed Effects:** Attracts warble flies in all habitats all day.

63. Unknown Herb

- **Class of Effect:** Irritant
- **Associated Trait:** AGI
- **Habitats:** Farm, Brushland

Odor Properties:

Source	Type	Clarity	Quality	Temperament	Agency	Tone
Covert	Bulb	Cloudy	Pungent	Bold	Body	Fragrant

- **Preparation:** Brush (remove dirt)
- **Poisonweed:** Squeeze
- **Method of Delivery:** ______________________
- **Effects:** ______________________
- **Poisonweed Effects:** ______________________

64. Lemonberry Root

- **Class of Effect:** Injurious
- **Associated Trait:** STR
- **Habitats:** Farm, Brushland

Odor Properties:

Source	Type	Clarity	Quality	Temperament	Agency	Tone
Covert	Root	Cloudy	Pungent	Bold	Body	Putrid

- **Preparation:** Squeeze
- **Poisonweed:** Brush (remove dirt)
- **Method of Delivery:** Eat
- **Effects:** Inflicts damage, 2d6 HP
- **Poisonweed Effects:** Toxic. Inflicts 2 HP poison damage per hour until cleared. DV=6 for toxin resistance check.

Murky Herbs

Murky herbs possess an intoxicating mix of exotic strangeness and austere purity.

65. Unknown Herb

- **Class of Effect:** Soporific
- **Associated Trait:** MYS
- **Habitats:** Oak Woodland, Pine Forest, Mountain Stream

Odor Properties:

Source	Type	Clarity	Quality	Temperament	Agency	Tone
Fungal	Cap	Murky	Minty	Shy	Mind	Fragrant

- **Preparation:** Lick
- **Poisonweed:** Crumble
- **Method of Delivery:** ______________________
- **Effects:** ______________________
- **Poisonweed Effects:** ______________________

66. Unknown Herb

- **Class of Effect:** Herbal
- **Associated Trait:** SML
- **Habitats:** Oak Woodland, Pine Forest, Mountain Stream

Odor Properties:

Source	Type	Clarity	Quality	Temperament	Agency	Tone
Fungal	Ball	Murky	Minty	Shy	Mind	Putrid

- **Preparation:** Crumble
- **Poisonweed:** Lick
- **Method of Delivery:** __________________________
- **Effects:** __________________________
- **Poisonweed Effects:** __________________________

67. Warble Cap

- **Class of Effect:** Medicinal
- **Associated Trait:** CON
- **Habitats:** Oak Woodland, Pine Forest, Mountain Stream

Odor Properties:

Source	Type	Clarity	Quality	Temperament	Agency	Tone
Fungal	Cap	Murky	Musky	Shy	Body	Fragrant

- **Preparation:** Chew (wet chew)
- **Poisonweed:** Claw
- **Method of Delivery:** Rub on body surface
- **Effects:** Drives out warbles imbedded in the skin
- **Poisonweed Effects:** Causes warbles to dig deeper into the host's flesh, inflicting an additional 3 HP damage for each warble.

68. Powderball

- **Class of Effect:** Defensive
- **Associated Trait:** SPD
- **Habitats:** Oak Woodland, Pine Forest, Mountain Stream

Odor Properties:

Source	Type	Clarity	Quality	Temperament	Agency	Tone
Fungal	Ball	Murky	Musky	Shy	Body	Putrid

- **Preparation:** Claw
- **Poisonweed:** Chew (wet chew)
- **Method of Delivery:** Breathe or allow spores in eyes
- **Effects:** Causes temporary blindness for 1 hour. Can be used against multiple opponents; aerial dispersal fills 2-meter front (8 hexes).
- **Poisonweed Effects:** Backfires and rebounds on user, to same effect.

69. Unknown Herb

- **Class of Effect:** Hypnotic
- **Associated Trait:** CHA
- **Habitats:** Oak Woodland, Pine Forest, Mountain Stream

Odor Properties:

Source	Type	Clarity	Quality	Temperament	Agency	Tone
Fungal	Cap	Murky	Acrid	Bold	Mind	Fragrant

- **Preparation:** Peel
- **Poisonweed:** Skin
- **Method of Delivery:** __________________________
- **Effects:** __________________________
- **Poisonweed Effects:** __________________________

70. Unknown Herb

- **Class of Effect:** Prophylactic
- **Associated Trait:** INT
- **Habitats:** Oak Woodland, Pine Forest, Mountain Stream

Odor Properties:

Source	Type	Clarity	Quality	Temperament	Agency	Tone
Fungal	Ball	Murky	Acrid	Bold	Mind	Putrid

- **Preparation:** Skin
- **Poisonweed:** Peel
- **Method of Delivery:** __________________________
- **Effects:** __________________________
- **Poisonweed Effects:** __________________________

71. Bloodcap

- **Class of Effect:** Irritant
- **Associated Trait:** AGI
- **Habitats:** Oak Woodland, Pine Forest, Mountain Stream

Odor Properties:

Source	Type	Clarity	Quality	Temperament	Agency	Tone
Fungal	Cap	Murky	Pungent	Bold	Body	Fragrant

- **Preparation:** Brush (remove dirt)
- **Poisonweed:** Squeeze
- **Method of Delivery:** Eat
- **Effects:** Causes excessive wound bleeding; doubles subsequent damage from any other cause for 1 hour
- **Poisonweed Effects:** Toxic. Inflicts 2 HP poison damage per hour until cleared. DV=6 for toxin resistance check.

72. Jump Ball

- **Class of Effect:** Injurious

- **Associated Trait:** STR
- **Habitats:** Oak Woodland, Pine Forest, Mountain Stream

Odor Properties:

Source	Type	Clarity	Quality	Temper-ament	Agency	Tone
Fungal	Ball	Murky	Pungent	Bold	Body	Putrid

- **Preparation:** Squeeze
- **Poisonweed:** Brush (remove dirt)
- **Method of Delivery:** Sniff spores
- **Effects:** Feeling of energy flows to leg muscles; doubles jumping height and distance for 1 hour. Dissipates if dispersed beyond user, so cannot be applied to multiple subjects.
- **Poisonweed Effects:** Causes weakness in leg muscles; reducing jumping height and distance by half.

73. Fluffneedle

- **Class of Effect:** Soporific
- **Associated Trait:** MYS
- **Habitats:** Orchard, Rocky Hillside

Odor Properties:

Source	Type	Clarity	Quality	Temper-ament	Agency	Tone
Floral	Fruit	Murky	Minty	Shy	Mind	Fragrant

- **Preparation:** Lick
- **Poisonweed:** Crumble
- **Method of Delivery:** Breathe seed fluff
- **Effects:** Seeds disperse in the air like a dandelion head; induces sleep in subjects up to 40 HP for 1 hour. Can be used against multiple opponents; aerial dispersal in 2-meter cone.
- **Poisonweed Effects:** Backfires and rebounds on user, to same effect.

74. Sunflower Dust

- **Class of Effect:** Herbal
- **Associated Trait:** SML
- **Habitats:** Orchard, Rocky Hillside

Odor Properties:

Source	Type	Clarity	Quality	Temper-ament	Agency	Tone
Floral	Flow-er	Murky	Minty	Shy	Mind	Putrid

- **Preparation:** Crumble
- **Poisonweed:** Lick
- **Method of Delivery:** Sprinkle on food or herbs
- **Effects:** Antitoxin; draws poison from food or herbs, rendering poisoned food edible and poisonous herbs nontoxic.

Has no effect on Poisonweed

- **Poisonweed Effects:** No effect. Food and herbs remain toxic.

75. Pumpkin Seeds

- **Class of Effect:** Medicinal
- **Associated Trait:** CON
- **Habitats:** Orchard, Rocky Hillside

Odor Properties:

Source	Type	Clarity	Quality	Temper-ament	Agency	Tone
Floral	Fruit	Murky	Musky	Shy	Body	Fragrant

- **Preparation:** Chew (wet chew)
- **Poisonweed:** Claw
- **Method of Delivery:** Eat
- **Effects:** Eradicates infestation by intestinal roundworms or liver flukes.
- **Poisonweed Effects:** Toxic. Inflicts 2 HP poison damage per hour until cleared. DV=6 for toxin resistance check.

76. Bounceberry Flower

- **Class of Effect:** Defensive
- **Associated Trait:** SPD
- **Habitats:** Orchard, Rocky Hillside

Odor Properties:

Source	Type	Clarity	Quality	Temper-ament	Agency	Tone
Floral	Flow-er	Cloudy	Musky	Shy	Body	Putrid

- **Preparation:** Claw
- **Poisonweed:** Chew (wet chew)
- **Method of Delivery:** Eat whole flower
- **Effects:** Subject feels sudden rush of energy; increases SPD Rating by +4 for 1 hour
- **Poisonweed Effects:** Toxic. Inflicts 2 HP poison damage per hour until cleared. DV=6 for toxin resistance check.

77. Purpleberry

- **Class of Effect:** Hypnotic
- **Associated Trait:** CHA
- **Habitats:** Orchard, Rocky Hillside

Odor Properties:

Source	Type	Clarity	Quality	Temper-ament	Agency	Tone
Floral	Fruit	Murky	Acrid	Bold	Mind	Fragrant

- **Preparation:** Peel
- **Poisonweed:** Skin
- **Method of Delivery:** Eat, or skin contact with juice

- **Effects:** Causes subject to experience fearful hallucination and lose contact with reality; GM should base hallucination on weakest Base Trait of the subject.
- **Poisonweed Effects:** If skin contact: Juice splashes on user during delivery, causing same fearful hallucination in user. If eaten: Toxic. Inflicts 2 HP poison damage per hour until cleared. DV=6 for toxin resistance check.

78. Unknown Herb

- **Class of Effect:** Prophylactic
- **Associated Trait:** INT
- **Habitats:** Orchard, Rocky Hillside

Odor Properties:

Source	Type	Clarity	Quality	Temper-ament	Agency	Tone
Floral	Flow-er	Murky	Acrid	Bold	Mind	Putrid

- **Preparation:** Skin
- **Poisonweed:** Peel
- **Method of Delivery:** _______________________________
- **Effects:** _______________________________
- **Poisonweed Effects:** _______________________________

79. Quickberry

- **Class of Effect:** Irritant
- **Associated Trait:** AGI
- **Habitats:** Orchard, Rocky Hillside

Odor Properties:

Source	Type	Clarity	Quality	Temper-ament	Agency	Tone
Floral	Fruit	Murky	Pun-gent	Bold	Body	Fragrant

- **Preparation:** Brush (remove dirt)
- **Poisonweed:** Squeeze
- **Method of Delivery:** Eat, or skin contact with juice
- **Effects:** Causes severe trembling; decreases AGI Rating of subject by –4 for 1 hour.
- **Poisonweed Effects:** If skin contact: Juice splashes on user during delivery, causing same trembling in user. If eaten: Toxic. Inflicts 2 HP poison damage per hour until cleared. DV=6 for toxin resistance check.

80. Delicate Flower

- **Class of Effect:** Injurious
- **Associated Trait:** STR
- **Habitats:** Orchard, Rocky Hillside

Odor Properties:

Source	Type	Clarity	Quality	Temper-ament	Agency	Tone
Floral	Flow-er	Murky	Pun-gent	Bold	Body	Putrid

- **Preparation:** Squeeze
- **Poisonweed:** Brush (remove dirt)
- **Method of Delivery:** Eat
- **Effects:** Fills subject with renewed energy; increases STR Rating by +3 for 1 hour. Dissipates if dispersed beyond user, so cannot be applied to multiple subjects.
- **Poisonweed Effects:** Opposite effect, decreasing STR Rating –3.

81. Lotus Leaf

- **Class of Effect:** Soporific
- **Associated Trait:** MYS
- **Habitats:** Grassland, Marsh, Suburb

Odor Properties:

Source	Type	Clarity	Quality	Temper-ament	Agency	Tone
Overt	Leaf	Murky	Minty	Shy	Mind	Fra-grant

- **Preparation:** Lick
- **Poisonweed:** Crumble
- **Method of Delivery:** Eat
- **Effects:** Induces sleep in subjects up to 60 HP for 1 hour
- **Poisonweed Effects:** Toxic. Inflicts 2 HP poison damage per hour until cleared. DV=6 for toxin resistance check.

82. Sunflower Sap

- **Class of Effect:** Herbal
- **Associated Trait:** SML
- **Habitats:** Grassland, Marsh, Suburb

Odor Properties:

Source	Type	Clarity	Quality	Temper-ament	Agency	Tone
Overt	Stem	Murky	Minty	Shy	Mind	Putrid

- **Preparation:** Crumble
- **Poisonweed:** Lick
- **Method of Delivery:** Sprinkle on surface of herb
- **Effects:** Dissolves Poisonweed, ruining it for any other use.
- **Poisonweed Effects:** No effect.

83. Lavender Leaf

- **Class of Effect:** Medicinal
- **Associated Trait:** CON
- **Habitats:** Grassland, Marsh, Suburb

Odor Properties:

Source	Type	Clarity	Quality	Temperament	Agency	Tone
Overt	Leaf	Cloudy	Musky	Shy	Body	Fragrant

- **Preparation:** Chew (wet chew)
- **Poisonweed:** Claw
- **Method of Delivery:** Eat
- **Effects:** Cures damage from blisters and burns, 2d6, stops further damage. At twice normal potency (requires Advanced preparation), cures Alopecia in Nibblers and Chatters.
- **Poisonweed Effects:** Toxic. Inflicts 2 HP poison damage per hour until cleared. DV=6 for toxin resistance check.

84. Unknown Herb

- **Class of Effect:** Defensive
- **Associated Trait:** SPD
- **Habitats:** Grassland, Marsh, Suburb

Odor Properties:

Source	Type	Clarity	Quality	Temperament	Agency	Tone
Overt	Stem	Murky	Musky	Shy	Body	Putrid

- **Preparation:** Claw
- **Poisonweed:** Chew (wet chew)
- **Method of Delivery:** ______________________
- **Effects:** ______________________
- **Poisonweed Effects:** ______________________

85. Unknown Herb

- **Class of Effect:** Hypnotic
- **Associated Trait:** CHA
- **Habitats:** Grassland, Marsh, Suburb

Odor Properties:

Source	Type	Clarity	Quality	Temperament	Agency	Tone
Overt	Leaf	Murky	Acrid	Bold	Mind	Fragrant

- **Preparation:** Peel
- **Poisonweed:** Skin
- **Method of Delivery:** ______________________
- **Effects:** ______________________
- **Poisonweed Effects:** ______________________

86. Rainbow Flower Sap

- **Class of Effect:** Prophylactic
- **Associated Trait:** INT
- **Habitats:** Grassland, Marsh, Suburb

Odor Properties:

Source	Type	Clarity	Quality	Temperament	Agency	Tone
Overt	Stem	Murky	Acrid	Bold	Mind	Putrid

- **Preparation:** Skin
- **Poisonweed:** Peel
- **Method of Delivery:** Lick sap as it oozes from stems
- **Effects:** Subject experiences a momentary sharpening of vision, as if zooming closer; increases INT Rating +2 for 1 hour
- **Poisonweed Effects:** Toxic. Inflicts 2 HP poison damage per hour until cleared. DV=6 for toxin resistance check.

87. Heart Leaf

- **Class of Effect:** Irritant
- **Associated Trait:** AGI
- **Habitats:** Grassland, Marsh, Suburb

Odor Properties:

Source	Type	Clarity	Quality	Temperament	Agency	Tone
Overt	Leaf	Murky	Pungent	Bold	Body	Fragrant

- **Preparation:** Brush (remove dirt)
- **Poisonweed:** Squeeze
- **Method of Delivery:** Eat
- **Effects:** Enhances concentration and focus, increases AGI Rating by +3 for 1 hour.
- **Poisonweed Effects:** Toxic. Inflicts 3 HP poison damage per hour until cleared. DV=8 for toxin resistance check.

88. Stinging Nettle

- **Class of Effect:** Injurious
- **Associated Trait:** STR
- **Habitats:** Grassland, Marsh, Suburb

Odor Properties:

Source	Type	Clarity	Quality	Temperament	Agency	Tone
Overt	Stem	Murky	Pungent	Bold	Body	Putrid

- **Preparation:** Squeeze
- **Poisonweed:** Brush (remove dirt)
- **Method of Delivery:** Contact with skin
- **Effects:** Painful contact with nettle hairs inflicts damage, 2d6 HP
- **Poisonweed Effects:** No effect.

89. Unknown Herb

- **Class of Effect:** Soporific
- **Associated Trait:** MYS

- **Habitats:** Farm, Brushland

Odor Properties:

Source	Type	Clarity	Quality	Temperament	Agency	Tone
Covert	Bulb	Murky	Minty	Shy	Mind	Fragrant

- **Preparation:** Lick
- **Poisonweed:** Crumble
- **Method of Delivery:** ___________________________
- **Effects:** ___________________________
- **Poisonweed Effects:** ___________________________

90. Fireroot

- **Class of Effect:** Herbal
- **Associated Trait:** SML
- **Habitats:** Farm, Brushland

Odor Properties:

Source	Type	Clarity	Quality	Temperament	Agency	Tone
Covert	Root	Murky	Minty	Shy	Mind	Putrid

- **Preparation:** Crumble
- **Poisonweed:** Lick
- **Method of Delivery:** Sprinkle on twigs and dried grass, then place in direct sunlight
- **Effects:** Spontaneously ignites, starting a small fire if placed in direct sunlight for 5 minutes.
- **Poisonweed Effects:** Flashes rather than igniting fire, causing temporary blindness in everyone within 1 meter for 10 minutes.

91. Blind Iris

- **Class of Effect:** Medicinal
- **Associated Trait:** CON
- **Habitats:** Farm, Brushland

Odor Properties:

Source	Type	Clarity	Quality	Temperament	Agency	Tone
Covert	Bulb	Murky	Musky	Shy	Body	Fragrant

- **Preparation:** Chew (wet chew)
- **Poisonweed:** Claw
- **Method of Delivery:** Eat
- **Effects:** Cures tularemia (the White Blindness); cures blindness caused by disease or herbs; cures White Blindness.
- **Poisonweed Effects:** Toxic. Inflicts 2 HP poison damage per hour until cleared. DV=6 for toxin resistance check.

92. Mandrake

- **Class of Effect:** Defensive
- **Associated Trait:** SPD
- **Habitats:** Farm, Brushland

Odor Properties:

Source	Type	Clarity	Quality	Temperament	Agency	Tone
Fungal	Root	Murky	Musky	Shy	Body	Putrid

- **Preparation:** Claw
- **Poisonweed:** Chew (wet chew)
- **Method of Delivery:** Eat or rub on body surface
- **Effects:** If rubbed on body: protects subject from injurious herbs. If eaten: causes subject to experience fearful hallucination and lose contact with reality. GM should base hallucination on weakest Base Trait of the subject
- **Poisonweed Effects:** If rubbed: inflicts 1d6 HP damage. If eaten: Toxic. Inflicts 2 HP poison damage per hour until cleared. DV=6 for toxin resistance check.

93. Unknown Herb

- **Class of Effect:** Hypnotic
- **Associated Trait:** CHA
- **Habitats:** Farm, Brushland

Odor Properties:

Source	Type	Clarity	Quality	Temperament	Agency	Tone
Covert	Bulb	Murky	Acrid	Bold	Mind	Fragrant

- **Preparation:** Peel
- **Poisonweed:** Skin
- **Method of Delivery:** ___________________________
- **Effects:** ___________________________
- **Poisonweed Effects:** ___________________________

94. Goldenrod Root

- **Class of Effect:** Prophylactic
- **Associated Trait:** INT
- **Habitats:** Farm, Brushland

Odor Properties:

Source	Type	Clarity	Quality	Temperament	Agency	Tone
Covert	Root	Murky	Acrid	Bold	Mind	Putrid

- **Preparation:** Skin
- **Poisonweed:** Peel
- **Method of Delivery:** Eat
- **Effects:** Halts the continuing effects of poison, but does not cure existing damage.

- **Poisonweed Effects:** Toxic. Inflicts 2 HP poison damage per hour until cleared. DV=6 for toxin resistance check.

95. Unknown Herb

- **Class of Effect:** Irritant
- **Associated Trait:** AGI
- **Habitats:** Farm, Brushland

Odor Properties:

Source	Type	Clarity	Quality	Temperament	Agency	Tone
Covert	Bulb	Murky	Pungent	Bold	Body	Fragrant

- **Preparation:** Brush (remove dirt)
- **Poisonweed:** Squeeze
- **Method of Delivery:** _______________
- **Effects:** _______________
- **Poisonweed Effects:** _______________

96. Sourroot

- **Class of Effect:** Injurious
- **Associated Trait:** STR
- **Habitats:** Farm, Brushland

Odor Properties:

Source	Type	Clarity	Quality	Temperament	Agency	Tone
Covert	Root	Murky	Pungent	Bold	Body	Putrid

- **Preparation:** Squeeze
- **Poisonweed:** Brush (remove dirt)
- **Method of Delivery:** Eat
- **Effects:** Inflicts damage, 3d6 HP
- **Poisonweed Effects:** Toxic. Inflicts 2 HP poison damage per hour until cleared. DV=6 for toxin resistance check.

Dense Herbs

Dense herbs appeal only to the most discerning Herbalists, bringing a cacophony of primitive refinement to the olfactory palate.

97. Wicked Mushroom

- **Class of Effect:** Soporific
- **Associated Trait:** MYS
- **Habitats:** Oak Woodland, Pine Forest, Mountain Stream

Odor Properties:

Source	Type	Clarity	Quality	Temperament	Agency	Tone
Fungal	Cap	Dense	Minty	Shy	Mind	Fragrant

- **Preparation:** Lick
- **Poisonweed:** Crumble
- **Method of Delivery:** Eat
- **Effects:** Subject experiences a feeling of oneness; increases MYS Rating by +2 for 1 hour.
- **Poisonweed Effects:** Toxic. Inflicts 2 HP poison damage per hour until cleared. DV=6 for toxin resistance check.

98. Unknown Herb

- **Class of Effect:** Herbal
- **Associated Trait:** SML
- **Habitats:** Oak Woodland, Pine Forest, Mountain Stream

Odor Properties:

Source	Type	Clarity	Quality	Temperament	Agency	Tone
Fungal	Ball	Dense	Minty	Shy	Mind	Putrid

- **Preparation:** Crumble
- **Poisonweed:** Lick
- **Method of Delivery:** _______________
- **Effects:** _______________
- **Poisonweed Effects:** _______________

99. Unknown Herb

- **Class of Effect:** Medicinal
- **Associated Trait:** CON
- **Habitats:** Oak Woodland, Pine Forest, Mountain Stream

Odor Properties:

Source	Type	Clarity	Quality	Temperament	Agency	Tone
Fungal	Cap	Dense	Musky	Shy	Body	Fragrant

- **Preparation:** Chew (wet chew)
- **Poisonweed:** Claw
- **Method of Delivery:** _______________
- **Effects:** _______________
- **Poisonweed Effects:** _______________

100. Unknown Herb

- **Class of Effect:** Defensive
- **Associated Trait:** SPD
- **Habitats:** Oak Woodland, Pine Forest, Mountain Stream

Odor Properties:

Source	Type	Clarity	Quality	Temperament	Agency	Tone
Fungal	Ball	Dense	Musky	Shy	Body	Putrid

- **Preparation:** Claw
- **Poisonweed:** Chew (wet chew)

- **Method of Delivery:** _______________________________
- **Effects:** _______________________________
- **Poisonweed Effects:** _______________________________

101. Snowcap

- **Class of Effect:** Hypnotic
- **Associated Trait:** CHA
- **Habitats:** Oak Woodland, Pine Forest, Mountain Stream

Odor Properties:

Source	Type	Clarity	Quality	Temperament	Agency	Tone
Fungal	Cap	Dense	Acrid	Bold	Mind	Fragrant

- **Preparation:** Peel
- **Poisonweed:** Skin
- **Method of Delivery:** Eat
- **Effects:** Fills subject with feeling of intense confidence; increases CHA Rating by +4 for 1 hour
- **Poisonweed Effects:** Toxic. Inflicts 2 HP poison damage per hour until cleared. DV=6 for toxin resistance check.

102. Foul Ball

- **Class of Effect:** Prophylactic
- **Associated Trait:** INT
- **Habitats:** Oak Woodland, Pine Forest, Mountain Stream

Odor Properties:

Source	Type	Clarity	Quality	Temperament	Agency	Tone
Fungal	Ball	Dense	Acrid	Bold	Mind	Putrid

- **Preparation:** Skin
- **Poisonweed:** Peel
- **Method of Delivery:** Smash on ground or subject, covering with spores
- **Effects:** The spores are very foul smelling, especially to most predatory mammals. Chasers, Stalkers, and Brutes are repelled from the area of a ground smash, or from the subject, for a distance of 50 meters for one hour. However, some carrion eaters (Coyote, Red Wolf, Wolverine, Grizzly Bear) are attracted by the smell from up to 500 meters away, and Turkey Vultures from several kilometers away.
- **Poisonweed Effects:** Attracts all ground predators up to 500 meters away.

103. Dung Fung

- **Class of Effect:** Irritant
- **Associated Trait:** AGI
- **Habitats:** Oak Woodland, Pine Forest, Mountain Stream

Odor Properties:

Source	Type	Clarity	Quality	Temperament	Agency	Tone
Fungal	Cap	Dense	Pungent	Bold	Body	Fragrant

- **Preparation:** Brush (remove dirt)
- **Poisonweed:** Squeeze
- **Method of Delivery:** Contact of head cap with skin
- **Effects:** Giant Pilobus head, with slender stalk that is almost transparent and a round head with a dark cap. Disturbance causes the dark cap to shoot up to 2 meters distant. Each cap sticks on contact, causing severe blisters and inflicting damage of 2 HP/minute for up to 10 minutes.
- **Poisonweed Effects:** Backfires and rebounds on user, to same effect.

104. Giant Puffball

- **Class of Effect:** Injurious
- **Associated Trait:** STR
- **Habitats:** Oak Woodland, Pine Forest, Mountain Stream

Odor Properties:

Source	Type	Clarity	Quality	Temperament	Agency	Tone
Fungal	Ball	Dense	Pungent	Bold	Body	Putrid

- **Preparation:** Squeeze
- **Poisonweed:** Brush (remove dirt)
- **Method of Delivery:** Breathe spores
- **Effects:** Explodes into a cloud of dust when smashed, which spreads in every direction for 2-meter radius. Exposure to the dust inflicts damage, 3d6 HP for each Pursuit/Combat round of exposure. The dust cloud lingers in the affected space for 1 minute.
- **Poisonweed Effects:** Fails to explode when smashed, lying dormant for 30 seconds (5 combat rounds), then exploding as normal.

105. Golden Rain (a.k.a. Golden Chain)

- **Class of Effect:** Soporific
- **Associated Trait:** MYS
- **Habitats:** Orchard, Rocky Hillside

Odor Properties:

Source	Type	Clarity	Quality	Temperament	Agency	Tone
Floral	Fruit	Dense	Minty	Shy	Mind	Fragrant

- **Preparation:** Lick
- **Poisonweed:** Crumble
- **Method of Delivery:** Breathe crushed seeds.
- **Effects:** Seeds turn to powder after preparation. Crushed

seed powder disperses in the air like pollen; induces sleep in subjects up to 60 HP for 1 hour. Can be used against multiple opponents; aerial dispersal in 2-meter cone.

- **Poisonweed Effects:** Backfires and rebounds on user, to same effect.

106. Carcass Flower

- **Class of Effect:** Herbal
- **Associated Trait:** SML
- **Habitats:** Orchard, Rocky Hillside

Odor Properties:

Source	Type	Clarity	Quality	Temperament	Agency	Tone
Floral	Flower	Dense	Minty	Shy	Mind	Putrid

- **Preparation:** Crumble
- **Poisonweed:** Lick
- **Method of Delivery:** Sprinkle on surface of herb
- **Effects:** Causes Poisonweed to revert into a Green herb of the same Source, which can then be used in normal herb remodelling. At twice normal potency (requires Advanced preparation), cures Leprosy in Armadillos and Rabies in all animals.
- **Poisonweed Effects:** No effect at either potency.

107. Unknown Herb

- **Class of Effect:** Medicinal
- **Associated Trait:** CON
- **Habitats:** Orchard, Rocky Hillside

Odor Properties:

Source	Type	Clarity	Quality	Temperament	Agency	Tone
Floral	Fruit	Dense	Musky	Shy	Body	Fragrant

- **Preparation:** Chew (wet chew)
- **Poisonweed:** Claw
- **Method of Delivery:** _______________
- **Effects:** _______________
- **Poisonweed Effects:** _______________

108. Hero Flower

- **Class of Effect:** Defensive
- **Associated Trait:** SPD
- **Habitats:** Orchard, Rocky Hillside

Odor Properties:

Source	Type	Clarity	Quality	Temperament	Agency	Tone
Floral	Flower	Dense	Musky	Shy	Body	Putrid

- **Preparation:** Claw

- **Poisonweed:** Chew (wet chew)
- **Method of Delivery:** Eat whole flower
- **Effects:** Subject feels rush of energy and enhanced concentration; increases AGI and SPD Ratings by +4 for 1 hour.
- **Poisonweed Effects:** Toxic. Inflicts 2 HP poison damage per hour until cleared. DV=6 for toxin resistance check.

109. Bitterberry

- **Class of Effect:** Hypnotic
- **Associated Trait:** CHA
- **Habitats:** Orchard, Rocky Hillside

Odor Properties:

Source	Type	Clarity	Quality	Temperament	Agency	Tone
Floral	Fruit	Dense	Acrid	Bold	Mind	Fragrant

- **Preparation:** Peel
- **Poisonweed:** Skin
- **Method of Delivery:** Eat, or skin contact with juice
- **Effects:** Causes confusion; subject acts upon first suggestion by herb user (83% likelihood; succeeds on d6 die roll of 2–6); herb user must speak the language of the subject.
- **Poisonweed Effects:** If skin contact: Juice splashes on user during delivery, causing user to act on first random suggestion by anyone on a d6 die roll of 1–5. If eaten: Toxic. Inflicts 2 HP poison damage per hour until cleared. DV=6 for toxin resistance check.

110. Pestflower

- **Class of Effect:** Prophylactic
- **Associated Trait:** INT
- **Habitats:** Orchard, Rocky Hillside

Odor Properties:

Source	Type	Clarity	Quality	Temperament	Agency	Tone
Floral	Flower	Dense	Acrid	Bold	Mind	Putrid

- **Preparation:** Skin
- **Poisonweed:** Peel
- **Method of Delivery:** Rub on body surface
- **Effects:** Repels all pests for 1 day and eradicates existing infestations of all external pests. At twice normal potency (requires Advanced preparation), also eliminates infestations by internal parasites, including brainworms.
- **Poisonweed Effects:** Attracts all pests except leeches in all habitats, and leeches in marsh, all day. No effect on internal parasites.

111. Unknown Herb

- **Class of Effect:** Irritant
- **Associated Trait:** AGI

- **Habitats:** Orchard, Rocky Hillside

Odor Properties:

Source	Type	Clarity	Quality	Temperament	Agency	Tone
Floral	Fruit	Dense	Pungent	Bold	Body	Fragrant

- **Preparation:** Brush (remove dirt)
- **Poisonweed:** Squeeze
- **Method of Delivery:** _______________________________
- **Effects:** _______________________________
- **Poisonweed Effects:** _______________________________

112. Unknown Herb

- **Class of Effect:** Injurious
- **Associated Trait:** STR
- **Habitats:** Orchard, Rocky Hillside

Odor Properties:

Source	Type	Clarity	Quality	Temperament	Agency	Tone
Floral	Flower	Dense	Pungent	Bold	Body	Putrid

- **Preparation:** Squeeze
- **Poisonweed:** Brush (remove dirt)
- **Method of Delivery:** _______________________________
- **Effects:** _______________________________
- **Poisonweed Effects:** _______________________________

113. Unknown Herb

- **Class of Effect:** Soporific
- **Associated Trait:** MYS
- **Habitats:** Grassland, Marsh, Suburb

Odor Properties:

Source	Type	Clarity	Quality	Temperament	Agency	Tone
Overt	Leaf	Dense	Minty	Shy	Mind	Fragrant

- **Preparation:** Lick
- **Poisonweed:** Crumble
- **Method of Delivery:** _______________________________
- **Effects:** _______________________________
- **Poisonweed Effects:** _______________________________

114. Truebark Dust

- **Class of Effect:** Herbal
- **Associated Trait:** SML
- **Habitats:** Grassland, Marsh, Suburb

Odor Properties:

Source	Type	Clarity	Quality	Temperament	Agency	Tone
Overt	Stem	Dense	Minty	Shy	Mind	Putrid

- **Preparation:** Crumble
- **Poisonweed:** Lick
- **Method of Delivery:** Sniff bark dust
- **Effects:** Sense of smell seems to brighten; increases SML Rating by +2 for 1 hour.
- **Poisonweed Effects:** Opposite effect, decreasing SML Rating −2.

115. Rabbit Weed

- **Class of Effect:** Medicinal
- **Associated Trait:** CON
- **Habitats:** Grassland, Marsh, Suburb

Odor Properties:

Source	Type	Clarity	Quality	Temperament	Agency	Tone
Overt	Leaf	Dense	Musky	Shy	Body	Fragrant

- **Preparation:** Chew (wet chew)
- **Poisonweed:** Claw
- **Method of Delivery:** Eat
- **Effects:** Cures any disease, but does not cure injuries caused by a disease
- **Poisonweed Effects:** Toxic. Inflicts 2 HP poison damage per hour until cleared. DV=6 for toxin resistance check.

116. Unknown Herb

- **Class of Effect:** Defensive
- **Associated Trait:** SPD
- **Habitats:** Grassland, Marsh, Suburb

Odor Properties:

Source	Type	Clarity	Quality	Temperament	Agency	Tone
Overt	Stem	Dense	Musky	Shy	Body	Putrid

- **Preparation:** Claw
- **Poisonweed:** Chew (wet chew)
- **Method of Delivery:** _______________________________
- **Effects:** _______________________________
- **Poisonweed Effects:** _______________________________

117. Unknown Herb

- **Class of Effect:** Hypnotic
- **Associated Trait:** CHA
- **Habitats:** Grassland, Marsh, Suburb

Odor Properties:

Source	Type	Clarity	Quality	Temperament	Agency	Tone
Overt	Leaf	Dense	Acrid	Bold	Mind	Fragrant

- **Preparation:** Peel
- **Poisonweed:** Skin
- **Method of Delivery:** _______________________________
- **Effects:** _______________________________
- **Poisonweed Effects:** _______________________________

118. Unknown Herb

- **Class of Effect:** Prophylactic
- **Associated Trait:** INT
- **Habitats:** Grassland, Marsh, Suburb

Odor Properties:

Source	Type	Clarity	Quality	Temperament	Agency	Tone
Overt	Stem	Dense	Acrid	Bold	Mind	Putrid

- **Preparation:** Skin
- **Poisonweed:** Peel
- **Method of Delivery:** _______________________________
- **Effects:** _______________________________
- **Poisonweed Effects:** _______________________________

119. Sugarleaf

- **Class of Effect:** Irritant
- **Associated Trait:** AGI
- **Habitats:** Grassland, Marsh, Suburb

Odor Properties:

Source	Type	Clarity	Quality	Temperament	Agency	Tone
Overt	Leaf	Dense	Pungent	Bold	Body	Fragrant

- **Preparation:** Brush (remove dirt)
- **Poisonweed:** Squeeze
- **Method of Delivery:** Eat
- **Effects:** Causes any movement by the subject to inflict intense pain, resulting in 1 HP damage for minor movement and 1d6 HP damage for any gross movement (such as changes of position or vigorous action). The effect is to produce voluntary paralysis for 10 minutes.
- **Poisonweed Effects:** Toxic. Inflicts 2 HP poison damage per hour until cleared. DV=6 for toxin resistance check.

120. Fire Nettle

- **Class of Effect:** Injurious
- **Associated Trait:** STR
- **Habitats:** Grassland, Marsh, Suburb

Odor Properties:

Source	Type	Clarity	Quality	Temperament	Agency	Tone
Overt	Stem	Dense	Pungent	Bold	Body	Putrid

- **Preparation:** Squeeze
- **Poisonweed:** Brush (remove dirt)
- **Method of Delivery:** Contact with skin
- **Effects:** Painful contact with nettle hairs inflicts damage, 3d6 HP
- **Poisonweed Effects:** No effect.

121. Death Lily

- **Class of Effect:** Soporific
- **Associated Trait:** MYS
- **Habitats:** Farm, Brushland

Odor Properties:

Source	Type	Clarity	Quality	Temperament	Agency	Tone
Covert	Bulb	Dense	Minty	Shy	Mind	Fragrant

- **Preparation:** Lick
- **Poisonweed:** Crumble
- **Method of Delivery:** Eat
- **Effects:** Induces sleep in any subject; causes subject to appear dead for 1 hour.
- **Poisonweed Effects:** Toxic. Inflicts 2 HP poison damage per hour until cleared. DV=6 for toxin resistance check.

122. Orchid Root

- **Class of Effect:** Herbal
- **Associated Trait:** SML
- **Habitats:** Farm, Brushland

Odor Properties:

Source	Type	Clarity	Quality	Temperament	Agency	Tone
Covert	Root	Dense	Minty	Shy	Mind	Putrid

- **Preparation:** Crumble
- **Poisonweed:** Lick
- **Method of Delivery:** Eat
- **Effects:** Protects from all herbs, including medicinal and curative herbs, and halts the ongoing effects of any herbs (such as prophylactics or herbs that boost trait ratings)
- **Poisonweed Effects:** Toxic. Inflicts 2 HP poison damage per hour until cleared. DV=6 for toxin resistance check.

123. Lifemelt Garlic

- **Class of Effect:** Medicinal
- **Associated Trait:** CON
- **Habitats:** Farm, Brushland

Odor Properties:

Source	Type	Clarity	Quality	Temperament	Agency	Tone
Covert	Bulb	Dense	Musky	Shy	Body	Fragrant

- **Preparation:** Chew (wet chew)
- **Poisonweed:** Claw
- **Method of Delivery:** Eat
- **Effects:** Drives out brainworms, but does not cure damage caused by brainworms
- **Poisonweed Effects:** Toxic. Inflicts 2 HP poison damage per hour until cleared. DV=6 for toxin resistance check.

124. Unknown Herb

- **Class of Effect:** Defensive
- **Associated Trait:** SPD
- **Habitats:** Farm, Brushland

Odor Properties:

Source	Type	Clarity	Quality	Temperament	Agency	Tone
Covert	Root	Dense	Musky	Shy	Body	Putrid

- **Preparation:** Claw
- **Poisonweed:** Chew (wet chew)
- **Method of Delivery:** _______________________
- **Effects:** _______________________
- **Poisonweed Effects:** _______________________

125. Unknown Herb

- **Class of Effect:** Hypnotic
- **Associated Trait:** CHA
- **Habitats:** Farm, Brushland

Odor Properties:

Source	Type	Clarity	Quality	Temperament	Agency	Tone
Covert	Bulb	Dense	Acrid	Bold	Mind	Fragrant

- **Preparation:** Peel
- **Poisonweed:** Skin
- **Method of Delivery:** _______________________
- **Effects:** _______________________
- **Poisonweed Effects:** _______________________

126. Arrowroot

- **Class of Effect:** Prophylactic
- **Associated Trait:** INT
- **Habitats:** Farm, Brushland

Odor Properties:

Source	Type	Clarity	Quality	Temperament	Agency	Tone
Covert	Root	Dense	Acrid	Bold	Mind	Putrid

- **Preparation:** Skin
- **Poisonweed:** Peel
- **Method of Delivery:** Eat
- **Effects.** Protects from all poisons, including toxic bites or stings from Crawlies or Snakes.
- **Poisonweed Effects.** Toxic. Inflicts 2 HP poison damage per hour until cleared. DV=6 for toxin resistance check.

127. Unknown Herb

- **Class of Effect:** Irritant
- **Associated Trait:** AGI
- **Habitats:** Farm, Brushland

Odor Properties:

Source	Type	Clarity	Quality	Temperament	Agency	Tone
Covert	Bulb	Dense	Pungent	Bold	Body	Fragrant

- **Preparation:** Brush (remove dirt)
- **Poisonweed:** Squeeze
- **Method of Delivery:** _______________________
- **Effects:** _______________________
- **Poisonweed Effects:** _______________________

128. Bitterroot

- **Class of Effect:** Injurious
- **Associated Trait:** STR
- **Habitats:** Farm, Brushland

Odor Properties:

Source	Type	Clarity	Quality	Temperament	Agency	Tone
Covert	Root	Dense	Pungent	Bold	Body	Putrid

- **Preparation:** Squeeze
- **Poisonweed:** Brush (remove dirt)
- **Method of Delivery:** Eat
- **Effects:** Inflicts damage, 4d6
- **Poisonweed Effects:** Toxic. Inflicts 2 HP poison damage per hour until cleared. DV=6 for toxin resistance check.

Appendix B: The Bestiary

The listings below provide detailed information about the traits, characteristics, special abilities, and habits of various animals that rabbits might encounter. Additional animals may be described in particular adventures.

Real animals vary in size. An adult raccoon, for instance, may weigh as little as 5 kilograms and as much as 25 kilograms, although most fall in the 5–10 kilograms range. To simplify, we provide a narrow range of adult body weight in the description of each animal. Each animal's CON Rating, which determines HP, also varies with body size. The following qualitative descriptors correspond to various ranges in body mass, CON, and HP. Ranges should be viewed as approximate.

Size	Mass (kilograms)	CON	HP
Tiny	< 1	< 4	< 20
Small	1-10	4-7	20-35
Medium	11-25	7-10	35-50
Large	26-50	10-15	50-75
Huge	> 50	> 15	> 75

Like PCs and NPCs, predators and other animals have the full range of eight traits. Levels in these traits increase as the animals grow older and more experienced. The Trait Ratings listed in each entry should be considered as Sub-Adults. Ratings should be adjusted downward 1 point for Juveniles, and upward 1 point for each step in age for older animals. Hit Points similarly should be adjusted downward 5 points for Juveniles, and upward 5 points for each step in age for older animals (double the HP adjustment if the base HP > 50). Obviously, this makes Apex Adult predators very serious threats in the game.

Abbreviations:

DV: Difficulty Value for player characters to spot that predator (or other animal)

iPD: Initial Pursuit Distance = hexes on pursuit board

Move: movement allowance = hexes on large-scale map (above ground) per 10 min; also the allowance for hexes per pursuit turn

Predators

Predators represent the major category of enemies that rabbits and other player characters must face. Different species of predators pose different risks, both because they possess a wide range of natural weapons and hunting tactics, and because some are larger, stronger, and faster than others. In B&B, five categories of predators are distinguished based on hunting styles: Chasers, Stalkers, Brutes, Cryptics, and Raptors. Although humans also occasionally hunt rabbits and can pose other kinds of threats to animals, they are treated as a completely different type of enemy.

Individual predators also can vary within each species. Although B&B generally does not draw gender distinctions, age differences can result in predators with very different abilities. Five age classes are recognized: Juveniles, Sub-Adults, Young Adults, Mature Adults, and Apex Adults. See Predator Encounters on how to determine the age of a predator that appears in a Wandering Encounter. However, the GM also should feel free to adjust the age class based on the general level and number of player characters in the party and their experience, or "batting record," during past encounters with predators.

Animals have been categorized on the basis of their basic behavior as a predator. Some species have been lumped with others merely for convenience. Ravens, for instance, are not true raptors, either taxonomically or functionally. But they hunt while flying, so we have grouped ravens with hawks, eagles, and owls.

Unless otherwise stated, Predators are initially very aggressive, but will become more defensive after they incur injuries at least equal to their CON Rating. If they lose half their HP, predators will break off the attack and attempt to flee from the battle board.

Chasers

Dogs and their relatives hunt by moving over terrain at a steady pace, running down their prey. In Combat, Chasers only Bite. Most Chasers speak the language of Dogs; Pine Martens speak the language of Weasels, and Ringtails speak the language of Ramblers.

Dogs, General Characteristics

Description: Dogs are chasers that have been domesticated and bred to enhance certain attributes. Along with Foxes, Coyotes, and Wolves, Dogs are members of the family Canidae. All the Canids are swift, long-legged runners; Coyotes and Wolves are especially well adapted for running down large prey, while Foxes (and Coyotes) are more adept at surprising smaller game. They have good vision, acute hearing, and an excellent sense of smell.

Habits: Dogs are quick to bark if they see rabbits, and give chase if they spot rabbits closer than 100 meters (2 large hexes). In combat, they may only Bite, but on an attack roll of 6, they also Shake for double damage.

Dog, Small (Terrier)

Description: Small, energetic dog (5–10 kilograms) such as a Jack Russell, Fox, or Rat Terrier. Bred mostly as a companion animal, they also have a reputation as effective vermin hunters.

Habits: Prone to barking, a terrier might chase a solitary bunny, but is more likely to run circles and bark at a group to sound the Intruder Alert. Allow Terriers to change facing by one hexside in each hex of movement at no additional cost. On a farm, this is likely to attract the attention of the Farmer or the Farmer's Wife (who may be considered either a Farmer or a Gardener in an encounter). In a Suburb, a barking terrier may attract the attention of 1–6 other dogs of various breeds.

Special Ability: Intruder Alert; Shake

Trait Statistics:	STR	SPD	INT	AGI	CON	MYS	SML	CHA
Rating:	2	3	4	2	5	2	4	4

Pursuit stats:	DV (to spot)	iPD	Move	Hit Points
	4	6	2	25

Dog, Medium (Border Collie)

Description: Medium-sized dog (15–20 kilograms), black-and-white with moderate fur. Bred as working dogs, and specifically for herding livestock such as sheep, Border Collies are regarded as one of the most intelligent dog breeds.

Habits: Border Collies were bred as herders. They are quick to respond to a group of animals, including small children, by nipping at their heels and attempting to drive them together into a compact group. If a Border Collie faces a group of 3 or more rabbits, it attempts to circle, driving stragglers back to a group in one hex. Allow Border Collies to change facing by one hexside in each hex of movement at no additional cost. The rabbits will not be harmed if they remain in one hex, but will be chased and attacked if they split up or flee faster than 1 hex per turn.

Special Ability: Intruder Alert; Shake

Trait Statistics:	STR	SPD	INT	AGI	CON	MYS	SML	CHA
Rating:	3	2	6	2	9	2	5	5

Pursuit stats:	DV (to spot)	iPD	Move	Hit Points
	4	10	4	45

Dog, Large (Retriever)

Description: Moderately large dogs (25–35 kilograms), including Labrador (Labs) and Golden Retrievers. Labs may be black, brown, or pale yellow, and Goldens are usually yellow or red.

Habits: Retrievers are even-tempered, sociable dogs. They typically are not aggressive unless protective of puppies or small human children. They are likely to investigate rabbits, approaching closely and sniffing, but are unlikely to attack or give chase UNLESS the rabbits run.

Special Ability: Shake

Trait Statistics:	STR	SPD	INT	AGI	CON	MYS	SML	CHA
Rating:	4	4	5	3	10	3	6	6

Pursuit stats:	DV (to spot)	iPD	Move	Hit Points
	4	10	6	50

Dog, Large (Doberman)

Description: A large dog (35–45 kilograms), muscular, with short black fur and brown points, and a very trim physique. The tails are usually docked, and the ears pointed. Bred as guard dogs, and often used as police or military dogs.

Habits: Dobermans are considered one of the more intelligent breeds and have a reputation for being intensely loyal, protective, and potentially aggressive. Dobermans should always be considered very dangerous, but usually attack only if rabbits encroach on a defended space.

Special Ability: Shake

Trait Statistics:	STR	SPD	INT	AGI	CON	MYS	SML	CHA
Rating:	4	5	5	4	15	3	5	4

Pursuit stats:	DV (to spot)	iPD	Move	Hit Points
	4	12	7	75

Dog, Huge (Rottweiler)

Description: A very large dog (50–60 kilograms) with short black fur and brown points. Unlike Dobermans, the tail and ears of Rottweilers are usually not altered. Originally bred as a working dog for pulling carts and herding, they also are used as search-and-rescue dogs and guard dogs.

Habits: Like Dobermans, Rottweilers have a reputation for extreme loyalty, protectiveness, and a high potential for aggression. They are fearless in most situations. They are exceptionally strong and surprisingly fast, and are likely to pursue rabbits if spotted.

Special Ability: Shake

Trait Statistics:	STR	SPD	INT	AGI	CON	MYS	SML	CHA
Rating:	5	4	4	4	18	3	5	4

Pursuit stats:	DV (to spot)	iPD	Move	Hit Points
	4	10	5	90

Red Fox

Description: A medium-sized Canid (10–15 kilograms), about the size of a spaniel. The coat may be red or black, but with black points, socks, and tail tip. Foxes have more pointed faces and bushier tails than other Canids.

Habits: Foxes are considered Chasers in the game, so they are limited to Biting in combat, with the ability to Shake after a successful Bite. However, they are more prone to surprising their prey than dogs or wolves, and attempt to approach with stealth until spotted, although lacking the advantage of true Stalking. Foxes are adept at hearing small animals such as mice under leaf litter or snow. They leap almost vertically into the air, then Pounce on prey with all four paws. During Pursuit, a Pounce allows the fox to advance one more hex and initiate combat. In Combat, a Pounce is a leaping attack that, if successful, can stun the Target for one combat round.

Special Ability: Pounce; Shake

Trait Statistics:	STR	SPD	INT	AGI	CON	MYS	SML	CHA
Rating:	2	4	5	4	8	3	6	6

Pursuit stats:	DV (to spot)	iPD		Move	Hit Points
	6	10		6	40

Gray Fox

Description: A small Canid (4–8 kilograms) with a slighter build and shorter than its red cousin. Gray Foxes are about the size of a terrier. They typically have a gray back, flecked with black and white, tawny fur on the neck and legs, and a black-striped tail.

Habits: Unlike all other dog relatives in the game, Gray Foxes are surprisingly adept at climbing trees (although with none of the agility of a Marten or Ringtail). Like Red Foxes, they are adept at hearing small animals such as mice under leaf litter or snow. They leap almost vertically into the air, then Pounce on prey with all four paws. During Pursuit, a Pounce allows the fox to advance one more hex and initiate combat. In Combat, a Pounce is a leaping attack that, if successful, can stun the Target for one combat round.

Special Ability: Pounce; Shake

Trait Statistics:	STR	SPD	INT	AGI	CON	MYS	SML	CHA
Rating:	2	4	4	3	6	3	7	5

Pursuit stats:	DV (to spot)	iPD		Move	Hit Points
6	10	6		30	

Coyote

Description: A medium-sized Canid (10–20 kilograms) about the size of a Border Collie. The most wide-ranging predator in North America, Coyotes are now found in all 50 states in the U.S. The fur may range from pale to dark, but usually is light gray mixed with brown or red. They are more muscular and longer legged than foxes, but not so robust as wolves.

Habits: Coyotes are very fleet pursuers, faster than any of the other ground predators. Like foxes, they also are adept at hearing small animals such as mice under leaf litter or snow. They leap almost vertically into the air, then Pounce on prey with all four paws. During Pursuit, a Pounce allows the fox to advance one more hex and initiate combat. In Combat, a Pounce is a leaping attack that, if successful, can stun the Target for one combat round.

Special Ability: Pounce; Shake

Trait Statistics:	STR	SPD	INT	AGI	CON	MYS	SML	CHA
Rating:	3	3	5	5	12	3	7	7

Pursuit stats:	DV (to spot)	iPD		Move	Hit Points
	4	14		9	60

Red Wolf

Description: A large, secretive Canid intermediate in form, size, and behavior between coyotes and gray wolves (25–35 kilograms). Originally native to the southeastern forests and marshes, it now is largely extirpated in the wild. Red wolves form monogamous pair bonds and are likely to hunt together with a partner.

Habits: Red wolves are likely to be encountered as a pair of adults, but may include juveniles. They attack and relentlessly pursue rabbits if spotted. If possible, they employ Teamwork in the hunt.

Special Ability: Teamwork; Shake

Trait Statistics:	STR	SPD	INT	AGI	CON	MYS	SML	CHA
Rating:	4	4	4	4	14	4	7	5

Pursuit stats:	DV (to spot)	iPD		Move	Hit Points
	4	12		8	70

Deer Wolf (Eastern Gray)

Description: A large Canid intermediate in size between a Coyote and Gray Wolf (25–30 kilograms). The Deer Wolf once was the most common wolf in eastern North America, but its range has been drastically reduced in the past century. Its appearance is similar to a Gray Wolf, but is smaller and more gracile, striking a balance between a typical wolf and coyote body form. Its actual taxonomy is still in dispute, sometimes considered a subspecies of gray wolf, or a hybrid between coyotes and gray wolves, or a separate species. In B&B, we consider Deer Wolves as a separate species with habits very similar to Red Wolves.

Habits: Deer wolves are likely to be encountered in small packs of 2–6 adults. If encountered, one or two peel off from the pack to pursue rabbits, but the entire pack is unlikely to pursue unless the party of rabbits is large or otherwise unusual (perhaps with large non-rabbit characters). If possible, they employ Teamwork in the hunt.

Special Ability: Teamwork; Shake

Trait Statistics:	STR	SPD	INT	AGI	CON	MYS	SML	CHA
Rating:	5	4	4	5	14	3	7	6

Pursuit stats:	DV (to spot)	iPD	Move	Hit Points
	4	12	8	70

Gray Wolf

Description: The largest wild Canid in the game (40–50 kilograms), although a bit smaller than a Rottweiler dog. The Gray Wolf, sometimes known as a Timber Wolf, is broader in the chest and more muscular than any of its lesser cousins, but still a long-legged and very fast pursuer. Wolves may be all-white or all-black, but usually have a coat of dark gray.

Habits: Although mated pairs may separate from a pack for part of the year, Gray Wolves typically are very social and found in large, multi-adult packs. Roll 1d6 + 2 to determine the number of adult wolves in a pack, with the two oldest (a male and female) being either Mature or Apex in age. Like Deer Wolves, they are quick to chase rabbits, but typically only one or two peel off from the pack to pursue rabbits, unless the party of rabbits is very large or unusual. They almost always employ Teamwork in a hunt.

Special Ability: Teamwork; Shake

Trait Statistics:	STR	SPD	INT	AGI	CON	MYS	SML	CHA
Rating:	6	5	6	6	18	3	6	7

Pursuit stats:	DV (to spot)	iPD	Move	Hit Points
	4	12	8	90

Pine Marten

Description: A small predator (1–2 kilograms) and a relative of weasels and ferrets. Martens have rich brown fur and bushy tails, with coal-black eyes and a face like a puppy. Their paws are equipped with long, semi-retractable claws, more like a cat than a weasel.

Habits: Martens are well adapted for arboreal life, and are as quick and agile when climbing trees as the squirrels they prefer as prey. Chases can become three-dimensional when pursuing a squirrel or chipmunk. They are also surprisingly swift when pursuing on the ground, but lack the special tricks (such as Fascinate!) of the stoats.

Special Ability: Tree Chase

Trait Statistics:	STR	SPD	INT	AGI	CON	MYS	SML	CHA
Rating:	3	3	4	4	7	2	4	2

Pursuit stats:	DV (to spot)	iPD	Move	Hit Points
	6	12	8	35

Ringtail

Description: A small relative of raccoons (1–2 kilograms) about the size of a house cat. Ringtails have a more slender build than raccoons, with a narrow, cat-like face and large eyes, and fox-like ears. The body is typically buff to dark brown, with a long, bushy tail as long as its body marked with black and white rings. The hind feet can be rotated like a squirrel, and the claws are short and semi-retractable, which makes them well suited for climbing trees and loose rocks.

Habits: Ringtails are usually nocturnal hunters, and are as comfortable pursuing prey in trees as on the ground. The long tail contributes to their exceptional balance on tree limbs or narrow ledges. It eats anything it can catch. If attacked, Ringtails spray a foul secretion in defense.

Special Ability: Tree Chase; Foul Spray

Trait Statistics:	STR	SPD	INT	AGI	CON	MYS	SML	CHA
Rating:	2	2	4	5	7	2	5	3

Pursuit stats:	DV (to spot)	iPD	Move	Hit Points
	6	10	5	35

Stalkers

Cats and Weasels hunt by stealth to sneak close, then pounce on their prey. Note special rules for placing Pursuit tokens for Stalkers. In Combat, Cats may Claw or Bite, and may Double Attack with Claw (with the Attack die reduced by two for the second attack). Stoats and Ferrets only Bite. However, note special rules after a successful bite by a Stoat. Small and large cats speak the language of Cats. Weasels, Ferrets and Mongooses speak the language of Weasels.

Cats, General Characteristics

Description: Cats are stalkers that have been domesticated as pets and pest killers. Along with Bobcat, Lynx, and Cougar, Cats are members of the family Felidae. All the Felids are crafty, patient hunters that attempt to approach without being detected as closely as possible before launching a final rush toward prey. Cats are adept mousers, but less adept against larger prey or birds in flight. Bobcats and Lynxes are particularly good at catching a bird as it takes flight. Cougars are well adapted to take down prey as large as an elk or moose, although they are not above catching a rabbit. All the Felids have excellent vision, at night as well as during the day, and acute hearing, but a relatively poor sense of smell among mammals.

Habits: Cats attempt to stalk a rabbit if possible, but will not give chase unless closer than 20 meters. In combat, cats may Claw or Bite, and may Double Attack with Claw. They are quick to give up pursuit.

House Cat (Persian)

Description: Small (5–7 kilograms) domestic cat found only near human habitation. Persians have long, white fur that is not very well suited for camouflage.

Habits: House Cats are pampered and overfed. They hunt for sport, not for food. They are very prone to distraction, and may

give up stalking if they notice movement in a different direction. On any attempt by a House Cat to use any other tactical maneuver during Pursuit, a 1d6 roll of 4 –6 indicates that the cat is distracted and runs off in a random direction. The Shiny effect applies even if the Cat is forced to switch Targets.

Special Ability/Weakness: Shiny

Trait Statistics:	STR	SPD	INT	AGI	CON	MYS	SML	CHA
Rating:	1	1	3	2	5	1	2	2

Pursuit stats:	DV (to spot)	iPD	Move	Hit Points
	6	6	2	25

Alley Cat (Tabby)

Description: Small (5 kilograms) domestic cat often found near human habitation, but which obtains part of its food from catching mice and rats. Tabbies come in a variety of coat colors, but most have some striped, spotted, or mottled combination of grays, browns, and black. All Tabbies have distinctive black markings on the face.

Habits: Alley cats often live dual lives, at times begging or stealing food, especially in towns, or spending part of the day indoor as pets, and at other times prowling the streets and roadsides for prey. They are notoriously territorial in towns, howling and "caterwauling," and often engaging in noisy fights. When injured during combat, Alley Cats may get Hissy.

Special Ability: Hissy

Trait Statistics:	STR	SPD	INT	AGI	CON	MYS	SML	CHA
Rating:	2	1	4	3	5	1	2	2

Pursuit stats:	DV (to spot)	iPD	Move	Hit Points
	6	6	3	25

Meezer Cat (Siamese)

Description: Small (5 kilograms) domestic cat often found near human habitation, with greater intelligence than other breeds. Typical coat color of a Siamese is seal point, with cream-colored fur and dark brown points on the ears, feet and tail.

Habits: Meezers are usually outgoing, curious, and highly vocal, with a loud, deep voice. Like Alley cats, they can be highly territorial, and get Hissy when injured in a fight.

Special Ability: Hissy

Trait Statistics:	STR	SPD	INT	AGI	CON	MYS	SML	CHA
Rating:	2	1	5	2	5	4	2	2

Pursuit stats:	DV (to spot)	iPD	Move	Hit Points
	6	8	3	25

Barn Cat (Black)

Description: Small (5 kilograms) domestic cat with all-black coat, possibly with white feet and/or white markings around the mouth and face, usually found on farms.

Habits: Barn cats have abundant experience catching mice and other small rodents. As proficient Mousers, they receive an AGI bonus of +2 when attacking prey smaller than a rabbit (such as a squirrel or chipmunk).

Special Ability: Mouser

Trait Statistics:	STR	SPD	INT	AGI	CON	MYS	SML	CHA
Rating:	2	2	4	3	5	1	2	1

Pursuit stats:	DV (to spot)	iPD	Move	Hit Points
	6	8	3	25

Polydactyl Cat (Calico)

Description: Small (5 kilograms) domestic cat with extra toes on the front and hind feet, all equipped with claws. Calico refers to the coat color, not the polydactyl feet. Calicos have large patches of black, white, and tawny fur, creating a tortoise-shell pattern. Also known as Tricolor cats, calicos are almost always female.

Habits: The extra toes on a Polydactyl Cat are not a hindrance, and in fact provide more claws for catching small prey. In consequence, Polydactlys are effective Mousers, and receive an AGI bonus of +2 when attacking prey smaller than a rabbit (such as a squirrel or chipmunk).

Special Ability: Mouser

Trait Statistics:	STR	SPD	INT	AGI	CON	MYS	SML	CHA
Rating:	4	1	3	3	5	2	2	2

Pursuit stats:	DV (to spot)	iPD	Move	Hit Points
	6	8	3	25

Farm Cat (Maine Coon)

Description: Maine Coons are one of the largest breeds of domestic cat (8–10 kilograms). They were bred to deal with agricultural pests, and often are favorites as working cats on a farm.

Habits: Like Barn cats, Maine Coons are adept Mousers and have abundant experience catching mice and other small rodents. They receive an AGI bonus of +2 when attacking prey smaller than a rabbit (such as a squirrel or chipmunk).

Special Ability: Mouser

Trait Statistics:	STR	SPD	INT	AGI	CON	MYS	SML	CHA
Rating:	2	1	4	3	5	1	2	4

Pursuit stats:	DV (to spot)	iPD	Move	Hit Points
	6	8	4	35

Feral Cat (Bengal)

Description: Feral cats are domestic breeds that have taken up life in the wild. Bengals are a breed (6 kilograms) that is especially well adapted for life in the wild. A hybrid that resulted from interbreeding between domestic cats and Asian leopard cats, Bengals have a tawny coat with dark rosettes and stripes that look very much like a miniature leopard. They are large for domestic cats, with long legs and needle-like claws.

Habits: Unlike most cats, Bengals are not reluctant to swim in water. They are excellent hunters, with jumping abilities that rival a Lynx.

Special Ability: Pounce

Trait Statistics:	STR	SPD	INT	AGI	CON	MYS	SML	CHA
Rating:	3	2	5	4	6	1	2	3

Pursuit stats:	DV (to spot)	iPD	Move	Hit Points
	8	8	4	30

Bobcat

Description: A wild cat of moderate size (10 kilograms) with spotted coat, tufted ears, and a stubby, black-tipped tail. Bobcats may be found in a wide range of habitats, from marshes to forests to scrubland and desert. Hares and rabbits are among its favored prey, as well as birds as large as a goose or swan.

Habits: Bobcats are most active around dawn and dusk (crepuscular). It is a classic stalker, approaching within 10 meters or less before launching a final attack. Like foxes, it is a master of Pouncing on small prey.

Special Ability: Pounce

Trait Statistics:	STR	SPD	INT	AGI	CON	MYS	SML	CHA
Rating:	3	3	5	5	8	1	2	4

Pursuit stats:	DV (to spot)	iPD	Move	Hit Points
	8	8	4	40

Ocelot

Description: A medium-sized cat (12 kilograms) native to Central and South America, the ocelot occasionally can be found as far north as the southwestern United States. It's fur is marked by a distinctive pattern of black, white, and tawny stripes and blotches running in line with its body axis. Not much bigger than a Bobcat, an Ocelot can quickly be distinguished by its smaller, rounded ears and a long tail.

Habits: Ocelots tend to be nocturnal, wandering widely as they hunt, stalking and pouncing on prey like other smaller cats. Favored prey are small mammals, including rabbits, rodents, opossums, and armadillos.

Special Ability: Pounce

Trait Statistics:	STR	SPD	INT	AGI	CON	MYS	SML	CHA
Rating:	3	5	5	5	9	2	2	4

Pursuit stats:	DV (to spot)	iPD	Move	Hit Points
	8	10	5	45

Lynx

Description: A larger cousin of the bobcat (15 kilograms), the Lynx also has a silvery brown coat, ears with long tufts, and a stubby tail. Lynxes are more common in alpine areas and the far north, where they hunt Snowshoe Hares, Grouse, and Ptarmigan.

Habits: Lynxes tend to be nocturnal, but are more likely to be active during the day in winter. Usually a solitary hunter, they are known to hunt in pairs.

Special Ability: Pounce

Trait Statistics:	STR	SPD	INT	AGI	CON	MYS	SML	CHA
Rating:	4	4	5	6	10	2	2	3

Pursuit stats:	DV (to spot)	iPD	Move	Hit Points
	8	10	6	50

Cougar (Mountain Lion)

Description: Also known as Mountain Lion, Puma, Panther, and Painter, the Cougar is the largest cat in North America (60 kilograms). Cougars are apex predators, capable of taking down prey as large as adult Elk and Moose, but often take smaller prey such as squirrels and rabbits. It also has the widest range of any feline predator, extending from the north tip of Canada to Tierra del Fuego at the southern tip of South America. In recent years, Cougars even have grown more common in suburbs and the fringes of large cities.

Habits: Despite its size and power, the Cougar is an ambush predator like other cats. It is a very adaptable predator: it eats anything it can catch and kill, and it can catch and kill virtually any other mammal in North America, except perhaps a Grizzly Bear. Although large prey may be killed by a suffocating bite to the throat, the typical killing bite is delivered to the neck, severing the 1st and 2nd vertebrae.

Special Ability: Nape Bite (x2)

Trait Statistics:	STR	SPD	INT	AGI	CON	MYS	SML	CHA
Rating:	8	6	6	8	24	2	2	3

Pursuit stats:	DV (to spot)	iPD	Move	Hit Points
	6	14	10	120

Weasels, General Characteristics

Description: Weasels and their relatives are members of the mammalian family Mustelidae. This is a large and varied family that includes stoats and weasels, ferrets, minks, otters, martens and fishers, skunks, badgers, and wolverines. A general feature of Mustelids is their long, lean body form and seemingly short legs. This body shape makes smaller members well suited to pursue prey into crevices and burrows, and predisposes larger species to be excellent diggers. They are remarkably agile, intelligent, and ferocious predators. All the Mustelids have good vision and hearing and an exceptional sense of smell.

Habits: Smaller Mustelids, up to the size of a Polecat, attempt to stalk potential prey. Stoats may use trickery to immobilize rabbits (see Fascinate!). Badgers are patient in laying siege to burrow systems, digging their prey out of underground refuges. Wolverines may sit and wait in hiding and ambush prey. In combat, all Weasel relatives Bite; Badger and Wolverine also have very powerful Claw attacks. Unlike cats, the claws are not retractable. Most Mustelids also prefer to kill prey with a killing bite delivered to the back of the skull. Except for Martens, they are quick to give up pursuit.

Stoat (Short-tailed Weasel)

Description: A small weasel (0.25 kilogram) with a varied coat that is typically reddish-brown in summer and snow white in winter, with a cream-colored throat and belly. The neck is long, contributing to the overall elongated appearance of the whole body.

Habits: The stoat is unusual in hunting prey that often is larger than itself. Although mice and other small rodents are favored, Stoats are well-known predators of rabbits and chickens. To hunt rabbits, it has been documented to employ a highly unorthodox tactic. Rather than relying on stealth to draw close, it becomes hyperactive, displaying erratic, frenetic, often acrobatic leaps, flips and flops. This energetic behavior (called the "weasel war dance" by some) has the effect of "mesmerizing" rabbits and other prey, causing them to freeze in place until the Stoat has maneuvered close enough to launch a serious attack.

Special Ability: Fascinate!; Nape Bite

Trait Statistics:	STR	SPD	INT	AGI	CON	MYS	SML	CHA
Rating:	1	3	4	3	4	4	4	2

Pursuit stats:	DV (to spot)	iPD	Move	Hit Points
	6	10	3	20

Big Stoat (Long-Tailed Weasel)

Description: The Long-Tailed Weasel is a larger cousin to Stoats, and hence is also known as a Big Stoat (0.5 kilogram). It is longer, with a longer, black-tipped tail, but otherwise is similar in both summer and winter coloring.

Habits: The Big Stoat's hunting habits are very similar to that of their smaller cousins. They can ambush prey, or use Fascinate! to briefly freeze them in their tracks. They attempt to climb onto the back of large prey and cling there until they can secure a bite to the head or neck.

Special Ability: Fascinate!; Nape Bite

Trait Statistics:	STR	SPD	INT	AGI	CON	MYS	SML	CHA
Rating:	1	2	5	4	5	3	4	2

Pursuit stats:	DV (to spot)	iPD	Move	Hit Points
	8	10	2	25

Ferret (European Polecat)

Description: The animal known to pet owners as a Ferret is a domesticated form of the European Polecat. Ferrets are out-sized versions of weasels (1.0 kilogram), with long, thin bodies and short legs, well suited for pursuing prey into burrows. (The Black-Footed Ferret, the only ferret native to North America, devotes most of its hunting effort in the burrow systems of Prairie Dogs.) Ferrets typically have cream-colored fur with black-tipped hairs, dark shoulders, neck, and tail, and a distinctive black mask.

Habits: Ferrets are ambush hunters and pursue prey into burrows, crevices, and other refuges. Domestic ferrets also can be trained to pursue and retrieve rabbits, rather like a hawk is used in falconry. Like weasels, they rely on a deadly bite to the neck and head to subdue prey.

Special Ability: Nape Bite

Trait Statistics:	STR	SPD	INT	AGI	CON	MYS	SML	CHA
Rating:	2	2	4	4	6	2	4	2

Pursuit stats:	DV (to spot)	iPD	Move	Hit Points
	6	12	8	30

Siberian Polecat

Description: Also known as the Steppe or Masked Polecat, the Siberian Polecat is a ferret species found in eastern Europe and central Asia. It is larger (3 kilograms) and more powerful than the more familiar Ferret (European Polecat). Coloration is similar to Ferrets.

Habits: The Siberian Polecat has a reputation for remaining in the same area until all available prey (such as ground squirrels) have been eradicated. It frequently hunts prey as large as rabbits, hares, and marmots, using the same ambush and pursuit techniques of other ferrets.

Special Ability: Nape Bite

Trait Statistics:	STR	SPD	INT	AGI	CON	MYS	SML	CHA
Rating:	3	5	4	4	7	2	4	2

Pursuit stats:	DV (to spot)	iPD	Move	Hit Points
	6	12	8	35

Mongooses, General Characteristics

Description: Superficially, Mongooses resemble weasels, but they are distantly related. Mustelids are considered more closely related to the Caniform (dog-like) clade of carnivores that includes dogs and bears, whereas the mongooses (Herpestids) are closer to cats and hyenas. Nevertheless, most mongooses have long, lean bodies like weasels, and are well adapted for pursuing prey into burrows and other refuges. Also like Stoats, Badgers, and Wolverines, Mongooses have a reputation for being fearless and ferocious.

Habits: In combat, Mongooses may only Bite. However, their fast reflexes permit them to move twice during combat, once before the attack, and again after the attack is delivered. This quickness contributes to their reputation as effective hunters of poisonous snakes.

Small Mongoose (Small Asian)

Description: The Small Asian Mongoose (0.5 kilogram), is native to southeast Asia, but has been introduced to Hawaii and throughout Central America and the Caribbean, where it has been a plague for native wildlife, especially birds. It has a long, lean body like a weasel, but is uniformly brown in coloration, lacking the cream-colored throat and belly of similar-sized Stoats.

Habits: Small Mongooses prey on many of the same animals as the Stoats and Ferrets, including small mammals and birds, as well as insects. They are more social than the weasels, often living in extended family groups in a common burrow system. They tend to be most active at night.

Special Ability: Extra Move

Trait Statistics:	STR	SPD	INT	AGI	CON	MYS	SML	CHA
Rating:	3	8	5	5	5	2	4	2

Pursuit stats:	DV (to spot)	iPD	Move	Hit Points
	6	10	6	25

Indian Mongoose (Gray)

Description: The Indian gray Mongoose resembles the Small Mongoose, but is twice the size (1.0 kilogram). It has a speckled iron-gray coloration, sometimes with reddish fur on the throat and legs. The tail is bushy, unlike any of the weasels. It is native to the Indian subcontinent, but also has been introduced to islands in the Caribbean and parts of the United States in a misguided effort to control poisonous snakes. Like other introduced mongoose species, it has had a severe and unintended impact on native bird species.

Habits: The hunting habits are similar to that of the Small Mongoose, with wide foraging and ambush attacks on prey that it flushes from hiding places.

Special Ability: Extra Move

Trait Statistics:	STR	SPD	INT	AGI	CON	MYS	SML	CHA
Rating:	5	8	6	6	6	2	5	2

Pursuit stats:	DV (to spot)	iPD	Move	Hit Points
	6	10	6	30

Ichneumon (Egyptian Gray)

Description: The largest and most fearsome of the mongooses (3 kilograms), the Egyptian Mongoose, also known as the Gray Mongoose or Ichneumon, is the size of a House Cat with the quickness of a Stoat, the tenacity of a Badger, and the attitude of a Wolverine.

Habits: The name "Ichneumon" means "tracker," and these mongooses have a strong reputation of following the scent of prey for kilometers. They range widely while hunting and may ambush, employ a strategem, or outright pursue prey when spotted. Unlike the other mongooses, Ichneumons are diurnal. They may be encountered as solitary hunters or in larger social groups, but do not coordinate their hunting like wolves or other pack hunters.

Special Ability: Extra Move

Trait Statistics:	STR	SPD	INT	AGI	CON	MYS	SML	CHA
Rating:	6	7	7	7	7	2	5	2

Pursuit stats:	DV (to spot)	iPD	Move	Hit Points
	6	12	7	35

Cryptics

Cryptics are snakes and other special predators that are seldom seen before they attack. Cryptic predators do not pursue prey; they lie in wait and strike without warning. For this reason, no iPD is given. Cryptics include a wide variety of different animals, including snakes, other reptiles, and large wading birds. See individual listings for the languages spoken by Cryptics.

Snakes, General Characteristics

Description: Most snakes, such as Racers and Garter snakes, are harmless and flee if disturbed. In North America, only the Pit Vipers and Coral Snakes are poisonous, and Coral Snakes are not aggressive or prone to biting, and do not prey on animals larger than a mouse. Pit Vipers, however, are important predators of small mammals. Two other listed snakes are constrictors, which kill their prey by squeezing with powerful coils of their body.

Habits: In combat, Snakes may only Bite. Constrictors bite and hold; they may begin constricting in the next combat round. Pit Vipers bite to inject venom, then release. Bites delivered to intended prey usually contain more venom than defensive bites; see specific descriptions for differences in damage by predatory and defensive bites. They speak the language of Coldies.

Gopher Snake

Description: Gopher snakes are medium to large snakes (0.5 kilogram), up to 1.8 meters long, that are found in a variety of habitats in North America. They have a gray or tawny coloration with large black blotches that closely resembles the patterning of a rattlesnake. The resemblance is probably not a coincidence, but rather an example of mimicry. When threatened, Gopher Snakes may coil, expand the neck closest to the head (making the head look triangular), and even rattle its tail against loose gravel to enhance the resemblance.

Habits: Gopher Snakes are non-poisonous, but have a strong, tenacious Bite. They are constrictors, so after securing a hold with a bite, they wrap their body around their prey and squeeze to kill. They may kill prey up to the size of a squirrel or baby rabbit.

Special Ability: Constrict

Trait Statistics:	STR	SPD	INT	AGI	CON	MYS	SML	CHA
Rating:	1	1	2	1	3	1	2	1

Pursuit stats:	DV (to spot)	iPD	Move	Hit Points
	6	—	1	15

Rattlesnake

Description: The 36 species of Rattlesnake native to the Americas range in size from tiny Pygmy Rattlesnakes (up to 60 centimeters) to Eastern Diamondbacks (more than 2 meters). Rattlesnakes in B&B may be considered similar to Western Diamondbacks, a large (1–2 meters; 2–6 kilograms), aggressive species with a broad geographic range. Assume a Juvenile is 1 meter long, with an additional 25 centimeters with each additional age step. Like the Gopher Snake, Rattlesnakes may vary from cream-colored to dark brown, with a mottled or striped pattern on the back. They are distinguished by a series of hollow rattles on the tip of the tail that creates a loud buzzing warning when the snake is disturbed.

Habits: Rattlesnakes may be encountered under a log or in a niche of stones during the day, but actively hunt at night. They possess heat-sensitive pits below the eyes (hence their name, "pit vipers") that can detect body heat signatures up to several meters distant. Defensive bites inject less toxin than bites delivered to intended prey. Juvenile and Sub-Adult rattlesnakes may take prey up to Squirrel size; Adults can prey on rabbits.

Special Ability: Poisonous Bite. In addition to normal damage, a successful predatory bite injects venom that continues to inflict 1d6 HP damage per hour for six hours. DV=10 for toxin resistance check, which if successful, reduces poison damage to 2 HP per hour. Poison damage also should be reduced to 2 HP per hour if the bite was defensive.

Trait Statistics:	STR	SPD	INT	AGI	CON	MYS	SML	CHA
Rating:	8	1	2	2	3	1	2	1

Pursuit stats:	DV (to spot)	iPD	Move	Hit Points
	8	—	1	15

Cottonmouth

Description: Also known as a Water Moccasin, the Cottonmouth is a pit viper frequently encountered in swamps, marshes, or near other water sources. Up to 80 centimeters in length (0.5 kilograms), they have a broad head like a rattlesnake, a dark, nearly black dorsal coloration, and a tail that lacks rattles. It takes its name from the bright white tissue that lines its mouth.

Habits: Cottonmouths are strong swimmers. They have a reputation for aggressiveness, but when disturbed typically gape, displaying its fangs and white mouth, while vibrating its tail. It hunts small mammals, reptiles, fish, and even carrion (so Feign Death will not succeed against a Cottonmouth). Juveniles may have a yellowish or greenish tail tip that is wriggled to lure prey (and possibly curious rabbits).

Special Ability: Poisonous Bite. In addition to normal damage, a successful bite injects venom that continues to inflict 3 HP damage per hour for six hours. DV=8 for toxin resistance check, which if successful, reduces poison damage to 1 HP per hour. Poison damage also should be reduced to 1 HP per hour if the bite was defensive.

Trait Statistics:	STR	SPD	INT	AGI	CON	MYS	SML	CHA
Rating:	5	1	2	1	3	1	2	1

Pursuit stats:	DV (to spot)	iPD	Move	Hit Points
	6	—	1	15

Copperhead

Description: Another pit viper that lacks rattles, Copperheads are modest-sized snakes (up to 1 meter; 0.2 kilogram) typically found woodland habitats. They have a broad head like other pit vipers and dorsal coloration consisting of alternating bands of light and darker brown that provide highly effective camouflage in leaf litter. They may prey on animals up to the size of a squirrel.

Habits: Copperheads are unlikely to harm rabbits unless disturbed, but are very hard to spot due to their excellent camouflage. If touched, they may vibrate the tail (with no rattles) and release a musk that smells like cucumbers. It can be found in a broad range of habitats, from semi-aquatic habitats such as marshes to arid, rocky hillsides.

Special Ability: Poisonous Bite. In addition to normal damage, a successful bite injects venom that continues to inflict 2 HP damage per hour for six hours. DV=6 for toxin resistance check, which if successful, eliminates poison damage. Poison damage should be reduced to 1 HP per hour if the bite was defensive.

Trait Statistics:	STR	SPD	INT	AGI	CON	MYS	SML	CHA
Rating:	4	1	2	1	3	1	2	1

Pursuit stats:	DV (to spot)	iPD	Move	Hit Points
	10	—	1	15

Python (Burmese)

Description: Although native to southeast Asia, Pythons have been introduced into south Florida and have expanded their range from there. They have a distinctive pattern of dark brown or reddish-brown blotches against a lighter brown dorsal coloration. They can grow to huge size (up to 4 meters; 35 kilograms). Juveniles should be considered as 2 meters in length, with an additional 0.5 meters for each age step for older snakes. They are very effective stealth predators of small mammals; by some reports, pythons have virtually eradicated rabbits in the Everglades. Pythons are usually found in habitats near water.

Habits: Pythons are relatively slow moving, but have excellent abilities to track by smell. They are equally comfortable climbing trees (with the aid of a prehensile tail) and swimming. They hunt by seizing prey, then wrapping coils around the prey and killing by constriction. They can take down prey up to the size of small deer and even alligators.

Special Ability: Constrict

Trait Statistics:	STR	SPD	INT	AGI	CON	MYS	SML	CHA
Rating:	3	1	4	3	20	2	3	5

Pursuit stats:	DV (to spot)	iPD	Move	Hit Points
	8	—	1	100

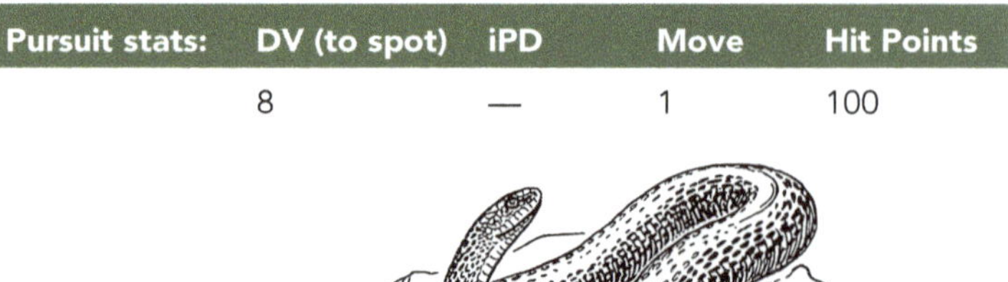

Other Reptiles, General Characteristics

Description: Two other reptilian predators are listed. Both are semi-aquatic and highly dependent on a nearby marsh, pond, or lake. Both the Snapping Turtle and Alligator are difficult to spot as they lie in wait, so are most dangerous before they are seen.

Habits: In combat, Snapping Turtles and Alligators bite in their initial attack. They attempt to drag seized prey underwater after a successful bite. Alligators also may slap enemies with the tail; treat a Tail-Slap the same as a paw-swipe from a Bear. They speak the language of Coldies.

Snapping Turtle

Description: A large (up to 10 kilograms) predatory turtle with sharp, beak-like jaws. The shell is smaller than pond turtles, giving it greater range of motion of the powerful forelegs. They are found almost exclusively in or near water, often hiding in sediment, reeds, or vegetation on the bank of a pond or river.

Habits: Snapping Turtles are stealth hunters, waiting for prey to approach within striking distance. The head and neck are highly flexible, extending nearly the length of the body. The attack strike is one of the fastest movements of any vertebrate; when the strike occurs underwater, the neck inflates, sucking prey into the mouth (a technique known as Gape-and-Suck). After biting, they hold onto the prey tenaciously, attempting to drag it into the water. They can prey on anything they can swallow, including animals as large as rabbits.

Special Ability: Drag; Dive Underwater; Unbreakable Grip

Trait Statistics:	STR	SPD	INT	AGI	CON	MYS	SML	CHA
Rating:	4	0	2	4	8	1	1	3

Pursuit stats:	DV (to spot)	iPD	Move	Hit Points
	10	—	1	40

Alligator

Description: Alligators can vary from under a meter to nearly 6 meters in length (up to 500 kilograms). Like Snapping Turtles, they are always found in or near water, often lurking just under the surface or floating quietly like a water-soaked log. The back is black or dark olive, and displays several rows of bumps or ridges. The belly is white, and the lining of the mouth white or light pink. The tail is flattened side-to-side and serves as the primary source of propulsion when swimming.

Habits: Alligators prefer to lie in wait near shore for potential prey to approach, often striking as the animal drinks from the water's edge. The attack rush can be very fast, with the alligator pursuing prey up to several meters ashore. After seizing large prey, the alligator attempts to return to water, dragging the prey underwater and spinning around its body axis to tear off chunks of meat. Large carcasses may be wedged underwater for later consumption. In close combat, alligators also can Slap with their tail. After laying her eggs in a mound of rotting vegetation, the mother lingers and defends the eggs and hatchlings from intruders. Protective mothers can be among the most dangerous of alligators.

Special Ability: Drag; Dive Underwater; Underwater Spin; Tail-Slap

Trait Statistics:	STR	SPD	INT	AGI	CON	MYS	SML	CHA
Rating:	5	3	3	4	36	2	1	3

Pursuit stats:	DV (to spot)	iPD	Move	Hit Points
	8	—	1	180

Large Wading Birds, General Characteristics

Description: Although seldom thought of a predators of mammals, large waders such as Egrets, Herons, and Cranes regularly take small mammals if the opportunity presents itself. All three are tall, long-legged birds, standing more than 1 meter high. They have long necks and long, sharp beaks that they use to spear fish, frogs, and other prey.

Habits: Although they are not camouflaged, all three are masters at standing motionless and moving without drawing attention so they can be overlooked by other animals passing quite near. This stalking ability is why they are difficult to spot. They attack by a sudden lunge with the head and neck, piercing their victim. A victim that is Skewered should immediately roll for shock. If the initial attack is not successful, they withdraw slowly, and if attacked, will fly. They speak the language of Waders.

Great Egret

Description: A large, long-legged heron with all-white feathers and a long yellow beak, the Great Egret stands 1 meter tall (up to 1.5 kilograms).

Habits: Great Egrets hunt almost exclusively in shallow water, sometimes right next to shore. They roost and nest in colonies in trees.

Special Ability: Skewer

Trait Statistics:	STR	SPD	INT	AGI	CON	MYS	SML	CHA
Rating:	3	3	4	5	3	2	1	4

Pursuit stats:	DV (to spot)	iPD	Move	Hit Points
	6	—	1	15

Great Blue Heron

Description: The largest North American heron is easily recognized by its white face, black head plumes, and blue-gray feathers on the back and tail. It stands 1.3 meters tall, with a wingspan of 2 meters (2.5 kilograms).

Habits: Like egrets, Great Blue Herons hunt almost exclusively in shallow water up to 0.5 meters deep. On occasion, they may fly low over the ground and stab at prey from the air. They roost and nest in colonies in trees.

Special Ability: Skewer

Trait Statistics:	STR	SPD	INT	AGI	CON	MYS	SML	CHA
Rating:	4	3	4	6	5	2	1	4

Pursuit stats:	DV (to spot)	iPD	Move	Hit Points
	8	—	1	25

Sandhill Crane

Description: Although unrelated to herons, Cranes are very large birds with a similar long-legged, spear-beaked appearance. Sandhill cranes are second only to Whooping Cranes as the largest bird in North America, standing 1.2 meters tall, with a wingspan of nearly 1.6 meters (3.5 kilograms). They bear a distinctive red cap on the head, uniformly gray body plumage, and tail feathers that droop, resembling a bustle.

Habits: Unlike the herons, Sandhill Cranes may forage in shallow water, marshy areas, or open prairies and meadows. They eat both vegetation (seeds, berries, cultivated foods) and live animals (fish, frogs, small mammals). Their fondness for eggs is likely the reason why they are often attacked by smaller birds, such as blackbirds. Cranes are often found in mated pairs, and can be seen (and heard) trumpeting in a duet as part of a bonding ritual. They nest on the ground.

Special Ability: Skewer

Trait Statistics:	STR	SPD	INT	AGI	CON	MYS	SML	CHA
Rating:	5	4	5	7	7	2	1	4

Pursuit stats:	DV (to spot)	iPD	Move	Hit Points
	8	—	1	35

Cryptic Mammals, General Characteristics

Description: Mink and Black Rats are listed here for different reasons. Mink are Mustelids, relatives of weasels, ferrets and martins. However, their fondness for water results in a hunting method that more closely resembles that of an Alligator or Snapping Turtle. Rats, on the other hand, are common residents in dark places, such as in or under human buildings, cliffs, rock piles, thick brush, and trees. Thus, both species are likely to be encountered when rabbits or other PCs wander too close.

Habits: Both Mink and Rats only Bite in combat. Mink are typically solitary hunters; Rats are usually encountered in groups. Mink speak the language of Weasels; Rats speak the language of Nibblers.

Mink

Description: A relative of Weasels and other Mustelids, Mink have rich reddish-brown fur, a long, sleek body, and short legs. They are about the size of a Ferret or Marten (1 kilogram). They may be found in woodland, grassland, or marsh, but never far from water. They may hunt on land by following streams and lakeshores, or in water by wading and swimming in search of both aquatic targets and potential prey near the water's edge. Rabbits are among their favorite prey, which they ambush near the water, pursue overland, and follow into burrows.

Habits: Mink are intelligent and agile hunters capable of pursuing with surprising speed for short distances like a Marten, or following prey into burrows like a Ferret. When prey are captured in or near water, they attempt to drag them into the water to subdue them.

Special Ability: Nape Bite; Drag; Dive Underwater

Trait Statistics:	STR	SPD	INT	AGI	CON	MYS	SML	CHA
Rating:	4	3	4	4	6	2	4	4

Pursuit stats:	DV (to spot)	iPD	Move	Hit Points
	8	4	6	30

Rats (Black)

Description: A dark-colored rat native to the Old World but introduced globally, where it has become a serious agricultural pest and vector of disease. It is smaller than the Brown Norway Rat, but more likely to aggregate in groups. Rats are omnivores, eating everything from seeds to crops to insects to carrion. A group may be bold enough to attack rabbits.

Habits: Black Rats are more social than Brown Rats, and may be found in groups that forage and nest in close proximity. They prefer to build nests in elevated locations such as building roofs, lofts in barns, or trees. They are excellent climbers, although not as agile as squirrels, and strong swimmers. When involved in combat, Rats can stack up to four per hex (as indicated on special tokens).

Special Ability: Group Attack

Trait Statistics:	STR	SPD	INT	AGI	CON	MYS	SML	CHA
Rating:	1	1	3	1	2	1	3	4

Pursuit stats:	DV (to spot)	iPD	Move	Hit Points
	4	—	1	10

Brutes

Large predators (or non-predator enemies) with great strength and stamina. All Brutes have the ability to Bite or Claw in Combat. Brutes include two main groups of predators: large Mustelids and Bears. A third group of large herbivores — Bulls and Bison — are included here for their notoriously bad temper. Badgers and Wolverines speak the language of Weasels. Bears speak the language of Ramblers. Bulls and Bison speak the language of Hoofers. See individual listings for descriptions and habits.

Badger

Description: The Badger of B&B is not the cute, cuddly European Badger made famous in stories of Peter Rabbit and The Wind in the Willows. This is the American Badger, a cantankerous and fearsome predator with a taste and talent for excavating burrowing animals. At just 8 kilograms, the Badger is not very big. Its short, splayed legs and a squat body make it look somewhat like a turtle that has lost its shell. But it brandishes powerful jaws and long claws equally useful for digging or rending flesh. It has very loose skin, making it difficult to gain purchase with tooth or claw, and nondescript gray fur marked only by black bars that frame its face and a white stripe running from nose to shoulders. Badgers are found throughout the dryland habitats of western North America, where they hunt for ground squirrels, prairie dogs, and other small mammals, including rabbits.

Habits: Badgers have a reputation for being ill-tempered, but it is probably more accurate to say they are fearless and not inclined to back down from larger creatures trying to threaten or intimidate. Like its African cousin (the Honey Badger), American Badgers have been known to repulse much larger predators, including bears and cougars. In a fight against a superior foe, a Badger tries to wedge itself between rocks or digs a shallow trench to protect its sides and belly. Unlike other predators, a Badger will not flee until it is reduced to 5 HP or fewer.

Special Ability: Rend

Trait Statistics:	STR	SPD	INT	AGI	CON	MYS	SML	CHA
Rating:	4	1	4	4	10	2	3	4

Pursuit stats:	DV (to spot)	iPD	Move	Hit Points
	4	6	3	50

Wolverine

Description: Wolverines are the Badger's bigger, badder cousin. They are covered in a rich, brown fur, with a broad rufous stripe that circles the highest point of the back. Wolverines stand taller than Badgers and are much larger (up to 20 kilograms), but still display a stocky appearance with short legs and head held low. Like Badgers, they have very powerful jaws and long claws. Found mostly in northern and alpine habitats, Wolverines subsist mostly on carrion, obtained from winter kills, raiding human traps, and stealing from Bears, Cougars, and Wolves. They also have been reported to hunt, usually by ambush, sometimes by dropping out of a tree on unsuspecting prey as large as deer.

Habits: Wolverines have the same never-back-down attitude of Badgers, with a twist: They also are likely to go on the offensive against larger predators to steal their food. Wolverines are known to drive Coyotes, Wolves, Cougars, Lynxes, and even Grizzly Bears away from a carcass. They are good diggers, but are not likely to engage in extensive excavation like a Badger. They also are good tree climbers.

Special Ability: Rend; Nape Bite

Trait Statistics:	STR	SPD	INT	AGI	CON	MYS	SML	CHA
Rating:	7	5	4	5	16	2	3	4

Pursuit stats:	DV (to spot)	iPD	Move	Hit Points
	4	8	4	80

Black Bear

Description: The more common and smaller bear of North America, Black Bears can vary greatly in size, with females considerably smaller (60 kilograms) and mature males much larger (up to 250 kilograms). They are covered in soft fur that typically is uniform in color, although they may be black, chocolate brown, or honey-colored. They frequent a broad range of habitats, preferring woodlands or brushland, usually in well-watered areas. The paws are large and surprisingly dexterous, but the claws are relatively short and rounded.

Habits: Black Bears are extremely powerful, able to tear fallen logs apart and flip over large stones (up to 150 kilograms) with one paw as they look for food. Their easy, ambling gait can mislead one into thinking they are slow-footed or slow-witted. In fact, they are very intelligent, particularly at solving puzzles. In Combat, Bears can Bite or Claw, and may stun an enemy with a Paw-Swipe.

Special Ability: Paw Swipe

Trait Statistics:	STR	SPD	INT	AGI	CON	MYS	SML	CHA
Rating:	8	1	5	3	30	4	8	4

Pursuit stats:	DV (to spot)	iPD	Move	Hit Points
	2	8	4	150

Grizzly Bear

Description: Grizzly Bears have traditionally been viewed as a distinct species, but now are recognized as a subspecies of Brown Bear. They are usually a lighter brown color than Black Bears, with fur that is light-tipped, giving it a "grizzled" appearance. Grizzlies can be distinguished by a distinctive hump at the shoulders, a scalloped facial profile, and long claws on the powerful forefeet. They are the largest predator in North America (unless one recognizes other races of Brown Bears, such as those on Kodiak Island, as different), with females up to 180 kilograms and mature males up to 700 kilograms. Standing on two legs, a big male may rise to 3 meters tall. Historically found throughout western North America, Grizzlies now are limited to the northern Rocky Mountains, western Canada, and Alaska.

Habits: Grizzlies are omnivores, but are known to be active hunters, taking animals as large as Moose and Bison, and of course fish in season. They also are effective hunters of small game, especially ground squirrels and marmots, which they can dig out of their burrows or overturn rocks to get at them. They can Bite or Claw in combat.

Special Ability: Paw Swipe

Trait Statistics:	STR	SPD	INT	AGI	CON	MYS	SML	CHA
Rating:	8	6	4	5	40	4	8	4

Pursuit stats:	DV (to spot)	iPD	Move	Hit Points
	2	10	8	200

Bull, young

Description: Unless otherwise specified by the Adventure or the GM, bulls may be considered to be typical black-and-white Holstein dairy cattle. Bulls are huge (1,000 kilograms) and powerful, and surprisingly fast on open ground.

Habits: Dairy bulls have a reputation for being more aggressive than bulls from beef-producing breeds. They are unpredictable in their behavior, seeming quite docile one moment and aggressive with intent to kill the next. Young bulls are especially unpredictable and may charge at the slightest provocation.

Special Ability: Hoof-Kick; Stomp; Horn Gore

Trait Statistics:	STR	SPD	INT	AGI	CON	MYS	SML	CHA
Rating:	6	5	1	2	40	2	3	2

Pursuit stats:	DV (to spot)	iPD	Move	Hit Points
	2	10	6	200

Bison

Description: Once a symbol of wildlife on the open plains, wild Bison are now restricted to reserves and national parks. Bison also may be kept on private farms and ranches, where they may interbreed with cattle (usually Hereford bulls) to produce beefalo. Bison are as large or larger than bovine Bulls (1,000 kilograms), and can be distinguished by the shaggy fur, huge, rounded head, and distinctive hump at the shoulders.

Habits: Usually found in groups or large herds, males often can be found alone or traveling in twos or threes. Bison bulls can be very aggressive; young bulls are especially unpredictable and may charge at the slightest provocation. When charging, a bull Bison is unlikely to stop for Minor obstacles. They are quite capable of crashing through ordinary fences, thickets, brambles, and similar barriers where rabbits might otherwise seek refuge.

Special Ability: Hoof-Kick; Stomp; Horn Gore

Trait Statistics:	STR	SPD	INT	AGI	CON	MYS	SML	CHA
Rating:	6	5	1	2	50	1	3	2

Pursuit stats:	DV (to spot)	iPD	Move	Hit Points
	2	10	5	250

Raptors

Birds of Prey hunt from the air, striking suddenly, often at great speed. Predatory birds of all kinds speak the language of Raptors. All aerial predators strike initially from the air. All but Ravens strike with their talons (Ravens strike with their beaks.) Vultures will not attack, but can easily be mistaken for a dangerous hawk or eagle. After a Raptor's first successful attack from the air, it must land and stay on the ground for one combat round before taking flight again. (Note that Great Blue Herons are classified here as Cryptics, not Raptors, but occasionally may stab at prey while flying low to the ground.)

Hawks, falcons, and eagles are diurnal predators, hunting only in the daytime. They have excellent eyesight and can spot rabbits from a great distance (> 100 meters). They may hunt as sit-and-wait predators, perched in a tree or atop a fencepost waiting to spot prey, or by methodically searching from the air. Few are able to sustain hovering flight, but others are able to pause in flight for a few seconds, often by turning into the wind (Osprey, Harrier, all Falcons, Barn Owl).

Owls are typically nocturnal or crepuscular (dawn and dusk) hunters, and remain perched at a roosting site or nest during the day. They have excellent vision in low light and highly acute hearing. (Barn Owls can strike a mouse in total darkness just from the sound of its footsteps.) They also have baffles on their wing feathers that muffle the sound of their flight; they can approach in almost complete silence.

Except for Harris Hawks, Caracara, and Golden Eagle (on occasion), the initial attack by a Raptor is from the air; if successful, the Raptor must stay on the ground for one combat round before taking flight again. Raptor attacks are considered Claw attacks.

Red-Tailed Hawk

Description: A large hawk (1.5 kilograms, 140-centimeter wingspan) easily recognized by a broad, red tail when it banks in the sky. It may be found in virtually any habitat, where it hunts almost any small game, from mice to jackrabbits. It has large talons arranged like all hawks — 3 toes forward, one back — with a hallux (back) claw nearly 3 centimeters long.

Habits: Red-tails may hunt from the air or from elevated perches such as the tops of fenceposts, telephone poles, or low branches of a tree. In flight, they typically cruise at intermediate height, diving vertically (stooping) on prey. They are hard to spot when perched, as they stand very still, and attack from a low angle, close to the ground. The main attack is by talon (Claw) from the air. On the ground, they may defend themselves by biting.

Special Ability: Aerial Attack

Trait Statistics:	STR	SPD	INT	AGI	CON	MYS	SML	CHA
Rating:	6	8	4	4	5	1	1	2

Pursuit stats:	DV (to spot)	iPD	Move	Hit Points
	4	14	17	25

Swainson's Hawk

Description: Similar in form and size to a Red-Tailed Hawk (1.5 kilograms, 130-centimeter wingspan), Swainson's Hawks can be distinguished by a dark "bib" on the chest. The plumage is dark brown dorsally, and may be white underneath (light phase) or dark rufous (dark phase). Swainson's hawks are found throughout western North America, where they prefer open country (grasslands, deserts, farm fields). They prefer to hunt small game, and specialize in ground squirrels.

Habits: Swainson's Hawks may hunt, like Red-Tails, from a perch, but are more likely to be seen soaring high in the sky as they search for prey. The attack is a steep dive from altitude, like a falcon.

Special Ability: Aerial Attack

Trait Statistics:	STR	SPD	INT	AGI	CON	MYS	SML	CHA
Rating:	5	8	3	4	5	2	1	2

Pursuit stats:	DV (to spot)	iPD	Move	Hit Points
	4	14	17	25

Harris Hawk

Description: A bit smaller than a Red-Tailed Hawk (1 kilograms, 120-centimeter wingspan), but with larger talons that allow them to take prey as large as a jackrabbit. They have all-dark plumage with rufous shoulders. Their range is limited to arid woodlands and deserts of the Southwest. They often may be seen perching together in the same tree or atop the same saguaro cactus, sometimes stacked atop one another, like an avian totem pole.

Habits: Harris Hawks are one of the few species of raptors documented to hunt cooperatively. For that reason, in B&B they are almost always encountered as a group (see Wandering Encounters). Unlike most other Raptors, except Caracara, they also are comfortable pursuing prey on the ground. A typical strategy is for a group of hawks to surround a bush where a rabbit has sought refuge, with some hawks acting as beaters to flush the rabbit, and others as hunters to seize it when it emerges. Although combat may be initiated on the ground, Talons are still used as their principal weapon (Claw attack).

Special Ability: Aerial Attack; Teamwork

Trait Statistics:	STR	SPD	INT	AGI	CON	MYS	SML	CHA
Rating:	4	8	6	3	4	2	1	2

Pursuit stats:	DV (to spot)	iPD	Move	Hit Points
	4	14	17	20

Harrier

Description: Harriers are medium-sized raptors with long wings (0.5 kilograms, 120-centimeter wingspan). Females are brown and males light gray in color. It preys on a variety of small game, including mice and voles, ground squirrels, rabbits, and ground nesting birds. In contrast to other hawks, Harriers have a distinctive facial disk similar to owls, which helps it to listen for its prey while in flight.

Habits: Harriers are low-speed raptors, and can be readily distinguished from other raptors by their pattern of flight. They hunt by coursing slowly over the ground in a wobbly flight, often no more than a meter or two above the ground. They are particularly common in open country such as Grassland or Marsh habitats (they are sometimes known as Marsh Hawks). In such country, they initially may be seen approaching from a considerable distance, but disappear behind low ridges and vegetation as they draw near. Rabbits should have an initial opportunity to spot when the hawk is 50–100 meters away. It attacks by appearing suddenly from behind a bush or tussock, then dropping vertically on its surprised prey. This ability to disappear and reappear in open country has given it another name: the Gray Ghost.

Special Ability: Surprise!; Aerial Attack

Trait Statistics:	STR	SPD	INT	AGI	CON	MYS	SML	CHA
Rating:	4	8	6	3	4	2	1	2

Pursuit stats:	DV (to spot)	iPD	Move	Hit Points
	2	12	8	20

Goshawk

Description: Goshawks are the largest of the Accipiter hawks in North America (1 kilogram), which include Sharp-Shinned and Cooper Hawks. It has relatively short, broad wings (100-centimeter wingspan) and a long, narrow tail, which favors maneuverability over speed in woodland habitats. Juveniles are brown and speckled; Adults are slate gray. They are adept at hunting other birds on the ground or in the air, as well as squirrels, rabbits and hares.

Habits: Goshawks are perch hunters that lurk in trees until they spot prey, then pursue in flight at breakneck speeds. They may pursue prey into thick vegetation without hesitation, apparently without regard to their own safety. The main attack is by Talon (Claw).

Special Ability: Aerial Attack

Trait Statistics:	STR	SPD	INT	AGI	CON	MYS	SML	CHA
Rating:	3	4	5	5	4	1	1	2

Pursuit stats:	DV (to spot)	iPD	Move	Hit Points
	6	14	10	20

Caracara

Description: Caracaras are odd-looking birds, looking like a long-legged buzzard with the face of a vulture. In fact, they are a large relative of falcons (1 kilogram; 130-centimeter wingspan), with distinctive black body plumage, white chest and neck, orange face, and black cap. They frequent open country, but can be found in woodlands. They are classed as a "carnivorous scavenger," preferring carrion but not above taking live prey when available. Small reptiles and birds are its most common prey, along with crabs, insects, and shellfish. They also steal food from other raptors.

Habits: Caracaras may soar high in the sky, searching for carcasses in the same manner as vultures, or they may hunt from a perch like a hawk. They also are known to hunt on foot, like a crow, turning over rocks and leaves as they search for small prey. Caracaras often are seen in small family groups, and like Harris Hawks, may pursue prey into a thicket on foot, although they do not hunt cooperatively. From the air or on the ground, their principal weapons are Talons.

Special Ability: Aerial Attack

Trait Statistics:	STR	SPD	INT	AGI	CON	MYS	SML	CHA
Rating:	2	2	4	2	5	1	1	2

Pursuit stats:	DV (to spot)	iPD	Move	Hit Points
	4	14	13	25

Prairie Falcon

Description: A large falcon (0.5 kilograms; 110-centimeter wingspan) found mostly in open, dryland habitats of western North America. It is similar to the Peregrine in appearance, with a faded, brown mask, and lighter coloration. Unlike other falcons that specialize in hunting birds, the Prairie Falcon prefers small mammals as prey.

Habits: Prairie Falcons hunt on the wing, searching from intermediate heights and stooping at great speed in a final attack. Although they are not camouflaged against an open sky, their lightning attack is often the first warning that they are near. They attack by Talon (Claw).

Special Ability: Aerial Attack

Trait Statistics:	STR	SPD	INT	AGI	CON	MYS	SML	CHA
Rating:	5	8	5	5	4	2	1	2

Pursuit stats:	DV (to spot)	iPD	Move	Hit Points
	4	14	20	20

Peregrine Falcon

Description: A large falcon (0.5 kilogram; 110-centimeter wingspan) found sparsely across most of North America, favoring mountains, coastlines, and other habitats with cliffs for nesting (including cities). It resembles the Prairie Falcon, but generally is darker in color, with a much more distinctive black mask. Also known as a Duck Hawk, the Peregrine is renowned for catching other birds on the wing. It rarely attacks mammalian prey, but if the opportunity presents itself ...

Habits: The Peregrine hunts from the air and attacks in a stoop at great speed; Peregrines have the distinction of holding the record for fastest flight: nearly 400 kilometers/hour in a steep dive. At such speed, striking prey could injure the falcon, so Peregrine's target a wing of their prey to disable it. When attacking prey on the ground, the dive levels out to parallel the ground, striking the target from the side rather than directly from above. The principal weapons in combat are its Talons.

Special Ability: Aerial Attack

Trait Statistics:	STR	SPD	INT	AGI	CON	MYS	SML	CHA
Rating:	4	6	5	5	4	1	1	2

Pursuit stats:	DV (to spot)	iPD	Move	Hit Points
	4	14	20	20

Osprey

Description: A fish-eating bird of prey smaller than an eagle but larger than other hawks (2 kilogram, 180-centimeter wingspan). Dark wings, a light breast and belly, and a black-and-white striped head distinguish it from other large raptors. It has a widespread range, but seldom is found far from standing bodies of water (ponds, lakes, estuaries, marshes). Although the vast bulk of its diet consists of fish, Ospreys also have been reported to take small mammals such as rabbits.

Habits: When hunting, an Osprey flies low over the water, plunging suddenly straight down to catch fish with both Talons. It may briefly submerge completely during the attack. To reduce wind drag, it habitually carries a fish headfirst in flight. When a fish is too big to carry, an Osprey may surfboard with the fish until it is beached. Attacks are only from the air, with Talons.

Special Ability: Aerial Attack

Trait Statistics:	STR	SPD	INT	AGI	CON	MYS	SML	CHA
Rating:	5	8	4	2	6	1	1	2

Pursuit stats:	DV (to spot)	iPD	Move	Hit Points
	2	14	12	30

Bald Eagle

Description: The largest true raptor in North America (5 kilogram; 230-centimeter wingspan). Bald Eagles are opportunistic feeders with a strong propensity for fishing. Adults have a distinctive black body and all-white head, although juveniles are more non-descript brown. Like Ospreys, they are seldom found far from standing water, including the ocean.

Habits: Bald Eagles capture fish by snagging prey swimming close to the surface, remaining in flight the whole time. They may congregate in great numbers along streams during runs of spawning salmon. They are as likely to eat carrion as to kill prey on their own, and they are adept at stealing food from other animals, including Osprey, Cormorants, Herons, Foxes, and Coyotes. Food stealing can quickly shift to predation, as Bald Eagles also are known to take other fishing birds as prey. They also target small- to medium-sized mammals, up to the size of beavers and deer fawns, as opportunities are available. Attacks are only from the air, with Talons.

Special Ability: Aerial Attack

Trait Statistics:	STR	SPD	INT	AGI	CON	MYS	SML	CHA
Rating:	6	4	4	3	8	2	1	3

Pursuit stats:	DV (to spot)	iPD	Move	Hit Points
	2	14	15	40

Golden Eagle

Description: Although the Golden Eagle is statistically smaller than a Bald Eagle (4 kilogram; 230-centimeter wingspan), it is a much more dangerous predator. It has a powerful beak and formidable talons, with a hallux (back) claw over 6 centimeters long. They favor open habitats and mountainous regions with rocky slopes throughout western North America (and across the steppes of Asia). Their preferred prey are small- to medium-sized mammals, including squirrels, rabbits, marmots, jackrabbits, and even sheep and goats. It is the most powerful aerial predator in North America, and one of the most powerful in the world.

Habits: Despite their size, Golden Eagles are adept fliers, showing both maneuverability and high speed in pursuit of prey. They may soar on thermals like vultures, or cruise under power at speeds of about 50 kilometers/hour; when diving on prey, they have been clocked at more than 300 kilometers/hour, nearly as fast as Peregrine Falcons. Hunting techniques can vary, including (a) soaring high in the air, then gliding to attack; (b) soaring high and diving almost vertically like a falcon; (c) covering the ground slowly before dropping suddenly on prey like a harrier; (d) initially gliding from a height, then twisting and turning around bushes and obstacles during powered flight in pursuit of prey such as a Jackrabbit; (e) flying low, gripping and holding on with powerful talons until the prey succumbs; (f) striking and releasing prey on precarious perches, such as cliff ledges, and retrieving the carcass at the bottom; and (g) approaching prey in a refuge (bush or burrow) and extracting with one foot. In all cases, the attack is by Talon.

Special Ability: Aerial Attack; Unbreakable Grip

Trait Statistics:	STR	SPD	INT	AGI	CON	MYS	SML	CHA
Rating:	8	6	6	6	8	2	1	3

Pursuit stats:	DV (to spot)	iPD	Move	Hit Points
	4	14	20	40

Barn Owl

Description: Medium-sized, long-legged owl with tawny back and brilliant white face and belly (0.5 kilogram; 90-centimeter wingspan). Barn Owls have a very wide distribution, on six continents, and avoid only the most extreme polar, alpine, and desert habitats. It particularly favors open farmland and grassland habitats for hunting. It roosts in places that offer cracks or crevices for a nest, including cliffs, tree cavities, and human buildings. Its diet includes bats, birds and insects, but consists mostly of small mammals up to the size of a Jackrabbit.

Habits: Barn Owls have excellent hearing and eyesight, and are often seen hunting in the late afternoon as well as at night. The hunting pattern is like a Harrier, coursing low over the ground in search of prey, then dropping vertically in attack. Attacks are only aerial, using Talons.

Special Ability: Nightvision; Surprise!; Aerial Attack

Trait Statistics:	STR	SPD	INT	AGI	CON	MYS	SML	CHA
Rating:	4	8	4	4	4	3	1	6

Pursuit stats:	DV (to spot)	iPD	Move	Hit Points
	8	12	8	20

Barred Owl

Description: Medium-sized owl, chocolate brown with dark eyes (0.75 kilogram; 120-centimeter wingspan). Barred Owls once were limited to woodlands of the eastern United States, but recently have expanded their range all the way to the Pacific Coast. Most often found in Orchards, Pine Forests, or Mountain Stream habitats. Prefers to hunt small mammals, up to the size of a rabbit.

Habits: An owl of woodlands, Barred Owls are sit-and-wait hunters, remaining silent (and invisible) as they perch on a low branch until prey is sighted, then launching into silent flight in a gliding attack. Only attacks from the air, with Talons.

Special Ability: Nightvision; Aerial Attack

Trait Statistics:	STR	SPD	INT	AGI	CON	MYS	SML	CHA
Rating:	5	5	4	5	5	3	1	5

Pursuit stats:	DV (to spot)	iPD	Move	Hit Points
	8	12	7	25

Great Horned Owl

Description: Large owl (1.5 kilograms; 150-centimeter wingspan). Distinguished by mottled brown coloration, with distinctive ear tufts and yellow eyes. Like most other owls, it has a prominent facial disk that is used to direct sound to the asymmetrically placed ears, and very large, powerful talons. The talons are arranged (like other owls) with two toes forward, two back, with 4-centimeter claws, and a grip strength nearly equal to a Golden Eagle.

Habits: Can be found in most habitats, from Farm to Mountain Stream, but most often encountered in Suburbs, Oak Woodlands, and Rocky Hillsides. Mostly nocturnal. May nest in trees, caves, cliff ledges, or on the ground. Rabbits are its favorite prey, but can take opossums, domestic cats, and other owls. It is known to defend its nest area violently, day or night. May hunt from a perch or fencepost, or while cruising in flight. Probably the most feared aerial predator, apart from Golden Eagles.

Special Ability: Nightvision; Aerial Attack; Unbreakable Grip

Trait Statistics:	STR	SPD	INT	AGI	CON	MYS	SML	CHA
Rating:	6	5	5	6	6	3	1	5

Pursuit stats:	DV (to spot)	iPD	Move	Hit Points
	8	10	6	30

Raven

Description: Large, black birds, like a Crow with a Roman nose (1 kilogram; 130-centimeter wingspan). Ravens are Corvids, cousins to Crows, Magpies, and Jays, and not true raptors. However, Ravens are adaptable and opportunistic omnivores, and kill prey when they have a chance. They are particularly adept at raiding nests for eggs or babies, snatching young rabbits, or stealing other valuable items such as Prized Food or herbs. They are common residents in forests as well as open country, rocky hillsides, and mountain regions.

Habits: Ravens often soar on thermals alongside Vultures, and compete with other scavengers at carcasses. What they lack in natural weapons they compensate for with trickery. Among the most intelligent of birds, Ravens are language experts. Their native language is Perchers, but they also can converse in Rabbit, Chatters, Nibblers, Dogs, Cats, and one other language for each age above Sub-Adult (determined by GM). They are not likely to engage in serious combat, preferring to snatch and fly, but when they attack, they use their large beak to hammer at sensitive targets and to bite (treat as a Bite attack).

Special Ability: Peck Eyes

Trait Statistics:	STR	SPD	INT	AGI	CON	MYS	SML	CHA
Rating:	4	6	6	2	3	3	1	5

Pursuit stats:	DV (to spot)	iPD	Move	Hit Points
	4	14	10	15

Vulture

Description: Vultures are listed with other Raptors for their general resemblance to soaring hawks and eagles, for their preference for eating meat, and for their language abilities. However, they should not be considered predators, and are included as Neutral Animals in Wandering Encounters. Vultures (based on Turkey Vultures) are large black birds with unfeathered red heads. They exclusively eat carrion, and can be seen searching for dead animals in almost all habitats.

Habits: Vultures are not aggressive. When threatened on the ground, they are slow to take flight. As a defense, they spew projectile vomit of partially digested rotten meat at their enemy.

Special Ability: Regurgitate

Trait Statistics:	STR	SPD	INT	AGI	CON	MYS	SML	CHA
Rating:	4	6	3	1	3	3	1	5

Pursuit stats:	DV (to spot)	iPD	Move	Hit Points
	4	14	10	15

Neutral Animals

Rabbits may encounter many animals in the world that pose no immediate threat. Some of these are designated as playable species: Raccoon, Jackrabbit, Chipmunk, Skunk, Porcupine, Opossum, Armadillo, and Squirrel. These and other non-predators are referred to as Neutral Animals. Players should note, however, that any particular neutral animal may be a potential ally, casually friendly, aloof and disinterested, or openly hostile. The animals described below do not represent a comprehensive list of possible neutrals that might be encountered. The animals that are listed below are included because they are common, and therefore likely to be encountered by rabbits in appropriate habitats, or because they possess unique attributes that could make encounters interesting. The descriptions also are abbreviated here; GMs may want to consult field guides to mammals, birds, or reptiles to find more complete descriptions of physical and behavioral attributes and listings of other species that could be included as neutral animals in the game.

As in our 5-part classification of predators, there is no strict taxonomic relationship among the following groups of animals. They are organized within the game by the language they speak.

Note that as non-predators, these neutral animals are not likely to pursue rabbits. They may be easily frightened, however. Rather than listing an initial pursuit distance (iPD), a Flight Distance (FD) is listed instead. In an encounter, a neutral animal may seek to hide or flee when one or more from the player's party approaches within this Flight Distance. A Difficulty Value (DV) also is provided to determine whether they flee. Roll 1d6; a result that exceeds the DV to flee indicates that they try to hide, retreat into a refuge, or run away.

Rabbit Relatives

Rabbits, Jackrabbits, Hares and Pikas. They speak the language of Rabbits.

Jackrabbit

Description: Available as a playable Non-rabbit species; profession: Herald; primary trait: SPD.

Habits: Generally wary and quick to take flight. Males can be aggressive in the Spring.

Special Ability: Jump Kick; Dash without tiring; Box

Trait Statistics:	STR	SPD	INT	AGI	CON	MYS	SML	CHA
Rating:	2	3	2	1	2	2	1	2

Pursuit stats:	DV (to spot)	¬FD	DV (to flee)	Move	Hit Points
	6	6	3	8	30

Pika

Description: Pikas are unusual rabbit relatives that live on rocky talus slopes high in the mountains. They have short ears and look a bit like overgrown hamsters. They are considered Tiny (0.35 kilogram).

Habits: Pikas gather grass in summer and build haystacks to dry for storage. When disturbed, they emit a high-pitched Alarm Call.

Special Ability: Alarm Call

Trait Statistics:	STR	SPD	INT	AGI	CON	MYS	SML	CHA
Rating:	1	2	2	2	1	2	2	3

Pursuit stats:	DV (to spot)	¬FD	DV (to flee)	Move	Hit Points
	6	6	2	1	15

Snowshoe Hare

Description: Snowshoe Hares are the Jackrabbits of the far north. Found in subarctic and high mountain regions, they have pelage that changes from brown in summer to white in winter, providing camouflage from Raptors, Lynx, and Coyotes year round. They take their name from their unusually long hind feet that allow them to run effectively in snow. Larger than a Rabbit but smaller than a Jackrabbit, they are considered Small (1.5 kilograms).

Habits: Habits are much like Rabbits and Jackrabbits. Like European Hares, they are noted for fighting with their forelegs while standing bipedally.

Special Ability: Jump Kick; Dash without tiring; Box

Trait Statistics:	STR	SPD	INT	AGI	CON	MYS	SML	CHA
Rating:	2	3	2	1	2	2	1	2

Pursuit stats:	DV (to spot)	¬FD	DV (to flee)	Move	Hit Points
	6	6	3	8	25

Weasel Relatives

Weasels are members of the family Mustelidae, a large and varied taxonomic group that includes stoats and weasels, ferrets and martens, skunks, minks, otters, badgers, and wolverines. For simplicity, we also have included here members of the Herpestidae — the mongooses. Although not closely related to weasels, the mongooses fill similar ecological roles. Most of the weasel relatives are listed under Predators. In B&B, all of these animals speak the language of Weasels.

Skunk

Description: Available as a playable Non-rabbit species; profession: Burglar; primary trait: AGI. With a stout body, short legs, and long fluffy tail, Skunks are unmistakable with long stripes of black and white. Skunks that are met during random encounters may be vectors of the rabies virus (1d6 roll of 1). Striped Skunks can grow quite big, the size of a house cat (5 kilograms); considered Small.

Habits: Skunks amble patiently, often in woodland or brushland habitats, searching for insects, grubs, eggs, and an occasional mouse or vole. When threatened, they can emit a foul spray either backward (Spray) or forward while standing on forelegs (Power Spray). Skunks are clever animals and highly manipulative, being able to break in or out of traps and other secure places.

Special Ability: Spray & Power Spray; manipulation bonus; Disassemble Man-Things

Trait Statistics:	STR	SPD	INT	AGI	CON	MYS	SML	CHA
Rating:	2	2	2	3	2	2	1	1

Pursuit stats:	DV (to spot)	¬FD	DV (to flee)	Move	Hit Points
	4	6	3	1	35

Otter

Description: A relative of weasels, ferrets, and martens, River Otters are never found far from rivers, lakes, or marshes. They are large for Mustelids (12 kilograms), and are considered Medium in size. They have short brown fur and a thick, muscular tail. The feet are webbed, providing the principal source of propulsion while swimming. The transparent nictitating membrane over the eye contributes to being nearsighted.

Habits: Otters have a well-deserved reputation for being curious, playful, and non-threatening. They pose little threat to adult rabbits, but might be tempted to snatch a baby. They are awkward when bounding on land, but supremely graceful on ice, snow, or riverbanks, or while swimming.

Special Ability: Dive Underwater

Trait Statistics:	STR	SPD	INT	AGI	CON	MYS	SML	CHA
Rating:	3	4	5	4	8	2	4	5

Pursuit stats:	DV (to spot)	¬FD	DV (to flee)	Move	Hit Points
	6	6	5	2	40

Chatters: Squirrels and their Relatives

Rodents constitute the largest order of mammals, making up about 40% of all living species. The rodents are taxonomically divided into five main groups; for convenience, we distinguish two in B&B: the Sciuromorphs (squirrels, chipmunks and their relatives) and all others (rats, mice, beavers, porcupines, etc.) Most of the members of the squirrel group are highly vocal, some with very sophisticated communication systems. In B&B, they speak the language of Chatters.

Bite [B]: All Chatters, standard bite only; no claw or kick.

Climb: Chipmunks, Tree Squirrels, and Flying Squirrels can climb trees, including canopy. Ground Squirrels can also climb trees, but preferentially try to run to a burrow. Marmots and Prairie Dogs can climb trees, but not canopy; and they are Vulnerable when in trees.

Glide [Pursuit & Combat]: Flying Squirrel, special move from treetop, canopy, or bush to any destination at same height (if within three hexes) or lower height (if within four hexes). Note that the flying squirrel must Climb to reach a greater height (and can go from treetop to canopy).

Alarm Call [Pursuit & Combat]: Ground Squirrel, Marmot, Prairie Dog. If any of these detects a predator, all animals (friendly, neutral, or hostile) on the board are aware of its location and general identity (ground predator, flying predator, or snake). The predator attacks with a −1 disadvantage (to AS) for 1d6 rounds.

Chipmunk

Description: Available as a playable Non-rabbit species; profession: Spy; primary trait: INT. Chipmunks are Tiny (50 grams), with brown fur and black-and-white stripes on the face and tail. Their primary food is seeds.

Habits: Chipmunks are quick and curious, and well adapted to climbing trees, brush, and even stiff flower stalks. As PCs, they have a number of special abilities associated with negotiating small or concealed spaces.

Special Ability: Quick Conceal; Automatic Stealth; Double Jump; Find Hidden Entry

Trait Statistics:	STR	SPD	INT	AGI	CON	MYS	SML	CHA
Rating:	1	2	3	2	1	2	2	2

Pursuit stats:	DV (to spot)	¬FD	DV (to flee)	Move	Hit Points
	4	6	4	1	10

Flying Squirrel

Description: With a fold of skin (patagium) that extends between forelegs and hind legs, and a wide, flat tail for guidance and balance, Flying Squirrels are very effective gliders, but cannot actually fly. They are smaller than ordinary tree squirrels (0.3 kilogram), and are considered Tiny.

Habits: Most squirrels are active in daylight, but Flying Squirrels are nocturnal. They glide from tree to tree in forest habitats, where they cache nuts and seeds much like other squirrels.

Special Ability: Glide

Trait Statistics:	STR	SPD	INT	AGI	CON	MYS	SML	CHA
Rating:	2	2	2	2	1	1	2	3

Pursuit stats:	DV (to spot)	¬FD	DV (to flee)	Move	Hit Points
	6	6	3	1	15

Ground Squirrel

Description: Ground squirrels are the burrowing counterpart of tree squirrels. They have nondescript brown fur and a short tail, and are a bit smaller than tree squirrels (0.5 kilogram). They can be found in a variety of habitats, including open grassland, farm fields, brushland, and rocky slopes.

Habits: Ground squirrels are social animals, living in dense populations or "colonies" consisting of dozens to thousands of individual burrow systems. They are good diggers, and good at scrambling over rocks, but not very good at climbing trees. When disturbed, they utter Alarm Calls and stand rigidly upright, which serves to warn all the Ground Squirrels in the vicinity. They also respond to alarms by other species, such as Blackbirds.

Special Ability: Alarm Call

Trait Statistics:	STR	SPD	INT	AGI	CON	MYS	SML	CHA
Rating:	2	2	2	2	1	1	2	2

Pursuit stats:	DV (to spot)	¬FD	DV (to flee)	Move	Hit Points
	4	6	3	1	15

Marmot

Description: Marmots are essentially overgrown Ground Squirrels (3 kilograms) with dark brown bodies, often with rusty fur at the shoulders or neck, a short bushy tail, and a white nose patch. Although associated with mountain meadows and rocky talus slopes, Yellow-Bellied Marmots also can be found in well-watered open country such as farm fields.

Habits: Marmots also are found in social aggregations, but are not as well integrated in a social network as Ground Squirrels and Prairie Dogs. They also emit a loud whistle as an Alarm Call when disturbed.

Special Ability: Alarm Call

Trait Statistics:	STR	SPD	INT	AGI	CON	MYS	SML	CHA
Rating:	3	2	2	2	3	1	2	2

Pursuit stats:	DV (to spot)	¬FD	DV (to flee)	Move	Hit Points
	4	6	3	1	30

Prairie Dog

Description: Prairie Dogs also are an overgrown Ground Squirrel (1.5 kilograms) with light tan fur and short tails.

Habits: Prairie Dogs live in large social groups — "Towns" — that can contain many thousands of individuals (one town was estimated to hold 400 million prairie dogs). Although towns can be quite extensive, individual animals live in small family groups or "Coteries." They employ sophisticated vocal communication, including Alarm Calls, and build complex, well-engineered, ventilated burrow systems.

Special Ability: Alarm Call

Trait Statistics:	STR	SPD	INT	AGI	CON	MYS	SML	CHA
Rating:	2	2	2	2	3	1	2	3

Pursuit stats:	DV (to spot)	¬FD	DV (to flee)	Move	Hit Points
	4	6	4	1	25

Tree Squirrel

Description: Available as a playable Non-rabbit species; profession: Grifter; primary trait: CHA. Tree squirrels include tiny Red Squirrels and large western Gray Squirrels; the tree squirrels in B&B are modeled after Fox Squirrels, with rusty brown fur (with black, melanistic morphs) and a long, bushy tail that aids in balance on tree limbs. Tree Squirrels are built for life in trees, and possess hind feet that can rotate 180 degrees, enabling the squirrel to hang upside down while clinging to a branch or tree trunk.

Habits: Tree Squirrels are clever and curious, and very industrious in collecting and caching acorns and other mast crops as a winter food store. Instead of creating a large cache of seeds and nuts like Chipmunks, Tree Squirrels bury individual food items and are able to recall the location of tens of thousands of buried items months later. Although they may vocalize when threatened by an enemy, they are more likely to climb a tree, shake their tail, and chatter, taunting their enemy. In a tree they are second only to Pine Martens in agility.

Special Ability: Tree Dash; Leap Acrobatically; Taunt; Lie & Cheat; count to 7

Trait Statistics:	STR	SPD	INT	AGI	CON	MYS	SML	CHA
Rating:	2	2	2	2	1	1	2	3

Pursuit stats:	DV (to spot)	¬FD	DV (to flee)	Move	Hit Points
	4	6	4	1	15

Nibblers: Rats and their relatives

All rodents other than Chatters are considered Nibblers. This is a varied assemblage, including aquatic (Beaver and Musk-rat), fossorial (Gopher), arboreal (Porcupine), as well as typical ground-dwelling Rats and Mice. Unlike squirrels, they rely more heavily on hearing and smell than vision, and generally lack complex communication. In B&B, they speak the language of Nibblers.

Beaver

Description: Beavers are the largest rodents in North America (20 kilograms), qualifying them as medium-sized mammals. They have rich brown fur, stocky build, and a flattened, nearly hairless tail. They consume the bark of saplings and thin-barked trees such as aspen, willow, alder, and birch. They are most common in marsh and mountain stream habitats.

Habits: Beavers are most famous for their engineering skills in constructing dams, water impoundments, and lodges with protected, underwater entrances. Their efforts modify the habitat, creating favorable niches for aquatic and emergent plants and the animals that use them. They are not fast, but are very good swimmers and quite strong, able to manipulate large branches and small trees in constructing dams and lodges. They also are noted for an alarm signal produced by slapping the water with their flat tail.

Special Ability: Dive Underwater

Trait Statistics:	STR	SPD	INT	AGI	CON	MYS	SML	CHA
Rating:	5	1	2	3	12	1	2	2

Pursuit stats:	DV (to spot)	¬FD	DV (to flee)	Move	Hit Points
	6	6	3	1	60

Gopher

Description: Gophers are small (0.25 kilogram) fossorial rodents that subsist on roots and tubers collected underground. They live and work underground, creating extensive tunnel systems as they forage. They have small eyes and large feet well adapted for digging, but are not as anatomically distinct as Moles. They are called Pocket Gophers for the fur-lined cheek pouches that are used to carry food items back to a central larder.

Habits: Pocket Gophers are solitary and seldom seen. They are outstanding diggers.

Special Ability: Fast Burrow

Trait Statistics:	STR	SPD	INT	AGI	CON	MYS	SML	CHA
Rating:	2	2	2	2	1	2	3	2

Pursuit stats:	DV (to spot)	¬FD	DV (to flee)	Move	Hit Points
	8	4	2	1	10

Kangaroo Rat

Description: Kangaroo Rats are small rodents (100 grams) typically found in arid habitats with sandy soil. They take their name from two outsized hind legs that allow them to hop bipedally like a kangaroo. They also have large eyes, a relatively short body, and a long tail, often much longer than the body.

Habits: Kangaroo Rats are strictly nocturnal, collecting seeds in fur-lined cheek pouches and returning them to a larder in a deep burrow. They locomote like kangaroos by hopping on their hind legs. Despite being burrow dwellers, the small forelegs render them poor diggers. They have poor resistance to heat, spending the hot desert days underground, but can extract all the water they need from succulent plants and metabolic physiology.

Special Ability: none

Trait Statistics:	STR	SPD	INT	AGI	CON	MYS	SML	CHA
Rating:	1	3	1	2	1	1	2	3

Pursuit stats:	DV (to spot)	¬FD	DV (to flee)	Move	Hit Points
	8	6	2	1	10

Mouse

Description: There are many kinds of mice. The generic mouse of B&B is modeled after a Deer Mouse, a common mouse native to North America. Deer mice are tiny rodents (25 grams) found in forest, brushland, and grassland habitats across North America. They also take up residence in human buildings, especially barns, alongside the common House Mouse. They have brown backs and white bellies, with large eyes.

Habits: Deer Mice nest in trees or tall vegetation, building completely enclosed nests that look like a domed bird nest. They have good senses of sight, hearing, and smell, and are active at night. They are not particularly social, but have overlapping home ranges and can achieve dense populations if food is plentiful.

Special Ability: none

Trait Statistics:	STR	SPD	INT	AGI	CON	MYS	SML	CHA
Rating:	1	2	1	2	1	1	2	2

Pursuit stats:	DV (to spot)	¬FD	DV (to flee)	Move	Hit Points
	8	6	2	1	10

Muskrat

Description: Muskrats are semi-aquatic rodents found in habitats with rivers, lakes, or ponds. They are sometimes mistaken for Beaver, although they are much smaller (2 kilograms) with a more slender, rat-like build.

Habits: Although they lack the engineering skills of Beavers, Muskrats do construct large nests consisting of mud and sticks with underwater entrances like a Beaver lodge. They are strong swimmers, using a lateral movement of the tail to assist in propelling them in water.

Special Ability: Dive Underwater

Trait Statistics:	STR	SPD	INT	AGI	CON	MYS	SML	CHA
Rating:	2	2	1	2	2	2	3	1

Pursuit stats:	DV (to spot)	¬FD	DV (to flee)	Move	Hit Points
	6	6	2	2	25

Nutria

Description: Nutria, also known as Coypu, are a semi-aquatic rodent native to South America that has been introduced to the United States and greatly expanded its range. They are intermediate in size between Muskrats and Beavers (8 kilograms), and can be distinguished by their round tail. They have food habits similar to muskrats.

Habits: Nutria lack the engineering skills of Beavers or even Muskrats. They dig tunnels in riverbanks for nests. They also have tremendous appetites to go along with a remarkable reproductive potential. Nutria habitats often can be recognized by patches entirely denuded of vegetation.

Special Ability: Dive Underwater

Trait Statistics:	STR	SPD	INT	AGI	CON	MYS	SML	CHA
Rating:	3	1	1	2	8	1	2	2

Pursuit stats:	DV (to spot)	¬FD	DV (to flee)	Move	Hit Points
	6	6	2	1	40

Packrat

Description: "Packrat" is a common name for Woodrats, which are rats native to the New World. They can be distinguished from Old World rats (such as Black Rats) by having tails with hair. A small rodent (0.5 kilogram), they typically inhabit woodland or brushland habitats, where they construct sometimes massive nests in trees.

Habits: Woodrats are good climbers and proficient at building large wooden nests in trees, niches in cliffs, or caves. They collect food items and store them in a central cache or middens. Packrats have an unusual attraction to shiny objects. While carrying one item, if they chance upon another desirable thing, they may drop the first item to "trade" it for the new thing. Middens sometimes contain dozens of discarded objects and "man-things."

Special Ability: Shiny

Trait Statistics:	STR	SPD	INT	AGI	CON	MYS	SML	CHA
Rating:	1	2	3	3	1	1	2	2

Pursuit stats:	DV (to spot)	¬FD	DV (to flee)	Move	Hit Points
	6	6	3	2	15

Porcupine

Description: Available as a playable Non-rabbit species; profession: Guardian; primary trait: CON. Porcupines are unmistakable, with the back and tail covered with long white quills. The quills are hollow hairs with sharp, barbed points that imbed in the skin of an attacker. They eat twigs, roots, and other vegetation.

Habits: Porcupines are excellent climbers, but neither fast nor agile in trees. Although a Porcupine cannot actually throw quills, it can position its body and rapidly shift position to make it seem as if the quills actually leapt off its body.

Special Ability: Bristle; Climb Trees; Throw Quills; Provide Antibiotic

Trait Statistics:	STR	SPD	INT	AGI	CON	MYS	SML	CHA
Rating:	2	1	2	1	3	2	2	2

Pursuit stats:	DV (to spot)	¬FD	DV (to flee)	Move	Hit Points
	6	3	2	1	45

Vole

Description: Voles are tiny rodents (30 grams) akin to mice, with rounded heads and shorter tails. Also known as meadow mice or field mice, Voles are commonly found in grassland habitats where they maintain a network of crisscrossing trails within their home range. Voles have a very high reproductive potential, which compensates for their popularity among many predators.

Habits: Voles may be active day or night, although they are mostly nocturnal in summer and diurnal in winter. Unlike most small mammals, both parents care for young, and adult voles can exhibit empathy for others. This high innate empathy is the source of their main special ability.

Special Ability: Serenity

Trait Statistics:	STR	SPD	INT	AGI	CON	MYS	SML	CHA
Rating:	1	2	1	2	3	1	2	2

Pursuit stats:	DV (to spot)	¬FD	DV (to flee)	Move	Hit Points
	8	6	2	1	10

Grubbers: Animals that Dig or Forage in the Ground

This grouping is a hodgepodge taxonomically, including unrelated animals that share a common habit of digging or nosing about in the ground or leaf litter. Most have a very highly-developed sense of smell. They speak the language of Grubbers.

Armadillo

Description: Available as a playable Non-rabbit species; profession: Trader; primary trait: SML. Armadillos are small to medium-sized mammals (5 kilograms). Armadillos are unique in being equipped with plates of armor consisting of hair and scale-covered bone that covers their head, back, and sides. When disturbed, they can roll up nearly into a ball to greatly reduce the risk of injury. Armadillos also are reproductively unique in producing identical quadruplets in every pregnancy. Armadillos are most common in woodland habitats where they forage, mostly by smell, for ants, termites, grubs, and worms. They have weak eyesight and are easily surprised.

Habits: Armadillos are weak swimmers, but are unafraid of water for two unusual abilities: (a) they can walk underwater; and (b) they can inflate gaps under their armor to create a raft. When surprised, Armadillos reflexively jump 1–2 meters straight up.

Special Ability: Roll Up; Armor; Find Hidden; Walk Underwater; Raft; immune to disease & pests

Trait Statistics:	STR	SPD	INT	AGI	CON	MYS	SML	CHA
Rating:	1	2	1	2	2	2	3	2

Pursuit stats:	DV (to spot)	¬FD	DV (to flee)	Move	Hit Points
	8	3	2	2	15

Javelina

Description: Also known as a Peccary or Skunk Pig, Javelinas are distant cousins to Pigs that live in arid regions of the Southwest. They bear a strong resemblance to pigs, albeit smaller (20 kilograms) with a leaner body build. The upper jaw is equipped with short, straight canine teeth, the tusks that are used to crush seeds and strip rinds from fruits. Javelinas are omnivores, foraging for roots, herbs, fruit, and insects. They have relatively poor vision, but have an excellent sense of smell.

Habits: The tusks serve as effective weapons in a defensive bite or Gore. Javelinas are social and form small herds. They rub each other with a strong, distinctive scent mark that can be detected dozens of meters away.

Special Ability: Tusk Gore

Trait Statistics:	STR	SPD	INT	AGI	CON	MYS	SML	CHA
Rating:	4	3	4	2	12	2	3	1

Pursuit stats:	DV (to spot)	¬FD	DV (to flee)	Move	Hit Points
	6	6	3	6	60

Mole

Description: A tiny fossorial mammal (75 grams) with gray or black fur and huge, oversized forepaws with strong claws for digging. Moles live an underground existence, digging both deep, permanent tunnels and temporary foraging tunnels through loose earth. They are active day or night as they search for earthworms. Excess soil is pushed to the surface, creating molehills. The eyes are tiny, with fused eyelids, useful only for distinguishing light and dark. They rely entirely on smell, hearing, and sensitivity to minute vibrations in the soil that they can sense with sensory hairs on their snout and tail.

Habits: Moles are voracious eaters, consuming nearly half their own body weight each day. They can dig burrows very quickly, especially in loose soil, but the tunnels tend to fill with loose dirt as they progress rather than remaining as open passageways.

Special Ability: Fast Burrow

Trait Statistics:	STR	SPD	INT	AGI	CON	MYS	SML	CHA
Rating:	1	1	1	1	1	4	4	2

Pursuit stats:	DV (to spot)	¬FD	DV (to flee)	Move	Hit Points
	8	6	3	1	10

Opossum

Description: Available as a playable Non-rabbit species; profession: Shaman; primary trait: MYS. The Virginia Opossum is the one marsupial native to North America. It is the size of a House Cat (5 kilograms), with grizzled, gray fur and a white face. The tail is hairless and prehensile, contributing to arboreal habit. As a Marsupial, young are born after a very brief gestation, then raised for two more months in two pouches located along the sides of the belly. Opossums are omnivores, eating fruits, insects, garbage, worms and mice, and they have a weakness for persimmons.

Habits: Opossums are best known for "playing possum"; in other words, feigning death. When threatened, they may attempt this ruse, or meet the threat with loud hissing and open jaws (Opossums have 50 teeth). They are excellent climbers, gripping limbs with all four feet and tail. They also have an excellent sense of smell, good hearing, but poor eyesight.

Special Ability: Feign Death; Rapid Breeding; Determine Function; Implant Thoughts

Trait Statistics:	STR	SPD	INT	AGI	CON	MYS	SML	CHA
Rating:	2	1	1	2	2	3	2	2

Pursuit stats:	DV (to spot)	¬FD	DV (to flee)	Move	Hit Points
	6	6	3	1	35

Pig

Description: Pigs are domestic animals derived from wild pigs in Europe. In North America, pigs that have escaped domestication and become feral thrive in woodlands of the Southeast. Feral pigs are sometimes called Razorbacks. They can grow to large size (75 kilograms). They are omnivores, eating vegetation, crops, acorns and other mast, frogs, turtles, eggs, and ground-nesting birds. They have an outstanding sense of smell and high intelligence.

Habits: Feral Pigs are equipped with curved tusks that can cause serious damage by Goring. Pigs are especially good at finding and identifying various fungi, including usable herbs.

Special Ability: Tusk Gore

Trait Statistics:	STR	SPD	INT	AGI	CON	MYS	SML	CHA
Rating:	4	3	4	2	18	2	4	1

Pursuit stats:	DV (to spot)	¬FD	DV (to flee)	Move	Hit Points
	4	6	3	3	90

Wild Boar

Description: Wild Boars are not feral Pigs, but rather the wild pig native to Europe and introduced to North America. They are massively built (150 kilograms) muscular animals with overdeveloped shoulders and underdeveloped hindquarters. The upper canine teeth grow continuously, forming long tusks that curve outward and upward from the jaw. The body is covered with short, stiff bristles. Along with Mongooses, they are among the animals most resistant to snake venom.

Habits: Male Boars may be solitary, but most Boars are found in social groups. They can be as ill-tempered as Bison, and are vicious fighters.

Special Ability: Tusk Gore

Trait Statistics:	STR	SPD	INT	AGI	CON	MYS	SML	CHA
Rating:	5	4	4	4	24	2	3	1

Pursuit stats:	DV (to spot)	¬FD	DV (to flee)	Move	Hit Points
	4	6	3	5	120

Ramblers: Animals not Built for Speed or Hiding

Ramblers include Raccoons and their cousins, the Coatis (also known as Coatimundis). Both are omnivores well adapted for climbing and nosing about to find food. They speak the language of Ramblers.

Coati

Description: A relative of Raccoons from Central and South America, Coatis are smaller, with a slender build and longer tail with less prominent bands. They are notable for having an elongated snout nearly as long as the head and a partial mask that gives the appearance of spectacles. Like Raccoons, Coatis have very dexterous hands and a prodigious sense of touch and smell with the flexible snout, which is used to root through leaf litter looking for insects and grubs. They are found in woodland habitats.

Habits: Coatis are social animals almost always found in moderate to large groups that forage together. They are good climbers, eating fruit in season. Although curious and outwardly docile, they can be fierce fighters if threatened, using both Bite and Claw attacks.

Special Ability: Double Bite.

Trait Statistics:	STR	SPD	INT	AGI	CON	MYS	SML	CHA
Rating:	2	2	3	3	9	1	2	1

Pursuit stats:	DV (to spot)	¬FD	DV (to flee)	Move	Hit Points
	4	6	3	2	45

Raccoon

Description: Available as a playable Non-rabbit species; profession: Bandit; primary trait: STR. Another familiar animal that is instantly recognizable, Raccoons are distinctive with a grizzled gray-brown coat, banded tail, and black mask on a white face. They are medium-sized mammals (12 kilograms), although the largest individuals verge on Large (26 kilograms). They have extremely dexterous front paws that they use in searching and manipulating food items. They are omnivorous, preferring woodlands, farms and woodlands, but also found in swamps, coastal marshes, and subalpine forests. Raccoons met during random encounters may be vectors of the rabies virus (1d6 roll of 1).

Habits: With good vision, hearing, and smell, Raccoons depend more on their sense of touch than most other mammals. They are noted for high intelligence and curiosity. They are good climbers, seeking trees or other vertical structures if threatened. They also increase their apparent size by stance and bristling, and produce an intimidating open-mouthed growl. Generally reluctant to fight, they are capable of standing up to a larger dog. In combat, they use Bite attacks.

Special Ability: Intimidate; Intruder Mode; Double Bite; carry while walking bipedally

Trait Statistics:	STR	SPD	INT	AGI	CON	MYS	SML	CHA
Rating:	3	2	2	2	2	1	2	1

Pursuit stats:	DV (to spot)	¬FD	DV (to flee)	Move	Hit Points
	6	6	3	2	45

Hoofers: Large, Long-Legged Grazers & Browsers

Ungulates are large, long-legged, herbivorous mammals that include relatives of Deer, Sheep and Goats, Cows, Antelope, and Horses. They speak the language Hoofers.

Bison

See under **Brutes**

Bull

See under **Brutes**

Cow

Description: The archetypal farm animal, cows in B&B may be considered as typical black-and-white Holstein dairy cattle unless otherwise specified by the Adventure or the GM. They are considered Huge (500 kilograms).

Habits: Generally slow moving and docile, but can become dangerous if frightened (as by lightning or large predators).

Special Ability: Hoof-Kick; Stomp; Horn Gore

Trait Statistics:	STR	SPD	INT	AGI	CON	MYS	SML	CHA
Rating:	3	4	1	1	36	2	2	2

Pursuit stats:	DV (to spot)	¬FD	DV (to flee)	Move	Hit Points
	2	6	3	2	180

Deer

Description: Two species of deer occupy eastern and western halves of North America: White-Tailed Deer in the east, and Mule Deer in the west. Although smaller and more gracile than cows, they also are considered Huge (100 kilograms). Males bear antlers that are shed and regrown each year. They prefer woodland, but can be found in any habitat.

Habits: Deer may be found alone or in larger herds. They are not aggressive, but can defend themselves with hoof and antlers.

Special Ability: Hoof-Kick; Stomp; Horn (Antler) Gore

Trait Statistics:	STR	SPD	INT	AGI	CON	MYS	SML	CHA
Rating:	2	4	2	2	20	1	2	2

Pursuit stats:	DV (to spot)	¬FD	DV (to flee)	Move	Hit Points
	4	8	3	7	100

Elk

Description: Elk, also known as Wapiti, are a much larger version of Deer (350 kilograms). They have a more robust, muscular appearance. Like Deer, males bear antlers that are shed and regrown each year. They also favor forest and subalpine habitats.

Habits: Elk also can be found as solitary individuals or in larger herds. Generally harmless, Elk can be formidable when defending themselves or calves, using hooves and antlers. Elk bugling can be heard for miles.

Special Ability: Hoof-Kick; Stomp; Horn (Antler) Gore

Trait Statistics:	STR	SPD	INT	AGI	CON	MYS	SML	CHA
Rating:	3	4	2	2	32	1	2	2

Pursuit stats:	DV (to spot)	¬FD	DV (to flee)	Move	Hit Points
	2	8	3	7	160

Goat

Description: Goats are domesticated animals bred for meat and milk. Rams can be quite large (70 kilograms). Both males and females are distinguished by short horns that generally curve backward, but in some breeds may twist in a variety of directions. Horns contribute to their favored means of self-defense: butting with the head.

Habits: Domestic goats are curious and agile, and generally harmless. They are able to balance on narrow footholds, allowing them to climb some trees and even fences. They are generally maintained in small flocks on farms, although goatherds may tend flocks in grassland habitats.

Special Ability: Hoof-Kick; Butt

Trait Statistics:	STR	SPD	INT	AGI	CON	MYS	SML	CHA
Rating:	2	3	2	2	18	1	2	2

Pursuit stats:	DV (to spot)	¬FD	DV (to flee)	Move	Hit Points
	2	8	3	6	90

Horse

Description: Horses are domesticated animals commonly found on farms and ranches. They also occur as Wild Horses, most of which originally derived from Spanish stock when they colonized the New World. Horses are long-legged grazers, but only distantly related to other Hoofers (cattle, deer, sheep or goats). Uniquely among all animals, they may be encountered carrying Humans (Ranchers).

Habits: Horses are generally peaceful grazers. Some may permit a small animal to ride upon their backs. But some can suddenly decide to chase and stomp small animals for no apparent reason. Their attitude can be determined by a CHA skill check against any PC that approaches.

Special Ability: Hoof-Kick; Stomp

Trait Statistics:	STR	SPD	INT	AGI	CON	MYS	SML	CHA
Rating:	3	5	2	2	36	1	2	3

Pursuit stats:	DV (to spot)	¬FD	DV (to flee)	Move	Hit Points
	2	8	3	8	180

Moose

Description: The largest members of the deer family (400 kilograms), Moose are truly huge, impressive animals. They can be quickly distinguished from Elk by a darker brown coloration and a distinctive, bulbous muzzle. Males bear antlers with broad, flat blades. Moose favor montane forests and marshes, especially near beaver ponds, where they forage for aquatic vegetation.

Habits: Moose generally are encountered alone or in small groups. Although they can seem placid, they can quickly become aggressive and are formidable fighters, using hooves and antlers.

Special Ability: Hoof-Kick; Stomp; Horn (Antler) Gore

Trait Statistics:	STR	SPD	INT	AGI	CON	MYS	SML	CHA
Rating:	4	3	2	3	34	1	2	2

Pursuit stats:	DV (to spot)	¬FD	DV (to flee)	Move	Hit Points
	2	8	3	6	170

Mountain Goat

Description: Mountain Goats are wild relatives of domestic Goats. Generally found only in mountain regions, they are larger than domestic Goats (100 kilograms), with shaggy white fur. They also have short, sharp horns that bend backward.

Habits: Mountain Goats are surefooted on rocky slopes, steep cliffs, and other places with treacherous footing. Billy goats (the males) can be quite aggressive, chasing or attacking without apparent reason.

Special Ability: Hoof-Kick; Butt

Trait Statistics:	STR	SPD	INT	AGI	CON	MYS	SML	CHA
Rating:	3	3	2	3	20	1	2	2

Pursuit stats:	DV (to spot)	¬FD	DV (to flee)	Move	Hit Points
	2	8	3	6	100

Pronghorn

Description: Pronghorn, which are widely and erroneously called antelope, are native to North America. They are the size of small deer (50 kilograms), with a tawny coat and distinctive white rump patch. The face is long and straight, with bold black and white markings, and the eyes are high on the head. Males and females have horns that consist of a tough sheath over a bony core, and thus is neither a true horn like cattle nor an antler like deer. Pronghorn can be found on open prairie and arid brushlands.

Habits: Pronghorn gather in mixed-sex herds that break into smaller groups in spring. They are built for running and can achieve speeds up to 90 kilometers/hour while negotiating uneven ground covered with bushes. (It is likely second only to Cheetahs in running speed.) They are more likely to avoid a fight than stand their ground.

Special Ability: Hoof-Kick; Stomp; Horn Gore

Trait Statistics:	STR	SPD	INT	AGI	CON	MYS	SML	CHA
Rating:	2	6	2	2	16	1	2	2

Pursuit stats:	DV (to spot)	¬FD	DV (to flee)	Move	Hit Points
	2	8	3	10	80

Sheep

Description: Sheep are a domesticated animal bred primarily for wool, but also for meat and milk. They are easily recognized by their thick wooly coat. Breeds vary greatly, but Sheep can be quite large (120 kilograms). Most domestic sheep are polled, lacking horns.

Habits: Domestic sheep are docile. Although they can Butt, they lack the natural armaments of Goats. When threatened, they are highly likely to cluster more tightly together in a flock and flee.

Special Ability: Hoof-Kick; Butt

Trait Statistics:	STR	SPD	INT	AGI	CON	MYS	SML	CHA
Rating:	1	3	1	1	18	1	2	2

Pursuit stats:	DV (to spot)	¬FD	DV (to flee)	Move	Hit Points
	2	8	3	6	90

Bats

Bats are one of the largest orders of mammals in species diversity, despite the fact that we are seldom aware of their presence. Bats are classified into two principal taxonomic groups: the microbats (Microchiroptera) and megabats (Megachiroptera). Nearly all of the microbats are small, nocturnal, insect-eating animals. In contrast, the megabats can be quite large, with fox-like faces, varied activity patterns, and food habits that include eating fruits and nectar. They all speak in the ultrasonic language of Bats (which no rabbit can speak).

Brown Bat

Description: A typical microbat, active in the evening as it hunts for moths and other flying insects. The Big Brown Bat, which is large for a microbat, weighs less than 30 grams.

Habits: Brown Bats are not hostile, and do not defend territories or roosting sites. They typically spend the day quietly roosting in a cave, tree hollow, or other dark cavity. Some may be host to the rabies virus (1d6 roll of 1), in which case they may attempt to bite if disturbed.

Special Ability: Echolocate

Trait Statistics:	STR	SPD	INT	AGI	CON	MYS	SML	CHA
Rating:	1	4	1	1	1	3	1	1

Pursuit stats:	DV (to spot)	¬FD	DV (to flee)	Move	Hit Points
	6	8	3	6	10

Fruit Bat

Description: Fruit Bats are a typical megabat, with large eyes and fox-like faces. Although not dangerous, they can be intimidating, with meter-long wingspans and weight nearly that of a rabbit (1 kilogram or more). They also may be a disease vector for rabies (1d6 roll of 1).

Habits: Fruit Bats typically are active just before and after sunset, gathering at fruit trees and berry bushes. Although most megabats do not apparently rely on ultrasound for navigation in darkness, echolocation has been reported in a few species so is included here.

Special Ability: Echolocate

Trait Statistics:	STR	SPD	INT	AGI	CON	MYS	SML	CHA
Rating:	1	4	2	1	2	2	2	1

Pursuit stats:	DV (to spot)	¬FD	DV (to flee)	Move	Hit Points
	4	8	3	6	15

Perchers: Songbirds and Their Relatives

Passerines, or Songbirds, make up about half of the avian species in the world. Nearly all are small, the largest being Ravens (listed under Raptors for their predatory habits). Many eat insects or seeds, although some specialize in finding fruits or other vegetation, and a few prey on reptiles, small mammals, and other birds. Most also display vocal communication; songs are used to advertise territories, while other calls can maintain flock cohesion, call attention to food, or sound the alarm that a predator is near. They speak the language of Perchers.

Blackbird

Description: The plumage of Blackbirds may be all black or, as in the familiar Red-Winged Blackbird, display bold patches of red feathers on the shoulders. With straight, sharp beaks, they probe under leaves and other obstacles for hidden insects. On territories, male blackbirds perch on prominent posts — saplings or bushes, or cattails in marshes — where they display and keep watch.

Habits: Blackbirds are notorious for harassing raptors, a behavior known as mobbing, in which they chase, dive-bomb, and pull feathers until the hawk or owl leaves the area. They also have a distinctive whistle used as an Alarm Call.

Special Ability: Alarm Call

Trait Statistics:	STR	SPD	INT	AGI	CON	MYS	SML	CHA
Rating:	1	3	3	1	1	1	1	3

Pursuit stats:	DV (to spot)	¬FD	DV (to flee)	Move	Hit Points
	4	8	3	12	10

Blue Jay

Description: Although many species of Jay are in North America, the Jay in B&B is modeled after the Steller's Jay of the western forests. They have distinctive blue plumage that grades to nearly black at the head and feathered crest. Jays eat insects, fruits and seeds, and relish mast crops, collecting acorns and pine nuts and storing them in caches.

Habits: Jays have a variety of vocalizations, including an Alarm Call to warn of predators. They also can effectively mimic the calls of raptors, especially Red-Tailed Hawks, causing other birds and small mammals to run for shelter.

Special Ability: Alarm Call

Trait Statistics:	STR	SPD	INT	AGI	CON	MYS	SML	CHA
Rating:	1	3	4	1	1	1	1	3

Pursuit stats:	DV (to spot)	¬FD	DV (to flee)	Move	Hit Points
	4	8	3	12	10

Crow

Description: The American Crow can be found throughout the United States and southern Canada. It is all black, much larger than a Blackbird, but with a more slender build and less-prominent beak than a Raven. They are omnivores and opportunists, as comfortable searching for food in woodland and farms as in the suburbs.

Habits: Crows are monogamous, but gather in huge flocks to roost at night (and probably to share information about food sources). They are capable of delivering a serious peck to vulnerable areas such as the eyes, but are not a threat to a healthy rabbit.

Special Ability: Peck Eyes

Trait Statistics:	STR	SPD	INT	AGI	CON	MYS	SML	CHA
Rating:	2	5	5	2	2	3	1	4

Pursuit stats:	DV (to spot)	¬FD	DV (to flee)	Move	Hit Points
	4	8	3	12	15

Magpie

Description: A black-and-white relative of Crows and Jays with a long iridescent tail. Generally prefers open habitats, including farms and suburbs. An opportunistic omnivore like Crows, and a carrion-eater like Ravens.

Habits: Noted for their intelligence, Magpies are the Raven-equivalent among Neutral animals. Like Ravens, Magpies are language experts. Their native language is Perchers, but they also can converse in Rabbit, Chatters, Nibblers, Dogs, Cats, and one other language for each age above Sub-Adult (determined by GM).

Special Ability: Shiny

Trait Statistics:	STR	SPD	INT	AGI	CON	MYS	SML	CHA
Rating:	1	4	5	1	2	2	1	4

Pursuit stats:	DV (to spot)	¬FD	DV (to flee)	Move	Hit Points
	4	8	3	12	15

Pigeon

Description: The Pigeon, or Rock Dove, is an introduced species to North America and familiar resident of urban and suburban areas. They nest on cliffs and rock ledges in the wild, but find rooftops and window ledges more than adequate in cities. Although seed and fruit-eaters in the wild, Pigeons subsist on scrounging for garbage near human habitation.

Habits: Pigeons gather and forage in noisy flocks, with much cooing and loud wing-clapping when they take flight. They are acrobatic in flight.

Special Ability: none

Trait Statistics:	STR	SPD	INT	AGI	CON	MYS	SML	CHA
Rating:	1	3	1	1	1	1	1	1

Pursuit stats:	DV (to spot)	¬FD	DV (to flee)	Move	Hit Points
	4	8	3	12	15

Robin

Description: The American Robin is a thrush with a brown back and red-orange breast. Living almost exclusively on earthworms, Robins are familiar fixtures on lawns and grassy meadows, where they can be seen cocking their heads to the side to listen for worms.

Habits: Robins are very good at finding and collecting earthworms, which might be used in trade with other animals.

Special Ability: none

Trait Statistics:	STR	SPD	INT	AGI	CON	MYS	SML	CHA
Rating:	1	3	2	1	1	1	1	2

Pursuit stats:	DV (to spot)	¬FD	DV (to flee)	Move	Hit Points
	4	8	3	12	10

Sparrow

Description: Sparrows are small seed-eating birds, generally brown or gray in coloration. There are many native species, and one important introduced species: House Sparrows (also known as English Sparrows).

Habits: Sparrows often gather in flocks to forage, but pair off to breed. Harmless, they can add more eyes and ears to spot enemies.

Special Ability: none

Trait Statistics:	STR	SPD	INT	AGI	CON	MYS	SML	CHA
Rating:	1	1	1	1	1	1	1	1

Pursuit stats:	DV (to spot)	¬FD	DV (to flee)	Move	Hit Points
	4	8	3	12	10

Woodpecker

Description: Woodpeckers are not songbirds, but are listed with them for their similar size and general appearance. Woodpeckers vary in size, from small Downy Woodpeckers to the probably extinct Ivory-Billed Woodpecker. Many have black-and-white plumage with patches of red on the head or breast. The Woodpecker of B&B is modeled after the Pileated Woodpecker, which is nearly the size of a crow, with a black body, white neck and face stripe, and bright red crest. They may be found in woodlands.

Habits: Pileated Woodpeckers drill and tear bark from trees in search of grubs. They have a loud call that sounds like something more appropriate in a jungle, and loud drumming on hollow logs or other resonant objects (rain gutters, metal rooftops). Woody Woodpecker was inspired by the Pileated.

Special Ability: Drill Wood

Trait Statistics:	STR	SPD	INT	AGI	CON	MYS	SML	CHA
Rating:	1	2	1	1	1	1	1	1

Pursuit stats:	DV (to spot)	¬FD	DV (to flee)	Move	Hit Points
	4	8	3	12	15

Strutters: Turkeys and Other Ground Birds

Heavy-bodied, ground-feeding birds that include a number of species subsequently domesticated and bred for meat or eggs. Collectively known as Galliform birds ("chicken-like"), they are called Strutters here because cocks typically show dramatic displays and courtship rituals when trying to attract females. Most species are polygamous, with a single cock defending a harem of hens from all rivals. Although all can fly, domesticated forms fly poorly and even wild Strutters typically fly only for a few hundred meters if startled. They speak the language of Strutters.

Chicken

Description: Chickens are the domesticated form of the Red Junglefowl native to southeast Asia. Chickens are a fixture on most farms, raised for their meat and eggs. They feed on seeds and insects, and "chicken scratch."

Habits: Most likely encountered while scratching around on the ground for bits of food. Hens are harmless, but Cocks brandish sharp spurs on their legs and can be quite aggressive, attacking with both beak (Bite) and spurs (Kick).

Special Ability: none

Trait Statistics:	STR	SPD	INT	AGI	CON	MYS	SML	CHA
Rating:	2	1	1	1	1	1	1	1

Pursuit stats:	DV (to spot)	¬FD	DV (to flee)	Move	Hit Points
	4	8	3	12	25

Grouse

Description: Sage Grouse are quite large, but Ruffed Grouse (the model for B&B) are small but chunky birds about twice the size of a Quail. Grouse have mottled, dark brown plumage that provides good camouflage in the forest habitats they prefer.

Habits: Grouse can be heard foot-drumming on hollow logs in Spring — their way to attract a mate. They often may be seen alone or in small groups, seldom in large coveys like Quail. When startled, they erupt into sudden flight, often startling any observer who might have been unaware of their presence.

Special Ability: none

Trait Statistics:	STR	SPD	INT	AGI	CON	MYS	SML	CHA
Rating:	1	1	1	1	1	1	1	1

Pursuit stats:	DV (to spot)	¬FD	DV (to flee)	Move	Hit Points
	8	8	3	12	15

Pheasant

Description: Ring-Necked Pheasants are introduced gamebirds in North America. Cocks are readily recognized by an iridescent blue-green head, bright red facial patch, golden feathers flecked with black, and long tail plumes. Females are mottled brown, with shorter tails. They feed and nest on the ground, and seldom fly unless flushed. They are common in open woodlands and grasslands.

Habits: Pheasants are notorious for taking flight without planning ahead, causing them to crash into fences, trees, or rivers. Generally harmless, although Cocks are armed with spurs on their legs.

Special Ability: none

Trait Statistics:	STR	SPD	INT	AGI	CON	MYS	SML	CHA
Rating:	2	1	1	2	2	1	1	1

Pursuit stats:	DV (to spot)	¬FD	DV (to flee)	Move	Hit Points
	6	8	3	12	25

Quail

Description: Quail are the smallest of the Strutters, about the weight of a Magpie, but with a stocky body and short tail. Quail are gray and brown, with white speckles, a black face mask, and a head plume or topknot that dangles forward.

Habits: Quail are often seen standing as sentinels on fenceposts or prominent rocks as a larger covey forages nearby. They may break into flight if flushed, but usually try to run away as something approaches.

Special Ability: none

Trait Statistics:	STR	SPD	INT	AGI	CON	MYS	SML	CHA
Rating:	1	1	1	1	1	1	1	1

Pursuit stats:	DV (to spot)	¬FD	DV (to flee)	Move	Hit Points
	6	8	3	12	15

Turkey

Description: Turkeys are the largest of the Galliform birds, with wild Turkeys about 5 kilograms and domesticated varieties up to 35 kilograms. Wild Turkeys favor woodlands, where they prefer mast crops (acorns, other nuts) in addition to a variety of insects in their diet. Like roosters, Tom Turkeys have sharp spurs on their legs.

Habits: As with Chickens, hens are relatively harmless, but Toms can be aggressive and inflict damage with their spurs. Wild Turkeys have a reputation for being wary and difficult to hunt.

Special Ability: none

Trait Statistics:	STR	SPD	INT	AGI	CON	MYS	SML	CHA
Rating:	2	1	1	3	3	1	1	1

Pursuit stats:	DV (to spot)	¬FD	DV (to flee)	Move	Hit Points
	4	8	3	12	35

Waders: Waterfowl and Wading Birds

This is a hodgepodge grouping including waterfowl such as ducks and geese, seabirds such as Gulls, and conventional waders such as Killdeer. The feature that unites them is their favored habitat, which is in or near standing water (pond, marsh, river or lake). They speak the language of Waders.

Duck

Description: The most familiar duck, and ancestor to domestic ducks, Mallards can be found across North America from ponds in city parks to estuaries and marshes to wilderness beaver ponds. Drakes display a distinctive iridescent green head, chestnut breast, and gray-and-black plumage on the wings and body. Females are mottled brown. Mallards may feed on seeds or insects on land, or dabble for aquatic plants while swimming. They seldom dive, unlike some other ducks.

Habits: Ducks are friendly and curious, but also cautious and defensive near the nest. They are excellent swimmers and strong fliers.

Special Ability: Swim

Trait Statistics:	STR	SPD	INT	AGI	CON	MYS	SML	CHA
Rating:	1	2	2	1	1	1	1	2

Pursuit stats:	DV (to spot)	¬FD	DV (to flee)	Move	Hit Points
	4	8	3	12	20

Goose

Description: Geese share many of the same qualities as ducks. The Canada Goose, the most common wild goose in North America, is a large bird (5 kilograms) with gray body, black head and body, and white patch that extends from the chin to the ear. They feed largely on grain and other vegetation, although insects also are taken. Like other waterfowl, they are migratory, and can be recognized when flying overhead by loud honking and V-formations.

Habits: Geese are monogamous and remain in family groups through most of the year. Adults can be very aggressive around the nest, chicks, or just of the family group, and attack by Biting and beating with the wings (treat like a blunt Claw attack).

Special Ability: Swim

Trait Statistics:	STR	SPD	INT	AGI	CON	MYS	SML	CHA
Rating:	3	2	2	3	3	1	1	2

Pursuit stats:	DV (to spot)	¬FD	DV (to flee)	Move	Hit Points
	4	8	3	12	35

Gull

Description: There are many species of gulls. Some live on seacoasts, others inland. One of the most common, seen in both settings across North America, is the Ring-Billed Gull, the model for Gulls in B&B. Gulls are highly adaptable omnivores. Different individuals may specialize in fishing, collecting earthworms, foraging for insects, scavenging through garbage, begging from humans, or stealing from other birds.

Habits: Gulls nest in large colonies, often on islands. They are intelligent and highly manipulative, turning over rocks and other objects as they search for food. Gulls may wait by refuse bins for humans to bring out garbage. Or they may seize clams and drop them from a height to crack shells. They are not ordinarily aggressive, but like Geese, can bite and beat an adversary with their wings.

Special Ability: Swim

Trait Statistics:	STR	SPD	INT	AGI	CON	MYS	SML	CHA
Rating:	2	3	3	3	2	1	1	2

Pursuit stats:	DV (to spot)	¬FD	DV (to flee)	Move	Hit Points
	4	8	3	12	20

Killdeer

Description: Although there are many wading birds, ranging from tiny sandpipers to large curlews and yellowlegs, the most familiar is likely the Killdeer. Killdeer are small, about the size of a Robin, with sand-colored back, white neck, and two distinctive black bands across the chest and neck. They frequent puddles, stream edges, rocky shorelines and meadows, where they forage for worms and other invertebrate prey.

Habits: Killdeer take their name from their distinctive vocal cry, "Kill Deer." They also are noteworthy in their habit to feign injury to draw a potential enemy away from the nest. The "nest" is little more than a scrape in gravel, with eggs camouflaged to look like pebbles. The Killdeer holds a wing down as if broken and cries plaintively as it limps farther and farther from the nest. Although they may look like an easy target for a predator, they are seldom caught during this act.

Special Ability: Feign Injury

Trait Statistics:	STR	SPD	INT	AGI	CON	MYS	SML	CHA
Rating:	1	2	2	1	1	3	1	3

Pursuit stats:	DV (to spot)	¬FD	DV (to flee)	Move	Hit Points
	4	8	3	12	10

Coldies: Reptiles and Amphibians

Reptiles and Amphibians are terrestrial vertebrates that are popularly known as "cold-blooded" animals (even though reptiles, in particular, are very good at using behavior to regulate their body temperature). Most are small, innocuous animals, which may have unusual abilities that could be of interest to an imaginative rabbit. They speak the language of Coldies.

Box Turtle

Description: A Box Turtle resembles a true Tortoise in appearance and habit. They are terrestrial, found in grassland, brushland, and semi-desert habitats. They have a strongly dome-shaped shell that affords complete withdrawal for protection. Box Turtles are omnivorous, eating any insect or other invertebrate it can catch.

Habits: Box Turtles are slow moving, relying on their Shell Armor for protection. They are effective diggers, excavating shallow, straight burrows that are often occupied by other animals.

Special Ability: Turtle Shell Armor — Any attack that hits the Tortoise incurs a damage reduction of 8 HP. Thus, any attack directed at a Tortoise must deliver 9 or more HP of damage or it has no effect.

Trait Statistics:	STR	SPD	INT	AGI	CON	MYS	SML	CHA
Rating:	1	1	1	1	5	1	1	1

Pursuit stats:	DV (to spot)	¬FD	DV (to flee)	Move	Hit Points
	6	6	4	1	25

Frog

Description: Frogs vary from tiny Treefrogs to great Bullfrogs. The frogs of B&B are modeled after Bullfrogs, although GMs may want to include other frogs for specific encounters. Bullfrogs are the largest frog in North America (0.5 kilogram; 15 centimeters long), with a large head and olive green coloration. Males have much larger tympani (eardrums) than females. It is native to eastern North America, but widely introduced through western states, where it frequents ponds, marshes and lakes. They are aggressive predators, feeding on other frogs, nestling birds, and mice as well as insects.

Habits: Bullfrogs are ambush predators, seizing prey with a leap and snap of their jaws. They are strong swimmers and noteworthy jumpers (up to 10 times their body length).

Special Ability: Dive Underwater

Trait Statistics:	STR	SPD	INT	AGI	CON	MYS	SML	CHA
Rating:	1	3	1	1	1	1	1	1

Pursuit stats:	DV (to spot)	¬FD	DV (to flee)	Move	Hit Points
	6	6	4	1	10

Garter Snake

Description: A harmless, medium-sized snake (1.2 meters) recognized by yellow stripes running the length of its brown or green body. They are not poisonous, although their saliva may be toxic to amphibians. They hunt insects, slugs, and are one of the few predators of Rough-skinned Newts, which are extremely toxic.

Habits: Garter Snakes spend the winter in massive aggregations that may contain hundreds or even thousands of snakes. Swarms also form when many males are attracted to a single female. The females carry eggs inside their bodies, giving birth to live young. Garter Snakes are excellent swimmers, and often are called Water Snakes.

Special Ability: none

Trait Statistics:	STR	SPD	INT	AGI	CON	MYS	SML	CHA
Rating:	1	2	1	1	1	1	2	1

Pursuit stats:	DV (to spot)	¬FD	DV (to flee)	Move	Hit Points
	8	6	4	2	10

Newt

Description: Newts are salamanders that are semi-aquatic, spending some time on land and much of their time in water. The Rough-Skinned Newt is a common example, with a chocolate brown back and bright orange belly. It can be found near shore or lying on the bottom of a pond or shallow lake. They are best known as one of the most toxic animals on the planet, containing a form of tetrodotoxin (same as Puffer Fish) in their skin. This neurotoxin blocks neural transmission, causing paralysis and asphyxiation. To advertise this defensive weapon, newts have a distinctive aposematic display where they curl their tail overhead and flop on one side, showing off the bright orange color of their undersides.

Habits: Slow-moving on land, but good swimmers, using an undulating movement of the body and tail for propulsion.

Special Ability: Poisonous Skin — If bitten, toxins in the newt's skin inflict 2d6 HP damage per hour for 6 hours. DV=12 for toxin resistance check, which if successful, reduces poison damage by half.

Trait Statistics:	STR	SPD	INT	AGI	CON	MYS	SML	CHA
Rating:	1	1	1	1	1	2	1	1

Pursuit stats:	DV (to spot)	¬FD	DV (to flee)	Move	Hit Points
	8	6	4	1	10

Pond Turtle

Description: A semi-aquatic turtle, including the familiar Red-Eared Slider that is commonly sold as pets. They can reach lengths up to 40 centimeters, with a shell that allows nearly complete withdrawal for protection. Turtles can be found in rivers, marshes, ponds and lakes in warmer habitats. They feed on aquatic plants.

Habits: They are slow swimmers and even slower moving out of the water, where they often can be seen basking on emergent logs.

Special Ability: Turtle Shell Armor; Dive Underwater

Trait Statistics:	STR	SPD	INT	AGI	CON	MYS	SML	CHA
Rating:	1	1	1	1	3	1	1	1

Pursuit stats:	DV (to spot)	¬FD	DV (to flee)	Move	Hit Points
	6	6	4	1	15

Racer

Description: Racers are medium-sized, fast-moving snakes (150 centimeters). They are distinguished by large eyes and black or green coloration. Active during the day, they are visual predators, moving through grassland, brushland, marsh, or suburban habitats as they search for insects, frogs, lizards, eggs, and small birds.

Habits: Racers are very fast moving, and capable of climbing bushes and small trees. They may hiss when threatened, but are more likely to flee. They are not poisonous.

Special Ability: Tree Dash

Trait Statistics:	STR	SPD	INT	AGI	CON	MYS	SML	CHA
Rating:	1	4	1	1	2	1	2	1

Pursuit stats:	DV (to spot)	¬FD	DV (to flee)	Move	Hit Points
	4	8	4	4	15

Skink

Description: Skinks are small, slender lizards with short legs (20-centimeters-long body + tail). Their smooth, slinky movement sometimes gives the appearance of a snake. Adults have alternating light and dark stripes running the length of the body and brown tails; Juveniles have bright blue tails. The tail is thought to attract the attention of attacking predators; a Skink can autotomize its tail, which continues to twitch and confuse the attacker as the Skink escapes. The tail can regenerate. Skinks prefer open habitats (Grassland, Oak Woodland, Rocky Slopes) and generally avoid deep forest.

Habits: Skinks are secretive, moving in and out of vegetation and leaf litter as they hunt for insects.

Special Ability: Tree Dash; Autotomy

Trait Statistics:	STR	SPD	INT	AGI	CON	MYS	SML	CHA
Rating:	1	3	1	1	1	1	1	1

Pursuit stats:	DV (to spot)	¬FD	DV (to flee)	Move	Hit Points
	4	6	4	3	10

Spiny Lizard

Description: A small, active lizard covered with spiny scales (20-centimeters-long body + tail). It frequents grasslands, brushlands, rocky slopes, oak woodlands, and pine forests, especially where there are prominent rocks. They are commonly seen basking in the sun on exposed rocks or fenceposts. The body and head may be gray to jet black, but the belly displays two lateral stripes of bright, iridescent blue, which are used as signals in territorial display.

Habits: Spiny Lizards are wickedly quick, seeking refuge in crevices or niches in rocks or trees. They are excellent climbers of trees and rocks. They are not poisonous (despite folklore to the contrary), but can deliver a good bite if captured.

Special Ability: Tree Dash

Trait Statistics:	STR	SPD	INT	AGI	CON	MYS	SML	CHA
Rating:	1	4	1	1	1	1	1	1

Pursuit stats:	DV (to spot)	¬FD	DV (to flee)	Move	Hit Points
	4	6	4	5	10

Toad

Description: A terrestrial relative of frogs, recognized by a brown coloration and warty skin (10 centimeters). It may be found in grassland, wet forests, oak woodland, and alpine meadows. Although terrestrial, it is never far from water. The warts on its skin are poison glands containing bufotoxin, which affects cardiovascular and neural function.

Habits: Toads are generally nocturnal. They are slow moving, progressing by walking or small hops. They may hide in burrows.

Special Ability: Poisonous Skin. If bitten, toxins in the toad's skin inflict 1d6 HP damage per hour for 3 hours. DV=8 for toxin resistance check. If licked, the toxins cause hallucinations.

Trait Statistics:	STR	SPD	INT	AGI	CON	MYS	SML	CHA
Rating:	1	1	1	1	3	1	1	1

Pursuit stats:	DV (to spot)	¬FD	DV (to flee)	Move	Hit Points
	4	6	4	1	15

Fishies: All Fish

Aquatic vertebrates, which include bony fishes and more primitive cartilaginous fishes. All obtain oxygen through gills, permitting them to stay underwater indefinitely. Fish are very diverse, but rabbits have few opportunities for encounters with them, so only a few of the most common kinds of fish are described

below. GMs are invited to expand on the list, particularly if Rabbits have interactions near intertidal or marine environments. All speak the language of Fishies.

Bass

Description: The Largemouth Bass is a large fish found in lakes with warm water (up to 11 kilograms; 75 centimeters). It is olive-green with (as its name implies) a wide mouth. They eat other fish, various invertebrates, and the occasional duckling.

Special Ability: none

Trait Statistics:	STR	SPD	INT	AGI	CON	MYS	SML	CHA
Rating:	3	3	1	3	3	1	1	1

Pursuit stats:	DV (to spot)	¬FD	DV (to flee)	Move	Hit Points
	4	4	3	2	15

Carp

Description: A freshwater fish found in ponds, shallow lakes, rivers, and marshes, where they feed on aquatic vegetation. Carp can grow quite large (40 kilograms; 120 centimeters). They are an invasive species in many habitats, where they compete with other fish and prey on fish and waterfowl. Domestic Carp include ornamental species (Koi). They also are raised in aquaculture like catfish.

Special Ability: none

Trait Statistics:	STR	SPD	INT	AGI	CON	MYS	SML	CHA
Rating:	2	2	1	2	2	1	1	1

Pursuit stats:	DV (to spot)	¬FD	DV (to flee)	Move	Hit Points
	4	4	3	2	10

Catfish

Description: Catfish are freshwater fish named for the barbels surrounding the mouth, which resemble cat whiskers. They are bottom feeders, generally preferring muddy substrates and tolerating murky water. The flattened head and barbels are adaptations for bottom feeding; the barbels aid in their sense of touch and perhaps chemical senses. Catfish also possess a strong spine in their dorsal fin, which can inflict wounds. They vary greatly in size, from 10 centimeters to more than 2 meters and 100 kilograms. The Brown Bullhead, a common species in ponds and lakes, is moderate in size (50 centimeters; 4 kilograms).

Special Ability: none

Trait Statistics:	STR	SPD	INT	AGI	CON	MYS	SML	CHA
Rating:	2	1	1	2	2	1	1	1

Pursuit stats:	DV (to spot)	¬FD	DV (to flee)	Move	Hit Points
	6	4	3	1	10

Lamprey

Description: Also known as Lamprey Eels, Lampreys are scale-less, boneless fish with a cartilaginous skeleton and a jawless sucking mouth (0.5 kilogram; 75 centimeters long). Lamprey migrate to sea as larvae, then return, like Salmon, to rivers as adults. They are carnivorous, usually considered parasitic rather than predators because they attach to the skin of other fish. They bore through the skin to suck blood, typically leaving gaping wounds that may lead to their death.

Special Ability: none

Trait Statistics:	STR	SPD	INT	AGI	CON	MYS	SML	CHA
Rating:	3	4	1	4	2	1	1	1

Pursuit stats:	DV (to spot)	¬FD	DV (to flee)	Move	Hit Points
	6	4	3	3	10

Sunfish

Description: A small fish (0.5 kilogram) related to Bass found in ponds and lakes with warm water. They prefer areas with abundant aquatic plants, where they feed on aquatic insects.

Special Ability: none

Trait Statistics:	STR	SPD	INT	AGI	CON	MYS	SML	CHA
Rating:	1	1	1	1	1	1	1	1

Pursuit stats:	DV (to spot)	¬FD	DV (to flee)	Move	Hit Points
	4	4	3	2	10

Trout

Description: Trout are fish of lakes and mountain streams with cold water. Fish in streams are generally smaller (2 kilograms) than lake fish (up to 9 kilograms). Trout that migrate to sea and return are called Steelhead and can be quite large (20 kilograms). They feed on aquatic insects and smaller fish.

Special Ability: none

Trait Statistics:	STR	SPD	INT	AGI	CON	MYS	SML	CHA
Rating:	2	4	2	3	2	1	1	1

Pursuit stats:	DV (to spot)	¬FD	DV (to flee)	Move	Hit Points
	4	4	3	3	10

Crawlies: Insects and Arthropods of All Kinds

Insects and other invertebrates are always present in all habitats and are too numerous to enumerate. The following listings include a handful of insects, arachnids, and other creepie-crawlies that might have interesting interactions with, or value to, rabbits and other player characters. GMs are encouraged to expand upon the list. All speak the language of Crawlies, which few Rabbits can master.

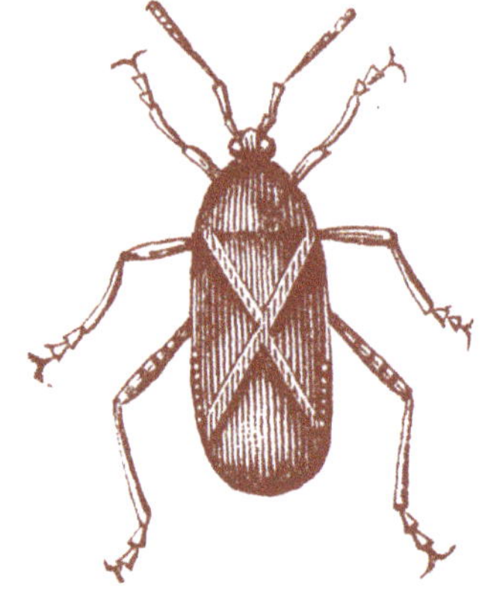

Ants

Description: Anthills may be found in any habitat. In Farm, Orchard, Grassland, Oak Woodland, or Mountain Stream, the ants are common sugar ants. They emit a foul odor when crushed, but otherwise are relatively harmless. In other habitats, you will find:

Acrobat Ant: Found in Brushlands. These ants habitually raise their abdomens over their head and thorax and can point the tip of the abdomen in almost any direction. When threatened, they release a venom from the abdomen that is toxic to other insects and noxious to other animals. Rabbits exposed to the venom incur 1d6 HP toxin damage. DV=8 for toxin resistance check.

Carpenter Ant: Found in Pine Forests, Suburbs. Large black ants that excavate galleries in wood. They are not poisonous, but have powerful jaws that deliver a painful nip. If a nest is disturbed, 1d6 ants attack and bite, for 1 HP damage each.

Fire Ant: Found in Marshes. Fire ants are aggressive ants with a red body. They are armed with a sting, and when disturbed will bite and then sting, injecting a painful toxin. If a nest is disturbed, 2d6 fire ants attack and sting, for 2 HP damage each. DV=8 for toxin resistance check, which if successful, only reduces damage top 1 HP per sting.

Harvester Ant: Found in Rocky Hillsides. Harvester ants collect seeds in hot, dry habitats. They may be red or black, and their nests may be recognized by being surrounded by an area cleared of all vegetation. Harvester Ants are armed with a sting and a very powerful venom. If a nest is disturbed, 2d6 ants attack and sting, inflicting 3 HP damage each. DV=10 for toxin resistance check, which if successful, only reduces damage to 2 HP per sting.

Habits: Harmless unless the nest is disturbed. All ants attack intruders to defend the nest.

Special Ability: Poisonous sting (some species).

Trait Statistics:	STR	SPD	INT	AGI	CON	MYS	SML	CHA
Rating:	1	1	1	1	1	1	1	1

Pursuit stats:	DV (to spot)	¬FD	DV (to flee)	Move	Hit Points
	4	2	4	1	1

Beetle

Description: Beetles come in a bewildering array of sizes, shapes, and even colors. In most habitats, rabbits are most likely to encounter ordinary black beetles. In Brushlands and Rocky Hillsides, however, they are more likely to encounter large darkling beetles, also known as "stink" beetles and "ass-in-the-air" beetles for their habit of raising the abdomen almost vertically.

Habits: Ordinary black beetles scurry away as quickly as they are discovered. Large Darkling beetles raise their abdomen, pointing it toward an intruder.

Special Ability: Noxious spray. If disturbed, the large Darkling beetle discharges a noxious chemical repellent that causes watery eyes and runny nose. The consequence of being sprayed is a brief reduction of INT Rating by −2 for 10 minutes.

Trait Statistics:	STR	SPD	INT	AGI	CON	MYS	SML	CHA
Rating:	1	1	1	1	3	1	1	1

Pursuit stats:	DV (to spot)	¬FD	DV (to flee)	Move	Hit Points
	6	2	4	1	1

Black Widow

Description: A shiny black spider with a red hourglass on the underside. Black Widows spin a tangled web to trap insect prey. They are usually found in dark, undisturbed places such as woodpiles, basements, tree cavities, or entrances to burrows or caves. They are highly toxic, causing severe pain, racing heart rate, and muscle spasms, but are rarely fatal to humans.

Habits: The Black Widow bites if its web is disturbed.

Special Ability: Poisonous bite that immediately inflicts 2d6 poison damage, with continuing 2 HP damage per hour for 12 hours. DV=6 for toxin resistance check, which if successful, limits initial injury to 1d6 HP and eliminates continuing poison damage.

Trait Statistics:	STR	SPD	INT	AGI	CON	MYS	SML	CHA
Rating:	3	1	1	1	1	1	1	1

Pursuit stats:	DV (to spot)	¬FD	DV (to flee)	Move	Hit Points
	6	2	4	1	1

Butterfly

Description: Colorful, slow-flying insects of the Order Lepidoptera. They move in a fluttering flight, often visiting flowers to collect nectar. Bright coloration of some, especially orange or red colors, often is an indication that they are toxic to eat. Their presence could be an indication of useful herbs.

Habits: Active during the day; harmless. They sometimes gather in groups at the edges of rain puddles or other wet soil, a behavior called "puddling," where they collect minerals and micronutrients.

Special Ability: none

Trait Statistics:	STR	SPD	INT	AGI	CON	MYS	SML	CHA
Rating:	1	2	1	1	1	1	1	5

Pursuit stats:	DV (to spot)	¬FD	DV (to flee)	Move	Hit Points
	2	2	4	4	1

Centipede

Description: Centipedes are voracious arthropod predators with many legs, one pair per segment of their body. Some are very fast moving; most have some kind of poisonous bite. Large Scolopendra centipedes can be up to 30 centimeters in length and capable of hunting frogs and small lizards.

Habits: Typically found in leaf litter or under logs or other objects in woodlands, brushlands, or forest habitats. They are mostly active at night.

Special Ability: Poisonous bite that immediately inflicts 1d6 poison damage, with continuing 1 HP damage per hour for 12 hours. DV=6 for toxin resistance check, which if successful, limits initial injury to 2 HP and eliminates continuing poison damage.

Trait Statistics:	STR	SPD	INT	AGI	CON	MYS	SML	CHA
Rating:	2	2	1	2	1	1	1	1

Pursuit stats:	DV (to spot)	¬FD	DV (to flee)	Move	Hit Points
	4	2	4	3	1

Cockroach

Description: A secretive insect, usually brown in color, with a flattened body. Cockroaches can fly, but usually are seen scurrying around in dark places. They may range from 2–5 centimeters in length, although giant cockroaches are known in other parts of the world nearly 10 centimeters long. They are reputed to withstand environmental extremes of heat, cold, and even radiation, but generally prefer warm, moist areas such as rotting vegetation, leaf litter, tree cavities, or dark corners of human habitations.

Habits: Cockroaches are weak fliers but fast runners and quickly scurry for cover if surprised. They can bite, but are not poisonous. Although they are not intelligent, they have an uncanny talent for finding the hidden entry into containers or lodging.

Special Ability: Find Hidden Entry

Trait Statistics:	STR	SPD	INT	AGI	CON	MYS	SML	CHA
Rating:	1	2	1	1	2	1	1	1

Pursuit stats:	DV (to spot)	¬FD	DV (to flee)	Move	Hit Points
	4	2	4	3	1

Dragonfly

Description: An insect of the Order Odonata, Dragonflies have two pairs of fixed wings that extend to the side, a slender body, and two very large compound, multifaceted eyes. They lay eggs in water, so they are usually seen in habitats near streams, ponds, marshes or lakes. They often are colored bright blue, green or red, and can be up to 10 centimeters long.

Habits: Dragonflies are excellent, acrobatic fliers that catch their prey on the wing. They have very good vision and quite wary.

Special Ability: none

Trait Statistics:	STR	SPD	INT	AGI	CON	MYS	SML	CHA
Rating:	1	4	1	1	1	1	1	2

Pursuit stats:	DV (to spot)	¬FD	DV (to flee)	Move	Hit Points
	4	2	4	8	1

Grasshopper

Description: A relative of crickets, cockroaches, and walking sticks, notable for having a greatly enlarged third pair of legs used for jumping. Grasshoppers can be quite large for insects, up to 10 centimeters long. They are voracious eaters, feeding on vegetation.

Habits: Grasshoppers can jump up to a meter. They are not social and usually live a solitary existence. Some species may undergo a rapid metamorphosis into a swarming morph, however, gathering in billions in a plague swarm that can devour crops and all other plants in their path.

Special Ability: none

Trait Statistics:	STR	SPD	INT	AGI	CON	MYS	SML	CHA
Rating:	1	3	1	1	1	1	1	1

Pursuit stats:	DV (to spot)	¬FD	DV (to flee)	Move	Hit Points
	6	4	4	2	1

Honeybees

Description: Honeybees build hives with honeycombs in hollow trees, crevices in cliffs, and sometimes human buildings.

Domesticated Honeybees also may be maintained on a Farm. Honeybees may be found in any habitat.

Habits: Honeybees are social insects that live in hives with a single queen and hundreds, sometimes thousands, of sterile workers. They are armed with a barbed sting that they use in defense of the hive. Unless the hive is threatened, they are not aggressive. If the hive is approached, roll 1d6 for number of stings. If the hive is damaged, roll an additional 3d6.

Special Ability: Poisonous sting that immediately inflicts 2 HP poison damage per sting. DV=8 for toxin resistance check, which if successful, limits initial injury to 1 HP. There is no continuing poison damage.

Trait Statistics:	STR	SPD	INT	AGI	CON	MYS	SML	CHA
Rating:	3	1	1	3	1	1	1	1

Pursuit stats:	DV (to spot)	¬FD	DV (to flee)	Move	Hit Points
	4	4	4	6	1

Millipede

Description: Herbivorous arthropods with many legs, two pairs per segment of their body. The body of a millipede is round in cross-section, unlike the flattened body of a centipede. The legs are underneath the body rather than splayed to the side, and move in waves of tiny steps, resulting in a very slow gait. Millipedes do not bite, but many can produce toxins or other chemical defenses (such as boiling cyanide), which is released when they are attacked.

Habits: If threatened, a millipede typically rolls into a tight spiral and may release chemical defenses. If eaten, treat a millipede's toxin like Poisonous Skin.

Special Ability: Poisonous Skin

Trait Statistics:	STR	SPD	INT	AGI	CON	MYS	SML	CHA
Rating:	1	1	1	1	1	1	1	1

Pursuit stats:	DV (to spot)	¬FD	DV (to flee)	Move	Hit Points
	6	2	4	1	1

Pillbug

Description: Pillbugs or Woodlice, sometimes called Sowbugs, are small arthropods related to crustaceans. They typically live in the leaf litter on the forest floor or in rotting vegetation. They feed on decaying vegetation.

Habits: When disturbed, Pillbugs roll up into a tight ball, where the exoskeleton provides a modest armor. When rolled up, they are almost perfect spheres, and might be used as play objects by young animals.

Special Ability: Roll Up

Trait Statistics:	STR	SPD	INT	AGI	CON	MYS	SML	CHA
Rating:	1	1	1	1	1	1	1	1

Pursuit stats:	DV (to spot)	¬FD	DV (to flee)	Move	Hit Points
	4	2	4	1	1

Scorpion

Description: A scorpion is an arachnid arthropod with prominent grasping pedipalps (pincers) and a segmented tail that is held in a curve above the back. The tail brandishes a sting that can deliver a potent poison. They often may be found under rocks or logs, or in rotting logs or other dark places.

Habits: Scorpions are very sensitive to vibration and can navigate well in darkness. They are usually active at night.

Special Ability: Poisonous sting that immediately inflicts 2d6 poison damage, with continuing 3 HP damage per hour for 12 hours. DV=8 for toxin resistance check, which if successful, limits initial injury to 1d6 HP and eliminates continuing poison damage.

Trait Statistics:	STR	SPD	INT	AGI	CON	MYS	SML	CHA
Rating:	6	1	1	5	1	1	1	1

Pursuit stats:	DV (to spot)	¬FD	DV (to flee)	Move	Hit Points
	8	2	4	2	1

Spider

Description: Apart from Black Widows and Tarantulas, which are listed separately, Spiders include any of the web-spinning arachnids. The typical garden spider is an Orb-weaver, producing an intricate radial web suspended between plant stalks or tree branches. Although all spiders are poisonous, most do not pose a serious threat.

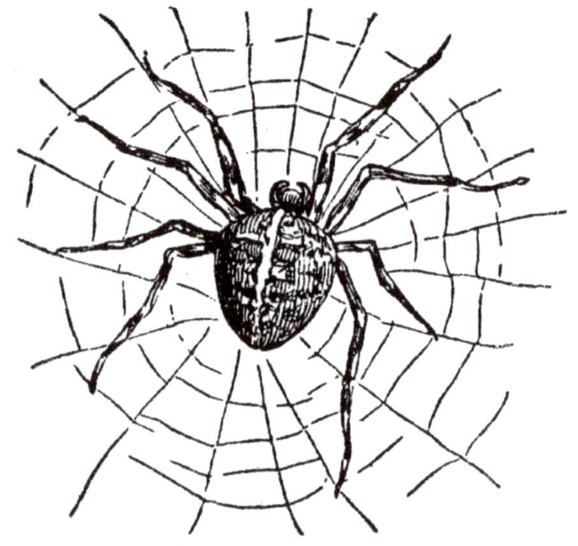

Habits: Spiders may be found in nearly all habitats. In arid regions, orb-weaving spiders are more common near water sources.

Special Ability: Poisonous bite that immediately inflicts 2 HP poison damage, with no further damage. DV=4 for toxin resistance check, which if successful, cancels any injury.

Trait Statistics:	STR	SPD	INT	AGI	CON	MYS	SML	CHA
Rating:	2	1	1	1	1	1	1	1

Pursuit stats:	DV (to spot)	¬FD	DV (to flee)	Move	Hit Points
	6	2	4	1	1

Tarantula

Description: A Tarantula is a very large terrestrial spider covered with black, brown, or red hair. They are slow-moving, taking deliberate steps with each leg. Tarantulas typically are found in dryland habitats, grasslands, and brushlands. The body may be up to 10 centimeters long, with a larger leg-span. Tarantulas have large chelicerae, which look like fangs and can deliver a poisonous bite. Although effective against their insect prey, Tarantulas are rarely aggressive.

Habits: Tarantulas are nocturnal hunters, but often can be seen wandering about in the day.

Special Ability: Poisonous bite that immediately inflicts 1d6 poison damage, with continuing 1 HP damage per hour for 12 hours. DV=6 for toxin resistance check, which if successful, limits initial injury to 2 HP and eliminates continuing poison damage.

Trait Statistics:	STR	SPD	INT	AGI	CON	MYS	SML	CHA
Rating:	6	1	1	1	1	1	1	1

Pursuit stats:	DV (to spot)	¬FD	DV (to flee)	Move	Hit Points
	4	2	4	1	1

Walking Stick

Description: A relative of Grasshoppers, Walking Sticks mimic the appearance of woody twigs, allowing them to go unnoticed. They move very slowly, often timing their movement to gusts of wind to avoid detection.

Habits: Excellent at deception, but otherwise harmless.

Special Ability: Quick Conceal

Trait Statistics:	STR	SPD	INT	AGI	CON	MYS	SML	CHA
Rating:	1	1	1	1	1	4	1	1

Pursuit stats:	DV (to spot)	¬FD	DV (to flee)	Move	Hit Points
	10	2	4	1	1

Wasps

Description: Wasps are predators and scavengers. Some nest in shallow burrows, some in nests constructed from mud, some from paper produced by chewing wood pulp. The model for Wasps in B&B are Bald Face Hornets, a particularly belligerent wasp that builds a large, multilayered paper nest. The nest, which can be as large as 50 centimeters in diameter, may be lodged in the crevice of a tree or hung openly from a tree branch. The Wasps, led by a primary queen assisted by secondary reproductives and hundreds of sterile daughters, are omnivorous, hunting other insects, consuming carrion, and scavenging refuse.

Habits: Most social wasps are vigorous in defending their nest, but Bald Faced Hornets are especially aggressive. Animals that approach the nest are vigorously attacked and stung repeatedly. In addition, they are unique in aiming at the eyes of attackers, and can squirt venom from the sting in an assailant's eyes to cause temporary blindness.

Special Ability: Poisonous sting. Wasps attack in a swarm, resulting in 2d6 stings that inflict 3 HP damage each. DV=10 for toxin resistance check, which if successful, only reduces damage to 2 HP per sting. Also, if attacked by Wasps, roll 2d6 to determine if they attempt to squirt venom in the eyes. A roll of 1 on either die indicates venom is squirted in one eye; a roll of 1 on both dice indicates temporary blindness lasting 1 hour in both eyes.

Trait Statistics:	STR	SPD	INT	AGI	CON	MYS	SML	CHA
Rating:	6	4	1	6	1	1	1	1

Pursuit stats:	DV (to spot)	¬FD	DV (to flee)	Move	Hit Points
	4	2	4	8	1

Worms

Eyeless, earless, legless invertebrates. Apart from pests and vectors of disease (e.g., Brainworms), the only worms that concern PCs are earthworms, which live in loose soil and are used as a commodity of exchange by some other animals. They have no language.

Earthworm (Nightcrawler, "Wriggler")

Description: Pink, 5–10 centimeters long, with segments along the body, Earthworms may be found burrowing in loose soil in most well-watered habitats. They may emerge at the surface after a heavy rain. They are a Prized Food item by many animals.

Special Ability: Fast Burrow

Trait Statistics:	STR	SPD	INT	AGI	CON	MYS	SML	CHA
Rating:	1	1	1	1	1	1	1	1

Pursuit stats:	DV (to spot)	¬FD	DV (to flee)	Move	Hit Points
	6	1	2	1	1

Humans

Humans are one species. But to rabbits and other animals, humans come in a bewildering range of sizes, shapes, and colors, with a staggering variety of second-skins (clothing), head-shells (hats), and other man-things (tools, machines, and other manufactured objects) at their disposal. Different classes of humans represent very different threats and opportunities when encountered by rabbits. Humans speak in jabbering vocalizations that no animal can understand.

Birdwatcher

Description: Featherless biped, with a head-shell, clumsy feet with no toes, and usually covered by a second skin that is brown or green. Often seen holding a man-thing (binoculars) to its face.

Habits: Birdwatchers pose little or no risk to rabbits. They spend most of their time looking up at trees, often holding a man-thing to their face. They may flail ineffectually if attacked.

Special Ability: none

Trait Statistics:	STR	SPD	INT	AGI	CON	MYS	SML	CHA
Rating:	3	1	10	1	20	0	0	0

Pursuit stats:	DV (to spot)	iPD	Move	Hit Points
	4	8	1	100

Boy

Description: Short, energetic, featherless biped, with fur on its head, clumsy feet with no toes, and usually covered by a second skin that is brightly colored. Often seen carrying a short stick (an actual stick) or a man-thing (action figure or toy gun).

Habits: Boys are immature humans with high levels of energy and curiosity. They pose a moderate risk to rabbits or other small animals. If they spot rabbits and can approach to within 10 meters, they may attempt to throw stones. A thrown stone hits with a standard 1d6 + AGI of the Boy vs. 1d6 + SPD of the target, inflicting 1–3 HP damage. Boys run away, vocalizing loudly, if hit for any damage.

Special Ability: Stone Throwing

Trait Statistics:	STR	SPD	INT	AGI	CON	MYS	SML	CHA
Rating:	2	1	8	2	15	0	0	0

Pursuit stats:	DV (to spot)	iPD	Move	Hit Points
	4	8	2	75

Farmer

Description: Featherless biped, with a head-shell, clumsy feet with no toes, and usually covered by a second skin that is blue or red. Often seen carrying a long stick (shotgun) or man-thing (large container).

Habits: Farmers pose a high risk to rabbits and other animals that may feed on human crops. If they spot rabbits and carry a shotgun, they may fire at distances up to 30 meters. The first shot always misses. Subsequent shots hit with a standard 1d6 + AGI of Farmer vs. 1d6 + SPD of target. Targets receive a +1 bonus to SPD if running. A hit causes 3d6 damage at 10 meters, 2d6 at 20 meters, and 1d6 at 30 meters.

Special Ability: Thunderstick (shotgun)

Trait Statistics:	STR	SPD	INT	AGI	CON	MYS	SML	CHA
Rating:	3	1	10	1	20	0	0	0

Pursuit stats:	DV (to spot)	iPD	Move	Hit Points
	4	8	1	100

Gardener

Description: Featherless biped, with long hair under a head-shell, clumsy feet with no toes, and usually covered by a second skin that is blue or red. Often seen carrying a long stick (rake or hoe) or man-thing (watering can).

Habits: Gardeners pose a moderate risk to rabbits and other small animals that may raid a garden. If they spot rabbits, they may attempt to throw rocks. A thrown stone hits with a standard 1d6 + AGI of the Gardener vs. 1d6 + SPD of the target, inflicting 1–3 HP damage. If attacked, a Gardener attempts to strike with a gardening tool up to one extra hex away from the target on a Battleboard. Hits with a garden tool inflict 1d6 damage.

Special Ability: Stone Throwing

Trait Statistics:	STR	SPD	INT	AGI	CON	MYS	SML	CHA
Rating:	3	1	10	1	20	0	0	0

Pursuit stats:	DV (to spot)	iPD	Move	Hit Points
	4	8	1	100

Girl

Description: Short, energetic, featherless biped, with fur on its head, clumsy feet with no toes, and usually covered by a second skin that is brightly colored. Often seen carrying a short stick (an actual stick) or man-thing (ball or toy doll).

Habits: Like Boys, Girls are immature humans with high levels of energy and curiosity. They pose a low risk to rabbits or other small animals. If they spot rabbits, Girls attempt to approach slowly, speaking softly, and often offering a handful of food. Girls scream if attacked, causing 1–3 hostile adults (Townie, Farmer, or Gardener) to appear.

Special Ability: none

Trait Statistics:	STR	SPD	INT	AGI	CON	MYS	SML	CHA
Rating:	2	1	8	1	15	0	0	0

Pursuit stats:	DV (to spot)	iPD	Move	Hit Points
	4	8	2	75

Hiker

Description: Featherless biped, with a head-shell, clumsy feet with no toes, and usually covered by a second skin that is brown or green. Often seen with a large hump on its back and carrying two long sticks (hiking poles).

Habits: Hikers pose low risk to rabbits. If they spot rabbits, they may stop and look. They may flail with the long sticks if attacked. Hits with a hiking pole cause 1–3 HP damage.

Special Ability: none

Trait Statistics:	STR	SPD	INT	AGI	CON	MYS	SML	CHA
Rating:	3	1	10	1	20	0	0	0

Pursuit stats:	DV (to spot)	iPD	Move	Hit Points
	4	8	1	100

Hunter

Description: Featherless biped, with a head-shell, clumsy feet with no toes, and usually covered by a second skin that is bright orange or green. Often seen carrying a long stick (rifle).

Habits: Hunters pose a very high risk to rabbits and jackrabbits, but not to other playable animals. If they spot rabbits, they may fire at distances up to 100 meters. The first shot always misses. Subsequent shots hit with a standard 1d6 + AGI of Hunter vs. 1d6 + SPD of target. Targets receive a +3 bonus to SPD if running. A hit causes 3d6 damage at all distances, with a 50% chance of being a Critical hit (attack roll of 4–6). If one rabbit is hit and immobilized, the Hunter ceases firing and attempts to carry the target away.

Special Ability: Thunderstick (rifle)

Trait Statistics:	STR	SPD	INT	AGI	CON	MYS	SML	CHA
Rating:	3	1	10	1	20	0	0	0

Pursuit stats:	DV (to spot)	iPD	Move	Hit Points
	6	8	1	100

Lumberjack

Description: Featherless biped, with a head-shell, clumsy feet with no toes, and usually covered by a second skin that is blue or red. Often seen carrying a man-thing (chainsaw or Pulaski [axe]).

Habits: Lumberjacks pose a low risk to rabbits. If they spot a rabbit, there is a small chance (1d6 roll of 1) that they throw stones. A thrown stone hits with a standard 1d6 + AGI of the Lumberjack vs. 1d6 + SPD of the target, inflicting 1–3 HP damage. If attacked, a Lumberjack attempts to strike with a carried tool. Hits with a chainsaw or Pulaski (axe) inflict 3d6 damage.

Special Ability: Stone Throwing

Trait Statistics:	STR	SPD	INT	AGI	CON	MYS	SML	CHA
Rating:	3	1	8	1	20	0	0	0

Pursuit stats:	DV (to spot)	iPD	Move	Hit Points
	4	8	1	100

Picnicker

Description: Featherless biped, with fur on its head, clumsy feet with no toes, and usually covered by a second skin that is brightly colored. Often seen carrying a bulky object (blanket or basket).

Habits: Picnickers pose low risk to rabbits. If they spot rabbits, they may stop and look. They may flail or throw objects ineffectually if attacked; 50% of thrown objects will be picnic food.

Special Ability: none

Trait Statistics:	STR	SPD	INT	AGI	CON	MYS	SML	CHA
Rating:	3	1	8	1	20	0	0	0

Pursuit stats:	DV (to spot)	iPD	Move	Hit Points
	4	8	1	100

Rancher

Description: Featherless biped, with a head-shell, clumsy feet with no toes, and usually covered by a second skin that is blue or red. Often seen carrying a long stick (rifle).

Habits: Ranchers pose moderate risk to varmints, including rabbits, jackrabbits, raccoons, porcupines, and squirrels, but not to other playable animals. If they spot rabbits, there is a 33% chance they may fire at distances up to 100 meters (1d6 roll of 1 or 2). The first shot always misses. Subsequent shots hit with a standard 1d6 + AGI of Hunter vs. 1d6 + SPD of target. Targets receive a +3 bonus to SPD if running. A hit causes 3d6 damage at all distances, with a 50% chance of being a Critical hit (attack roll of 4–6). A Rancher will not stop shooting until all rabbits are gone.

Special Ability: Thunderstick (rifle)

Trait Statistics:	STR	SPD	INT	AGI	CON	MYS	SML	CHA
Rating:	3	1	10	1	20	0	0	0

Pursuit stats:	DV (to spot)	iPD	Move	Hit Points
	4	8	1	100

Ranger

Description: Featherless biped, with a head-shell, clumsy feet with no toes, and usually covered by a second skin that is brown or green. Often seen carrying a long stick (rifle).

Habits: Rangers may be Game Wardens or Forest Rangers. Either kind of Ranger poses low risk to rabbits. If they spot rabbits, they may stop and look. If attacked, they throw part of their second skin (jacket) on the attacker to subdue it. Successful capture is determined by a 1d6 + AGI of Ranger vs. 1d6 + SPD of rabbit. Captured targets are transferred to a cage and transported away. There is a 50% chance of the rabbit escaping during the transfer to a cage (1d6 roll of 4–6).

Special Ability: Capture

Trait Statistics:	STR	SPD	INT	AGI	CON	MYS	SML	CHA
Rating:	3	1	12	1	20	0	0	0

Pursuit stats:	DV (to spot)	iPD	Move	Hit Points
	4	8	1	100

Sportsman

Description: Featherless biped, with a head-shell, clumsy feet with no toes, and usually covered by a second skin that looks like leaves. Often seen carrying a long stick (rifle or fishing pole).

Habits: Sportsmen pose either low or very high risk to rabbits. Roll 1d6 upon encountering a Sportsman: 1–3 indicates it carries a rifle; 4–6 indicates a fishing pole. A fisherman will not attack. A rifle-toting Sportsman, however, shoots any small animal, including all playable characters, if spotted. The first shot always misses. Subsequent shots hit with a standard 1d6 + AGI of Sportsman vs. 1d6 + SPD of target. Targets receive a +3 bonus to SPD if running. A hit causes 3d6 damage at all distances, with a 50% chance of being a Critical hit (attack roll of 4–6). A Sportsman will not stop shooting until all rabbits are gone.

Special Ability: Thunderstick (rifle)

Trait Statistics:	STR	SPD	INT	AGI	CON	MYS	SML	CHA
Rating:	3	1	10	1	20	0	0	0

Pursuit stats:	DV (to spot)	iPD	Move	Hit Points
	4	8	1	100

Townie

Description: Featherless biped, with fur on its head, clumsy feet with no toes, and usually covered by a second skin that is brightly colored. Often seen carrying a bulky object (shopping bag).

Habits: Picnickers pose low risk to rabbits. If they spot rabbits, they may stop and look. They may flail or throw objects ineffectually if attacked; 50% of thrown objects will be items from their shopping bag, including cans, bottles, or packaged food.

Special Ability: none

Trait Statistics:	STR	SPD	INT	AGI	CON	MYS	SML	CHA
Rating:	3	1	6	1	20	0	0	0

Pursuit stats:	DV (to spot)	iPD	Move	Hit Points
	2	8	1	100

Trapper

Description: Featherless biped, with a head-shell, clumsy feet with no toes, and usually covered by a second skin that looks like leaves. Often seen carrying a man-thing (axe or trap).

Habits: Trappers pose high risk to rabbits, but not during encounters. Their real threat stems from traps they lay. If a Trapper spots rabbits, he tries to slip away unnoticed. However, traps will be set in the immediate vicinity. The GM secretly places 1d6 traps on the appropriate Battleboard (Marsh or Pine Forest). Randomly place the party on and around one of the six numbered hexes. Rabbits must successfully leave the board at the exit arrows to move on.

Special Ability: none

Trait Statistics:	STR	SPD	INT	AGI	CON	MYS	SML	CHA
Rating:	3	1	12	1	5	0	0	0

Pursuit stats:	DV (to spot)	iPD	Move	Hit Points
	6	8	1	100

Beasts of Folklore and Legend

Tall tales, folklore, myths, and legends are replete with "fearsome critters": fantastic beasts, birds, and serpents with unusual, and sometimes magical, abilities. The following critters include a collection from North American folklore, notably from the tales of Paul Bunyan and Pecos Bill. All cultures contain references to such creatures, however, and GMs should feel free to adapt fearsome critters from other traditions, using the following examples as a guide. Legendary beasts speak a variety of different language, as specified in each description.

Agropelter

Description: The Agropelter is a medium-sized ape-like creature with a slender, wiry body and thin, whip-like arms that are strong enough to break off dead branches and bark from trees. Even during an encounter, it is seldom seen as more than a shadow.

Habits: Agropelters live exclusively in conifer forests such as pine woods, preferring trees with an abundance of dead branches. A cryptic night hunter, the Agropelter waits for prey to walk underneath its perch in a tree, then hurls branches, chunks of bark, and cones down on the unwary victim. Its preferred prey are woodpeckers, tree squirrels, and other small animals that make their homes in pine trees. But it is not above taking an occasional rabbit if one should pass under its perch. Agropelters speak the language of Chatters.

Special Ability: Stone (Branch) Throwing.

Trait Statistics:	STR	SPD	INT	AGI	CON	MYS	SML	CHA
Rating:	6	2	4	5	15	5	2	0

Pursuit stats:	DV (to spot)	iPD	Move	Hit Points
	8	8	3	75

Azeban

Description: A trickster of Native American mythology, the Azeban can be mistaken for an ordinary Raccoon. The Azeban is not dangerous or evil, but can be foolish or mischievous to the point of causing trouble for rabbits. It is most often found in open woodlands or orchards.

Habits: When encountered, the Azeban may try to trick player characters in order to obtain food, herbs, or favors. One common trick is the "Damsel-in-Distress," where a female Azeban pretends to be fleeing from a dangerous enemy and pleads for help. She may even carry an infant to bolster the ruse, but the "infant" may be a doll made from straw and pitch that can entangle a creature that offers to help, enabling the Azeban to steal herbs and other items of value. Another trick is the "Pigeon Drop," where the Azeban tries to persuade the PCs to place their herbs in a safe place (a large snail shell) along with the Azeban's herbs to protect them from Coatis, which are known to be herb thieves. If they agree, the Azeban tells the PCs to take the shell to a meeting place, but secretly switches the snail shell for an empty one, thereby stealing all their herbs. A third ploy is to secretly expose intended victims to Falseflower Dust, causing them to mistake true herbs for toxic Poisonweed (and vice versa). The Azeban then may offer to exchange Poisonweed for

true herbs or other valuable commodities. Azeban speaks the language of Ramblers.

Special Ability: Persuasion. Based on CHA Rating, the Azeban can be persuasive even against a hostile target.

Trait Statistics:	STR	SPD	INT	AGI	CON	MYS	SML	CHA
Rating:	4	3	6	6	10	4	2	7

Pursuit stats:	DV (to spot)	iPD	Move	Hit Points
	6	8	2	50

Caladrius

Description: The Caladrius is a small bird white as new-fallen snow. It looks similar to a pigeon, but is a solitary creature, never gathering in flocks. It may be found on the rooftops of human dwellings or under bridges. Caladrii speak the language of Perchers.

Habits: The Caladrius is never found far from human dwellings where it may be seen perching on the edge of rooftops or under bridges. If a Caladrius is tricked or persuaded into looking directly into the eyes of an animal that is sick or injured, its stare absorbs the malady from the victim, completely healing its wounds or curing its disease. If attacked, however, its evil glance can have the opposite effect, causing 2d6 HP injury in its attacker.

Special Ability: Empathic Heal or Hurt.

Trait Statistics:	STR	SPD	INT	AGI	CON	MYS	SML	CHA
Rating:	3	3	3	6	6	4	2	6

Pursuit stats:	DV (to spot)	iPD	Move	Hit Points
	8	8	12	30

Chupacabra

Description: Named for being a "goat sucker," the Chupacabra is a fearsome beast the size of a huge dog or small bear, but with a slender body covered with little or no fur. A fearsome row of spines run down its back from neck to tail. The tail, like the legs, is long and skinny. The Chupacabra can be detected when close by its rank, sulfurous odor. Chupacabras speak the language of Dogs.

Habits: The Chupacabra is a predator with the habits of a vampire. It is a nocturnal hunter that slashes its prey with long claws and drinks blood. It can run very fast on four legs, but can stand upright, almost like a human.

Special Ability: Paw Swipe

Trait Statistics:	STR	SPD	INT	AGI	CON	MYS	SML	CHA
Rating:	8	6	5	6	30	4	8	4

Pursuit stats:	DV (to spot)	iPD	Move	Hit Points
	6	10	8	150

Dingmaul

Description: The Dingmaul, otherwise known as a Plunkus or Ball-Tailed Cat, is a dangerous predator of the high pine forest. Although superficially feline in appearance, its body is covered in fine, hair-like scales that reveal its true reptilian nature. It has four legs equipped with claws that enable it to climb trees with the ease of a squirrel. Its tail, however, is its most unusual feature. Reaching lengths up to 3 meters, the slender, muscular tail terminates in a bony ball that is smooth and polished on one side, and bears sharp, curved spikes on the other. Dingmauls speak the language of Cats.

Habits: Like many forest predators, the Dingmaul is an ambush predator that waits for prey while lying motionless on a low overhanging branch. The tail is used as the primary weapon. Prey is first stunned by a tail flick, using the smooth side of the ball as a club. When senseless, the prey then is seized by the hooked spikes on the other side of the ball and drawn up into the tree. When attacked, the Dingmaul defends itself by lashing out with either side of its tail ball, striking enemies up to 2 meters away.

Special Ability: Tail-Slap.

Trait Statistics:	STR	SPD	INT	AGI	CON	MYS	SML	CHA
Rating:	8	6	6	8	24	2	2	3

Pursuit stats:	DV (to spot)	iPD	Move	Hit Points
	8	14	6	120

Flying Wolf (Ahool)

Description: A large bat, resembling a large fruit bat or flying fox. It is known as Ahool for its distinctive, plaintive cry (*"ahoooooool"*), which also sounds like the howl of a wolf. It has large dark eyes, sharp grasping claws on the wings, and a wingspan of nearly a meter. Its jaws are filled with razor-sharp teeth, including four long fangs that can deliver a severe bite.

Habits: Although an individual Flying Wolf is capable of attacking and injuring an animal the size of a rabbit, it is not powerful enough to carry the weight of a rabbit in flight. However, Flying Wolves are seldom found alone, as they hunt in small groups (1–6). Working together, two or three may seize a larger prey and carry it to a lofty perch, usually near the top of a tree or on a rocky ledge. It is a nocturnal hunter, hunting in mountainous areas close to the caves where it sleeps through the day. Flying Wolves speak the language of Bats.

Special Ability: Aerial attack; Teamwork.

Trait Statistics:	STR	SPD	INT	AGI	CON	MYS	SML	CHA
Rating:	4	8	6	3	6	2	1	2

Pursuit stats:	DV (to spot)	iPD	Move	Hit Points
	6	14	17	30

Hoop Snake

Description: A large predatory snake, up to 150 centimeters long, that inhabits flatland such as grassy prairies. Unlike other snakes, the Hoop Snake can grasp its tail in its mouth, creating a circular hoop that can roll at great speed over level ground. The tip of the tail is stiff and horny, forming a sharp spike that serves as its principal weapon. The tail may be tipped with venom.

Habits: In pursuit of prey, the Hoop Snake suddenly extends its body at the last moment before contact, attacking its prey with its spike-like tail. If attacked from the sides, the Hoop Snake coils like a Rattlesnake, but holds its tail up instead of its head, ready to strike. Although it is capable of biting, it has no fangs to inject venom and can cause only modest injury by biting. Hoop Snakes speak the language of Coldies.

Special Ability: Tail-Slap

Trait Statistics:	STR	SPD	INT	AGI	CON	MYS	SML	CHA
Rating:	8	4	2	4	6	1	2	1

Pursuit stats:	DV (to spot)	iPD	Move	Hit Points
	8	8	8	30

Jackalope

Description: A creature believed to be related to rabbits and hares and having the general form of a large jackrabbit, but which displays forked antlers much like a pronghorn antelope.

Habits: The Jackalope dwells in open grasslands, and sometimes can be seen in small groups of two or three. It is a shy creature, most often active at night and seldom aggressive. It is a swift runner and attempts to flee when threatened. However, the Jackalope can charge when cornered, using its antlers to inflict serious injury (4d6 HP). Jackalope speak the language of Rabbits.

Special Ability: Jump Kick; Dash without Tiring; Horn (Antler) Gore

Trait Statistics:	STR	SPD	INT	AGI	CON	MYS	SML	CHA
Rating:	2	5	2	3	6	2	1	2

Pursuit stats:	DV (to spot)	iPD	Move	Hit Points
	6	8	9	30

Jaculus

Description: Neither lizard nor snake, this reptilian creature has a long, serpent-like body with strong hind legs resembling a kangaroo. Lacking forelegs, it has a pair of bat-like wings. The Jaculus is no larger than a house cat, but is known to attack animals many times its size. It is not venomous, but has an arrow-shaped head that pierces its prey, allowing it to attack an enemy from the inside. Jaculi speak the language of Coldies.

Habits: The Jaculus is an ambush predator that waits for prey among the branches of trees, especially in oak woodlands. When a potential victim is spotted, the Jaculus launches itself from the tree with great force, gathering speed with its wings, then folding the wings against its body at the last moment as its head strikes and penetrates its victim. The initial attack is often sufficient to overcome its prey, but the Jaculus is quite capable of inflicting further injury by biting at internal parts and ripping with its powerful hind legs. It is most active during the day, and is difficult to distinguish from a dead branch, with owls or other birds sometimes roosting upon its back during the night.

Special Ability: Aerial Attack; Skewer.

Trait Statistics:	STR	SPD	INT	AGI	CON	MYS	SML	CHA
Rating:	6	4	5	7	8	2	1	4

Pursuit stats:	DV (to spot)	iPD	Move	Hit Points
	6	8	10	40

Lavellan

Description: The Lavellan is a rodent-like creature about the size and shape of a Muskrat. Although it looks relatively harmless, the Lavellan is a voracious predator, and might be more accurately described as a giant water shrew. It has small eyes and a long snout, suggesting that it relies more on its acute sense of smell than its vision to find prey. The slender muzzle is deceptive, however, as it conceals jaws with sharp teeth that can inject a powerful venom. It is said that the Lavellan can project a venomous spray over a distance up to 2 meters.

Habits: Like a shrew or stoat, the Lavellan is constantly on the move looking for prey in its native swamp and marsh habitat. It is as comfortable in the water as on land, and moves easily between them as it hunts. When it spots prey, it attacks without hesitation or fear, even if outnumbered. In the frenzy of combat, it typically switches targets after each attack, attempting to bite all of its enemies, then retreats into the water to allow the poison to finish the job. It is active day or night. Lavellans speak the language of Nibblers.

Special Ability: Poison Spray. (The spray is projected in a stream in a straight line from the Lavellan up to 2 hexes toward the Target. The poison acts on skin contact, with an effect like Stinging Nettle. The effect lasts for 3 consecutive combat rounds, or until treated by herbs.)

Trait Statistics:	STR	SPD	INT	AGI	CON	MYS	SML	CHA
Rating:	5	4	3	5	10	2	6	4

Pursuit stats:	DV (to spot)	iPD	Move	Hit Points
	6	6	4	50

Rat King

Description: A Rat King is an unlikely looking creature that resembles a collection of individual rats joined by their intertwined and knotted tails. They are not born, per se, but arise from the accidental (or in some cases, intentional) entanglement of several rats with hair, gum, or other sticky substances. A Rat King may be made up by as few as three or by as many as 12 rats that act in a coordinated fashion toward a common purpose.

Habits: It is said that a Rat King possesses a single mind that bestows it with great power to feel the raw sensations of individual rats and other small animals. A Rat King with 3–5 constituent rats can command rats and smaller rodents (Nibblers). Larger Rat Kings can read the perceptions and command individual animals up to 5 HP per constituent rat. Thus, a 10-rat Rat King could command an animal up to 50 HP. Rat Kings are never found far from human habitation. Rat Kings speak the language of Nibblers.

Special Ability: Enthrall Nibblers. (Used like an Enthrall ability of Storytellers to control the behavior of small rodents, up to the size of a Squirrel. The Rat King need not be present for the follower to continue acting faithfully. The effect is broken only if the follower loses half its hit points, or if the Rat King receives any injury.)

Telesthesia. The Rat King can sense perceptions of other animals within 30 meters, regardless of barriers separating them.

Trait Statistics:	STR	SPD	INT	AGI	CON	MYS	SML	CHA
Rating:	3	1	1	3	8	8	3	6

Pursuit stats:	DV (to spot)	iPD	Move	Hit Points
	6	6	2	40

Sidehill Gouger

Description: The Sidehill Gouger is a medium-sized coyote-like animal about the size of a Border Collie that dwells on steep hillsides. They have four legs, but two legs on one side of the body are shorter than the two legs on the opposite side, enabling them to move rapidly across steep slopes while keeping their body level. Gougers come in left- and right-legged varieties (clockwise and counterclockwise) and retreat into hillside burrows at night.

Habits: Gougers are very fast at traversing slopes in their preferred direction, but cannot turn around or run in the opposite direction (with their short legs on the downhill side). If they slip and fall to level ground, they are likely to run in circles until exhausted. When a left- and right-legged Gouger meet, they may fight to the death, because neither can turn around. Occasionally, however, they have been reported to cooperate, each holding on to the body of the other, with the longer legs of both to the outside, enabling them to traverse any terrain, albeit at a slow, stumbling pace. Sidehill Gougers speak the language of Dogs.

Special Ability: Shake

Trait Statistics:	STR	SPD	INT	AGI	CON	MYS	SML	CHA
Rating:	3	3	5	5	12	3	7	7

Pursuit stats:	DV (to spot)	iPD	Move	Hit Points
	4	14	9	60

Skvader

Description: Originally a resident of Scandinavia, the Skvader is believed to have been introduced to North America by the Vikings. It looks like an ordinary rabbit, with normal legs, body, and ears, but also possesses two fully feathered wings and a feathered tail more closely resembling a grouse.

Habits: An exceedingly shy creature that seldom ventures far from its preferred montane habitat, often near mountain streams and forest. It is reputed to be as swift as a rabbit, but is more likely to take flight (literally) if threatened. Rarely, a female Skvader may interbreed with a male Jackalope to produce a hybrid creature with both antlers and wings called a Wolpertinger. A young Wolpertinger is said to be extremely protective of its mother, launching attacks like a stooping falcon to impale enemies on its antlers. Skvaders speak the language of Rabbits.

Special Ability: Aerial Attack

Trait Statistics:	STR	SPD	INT	AGI	CON	MYS	SML	CHA
Rating:	2	3	2	1	2	2	1	2

Pursuit stats:	DV (to spot)	iPD	Move	Hit Points
	8	8	12	25

Slide-Rock Bolter

Description: An almost indescribable horror of a creature, the Slide-Rock Bolter is legless, with a long, tapering body, a massive head with a gaping mouth, and tiny eyes. Its body often is partially buried or obscured by the loose talus where it dwells, and its head may be mistaken for a large boulder. Smaller specimens may be a little over a meter in length, but older adults can be twice as long.

Habits: Having no legs, the Bolter cannot actually pursue prey. Instead, it remains motionless on the steep slopes of a rocky hillside, waiting for unsuspecting prey to pass below. At the right time, it releases its slender body and slides down the slope. Its first (and only) attack is often sufficient to severely injure one or more victims in its path, often causing other rocks to fall and adding to the general confusion and potential injury. Bolters speak the language of Coldies.

Special Ability: Tusk Gore

Trait Statistics:	STR	SPD	INT	AGI	CON	MYS	SML	CHA
Rating:	3	1	4	3	20	2	3	5

Pursuit stats:	DV (to spot)	iPD	Move	Hit Points
	8	8	1	100

Tree Octopus

Description: An amphibious creature that looks exactly like a Pacific giant octopus, but which spends much of its adult life in temperate rainforests. Their eight arms make them surprisingly agile in negotiating tree branches, and their soft bodies allow them to squeeze into the smallest cracks and crannies in search of prey. Although its skin is specialized to reduce desiccation, it cannot survive for long in hot or dry conditions.

Habits: Young octopi hatch from eggs in a marine environment and grow up on a typical diet of crabs, fish, and other small prey. Upon reaching adulthood, however, an octopus migrates into streams to ponds and marshes, eventually climbing out of the water seeking moist habitats with abundant trees. They avoid the heat of the day and are most active at night. The adult Tree Octopus retains a carnivorous habit, taking birds and small mammals up to the size of a rabbit. A common tactic is to drop vertically from an overhanging branch, quickly enveloping its prey in a tangle of arms. Curiously, they also have developed a fondness for red delicious apples, so they commonly may be found in orchards. Tree Octopi speak the language of Fishies.

Special Ability: Unbreakable Grip

Trait Statistics:	STR	SPD	INT	AGI	CON	MYS	SML	CHA
Rating:	6	5	5	6	6	3	1	2

Pursuit stats:	DV (to spot)	iPD	Move	Hit Points
	8	4	6	30

Triffid

Description: A tall, mobile, highly poisonous plant, the triffid possesses a single, broad flower head that resembles a large sunflower. A coiled tendril inside the flower can be flicked out, reaching up to 2 meters. The tip of the tendril is coated with a powerful contact poison that can cause blindness (if striking the eyes), immobility (if striking the legs), or injury (if striking the body). The flower head is supported by a long, woody stalk 1–2 meters high. At the base of the stalk is a large bulb covered with small, hair-like roots. Three woody tubers extend from the bulb, supporting the entire plant in a wobbly tripod arrangement. The plant is capable of rocking back and forth on these tubers, effectively "walking" at a slow pace over unobstructed ground.

Habits: The Triffid is carnivorous, but is too slow to pursue its prey, relying instead on camouflage and stealth to strike with little warning. It may become excited on sensing nearby prey, and can make a rattling noise with its tubers that sounds similar to crickets or the buzzing of a rattlesnake. To enhance its stealth, it frequents areas of thick undergrowth, and is most active at night. Triffids speak a language that no animal can understand.

Special Ability: Tendril Slap (treat like a Tail Slap to determine a hit.) If eyes are unprotected, roll 1d6 to determine what is hit: 1–2 = Eyes, causing temporary blindness for 1 day; 3–4 = Legs, causing immobility for 1 hour; 5–6 = Body, causing 2d6 Poison damage. If hit, the victim may roll for a toxin resistance check, DV=10, which if successful, reduces damage to 1d6, with no blindness or immobility.

Trait Statistics:	STR	SPD	INT	AGI	CON	MYS	SML	CHA
Rating:	3	1	1	6	8	1	1	1

Pursuit stats:	DV (to spot)	iPD	Move	Hit Points
	4	4	1	40

Tripodero

Description: Typically seen around open areas where humans dig in the earth and move heavy sticks and stones to make their dwellings. It stands on three straight legs and possesses a long, tubular mouth, cheek pouches, and an acute visual sense.

Habits: The Tripodero lives in areas of thick brush, where it waits quietly for prey. When it spies its quarry, it slowly extends its legs, reaching a height of 2 meters or more. The tripodero carries hardened clay pellets or small stones in its cheeks, and can fire these through its tubular mouth like a blowgun with accuracy over distances up to 20 meters. Victims may be stunned or knocked senseless if struck by a Tripodero pellet. Tripoderos speak a language that no animal can understand.

Special Ability: Stone Throwing. A thrown stone hits with a standard 1d6 + AGI of the Tripodero vs. 1d6 + SPD of the target. A hit inflicts 1–3 HP damage and a chance to stun; roll 1d6 again, a 1 indicates the target is stunned for 1 full combat round.

Trait Statistics:	STR	SPD	INT	AGI	CON	MYS	SML	CHA
Rating:	2	1	4	6	10	2	1	2

Pursuit stats:	DV (to spot)	iPD	Move	Hit Points
	6	8	2	50

Whirling Whimpus

Description: The Whirling Whimpus is a medium-sized mammal about the size of a Beaver but closely resembling the cartoon depiction of a Tasmanian Devil. The front legs are long and powerful, with broad, flat paws. But the hind legs are fused into a single stout hoof. When alarmed or hunting, the Whimpus twirls on its single hind hoof, achieving fantastic rotational speed. When whirling, it cannot be distinguished from a dust devil or small whirlwind. Although it is easy to spot in this form, especially across the open farm fields where it prefers to hunt, its resemblance to a weather feature provides an effective camouflage for its true predatory nature.

Habits: The Whimpus actively hunts while whirling, and if surprised at rest immediately begins to whirl, reaching top speed in a dozen seconds. It is only dangerous when whirling, when it reaches out with its long forelegs, striking a target repeatedly like a flail. An enemy may be struck as many as 6 times in a single attack. Whirling Whimpuses speak the language of Hoofers.

Special Ability: Whirling Attack (see description above)

Trait Statistics:	STR	SPD	INT	AGI	CON	MYS	SML	CHA
Rating:	4	8	4	6	10	2	3	4

Pursuit stats:	DV (to spot)	iPD	Move	Hit Points
	4	6	5	50

Appendix C: Player Aids

- Player Reference Sheet
- Character Cards — Rabbits
- Character Cards — Non-Rabbits
- Quick Reference Guide to Traps
- Black Adder's Honeycomb of Herbal Lore
- Quick Reference Guide to Herbs, Properties, Preparations, & Effects
- Quick Reference Guide to the Bestiary: Predators and Neutral Animals
- Pursuit Board & Key
- Battleboards for 10 habitats & Key
- Battleboards for Burrow & 2 expansions
- Map of Coneylaeth
- Map for Ice-Crack mini-game
- Token Sheets for Rabbits, Non-Rabbit PCs, NPCs, Predators
- Token Sheets for trap clues & hidden items
- Herb Search Map
- Combat Tactics Cards
- Handicap Markers for Combat Tactics Cards

Player Reference Sheet: All Characters

Primary Traits

STR	Fighter	Bandit (Raccoon)
SPD	Runner	Herald (Jackrabbit)
INT	Scout	Spy (Chipmunk)
AGI	Maverick	Burglar (Skunk)
CON	Empath	Guardian (Porcupine)
MYS	Seer	Shaman (Opossum)
SML	Herbalist	Trader (Armadillo)
CHA	Storyteller	Grifter (Squirrel)

Calculating Trait Ratings

Trait Value	Trait Base Bonus	Maximum Trait Level
6 or less	+0	4
7-12	+0	5
13-15	+1	6
16-17	+2	7
18 or more	+3	8

Trait Rating = Trait Base Bonus + Current Trait Level

Advancing Levels

Start at Level 0 in all Traits except for Primary Trait and one additional (which start at Level 1). Spend Advancement Points (AP) to increase levels: 1 AP to reach Level 1, 2 more AP to reach Level 2, 3 more AP to reach Level 3, etc. You gain special abilities in your profession when the level of your Primary Trait reaches Level 3, and again at Level 6.

Combat

Initiative is based on **SPD** Rating (highest goes first); aggressor gets +1 in first round. In sequence, each character takes a Move/Action turn (based on settings on CTC) and resolves the results. May move before action or move after action; no double move or double action unless by a special ability. Rabbits have a number of Move Points = **SPD** Rating + 2. Movement may be affected by special abilities, terrain and handicaps. There are special rules for changing facing and for movement underground.

Combat Tactics Card (CTC)

Before starting combat, fill in your **AGI**, **SPD** and **STR** Trait Bonuses and Ratings. Enter your MP value in that space. If you have any special tactics, fill those in as well. During the combat round, the first time you attack or are attacked, indicate the Combat Tactic you will use (place a marker in the box). Set your Attack and Defend dice by rolling 2d6 and placing one die in Attack and the other in Defend. (Note: If you are emphasizing attack, place the higher die there; if more cautious, place the higher die in Defend.)

After your attack, reduce your Attack die by 1. After each time that you are attacked, reduce your Defend die by 1. If either reaches 0, remove the die from the CTC (there are no negative values for Attack and Defend dice). If you receive Handicaps, place those markers in the Handicap box. If you ever choose Flee, you must maintain that tactic until until you leave the battleboard.

When your turn comes around again, select your next combat tactic, and reroll 2d6, placing one die in Attack and the other in Defend.

- **Combat Tactics available to all:**
- **Kick [K]:** A Kick may be directed at any of the three adjacent hexes behind the attacker.
  - [PS] Core Damage, plus a chance of Critical [Roll 6], Special = defender is Vulnerable.
  - [OPT] Push Back: Core Damage, plus a chance to push target away one hex [Roll 6]
  - [OPT] Hop Forward: Core Damage, plus a chance to hop forward one hex away from target [Roll 6]
- **Bite [B]:** A Bite may be directed at the adjacent hex directly ahead of the attacker.
  - [PS] Core Damage.
  - [OPT] Bite and Hold: Core Damage, plus a chance to Hold [Roll 5,6]; attacker is Vulnerable.
  - [OPT] Vicious Bite: Core Damage, plus a chance of Critical [Roll 6], Special = Bleeding; attacker is Vulnerable.
- **Claw [C]:** A Claw may be directed at any of the three adjacent hexes ahead of the attacker.
  - [PS] Core Damage.
  - [OPT] Cuff: One point of damage, considered non-hostile. Attacker is Wary.
  - [OPT] Vicious Claw: Core Damage, plus a chance of Critical [Roll 6]; attacker is Vulnerable.
- **Dodge [D]:** A Dodge is defensive in nature; no target is necessary.
  - [PS] Increase Defense Score by 2.
  - [OPT] Use Pause: The intent is to do something else during your turn, such as use an herb on self, eat, groom, etc. Increase Defense Score by 1.
  - [OPT] Flee: You disengage from the fight and attempt to flee the battleboard. For the remainder of combat, you may not perform any other action. Increase Defense Score by 3 while still on the board.
- **Submit [S]:** When one rabbit submits to another, the dominant rabbit will stop fighting and not go on to injure the submissive rabbit.
  - [PS] Stop fighting and assume a submissive posture. Submissive rabbit is doubly Vulnerable.
  - [OPT] Feign Death: Stop fighting and appear to be dead.
  - [OPT] Feign Disease: Stop fighting and appear to be diseased, by markedly unusual behavior.

Attack and Defense Scores

Attack Score = Attack Die + **AGI** Rating (of attacker).

Defense Score = Defend Die + **SPD** Rating (of defender).

Core Damage = **STR** Rating + 1d6; some tactics may yield additional damage or the chance of a critical hit.

Player Reference Sheet

Rabbits

Calculating Hit Points (HP)

A starting rabbit has HP = CON Base Bonus + 8. With each new CON Level, add CON Base Bonus + 5.

Some Special Abilities of Rabbits (≤ Level 3)

- Fighters may Rip after a successful Bite.
- At **STR** Level 3, Fighters may Double Attack in Combat.
- Runners may **Speed Burst**, enabling an extra full movement at any time during combat, at the cost of 1 HP.
- At **SPD** Level 3, Runners may combine Dodge and Attack in Combat.
- Scouts may Evaluate Opponent, learning the combat stats (**STR**, **SPD**, **AGI** Rating & **HP**) for one opponent.
- At **INT** Level 3, Scouts may passively detect Stalker or Cryptic predators.
- At **AGI** Level 1, Mavericks may carry an additional number of objects equal to their AGI Rating.
- At **AGI** Level 3, Mavericks may steal items, including food or herbs, in combat.
- At **AGI** Level 3, Mavericks may do a three-legged carry.
- Empaths may use Empathic Heal (Laying On Paws).
- At **CON** Level 3, Empaths may use Empathic Hurt in combat.
- Seers may enter trances.
- At **MYS** Level 3, Seers may use Luck, # of times a day up to their **MYS** Base Bonus (minimum 1).
- Herbalists may Apply Herbs in combat.
- At **SML** Level 3, Herbalists may perform Advanced Preparation of herbs.
- Storytellers may learn two languages for each point of their **CHA** Rating.
- At **CHA** Level 3, Storytellers may Confuse, in combat .

- Rabbits can only count to 4.
- Be vigilant about pests; Groom often.
- The lead member of the party may passively detect Chasers, Brutes, or Raptors. Anyone may declare a search by Posting, which increases the chance of spotting a predator.
- The lead member also may passively detect trap clues, hazards, or pests. Scouts have an advantage in all spotting.
- To use herbs, you must prepare them first. To prepare them correctly, you must recognize their odor Type, Clarity and Quality. Incorrect preparation can create Poisonweed.
- You must know the language of another animal to communicate effectively. If the language is not known, you may pantomime.

Non-Rabbits

Traits of Non-Rabbit Characters

Animal	STR	SPD	INT	AGI	CON	MYS	SML	CHA
Raccoon	**4d6**					2d6		2d6
Jackrabbit		**4d6**		2d6			2d6	
Chipmunk	2d6		**4d6**		2d6			
Skunk				**4d6**			2d6	2d6
Porcupine		2d6		2d6	**4d6**			
Opossum		2d6	2d6			**4d6**		
Armadillo	2d6		2d6				**4d6**	
Squirrel					2d6	2d6		**4d6**

* Blank cells in the table indicate a roll of 3d6.

Calculating Hit Points (HP)

Species	HP for Starting Character	HPs added for each CON Level
Rabbit	8 + **CON** Base Bonus	5 + **CON** Base Bonus
Raccoon	15 + **CON** Base Bonus	7 + **CON** Base Bonus
Jackrabbit	8 + **CON** Base Bonus	5 + **CON** Base Bonus
Chipmunk	5 + **CON** Base Bonus	3 + **CON** Base Bonus
Skunk	10 + **CON** Base Bonus	6 + **CON** Base Bonus
Porcupine	18 + **CON** Base Bonus	8 + **CON** Base Bonus
Opossum	10 + **CON** Base Bonus	6 + **CON** Base Bonus
Armadillo	10 + **CON** Base Bonus	6 + **CON** Base Bonus
Gray Squirrel	6 + **CON** Base Bonus	4 + **CON** Base Bonus

Some Special Abilities of Non-Rabbits (≤ Level 3)

- Bandits may Intimidate in pursuit, and use Intruder Mode.
- At **STR** Level 3, Bandits may Double Bite in combat.
- Heralds may Jump Kick in pursuit, and Dash Without Tiring.
- At **SPD** Level 3, Heralds may Box in combat.
- Spies may Quick Conceal, and use Automatic Stealth Mode.
- At **INT** Level 3, Spies may Double Jump in Combat.
- Burglars may Spray, and gain Manipulation Bonus (+2 AGI).
- At **AGI** Level 3, Burglars may Power Spray in combat.
- Guardians may Bristle.
- At **CON** Level 3, Guardians may Throw Quills in combat.
- Shamans may Feign Death, and may engage in Rapid Breeding.
- At **MYS** Level 3, Shamans may Determine Function.
- Traders may Roll Up, and have Natural Armor.
- Traders have an ability to Find Hidden.
- At **SML** Level 3, Traders may Walk Underwater or Raft.
- At **SML** Level 3, Traders may Claw in combat for double damage.
- Grifters may Tree Dash, Leap Acrobatically, or Taunt.
- At **CHA** Level 3, Grifters may Lie & Cheat without detection.

The Herbalist

STR Rating for Damage & jumping.
SPD Rating for Defense, climbing, swimming.
AGI Rating for Attack, carrying, and disarming traps.
CON Rating for Hit Points.

Smell (SML)

Special Abilities

- In Pursuit, Herbalists may Disperse Herb.
- In Combat, Herbalists may Apply Herbs.
- At **SML** Level 3, Herbalists may perform Advanced Preparation of Herbs (see Herb rules)
- AT **SML** Level 6, Herbalists may attempt to Remodel Herbs (see Herb rules)

Hawksbeard the Herbalist

I have secret knowledge, passed down through generations, of the diversity of plants and the ways to prepare them. I can produce herbs that protect and heal, as well as those that confuse and injure. Clearly this powerful lore cannot be passed on to every rabbit, due to its possible abuse. My nose is a powerful tool in this endeavor, and also allows me great investigative and tracking skills. If you are ready to cleanse the horrors of the world with precious herbs, take an Herbalist as a mate.

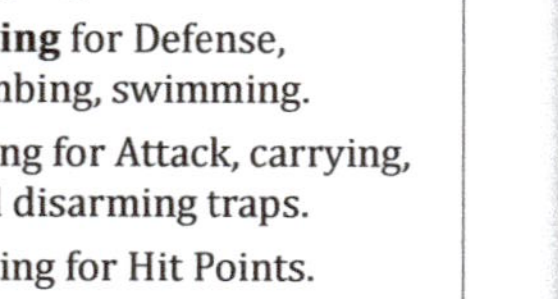

The Scout

STR Rating for Damage & jumping.
SPD Rating for Defense, climbing, swimming.
AGI Rating for Attack, carrying, and disarming traps.
CON Rating for Hit Points.

Intelligence (INT)

Special Abilities

- In Pursuit, Scouts may use Flash Tail to Confound.
- Scouts get **INT** Rating Bonus (instead of **INT** Base Bonus) for passively spotting ordinary predators, trap clues, or pests. With an active examination, a Scout always detects pests.
- In Combat, Scouts may Evaluate Opponent.
- At **INT** Level 3, Scouts may passively detect Stalker or Cryptic predators.
- At **INT** Level 6, Scouts may attempt to understand the function of man-things.

Sweetbriar the Scout

Any rabbit with a brain immediately realizes that Scouts are the best profession. Our high intelligence makes us key in recognizing all sorts of threats, be they predators, traps, pests, or other hazards of nature. Our wits are are often called on to lead exploratory parties. All the better if you enjoy adventure tinged with a little fear, because we are usually the first to encounter danger. Our bravery in the face of risk has been celebrated in many classic stories of rabbit heroes. If you want your kits to be clever, pick one of us for a mate.

The Fighter

STR Rating for Damage & jumping.
SPD Rating for Defense, climbing, swimming.
AGI Rating for Attack, carrying, and disarming traps.
CON Rating for Hit Points.

Strength (STR)

Special Abilities

- In Pursuit, Fighters may Vault over obstacles
- In Combat, Fighters may Rip after a successful Bite
- At **STR** Level 3, Fighters may Vault over Major Obstacles in Pursuit.
- At **STR** Level 3, Fighters may Double Attack in Combat.
- At **STR** Level 6, Fighters may attempt Killing Blow in Combat.

Mugwort the Fighter

Clearly the strongest rabbits should rule the warren, and that is why being a Fighter is the best. Fearlessly we rush into every battle, prepared to give our lives to protect the Warren. There is nothing like the satisfaction of ruthless claws, bites, and rips, watching our foes collapse before our onslaught or flee in terror. We can take on the most powerful foes, secure in our knowledge that our fighting tactics and massive damage are likely to win the day. Why, any mate would be honored to breed with one of us, as our kits are also likely to burst with strength.

The Empath

STR Rating for Damage & jumping.
SPD Rating for Defense, climbing, swimming.
AGI Rating for Attack, carrying, and disarming traps.
CON Rating for Hit Points.

Constitution (CON)

Ragged Robin the Empath

I have always been attuned to other rabbits, feeling their emotions and their pains. I can ease their pain by taking it upon myself. I care about others. Fortunately, my inner strength and health are usually strong. If you wish a nurturing parent for your kits, and for them to have sound bodies, then consider an Empath as a mate.

Special Abilities

- In Pursuit, Empath may use Second Wind.
- Empaths may use Empathic Heal (Laying On Paws).
- At **CON** Level 3, Empaths may use Empathic Hurt in combat
- At **CON** Level 6, Empaths may attempt Restore to Life.

The Runner

Speed (SPD)

Special Abilities

- In Pursuit, Runners may use the Combo maneuver.
- In Combat, Runners may Speed Burst.
- At **SPD** Level 3, Runners may combine Dodge and Attack in Combat.
- At **SPD** Level 6, Runners may attempt Intercept in Combat.

Speedwell the Runner

The fleetest rabbits have always been honored, in all the legendary tales. It is not just that we win all the races, but we also excel in combat due to great defensive skills. At times we are called on to lure the predators away from weaker rabbits, confident in our ability to outrun them until they have been led far away and we can then duck into cover. Often the Warren chooses a Runner as a leader, prizing our speedy nature. And if you want your kits to survive to adulthood, you could do worse than choosing a Runner as a mate.

STR Rating for Damage & jumping.

SPD Rating for Defense, climbing, swimming.

AGI Rating for Attack, carrying, and disarming traps.

CON Rating for Hit Points.

The Maverick

STR Rating for Damage & jumping.

SPD Rating for Defense, climbing, swimming.

AGI Rating for Attack, carrying, and disarming traps.

CON Rating for Hit Points.

Agility (AGI)

Periwinkle the Maverick

Guess what I am holding in my paw? It could be some hard-to-get prime food, a piece taken from a disabled trap, a thorn I could use as a weapon, or a mysterious man-thing. We are the masters of manipulation and construction. We can gain passage through obstacles that no other rabbit can pass, due to our extraordinary agility. We are the best way to figure out the workings of man-stuff that was designed for hands instead of paws. And just for fun, we are also skilled in disguise. Your life will never be dull if you choose a Maverick as a mate.

Special Abilities

- In Pursuit, Mavericks may use Tumble.
- Mavericks may carry an additional number of objects equal to their AGI Rating.
  - At **AGI** Level 3, Mavericks may attempt to steal items, including food or herbs, in combat.
    - At **AGI** Level 3, Mavericks may carry an additional item by gripping it with one paw and walking or three-legged.
    - AT **AGI** Level 6, Mavericks may grip and handle man-things, by using paw and mouth, or both paws.

The Storyteller

Charisma (CHA)

Moxieplum the Storyteller

There was once a rabbit who could captivate the warren with tales of adventure, and danger, and romance. Such are the carriers of lore and tradition, passed on from generation to generation. Do you wish your kits to be guided by the moral stories, hear of a thousand enemies, fantasize about heroes? Then turn your ears towards a Storyteller.

Special Abilities

- In Pursuit, Storytellers may Encourage.
- Storytellers may learn two languages for each point of their CHA Rating (beyond the automatic rabbit language).
- At **CHA** Level 3, Storytellers may attempt to Confuse, in combat.
- AT **CHA** Level 6, Storytellers may attempt to Enthrall.

STR Rating for Damage & jumping.
SPD Rating for Defense, climbing, swimming.
AGI Rating for Attack, carrying, and disarming traps.
CON Rating for Hit Points.

The Seer

Mysticism (MYS)

Moonseed the Seer

Have I met you before? You look familiar, but we may have never met… yet. Sometimes I see things that have not come to pass, and sometimes they never do. It is difficult to describe. I will not tell you who your mate will be; you must discover that for yourself.

Special Abilities

- In Pursuit or Combat, Seers may Feign Disease.
- Seers may enter trances. See Trance rules for details.
- At **MYS** Level 3, Seers may use Luck, a number of times a day not to exceed their **MYS** Rating. See Luck rules for details.
- AT **MYS** Level 6, Seers may attempt to Tempt Fate, once a day.

STR Rating for Damage & jumping.
SPD Rating for Defense, climbing, swimming.
AGI Rating for Attack, carrying, and disarming traps.
CON Rating for Hit Points.

Raccoon

STR Rating for Damage & jumping.

SPD Rating for Defense, climbing, swimming.

AGI Rating for Attack, carrying, and disarming traps.

CON Rating for Hit Points.

Special Abilities

- In Pursuit, Bandits may Intimidate.
- Bandits may use Intruder Mode.
- Bandits can climb trees.
- Bandits are good diggers.
- At **STR** Level 3, Bandits may Double Bite in combat.
- At **STR** Level 6, Bandits may carry a large object or animal while walking bipedally.

The Bandit

Strength (STR)

About Bandits, Mugwort the rabbit says:

I suppose a Trash Panda isn't bad to have with you in a tight spot, what with long eye-teeth and serious attitude. But all that twittering? And what's with washing their food? Can't they just eat grass like a normal animal?

The Herald

Speed (SPD)

Special Abilities

- In Pursuit, Heralds may Jump Kick.
- Heralds may Dash Without Tiring.
- Heralds cannot climb trees.
- Heralds are good diggers.
- At **SPD** Level 3, Heralds may Box in combat
- At **SPD** Level 6, Heralds may Jump Kick in combat.

About Heralds, Speedwell the rabbit says:

As swift as a fox, and a fine boxer. But Jacks lack the finesse of a true rabbit. They are all ears and no nose.

Jackrabbit

STR Rating for Damage & jumping.

SPD Rating for Defense, climbing, swimming.

AGI Rating for Attack, carrying, and disarming traps.

CON Rating for Hit Points.

The Burglar

Skunk

Agility (AGI)

STR Rating for Damage & jumping.
SPD Rating for Defense, climbing, swimming.
AGI Rating for Attack, carrying, and disarming traps.
CON Rating for Hit Points.

Special Abilities

- In Pursuit, Burglars may Spray.
- Burglars have Manipulation Bonus (+2 to **AGI** Rating for opening small containers).
- Burglars cannot climb trees.
- Burglars are good diggers.
- At **AGI** Level 3, Burglars may Power Spray in combat (forward shooting range 3 from handstand).
- At **AGI** Level 6, Burglars may Disassemble Man-Things.

About Burglars, Periwinkle the rabbit says:
Oh, I wish I had the fingers of a Stink-Kitty. Those essence peddlers are so good with their hands, they can fiddle a tight, twisty man-thing out of a big, clanky man-thing. Handy to have around, as long as they stay down wind.

The Spy

Chipmunk

Intelligence (INT)

STR Rating for Damage & jumping.
SPD Rating for Defense, climbing, swimming.
AGI Rating for Attack, carrying, and disarming traps.
CON Rating for Hit Points.

About Spies, Sweetbriar the rabbit says:
I'll admit the little striped mice are good at getting into cracks and crannies. And they are sneaky buggers. But what are they saving all those seeds for?

Special Abilities

- In Pursuit or Combat, Spies may Quick Conceal.
- Spies may use Automatic Stealth Mode.
- Spies can climb trees, including tree canopies.
- Spies are weak diggers.
- Spies get a facing change bonus in combat.
- At **INT** Level 3, Spies may Double Jump in combat.
- At **INT** Level 6, Spies may Find Hidden Entry.

Porcupine

The Guardian

Constitution (CON)

STR Rating for Damage & jumping.

SPD Rating for Defense, climbing, swimming.

AGI Rating for Attack, carrying, and disarming traps.

CON Rating for Hit Points.

Special Abilities

- In Pursuit, Guardians may Bristle.
- Guardians can climb trees.
- Guardians are weak diggers.
- At **CON** Level 3, Guardians may Throw Quills in combat (not actually thrown).
- At **CON** Level 6, Guardians may Provide Antibiotic by use of a quill injection, to cure disease.

About Guardians, Ragged Robin the rabbit says:

Quill-Pigs are an odd sort. They are slow and clumsy, but good in trees, and I can't think of a better friend to have your back when a Badger visits your burrow.

Opossum

The Shaman

Mysticism (MYS)

STR Rating for Damage & jumping.

SPD Rating for Defense, climbing, swimming.

AGI Rating for Attack, carrying, and disarming traps.

CON Rating for Hit Points.

Special Abilities

- In Pursuit or Combat, Shamans may Feign Death.
- Shamans may engage in Rapid Breeding.
- Shamans can climb trees.
- Shamans are good diggers.
- At **MYS** Level 3, Shamans may Determine Function.
- At **MYS** Level 6, Shamans may attempt to Implant Thoughts.

About Shamans, Moonseed the rabbit says:

I have the highest regard for White Dogs. Many think them dim-witted and slow. But I know possums to have a different way of knowing, feeling more than thinking. They should leave their children at home, though.

The Trader

Armadillo

STR **Rating** for Damage & jumping.
SPD **Rating** for Defense, climbing, swimming.
AGI Rating for Attack, carrying, and disarming traps.
CON Rating for Hit Points.

Smell (SML)

Special Abilities

- In Pursuit or Combat, Traders may Roll Up.
- In Combat, Traders have Natural Armor that reduces damage.
- Traders have an increased ability to Find Hidden.
- Traders cannot climb trees.
- Traders are exceptional diggers.
- Traders cannot Bite in combat.
- At **CON** Level 3, Traders may Walk Underwater or Raft.

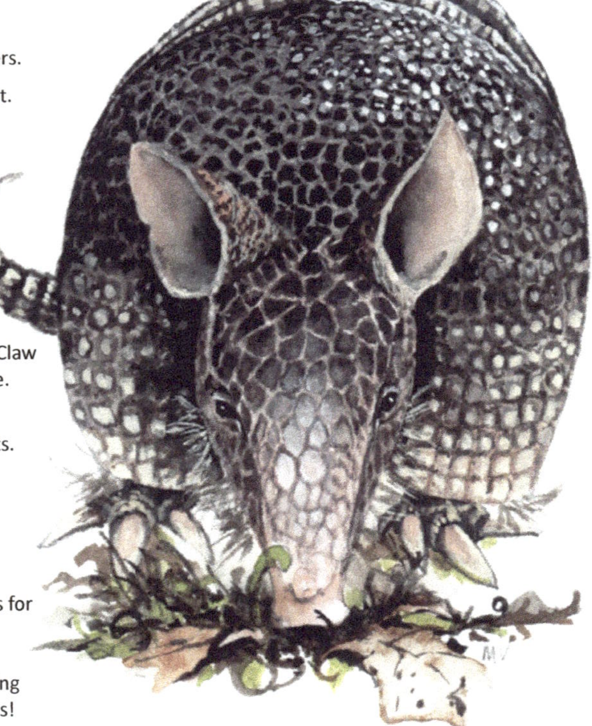

- At **SML** Level 3, Traders may Claw in combat for double damage.
- At **SML** Level 6, Traders are immune to diseases and pests.

About Traders, Hawksbeard the rabbit says:

I'm always wanting odds and ends for working my herbs, and there is nothing like a visit to the nearest Turtle-Rabbit if you need something to trade. And they work for worms! Don't let one run across a man-path, though. It is not pretty.

The Grifter

About Grifters, Moxieplum the rabbit says:

It's a scandal! Simply disgraceful the way those nut smugglers carry on, dashing up a tree to taunt and heckle. They are just fancy rats, I say. Oh, they chatter a good deal, but give me an honest story any day, without all the tail waggling.

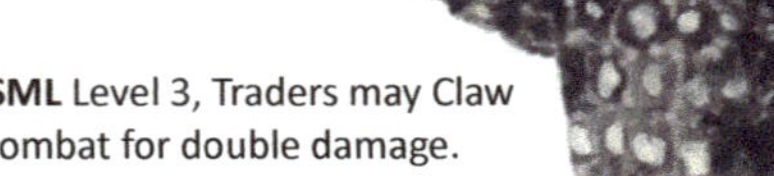

Special Abilities

- In Pursuit, Grifters may Tree Dash
- In Combat, Grifters may Leap Acrobatically.
- In Combat, Grifters may Taunt.
- Grifters can climb trees, including tree canopies.
- Grifters are weak diggers.
- Grifters get a facing change bonus in combat.
- At **CHA** Level 3, Grifters may Lie and Cheat without detection.
- At **CHA** Level 6, may count to seven (beyond seven is a thousand).

Charisma (CHA)

Squirrel

STR **Rating** for Damage & jumping.
SPD **Rating** for Defense, climbing, swimming.
AGI Rating for Attack, carrying, and disarming traps.
CON Rating for Hit Points.

Bunnies & Burrows

(Rabbit)

Name ______________________________ Gender F ☐ M ☐

Player Name ______________________________

Profession:
○ Fighter ○ Scout ○ Empath ○ Herbalist
○ Runner ○ Maverick ○ Seer ○ Storyteller

Traits

Base Scores
Roll 3 6-sided dice (3d6); see rules for details.

Base Bonus
+1 for scores 13-15, +2 for 16-17, +3 for 18+

Max Levels
Base <7 = 4, 7-12 =5, 13-15 = 6, 16-17 = 7, 18+ = 8

	Base	Bonus	Level 1 2 3 4 5 6 7 8	Trait Ratings (Level + Base Bonus)
Strength (STR)				STR
Speed (SPD)				SPD
Intelligence (INT)				INT
Agility (AGI)				AGI
Constitution (CON)				CON
Mysticism (MYS)				MYS
Smell (SML)				SML
Charisma (CHA)				CHA

Hit Points — Max ____ changes ____

Advancement Points — Earned ____ Unspent ____

Movement Points ____

Injuries
☐ ☐
☐ ☐
☐ ☐
☐

Pursuit Tactics
Basic
☐ Speed Burst ☐ Pass Between
☐ Zig-Zag ☐ Twist
☐ Dust Up ☐ Freeze
☐ Jink ☐ Last Ditch (SPD, INT, or CON)

Special
☐ ______________________________

Languages
☒ Rabbits ☐ Hoofers
☐ Nibblers ☐ Raptors
☐ Chatters ☐ Perchers
☐ Grubbers ☐ Strutters
☐ Ramblers ☐ Waders
☐ Weasels ☐ Coldies
☐ Dogs ☐ Fishies
☐ Cats ☐ Crawlies

Bunnies & Burrows

Name ______________________________ Gender F ☐ M ☐

Animal Species ______________________________

Player Name ______________________________

Profession:
○ Bandit ○ Herald ○ Spy ○ Burglar
○ Guardian ○ Shaman ○ Trader ○ Grifter

Traits

Base Scores
Roll 2-4 6-sided dice; varies with profession; see rules for details.

Base Bonus
+1 for scores 13-15, +2 for 16-17, +3 for 18+

Max Levels
Base <7 = 4, 7-12 =5, 13-15 = 6, 16-17 = 7, 18+ = 8

	Base	Bonus	Level 1 2 3 4 5 6 7 8	Trait Ratings (Level + Base Bonus)
Strength (STR)				STR
Speed (SPD)				SPD
Intelligence (INT)				INT
Agility (AGI)				AGI
Constitution (CON)				CON
Mysticism (MYS)				MYS
Smell (SML)				SML
Charisma (CHA)				CHA

Hit Points — Max ____ changes ____

Advancement Points — Earned ____ Unspent ____

Movement Points ____

Injuries
☐ ☐
☐ ☐
☐ ☐
☐

Pursuit Tactics
Basic
☐ Speed Burst ☐ Pass Between
☐ Zig-Zag ☐ Twist
☐ Dust Up ☐ Freeze
☐ Jink ☐ Last Ditch (SPD, INT, or CON)

Special
☐ ______________________________

Languages
☒ Rabbits ☐ Hoofers
☐ Nibblers ☐ Raptors
☐ Chatters ☐ Perchers
☐ Grubbers ☐ Strutters
☐ Ramblers ☐ Waders
☐ Weasels ☐ Coldies
☐ Dogs ☐ Fishies
☐ Cats ☐ Crawlies

Quick Reference Guide to Traps

Rabbits have a chance to notice a trap clue when they approach a hidden trap.

- The first opportunity is for the lead rabbit, or any Scout, to detect the trap clue with a passive INT skill check that exceeds the concealment DV of the trap.
- Nearby trap clues may be discovered if rabbits actively search by Posting.
- Trap clues also may be discovered as rabbits move about the Battleboard, encountering bait items, clues, and possibly springing the trap. See the *Trap Snapper* mini-game for details.

Traps

Trap Type	Conceal DV	Disarm DV	Clue 1	Clue 2	Optional Clue
Snare	4	2	Length of Vine	2nd Length of Vine	—
Live Trap	2	4	Bait Item	Shaded Hex	—
Box Trap	4	4	Bait Item	Stick	—
Pit Trap	6	4	Bait Item	Disturbed Earth	2nd Disturbed Earth
Pit and Stakes Trap	6	6	Stick	Disturbed Earth	2nd Disturbed Earth
Foot Trap	6	4	Glint of Metal	Bait Item	—
Net and Sapling	6	6	Length of Vine	Bait Item	2nd Length of Vine
Crossbow Trap	8	6	Length of Vine	Glint of Metal	2nd Length of Vine
Beartooth	6	8	Glint of Metal	2nd Glint of Metal	—
Deadfall	4	8	Stick	Shaded Hex	2nd Shaded Hex

Rabbit Actions

- Kick dirt to any one adjacent hex.
- Poke stick into any one adjacent hex.
- Throw rock into any one adjacent hex.
- Chew vine in current or any one adjacent hex.
- Kick object in any one adjacent hex.
- Pull object in any one adjacent hex.
- Jump onto object in any one adjacent hex (and move to that hex).
- Post: All clue tokens that are one or two hexes away are turned face up.

Black Adder's Honeycomb of Herbal Lore

Temperament:			Shy (–)			Bold (+)		
Agency:		Mind (+)	Body (–)	Mind (+)	Body (–)			
Quality:		Minty		Musky		Acrid		Pungent
Tone:	Fragrant (+)	Putrid (–)	Fragrant (+)	Putrid (–)	Fragrant (+)	Putrid (–)	Fragrant (+)	Putrid (–)
Assoc. Trait:	MYS	SML	CON	SPD	CHA	INT	AGI	STR
Class of Effect:	Soporific	Herbal	Medicinal	Defensive	Hypnotic	Prophylactic	Irritant	Injurious
Clarity / Source	Lick	Crumble	Chew	Claw	Peel	Skin	Brush	Squeeze

Green	Fungal	I.	Bracket Fungus
	Floral	II.	Juniper Berry
	Overt	III.	Bracken Fern Frond
	Covert	IV.	Ground Pine (clubmoss)

		No.	Type	No.	Type	No.	Type	No.	Type	No.	Type	No.	Type	No.	Type	No.	Type
Clear	Fungal	1	cap	2	stump-ball	3	cap	4	ball	5	golden bolete	6	ball	7	poison mushroom	8	ruff-ball
	Floral	9	fluffy-head	10	flower	11	redberry	12	flower	13	fruit	14	mosquito flower	15	joint-pine cone	16	lemon-berry flower
	Overt	17	leaf	18	willow bark	19	willow leaves	20	stem	21	locoweed	22	tickweed	23	scritchweed	24	prickly nettle
	Covert	25	bulb	26	white snakeroot	27	woodsorrel bulb	28	quickberry root	29	mad iris	30	flea root	31	bulb	32	root
Cloudy	Fungal	33	cap	34	ball	35	jelly button	36	snuffball	37	cap	38	ball	39	bitter mushroom	40	tuffball
	Floral	41	poppy puff	42	false-flower dust	43	bounceberry	44	cacomistletoe	45	razzleberry	46	leech flower	47	lemonberry	48	flower
	Overt	49	leaf	50	truebark	51	burning nettle	52	dodgeweed	53	black snakeroot	54	mite weed	55	leaf	56	biting nettle
	Covert	57	slumberlily	58	root	59	wild garlic	60	root	61	bulb	62	warble root	63	bulb	64	lemon-berry root
Murky	Fungal	65	cap	66	ball	67	warble cap	68	powderball	69	cap	70	ball	71	blood-cap	72	jump ball
	Floral	73	fluff-needle	74	sunflower dust	75	pumpkin seeds	76	bounceberry flower	77	purpleberry	78	flower	79	quickberry	80	delicate flower
	Overt	81	lotus leaf	82	sunflower sap	83	lavender leaf	84	stem	85	leaf	86	rainbow flower sap	87	heart leaf	88	stinging nettle
	Covert	89	bulb	90	fireroot	91	blind iris	92	mandrake	93	bulb	94	goldenrod root	95	bulb	96	sourroot

		No.	Type	No.	Type	No.	Type	No.	Type	No.	Type	No.	Type	No.	Type	No.	Type
Dense	Fungal	97	wicked mushroom	98	ball	99	cap	100	ball	101	snowcap	102	foul ball	103	dung fung	104	giant puffball
	Floral	105	golden rain	106	carcass flower	107	fruit	108	hero flower	109	bitterberry	110	pestflower	111	fruit	112	flower
	Overt	113	leaf	114	truebark dust	115	rabbit weed	116	stem	117	leaf	118	stem	119	sugarleaf	120	fire nettle
	Covert	121	death lily	122	orchid root	123	lifemelt garlic	124	root	125	bulb	126	arrowroot	127	bulb	128	bitterroot

Quick Reference Guide to Herbs, Properties, Preparations, and Effects

Clear Odor Clarity

#	Herb	Effect Class	Trait	Habitat	Source	Type	Quality	Tone	Prep.	Delivery	Effect
2	Stumpball	Herbal	SML	Oak Forest, Pine Wood, Mtn. Stream	Fungal	Ball	Minty	Putrid	Crumble	Breathe	reduces SML −1
5	Golden Bolete	Hypnotic	CHA	Oak Forest, Pine Wood, Mtn. Stream	Fungal	Cap	Acrid	Fragrant	Peel	Eat	increases CHA +1
7	Poison Mush-room	Irritant	AGI	Oak Forest, Pine Wood, Mtn. Stream	Fungal	Cap	Pungent	Fragrant	Brush	Eat	1d6 damage
8	Ruffball	Injurious	STR	Oak Forest, Pine Wood, Mtn. Stream	Fungal	Ball	Pungent	Putrid	Squeeze	Breathe	increases STR +1
9	Fluffy-head	Soporific	MYS	Orchard, Rocky Hillside	Floral	Fruit	Minty	Fragrant	Lick	Contact	reduces AGI −1
11	Redberry	Medicinal	CON	Orchard, Rocky Hillside	Floral	Fruit	Musky	Fragrant	Chew	Contact	cure wounds SML*
14	Mosquito Flower	Prophy-lactic	INT	Orchard, Rocky Hillside	Floral	Flower	Acrid	Putrid	Skin	Rub	repels mosquitoes
15	Joint-pine Cone	Irritant	AGI	Orchard, Rocky Hillside	Floral	Fruit	Pungent	Fragrant	Brush	Eat	Increases AGI +1
16	Lemon-berry Flower	Injurious	STR	Orchard, Rocky Hillside	Floral	Flower	Pungent	Putrid	Squeeze	Eat	SML* damage
18	Willow Bark	Herbal	SML	Grassland, Marsh, Suburb	Overt	Stem	Minty	Putrid	Crumble	Sprinkle	detects poison
19	Willow Leaves	Medicinal	CON	Grassland, Marsh, Suburb	Overt	Leaf	Musky	Fragrant	Chew	Eat	reduces pain; cures fever & snuffles
21	Loco-weed	Hypnotic	CHA	Grassland, Marsh, Suburb	Overt	Leaf	Acrid	Mind	Peel	Eat	irrational behavior
22	Tickweed	Prophy-lactic	INT	Grassland, Marsh, Suburb	Overt	Stem	Acrid	Putrid	Skin	Rub	repels ticks
23	Scritch-weed	Irritant	AGI	Grassland, Marsh, Suburb	Overt	Leaf	Pungent	Fragrant	Brush	Eat	causes itching; reduces SPD −1
24	Prickly Nettle	Injurious	STR	Grassland, Marsh, Suburb	Overt	Leaf	Pungent	Putrid	Squeeze	Contact	3 HP damage
26	White Snakeroot	Herbal	SML	Farm, Brush-land	Covert	Root	Minty	Putrid	Crumble	Tongue	3 HP damage; iden-tify herb C & Q
27	Woodsor-rel Bulb	Medicinal	CON	Farm, Brush-land	Covert	Bulb	Musky	Fragrant	Chew	Eat	counters irritant herbs
28	Quickber-ry Root	Defensive	SPD	Farm, Brush-land	Covert	Root	Musky	Putrid	Claw	Eat	increases SPD +1; decreases AGI −1
29	Mad Iris	Hypnotic	CHA	Farm, Brush-land	Covert	Bulb	Acrid	Fragrant	Peel	Eat	attack at random
30	Flea Root	Prophy-lactic	INT	Farm, Brush-land	Covert	Root	Acrid	Putrid	Skin	Rub	repels fleas

Cloudy Odor Clarity

#	Herb	Effect Class	Trait	Habitat	Source	Type	Quality	Tone	Prep.	Delivery	Effect
35	Jelly Button	Medicinal	CON	Oak Forest, Pine Wood, Mtn. Stream	Fungal	Cap	Musky	Fragrant	Chew	Eat	cures shakes
36	Snuffball	Defensive	SPD	Oak Forest, Pine Wood, Mtn. Stream	Fungal	Ball	Musky	Putrid	Claw	Breathe	causes sneezing; renders immobile
39	Bitter Mushroom	Irritant	AGI	Oak Forest, Pine Wood, Mtn. Stream	Fungal	Cap	Pungent	Fragrant	Brush	Eat	increases AGI +2
40	Tuffball	Injurious	STR	Oak Forest, Pine Wood, Mtn. Stream	Fungal	Ball	Pungent	Putrid	Squeeze	Breathe	increases STR +2
41	Poppy Puff	Soporific	MYS	Orchard, Rocky Hillside	Floral	Fruit	Minty	Mind	Lick	Breathe	induces sleep ≤ 25 HP
42	False-flower Dust	Herbal	SML	Orchard, Rocky Hillside	Floral	Flower	Minty	Putrid	Crumble	Breathe	mistake true herbs for poisonweed
43	Bounce-berry	Medicinal	CON	Orchard, Rocky Hillside	Floral	Fruit	Musky	Fragrant	Chew	Eat	increases CON +2
44	Cacomis-tletoe	Defensive	SPD	Orchard, Rocky Hillside	Floral	Flower	Musky	Putrid	Claw	Eat	increases SPD +2; +4 for climbing
45	Razzle-berry	Hypnotic	CHA	Orchard, Rocky Hillside	Floral	Fruit	Acrid	Fragrant	Peel	Eat	acts upon suggestion (50%)
46	Leech Flower	Prophylactic	INT	Orchard, Rocky Hillside	Floral	Flower	Acrid	Putrid	Skin	Rub	repels leeches
47	Lemon-berry	Irritant	AGI	Orchard, Rocky Hillside	Floral	Fruit	Pungent	Fragrant	Brush	Contact	blisters damage 1 HP/min
50	Truebark	Herbal	SML	Grassland, Marsh, Suburb	Overt	Stem	Minty	Putrid	Crumble	Sprinkle	detects poisonweed
51	Burning Nettle	Medicinal	CON	Grassland, Marsh, Suburb	Overt	Leaf	Musky	Fragrant	Chew	Contact	cures wounds 1d6 + SML*
52	Dodge-weed	Defensive	SPD	Grassland, Marsh, Suburb	Overt	Stem	Musky	Putrid	Claw	Eat	increases SPD +2; cures bumblefoot
53	Black Snake-root	Hypnotic	CHA	Grassland, Marsh, Suburb	Overt	Leaf	Acrid	Fragrant	Peel	Eat	3 HP damage; increases CHA +2
54	Mite Weed	Prophylactic	INT	Grassland, Marsh, Suburb	Overt	Stem	Acrid	Putrid	Skin	Rub	repels mites
56	Biting Nettle	Injurious	STR	Farm, Brushland	Covert	Stem	Pungent	Putrid	Squeeze	Contact	1d6 damage
57	Slumber-lily	Soporific	MYS	Farm, Brushland	Covert	Bulb	Minty	Fragrant	Lick	Eat	induces sleep ≤ 40 HP
59	Wild Garlic	Medicinal	CON	Farm, Brushland	Covert	Bulb	Musky	Fragrant	Chew	Eat	cures poison SML*; eradicates flukes
62	Warble Root	Prophylactic	INT	Farm, Brushland	Covert	Root	Acrid	Putrid	Skin	Rub	repels warble flies
64	Lemon-berry Root	Injurious	STR	Farm, Brushland	Covert	Root	Pungent	Putrid	Squeeze	Eat	1d6 + SML* damage

#	Herb	Effect Class	Trait	Habitat	Source	Type	Quality	Tone	Prep.	Delivery	Effect
67	Warble Cap	Medicinal	CON	Oak Forest, Pine Wood, Mtn. Stream	Fungal	Cap	Musky	Fragrant	Chew	Rub	drives out warbles
68	Powderball	Defensive	SPD	Oak Forest, Pine Wood, Mtn. Stream	Fungal	Ball	Musky	Putrid	Claw	Breathe	temporary blindness
71	Bloodcap	Irritant	AGI	Oak Forest, Pine Wood, Mtn. Stream	Fungal	Cap	Pungent	Fragrant	Brush	Eat	wound bleeding; see Combat
72	Jump Ball	Injurious	STR	Oak Forest, Pine Wood, Mtn. Stream	Fungal	Ball	Pungent	Putrid	Squeeze	Sniff	2x jumping distance
73	Fluffneedle	Soporific	MYS	Orchard, Rocky Hillside	Floral	Fruit	Minty	Fragrant	Lick	Breathe	induces sleep ≤ 40 HP
74	Sunflower Dust	Herbal	SML	Orchard, Rocky Hillside	Floral	Flower	Minty	Putrid	Crumble	Sprinkle	draws poison from food or herbs
75	Pumpkin Seeds	Medicinal	CON	Orchard, Rocky Hillside	Floral	Fruit	Musky	Fragrant	Chew	Eat	eradicates intestinal roundworms
76	Bounceberry Flower	Defensive	SPD	Orchard, Rocky Hillside	Floral	Flower	Musky	Putrid	Claw	Eat	increases SPD +3
77	Purpleberry	Hypnotic	CHA	Orchard, Rocky Hillside	Floral	Fruit	Acrid	Fragrant	Peel	Contact	causes hallucination
79	Quickberry	Irritant	AGI	Orchard, Rocky Hillside	Floral	Fruit	Pungent	Fragrant	Brush	Eat	trembling; decreases AGI −3
80	Delicate Flower	Injurious	STR	Orchard, Rocky Hillside	Floral	Flower	Pungent	Putrid	Squeeze	Eat	increases STR + 3
81	Lotus Leaf	Soporific	MYS	Grassland, Marsh, Suburb	Overt	Leaf	Minty	Fragrant	Lick	Eat	induces sleep ≤ 60 HP
82	Sunflower Sap	Herbal	SML	Grassland, Marsh, Suburb	Overt	Stem	Minty	Putrid	Crumble	Sprinkle	dissolves poisonweed
83	Lavender Leaf	Medicinal	CON	Grassland, Marsh, Suburb	Overt	Leaf	Musky	Fragrant	Chew	Eat	cures blisters & burns 2d6, & alopecia
86	Rainbow Flower Sap	Prophylactic	INT	Grassland, Marsh, Suburb	Overt	Stem	Acrid	Putrid	Skin	Lick	increases INT +3
87	Heart Leaf	Irritant	AGI	Grassland, Marsh, Suburb	Overt	Leaf	Pungent	Fragrant	Brush	Eat	Increase AGI +3
88	Stinging Nettle	Injurious	STR	Grassland, Marsh, Suburb	Overt	Stem	Pungent	Putrid	Squeeze	Contact	1d6 + SML* damage
90	Fireroot	Herbal	SML	Farm, Brushland	Covert	Root	Minty	Putrid	Crumble	Sprinkle	ignites fire in direct sun
91	Blind Iris	Medicinal	CON	Farm, Brushland	Covert	Bulb	Musky	Fragrant	Chew	Eat	cures tularemia, blindness
92	Mandrake	Defensive	SPD	Farm, Brushland	Covert	Root	Musky	Putrid	Claw	Rub/Eat	rub: protect from injurious herbs; eat: causes hallucinations
94	Goldenrod Root	Prophylactic	INT	Farm, Brushland	Covert	Root	Acrid	Putrid	Skin	Eat	halts effects of poison
96	Sourroot	Injurious	STR	Farm, Brushland	Covert	Root	Pungent	Putrid	Squeeze	Eat	2d6 + SML* damage

Dense Odor Clarity

#	Herb	Effect Class	Trait	Habitat	Source	Type	Quality	Tone	Prep.	Delivery	Effect
97	Wicked Mushroom	Soporific	MYS	Oak Forest, Pine Wood, Mtn. Stream	Fungal	Cap	Minty	Fragrant	Lick	Eat	increases MYS +2
101	Snowcap	Hypnotic	CHA	Oak Forest, Pine Wood, Mtn. Stream	Fungal	Cap	Acrid	Mind	Peel	Eat	increases CHA +4
102	Foul Ball	Prophylactic	INT	Oak Forest, Pine Wood, Mtn. Stream	Fungal	Ball	Acrid	Putrid	Skin	Breathe	repel predators; attract carrion eaters
103	Dung Fung	Irritant	AGI	Oak Forest, Pine Wood, Mtn. Stream	Fungal	Cap	Pungent	Fragrant	Brush	Contact	blisters damage 2 HP/minute
104	Giant Puffball	Injurious	STR	Oak Forest, Pine Wood, Mtn. Stream	Fungal	Ball	Pungent	Putrid	Squeeze	Breathe	explodes when smashed, 3d6 damage
105	Golden Rain	Soporific	MYS	Orchard, Rocky Hillside	Floral	Fruit	Minty	Fragrant	Lick	Breathe	induces sleep ≤ 60 HP
106	Carcass Flower	Herbal	SML	Orchard, Rocky Hillside	Floral	Flower	Minty	Putrid	Crumble	Sprinkle	p.weed to green; cures leprosy, rabies
108	Hero Flower	Defensive	SPD	Orchard, Rocky Hillside	Floral	Flower	Musky	Putrid	Claw	Eat	increases AGI & SPD +3
109	Bitterberry	Hypnotic	CHA	Orchard, Rocky Hillside	Floral	Fruit	Acrid	Fragrant	Peel	Contact	acts upon suggestion (83%)
110	Pestflower	Prophylactic	INT	Orchard, Rocky Hillside	Floral	Flower	Acrid	Putrid	Skin	Rub	repels all pests; eradicates parasites
114	Truebark Dust	Herbal	SML	Grassland, Marsh, Suburb	Overt	Stem	Minty	Putrid	Crumble	Sniff	increases SML +2
115	Rabbit Weed	Medicinal	CON	Grassland, Marsh, Suburb	Overt	Leaf	Musky	Fragrant	Chew	Eat	cures any disease
119	Sugarleaf	Irritant	AGI	Grassland, Marsh, Suburb	Overt	Leaf	Pungent	Fragrant	Brush	Eat	damage if moving; effective paralysis
120	Fire Nettle	Injurious	STR	Grassland, Marsh, Suburb	Overt	Stem	Pungent	Putrid	Squeeze	Contact	2d6 + SML* damage
121	Death Lily	Soporific	MYS	Farm, Brushland	Covert	Bulb	Minty	Fragrant	Lick	Eat	induces sleep in any; appears dead
122	Orchid Root	Herbal	SML	Farm, Brushland	Covert	Root	Minty	Putrid	Crumble	Eat	protects from all herbs
123	Lifemelt Garlic	Medicinal	CON	Farm, Brushland	Covert	Bulb	Musky	Fragrant	Chew	Eat	drives out brainworms
126	Arrowroot	Prophylactic	INT	Farm, Brushland	Covert	Root	Acrid	Putrid	Skin	Eat	protects from all poisons
128	Bitterroot	Injurious	STR	Farm, Brushland	Covert	Root	Pungent	Putrid	Squeeze	Eat	3d6 + SML* damage

* Effects that list "SML*" add the SML Rating of the herbalist that prepared the herb, not the user, to the die roll.

Quick Reference Guide to the Bestiary: Predators and Neutral Animals

Predators

Chasers

Species	Spot DV	iPD	MP	HP	STR	SPD	INT	AGI	CON	MYS	SML	CHA	Special Ability
Dog, small (Terrier)	4	6	2	25	2	3	4	2	5	2	4	4	Intruder Alert; Shake
Dog, medium (Border Collie)	4	10	4	45	3	2	6	2	9	2	5	5	Intruder Alert; Shake
Dog, large (Retriever)	4	10	6	50	4	4	5	3	10	3	6	6	Shake
Dog, large (Doberman)	4	12	7	75	4	5	5	4	15	3	5	4	Shake
Dog, huge (Rottweiler)	4	10	5	90	5	4	4	4	18	3	5	4	Shake
Red Fox	6	10	6	40	2	4	5	4	8	3	6	6	Pounce; Shake
Gray Fox	6	10	6	30	2	4	4	3	6	3	7	5	Pounce; Shake
Coyote	4	14	9	60	3	3	5	5	12	3	7	7	Pounce; Shake
Red Wolf	4	12	8	70	4	4	4	4	14	4	7	5	Teamwork; Shake
Deer Wolf	4	12	8	70	5	4	4	5	14	3	7	6	Teamwork; Shake
Gray Wolf	4	12	8	90	6	5	6	6	18	3	6	7	Teamwork; Shake
Pine Marten	6	12	8	35	3	3	4	4	7	2	4	2	Tree Chase
Ringtail	6	10	5	35	2	2	4	5	7	2	5	3	Tree Chase; Foul Spray

Stalkers

Species	Spot DV	iPD	MP	HP	STR	SPD	INT	AGI	CON	MYS	SML	CHA	Special Ability
House Cat (Persian)	6	6	2	25	1	1	3	2	5	1	2	2	Shiny
Alley Cat (Tabby)	6	6	3	25	2	1	4	3	5	1	2	2	Hissy
Meezer Cat (Siamese)	6	8	3	25	2	1	5	2	5	4	2	2	Hissy
Barn Cat (Black)	6	8	3	25	2	2	4	3	5	1	2	1	Mouser
Polydactyl Cat (Calico)	6	8	3	25	4	1	3	3	5	2	2	2	Mouser
Farm Cat (Maine Coon)	6	8	4	35	2	1	4	3	5	1	2	4	Mouser
Feral Cat (Bengal)	8	8	4	30	3	2	5	4	6	1	2	3	Pounce
Bobcat	8	8	4	40	3	3	5	5	8	1	2	4	Pounce
Ocelot	8	10	5	45	3	5	5	5	9	2	2	4	Pounce

Species	Spot DV	iPD	MP	HP	STR	SPD	INT	AGI	CON	MYS	SML	CHA	Special Ability
Lynx	8	10	6	50	4	4	5	6	10	2	2	3	Pounce
Cougar (Mountain Lion)	6	14	10	120	8	6	6	8	24	2	2	3	Nape Bite (x2 damage)
Stoat	6	10	3	20	1	3	4	3	4	4	4	2	Fascinate; Nape Bite
Big Stoat	8	10	2	25	1	2	5	4	5	3	4	2	Fascinate; Nape Bite
Ferret (European Polecat)	6	12	8	30	2	2	4	4	6	2	4	2	Nape Bite
Siberian Polecat	6	12	8	35	3	5	4	4	7	2	4	2	Nape Bite
Small Mongoose (Small Asian)	6	10	6	25	3	8	5	5	5	2	4	2	Extra Move
Indian Mongoose (Gray)	6	10	6	30	5	8	6	6	6	2	5	2	Extra Move
Ichneumon (Egyptian Gray)	6	12	7	35	6	7	7	7	7	2	5	2	Extra Move

Cryptics (do not engage in Pursuit)

Species	Spot DV	iPD	MP	HP	STR	SPD	INT	AGI	CON	MYS	SML	CHA	Special Ability
Gopher Snake	6	1	15	1	1	2	1	3	1	2	1		Constrict
Rattlesnake	8	1	15	8	1	2	2	3	1	2	1		Poisonous Bite
Cottonmouth	6	1	15	5	1	2	1	3	1	2	1		Poisonous Bite
Copperhead	10	1	15	4	1	2	1	3	1	2	1		Poisonous Bite
Python (Burmese)	8	1	100	3	1	4	3	20	2	3	5		Constrict
Snapping Turtle	10	1	40	4	0	2	4	8	1	1	3		Drag; Dive Underwater; Unbreakable Grip
Alligator	8	1	180	5	3	3	4	36	2	1	3		Drag; Dive Underwater; Underwater Spin; Tail-Slap
Great Egret	6	1	15	3	3	4	5	3	2	1	4		Skewer
Great Blue Heron	8	1	25	4	3	4	6	5	2	1	4		Skewer
Sandhill Crane	8	1	35	5	4	5	7	7	2	1	4		Skewer
Mink	8	4	6	30	4	3	4	4	6	2	4	4	Nape Bite; Drag; Dive Underwater
Rats (Black)	4	1	10	1	1	3	1	2	1	3	4		Group Attack

Brutes

Species	Spot DV	iPD	MP	HP	STR	SPD	INT	AGI	CON	MYS	SML	CHA	Special Ability
Badger	4	6	3	50	4	1	4	4	10	2	3	4	Rend
Wolverine	4	8	4	80	7	5	4	5	16	2	3	4	Rend; Nape Bite
Black Bear	2	8	4	150	8	1	5	3	30	4	8	4	Paw Swipe

Species	Spot DV	iPD	MP	HP	STR	SPD	INT	AGI	CON	MYS	SML	CHA	Special Ability
Grizzly Bear	2	10	8	200	8	6	4	5	40	4	8	4	Paw Swipe
Bull, young	2	10	6	200	6	5	1	2	40	2	3	2	Hoof-Kick; Stomp; Horn Gore
Bison	2	10	5	250	6	5	1	2	50	1	3	2	Hoof-Kick; Stomp; Horn Gore

Raptors

Species	Spot DV	iPD	MP	HP	STR	SPD	INT	AGI	CON	MYS	SML	CHA	Special Ability
Red-tailed Hawk	4	14	17	25	6	8	4	4	5	1	2	2	Aerial Attack
Swainson's Hawk	4	14	17	25	5	8	3	4	5	2	1	2	Aerial Attack
Harris Hawk	4	14	17	20	4	8	6	3	4	2	1	2	Aerial Attack; Teamwork
Harrier	2	12	8	20	4	8	6	3	4	2	1	2	Surprise; Aerial Attack
Goshawk	6	14	10	20	3	4	5	5	4	1	1	2	Aerial Attack
Caracara	4	14	13	25	2	2	4	2	5	1	1	2	Aerial Attack
Prairie Falcon	4	14	20	20	5	8	5	5	4	2	1	2	Aerial Attack
Peregrine Falcon	4	14	20	20	4	6	5	5	4	1	1	2	Aerial Attack
Osprey	2	14	12	30	5	8	4	2	6	1	1	2	Aerial Attack
Bald Eagle	2	14	15	40	6	4	4	3	8	2	1	3	Aerial Attack
Golden Eagle	4	14	20	40	8	6	6	6	8	2	1	3	Aerial Attack; Unbreakable Grip
Barn Owl	8	12	8	20	4	8	4	4	4	3	1	6	Nightvision; Surprise; Aerial Attack
Barred Owl	8	12	7	25	5	5	4	5	5	3	1	5	Nightvision; Aerial Attack
Great Horned Owl	8	10	6	30	6	5	5	6	6	3	1	5	Nightvision; Aerial Attack; Unbreakable Grip
Raven	4	14	10	15	4	6	6	2	3	3	1	5	Peck Eyes
Vulture	4	14	10	15	4	6	3	1	3	3	1	5	Regurgitate

Neutral Animals

Rabbit Relatives

Species	Spot DV	FD	Flee DV	MP	HP	STR	SPD	INT	AGI	CON	MYS	SML	CHA	Special Ability
Jackrabbit	6	6	3	8	30	2	3	2	1	2	2	1	2	Jump Kick; Dash without Tiring; Box
Pika	6	6	2	1	15	1	2	2	2	1	2	2	3	Alarm Call
Snowshoe Hare	6	6	3	8	25	2	3	2	1	2	2	1	2	Jump Kick; Dash without Tiring; Box

Weasel Relatives

Species	Spot DV	FD	Flee DV	MP	HP	STR	SPD	INT	AGI	CON	MYS	SML	CHA	Special Ability
Skunk	4	6	3	1	35	2	2	2	3	2	2	1	1	Spray & Power Spray; manipulatio bonus; Disassemble Man-Things
Otter	6	6	5	2	40	3	4	5	4	8	2	4	5	Dive Underwater

Chatters: Squirrels and their Relatives

Species	Spot DV	FD	Flee DV	MP	HP	STR	SPD	INT	AGI	CON	MYS	SML	CHA	Special Ability
Chipmunk	4	6	4	1	10	1	2	3	2	1	2	2	2	Quick Conceal; Automatic Stealth; Double Jump; Find Hidden Entry
Flying Squirrel	6	6	3	1	15	2	2	2	2	1	1	2	3	Glide
Ground Squirrel	4	6	3	1	15	2	2	2	2	1	1	2	2	Alarm Call
Marmot	4	6	3	1	30	3	2	2	2	3	1	2	2	Alarm Call
Prairie Dog	4	6	4	1	25	2	2	2	2	3	1	2	3	Alarm Call
Tree Squirrel	4	6	4	1	15	2	2	2	2	1	1	2	3	Tree Dash; Leap Acrobatically; Taunt; Lie & Cheat; count to 7

Nibblers: Rats and their Relatives

Species	Spot DV	FD	Flee DV	MP	HP	STR	SPD	INT	AGI	CON	MYS	SML	CHA	Special Ability
Beaver	6	6	3	1	60	5	1	2	3	12	1	2	2	Dive Underwater
Gopher	8	4	2	1	10	2	2	2	2	1	2	3	2	Fast Burrow
Kangaroo Rat	8	6	2	1	10	1	3	1	2	1	1	2	3	none
Mouse	8	6	2	1	10	1	2	1	2	1	1	2	2	none
Muskrat	6	6	2	2	25	2	2	1	2	2	2	3	1	Dive Underwater
Nutria	6	6	2	1	40	3	1	1	2	8	1	2	2	Dive Underwater
Packrat	6	6	3	2	15	1	2	3	3	1	1	2	2	Shiny
Porcupine	6	3	2	1	45	2	1	2	1	3	2	2	2	Bristle; Climb Trees; Throw Quills; Provide Antibiotic
Vole	8	6	2	1	10	1	2	1	2	3	1	2	2	Serenity

Grubbers: animals that dig or forage in the ground

Species	Spot DV	FD	Flee DV	MP	HP	STR	SPD	INT	AGI	CON	MYS	SML	CHA	Special Ability
Armadillo	8	3	2	2	15	1	2	1	2	2	2	3	2	Roll Up; Armor; Find Hidden; Walk Underwater; Raft; immune to disease & pests
Javelina	6	6	3	6	60	4	3	4	2	12	2	3	1	Tusk Gore

Species	Spot DV	FD	Flee DV	MP	HP	STR	SPD	INT	AGI	CON	MYS	SML	CHA	Special Ability
Mole	8	6	3	1	10	1	1	1	1	1	4	4	2	Fast Burrow
Opossum	6	6	3	1	35	2	1	1	2	2	3	2	2	Feign Death; Rapid Breeding; Determine Function; Implant Thoughts
Pig	4	6	3	3	90	4	3	4	2	18	2	4	1	Tusk Gore
Wild Boar	4	6	3	5	120	5	4	4	4	24	2	3	1	Tusk Gore

Ramblers: Animals Not Built for Speed or Hiding

Species	Spot DV	FD	Flee DV	MP	HP	STR	SPD	INT	AGI	CON	MYS	SML	CHA	Special Ability
Coati	4	6	3	2	45	2	2	3	3	9	1	2	1	Double Bite
Raccoon	6	6	3	2	45	3	2	2	2	2	1	2	1	Intimidate; Intruder Mode; Double Bite; carry while walking bipedally

Hoofers: large, long-legged grazers & browsers

Species	Spot DV	FD	Flee DV	MP	HP	STR	SPD	INT	AGI	CON	MYS	SML	CHA	Special Ability
Cow	2	6	3	2	180	3	4	1	1	36	2	2	2	Hoof-Kick; Stomp; Horn Gore
Deer	4	8	3	7	100	2	4	2	2	20	1	2	2	Hoof-Kick; Stomp; Horn Gore
Elk	2	8	3	7	160	3	4	2	2	32	1	2	2	Hoof-Kick; Stomp; Horn Gore
Goat	2	8	3	6	90	2	3	2	2	18	1	2	2	Hoof-Kick; Butt
Horse	2	8	3	8	180	3	5	2	2	36	1	2	3	Hoof-Kick; Stomp
Moose	2	8	3	6	170	4	3	2	3	34	1	2	2	Hoof-Kick; Stomp; Horn Gore
Mountain Goat	2	8	3	6	100	3	3	2	3	20	1	2	2	Hoof-Kick; Butt
Pronghorn	2	8	3	10	80	2	6	2	2	16	1	2	2	Hoof-Kick; Stomp; Horn Gore
Sheep	2	8	3	6	90	1	3	1	1	18	1	2	2	Hoof-Kick; Butt

Bats

Species	Spot DV	FD	Flee DV	MP	HP	STR	SPD	INT	AGI	CON	MYS	SML	CHA	Special Ability
Brown Bat	6	8	3	6	10	1	4	1	1	1	3	1	1	Echolocate
Fruit Bat	4	8	3	6	15	1	4	2	1	2	2	2	1	Echolocate

Perchers: Songbirds and Their Relatives

Species	Spot DV	FD	Flee DV	MP	HP	STR	SPD	INT	AGI	CON	MYS	SML	CHA	Special Ability
Blackbird	4	8	3	12	10	1	3	3	1	1	1	1	3	Alarm Call
Blue Jay	4	8	3	12	10	1	3	4	1	1	1	1	3	Alarm Call
Crow	4	8	3	12	15	2	5	5	2	2	3	1	4	Peck Eyes
Magpie	4	8	3	12	15	1	4	5	1	2	2	1	4	Shiny
Pigeon	4	8	3	12	10	1	3	2	1	1	1	1	2	none
Robin	4	8	3	12	10	1	3	2	1	1	1	1	2	none
Sparrow	4	8	3	12	10	1	1	1	1	1	1	1	1	none
Woodpecker	4	8	3	12	15	1	2	1	1	1	1	1	1	Drill Wood

Strutters: Turkeys and other ground birds

Species	Spot DV	FD	Flee DV	MP	HP	STR	SPD	INT	AGI	CON	MYS	SML	CHA	Special Ability
Chicken	4	8	3	12	25	2	1	1	1	1	1	1	1	none
Grouse	8	8	3	12	15	1	1	1	1	1	1	1	1	none
Pheasant	6	8	3	12	25	2	1	1	2	2	1	1	1	none
Quail	6	8	3	12	15	1	1	1	1	1	1	1	1	none
Turkey	4	8	3	12	35	2	1	1	3	3	1	1	1	none

Waders: Waterfowl and Wading Birds

Species	Spot DV	FD	Flee DV	MP	HP	STR	SPD	INT	AGI	CON	MYS	SML	CHA	Special Ability
Duck	4	8	3	12	20	1	2	2	1	1	1	1	2	Swim
Goose	4	8	3	12	35	3	2	2	3	3	1	1	2	Swim
Gull	4	8	3	12	20	2	3	3	3	2	1	1	2	Swim
Killdeeer	4	8	3	12	20	1	2	2	1	1	3	1	3	Feign Injury

Coldies: Reptiles and Amphibians

Species	Spot DV	FD	Flee DV	MP	HP	STR	SPD	INT	AGI	CON	MYS	SML	CHA	Special Ability
Box Turtle	6	6	4	1	25	1	1	1	1	5	1	1	1	Turtle Shell Armor
Frog	6	6	4	1	10	1	3	1	1	1	1	1	1	Dive Underwater
Garter Snake	8	6	4	2	10	1	2	1	1	1	1	2	1	none
Newt	8	6	4	1	10	1	1	1	1	1	2	1	1	Poisonous Skin
Pond Turtle	6	6	4	1	15	1	1	1	1	3	1	1	1	Turtle Shell Armor; Dive Underwater
Racer	4	8	4	4	15	1	4	1	1	2	1	2	1	Tree Dash
Skink	4	6	4	3	10	1	3	1	1	1	1	1	1	Tree Dash; Autotomy
Spiny Lizard	4	6	4	5	10	1	4	1	1	1	1	1	1	Tree Dash

Species	Spot DV	FD	Flee DV	MP	HP	STR	SPD	INT	AGI	CON	MYS	SML	CHA	Special Ability
Toad	4	6	4	1	15	1	1	1	1	3	1	1	1	Poisonous Skin

Fishies: All Fish

Species	Spot DV	FD	Flee DV	MP	HP	STR	SPD	INT	AGI	CON	MYS	SML	CHA	Special Ability
Bass	4	4	3	2	15	3	3	1	3	3	1	1	1	none
Carp	4	4	3	2	15	3	3	1	3	3	1	1	1	none
Catfish	6	4	3	1	10	2	1	2	2	2	1	1	1	none
Lamprey	6	4	3	3	10	2	1	1	2	2	1	1	1	none
Sunfish	4	4	3	2	10	1	1	1	1	1	1	1	1	none
Trout	4	4	3	2	10	2	4	2	3	2	1	1	1	none

Crawlies: Insects and Arthropods of All Kinds

Species	Spot DV	FD	Flee DV	MP	HP	STR	SPD	INT	AGI	CON	MYS	SML	CHA	Special Ability
Ants, Acrobat	4	2	4	1	1	1	1	1	1	1	1	1	1	Poisonous Sting
Ants, Carpenter	4	2	4	1	1	1	1	1	1	1	1	1	1	none
Ants, Fire	4	2	4	1	1	1	1	1	1	1	1	1	1	Poisonous Sting
Ants, Harvester	4	2	4	1	1	1	1	1	1	1	1	1	1	Poisonous Sting
Beetle (Darkling)	6	2	4	1	1	1	1	1	1	3	1	1	1	Noxious Spray
Black Widow Spider	6	2	4	1	1	3	1	1	1	1	1	1	1	Poisonous Bite
Butterfly	2	2	4	4	1	1	2	1	1	1	1	1	5	none
Centipede	4	2	4	3	1	2	2	1	2	1	1	1	1	Poisonous Bite
Cockroach	4	2	4	3	1	1	2	1	1	2	1	1	1	Find Hidden Entry
Dragonfly	4	2	4	8	1	1	4	1	1	1	1	1	2	none
Grasshopper	6	4	4	2	1	1	3	1	1	1	1	1	1	none
Honeybees	4	4	4	6	1	3	1	1	3	1	1	1	1	Poisonous Sting
Millipede	6	2	4	1	1	1	1	1	1	1	1	1	1	Poisonous Skin
Pillbug	4	2	4	1	1	1	1	1	1	1	1	1	1	Roll Up
Scorpion	8	2	4	2	1	6	1	1	5	1	1	1	1	Poisonous Sting
Spider	6	2	4	1	1	2	1	1	1	1	1	1	1	Poisonous Bite
Tarantula	4	2	4	1	1	6	1	1	1	1	1	1	1	Poisonous Bite
Walking Stick	10	2	4	1	1	1	1	1	1	1	4	1	1	Quick Conceal
Wasps	4	2	4	8	1	6	4	1	6	1	1	1	1	Poisonous Sting

Worms

Species	Spot DV	FD	Flee DV	MP	HP	STR	SPD	INT	AGI	CON	MYS	SML	CHA	Special Ability
Earthworm (Nightcrawler)	6	1	2	1	1	1	1	1	1	1	1	1	1	Fast Burrow

Special Creatures

Humans

Type	Spot DV	iPD	MP	HP	STR	SPD	INT	AGI	CON	MYS	SML	CHA	Special Ability
Birdwatcher	4	8	1	100	3	1	10	1	20	0	0	0	none
Boy	4	8	2	75	2	1	8	2	15	0	0	0	Stone Throwing
Farmer	4	8	1	100	3	1	10	1	20	0	0	0	Thunderstick
Gardener	4	8	1	100	3	1	10	1	20	0	0	0	Stone Throwing
Girl	4	8	2	75	2	1	8	1	15	0	0	0	none
Hiker	4	8	1	100	3	1	10	1	20	0	0	0	none
Hunter	6	8	1	100	3	1	10	1	20	0	0	0	Thunderstick
Lumberjack	4	8	1	100	3	1	8	1	20	0	0	0	Stone Throwing
Picnicker	4	8	1	100	3	1	8	1	20	0	0	0	none
Rancher	4	8	1	100	3	1	10	1	20	0	0	0	Thunderstick
Ranger	4	8	1	100	3	1	12	1	20	0	0	0	Capture
Sportsman	4	8	1	100	3	1	10	1	20	0	0	0	Thunderstick
Townie	2	8	1	100	3	1	6	1	20	0	0	0	none
Trapper	6	8	1	100	3	1	12	1	5	0	0	0	none

Beasts of Folklore and Legend

Species	Spot DV	iPD	MP	HP	STR	SPD	INT	AGI	CON	MYS	SML	CHA	Special Ability
Agropelter	8	8	3	75	6	2	4	5	15	5	2	0	Stone (Branch) Throwing
Azeban	6	8	2	50	4	3	6	6	10	4	2	7	Persuasion
Caladrius	8	8	12	30	3	3	3	6	6	4	2	6	Empathic Heal or Hurt
Chupacabra	6	10	8	150	8	6	5	6	30	4	8	4	Paw Swipe
Dingmaul	8	14	6	120	8	6	6	8	24	2	2	3	Tail-Slap
Flying Wolf (Ahool)	6	14	17	30	4	8	6	3	6	2	1	2	Aerial Attack; Teamwork
Hoop Snake	8	8	8	30	8	4	2	4	6	1	2	1	Tail-Slap
Jackalope	6	8	9	30	2	5	2	3	6	2	1	2	Jump Kick; Dash without Tiring; Horn Gore
Jaculus	6	8	10	40	6	4	5	7	8	2	1	4	Aerial Attack; Skewer
Lavellan	6	6	4	50	5	4	3	5	10	2	6	4	Poison Spray

Species	Spot DV	iPD	MP	HP	STR	SPD	INT	AGI	CON	MYS	SML	CHA	Special Ability
Rat King	6	6	2	40	3	1	1	3	8	8	3	6	Enthrall Nibblers; Telesthesia
Sidehill Gouger	4	14	9	60	3	3	5	5	12	3	7	7	Shake
Skvader	8	8	12	25	2	3	2	1	2	2	1	2	Aerial Attack
Slide-Rock Bolter	8	8	1	100	3	1	4	3	20	2	3	5	Tusk Gore
Tree Octopus	8	4	6	30	6	5	5	6	6	3	1	2	Unbreakable Grip
Triffid	4	4	1	40	3	1	1	6	8	1	1	1	Tendril Slap
Tripodero	6	8	2	50	2	1	4	6	10	2	1	2	Stone Throwing
Whirling Whimpus	4	6	5	50	4	8	4	6	10	2	3	4	Whirling Attack

Pursuit Board & Key

The green hexes on the left side of the board represent safe refuge. Small green bush symbols indicate the presence of obstacles that may impede a fleeing rabbit or its pursuer, or offer a temporary refuge. Both Pursuers and Fugitives can move through any open hex (yellow), including hexes that contain obstacles, but only Fugitives may enter refuge hexes (green). Fugitives must begin Pursuit within 2 hexes of the midline, as indicated by darker yellow hexes. Fugitives may not leave the Pursuit Board, except as the result of a Last Ditch special tactic.

The red icons represent the starting position(s) of the Pursuer(s), whether predators or hostile rabbits. Initial positions of Fugitives (the rabbits and their allies being chased) are determined based on initial pursuit distance (iPD) that separates them from their Pursuers at the outset of the encounter.

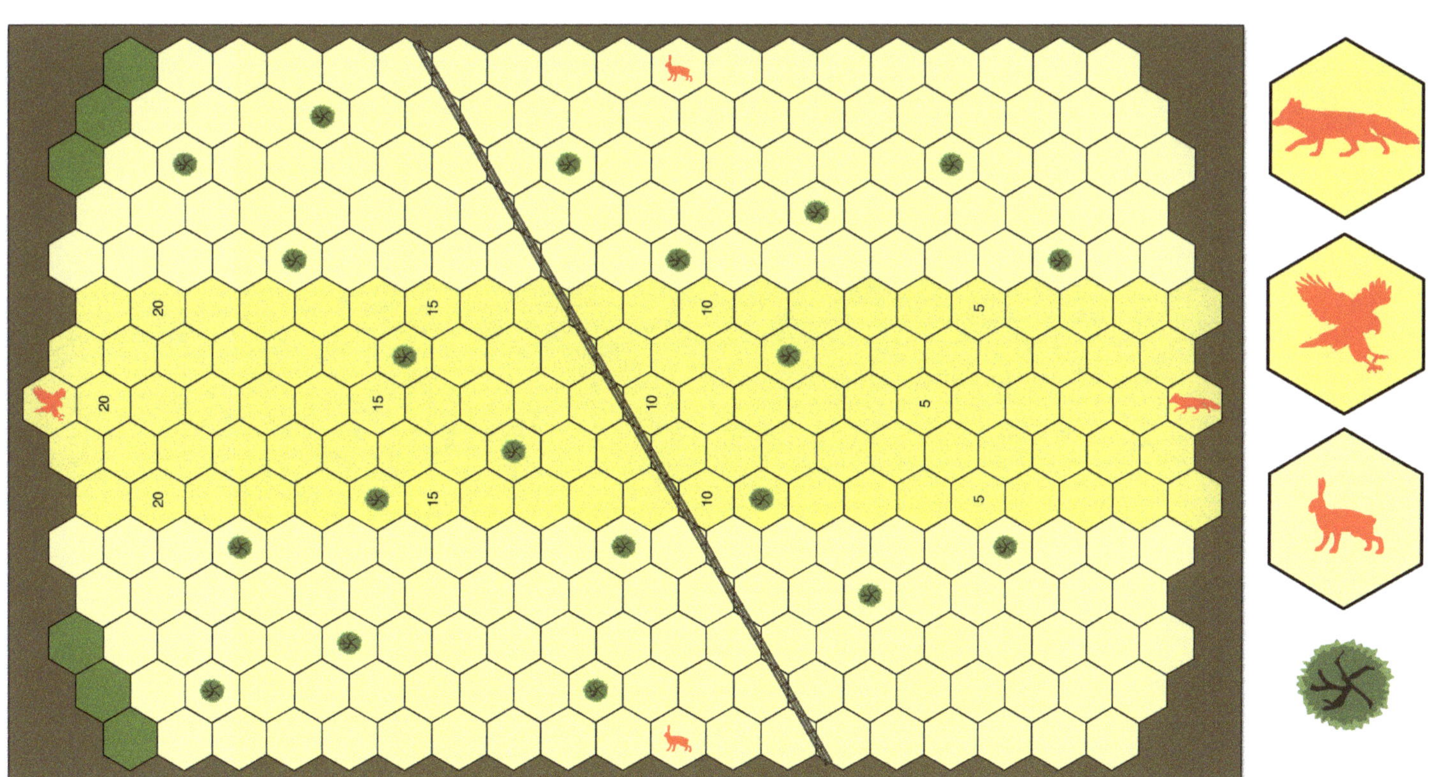

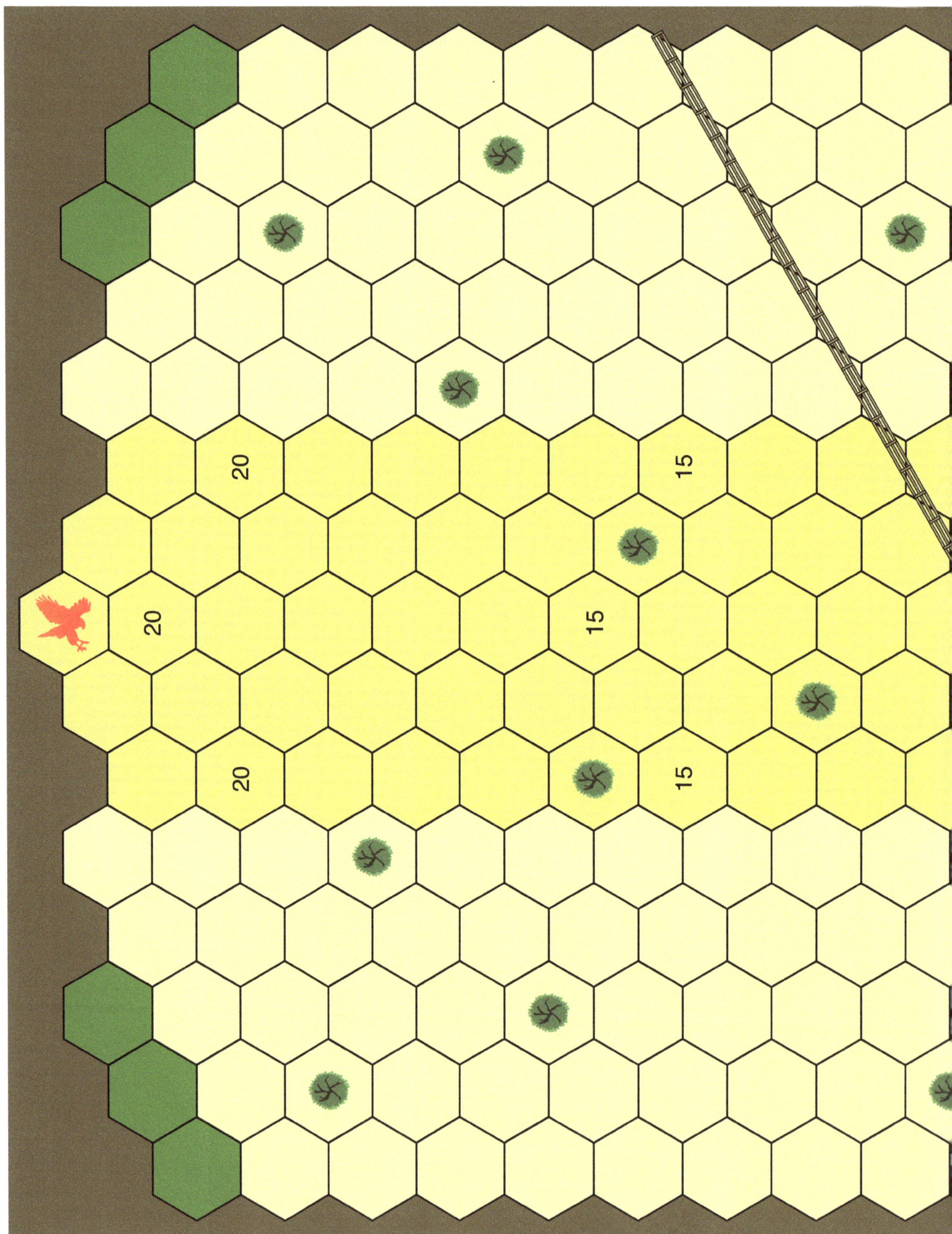

20
20
20
20
15
15
15
15

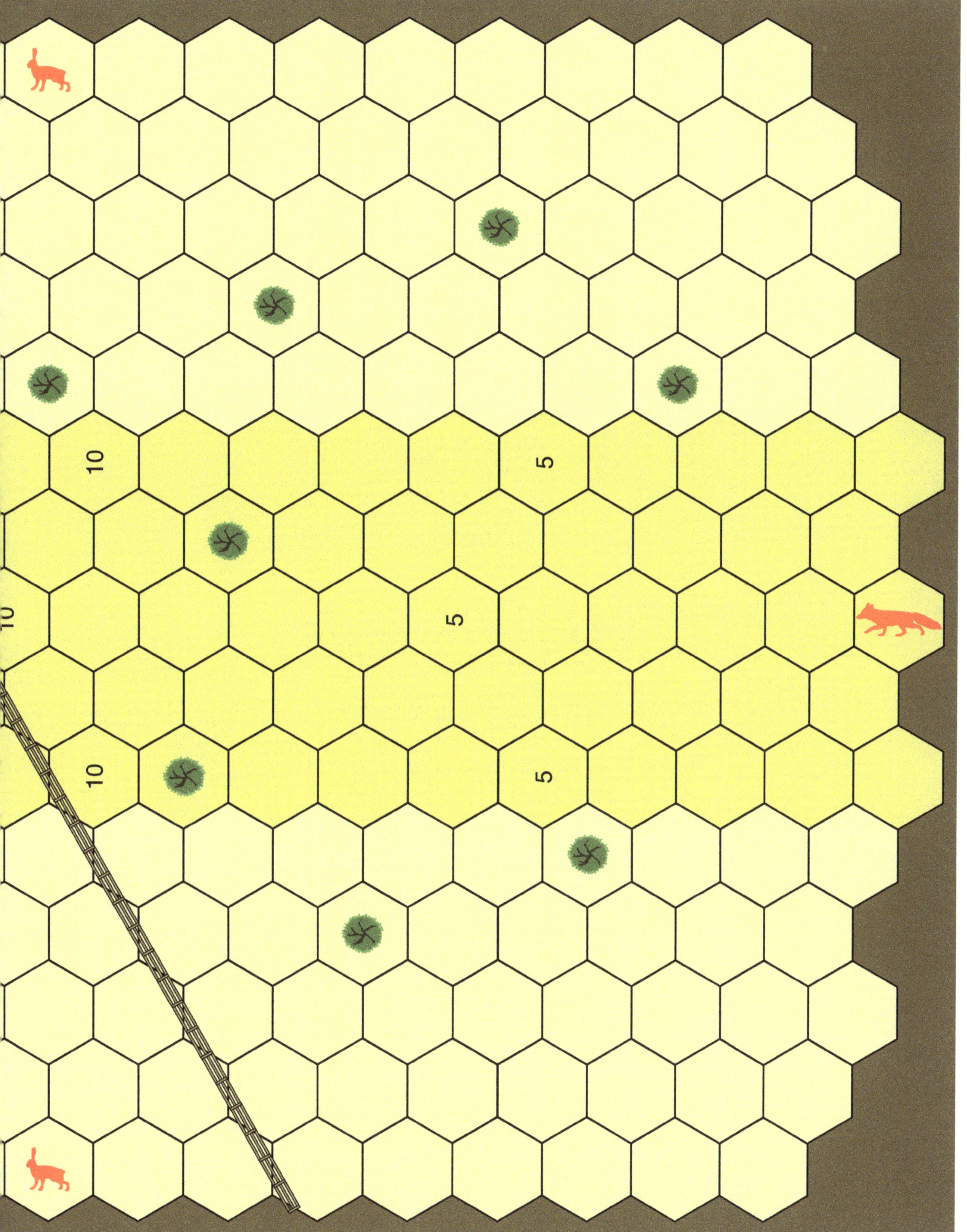

10
10
10
10
5
5
5

Battleboards for 10 Habitats & Key

All Battleboards

- Exit arrows (blue) at southwest and southeast corners; cannot leave or enter by any other edge.
- red dashed line around tree hex: cost one extra MP (+1) to enter hex of tree trunk.
- trunk or canopy of any tree requires Climb ability; yellow bird indicates access to climb up from ground.

Farm

- Garden surrounded by woven wire fence (red lines) that cannot be climbed or bitten through, buried one-half meter deep.
- Southern edge of garden walled with stone.
- Doghouse on northern edge, next to #1, costs +1 MP to enter.
- Can move under bed of pickup truck; to enter bed, requires Jump or Climb ability (indicate with Canopy token).
- garden includes variety of vegetables.

Orchard

- canopy of each tree extends into adjacent spaces.
- moving from canopy to canopy requires jump of 1 meter.

Marsh

- blue dashed line around hex: cost +1 MP to exit, treat whole hex as a hazard (Quicksand).
- hexes with rabbit footprints: boggy ground offers poor footing, costs +1 MP to exit.
- partial dashed red line (#2), costs +1 MP to cross either direction.
- foot path (with footprints) bears man smell.
- broken bridge: requires a leap of 1 meter to cross safely; leap of one-half to 1 meter may slip into water on 1d6 roll of 1–3.
- full stream hex: full hexes require all remaining MP to wade across, or STR 3+ to jump.
- narrow streams along hex borders: require +3 MP to wade across or leap of one-half meter.

Grassland

- double red dashed line, between bush and boulder: costs all remaining MP to cross.
- full stream hex: full hexes require all remaining MP to wade across, or STR 3+ to jump.
- hollow log may be entered by rabbit or smaller at either end: costs 1 MP to enter and 1 MP to exit; treat walking on top as hazard (Slip & Fall), +1 MP to exit.
- blue dashed line around ant nest in northeast quadrant: handicap, determine which kind of ant at random (Acrobat, Fire, Harvester); 1 extra MP to exit.
- burrow in northwest quadrant: requires 1 extra MP to enter; may be duck hole (1 meter deep, no chambers) or full burrow (continue with Burrow Battleboard).

Oak Woodland

- double red dashed lines: hollow log, costs all remaining MP to cross northeast to southwest.
- double red dashed lines: costs all remaining MP to pass between small tree and boulder.
- hollow log may be entered at either end: costs 1 MP to enter and 1 MP to exit (without passing through either hex in between).
- piles of leaves are deep enough to hide a rabbit or smaller, or a rabbit-sized object; offer poor footing (rabbit footprints); +1 MP to exit.
- fairy ring around tree in northeast quadrant contains mushrooms: determine whether edible or poison at random.

Brushland

- double red dashed lines: heavy brush, requires all remaining MP to cross.

Rocky Hillside

- double red dashed lines: dense brush or tree, costs 1 extra MP to cross.
- cliff faces along hex edges: cannot be climbed; can jump down for 2d6 damage, or land in bush for 1d6 damage.
- large tree in center can be climbed up or down; permits access between middle and top terrace.
- rocky trails: loose rocks; treat as a hazard (talus slope).
- burrow & cave in northwest quadrant are connected: requires all extra MP to pass between middle and top terrace.

Mountain Stream

- blue dashed lines around Beaver dam and northwestern rock: treat whole hex as a hazard (Slip & Fall).
- double red dashed line: costs all remaining MP to cross.
- full stream hex: full hexes require all remaining MP to wade across, or STR 3+ to jump.
- Cave in northeast requires 1 extra MP to enter; continue underground using burrow Battleboard, entering at southwestern corner.
- center island is a Beaver Lodge. Entrance is in one of 3 hexes along northern side or 3 hexes along southern side of island (determine at random). Wet logs of lodge offer poor footing (shown by rabbit footprints); +1 MP to exit.
- crossing the stream at the northwestern rock involves 2 leaps of one-half meter, requiring STR 1 or greater.

Suburb

- double red dashed lines: require all remaining MP to cross.
- dark brown fence along southern edge has heavy wooden planks and cannot be crossed.
- white picket fence offers no obstacle to movement by rabbit or smaller, 3 extra MP to cross by larger up to raccoon size; cannot be crossed by large dog.
- doghouse on western edge, next to #2, costs +1 MP to enter.
- gray zones are concrete, bar any digging.
- food on picnic table includes vegetables and fruit; climbing access from any of 4 hexes with table; use canopy token to indicate on table, otherwise underneath.
- pond contains large carp.

Pine Forest

- partial red dashed line: cost +1 MP to cross either direction.
- double red dashed lines: fallen tree branch, costs all remaining MP to cross northeast to southwest.
- hollow log in southwest quadrant may be entered at either end: costs 1 MP to enter and 1 MP to exit, without passing through hex in between.
- piles of leaves are deep enough to hide a rabbit or smaller, or a rabbit-sized object; offer poor footing (rabbit footprints); +1 MP to exit.

Battleboards for Burrow & Extensions

Main Burrow

- Burrow Exits at southwestern and southeastern corners.
- If no extensions are added, east and west edges are solid.
- Three shades indicate relative depth: lightest shade is shallow (1 meter); medium brown is intermediate (2–3 meters); dark brown is deep (4–5 meters).
- wavy arrows between hexes: tunnel slopes down

Burrow Extensions

- Burrow half-sheets can align with eastern or western edge of main burrow Battleboard. Can be cut in half, or rotated 180 degrees, to use either half.
- Single entrance to each half-sheet are at intermediate depth (medium brown). No other exits, although some chambers are shallow (light shade).

Battleboard — Brushland

Battleboard — Grassland

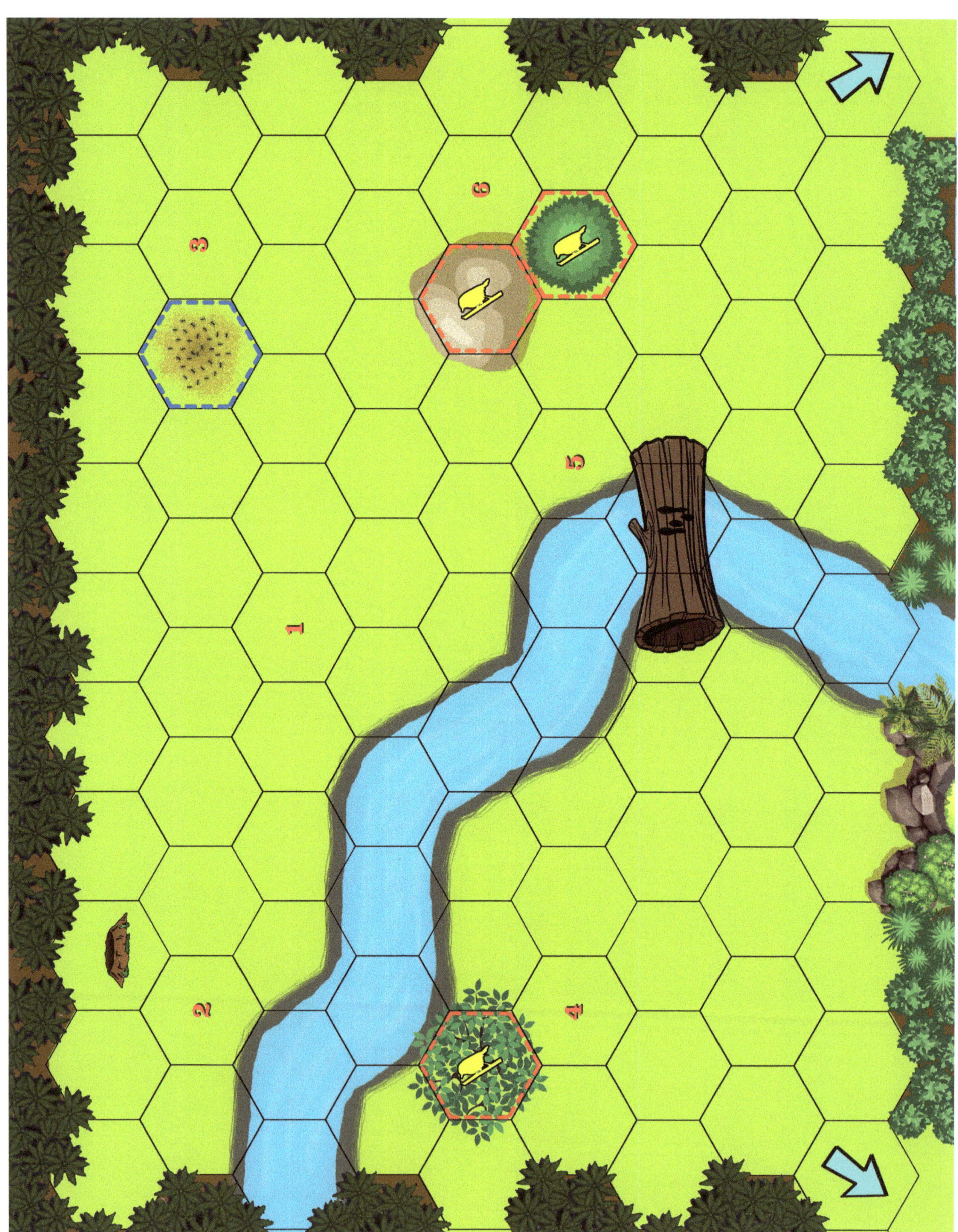

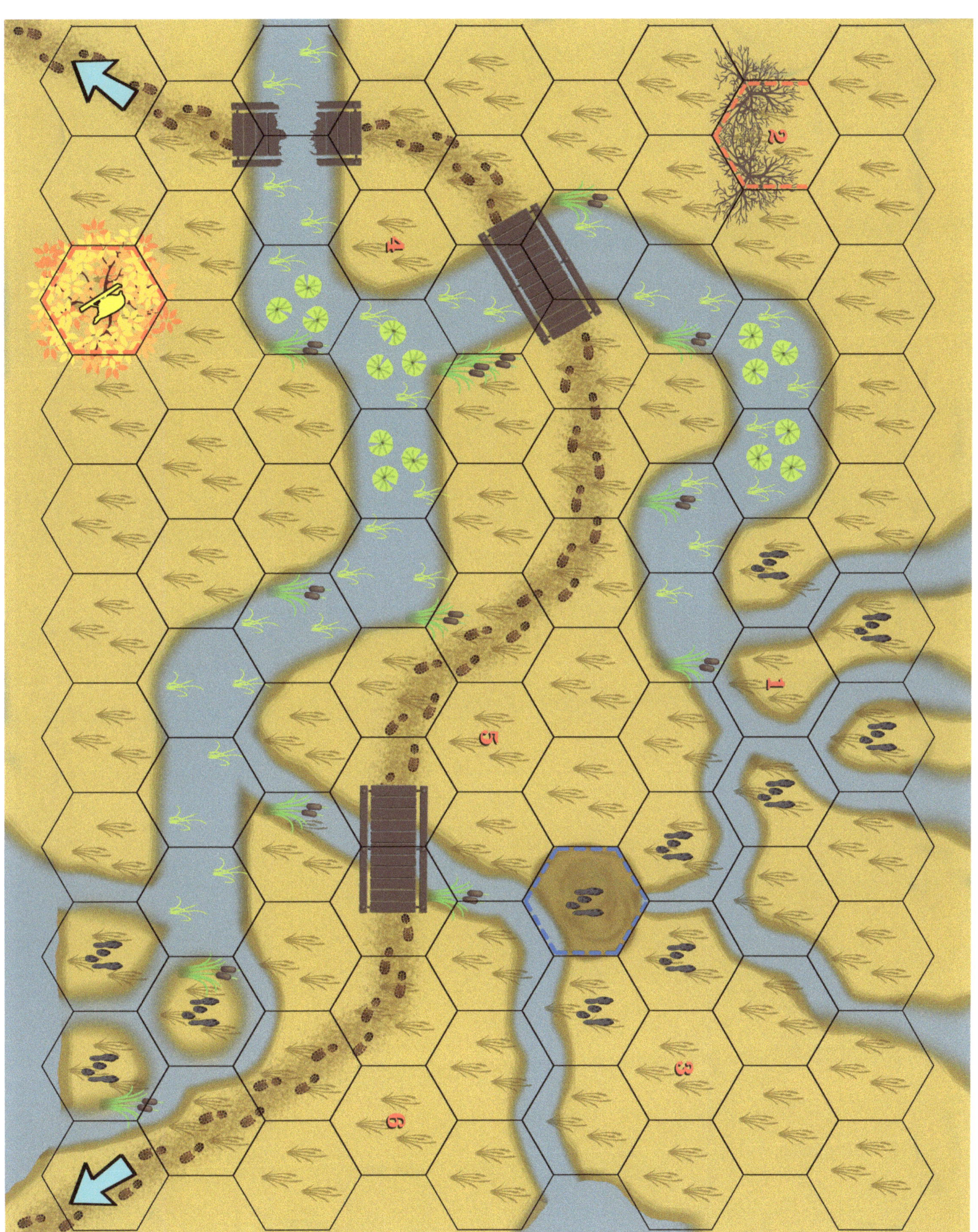

2
4
1
5
6
3

Battleboard – Mountain Stream

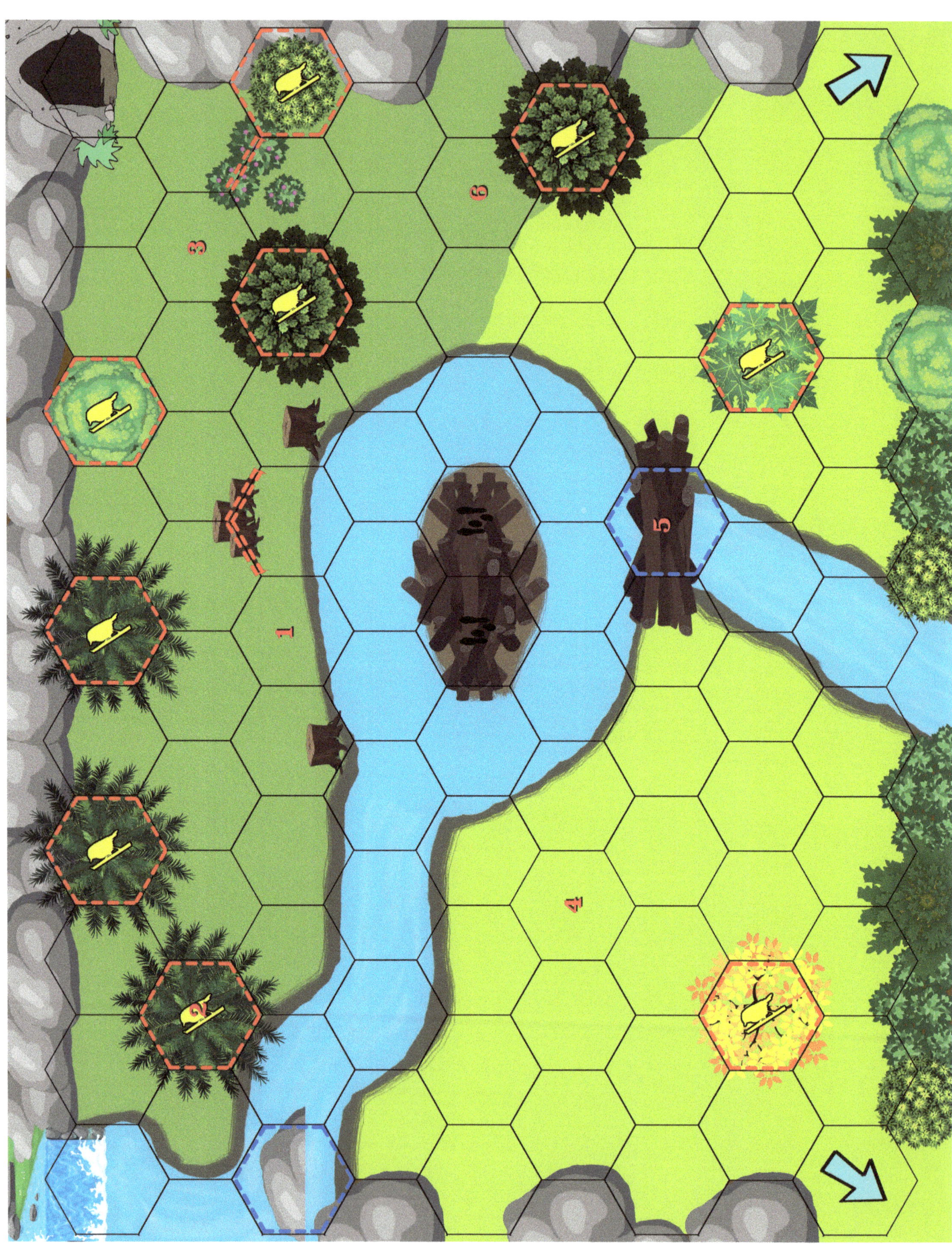

Battleboard — Orchard

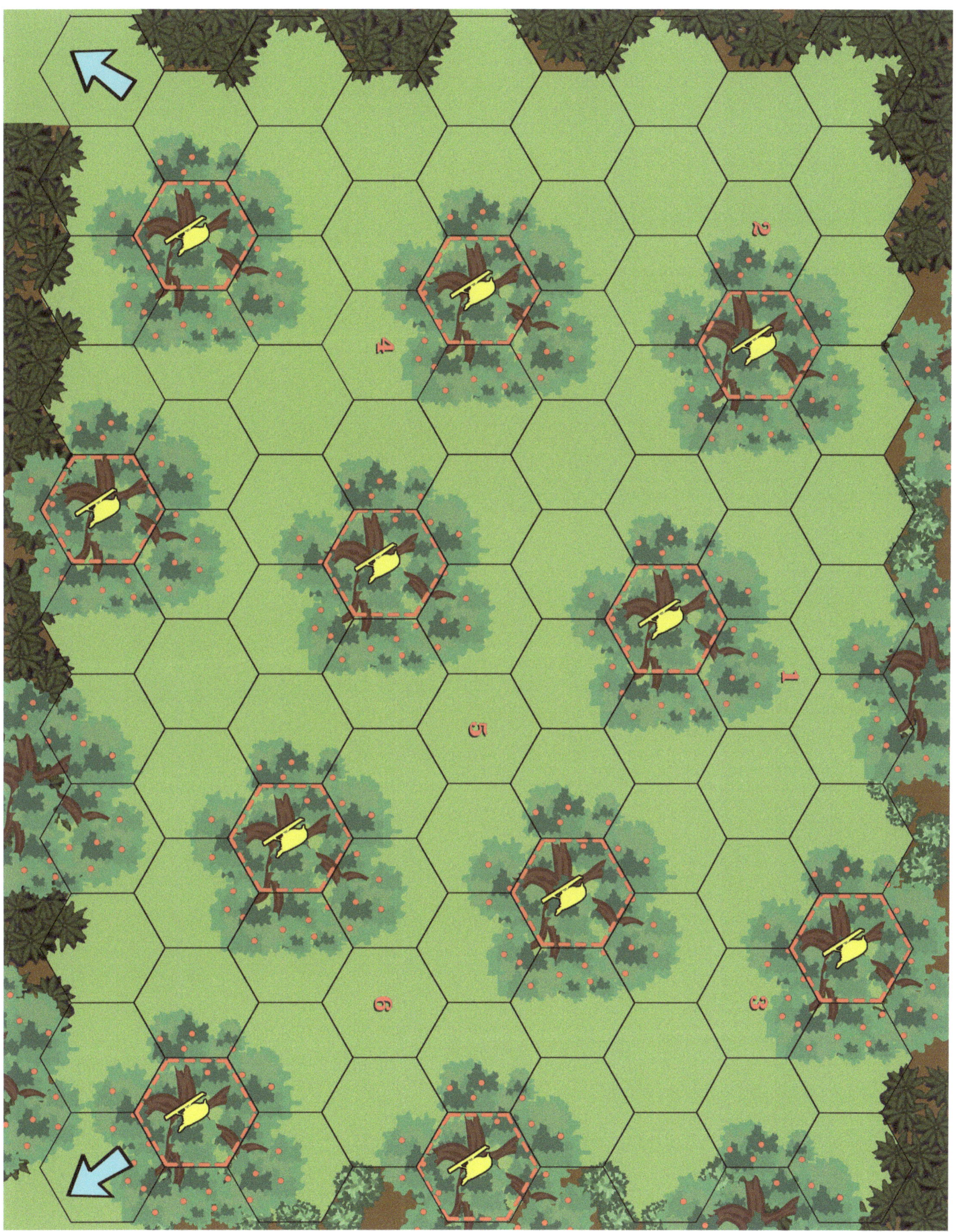

Battleboard — Pine Forest

Battleboard — Rocky Hillside

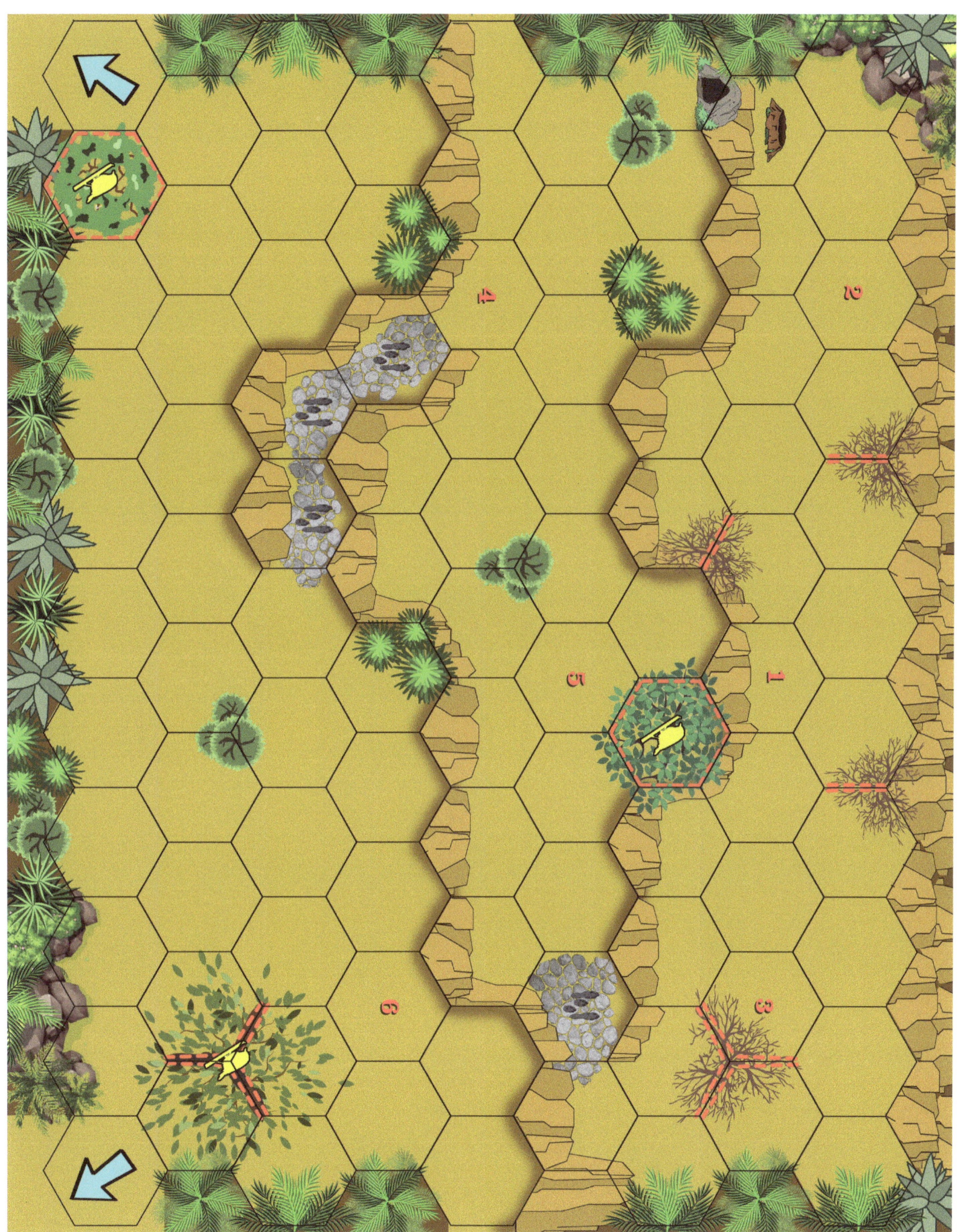

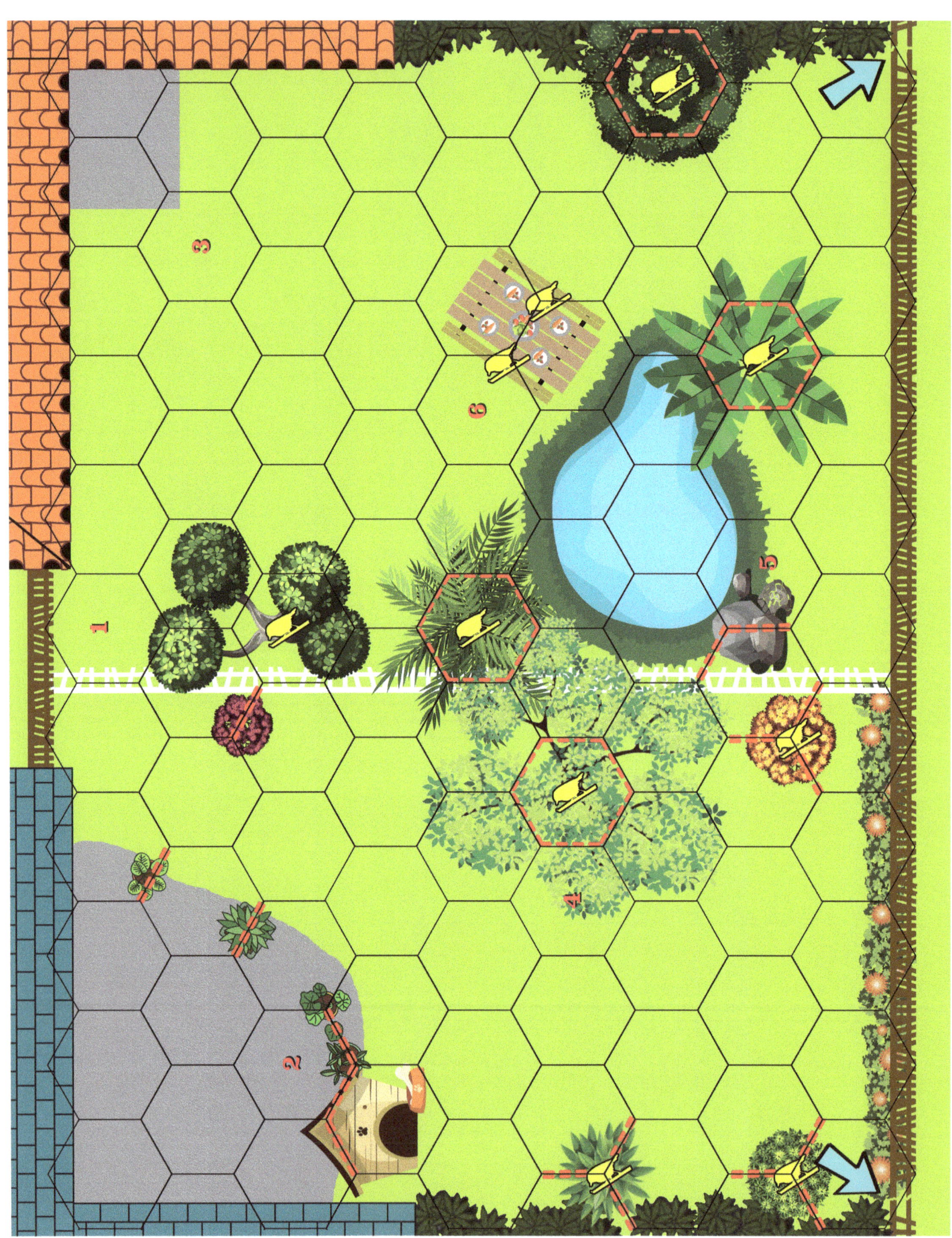

Battleboard — Woodland

Battleboard — Burrow

Ice Crack playing sheet

Bunnies & Burrows
The Fields and Forests of
Coneylaeth

Tokens for Combat, Pursuit, and Mini-Games

Pursuit, Combat, Herb search, and other parts of **Bunnies & Burrows** are best played with the use of markers or tokens representing characters and artifacts in the game. These tokens are provided on separate sheets, but are reprinted here for reference.

Character tokens represent the 8 professions of rabbits and the 8 professions of playable non-rabbit animals. The tokens are color-coded based on the primary trait of the profession and bear unique silhouettes of rabbits and other species. An additional set of 8 tokens are provided that depict a rabbit from overhead view. Players may find these more convenient for use during Pursuit.

Both player and predator tokens are arrow-shaped, to render facing direction clear. Predator tokens additionally display essential stats necessary for conducting most aspects of combat. The name of the predator is displayed at bottom right, printed along the back edge. Black print is relevant for Combat; Blue print is used for Pursuit. Proceeding clockwise from the name, the two numbers at lower left show Pursuit movement allowance (MP) and INT Rating (which limits the number of special tactics that may be used during Pursuit). At the point of the arrow on the left side is the predator's SPD Rating, required for defense. At upper left are AGI and STR Ratings used for calculating Attack Score and damage. Finally, at upper right are the predator's hit points (HP). Remember, all these stats represent a Sub-Adult predator; combat stats and HP increase with older predators.

Character Tokens for Combat and Pursuit

Predator Tokens

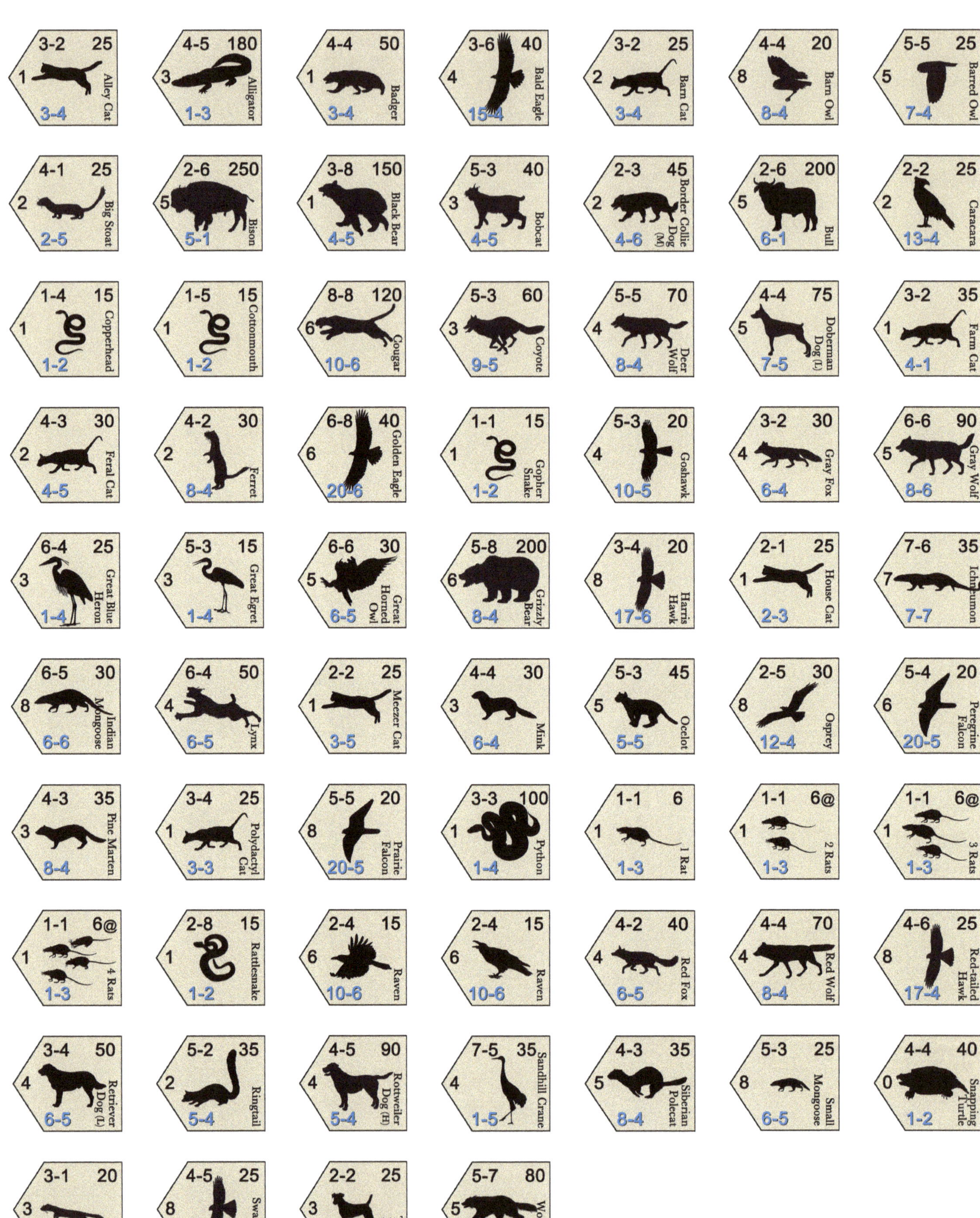

Pursuit Obstacles, Herb Search

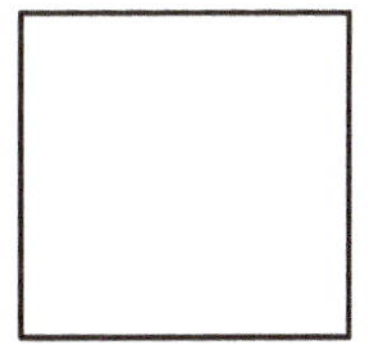      

Clear Herb 

Cloudy Herb 

Dense Herb 

Green Herb 

Murky Herb 

Garden Raid Tokens

Apple 

Carrots 

Corn 

Disturbed Earth 

Eggplant 

Garlic 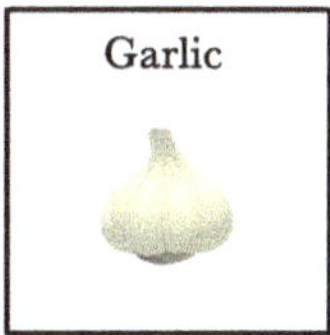

Glint of Metal 

Length of Vine 

Lettuce 

Melon 

Onion 

Peas 

Peppers 

Pumpkin 

Squash 

Stick 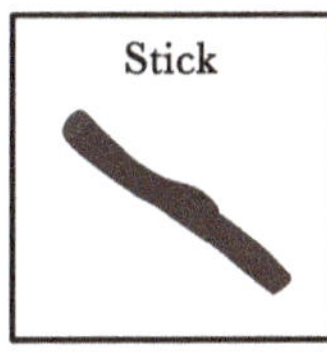

Strawberries 

Tomato 

Herb Search Map

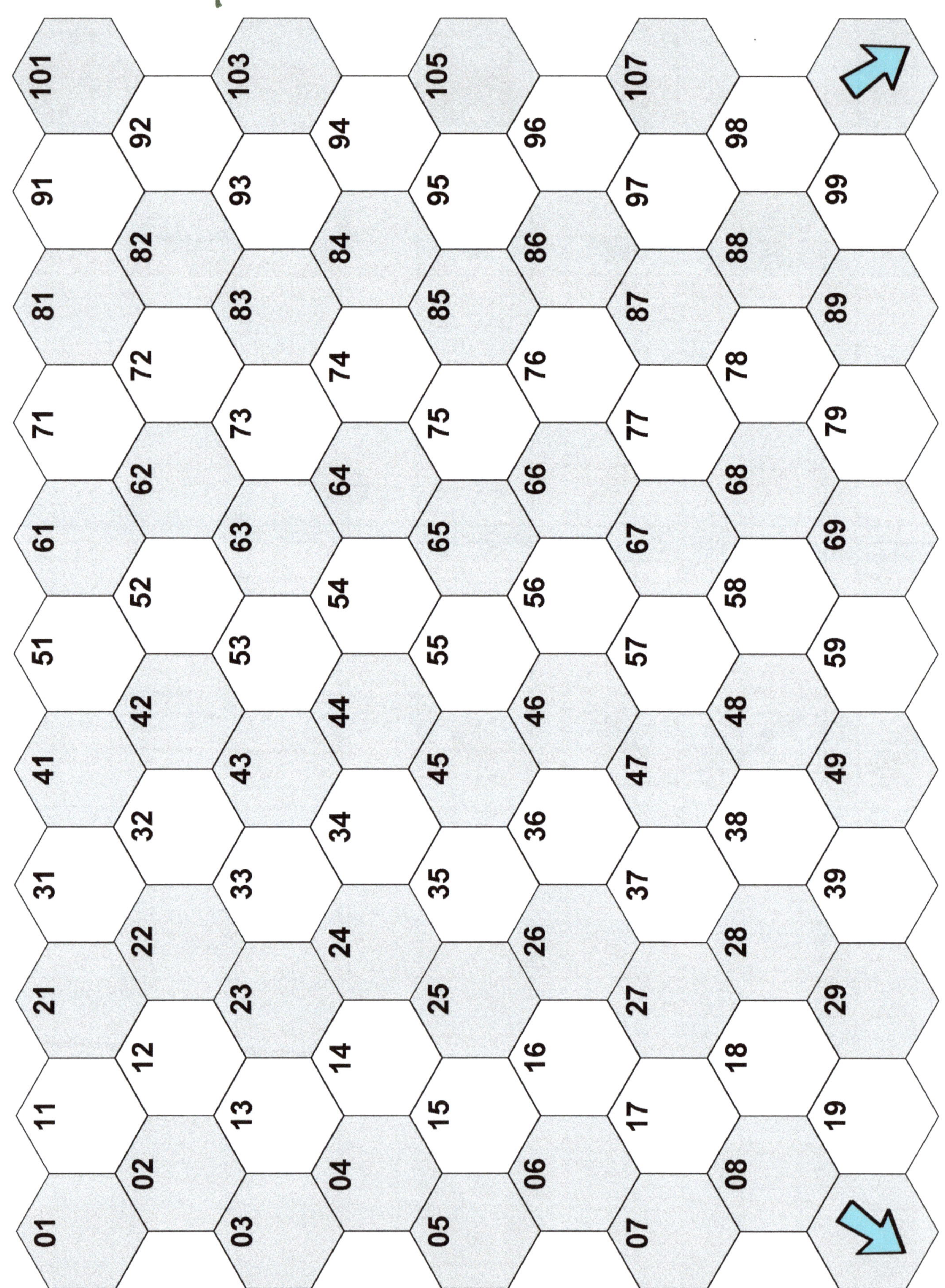

Combat Tactics Cards

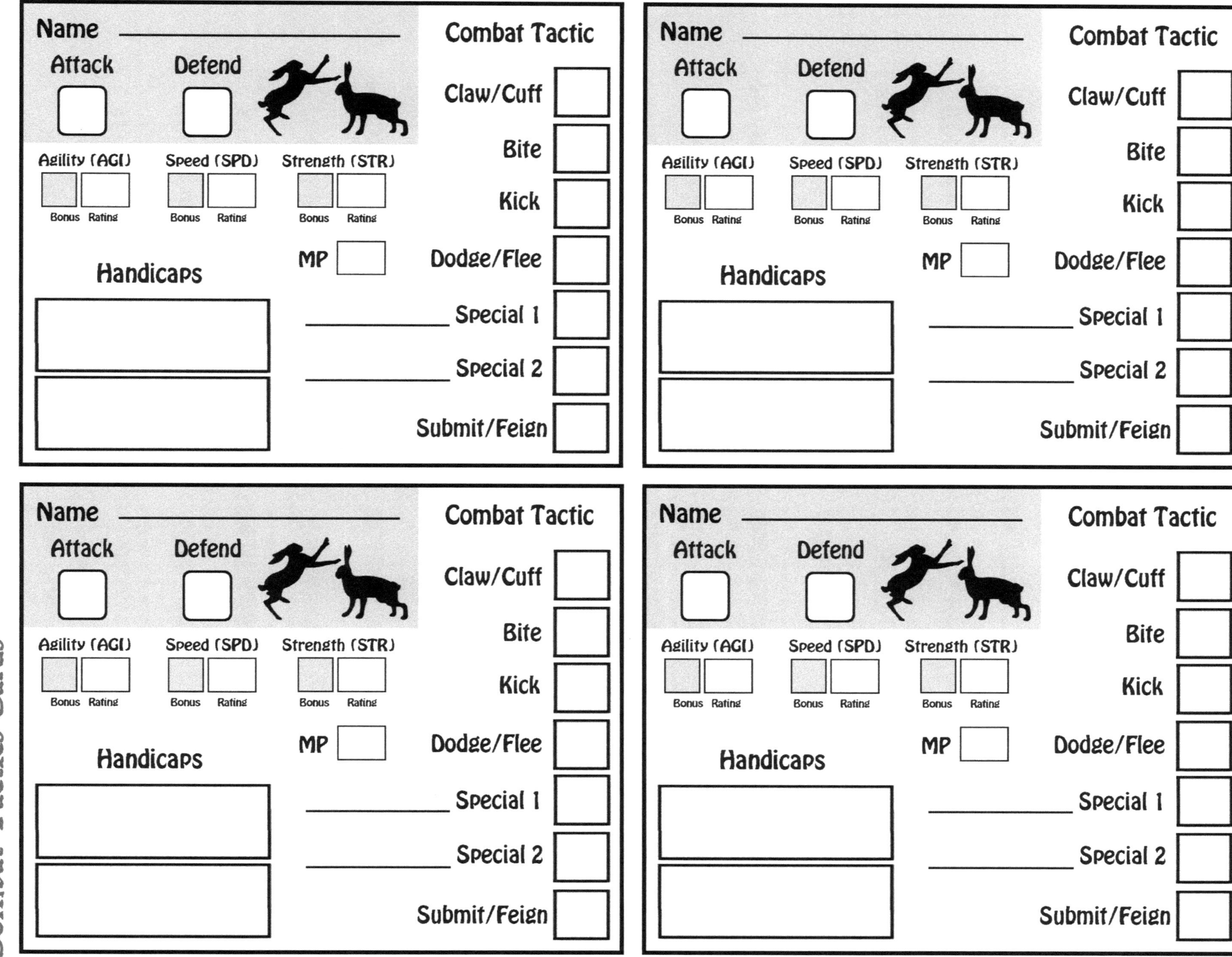

Handicap Markers for Combat Tactics Card

ANTS 3 HP damage/round	**ASLEEP** immobile 1d6 rounds	**CONFUSED** no attack 1 round	**DISEASED** see specific disease
ENTHRALLED ally with Storyteller	**FASCINATED** approach 1d6 rounds	**HELD** immobile; -2 on all actions	**IN SHOCK** immobile, DS=0 for 1d6 rounds
POISONED -1 MP; -1 HP/round	**QUILLED** AGI -1 or -2	**SNEEZING** no attack; random move 1d6 rounds	**SPRAYED** -3 MP; +1 MP/round
STUNNED immobile 1 round	**VULNERABLE** DS -1/ V marker for 1 round	**VULNERABLE** DS -1/ V marker for 1 round	**VULNERABLE** DS -1/ V marker for 1 round
Jaw Injury -1 STR	**Hindleg Injury** -1 SPD	**Eye Injury** -1 INT	**Foreleg Injury** -1 AGI
Persistent Disease -1 CON	**Emotional Trauma** -1 MYS	**Nose Injury** -1 SML	**Ear Injury** -1 CHA
ANTS 3 HP damage/round	**ASLEEP** immobile 1d6 rounds	**CONFUSED** no attack 1 round	**DISEASED** see specific disease
ENTHRALLED ally with Storyteller	**FASCINATED** approach 1d6 rounds	**HELD** -2 on all actions	**IN SHOCK** immobile, DS=0 for 1d6 rounds
POISONED -1 MP; -1 HP/round	**QUILLED** AGI -1 or -2	**SNEEZING** no attack; random move 1d6 rounds	**SPRAYED** -3 MP; +1 MP/round
STUNNED immobile 1 round	**VULNERABLE** DS -1/ V marker for 1 round	**VULNERABLE** DS -1/ V marker for 1 round	**VULNERABLE** DS -1/ V marker for 1 round
Jaw Injury -1 STR	**Hindleg Injury** -1 SPD	**Eye Injury** -1 INT	**Foreleg Injury** -1 AGI
Persistent Disease -1 CON	**Emotional Trauma** -1 MYS	**Nose Injury** -1 SML	**Ear Injury** -1 CHA
ANTS 3 HP damage/round	**ASLEEP** immobile 1d6 rounds	**CONFUSED** no attack 1 round	**DISEASED** see specific disease
ENTHRALLED ally with Storyteller	**FASCINATED** approach 1d6 rounds	**HELD** immobile; -2 on all actions	**IN SHOCK** immobile, DS=0 for 1d6 rounds
POISONED -1 MP; -1 HP/round	**QUILLED** AGI -1 or -2	**SNEEZING** no attack; random move 1d6 rounds	**SPRAYED** -3 MP; +1 MP/round
STUNNED immobile 1 round	**VULNERABLE** DS -1/ V marker for 1 round	**VULNERABLE** DS -1/ V marker for 1 round	**VULNERABLE** DS -1/ V marker for 1 round
Jaw Injury -1 STR	**Hindleg Injury** -1 SPD	**Eye Injury** -1 INT	**Foreleg Injury** -1 AGI
Persistent Disease -1 CON	**Emotional Trauma** -1 MYS	**Nose Injury** -1 SML	**Ear Injury** -1 CHA
TAUNTED move toward Taunter	**TAUNTED** move toward Taunter	**TAUNTED** move toward Taunter	**TAUNTED** move toward Taunter

Acknowledgements

I must give great thanks to all those who played various stages of this version of B&B, including members of the Royal Dragoon Guard (Fort Shorncliffe RMA and Sandgate Castle RMA Home Guard), players at North Texas RPG Con and ChupacabraCon, and participants in demonstrations for Round Rock High School and Austin Community College. Particular gratitude goes to Jeff Dee, Talzhemir Mrr, Ben Burns, Matt Sheffield, Marshall Mahurin, Jim Wampler, Liz and Mike Stewart, Edwin Stahlnecker and John Lile, all of whom gave me valued and detailed feedback. And of course, hearty thanks to Judy, my wife of 56 years, for supporting (and tolerating) me throughout this effort.

— *B. Dennis Sustare*

I'd like to express my thanks to my father, Calvin, who instilled a love for natural things, and to two professors of zoology, Robert M. ("Doc") Storm and Jack P. Hailman (Jack was graduate mentor to both Dennis and myself), who fostered an abiding respect for detailed observation. More proximate to this project, I thank my daughter Amanda and grandson Elijah for critiquing some game elements, my son John for creative brainstorming, and my wife Karen, (merely of 44 years), who always encouraged my creative endeavors despite my four-decade career of empirical research.

— *Scott R. Robinson*